AFFINITY FOR WAR

The Petralist – Book 4

AFFINITY FOR WAR

The Petralist – Book 4

FRANK MORIN

 Whipsaw Press

Affinity for War
Book 4 of the Petralist

ISBN: 978-1-946910-04-2

A Whipsaw Press Original

Edited by Joshua Essoe
(http://www.joshuaessoe.com/)

Cover art by Brad Fraunfelter
(http://www.bfillustration.com/)

Illustrations by Jared Blando
(http://www.theredepic.com/)

Book design by Kathryn Morin

First Whipsaw printing July 2018

Acknowledgements

Book four is here! I'll just say "Wow".

- Wow for the epic length. This book is about 30% longer than *No Stone Unturned*, and it refuses to shorten any further.
- Wow for the amazing new adventures I can barely believe, even though I'm the one recording it all.
- Wow for how this book pushed me to the limits in this epic ten-month writing and editing saga.
- Wow for the finished product.

As usual, no book is written in a vacuum, and I have to take a moment to thank the great team supporting, encouraging, and assisting in the work. My kids remain my most enthusiastic core supporters, and my lovely wife Jenny inspires me every single day.

My Fast Rollers team and Story Squad play a more critical role than they know. Thanks to them and to my beta readers for your dedication to this series and your undying enthusiasm. A particular thanks to Eve Ledesma and Joshua Lee for their detailed feedback above and beyond all others.

I hadn't thought Brad Fraunfelter could wow me with a new cover more than he had with the last one, but he did it yet again. The depth of his skill and his dedication to excellence are the marks of a true master craftsman.

And I blame Joshua Essoe for forcing me to dig deeper than ever to produce the best Petralist novel by far. Edits ended up taking a lot longer than I had hoped, but I couldn't rest until I made this story the best it could be. Joshua's insightful comments and unrelenting demand for clarity helped me shape the ultimate journey for Connor and his friends.

I know you've been anxious to get your hands on this story.

I hope you enjoy devouring it as much as I enjoyed crafting it.

The Northern Reaches
Varvakis
Orlov
Platov
River Angara
Lake Pyasino
Krashnov
River Glenet
Valeska Rivera
Althing
Jagdish
Granadure
Edduritz
Dagmanson
Ranok
Finnlangur
Ravinder
R. Baol
R. Bergrin
River Sanjit
Prahalad
Obrion
R. Macantacht
Donleavy
The Broken Water
Maninder
The Western Sea
The Eastern Sea
Sea of Olcan
Zehravad
Ozlem
Hayreddin
Murex
Tabnit
Mahzun
Tabnit
Brando
The Known World

GRANADURE
GRANITE MINE
ALASDAIR
QUARTZ ZINC GOLD MINE
THE WICK
PUMICE MINE
BASALT MINE
MARBLE MINE
MERKLAND
SLATE MINE
OBRION
SAOL RIVER
CRANN
TRODAIRE
DONLEAVY
MACANTACHT RIVER
FREASTAL
GRANITE MINE
BASALT MINE
GRANITE MINE
CASUR
MULRENNAN
CARRAIG
DEIFUR
LIMESTONE MINE
RAINEACH
LAIGE
SANDSTONE MINES
CHOSTALAN
SPEIRMOR
RADHARC
THE DESERT
BLANDO
THE LANDS OF
OBRION
N
W
E
S

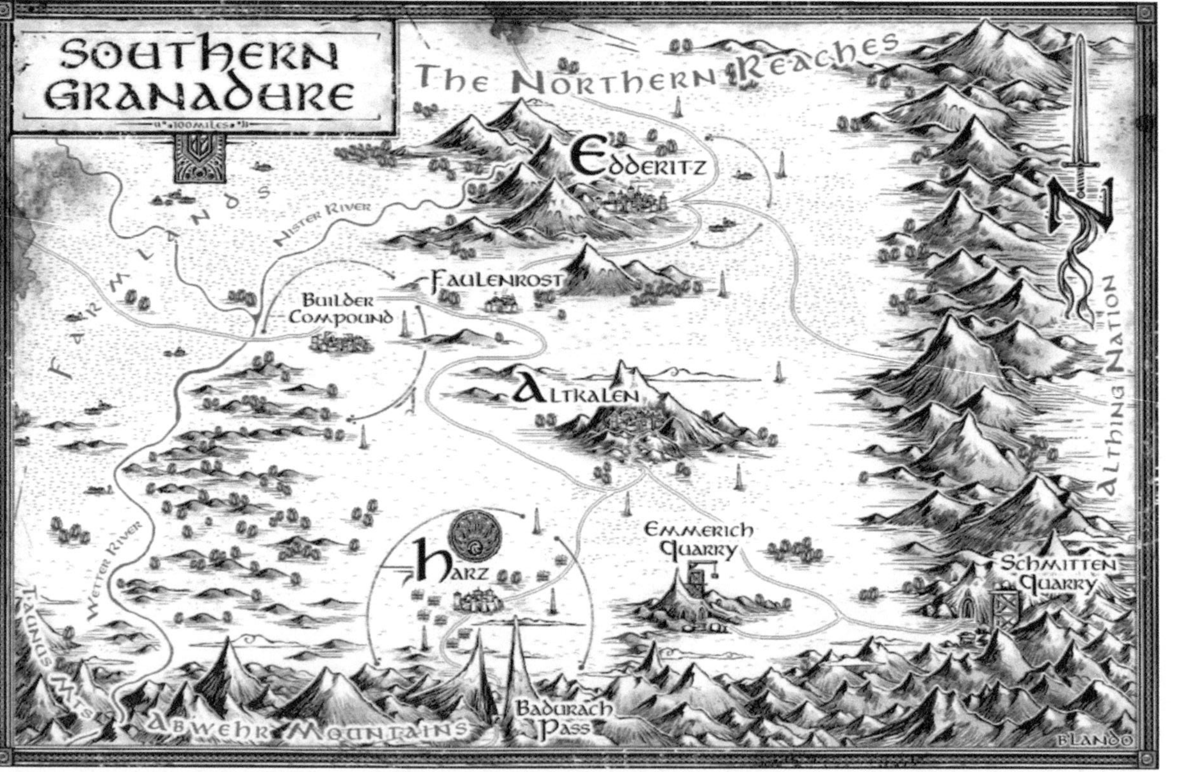

Southern Granadure
100 Miles
The Northern Reaches
Edderitz
Farm Lands
Nister River
Faulenrost
Builder Compound
Altkalen
Wetter River
Harz
Emmerich Quarry
Schmitten Quarry
Althing Nation
Taunus Mts
Abwehr Mountains
Badurach Pass
Blando

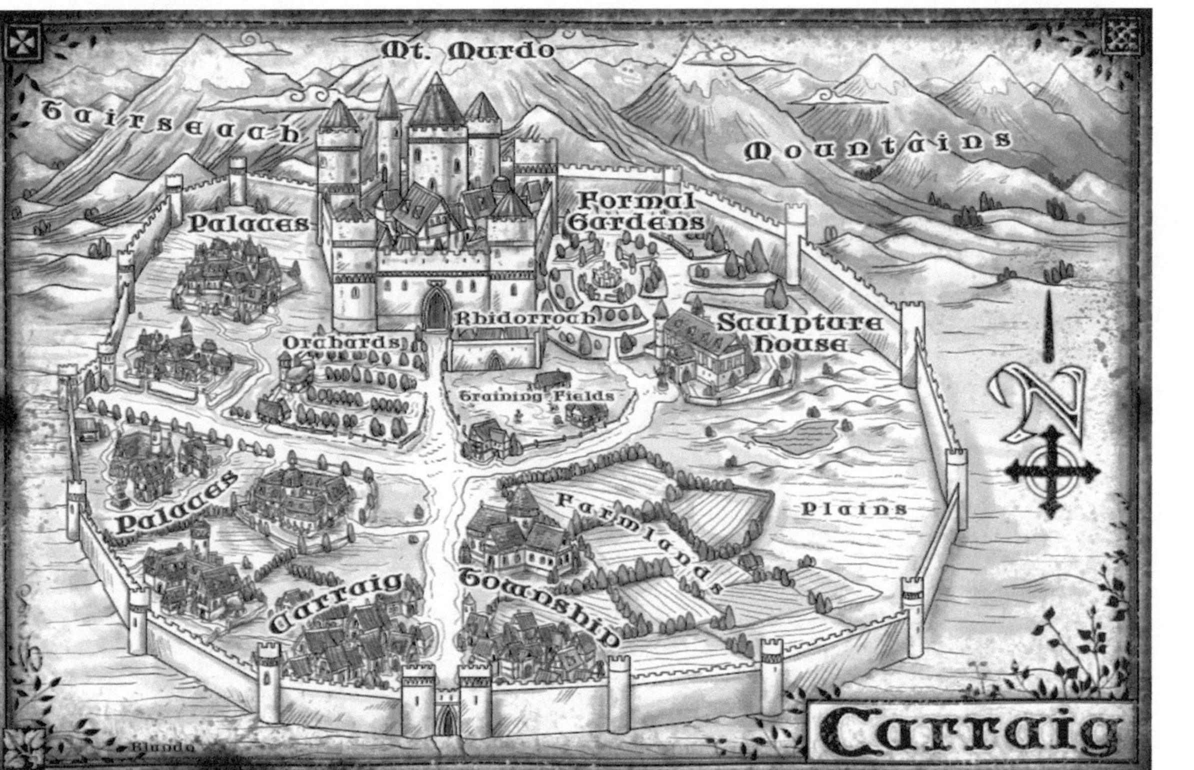

Mt. Murdo
Tairseach
Mountains
Palaces
Formal Gardens
Rhidorroch
Sculpture House
Orchards
Training Fields
Palaces
Farmlands
Plains
Carraig Township
N
Carraig

Wick Tor
loch Sholto
Mount Alasdair
Mount Ingram
loch Kadhar
Upper Wick
Alasdair
Powder house
Lord Gavin's Manor house
River Barges
Loch Wick
Lower Wick
the Valley
BLANDÖ
N
The Lands of Alasdair

CHAPTER ONE

"The north wind drives away the rain, but only he who tills the earth can enjoy the harvest."

~Gregor

Connor laughed with the thrill of clinging with all his might to the hand rails on the back of the Swift. Verena tore into the sky, taking them up in a nearly-vertical ascent. The amazingly nimble little craft roared, every thruster thrown wide. If Connor wasn't tapping granite strength, he never would have managed to hold on.

He was free in a way he'd never been his entire life, and for a moment, he could almost believe nothing would ever interrupt that glorious feeling.

Except for maybe the looming war.

"Are you still with me?" Verena called, glancing back at him from the pilot seat.

Only her head extended above the armored plating protecting her on every side. The Swift was little more than a flying, armored chair, with quartzite thrusters attached on every plane, allowing Verena to spin, twist, and roll in any direction. And of course, the many deadly mechanicals built into the craft transformed it into a unique battle platform.

"You can't ditch me," Connor grinned.

She pushed up the visor of her helmet as she slowed, banked to the left, and entered a concealing cloud bank. "Is that a challenge?"

Her bright blue eyes sparkled with humor, and her cute, heart-shaped face was very distracting. He knew not to underestimate her, though, so he lifted one hand in a placating gesture. "Maybe once we're safely out of Obrion."

They had both risked too much to escape the Carraig. Falling from over two thousand feet would definitely dent his plans to reach Granadure with her. They had crossed half of

Obrion in recent days and were almost back to the northern border and Alasdair.

As they slowed to a hover in the clouds, surrounded by the gossamer tendrils of mist that concealed them from prying eyes, Hamish banked in close to their right side. In his amazing Builder battle suit, he was as agile as the Swift in the air, and just as deadly.

Jean clung to his back, her long, blonde braid snapping in the wind. While flying, she replaced her normal blue dress with a pair of heavy leather trousers, wore a pair of long-vision goggles to protect her eyes, and seemed unable to keep from laughing.

"Think anyone saw us?" Hamish asked.

"I doubt it," Connor said.

Merkland was still far enough away that even Pathfinders on the famous white walls would have a hard time spotting them. They had waited to leave the river until they turned into the Lower Wick from the mighty Macantact.

As Verena ghosted southwest over the rolling, forested hills toward Merkland, Hamish drifted closer. Connor helped Jean transfer to the top of the storage box at the rear of the Swift beside him.

She extended one hand, trailing it through the clouds. "It's like the mists that rise from the Wick on cool mornings."

Hamish rolled onto his back and spread both arms wide. "Wait till we fly through a thunderhead cloud. They're so full of water, it's like flying through the river."

"Aren't you worried about getting struck by lightning?" Jean asked.

"Don't talk with Hamish about lightning," Verena said with a groan. "He once flew into a thunder cloud carrying a pastry on an iron stick. Lightning nearly took off his hand."

"You didn't!" Jean gasped.

Hamish shrugged. "There's got to be a way to use all that charbroiling energy to cook dinner."

Connor said, "Cook your brain, more like it."

"There's Merkland," Verena interrupted, pointing to their left.

She slowed to a hover, and the steady hissing of the thrusters would be dispelled through the clouds. Hopefully any listening Pathfinders would mistake the sound for a distant breeze. The Swift was painted mottled gray and white, which turned it nearly invisible in just about any sky. As long as they remained in the clouds, they should be safe from discovery.

They spent a moment studying the panoramic vista through the misty clouds. The low hills flanking the Wick changed to flat farmlands that spread for miles around Merkland. The mighty fortress, seat of High Lord Dougal's realm, was built on a flat-topped bluff overlooking the junction of the Lower Wick and the mighty Macantact rivers. The famous white granite walls towered thirty feet, broken by two huge gates on the landward sides.

The many spires of Dougal's central palace would have seemed wondrous if Connor hadn't just spent months living at the Carraig. The inner city was so packed with soaring towers that Merkland looked like a humble village in comparison.

Well, it would if the Carraig hadn't just been thoroughly smashed by a raging elfonnel. The memory of that desperate day, full of terror and death, had lingered with Connor ever since Shona had freed him from her service and sent him away with Verena.

Surprisingly, the memory that clung to him the most from that terrible day was not witnessing Declan's heroic sacrifice, finding the dead, savaged bodies inside the monster's stomach, or the shattered plain and falling buildings. Even though he'd taken command of all of the combined armed forces, ascended through the threshold with soapstone, and unlocked incredible new powers, it was the unrivaled sense of glory he'd enjoyed that haunted his dreams.

He had become a rampager.

That memory chilled him again as he thought about it. Daring porphyry and the agonizing transformation into a rampager had been a last, desperate ploy to escape Dougal's control and face the unrivaled power of the elfonnel. As a rampager, he'd been stronger than the mightiest Boulder, as fast as a fracked Strider, and able to take the fight to the elfonnel.

When he remembered that experience, he found himself yearning for more porphyry and for an excuse to tempt the transformation again. That yearning had awakened him from sleep several times, and it returned in quiet moments when he let his thoughts wander. Even though he was out of porphyry, he found himself thinking of situations when it might be necessary.

His best defense against such disturbing yearnings was to think about Verena. Her face, her smile, and her minty lips always helped ground him.

Connor sucked on the little piece of quartzite already wedged into his cheek, focusing his thoughts on the liquid warmth of quartzite power pooling in the center of his head. With a simple thought, he directed some of that power to his eyes.

He winced at a brief, sharp stab of pain. Even though he expected it, he still rubbed one eye with a finger, marveling anew at how the soft orb had transformed into hard, faceted crystal. He blinked a couple of times, then looked out over a world turned marvelous.

The beautiful landscape seemed to glow, and he drank in the deeper hues now visible. Quartzite enhanced colors with deeper reds and more vibrant blues and purples, invisible to unenhanced eyes. As he focused on the distant Merkland Torr, his vision swept down like a diving hawk and he clutched the hand rails harder as his stomach lurched.

As he scanned the castle, it seemed as if he was hovering only a few feet above the walls instead of nearly a mile overhead and three miles distant. Soldiers manned the parapets, and he picked out three Sentries and four Pathfinders.

They were not looking at the sky. Most of them were turned toward the north where an army was issuing through the huge main gates, ten abreast, marching into the wide plain north of town.

"Do you see the army?" Verena asked.

"I'm staring at one captain's warty nose right now."

She chuckled. "I can't zoom in quite that far."

She had activated the quartzite embedded in her visor, enabling her long-vision goggles, which did a remarkable job of imitating Pathfinder vision. She had explained that for Builders, releasing the air power of quartzite was easy, but affecting the senses was far more challenging. For Petralists, just the opposite held true.

The constant smile Jean wore while flying faded as she peered at the distant army. "Are they heading toward Alasdair?"

Verena reached back and touched Jean's goggles, activating the long-vision aspect. "I set your zoom factor to about eight times normal. Close things will seem gigantic, but you should get a pretty good view of what's going on down there."

They watched the army for a few minutes before Jean said, "The walls really are made of Alasdair White."

"They are," Connor confirmed.

He'd seen the fortress on his journey south months ago, on his way toward Raineach and his Aunt Ailsa. At that time, those gleaming white granite walls had seemed like one of the wonders of the world.

Hamish whistled softly. "What a fortune to stack into walls."

Verena said, "I've heard that it's all builded stone."

"You can't be serious," Hamish exclaimed. "They kill Builders in Obrion. There's no one to maintain it."

"It's one of the wonders from the Age of Discovery before the great purge," Verena said.

"What does touching granite with your powers do?" Jean asked.

Hamish said, "Hardens it. Like the projectiles in the speedslings. They become nearly indestructible."

Among the impressive armaments the Swift carried were a pair of extra-long speedslings, mounted to either side of the bottom of the chair. Verena could unleash thousands of deadly little hornets in a matter of seconds. Hamish carried a much smaller version of the weapon in a holster on his hip.

Verena added "The mystery is how the wall still stands. Even if they only opened a tiny fraction of the stones' power, it should have all been spent by now. So much was lost during the purge."

Hamish pivoted and pointed toward the south. "What is that?"

Something that vaguely resembled a long, narrow house was approaching Merkland along the main highway, moving at remarkable speed.

Connor focused on it and frowned. "It's sliding up a set of iron rails built beside the road."

Verena said with a note of excitement in her voice, "That's the speedcaravan."

CHAPTER TWO

"The heart of the mountain is but a dormant volcano, but fires rage only after a spark is struck."

~Ilse

I ve heard of the speedcaravan," Connor said, studying the fast-moving vehicle with even more interest.

Verena pivoted the Swift to improve their view. "It's one of the few remaining Builder inventions that has survived since the Age of Discovery. That's the last working one. It runs from Merkland, down half the length of Obrion, to Donleavy. How it's still operational after three hundred years is a mystery. We've started trying to build new routes in Obrion, but track maintenance is causing a ton of problems."

"Wish we could study it," Hamish said.

Verena shook her head. "Only high officials ride them. There's a good chance Dougal is aboard."

"He made good time." Connor wouldn't have expected anyone else could have crossed Obrion as fast as they had.

Hamish's tone turned eager. "We could attack. They'd never expect a strike from the air."

It was tempting. Dougal was the driving force behind Obrion's war effort. Connor had sensed his determination to unleash death and destruction upon Granadure. He didn't like the idea of killing anyone, but if they could remove Dougal, how many lives would they save?

"Tempting," Verena said, as if reading Connor's mind. "But we've seen enough. Let's get back to Kilian."

Hamish grumbled something under his breath as Verena banked away, but did not protest. Connor was glad they were leaving. He didn't want to spend any time near Dougal. The man had tried to take over his mind during the battle against the elfonnel. He didn't want to think about that terrifying experience. He wanted to enjoy his new-found freedom for a while.

"You don't feel any connection, do you?" Jean asked.

"No, and I don't want to. I don't have any more porphyry so I can't fight him off again."

Verena said, "We'll have to see if the charred porphyry powder we have at the Builder compound works."

"You have more?" Connor exclaimed, grabbing her shoulder harder than he intended. Knowing they had access to more triggered an intense yearning for it. He felt a mighty urge to skip the visit to Alasdair altogether in order to get it sooner.

"I don't think it would be wise for you to take any more," Verena said slowly, twisting to look at him. Her voice sounded concerned. "We interviewed the captured rampagers, and they were slaves to that powder. They would have done anything to get more. I don't think I want to see you like that."

Connor released her and took a deep breath. The intensity of that sudden craving unnerved him. "We don't have any here anyway," he said, more to help himself relax than for anyone else.

As they soared back toward the Wick, Verena said, "At least we know the speedcaravan is back. The army seemed to be heading north toward the border. If Dougal is aboard, he's probably headed up to the pass to oversee the army."

"Does that mean the war's about to start?" Jean asked worriedly.

Verena shrugged. "Maybe. But we could get the first real snows of winter any day. That would make invasion difficult, even for Petralists."

Hamish glanced back at the speedcaravan and frowned. "Wish I had that latest bomb Dierk's been working on."

"Would you really kill everyone in that caravan without knowing who they are?" Verena asked.

Hamish sighed. "No. I don't want to kill anyone but Dougal."

"We'll deal with him," Connor assured him.

He was happy that his friends shared his reluctance about killing. Bash fighting was the best fun in the world, but the looming war would be different.

After a moment, Verena said, "I'm starting to worry about how many men Dougal has marshaled. We saw at least twenty thousand troops already at the pass a couple weeks ago."

"That's a lot of soldiers," Jean whispered.

"Granadure's got roughly the same already marshaled on the Badurach side of the pass," Hamish said.

Verena added, "And there are reinforcements gathering at Harz fortress and the trading center of Altkalen. I suspect there are reinforcement armies assembling in Obrion at every high lord's capital. If war breaks out, both sides could marshal upwards of a hundred thousand soldiers."

The thought of so many armed men and women trying to kill each other, led by hundreds of mighty Petralists who could literally rip the landscape apart, made Connor feel insignificant. He couldn't comprehend why so many people seemed so eager to rush into such destruction.

It would be better if nations settled arguments with pie eating contests. There would probably be a lot more wars in that case, but everyone would have a lot more fun.

Verena accelerated and called back, "Jean, are you going to ride with us?"

Jean shook her head, already grinning in a wild way that seemed so unlike her. She shouted, "Hamish, catch!"

She jumped off the Swift.

The move so surprised Connor that he nearly jumped off to catch her. He only just remembered that would only mean Verena would have to pluck two people out of the air.

Hamish reacted so fast, he must have been expecting the move. With an explosion of air from the thrusters built into the chest, arms, and even the hands of his suit, Hamish twisted hard over. He shot across the distance, catching Jean before she could fall out of the clouds and risk giving them away to any watchful Pathfinders.

The two spiraled a few yards lower before his increased thrusters pulled them higher again. Twined together and laughing, they rose into the clouds until the mists obscured them from view.

"I'm starting to think Hamish is a bad influence on her," Connor said.

Verena grinned at him, her visor still raised. "What's the matter, Connor? They're just having a little fun."

"I thought you understood Hamish's history. For years he was famous for falling and dropping things."

"I think he's motivated enough not to drop Jean," Verena said with a chuckle. "Now kiss me and stop being a mother hen."

Connor eagerly obliged. He loved Verena's soft, minty lips. He loved even more the fact that she hadn't pressured him to kiss her too much since they escaped the Carraig. Shona had used her beauty as a tool to try controlling him. He'd escaped her service, but still hesitated to focus too much on the physical attraction he felt with Verena.

Their relationship was deepening, and he loved spending time with her. They seemed to never run out of things to say, and her presence was a constant comfort that helped wash away the challenging, negative experiences he'd recently been through. He wasn't sure what life held in store, but he didn't doubt for a minute that Verena would be a part of it.

Hamish descended nearby, with Jean clinging to his back. They waved, and Hamish accelerated through the clouds back to the northeast. Verena gave chase, and Connor grinned as the wind tore at his face. It didn't draw tears from his Pathfinder-hardened eyes, so he kept the quartzite applied until they passed the hills concealing the Lower Wick from the environs around Merkland. Only then did they begin a slow glide down toward the Wick.

Two miles upriver, Verena slowed further and dropped to glide inches above the smooth, steadily-flowing river. Connor leaned down and draped a hand into the waters, focusing on his soapstone affinity. He had downed a mixture of soapstone powder and water earlier. Envisioning the gateway to the element like a watery doorway in his mind, he thrust his senses through.

The gateway opened easily to his mind. Water had been the first element he established affinity with, and it was still his most reliable tertiary power. His senses radiated out through the river and he quested for the hidden team.

Kilian was shielding. Connor didn't know the technique yet, and he wondered if it was similar to shielding with slate on solid ground. He was eager to learn it. Despite seeing the river through soapstone senses clearly enough that he could map the contours of the bottom or count the fish swimming within a hundred yards, he felt no indication of Kilian lurking beneath the surface.

That didn't mean Kilian couldn't sense him.

Connor withdrew his senses and lifted his hand from the water. "I'm sure he felt that."

"Did you sense him this time?" she asked.

"No."

"I bet he's upriver at least another quarter mile."

"I doubt it."

Just then, the waters of the Wick fifty feet behind them began to bubble and spray. A glistening, silver-hulled ship made entirely of water lifted to the surface. The rest of their party sat on six watery, throne-like chairs set in a half circle on the deck. Even though they had been traveling submerged, riding on chairs made of water, they looked completely dry.

Soapstone was so much fun.

"I should have sensed him that close," Connor grumbled as Verena banked around and settled the Swift to the small aft deck, directly behind the Grandurians. Hamish landed a few seconds later, and four more watery chairs rose from the deck and joined the half-circle.

"How did it go?" Kilian asked as they shed their thick flying leathers and Jean helped Hamish strip out of his suit. The Dawnus sat in a chair more reclined than the others, one leg thrown over the arm, looking completely relaxed, despite the effort of maintaining the ship.

They had met up with Kilian just as they reached the Macantact River. He had never explained how he knew to find them there. He had only said that he'd sensed the rise of the elfonnel while he was preparing to infiltrate Merkland on his hunt for Dougal. He'd abandoned his lone assault and rushed downriver instead.

Verena dropped into a chair beside Captain Ilse. The slender, raven-haired captain led the Grandurian special team that had been assigned to help Connor escape from the Carraig, or kill him if he wouldn't come. They had figured out how to get along, and now Connor cautiously considered her a friend. He took the chair on Verena's other side.

Verena said, "Reinforcements are marching from Merkland, heading for the pass."

The other four members of Ilse's team leaned forward to listen. Hulking Erich and his shapely twin sister Anika radiated power even when not tapping granite. Dietmar, the fearless Wingrunner, shifted on his seat, as if barely restraining the urge to run across the surface of the river in a fracked sprint and race them to Alasdair. Margrit, the team's Longseer, sat primly on her chair, blue dress smooth and proper, wide-brimmed hat tipped back enough for Connor to glimpse her eyes. They glittered even when not tapping quartzite.

"How many?" Kilian asked.

"About four thousand, with companies of Petralists leading the way," Connor said.

Ilse pursed her lips. "The pass will now have roughly as many men as that army we spotted massing outside of Crann."

"Do you think they'll wait for more reinforcements?" Connor asked.

They had slipped past the huge metropolis of Crann two nights ago and had scouted it just as they had Merkland. Merkland could fit inside of Crann a dozen times.

They had estimated close to twenty-five thousand troops camped north of the city, their hundreds of campfires like a blanket of twinkling stars in the darkness. Connor had spotted the standards of six high lords snapping in the breeze on poles positioned around the huge, well-lit command tent. Obrion was indeed marshaling for war.

Verena added, "The speedcaravan was just arriving."

Kilian sat up straighter, his blue eyes intent. "Was Dougal aboard?"

"We didn't go down and verify," Hamish grumbled. "Some people thought it was too dangerous to attack."

Kilian said, "Wise choice. Dougal would not travel these days without powerful guards. Gregor is almost always in his company, and from what you told me, he had other senior Petralists stationed at the Carraig who might have returned with him."

"They wouldn't have seen us coming," Hamish insisted.

"Let's not start that again," Verena said.

"I prefer he not know our location," Kilian said. "Your attack might have surprised him. You might even have killed him or some of his guards. But at this point, such an attack might have served as the final excuse Obrion needs to launch a full invasion."

Hamish looked surprised. "Didn't think of that."

"It's always wise to take the time to think things through before leaping into life or death decisions," Kilian said in the tone of a teacher. Then he added, "We may have to call for reinforcements from Harz."

Ilse asked, "Do you have word on how many troops Altkalen has ready?"

Kilian shook his head. "One of many reports I need to read when we return to the Builder compound."

He waved them all to take their seats. "I'm afraid your homecoming visit will have to be brief."

"We should stay overnight at least," Jean pleaded.

"I wish we could, but half a day is the most we can spare."

While Jean continued to argue for more time, Connor shared a concerned look with Hamish. His greatest worry since escaping the Carraig was the safety of his family.

Shona might have set him free, but High Lord Dougal had made it clear he intended to use Connor as the hammer against Granadure. He couldn't imagine Dougal not sending soldiers to Alasdair to watch his family. Or worse, capture and torture them as leverage against Connor.

"We'll make the best of it," he told Jean.

He swore that if they spotted soldiers marching against Alasdair, then come hammers or high waters, he'd stay and defend his family, no matter what Kilian decided.

Kilian was already pulling the water craft below the surface. As the river bubbled up all around them, they accelerated upriver and sank to fifteen feet. An open bubble of air formed above the deck, shielding them from the flowing water. Kilian might look like an average, middle-aged man, with piercing blue eyes and blue-tinged, dark hair, but under that easy smile and relaxed manner lurked perhaps the most powerful Petralist alive. Connor wasn't sure how old Kilian might be, but he'd learned enough while prying into ancient secrets at the Carraig to suspect he'd been around a very long time.

That made Kilian a curious mystery. Connor loved the underwater form of travel, and he hoped to learn deeper Petralist secrets. He hoped Kilian would be willing to share that knowledge, but wondered what price he would exact in return.

Chapter Three

"The mightiest pedra can fall to a child's knife when distracted by the hunter and his arrow, but Time most beloved is grasped like water dripping from a cauldron."

~Connor

Connor relaxed on the soft, throne-like chair of water as they slid upriver. Kilian again lounged with one leg thrown over the arm of his chair. A smile tugged at the corners of his mouth as he listened to Hamish, who was regaling the group with stories of his favorite Sogail feast.

"You did not eat that entire bird," Jean corrected through a laugh. The two sat close together, holding hands.

Connor couldn't blame them. He loved the feel of Verena's warm fingers twined with his. Spending time with Verena was easy, and he could relax and just be himself.

The contrast with Shona was striking. Lady Shona might be beautiful and graceful and politically powerful, but spending time with her had always felt like battling a pedra.

Verena said, "I wish we were arriving in Alasdair during this Sogail feast. It sounds like quite a party."

"It is," Connor assured her. "Everyone celebrates their age-day, and there's no other feast half as good. Not even the harvest feast can top it."

"We probably just missed that one," Hamish grumbled.

Jean nodded, then pushed her thick hair back from her face. She'd shaken out the braid so it fell in loose, golden waves halfway down her back. "The crops got planted more or less on time this year, despite the rebuilding challenges and the chaos from that flood. Harvest should have happened on time."

Connor was glad the village had recovered so well from the devastating flood that he had unleashed upon the valley when he blew the cliff above Lord Gavin's manor. If he hadn't, the resulting pitched battle would probably have leveled the town and claimed the lives of everyone he knew. He wondered if the villagers understood that.

He'd find out soon enough. They would arrive in Alasdair by morning. Despite their rapid pace, Connor had to stop himself from tapping soapstone and adding the force of his affinity to Kilian's to drive them faster. He'd been gone for months, and now that they were so close, he couldn't wait to get home.

Hamish grinned. "Still, there will be plenty of food with harvest finished. This time of year, everyone's always looking for an excuse to celebrate something."

"Is many good," said Erich, the hulking Rumbler, in his thick Grandurian accent. He stabbed a meaty finger at his own chest. "I eat many best champion."

"What?" Connor frowned as he struggled to understand that one. Erich was one of the deadliest fighters Connor knew, but when he spoke Obrioner, he sounded like he'd squashed too much of his brains between all those muscles.

Anika explained, "He is say that in many big eats, he is always champion."

She might be smiling, but Connor did not let her relaxed demeanor fool him. When she tapped her granite Petralist affinity and transformed into the perfectly sculpted, stone-like fighting goddess, she scared him more than just about anyone.

Captain Ilse chuckled. "Remind me to continue your Obrioner lessons." Unlike the blonde siblings, she spoke Obrioner with almost no accent.

"We'll get a feast for sure," Hamish assured Erich, rubbing his hands together in expectation. "Our return will be the perfect excuse to celebrate, and I challenge you to an eating contest."

Erich grinned. "Little man, no stomach big."

"Don't let his size fool you," Jean assured Erich. "Hamish can eat more than any three other people I've ever met."

"Is many good challenge," Erich said, looking eager for the contest.

The bland travel rations they'd been eating in recent days probably stoked his enthusiasm. Connor wondered if Alasdair had enough food stored for the winter to survive an all-out food duel between those two.

Hamish's legendary appetite had only grown in recent months, fueled by his arms practice and Builder duties. He'd grown from a gangly, clumsy youth into a strong, competent warrior. Jean certainly seemed to appreciate the changes.

Jean asked, "Do you realize we've been gone longer than anyone ever, except for those taken by the curse hunters?"

Those poor few, like Connor's uncle Martys, who had been taken as a child, were never heard from again.

"That's why the feast will be bigger than ever," Hamish assured her.

"I hope so," she said.

Connor said, "Me too. I could eat a torc. Let's just hope we can avoid a riot when everyone sees who we're traveling with."

Kilian said, "Your parents seemed unusually competent. As long as we avoid your local lord, I am confident we can find a way to get along."

Erich and Anika both shrugged. They didn't look concerned. Of course, with their granite-enhanced strength, the villagers posed no real threat. No one there possessed any Petralist affinity. The two siblings could level all of Alasdair and beat down any resistance without breaking a sweat.

Ilse said, "My only concern is that Dougal has already stationed soldiers there."

"When I left to serve Lady Shona at the Carraig, everyone High Lord Dougal had sent to assist with rebuilding was already gone," Jean assured her.

"That does not mean he has not sent soldiers to watch your families," Ilse said.

"Then we deal with them," Connor said, his tone hard. Nothing prevented him from fighting for them any longer.

Shona had once threatened to enslave his entire family if he refused her bidding, but she had released him at the end. That still shocked him, and he had to wonder if the decision was part of some intricate, subtle geall she was still playing. He just couldn't imagine how.

Shona had claimed that she couldn't bear the thought of sharing him with women from all the high noble houses as the king had authorized. That unexpected gesture suggested that deep down Shona really did care for him as a person and not just the tool she needed to further her ambitions. Still, Connor worried that she would regret the choice. His family would pay the price if she did.

His feelings for Shona were complex, and at times contradictory, but Dougal represented a clear threat. The more Connor thought about it, the more he realized that escape was but the first and perhaps easiest part of his future. Somehow he had to convince his family of the danger.

Worrying was even less helpful than guarding the oven in Hamish's house, right before dinner. He would assess the situation when they arrived. Then he'd deal with it.

So for the moment, Connor tapped soapstone. He allowed his water senses to slip through his chair and explore the rest of the open space above the deck, then the craft that supported their chairs. He tried to gain a sense of how Kilian was keeping it intact and rushing upriver so easily.

Verena noticed him glancing down at their craft and said, "What are you looking at?"

"Just studying this water boat."

She grimaced. "The right word's important, and that's not it."

Hamish broke off from a discussion with Erich about how to rate the best sweetbreads. "Let's call it the swim-dunk!"

Erich grunted, "Better call it Swim-no-swim."

"We could just call it the underwater Slide," Jean suggested.

"That's still not right, but it'll do for now," Verena said.

They'd have plenty of time to think about it. Travel by river underwater was a brilliant idea. Flying was faster, although not everyone could fit on the Swift. Some of Dougal's forces had learned to start scanning the skies for windriders, and only a Spitter might notice their fast, clandestine progress underwater. With Kilian's shielding ability, Connor doubted anyone would sense them.

"I want to try running the Slide," Connor announced.

"Do you feel you're ready?" Kilian asked.

"Let's find out."

"Very well. Give it a try."

Captain Ilse, who did not look comfortable so long separated from the earth, gave him a concerned look. "I don't feel like getting wet, boy."

Connor gave her a confident smile. "Trust me."

"I don't really feel like getting wet either," Verena said uneasily.

"I know water," Connor assured her.

Eager to do something besides counting the seconds until they stopped for the night, he again tapped soapstone. His senses connected with the water, expanded across the length of the Slide's hull, then into the river.

For a second he felt one with the waters, could feel the power of the Wick as hundreds of thousands of gallons of water pushed ever downward toward Merkland and the Macantact. That power, that unrelenting strength of the river was his strength. The fish darting through the waters tickled at his mind, and he could have pointed to every single one of them.

He gasped and Verena started, her expression worried as she glanced at the roof of the bubble. "What?"

"Some of the fish in here are so much bigger than anything we've ever caught."

Hamish said, "Like that one that got away from me a couple summers back."

Jean rolled her eyes. "The big fish always get away, Hamish."

Connor focused on their craft. It slid through the water with remarkable ease. He sensed Kilian's presence in the waters, although only at the very front of the bubble and along the hull. That was a little strange, but Connor was too excited to prove himself to the mighty Dawnus and to his friends to worry about it.

So he thrust fingers of thought around the Slide and seized control of it. Kilian let him take it, his influence fading, as if through an invisible sieve.

Connor grinned, and for a second he was master of the Slide.

Then the roof collapsed.

Chapter Four

"Experience ever graces the world with the dawn of a new day, and one with eyes to see may appreciate each precious gift."

~Sentry class teacher

Connor's moment of victory didn't exactly get rained on. More like swept away in a flood.

As the roof collapsed and water poured into the bubble, Verena managed to punch him in the ribs before getting tumbled off her seat. It only took a few seconds to seize the waters, form a new bubble over the hull of the Slide, drag his friends back to their seats, and drain the water out of everyone's clothing. Ilse still glared at him like she was seriously contemplating violence.

Connor glanced at Kilian, who had allowed him to fix the mess. Kilian only raised a single eyebrow in question, but Connor couldn't explain what had gone wrong, and that only embarrassed him further.

Since his ascension, his control with soapstone had improved dramatically. When he had taken control of the water, the hull of the Slide had responded immediately to his will, but he didn't understand why the roof of the bubble had slipped through his watery fingers.

"That could have gone better," Hamish laughed. He fished a sweetbread out of a pouch at his belt and looked delighted that it wasn't soggy. "You sure you don't want me to help?"

Verena laughed, and the sound was like music to Connor's ears. "Oh, Hamish, you'd drown us if you activated soapstone in the middle of this river."

"I'm not that bad," he grumbled, then took an enormous bite.

Jean patted his hand. "It was nice of you to offer, Hamish, but I think Connor has it under control." She hesitated. "You do, don't you?"

Connor glanced again at Kilian. "What did I miss?"

"What does it feel like you missed?" Little waves began crashing inside of Kilian's eyes, the foaming movement changing them from deep blue to frothy white, then back again.

Connor thought about it as he fine-tuned the angles of their chairs. Their speed had slowed to a crawl, so he increased it again, driving the Slide through the Lower Wick. It seemed a lot more difficult than when Kilian had done it, and the protective bubble over the deck began to vibrate as they accelerated. Verena and Ilse weren't the only two who cast uneasy glances around.

"You're going to exhaust yourself trying to move all this water all the miles up to Alasdair," Kilian said.

"If I don't move it, we'll never get there."

Kilian shook his head. "You've got great talent with water, but you don't really understand it yet. We're moving upriver. The idea isn't to hold the Slide and this bubble of air like a ball underwater. All you need to do is push the hull and split the waters in front of us. The rest takes care of itself."

"How? The ceiling will collapse again if I let it go."

"Don't!" Ilse growled, and Verena covered her nose.

"Watch me again and pay more attention," Kilian directed.

His will slipped into the waters and smoothly plucked them away from Connor. As much as Connor had progressed with soapstone, he still had a lot to learn. The Slide accelerated upriver, the vibrations in the roof bubble faded away, and the ride smoothed out.

Connor let his water senses flow around the Slide and the bubble, studying what Kilian was doing. It took a moment before he understood. "That's amazing."

"Then you do it," Kilian said.

"Here we go," Hamish said, pulling on his helmet.

Verena lifted a piece of quartzite, probably planning to create a shield of air to protect herself when the roof collapsed. Jean scuttled to her side to share it. Dietmar looked like he was considering fracking and making a break for the surface. Erich just took a deep breath and held it.

Their lack of confidence might be justified, but it wasn't helpful. Connor was tempted to drench them. As fun as that might be, it would only reinforce their doubt. So he took control of the Slide again, and this time the ceiling only rippled a little.

He was tempted to open a drip over Ilse's head, but she'd probably order Erich and Anika to throw him right out of the river. Verena gave him an encouraging smile, but did not put away her quartzite.

This time Connor gripped the hull of the slide and imagined an invisible knife rising from the bow. The blade split the waters of the Wick, allowing their craft to slide through the opening it tore through the moving waters. He extended the blade at an angle above the prow of the Slide and experimented with its width until the waters split far enough for them to slip through the gap before closing again behind.

Kilian was right. He didn't have to control the ceiling. There wasn't a ceiling at all, just a temporary gap in the waters that they slipped through. He grinned as the process became smooth and stable, and took far less effort to maintain.

Once he settle the Slide into a constant pace, keeping it in the center of the river, ten feet below the surface, his thoughts returned to their upcoming visit home. His excitement grew, and he was tempted to accelerate.

It would feel so good to talk things over with his parents, but he worried they wouldn't be ready to accept the danger that faced them. For generations, nothing ever changed in Alasdair, but he feared a storm was coming that threatened to sweep away everyone he loved.

He had no idea how to stop it.

Chapter Five

"The moth who draws close usually comprehends the danger of the flame only in the act of being consumed."

~Evander

As much as Connor wanted to push through the night to reach Alasdair, bursting into the sleeping town in company with Grandurians might not be the best way to kick off his homecoming. So when he reached a section of river that he recognized shortly before nightfall, he drew the Slide to the shore.

"How close are we?" Hamish asked as Connor pulled the craft to the surface and slid their chairs off the deck and over to the bank.

"Maybe an hour at the speed we've been going."

Ilse seemed thrilled to get off the water, and she immediately raised a Sapper tower and looked determined to remain there for the evening. Steep, forested hills rose on both sides of the river, and a well-marked trail cut through the trees not far from the bank, heading north toward Alasdair.

Verena said, "Hey, I know this place. Connor, this is where we first met."

"Yeah, that night you kidnapped me."

Verena slipped an arm around his waist, snuggling under the crook of his arm the way he loved. "So many things would've been different if we hadn't stopped that barge."

"Praise Tallan's memory you did," Kilian said.

Connor shuddered to consider how different his life might have been, but for that meeting. "I would have pledged service to High Lord Dougal."

Verena grimaced. "Shona would have owned you."

No doubt he would have eagerly accepted Shona's manipulations if not for the truths he'd learned during that conflict around Alasdair. After dinner, as he rolled into his blanket near the fire, Connor thought about that. The last few months had been very difficult. He and his friends had risked their lives multiple times. And yet, the alternative would've been so much worse.

He slept deeply, and it seemed only a moment later when he felt roughly shaken awake. He groaned, "Let me sleep another minute."

The shaking intensified, and he realized with a start that the entire ground was moving.

Connor sat bolt upright and glanced around. In the soft light of early morning, the ground was bucking and rolling like a wave on the Wick. The air vibrated with a low-pitched groaning that emanated from the ground. Trees began to shake, shedding leaves like rain, and the air smelled sharp, as if a bag of spices had been opened nearby.

"What's going on?" Verena cried. She tried to stand, but fell back to her knees.

Hamish awoke with a start, shouting, "Two donuts aren't enough!" Then he looked around in confusion. "Aw, that was such a good dream."

"Earthquake," Jean said, still lying prone, her voice completely calm. "This one feels stronger than the others."

"I'm not waiting for a tree to fall on me." Verena scurried on hands and knees to the Swift. She threw herself into the pilot seat, and the quartzite thrusters roared to life. The nimble little craft shot into the air, then banked around to hover about twenty feet above them.

"You don't care if I get crushed by a tree?" Connor called.

"As if a tree could hurt you," Verena shouted above the groaning of the earth and the snapping of branches in the forest. "You've probably already absorbed granite."

"Uh. Of course."

That was a good idea. Connor shoved a finger into the pouch of granite powder at his belt. He didn't have a large supply, so he only absorbed a little through his skin. The itch of granite flowed up his arm, like a dozen insects crawling under the skin.

He ignored the urge to scratch. He had established affinity to granite as a child, without even knowing what that meant, and the curse was as familiar to him as breathing.

Ilse's ten-foot earthen tower slid closer to the group. The shaking of the ground subsided directly under them as she exerted her earth affinity and created a small oasis of calm. Earth vibrated all around, rattling pebbles and sticks.

Ilse said, "Jean is right. The heart of the quake lies somewhere near Alasdair."

Connor snatched a piece of slate from his belt pouch, pressed his hand to the ground, and envisioned the gateway to earth in his mind. He liked to imagine it as a shallow, sunken pit, lined with slate stones, engraved with silver script of some of his favorite obscure Sentry speak.

The doorway opened to his mind and his earth senses radiated into the ground. The earth tasted like a sore tooth, and the groaning that shook the clearing was bubbling up from the depths. He couldn't pinpoint the source like Ilse had, though.

The earthquake subsided a few seconds later, and Connor withdrew his connection, pondering what he had felt. The earth was not alive like people, but why then did it feel like it was in agony? What was the source of his earth powers? How did slate link him to that vast strength? He hadn't wondered about that before, but the earthquake had shaken the ground to its roots, and for the first time he realized the top layer was perhaps more like a thick skin over the planet.

He wasn't sure he wanted to know what was underneath.

"We need to get to Alasdair," Hamish said. He jumped up and began to pull on boots, hopping from one foot to the other and nearly tripping himself. "What if people are hurt?"

"You said there were earthquakes before, right?" Connor asked as the rest of the group quickly packed their meager supplies.

Jean said, "They started shortly after you left, but they weren't this severe."

Ilse said, "We're several miles south of Alasdair, so the shaking was most likely worse for them."

"I hope Gran is okay," Jean said with a worried frown. Then she moved to help Hamish with the buckles of his flying suit.

Verena settled the Swift to the ground nearby as gently as a hummingbird landing on a flower.

Hamish took Jean's hand. "Let's go. We can get to Alasdair faster by air."

Of course he was right. They crammed their blankets into the supply box at the back of the Swift, then Connor climbed aboard.

"Ready?" Verena asked, pulling on her helmet and snapping down the visor.

"Ready."

The thrusters came to life again, creating a rushing gale of fresh wind that smelled like the high country, and the Swift eased off the ground.

"We'll meet you in the village," Kilian said. "Perhaps it's good for you to arrive first and warn them we mean no harm."

Connor waved, and Verena rose above the trees. Hamish and Jean were already soaring out over the river. Connor crouched on the supply box, one hand resting on Verena's shoulder. He loved flying with her. Verena seemed more bird than human in the air, and they both smiled as they rose over a hundred feet into the cool morning sky and soared upriver.

Connor glanced back as they banked around the first turn. The elegant hull of the Slide had already formed, and it was gliding on the surface of the river, leaving no trace of its passing.

Verena accelerated to catch up with Hamish. At their pace, they'd reach the town before the cutters headed for the quarry. Most of the townsfolk would have already been awake before the earthquake struck, although Connor doubted Lord Gavin and his shrewish wife, Lady Isobel, would bother to rise and check on their people.

His excitement grew and overshadowed his worry, but then they rounded a long, gentle bend and the forest simply ended. Trees, broken and stripped of branches, lay in enormous piles flanking the river. Some of the piles of tangled wood reared over fifty feet and stretched for hundreds more, rivaling the hills that hemmed them in along the banks. The mass of bleached, dead trees seemed to watch in silent accusation as Connor passed.

He had killed them. The flood he'd unleashed from Loch Sholto when he broke the mountain had thundered down the valley along the river. The back wave had swept away most of the buildings in Alasdair. Luckily, everyone had already fled. He'd been driven to make the desperate choice, but seeing the destruction again was a stark reminder that consequences were often ugly when Petralists clashed.

As they continued farther north, the piles of timber began to shrink. It looked like villagers were harvesting the wood.

Then they soared over a tight bend in the river, and the steep hills on their left fell away, revealing the fertile expanse of the wide Alasdair valley. Connor's mood lifted with the sight of the green, well-tended fields stretching away toward the western mountains.

He wedged a tiny piece of quartzite into his cheek and sucked on it. The liquid warmth of quartzite pooled in the center of his head, and he applied some of it to his eyes. They transformed and the beautiful Alasdair valley glittered in his enhanced vision.

Wherever he looked, his gaze swooped closer, picking out fantastic details of objects over a mile distant, as if he was bending close over them. Colors intensified, and the air shone with hues not visible to unenhanced sight.

Memories flooded in with each sight. He and Hamish had explored every inch of this area as kids. Looking out over the valley, he felt a deep contentment. He was home.

His memory did not match the scarred landscape to their right, though. In the past, a long slope paralleling the river had led up to Lord Gavin's plateau, which lorded over the last half mile of river before the final turn revealed Loch Wich and the town itself.

Now the slope was stripped away, and all that remained of the plateau was steep-sided rock, over a hundred feet high, scraped raw by the floods. It clung to the bank of the river like an open wound at the base of Alasdair Mountain. Nothing green grew on the scarred, rocky hillside, and Connor was not surprised that Lord Gavin had not tried to rebuild there.

From a height of a couple hundred feet above the river, Connor enjoyed a clear view of the barren top of that rocky hill. He was surprised to note that all signs of Lord Gavin's manor were gone.

That was weird. He saw no sign of the basements of the ruined manor house. An enormous hole should be there, or maybe a small pond if it had filled with water, but it was simply gone.

"They covered it up," he exclaimed after another moment's study.

"What?" Verena asked.

He pointed at the plateau. "They covered up the basements with a screen of rock."

"Why would they do that?"

"I have no idea."

Verena banked the Swift closer to Hamish so they could ask Jean about it, but Connor noticed a pair of figures standing on a ledge on the flank of Alasdair Mountain, which rose above the plateau. Half of the steep, front face of that slope was simply gone, destroyed by Connor's flood. A new switchback road had been built up the remaining steep section to connect to Quarry Road, which led around to the back side of Wick Torr to the quarry on the opposite side of that peak. Two boys from town were standing at the summit of that switchback road, waving a lighted torch.

"Even more interesting, why do they have scouts posted on the mountain?" He pointed.

"We could go ask them what they're doing," Hamish suggested.

"They're warning the town of our approach," Verena said.

"How do you know?" Hamish asked.

"It's the only thing that makes sense."

"I wanted to surprise them," Hamish grumbled.

He accelerated into a long, shallow dive toward the town, which was just coming into view. The north edge of the plateau connected with the towering cliff of Wick Torr, and a road descended from there toward the town, which was built right beneath the massive cliff.

As Verena accelerated after Hamish, Connor drank in the sight of the town. Where Lord Gavin's plateau was a scarred ruin, Alasdair looked intact and full of life. The light of the morning sun, just cresting the distant eastern mountains, illuminated the town in full morning glory.

The last time Connor had seen Alasdair, it had been a gutted ruin, swept clean by the flood. Now the township, enclosed within the solid granite outer walls of the original quarry, was packed with buildings and people.

Alasdair stretched for just over a quarter mile, with Market Street splitting it down the middle between East Gate and the distant Wall Gate. Three other streets paralleled Market Street, with avenues linking them together and breaking the town into regular blocks.

Thankfully he saw no signs of damage from the recent earthquake. People were moving about, but not in their usual early morning patterns. It took him a moment to realize what they were doing.

They were preparing for battle.

The truth shocked him. Men were rushing toward both gates. Women and children were massing in several groups along Wall Street, preparing ladders to scramble over the long river-facing wall to escape the town.

"They think we're coming to attack," Connor exclaimed.

Verena repeated his words to Hamish through her speakstone.

Hamish slowed to a hover to let them catch up. "Jean, why didn't you warn us about their new signal lookout? They're going to be in a panic. They don't know it's us."

"I didn't know. None of this was in place when I left."

Connor said, "Well, let's get down there and calm them down."

As they resumed their dive, Connor decided it was good the townsfolk were ready to act. It looked like armed conflict had indeed created change in Alasdair. He hoped that meant they'd be willing to see reason and recognize the danger that might already be moving against them.

"Where do you want to land?" Verena asked as they swooped toward the town and the men massed at East Gate.

"Just outside the gate."

His father, Hendry, stood in the center of the assembled men, the Ashlar hammer held comfortably in his hand. The sight of his dad filled Connor with joy. His father looked the same. Perhaps with a few more worry lines, but just as calmly capable as ever.

To either side, the strong men of Alasdair stood ready to meet the threat, hefting axes, hammers, and even a few spears. Half a dozen others, carrying bows and quivers laden with arrows, were scrambling onto roofs with the best field of fire.

They landed together about fifty feet from East Gate. Connor didn't wait for the Swift to touch down, but leaped off and rushed toward the waiting villagers. Jean slid off of Hamish's back and outran him, her long blond hair streaming out behind.

They recognized her immediately and Hendry called, "Jean? Is that really you?"

Connor waved, drawing his father's attention. "Dad!"

"Connor!" His father shouted and broke into a run.

Chapter Six

"A brick may build or destroy, but the hand that throws it chooses to make it a missile."

~Evander

As Connor ran to meet his father, Hamish launched back into the air and soared overhead, shouting, "Hey, dad!" He waved so hard with his helmet that he nearly knocked himself out of the air. He collided with his father as he landed and the two of them nearly went down together. They hugged and laughed, breaking the grim mood at the gate.

Connor met his father in a fierce hug about twenty feet from the gate, and for a moment, all was right with the world. When his father finally eased his hold, he pushed Connor back and gripped his shoulders with powerful hands. He looked close to tears. The two of them began laughing and talking at the same time.

"Connor! It's so good to see you, Son. Your mother will be so excited to see you."

"Where is she?"

"She's leading one of the run groups. That reminds me. We need to send the all clear signal."

Hendry waved at one of the old timers, a wizened fellow named Clifden, who stood atop the wall beside the gate. The man acknowledged with a smart salute and a gap-toothed smile. Then he raised his bladder pipe to his lips and blew a piercing, descending scale.

"What is that thing?" Verena asked as she joined them, wincing at the sound. "What a strange instrument."

She was right. The bladder pipe was a long, straight, wooden instrument, with the reed at the top enclosed by a pig bladder. When Clifden blew into the bladder it inflated, creating a sort of air reserve that provided a constant flow down through the instrument. The bladder pipe made a loud, distinctive sound, kind of a screeching younger cousin to the big bag pipes used by the hillmen south of Merkland.

"Clifden hasn't gotten to play so much in years," Hendry said with a smile. "Assigning him the task of town signaler was your mother's idea."

"Dad, you might remember Verena," Connor said, suddenly nervous as he made the introduction.

His father gave her a smile and extended a hand in welcome. "How could I forget?"

Verena ignored his extended hand and hugged him instead. "It's good to see you again, Ashlar."

Jean joined them, and Hendry hugged her in turn. "It warms my heart to see you again, lass."

Jean beamed. "It's good to be home, even if only for a little while."

Hendry's smile faded. "Let's not talk of leaving till later."

Connor asked, "Is everyone all right? We felt the earthquake downriver."

Hendry nodded. "Fine. All fine. The earthquakes are strange. Started not long after you left, but most have been small. This morning's quake was the strongest yet." He gestured toward the nearby towering cliff. "Even dislodged a few rocks from the torr, but nothing serious."

Connor shuddered to think what might happen if the cliff broke free. It could flatten the town and kill everyone in one tragic moment. He'd grown up in the shadow of the torr and had always felt its looming presence a comforting shield against the fierce storms that raged down from Mount Ingram. Now the huge cliff held a sense of new menace.

"I'm glad everyone's all right," he said.

"The town is secure," his father assured him. "The only tangible result of the earthquakes is a strange cracking that began in the floor of the quarry after the last one."

Connor asked, "How can the quarry floor crack? It's solid granite."

His father shrugged and turned, draping his arms across Connor's and Verena's shoulders. "It's nothing to worry about, Son. With the war looming and rebuilding costs to help defray, quotas are higher than ever. We haven't bothered to cut out the weakened areas yet."

They didn't have time to discuss the quarry, quotas, or anything else. A crowd of eager villagers swarmed around them, and Connor spent the next several minutes greeting everyone and fielding dozens of questions. His parents had maintained the lie that he had died in the flood, even though Dougal knew the truth.

Some villagers stared at him with awe, and he heard several whisper, "Guardians" or "curse". He gave vague answers to their many questions as the happy crowd moved into the town proper, down Market Street, and poured into the central square.

Word of their arrival had already spread across the town, and villagers flooded into the square from every side in a joyous wave. It felt great to be home, and Connor was thrilled to see how much of the town had already been rebuilt. New shops lined Market Street, and he glimpsed rows of new homes beyond. Alasdair had risen from the dead even more dramatically than he had.

Everywhere he looked, Connor saw faces he'd known his whole life, and he felt a deep sense of contentment as he exchanged enthusiastic greetings with friends and old neighbors. Hamish's laugh rang above the crowd, and at one point he rose into the air, thrusters lifting him and four of his younger siblings, who shrieked with delight as they clung to his shoulders and back. The youngest was already pulling a breadstick out of one of Hamish's waist pouches.

"Tallan's hoary toes, how is he doing that?" Clifden exclaimed, making a warding gesture with his bladder pipe.

"It's powered by Builder magic," Connor explained.

Clifden huffed and sidled farther from Hamish.

Jean was nearly overrun by enthusiastic villagers. Her only family was her grandmother, Mhairi, but everyone loved her.

"Connor!" His mother's voice cut through the din and Connor turned to see Lilias barreling through the crowd, followed by his younger siblings.

He rushed to her, grinning so wide it felt like his jaw might split, but at the same time, he found it hard to speak. His mother gave the best hugs in the world, and she had been saving up. Connor could have enjoyed that embrace for a lot longer, but his younger siblings tackled him, shrieking with excitement, and clamoring for attention.

Blair had grown a lot and looked more like their dad than ever. He already stood as tall as Connor, and his voice had deepened to a rich baritone. He slapped Connor on the back. "Welcome home, Connor. I hope you're not going to wreck everything again."

"Not this time."

Eight year-old Roderick, the only blonde of the family, didn't say anything, but just clung to Connor like he was afraid he was about to disappear. The baby, Fiona, who looked big enough now to be walking and talking, clutched at their mother, not trusting Connor yet. He doubted she even remembered him.

Four year-old Wallace, who looked like a miniature copy of Blair, bounced on his toes enthusiastically. "Connor! Do something with your curse for me."

A few of the nearby villagers shuffled back, their grins fading. Everyone knew Connor was cursed, but that didn't mean they wanted to admit it out loud.

Connor dropped to one knee beside Wallace. "What would you like me to do?"

"Make me a pedra!" Wallace exclaimed.

"I'm not very good at pedras," Connor said, thinking of the great stone pedra that Kilian and Ilse had conjured during the battles of Alasdair. "But I might be able to do a squirrel a little later."

Wallace thought about that for a moment. "As long as it breathes fire."

"I like this boy," Verena laughed.

Connor's father began to speak, but he was interrupted by Stuart. Connor blinked in surprise when he saw how big Stuart had grown. He celebrated the same age day as Connor, Hamish, and Jean, but he had always been the biggest of them. In the months since they'd left, he'd grown even more, packing on muscle and several inches of height.

Connor grinned at him, but Stuart barely glanced in his direction. He made a sharp salute and gestured toward Wall Gate. "Ashlar, I've got another scout report. We've got Grandurians coming upriver fast."

"Dad, they're with us," Connor interrupted.

Stuart did look at him then, and his expression was not friendly. "You dare bring enemies here, Connor?"

"They're not here to fight," Connor insisted.

"I saw them myself," Stuart said, and he pulled out of his pocket a squat, circular device made of bright, shining brass. "I've got the new spyglass, and I recognized them. It's Kilian and that Captain Ilse."

That sparked cries of alarm from nearby villagers, but Connor shouted above them. "It's all right. They're here with me."

"Why would you bring them here?" his mother demanded.

"Several reasons. We have a lot to talk about. But for now, know they're friends."

Stuart growled, "They weren't friends last time, or did you forget all about that while you've been away on holiday?"

"Hardly a holiday," Connor said, forcing down a growing irritation at Stuart's hostility. "We made it back here alive only because of them."

Hamish joined him, two siblings still riding on his shoulders. "And I've been living with them. They've trained me to become a Builder."

"Against the law," Stuart growled. When Jean joined Hamish and took his hand in hers, Stuart's scowl deepened.

Hamish grinned and clapped Stuart on the shoulder. "Missed you too, blockhead."

Stuart raised a fist, but Jean placed a hand on his arm. "They are our friends." His anger fizzled and he stared at Jean with a look of unabashed adoration.

Connor felt sorry for him. He didn't have a chance.

The villagers still seemed nervous, and it took all of the persuasive powers of Connor, Hamish, and Jean combined to convince them that the Grandurians were not a threat. Finally Hendry agreed to allow them into the village as Connor's guests.

"But no fighting," Lilias warned.

"I promise they're not here to fight," Connor said.

Many of the villagers still looked doubtful, but they calmed down when Hendry told them it would be all right. Connor was impressed. As Ashlar, Hendry had always had a lot of influence in town, but now people treated him more like the lord of Alasdair than they ever had Lord Gavin. He was the one who had led them through their difficult times.

The women's circle and town council still decided to assemble at Wall Gate to formally greet the newcomers, with most of the other villagers crowded around behind. Connor, Hamish, and Jean waited at the front of the group with their parents. Verena headed to the quay to escort Kilian and the others to the town.

"I still have half a mind to send the children to the bolt hole," Lilias said nervously as Kilian drew the glittering Slide to the quay.

"What is that?" Connor asked.

"Not something you can talk about with your Grandurian girl," Hamish's father, Amhain, cautioned.

"Verena is not an enemy," Connor said.

"On your word," Amhain said, but didn't sound convinced.

He was tall, although Hamish was now taller. Amhain lacked the bulk of Hendry and the cutters. His was a lanky strength, honed from years of working the lift crank at the quarry. He carried a spear that looked like it had been made out of a pitchfork.

Hendry said, "Your girl is not from Alasdair, Son. You need to trust us and keep what we're going to share with you private. Can you do that?"

Connor hated the thought of keeping secrets from Verena, but he could see they were determined, so he nodded. "You have my word."

"And mine," Hamish said. "So what is the bolt hole?"

"Lord Gavin's old manor house," Hendry explained.

"I saw that someone had covered over the basements," Connor said.

His father gave him a sharp look. "No one's supposed to notice that. The secret is no good if people know it's there."

"I doubt anyone else would. I saw it from the air, and I was using quartzite."

At his father's puzzled look, Connor explained. "Quartzite enhances my vision like a Pathfinder. Even with enhanced eyes, I had to study the rock face. If I hadn't known there was supposed to be a hole there, I never would have figured it out."

"That's good to know. We don't want anyone to have any reason to go up there. It's just a barren pile of rock now."

"So you're using the basements?" Jean asked.

"Aye," Amhain said proudly. "We've rebuilt them. We've got bedrooms, water and food storage, and a cooking and eating hall."

"All underground and unknown by anyone outside of Alasdair," Hendry said.

Connor said, "That's amazing. When did you have time to do all that?"

His father said, "We've had a couple men in shifts working on it for months. With the war brewing, we've increased the effort. We're even working on a tunnel to connect it to town. Never know when we might have to escape another hostile force."

Connor nodded. "I think the time is coming."

"We'll be ready," his father insisted.

"Lord Gavin and Lady Isobel have no idea," Amhain added, his tone derisive. "Barely ever leave that fancy new manor house. Just bemoan their hard life and write letters to Dougal every day asking for more help, even though he paid for nearly the entire rebuilding."

"Dougal may not be so generous in the future," Connor warned. He suspected Dougal's generosity had been motivated more to bolster Shona's claim on his allegiance than out of simple interest in getting the quarry back up to production as quickly as possible.

The bolt hole might be the perfect first step in securing the village if Dougal sent hostile forces against the town. It wouldn't offer a final solution, but it was a good start.

Kilian brought the Slide to a halt at the edge of the nearest stone quay that jutted out into the loch. The village sat about thirty feet above the river and a couple hundred feet to the east of the loch. The road descended from Wall Gate in a gentle slope, past the blocking yard where granite blocks were lowered down the towering cliff of Wick Torr from the quarry for processing. It skirted the edge of the loch, then rose slightly again to the steep-roofed Powder House. There Hendry finished processing the precious white granite into powder for shipping down to Merkland.

On the far side of the Powder House, a small wooden foot bridge had been added across the bubbling Upper Wick as it emptied into the loch. Jean had mentioned once that Lord Gavin's new manor house was across the river, so that made sense. Lady Isobel would never be expected to hop across the stepping stones that had served the villagers for generations.

As Kilian led Ilse and her team up the road from the quay, Connor led a group of village leaders, including his parents, to meet them. When they stopped a few paces from the Grandurians, Verena joined him and took his hand in hers.

"Dad, Mom, you probably remember Kilian and this company from last year."

Hendry and Lilias nodded in unison, their expressions unreadable. Amhain openly scowled.

"I remember them," Hendry said in a neutral tone. "Last time they visited, we didn't exactly get along, and they made a nuisance of themselves."

Kilian extended his hand, a friendly smile on his face. "This time we did not come to fight."

"So my son claims," Hendry said. "I heard you helped save Connor, and you've sheltered Hamish and treated him well. For that, and for returning them to us today, I thank you. You're welcome in my house."

He took the proffered hand and Kilian said, "I've always liked this town." He glanced at the men still massed at Wall Gate. "I respect those willing to take responsibility for their own defense. I am honored to enter as your guest."

"Welcome to Alasdair," Lilias said, speaking for the women's circle. "And thank you for helping my son."

Captain Ilse said, "We met under difficult circumstances last time, but in the months since, your son has demonstrated remarkable courage and resourcefulness. You trained him well."

"Come on, then," Hamish beckoned, breaking the rather formal mood. "No one's had breakfast yet, and there's a feast to plan."

Most of the villagers followed them back to the town square, curiosity replacing worry once they saw the Grandurians didn't immediately attack. In the square, young Wallace dared approach Ilse, his expression serious. "You better not break things again lady, or my uncle will beat you up."

Connor sighed. He really had been gone too long. He ruffled Wallace's hair. "Hey, I'm your brother, not your uncle."

Wallace gave him a disgusted look. "I know who you are, Connor." The boy turned and pointed behind Lilias. "He's the uncle."

Connor turned and saw a stranger approaching. The burly fellow walked like a soldier, although he carried no visible weapon. His gaze was locked on Ilse, and Connor had seen that same eager expression countless times at the Carraig. The man was ready to fight.

The man grinned at Connor. "Tallan's napping with the cookie jar unlocked, he is." He clapped Connor on the shoulder. "Long may yer chimney smoke, laddie. I'm your uncle Martys."

Connor gaped and glanced at his father, who nodded and smiled. "He is."

"Uncle Martys?" Connor took the man's extended hand. His uncle had a strong grip, his big hands calloused from his soldier's life. Everyone knew the story of Martys, the young boy who had been taken away to serve High Lord Dougal, and never seen again.

"You're a Guardian?" Connor asked.

"Aye, lad," Martys said, his gaze drifting back to the Grandurians. "And I'm about to go to war."

Chapter Seven

"Authorization alone, granted by authority beyond my own, grants access to exit."

~Declan

Connor tensed. Martys was a Guardian, sworn to Dougal. He had never imagined he might actually meet his lost uncle, only to beat him senseless ten seconds later. Ilse did not look outwardly concerned, but Erich and Anika both perked up at the suggestion of a potential fight.

Uncle Martys was a big man, as tall as Hendry, with broad shoulders and huge hands. His brown hair was cut short like most soldiers. He wore heavy, blue canvas trousers and a green shirt. Dougal's colors. His stance seemed relaxed, but his dark brown eyes were locked on Ilse.

"Don't you dare start a fight," Lilias said before Connor could interject. "My boy just got home, and we're going to have a party."

Martys laughed, and his manner shifted subtly, the threat of danger evaporating. "Fighting before breakfast? Shame on you, Lilias for suggesting such a thing. Dinnae get yerself into a high doh, bonnie sister. I was just saying that after I get back to Merkland, I'm heading for the front." He winked at Anika. "Although I'm hoping I run into you again when the fighting starts, lass. I've heard Grandurian women like to wrestle."

Anika sniffed. "No many good wrestle in Obrion."

Erich took a threatening step forward, his expression darkening. "I like break Guardians too."

"I won't warn you again." Lilias drew a long wooden cooking spoon from the rear of her apron and waved it at Erich like a sword. "No fighting, or you get no breakfast."

Erich grinned down at her. "Is legend you lovely cook. No fight. Many eat."

Lilias actually flushed. "Well I doubt breakfast will be legendary, but I promise we'll have plenty."

"Good," Hamish said, clapping Erich on the shoulder. "We've got a bet on to see who can eat the most."

Lilias paled as she looked from Hamish to the huge Erich. "Oh, my."

Hendry laughed and raised his voice so everyone could hear. "Today we celebrate! Break out the tables. At noon, we feast!"

Connor suspected the villagers of Alasdair had not found many excuses to celebrate in recent months. They welcomed Hendry's announcement with enthusiasm. Women scurried off to gather food, while men formed teams to assemble the long Sogail feasting tables in the central square. Common linn were used to accepting things they weren't allowed to change, so they shifted readily from lingering distrust of the Grandurians to eager preparations for the feast.

Hendry said, "In the meantime, you're all invited to our house for breakfast."

"Not Hamish," Amhain said. "He's coming home with us."

Peigi, Hamish's mother, a petite, willowy woman with graying brown hair joined her husband and peered up at Erich. "You come along too, young man. I've got a few other children who will want to participate in that eating challenge. It's not every day we get to vanquish Grandurians at the breakfast table."

Erich gave her a deep bow. "I follow." Then he bowed to Lilias and added, "I come eat your house later."

She looked like she wanted to clarify what he meant, but wasn't sure she really wanted to.

Anika said, "I come too. Witness mighty duel."

The entire group set off, surrounded by Hamish's many siblings. Jean called after them, "I'll see you later, Hamish. I've got to visit with Gran."

"Oh posh, dear," Mhairi chided Jean. "Young men do better when you leave them for a time." The two of them headed for the healer house arm in arm. Mhairi stood a full head shorter than Jean, but despite her age she still moved with the same spry energy.

"The rest of you will join us," Lilias told Kilian. He bowed over her hand, and she blushed. Then she took Verena's hand and said, "And you too, of course, dear."

She headed toward Wall Street and their home, towing Verena along, with the rest of the group trailing.

Martys fell in beside Kilian and said, "So ye've returned to the scene of the crime, have ye?"

"No. The crime was committed in Merkland by your High Lord Dougal."

"I dinnae ken that, but I've walked the world long enough to know there's a story for every side. Regale me, Grandurian, and see if ye can convince me ye dinnae have yer head out the window."

Kilian chuckled. "You're an interesting man, Martys. Most Guardians I've met can't think past the start of the next bash fight."

That was an understatement. Even Tomas and Cameron, the two Fast Rollers in Rory's company who had helped train Connor, loved bash fighting more than eating.

Martys shrugged. "Bash fighting has a way of arriving when it will, and I'll give it laldy when it comes, but we've agreed no fighting afore breakfast. So let's hear yer justification for taking the fight to my home town last year."

"Very well," Kilian said, and the two began to discuss the situation that led up to the battles of Alasdair. Uncle Martys seemed content to talk for the moment, and Kilian seemed to enjoy the conversation.

So Connor drew his father back from the rest of the group so they could talk. "Dad, it's good to be home."

Hendry smiled. "You timing couldn't be better. Martys arrived just yesterday. We're still getting to know him."

"I'm glad I got to meet him." Even though the presence of a Guardian complicated the visit, Connor was eager to ask Martys about his life of service to Dougal.

Their home was the last building on Wall Street, set close to the corner where the river wall met the eastern wall. One of the few structures that had survived the flood, it had once been the biggest house on the street.

At two stories, it was tall enough to see over the wall. The ground floor was constructed of good quality grout stone, with the second story made of wood. Compared to the new homes now lining the street it didn't look so fine or grand in comparison, but it was home.

When they arrived, Connor's siblings talked over each other in their excitement to show Connor everything. They told him all about the rebuilding, the earthquakes, and the new Ashlar hammer gifted to Hendry by High Lord Dougal himself.

Memories flooded Connor when he stepped across the threshold. The house looked almost exactly the same. Lilias stopped in the kitchen with Verena. It smelled of fresh-baked bread and the rows of his mother's spice jars.

The rest of them moved to the main living room, although Connor followed his brothers on a tour of the house. The loft was still crowded with their beds and more clothing strewn on the floor than in the bank of drawers. It smelled like boy feet, and Connor was sure if he looked under Wallace's bunk, he'd find a jar with a captured frog inside and a hole drilled through the lid.

Uncle Martys and Hendry sat in padded wooden armchairs in the main room along with the Grandurians. Connor and his chattering siblings joined them once they finished wandering through the house. Martys was so recently returned, he soon captured everyone's attention with his lilting brogue and unusual turn of phrase, punctuated by ready laughter. Even Blair, Connor's ever-serious younger brother, was soon laughing at Martys' tales of Guardian life.

Kilian's easy smile soon calmed the boys' nerves about Grandurians in the house, and they began asking him questions about Granadure. The children took to Dietmar immediately, and they were endlessly fascinated by Margrit's glowing eyes.

Even Ilse, who seemed to prefer watching more than talking, couldn't escape attention. Wallace dropped to his knees beside her chair and stared up at her with open curiosity. "Are you a soldier?"

"I am."

"Do you kill people?"

For once, she actually looked unsure how to respond, and Connor said, "That's not really a question you ask people."

"Because killing is bad?"

Ilse nodded. "Usually. My job is to protect my country against evil. Sometimes that means we have to fight."

Wallace nodded, his expression serious. "Like when Connor had to fight you."

She smiled. "Your brother and I have learned that we fight for the same things."

Wallace turned a startled look on Connor. "You're Grandurian now?"

The outburst caught everyone's attention, and the room fell silent as the others turned to listen.

"No." Connor keenly felt the weight of everyone's eyes on him. This wasn't how he had planned to talk about future plans with his family, but it was an opportunity he couldn't miss. "I'll always be Obrioner, but there are evil men in Obrion who are trying to start a war that will kill a lot of people and cause a lot of suffering. I plan to help stop it."

"What's for ye'll no go by ye," Martys said solemnly.

"What does that mean?" Ilse asked. She had not yet cracked a smile at his stories, and seemed intent on maintaining her guard around him.

"My head's mince," Martys chuckled, rapping his noggin. "I forgot ye wouldn't understand the pure language when ye hear it, lass. That saying means what will happen will happen." He gestured at Connor. "I respect yer goals, Connor me boy, but this war is a coming, and I dinnae ken you or Tallan himself can do nothing to stop it."

"It's worth a try," Connor insisted.

He wasn't sure yet what he planned to do. He needed to spread the truth about patronage, but didn't know how to do that either. When Guardians knew the truth, Connor fully expected them to revolt. That would cripple the invasion plan, but would it plunge Obrion into civil war? Would Granadure invade in turn when they saw Obrion weakened?

Martys said, "Aye, that may be, lad. But to most folks in Obrion, these here Grandurians are worse than a tattyboggle, an' when the high lords say it be time for war, there be few willin' to test the waters fer snakes afore they jump in, hogs to the wind."

"There are many in Granadure who see war as inevitable too," Kilian said. "But it's always worth the effort to try stopping the fight before it begins."

Martys saluted him. "If a skinny malinky long-legs like yerself tries ta stop this war, I'm afraid one clean shirt'll do ye."

"And what does that mean?" Ilse asked, and Connor was glad she did. He didn't understand half of what his uncle said.

"It means that I don't think ye'll last long if ye try standing between the armies. Dinnae bother bringing a change of clothes on that trip. Ye'll be dead afore ye need another clean shirt."

"And I think we've had enough talk of war and death before breakfast," Lilias broke in with a frown.

Connor hadn't even seen her enter the room. She and Verena joined the group, and she announced, "Breakfast is nearly ready. Some of the ladies from the women's circle came to help. Neasa herself brought over a tray of sweetbreads."

Connor's brothers oohed over that and Connor explained, "Best baker in the world."

"I hope you're right," Martys said. "I've traveled the length and breadth of Obrion, and I've tasted the best of the best from the best in many cities."

"I didn't realize Guardians traveled so much," Connor said. From what he understood, most Guardians were stationed within their own high lord's realm, and rarely left their assigned post.

Martys shrugged. "Not many do, but High Lord Dougal is an exceptional ruler." He made a tiny bow toward Ilse. "I know ye don't agree, but hold yer biscuits afore ye judge."

Ilse said, "I am not one to insult the beliefs of those who invite me into their home, no matter how much I may disagree."

"Good on ye, lassie," Martys beamed. "My good high lord knows the importance of establishing relations between the realms, and he assigned me to the security detail of one of his representatives. Let me tell ye all the tale of the time we traveled all the way down to Radharc, on the borders of the endless desert. Ye won't believe what they eat down there."

"Save that story for after breakfast," Lilias said. "Time to eat."

Chapter Eight

"Sunlight filtering through a cloudy sky is fractured into many bands, but is all the same light."

~Evander

Neasa and four other local women carried in a feast while they wedged extra chairs around the long wooden table in the dining room. Soon it groaned under the weight of sweetbreads, hard boiled eggs, and porridge. Pitchers of milk and fresh-squeezed apple juice were wedged in between platters of boiled ham, sausage links, and immense piles of bacon.

For several minutes, talking faded away as they feasted. Connor tried to tell himself to slow down after his third plate. He needed to save room for the lunch feast. Then Verena passed him the platter of sausages, and he had to eat just one more. Or maybe three.

After the simple fare they'd survived on for the past several days, the food tasted divine. Besides, he wouldn't get to breakfast again with his family for Tallan only knew how long.

They annihilated all that food. His younger brothers even licked the plates, despite his mother's hissed reminders to watch their manners. Connor sat back with a sigh, so full his stomach ached. He was tempted to tap a little granite to help.

He glanced at Verena and she smiled. "That was amazing."

"Best breakfast I've had in months," Martys said, slapping his stomach, and the others clamored agreement.

Hendry rose. "After a feeding like that, I think it best we tour the town to help restore our appetites for lunch."

Connor only wanted to curl up and take a nap, but Verena grabbed his hand and led him out after everyone else. The warm autumn morning had chased away the worst of the chill, and the sky sparkled with intense blue.

They met Hamish and his family exiting their home too. Hamish raised his hands in victory. "I have vanquished the mighty Erich!"

His family talked over each other, all trying to describe the epic food duel at the same time. Amhain looked proud, while Peigi looked shocked by how much food they had consumed. Erich looked a bit sick, and walking seemed to pain him. Anika looked disgusted and slapped his stomach hard enough to make him wince.

"How is possible little man eat so much?" Erich moaned.

"Practice and discipline," Hamish said solemnly. "You've got to embrace the food, Erich, just as deeply as you embrace granite in a bash fight."

Anika grinned and clapped Hamish on the shoulder. "You great victory, Builder boy. Food wrestle today much glory."

"Thanks." Hamish was wise enough to look nervous standing so close to her.

"That's my boy," Amhain said, glowing with pride.

Hamish's gangly, blonde, thirteen year-old sister looked awed. "Hamish finished eighty-five slices of bacon, twenty-nine eggs, forty-seven sausages--"

"And sixty-two sweetbreads!" Hamish finished.

Verena gaped. "You should have exploded!"

Hamish patted his armored midsection and grinned. "I probably would have if I hadn't still been wearing my suit."

Connor laughed. "Where did all the bacon come from?"

Peigi smiled. "We received five tons of smoked bacon with the rebuilding supplies."

"Five tons?" Connor exclaimed. He'd never heard of so much bacon in one place.

Amhain grinned. "That food was probably supposed to go to the front lines."

Hamish and his family decided to join them on a tour of the town. As the happy group headed for the distant western wall, where they'd make the turn toward Wall Gate, Hendry and Lilias pulled Connor to the back of the group.

Lilias extracted from a pocket of her apron a folded parchment. "We received a letter from Ailsa last week, explaining some of what you've been through, Son. It's a wonder you survived."

His father gave him a solemn look. "Connor, why don't you share the real reason you came home?"

"I want to take you away with me."

"Impossible," Hendry said simply.

That single word shattered Connor's carefully-built hope that his parents would see reason. "But Dad, Dougal is probably going to send soldiers to take you all to use you as leverage against me."

"So you want us to run?" his father asked. "And abandon the village and our responsibilities at the time we're needed the most?"

"You won't do anyone any good in chains," Connor pointed out.

"You want us to leave our home after we've worked so hard to rebuild here?" Lilias asked.

"If that's what it takes to keep you safe, yes." Connor felt a growing sense of frustration. "I know what I'm talking about. You have to trust me."

Hendry said, "We do trust you, Son, but we can't leave. Not yet."

"We see the danger," his mother assured him. "But most of the village won't recognize it. High Lord Dougal is very popular here after all he did to help us rebuild." She hesitated before adding, "Most people would think your serving him in whatever way he deems right is your duty, rightly owed to our high lord."

"That's because they don't understand that everything is a lie. Patronage is a lie. The high lords use it to keep Guardians like Martys enslaved. Our entire society is based on that lie."

Hendry glanced at his brother, who walked about fifty feet ahead of them, chatting with Amhain. "That's a dangerous truth."

"I know. It could break Obrion apart."

Lilias frowned. "Are you sure you're the one who has to take the awful risk of spreading that news?"

"Who else could do it?"

"Why not your Grandurian friends," his father suggested. "Seeing Obrion weakened right now would help them, wouldn't it?"

"No one would believe them. They'd think it's just a Grandurian lie, calculated to weaken us when we need to be strongest."

His father nodded. "Probably."

Connor told them, "I have to be involved. I'm Blood of the Tallan."

His mother made a warding sign. "Do you have to say that?"

"My curse is not a curse. The whole concept of curses is a lie. Commoners with curses are Petralists, just like noble born. They don't want us to know. I'm a common linn, with the very curse they want so badly. I'm the one who can make people listen."

"That'll infuriate High Lord Dougal," Hendry said with a grimace.

"Exactly. That's why you have to come. The rest of the village should be safe."

"How can you be sure?" Hendry asked.

Connor hesitated. "Nothing is sure, but it makes sense."

Hendry said, "We may live in a secluded village, but I've seen enough to know that high lords don't have to make sense."

"And you're forgetting our responsibilities," Lilias added. "Your father is Ashlar, and I'm head of the women's circle. We can't just abandon everyone in a time of crisis."

"If you come, you could spare everyone greater danger."

"Or we might be leaving them to face the greatest danger in Alasdair's history alone," Hendry countered. "We can't do that, Son."

"But if Dougal's soldiers take you, he might torture you, torture the whole family, just to get to me," Connor said, hating to have to speak the words aloud.

His mother took his hands in hers. "No one knows what will come, but you cannot give in to evil, Son."

Connor shook his head. "I couldn't let him hurt you." The very thought tore at his heart.

"Surrendering would result in many more getting hurt, wouldn't it?" his mother asked.

When he nodded, she gripped his hands with fierce strength. "Then you must swear never to surrender. Swear to me."

He was taken aback by her intensity. When he hesitated, she squeezed his hands hard enough to hurt. "Swear it to me, Connor."

"I won't have to if you come with me," he countered.

His father said, "We cannot leave, but we're not fools. You know we've got the scouts in place. Stuart uses the town boys who are too young to have assigned vocations. Lord Gavin pays them no heed, but they have sharp eyes. If we see an armed party heading upriver, we'll head for the bolt hole until they're gone."

"But you might not have time to get everyone out," Connor pointed out.

Hendry said, "That's true, but as you just suggested, the greatest threat is to our family, Amhain's family, and perhaps Mhairi. Those few of us could perhaps reach the bolt hole in time."

"Would you really?" Connor gave him a doubtful look. "You'd run and leave the rest of the village defenseless?"

"If we knew the threat was directed against us," his mother insisted. "We could send instructions from the bolt hole to the other villagers."

"And what if Dougal has a Pathfinder? They'd discover what you were doing."

"We'll think of something," Hendry insisted.

Connor wanted to rage at their stubbornness, but shouting wouldn't help. They wouldn't leave. Not yet. Using the bolt hole offered at least a shadow of hope, and he clung to it to keep from despairing. Then he got an idea.

He beckoned Verena over. She'd been walking at the tail of the group beside Roderick.

"They won't go," he told Verena when she joined them.

"I shouldn't be surprised you've already talked about whisking us away from our homes with your promised one." Lilias said as Verena took Connor's hand in hers.

"Mom, we're not promised," Connor said, feeling color rise in his cheeks. Why did moms have to be so embarrassing?

Lilias sighed. "It's only a matter of time. I wish I had more time to get to know you, dear."

Verena said, "You should come with us. It'll be safer that way, and we can talk all you want."

"Oh, you do know how to tempt a mother."

"But we've already gone over all that," Hendry cut in. "Is that why you invited her over?"

Connor shook his head. "Verena, they've at least agreed to hide if Dougal sends soldiers. They've got the scouts in place, but the challenge will be communication."

She immediately saw his point. "I can spare perhaps three pairs of speakstones, Connor. That's all I've got."

"It'll be enough." He squeezed her hand in thanks. Their supply of power stones was low, and most of the quartzite was dedicated to powering the Swift and Hamish's suit. Offering up even three pairs of small stones was a meaningful sacrifice.

"What are speakstones?" Hendry asked.

"They allow communication over distance," Verena said. "I'll show you how they work before we leave."

"Make sure no one mentions them around Martys, or any of Dougal's people," Connor warned. "They're Builder inventions, so they're highly illegal."

"We know how to be careful," his mother assured him. "Besides, they're not the first contraband stone we've kept secret."

She drew from a deep pocket of her dress a small leather pouch and handed it to him. "Ailsa sent these with that letter. She said you'd need them when you eventually returned."

The pouch contained power stones for all of his affinities, except granite.

His father handed him another pouch, filled with precious powdered granite. "I quarried this in secret for you."

"Thank you," he said as he reverently took the powder. Preparing powder on the side was a huge risk.

"Since you won't leave, there's one other thing I can do to help shield you all from High Lord Dougal," Connor said.

"Now don't go killing high lords," his mother warned.

"I'll kill him if I have to," Connor promised.

Especially if Dougal threatened his family. He'd seen enough death to hate the thought of killing anyone, but he had seen enough of evil to know that sometimes there was no other way.

"But that's not what I have in mind. I'm going to take all the Cutter tools."

CHAPTER NINE

*"The impetuous youth may, when motivated by a greater cause, bend
their will to study of import worthy of greatest efforts."*

~Evander

Connor's parents argued against the plan, but Connor
insisted. "I need Dougal's people to see that I not only
broke with him, but I betrayed my family and the town,
and left you all facing winter with no means to fulfill
your duty."

"And no way to supply the stones that are so critical to
the war effort," Verena added.

Connor nodded. "It might be enough to convince
Dougal's men that kidnapping you won't give them the leverage
they're looking for."

Hendry said, "I see your point, but are you really ready to
cripple your homeland in a time of war?"

"There won't be a war if no one invades," Connor said.

Verena said, "And I guarantee Dougal can get replacement
tools. Sabotaging enemy quarries is fairly standard practice in a time
of war. No doubt he's got a stockpile of spare chisels, and even a
few hammers in a closely guarded vault in Merkland."

Lilias wrung her hands. "I still don't like it."

"It's a necessary act," Connor assured her. "But you can't
tell anyone else. In order to fool Dougal's men, the rest of the
town needs to believe I'm really stealing from them."

Lilias said, "Oh, Son, you'll destroy your good name
forever."

He shrugged to hide how much the thought hurt. He loved
Alasdair, but that was why he had to do it. "It's worth the price."

They looked like they wanted to protest more, but didn't
have a good argument against the idea. They rejoined the rest of the
group in exploring the town, and Connor tried to soak it all in. Even

if he didn't steal the chisels, he could never return to the simple life of Alasdair, but maybe he could save their homes for them.

As they walked, most of the adults gave the Grandurians a wide berth, but children soon flocked around them, eager to view the foreigners up close. They called out an unending stream of questions.

"What's Granadure like?" Hamish's five year-old brother, Grier, asked Ilse at the same time that eleven year-old Neilina asked Erich, "How'd you get so big if you can't even out-eat my brother?" And nine year-old Ammie tugged on Anika's sleeve. "Have you ever eaten a frog?"

When they reached the Healer house on Cliff Street that ran close to the base of the towering Wick Torr, Jean joined them. She greeted Hamish with a kiss, and his younger siblings chortled with laughter. Ammie asked if she had to give him one of Mhairi's tonics after every kiss.

Connor followed along, hand in hand with Verena, enjoying the stroll and the chance to absorb the feel of the town. It might be almost entirely new, but the scents and sounds were the same, the faces ones he knew so well. He already felt distanced from it, though, and the thought saddened him.

"What's wrong?" Verena asked gently.

"It's just. . ." He trailed off and gestured around them. "I've been realizing that this won't ever be my home again. Not really."

"I felt the same way the last time I visited my family. It was fun to visit, but the Builder compound is my real home."

Connor appreciated that she understood. He was happy she would be at his side as they headed into Granadure and whatever life threw at them there.

The rest of the morning passed far too quickly, filled with pleasant conversation and the easy contentment that came when surrounded by loved ones. Preparations for the grand feast took until an hour past noon, but all too soon they took their places at the head table in the market square.

Villagers crowded the heavy Sogail feasting tables, which were piled high with food. Meats and breads and cakes vied for space with puddings and vegetables and mountains of bacon. The sight of it all rekindled Connor's appetite, and he vowed to eat as much as Hamish.

Hendry rose once everyone was assembled, and quiet fell instantly. Again Connor marveled at how much his influence had grown in the past few months. He gave a little speech welcoming

Connor, Hamish, and Jean home, but he was wise enough to keep it short. Speeches before big meals forced people to wait to eat, and speeches afterward were excuses to nap.

He finished with, "As my brother likes to say, give it laldy!"

Villagers cheered, banging tables with knives or tankards. The phrase was not used much in town, but Connor suspected it might suddenly become popular again. It was a good way for his father to help link his brother back to the town again.

Connor dug in with everyone else, despite the huge breakfast. Hamish ate with great enthusiasm too, but far slower than normal. It appeared he had reached even his astonishing limit. More than one sweetbread got slipped into the bulging pouch at his belt.

Only when the feasting began to slow did Connor decide it was time. He hadn't wanted to waste a good meal, and with everyone full to bursting, they'd be less likely to grow belligerent.

Connor slipped a tiny piece of marble into his mouth and wedged it under his tongue. He sucked on it, and the spicy burn seeped into his tongue. He loved that initial burst of spicy flavor before it grew to painful intensity.

Imagining the gateway to elemental fire as a doorway in his mind, fashioned of white-hot, billowing flames, Connor extended his senses through and connected with fire. The tiny flames of Sogail candles burning at every table glowed in his mind, and he rose from his seat, grinning with the elation that came with walking with elemental fire.

He made a point to not draw too deep from the marble. Under the influence of fire, he could easily become reckless, but when tightly controlled, it offered exactly what he needed.

Most people were too engrossed in the feasting and their own conversations to notice him rise. So Connor reached out with fingers of thought, snatched the little flames of the Sogail candles, and pulled. Streams of fire arced into the air from the candles and drew every eye as they shot across the square and began spiraling around his fingers like long, fiery serpents.

"Thank you all for welcoming us with such legendary hospitality," Connor spoke loudly into the quiet. A few people cheered, but fell silent when others did not join in.

Connor hated to scare them, but he needed that fear. So he sent the streamers of fire shooting into the air and rippling around the market square. Even though they passed several feet above everyone's heads, many people ducked, looking nervous.

Stuart rose, glaring. "You're wrecking the feast, Connor."

"I'm just getting started."

He sent a stream of fire flicking in front of Stuart's eyes. Stuart recoiled, tripped over his bench, and sprawled on his backside between the tables.

"I'd say I'm sorry about that," Connor said, forcing his tone to turn cold. "But I'm just not." The crowd was turning angry, and success had never felt so bad. "In fact, now that we've eaten our fill and taken advantage of your hospitality, it's time to go. As you know, Obrion is on the brink of war with Granadure. What you might not know is that High Lord Dougal is my enemy."

A gasp rippled through the crowd, and Uncle Martys, who sat several seats away from Connor said, "Those be dangerous words, laddie."

"High Lord Dougal is a liar," Connor spoke directly to Martys. "He's already killed people in Obrion, and he plans to kill many more."

Martys slowly rose from his seat. "You picked an unfortunate time to insist on a fight, lad, but then again, I only promised not to fight before breakfast. I guess making it until after lunchtime isn't bad."

Connor hated to antagonize his uncle, but Martys could bring word back to Dougal and help convince him to leave the family alone. "I wish you'd picked a different time to come home, Uncle. Because I'm leaving to fight Dougal, and I'm taking all the cutter tools with me."

Villagers shouted in shock, and the cutters all leaped to their feet, cursing and defiant. Even Hendry rose, his expression furious. Amhain brandished his knife like he wished it was a sword.

Martys's skin faded to gray as he tapped granite, and his already-impressive bulk increased. His muscles hardened and shifted to sculpted lines that strained the limits of his shirt. "Hendry, Lilias, get the children out of here. I'll take care of this."

Connor waited for his family and Hamish's to move away. Hamish had to drag his angry father from the table. Soon only Martys faced Connor.

Most of the villagers had drawn back a bit, but remained in the square, curious to witness the fight. They waited too long, because at a gesture from Kilian, Ilse led her team away from the head table to position themselves at each of the main exits.

When people realized what they were doing, curiosity turned to fear. Now Martys really was their one hope for salvation.

"Stand down, Uncle," Connor told him. He pulled off his own shirt and tapped granite. His skin too faded and his muscles expanded, transforming him into a perfectly sculpted living statue. Many villagers gaped. Knowing he was cursed and seeing him transform were two entirely different things.

Martys shook his head, a little smile playing across his lips. "Son, I've been a Guardian since before you were a glimmer in your daddy's eyes. Bash fighting is what I do."

Connor shrugged, loving the play of his enormous muscles. "I hate to see an old man get beat, Uncle, but I can't show you mercy even if you hobble into battle using a cane."

Martys laughed, a wild look coming into his eyes, and charged.

CHAPTER TEN

"The mountain may withstand the assault of ages, but crumble in a single moment."

~Evander

Connor was tempted to let himself enjoy a little bash fighting, but he needed to make the villagers fear him and prove to them that he was a deranged threat to the town. So he drew deep from marble, triggering an intense burning sensation in his mouth as he used the little stone under his tongue to create new flames.

He threw out his hands, and sheets of flame whipped around Martys, who tried plunging through the fire. It was a brave, but stupid move. Connor seized him with the flames, wrapping them around his wrists and ankles, and yanking Martys out of the air.

Martys crashed into the head table, his stone-hardened weight smashing it to pieces. Connor caught the flying wood with his flames and used them as more fuel. Martys shouted curses, but was unable to break free. His stone-hardened skin protected him from burning, although the fiery bonds left black singe marks on his skin.

Normal flames couldn't act as physical barriers like that, but when manipulated by a Petralist, somehow they could. Connor didn't understand how it worked, but he'd seen it many times and counted on those unique, magical properties.

He raised a fist and drew the bound Martys into the air to face him. Martys glared, displaying no fear, only a burning desire to reach Connor and beat on him with unrestrained fury.

"I respect your strength, Uncle, but you can't beat elemental power."

Martys's fury melted away, replaced by a look of humor. He spoke in a low whisper, barely loud enough for Connor to hear. "Do ye think me daft, laddie? Of course I know that, but we had to give everyone a show, didn't we?"

For a second Connor wasn't sure what to say. Martys was hanging in the air, back to the crowd, so no one else could have seen or heard. Martys's bulk and the flames billowing around Connor effectively concealed his reaction too.

"Snap out of it, lad," Martys hissed. "Or ye'll give up the whole deception."

"You're not reacting the way I need you to," Connor growled.

"It's clear as a mountain loch that ye cannae stay, lad. I see what ye be doing, and I salute ye for it, but I've got my part to play to make it work. So punch me block a good ringer. We can talk once ye kidnap me."

Connor wasn't sure what to do, so he took his uncle's advice and punched him in the side of the head. The crack of his granite-hardened fist slamming into Martys's rock-like skull rang across the clearing and silenced the shouting. Villagers stared in mute terror as Connor released Martys, allowing him to slump motionless to the ground.

No one spoke, but all eyes turned as Hendry stepped a couple paces out of the crowd, flanked by Lilias, Amhain, and Peigi. He spoke softly, but his voice carried easily across the quiet square.

"You're a disgrace to Alasdair, Son."

Even though he knew his father was playing a necessary part, the words seared Connor's heart. He forced himself not to flinch, made himself meet his father's gaze with unblinking, cold detachment.

"Bring me those chisels, Dad, and your hammer. Don't make me ask twice."

Many of the townsfolk looked ready to burst with rage, but no one dared move. They were powerless against Connor's Petralist powers.

Hendry turned to face the crowd. "Cutters, bring me your chisels."

"You can't be serious," Stuart exclaimed.

"They're not worth your lives, and today they cost me my son."

Stuart looked like he planned to fight instead of surrendering his precious chisel. Connor didn't blame him. If High Lord Dougal didn't provide replacements, they'd default on existing loans.

Many of the families now glaring at him could end up enslaved to pay the debt. He might not be striking at them with granite-hardened fists, but he was delivering a potentially killing blow to the town all the same.

Within minutes, the angry cutters fetched the long diorite chisels and placed them on the nearest table. The pile of precious black-and-white stone tools represented the town's true wealth, the very meaning of their existence.

Before placing his chisel down, Stuart snarled, "You're a traitor, Connor. I hope High Lord Dougal tracks you down like the unclaimed animal you are and rips your heart out."

A murmur of agreement rippled across the crowd. He'd accomplished exactly what he had hoped to. Why did he feel so rotten?

So he winked at Stuart. "High Lord Dougal is a villain, a liar, and a murderer. He's the one who had better watch out."

"Don't go insulting good High Lord Dougal," cried Neasa, the fat baker. "He's done nothing but good by our town." Many voices raised in agreement. "He even gifted your own daddy a new hammer!"

Connor forced himself to say, "And I'll put it to good use."

Hendry returned then, carrying the precious Ashlar hammer. He did not put it down on the table, but approached Connor and extended it to him.

Unlike the hammer Connor had watched his father wield all his life, this one wasn't worn from generations of use. The fact that his father was willing to play along, to trust him, and to part with the precious tool, nearly brought tears to Connor's eyes.

"I can't take this, Dad," he whispered.

"You have to. Like you said, it's our best hope. Use it well until the day you return it."

Connor took it and met his father's gaze. "I will."

Then he motioned to Captain Ilse. "Gather up those chisels. Let's go. And take Martys too."

"You're going to kill him?" Stuart demanded.

"The less you know, the fewer nightmares you'll have."

Kilian didn't look pleased when Erich hoisted the still-unconscious Martys onto one beefy shoulder. With a leaden heart, Connor turned and led the way toward East Gate.

Shouted curses began behind them, led by Stuart and Amhain, but the villagers did not pursue them. Hamish walked in dejected silence beside Connor, while Verena walked on his other side and slipped one warm hand into his.

"They wouldn't leave," Hamish said, shaking his head. "Thought me daft to even suggest it. Just wish I could have told them the truth."

"You're dad's no actor," Connor reminded him. "He never could have played the part, and everyone would have realized the whole thing was a sham."

Hamish growled, "I still don't have to like it."

Jean appeared around the next corner with Mhairi. Connor tensed for another tongue lashing. Mhairi in a fit of anger was as terrifying as Anika max-tapping granite.

Mhairi only shook her head slowly. "I always say we should look deep and see clear before making decisions. On the face of it, you've all just struck at the heart of our town's very livelihood, but I know you." She looked form Connor to Hamish, then patted Jean's cheek. "You young-uns have done something hard, but I believe you've done the right thing. Safety go with you."

With the traditional blessing delivered, she pulled Jean into a fierce hug. Tears stood in Jean's eyes as she hugged her grandmother. "I'll miss you, Gran."

Mhairi looked to Hamish. "If you let anything happen to my girl, I'll whip you from here to Donleavy, boy."

"I'll keep her safe," Hamish promised.

Mhairi gave him a rare, warm smile. "I know you will, lad."

She then kissed Connor's cheek. "Take our hope with you, son. Be brave and remember why you did what you did today, and you won't stray from the right path."

"Thank you." He should have known they'd never fool Mhairi.

Then she poked Martys in the ribs. "You can stop play-acting now, boy."

Martys sighed. "Was I doing such a poor job of it?"

Erich dumped him to the ground as Mhairi shook her head. "Nay. I'm sure you fooled everyone who needed to be."

"That's why you brought him along," Kilian said as Martys rose. "But to what end?"

"Because I'm coming with you," Martys said.

"I don't think so," Kilian said, and Erich grinned, ready for a bash fight.

Connor said, "Uncle Martys, I actually need you to go back to Merkland and tell Dougal how deranged I am, how evil I've become, and how everyone in town hates me."

"Aye, twas a magnificent performance, but I'm not leaving until I know the truth."

"The truth about what?" Kilian asked with a frown.

"All this," Martys said, gesturing around the group. "I pay attention, and I hear things. Connor helped clear up the mess here last year, then he appeared at the Carraig leading his own army, and all signs pointed to marriage to Lady Shona herself. Then I find him suddenly here, on the run from our high lord, in company with Grandurians, swearing my liege is a liar and a murderer."

"You're well connected, Uncle."

"Like I said, I travel in company with some important people. I know the war's coming, but now you lot say you think you can stop it. And you, laddie, you've broken with your high lord, but no have turned unclaimed."

"What if I told you I won't? What if I told you patronage is a lie?"

Martys blinked, looking as surprised as Connor expected. For a second, he even looked angry. "That's a powerful big lump of coal to swallow, laddie. I'm thinking yer head's out the window on this one."

Connor shook his head. "We don't have time to explain everything now, but I promise you that patronage is a lie. You've been enslaved to Dougal's service your whole life for nothing."

"We need to go," Kilian said.

"And I'm going with ye," Martys insisted.

"You are willing to betray your nation?" Captain Ilse asked.

Martys scratched his head. "Well, if what Connor just said is true, maybe betraying my country is the best patriotism, eh?"

"That's a quick change of heart from a man who's served all his life," Kilian pointed out suspiciously.

Martys shrugged. "Some of me work I enjoy, but it's a sore fight for half a loaf, don't ye know?"

"And what exactly does that mean?" Ilse asked with a hint of annoyance in her voice.

"Work hard all yer life, but get less than half of what ye deserve is about what I'm used to. Either Connor is telling the truth, and I'd be daft not to join the revolution now. Or he's corked and spun till his head's sprung a leak. That'd be your fault, and I'd be daft twice over if I left him in your company without protection."

"I don't need protection," Connor said, although he felt moved by Martys's show of support.

Martys shook his head. "Ye're family, laddie. I no have enjoyed much of that in me life, so I figure I owe ye. I'm sticking to you like flies to fresh dung until I sort out the truth."

Jean grimaced at the analogy, but Hamish looked like he was filing it away for future use.

"That's assuming I allow you to come," Kilian said in a tone that made it clear he was leaning more toward unleashing the siblings.

Martys shrugged. "I dinnae plan to play dead twice in one day, so I come, or we fight until some of us be dead for real."

"I can leave you any way I choose," Kilian said, and fires ignited in his eyes.

"Perhaps," Martys said, looking unimpressed. "But will ye murder me in cold blood then? Because if you let me live, I'd have to assume ye're lying and confusing my nephew, and I'd be obliged to explain to my lord Dougal all about yer little plot."

"No." Connor hadn't just suffered through that horrible experience only for Martys to waste the effort. But he couldn't condone murder either.

He met Kilian's gaze. "We take him with us."

"This is a mistake," Ilse said.

"I won't let you murder him," Connor said. "And I won't let him waste what we just accomplished here. So we take him with us."

Kilian leaned a bit closer to Martys, the flames growing white hot in his eyes. "Don't make me regret not killing you now."

Martys clapped him on the shoulder. "You do right by Connor and you and I will get along."

Kilian grunted and turned away. "We've wasted too much time already."

Martys winked at Connor. "I just so happen to have my pack stashed over by the gate. I can pick it up on the way out."

Uncle Martys was proving far more fascinating than Connor had expected. He wondered how long it would take for Martys to regret forcing his way into the group, but until then he was looking forward to getting to know him better.

They exited East Gate without further delay, but just as Verena was settling into the pilot seat of the Swift, fast movement caught Connor's eye.

"Strider," he warned, and tapped granite. The others reacted just as quickly, falling into fighting stances.

The Strider, dressed in Dougal's colors, skidded to a stop nearby, and Connor recognized him.

"Donald?" The man was the head Strider in Captain Rory's Fast Roller company.

Donald waved. "Hello, Connor. I thought I might find you here."

CHAPTER ELEVEN

"The fires may ravage the sun-dried forest, but reunion gladdens the heart with a deeper flame."

~Evander

Connor grabbed Donald's arm. "Has Dougal sent an army against Alasdair?"

"Easy, lad," Donald said, wincing at the pressure. "I am alone."

Connor sighed with relief and let go. "Sorry. I wasn't expecting to see you today."

"I just arrived in Merkland yesterday on the speedcaravan. I was dispatched after the earthquake. My official mission is to check on the town and verify the quarry is undamaged."

"It's undamaged, but production is about to suffer," Connor told him, gesturing at the canvas sack full of chisels that Anika carried. He had kept the Ashlar hammer.

Donald nodded. "Might be the first quarry struck on this side of the border, but I'm pretty sure at least one raiding party's been sent into Granadure to try to accomplish the same thing."

Kilian exchanged a glance with Ilse. "Why would you share such intelligence with us?"

Donald shrugged. "By the time you get back, you'll probably have a report about it waiting for you. I'll pass word along about the attack here. Don't worry."

"What was the real reason you came?" Connor asked.

"And are more coming?" Hamish demanded.

Donald shook his head. "Everyone I saw was headed for the front, but I don't make those decisions." He pulled a rolled parchment out of his leather jacket and handed it across. "This is for you."

"From Captain Rory?" Connor asked.

Donald shook his head. "Rory and the rest of the company are heading for the front, along with High Lord Dougal, Lady Shona, and most of the senior officials."

"Again you share intelligence with us. Why?" Ilse asked.

"I was ordered to." Donald glanced at the Grandurians looming around him, and for the first time looking a bit nervous. "You all helped at the Carraig. It was easy to guess you might pass through here on your way out of the country. If I caught up to you, High Lord Dougal ordered me to tell you to inform Kilian that he was heading for the front to take command, and that the day of reckoning is upon you."

Kilian grunted. "He really does like to grandstand."

"Lady Shona gave me that letter for you," Donald told Connor.

He glanced at it more closely. Verena took a step closer and looked like she wanted to burn it.

Donald turned to Anika. "And Captain Rory asked me to say hello."

Anika grinned, grabbed Donald by the shoulders, and lifted him off the ground. "Tell mine capitain--"

She drew Donald closer, as if to pass a kiss to Rory through him, but he shouted, "Whoa! Hold on, miss. I get it, really. I'll tell him."

Laughing, Anika placed Donald back on the ground, and he quickly retreated a few steps.

Martys looked at her with new interest. "Captain Rory, eh?"

"You know him?" Connor asked.

"By reputation."

Anika said, "Capitain has strongest hands."

Martys sighed. "Guess I need to find another girl to wrestle."

Kilian spoke to Donald. "Has the order to invade been given?"

"Not that I'm aware. And I'm not authorized to say anything more about that." He glanced at Connor. "I'm sorry to see you forced to run like this. Captain Rory said if I saw you to tell you he understands, but he cautions you not to join the fighting against your homeland. We cannot show mercy on the battlefield."

"I understand." Connor hesitated then asked, "If I give you a message for Rory, are you duty bound to share it with High Lord Dougal too?"

"I report to Captain Rory, and I give my reports to him directly. If he chooses to share information further up the command chain, that is up to him, isn't it?"

"Tell your captain that my intention is to find a way to stop the war, if possible."

Donald gave him an incredulous look and Martys said, "I've tried to tell him, but he's one of those young kids who thinks he can change the world."

"He just might manage it," Donald said.

"Tell Rory that Dougal is my enemy, not Obrion."

Donald nodded. "I'll tell him."

"And make sure he knows that we've broken with Alasdair, stolen their tools in an attempt to disrupt the flow of stone to fuel his Petralists, and we will never return."

Donald nodded again, turned to go, then looked back. "Good luck, Connor."

Then he sped back into town.

Martys chuckled. "Life is never dull around you, nephew. I'll give you that."

"We need to get back over the border," Kilian said.

"These last mountains are difficult, but not impossible," Ilse said. "I can create bridges to get over the chasms."

"I need to move faster." Kilian glanced at the Swift.

Verena said, "I can't carry everyone."

"I know. We'll have to split the party," Kilian said with a frown. "You and Hamish will fly Connor, Jean, and myself north with all possible speed. Ilse, you take the rest of the team overland and meet us at the Builder compound. Try not to kill Martys before you arrive."

"I'm going with Connor," Martys insisted.

Verena shook her head. "No. The Swift's not a troop transport. We'll be lucky to make it without running out of quartzite as it is."

Connor turned away from them as they finalized details. He considered the letter from Shona for a moment, not sure if he should burn it or read it.

Shona had a way of twisting things in his mind and his heart, making it hard to think straight. Then again, she had freed him at the last. That fact was enough for his curiosity to win out. He unrolled the parchment.

Dearest Connor,

I hope this letter finds you somehow. I know you have to leave, and I can't imagine how hard it is for you, but surely you'll stop in Alasdair one final time before escaping the insanity that has swallowed up our lives.

Oh Connor, I already miss you more than those dark days when I thought you dead. To think we got a second chance to correct those first dreadful mistakes, that we came so close to accomplishing everything we had dreamed of, only to be separated again by such awful circumstances. It is almost more than I can bear.

Don't hate me, Connor. I think by now you know me enough to understand that I am as much a prisoner in my life as you nearly were. Together, it might have been bearable, but now my life stretches before me, grim and dark, and full of choices forced upon me by my birth, the demands of my station, and my duty to my father, my house, and my people. Your courage and unwavering loyalty inspire me, Connor, and I promise to press on, despite the challenges.

Be cautious, my Guardian. You are in company with perhaps the most dangerous people on the planet. I know you have reason to mistrust my father, but know that I want only what is best for you. The Grandurians have promised you fairness and truth and even love, but they are not the saints they pretend to be.

Be watchful, Connor, and when the lies begin to be revealed, know that I understand why you had to leave, why I had to send you into that deadly peril. Know also that I am here for you always, and when you are ready to return to my side, do not hesitate. Come to me, and together we can set all things right.

With love and hope,
Shona.

Connor read the letter twice, not quite believing it. Verena joined him, slipped under his arm, and read it too.

"That woman," Verena growled. When Connor did not immediately reply, she glanced at him, a look of concern on her face. "You don't believe that rubbish, do you?"

"With Shona, it's hard to know what to believe," Connor admitted.

"You should have burned it. She twists everything."

Connor smiled. "She says the same thing about you."

The attempt at levity failed and withered to ash under her glare. "What she says does not change the fact that I'm right, and she's a poisonous viper."

"Sorry," he apologized quickly. Clearly Verena would see nothing about Shona as a source for humor.

He had always thought of Shona more like a hunting pedra, beautiful, graceful, and absolutely deadly. He rolled up the letter and tucked it into his shirt.

Verena didn't look happy about that. She was probably right that he should just burn it, but he needed time to think. At least some of what Shona said in the letter was true, but the trick was knowing which parts were lies or carefully-crafted half-truths.

Hamish landed a moment later in a whoosh of thrusters. Connor hadn't even noticed him take off. He carried a couple of planks and some nails. Connor hated to use his father's hammer for anything as mundane as pounding nails, but it was the best tool for the job.

"Let me," Martys said, taking the hammer and nails from him and quickly fashioning a sturdy platform atop the supply box at the back of the Swift.

Connor decided it was probably good that he wasn't the one wielding his father's hammer. Accidentally triggering its diorite power would blow up the Swift, scatter their party, and probably wreck half the town again.

Definitely not the way he planned to end the day.

"This way, you'll still be able to access what's inside," Martys pointed out when he finished, a surprisingly short time later.

"You're very good with those tools," Hamish said, admiring the handiwork.

"If you'd built it, we'd have fallen off before we reached the top of the Torr," Connor told him.

Hamish barked a laugh. "And for growing up in a house with a hammer, you probably would have nailed your feet to the ground."

"Time to go," Kilian said. He looked impatient to leave.

Martys gripped Connor's hand. "Have a care, lad."

"I'll see you in a few days. Try not to fight with them. I want you to arrive in one piece."

Martys chuckled. "And deprive those two a good bash fight?"

He trotted after Ilse and her team, who were heading for the path up toward Quarry Road to begin their landward trek toward Mount Ingram and the border beyond.

"Let's go, Connor," Verena called.

He jumped onto the plank at the back of the Swift with Kilian, and Verena opened up the thrusters and lifted off the ground. Hamish, with Jean clinging to his back, swooped in close as they rose above Wick Torr. "Granadure, here we come!"

Connor glanced back down at Alasdair, trying to memorize every detail.

He did not expect to ever see Alasdair again.

Chapter Twelve

"Victory is weighed on scales of success, not solely upon the heartstrings of the martyr."

~Anton

There it is," Verena said, slowing the Swift and hovering about a thousand feet in the air above the southern end of a long, green valley that extended several miles to the northwest.

Connor leaned closer to hear her better. The movement gave Kilian and Jean a little more space, perched on either side of him on the narrow platform.

Hamish flew beside them, reclining on his left side in the air and easily keeping pace with the heavily-loaded Swift. At one point he had actually started snoring, but then he pitched down toward the ground, and with a startled squawk, woke up and stabilized his flight.

He had carried Jean quite a bit of the way, but they had learned that they could travel farther faster by shifting her every hour back to the Swift. Kilian had pushed them hard ever since they soared over the mountains dividing Obrion from Granadure. He was eager to return to his office and catch up on the current state of things.

It was often cold in the heights, and they lacked enough flying leathers to keep them all warm. Kilian had placed a hand on Jean's shoulder every time she started shivering and shared heat with her. He had taught Connor how to maintain a low marble burn to keep himself warm. With that minuscule amount of marble being consumed, he maintained a mouth-watering spicy taste that made him constantly hungry.

The precious diorite chisels were packed in the storage box, under the platform where he stood. His father's hammer was clipped to his belt. He had fingered it as they flew through the long hours of the day, convincing himself that taking it had been the right thing.

Hamish drifted close and pushed up his visor. He was already chewing on a breadstick, and like a best friend should, he tossed one to Connor. "Nearly home. Can't wait to see what's for dinner."

The casual comment startled Connor. Did Hamish really think of the Builder compound as home? Would Connor find home there too?

"What do you think?" Verena asked.

After a brief hesitation, Jean said, "The valley is lovely."

That was a nice way to put it. The Builder compound itself was a sprawling mass of buildings clustered in the center of the wide, green expanse. Buildings of every size and type of construction crowded together around a massive, central structure. It sported perhaps a dozen additions of varying sizes, shapes and heights, turning it into a bizarre construct unlike anything Connor had seen. The strange structure looked like it had gotten hungry and started eating nearby buildings.

"That's the dining hall," Hamish said, pointing. "Beautiful."

Verena eased open the rear thrusters, drifting over the valley and taking them on a gentle arc around the compound. She descended toward one huge, blocky structure on the north end of the jumble. "That's our main research facility."

The building faced north toward the fields of tall grasses, still green despite the late season, and long empty fields of brown dirt and the stalks of harvested crops. Groves of hardwoods, bare of leaves, were scattered between fields. Several miles in the distance, a thin strip of blue suggested a river along the northern boundary of the valley.

The high, north-facing wall of the research facility was filled with huge, square, sliding doors, twenty feet to a side. They towered over a wide, paved courtyard.

Half a dozen long, low buildings, running in parallel lines north to south formed a western barrier to the Builder compound, as if trying to hold in the sprawling mass of buildings.

Connor pointed toward them. "What are those, the ones that look like they were actually planned?"

"Warehouses. They hold all the finalized mechanicals," Verena said. Then she glanced over her shoulder at him. "What do you mean planned?"

Connor shrugged. "Well, the rest of the compound seems to have been dropped out of the back of a flying wagon and then used where they landed."

Hamish laughed and rolled an entire backward somersault. "Yeah. Never thought of it that way. Most of the time, we were so focused on research and crafting new mechanicals, I never really noticed how crazy this place is."

"That's because it started small and grew a lot faster than anyone expected. It completely took over the town that used to be here," Verena explained, looking out over the buildings with a little smile on her lips. "I think there are plans to straighten things out, but we just haven't had time."

Kilian said, "We'll get around to it. For now, we have to stop a war."

Hamish said, "I didn't even know there was a town here before. I thought the nearest town was Faulenrost."

He pointed to the east, toward rows of low hills that rose from the edge of the valley about a mile away. Nestled in the rising folds of land, Connor could make out a picturesque little town. From what Verena had told him, the capital city of Granadure, Edderitz, lay to the northeast, beyond the snow-capped mountains that reared behind Faulenrost. He hoped to visit it some day.

Verena was nodding. "It wasn't much of a town, but Schwinkendorf has been around for over two hundred years."

"So that's why they gave the new road that stupid name," Hamish said.

They had flown over the wide, even road the last few miles. Verena had explained it was a new highway being built between the compound and Edderitz. There were plans to add a new speedcaravan line near that road to facilitate moving mechanicals and supplies.

"There's always a reason for things," Verena said.

Hamish drifted around to the back of the Swift, and Jean swung onto his back. She'd done it enough times that she didn't even look bothered by the three-hundred-foot drop below them.

Hamish was still chuckling. "No wonder you just called this place the Builder compound. What a ridiculous name."

"Don't make fun," Verena chided as she adjusted to the shift in weight from Jean's departure. "It was named after the man who originally founded it, Vinzenz Schwinkendorf."

"Who was he?" Hamish asked.

"He was only the greatest chef in Granadure two hundred years ago."

"Really?" This time Hamish sounded interested.

"Oh, yes. He was the king's own chef. In fact, I was told once that the book of his greatest recipes was kept somewhere here, but it's been lost."

"No," Hamish breathed, glancing around as they descended the last hundred feet toward the courtyard of the research building. "How could something so important get lost?"

Verena shrugged. "I have no idea. It could be anywhere, though."

"It's a pity, really," Kilian agreed. "Old Vinzenz was really amazing."

"You knew him?" Connor asked, awed that someone could have lived so long.

"I've known a lot of people, but today we have work to do."

Verena gently landed the Swift, and Connor was happy to jump off. He enjoyed flying with Verena, but he preferred walking with her, holding hands or letting her nestle under his arm.

The nearest immense door rolled up on concealed hinges, revealing a cavernous room beyond. A skinny Builder with glasses, wearing a long, tan jacket, rushed out, beaming with excitement. A girl of maybe fourteen, with thick, black hair, trailed him. Connor remembered meeting the man in Alasdair during the battles, but didn't remember his name.

"Dierk!" Hamish rushed over to pump the man's hand. "What's for lunch?"

"I took the liberty of ordering something," Dierk said.

"Excellent!" Hamish grinned at the girl, who had sidled up beside Dierk. "Hello, Ingrid. How's your training going?"

She blushed and dropped her gaze, mumbling something that Connor couldn't hear. She turned away and rushed to Verena, gripping her hands and looking at her with wide-eyed excitement. "Oh, Builder Verena. It's so good to see you again! I've started flying with Uncle Dierk."

Verena gave her a warm hug. "I can't wait to fly with you."

"Really?" Ingrid exclaimed, but then her smile faded and she added. "I'm sorry, Builder Verena, but I'm just about to leave. I'm catching a ride down to the pass with the windrider transporting the latest bomb." Her expression lifted again and she finished excitedly. "I've been working with the ear scouts at the front."

"That's a very important post," Verena assured her, and Ingrid beamed even wider.

"I don't like her posted at the pass," Dierk admitted. "But we're so desperately short of Builders, and she's got a real gift with the speakstones."

"Congratulations, Ingrid," Hamish said, extending a hand toward her. She looked up at him for a moment, but immediately blushed and looked down. She started reaching out to accept his hand, but then drew back again.

She seemed completely unable to handle speaking with him. Connor smiled to see it. She'd probably realized that his hands weren't usually all that clean.

Dierk bowed to Jean. "I remember you, Lady Jean. Your bravery in rallying your town was inspiring."

"It's a pleasure," Jean said with a smile. She also greeted Ingrid, who curtsied graciously. When Hamish took Jean's hand and pulled her closer to point at something inside the building, only Connor noticed Ingrid's brief glare at Jean's back.

"There is much to be done," Kilian said. "I'll need to see troop reports, distribution records for the mechanicals, and updates on latest intelligence from the pass." He looked at Verena. "You and Hamish get settled and get up to speed on the current manufacturing situation."

"Of course," Verena said.

Dierk chased after Kilian as the Dawnus marched into the cavernous room inside the building. "Come along Ingrid, or you'll miss your ride to the front."

Hamish took Jean's hand. "Come on. I'll show you my workshop."

"Great," Jean grinned, and the two headed inside.

"Do you have time to show me around?" Connor asked Verena. "Or do you have too much work to catch up on?"

"It's waited this long," she said, grinning. "I want to show you my workshop."

She hopped back into the Swift and rose into a hover. "We'll go in through the outer door to my shop. Come on."

Connor jumped onto the back, and she sidled sideways, down the long row of huge rolling doors to the second-to-last one. He jumped off and, ignoring the thick chain used to slowly crank open the door, he tapped granite strength, grabbed the massive door and heaved. It rumbled up the track, rattling the chain, and slammed against the stop. He cringed. He'd heaved a little harder than needed.

Verena didn't seem to mind. She smiled as she flew the Swift inside. "It's good to be home."

Chapter Thirteen

"The storms of time obscure and conceal more than the snows of a winter tempest, and the days subsequent to war are turbulent and full of chaos."

~Evander

Verena's enormous workroom was well organized, with rows of tables and materials laid out with precision. An enormous windrider flying wagon with a broken runner on the left side sat leaning heavily over near the outer door.

Verena nodded at it. "A work in progress."

Connor slid a hand along the polished wooden rail as he walked past. The beautifully crafted wagon was longer than a hauling wagon from Alasdair. This one was configured with benches for troop transport, and could probably carry at least fifty soldiers. A high bench ran across the front for the pilot, with several quartzite-inlaid levers for controlling the thrusters. The lift thrusters underneath were ten times bigger than the ones powering the Swift.

"What do you think of Granadure so far?" Verena asked as they walked deeper into the workroom, an eager note in her voice.

"I like what I've seen, but I haven't seen much," he admitted. The landscape was rugged and beautiful, and snow already clung to the higher peaks. They hadn't passed any major settlements, but the small villages he'd glimpsed had looked remarkably similar to Obrioner towns. Part of him had expected something more foreign. "I'm looking forward to exploring the Builder compound."

"I plan to show you everything. You're going to love it."

Connor paused near the inner door at a table covered with gauntlets of all shapes, sizes, and materials. He picked one up and examined it. "These are for that slippery coal stone, right?"

Verena nodded. "Blind coal. This is where I designed the protective gauntlets."

"I'm glad you brought a pair with you to the Carraig." Connor thought back to that terrifying moment when the elfonnel had lunged and swallowed her. "If you hadn't. . ."

He couldn't finish the thought.

She drew close and hugged him. "Without the gauntlets and the shieldstone, I would have been long gone before you found me."

Connor held her as she trembled against him. He had followed her into the monster and saved her from its sludge-like stomach acid. They had barely escaped with their lives.

"There's so much to do, Connor," Verena said softly. "And some days I wonder if we'll get it all done before the war starts. Once the fighting begins, I don't see how we're going to stop it before a lot of people get killed."

"We'll figure it out."

She sighed. "Kilian believes he has to kill Dougal to stop him."

"He might have to. And somehow I have to spread the truth about patronage. We might be able to use that to drive the Guardians away from their high lords."

"Are you ready to deal with civil war?"

"I worry it'll come to that. Would that be better than an invasion? Either way, a lot of people are going to die."

Verena considered that as she released him and paced away. "We'll figure it out, Connor. We made it this far together, so I have to believe we can."

"Do you think removing Dougal would really open the door to lasting peace?" he asked.

"Maybe." She sighed, a wistful sound. "Wouldn't it be nice to have some quiet time to relax?"

"That would be a welcome change," Connor agreed.

He hadn't felt truly relaxed since before the battles of Alasdair. The intrigue at the Carraig was not conducive to relaxation. Nor were Shona's constant manipulations.

Verena said, "When we win peace, I'll show you around Granadure. We can stop by Edderitz. My family will be so excited to meet you."

"I'd like that," Connor admitted. Even though they'd left most of the town of Alasdair hating them, he was happy his parents had gotten to know Verena a little. He had never really thought about her family, and he suddenly felt eager to meet them. "Tell me about your family."

She shrugged. "They're kind of boring, honestly. Most of them are stuck at court and busy running the country."

"Really? They're nobility?" That surprised him, and not in a good way.

She nodded. "Being related to the queen carries a lot of responsibility. If not for my Builder powers and work here, I'd probably be stuck in the palace too." She shuddered at the thought.

Connor's smile faded, and he felt a cold, sinking feeling in his gut. He'd just spent so much time escaping Shona, the Carraig, and the intrigues of nobility. "Why didn't you tell me you're royalty?"

She shrugged. "It doesn't matter. I'm a Builder. That's all that's important."

"It might," he said, trying to quell the dark whispers of doubt that began creeping into his mind. Shona had warned him in her letter to be on alert, to watch for the truth to finally be revealed. Had she known? What else might she know? "Royalty makes me nervous."

Understanding dawned in her eyes and she took his hands in her warm ones. "Oh, Connor, they're nothing like Shona and the nobles of Obrion. They won't try manipulating you like that."

"But they're going to want me to do things for them, won't they?"

"Nothing more than they should," Verena said, looking puzzled. "You're here, so of course, you'll help."

"Help how?" Connor asked, an edge of suspicion creeping into his voice.

He hated to think Shona might actually have been sincere in her warning. He wanted to hate Shona, wanted to love Verena unconditionally, but his time spent at the Carraig had taught him to remain on his guard.

Verena shrugged. "I don't know any specifics, Connor." She gave him a reassuring smile. "We risked so much to get here. You know you're safe with me, but we don't live in a world without others. Our powers, our family connections, they all tether us to duty and responsibility."

That was true enough. His connections to his family were a constant worry in the back of his mind. Had he done enough to break with them, or had he left them to suffer at Dougal's hands? It made sense that Verena faced similar duty, but was her duty to bring him to them so they could use him?

Verena added softly, "Connor, you're right. Everyone expects great things from you because you can do great things. It would be insulting if no one asked. And it's insulting to this country that's sheltering you if you don't want to help it."

"I want to help," he assured her. "I've just had too many people trying to manipulate me and my powers to trust people I don't know."

"I'm not manipulating you, and I vouch for my family."

Connor nodded slowly. "All right. I'll trust you until I meet them."

"I think you're being a little paranoid," she said with a smile and a playful jab to his ribs.

He nodded. "It's a habit that's kept me alive."

"Don't forget that we've kept each other alive, Connor. You can trust what we have together."

He did trust her. He forced away the insidious whispers of doubt and squashed the voice of warning that was sounding in the back of his mind from his Carraig-tuned senses. Surely he'd left that kind of political intrigue behind and could enjoy a simpler life in Granadure.

Connor pulled her to him and as they embraced the feel of her in his arms helped dispel his worries. He would keep an open mind about her family until they gave him reason to doubt.

After a moment, she eased back in his arms and stared up at him, her expression questioning. "Are we all right?"

He nodded. "We are. And I hope I'll be all right with your family."

She smiled and rose up on tip toe to kiss him lightly on the lips.

"So, what next?" Connor asked, looking around the workroom.

Verena pulled a wooden box from under one of the workbenches and extracted a hammer and a pry bar. "Now we rip that annoying platform off of the Swift."

CHAPTER FOURTEEN

"The whisper of a Pathfinder can cross the plateau, but a single rain cloud may trigger the flash flood."

~Redmund

Jean followed Hamish into his cavernous workroom. The cluttered space reflected the often-transitory focus of his mind. Work spaces were scattered around the huge room, like independent islands made up of several tables, flanked by shelves, cabinets, and crates. Every surface was crammed with gear. Tools, random articles of clothing, dishes, and piles of partially-assembled mechanicals seemed dropped at random.

Rocks were piled everywhere, from large quartzite stones to tiny pebbles. She spotted four separate caches of sweetbreads. They looked stale, but that had never stopped Hamish before. Close to the huge sliding outer door was a broken down windrider and piles of rubble, as if he smashed furniture when he got bored. A tiled room with no front wall was situated in another corner, with several large watermelons positioned on the tile floor.

Dierk had mentioned that there weren't a lot of Builders, and most were stationed at the front to assist the army. Jean had been a little surprised to learn that Hamish was already considered one of the lead researchers. Along with Verena, he explored new concepts and developed new mechanicals while most of the other Builders, under the direction of Dierk, spent the majority of their time in production of existing mechanical designs.

"What do you think?" Hamish asked as he led her to the biggest work area in the center of the room. He spread his arms and turned a slow circle. "This is home. The best place on earth. This is where all the fun happens."

"Even better than the dining hall?" she teased.

"The dining hall is a special place, but here I build things. There I just eat things."

Jean pressed a hand to his forehead. "Are you feeling all right?"

Hamish laughed. "I can eat here too." He dragged a large wooden trunk from under the nearest work table. "This thing is full of emergency rations. When I've got a really difficult problem to figure out, I need immediate access to food."

Jean smiled. "I take notes."

Hamish took her hand and together they explored the various work areas. Several were for enhancements to existing mechanicals. He pointed to a blocky helmet and said, "I'm taking the concept of a healthbed and trying to make it work as a portable healing helmet."

"Healthbed?"

"One of the first Builder inventions," he explained. "Sandstone beds, with the release rate opened a fraction. Anyone sleeping on the beds is surrounded by healing energy. They can heal from wounds ten times faster than normal."

"I need to see one of those," Jean said, eager to explore combining the use of such a bed with her remedies. The results could be miraculous.

Hamish led her to another table piled with quartzite stones roughly cut into different geometric shapes. "Here I'm exploring whether or not the shape of a shieldstone affects the size, shape, and effectiveness of the shields they produce."

In the central work area, he showed her a new mechanical he was working on. He'd wound a long, slender rope inside a cube-like metal framework, lined with quartzite. A type of hinged grappling hook with inward-curving teeth was attached to the end of the rope.

Hamish patted the cube with a smile. "This is going to be the yanksnatcher."

"What does it do?"

He picked it up and moved around the tables and aimed the grapple at the distant windrider. The quartzite lining the box activated with a whoosh and the grapple shot out, dragging the unwinding rope behind. It slammed into the side of the windrider with a loud bang, then clattered to the floor.

As Hamish began winding the rope back in with a small hand crank, he shrugged. "It's not finished. The plan is for that hinged grapple mouth to catch onto whatever it hits and lock into place."

"That's a clever idea. A soldier could scale a wall or a cliff so much faster with that."

"Or I could score the last cinnamon roll from across the dining hall."

Jean smiled, imagining what the grapple would do to an unsuspecting pastry. "You should talk with a blacksmith. They might be able to suggest a spring to help with the coiling."

"Of course," Hamish laughed, giving her a quick kiss. "You're brilliant!"

As they discussed ideas for getting the grapple end to close and lock, Hamish led her to a metal construct nearly five feet tall. Its thick steel sides tapered down to a small box. The little compartment was lined with soapstone, and a heavy steel plug hung by a chain above the opening. "This is the smash packer."

"What does it do?"

"I'll show you." Hamish threw back the lid to a nearby wooden box and drew out of it an entire loaf of rather stale bread. He shoved it into the little opening, squashing it terribly to make it fit. Then he touched a quartzite block attached to the top of the hanging plug.

Air howled out of the little stone, rattling the chain as it sought to drive the plug down the tapered sides. Hamish released the restraining lever, and the plug drove down the smashpacker with astonishing speed, slamming into the doomed bread.

When Hamish shuttered the quartzite and cranked back the plug, he drew forth a perfect little cube of bread, about the size of an eyeball, but square.

"Behold," Hamish declared, handing the little cube to her with a bow. It was a bit heavier than she expected, and very dense.

"Go ahead, try it," Hamish urged.

Jean wasn't entirely sure she wanted to put that thing into her mouth, but Hamish looked so eager she couldn't resist. It tasted remarkably good, with a surprisingly vibrant flavor.

"Don't bite too hard," Hamish cautioned. "The smash packer super-condenses everything, so you've got to eat it slowly. It'll soften up in a few seconds."

"This is amazing," Jean said, and she meant it. The flavor intensified as she worked at the cube with her teeth, becoming more savory every second.

Hamish pulled a drawer out of a nearby cabinet and showed her dozens of smash-packed cubes of varying colors. "These are all different meals I've smashpacked. These cubes last for weeks before going bad, and you can carry around a week's worth of meals easily. It could change the way we feed troops."

Jean nodded as she scanned the piles of little cubes. One of the biggest challenges for armies was maintaining supply lines and ensuring their troops ate well. "This is amazing!"

"It's working better than this thing." Hamish led her to another table where a strange contraption rested. It looked like a small grill plate, fastened over a bed of marble, with a thin mesh wire forming a box over the top.

"What is it?"

"I'm hoping it will become the lunchifier. The goal is to super-fast fry foods when we're on long flights, but so far all I've managed is to super-fast burn things to a crisp."

"I'll work on it with you," Jean offered.

When they reached the back half of the room, Jean pointed to a bunch of debris in one corner that looked like a chair had been smashed to pieces. "What have you been doing there?"

"I'm studying diorite. I'm trying to figure out the most subtle uses of its explosive power."

Jean laughed. "Diorite is not exactly subtle, Hamish."

"That's exactly what Verena said," Hamish said with a shake of his head. "You're spending too much time with her."

"I'm spending too much time with you," she teased.

"Not nearly enough," he replied with a smile.

Hamish crossed to a locked cabinet and fetched a tray that contained twelve throwing darts, each with a single grain of sand secured to the tip. "See?" He touched the tip with a finger, then threw it at a nearby overturned chair.

The chair exploded.

The cavernous room seemed to enjoy echoing the thunderous report, and Jean covered her ears.

Hamish grinned. "See. One grain of diorite. Subtle."

"Oh, Hamish, I've missed the way you think."

He next took her to a work area dedicated to his flying suit, which he'd already hung on its custom rack. Jean marveled anew at the amazing craftsmanship. "You really came up with all of this on your own?"

"Pretty much." Hamish fingered the overlapping rows of leaf-shaped granite plates in the breastplate. "Verena did help some."

Jean could barely believe it. Hamish usually lacked the staying power to take a flash of brilliance to completion. His mind worked like lightning, with intense, momentary bursts of ideas. To construct that suit, he had learned to focus his mind more like a fireplace of stoked coals, maintaining a steady burn for the long term.

She felt immensely proud of him.

The suit fit Hamish's personality as perfectly as it did his body. In the air, Hamish was like a bird. A very deadly bird. His Builder powers had unlocked an entirely different aspect of his personality, one that she wanted to explore.

As Hamish began explaining the various thrusters, weapons, and components built into the suit, Jean felt awed that he had managed to integrate such a complex mechanical and make it work so well. "How did you figure out the optimal amount of water to include in that water bladder?"

Hamish shrugged. "I designed the outer layer first, then added the inner jacket. The water bladder fills what's left in between. It seems to have enough of the Bash-Hurt-Disbursal property I need."

"Is that another new word?"

Hamish grinned and nodded. "It means the water absorbs the shock of the impact and spreads it around, dispersing its effect. I invented that term. Pretty good, huh?"

When Jean hesitated, Hamish sighed. "I'm not nearly as good at it as Verena, but I'm getting better. You should have heard some of my early ideas."

"I'll take your word for that. How about all of these thrusters? How did you determine the optimal size of the quartzite blocks for best thrust force without having too much weight?"

Hamish shrugged again. "I used blocks that would fit the boots without getting in the way."

"Okay," Jean said slowly, fighting a frown. "You also have that tiny speedsling on your hip. How did you figure out what the best size was for managing the weight and size against the amount of ammunition you could carry?"

"Easy. That particular speedsling fit my hand best, but when I was cutting it smaller, I sort of knocked the table over and it broke the barrel. I smoothed the edges to make it work."

"So you didn't really do much testing?"

"Of course, I did. I flew it before we fought those rampagers and I told you we already tested the bash-hurt-disbursal property. It works, so why muddle it up with extra thinking?"

It was oddly comforting to know that under the new, amazing Hamish was the old, adorable one she had grown to love. "You and I are going to review every aspect of this suit, and I'm going to teach you how to properly test and calibrate it."

"Why?"

"Because together we can make it better. A lot better."

"But you've never built mechanicals before."

"I've developed tonics and medicines, and that requires the same kind of rigorous testing to make sure I don't hurt someone or fail to cure the disease." She placed a hand on his arm. "Hamish, if we do this right we can probably make this suit twice as powerful."

"Have I told you yet today that I love you?" Hamish laughed as he wrapped her in a hug.

Then he snapped his fingers and rushed over to the work table where he stored his emergency rations. "I need to check something."

Ignoring the crate of rations, he instead extracted a small wooden box, placed it on the table, and opened the lid. The inner compartment was very small and Hamish extracted from it a small glass bottle with a locking lid.

He held it up for her to see. "I left this cream here before I left."

Jean grimaced. "Don't open it. It'll be gross by now."

"This crate is packed with sawdust to insulate it." He reached into the box and extracted a tiny piece of soapstone, ringed with ice. "It's part of an experiment to explore cooling food. Kind of the opposite of the heatstone ovens. With soapstone we manipulate water. Ice is harder to manage, but it's possible. I left it here with the release rate open just a fraction to keep the cream cool until I came back."

Jean touched the bottle and it was quite cold. In the winter, when they left cream outside, it did tend to last longer. Still not sure it was a good idea, she opened the lid and sniffed.

"It actually doesn't smell bad."

Hamish took the bottle and drank a long gulp.

"Wait! You're not even sure that's okay."

He shrugged. "It tastes all right. So I guess it's okay. I need a cookie, though."

Jean shook her head. "You're incorrigible."

"I think Verena had some cookies stashed in a cupboard. Let's go visit her workroom."

CHAPTER FIFTEEN

"Suspicion, like the invisible canker, rots the foundation before bedrock can be made secure."

~Evander

Verena pried off the planks from the supply box on the Swift and surveyed her precious craft. No doubt they'd have to leave again soon, but they needed a better travel plan. Access to the skies granted them unparalleled mobility, but that little platform was not the answer.

She paced around the armored Swift, surveying it for damage. Placing her hands on the main controls, she flicked her Builder senses through the Swift's many components, noting the power levels available in the various thrusters. She had already ordered several hundred hornets to refill the deadly speedslings slung along the underside of the craft.

Standing across from her, Connor placed his hands over hers. "I wish I could feel what you do in the stones."

"And sometimes I wish I could establish affinity with them like you," she admitted.

He smiled, and she felt relieved that he seemed to have accepted her connection with the royal house, at least for now. She should have considered how he might respond to learning that, but it was a fact, and she couldn't hide from it. She loved her family, and she was sure he would come to love them too.

Of course, they didn't know anything about him yet. How would her father and mother react to the fact that she'd fallen in love with an Obrioner? The fact still amazed her too. How would her siblings react, especially her brother Vinzenz? She worried he'd forget he was a Healer when he found out about Connor and instead take up the responsibility of issuing an honor duel as any self-respecting Rumbler would in defense of his sister.

Family could really make things difficult sometimes.

As she considered the potential ramifications of her relationship with Connor, she again marveled that the two of them had fallen in love instead of becoming bitter enemies. She had been ordered to use Connor to gather information about the enemy in those critical first days around Alasdair. She had welcomed the assignment, had already been interested in learning more about him.

No one had been more surprised than she had when their adventures had thrown them together and the relationship had grown into something special. It had taken him a while to choose the right course, but when he had, his heroic actions to save his family, his village, and her life had inspired her.

She hated to think about everything he must have suffered at the Carraig under Shona's influence, surrounded by all of those Petralists with their intrigues and lack of honor. If only she could continue hating Shona with the pure, undefiled fury that she had for so long. In the end, Shona had let Connor go.

Had Shona undergone the same internal transformation that she had? Was that why she wrote that infuriating letter? She still seemed intent on twisting his heart. What else was she planning?

Verena returned to the supply box at the rear of the Swift, flipped it open, and began extracting the pitiful number of resupply blocks remaining. Had they stayed out much longer, they would have faced the serious risk of getting stranded in enemy territory.

At the bottom of the box, she found a piece of slate. It was the stone that she had snatched up during the crazy battle against the elfonnel. She had caught it out of pure reflex as Ivor raced with her across that strange stone ceiling that had concealed the ancient city under the plain.

She had initially planned to throw it back at the elfonnel in an attempt to help slow it down, but the stone's power had already been activated. It felt strange though, so she had held onto it, intending to study it further. During the busy days since they escaped the Carraig, she had forgotten all about it.

"You should have left that platform on," Hamish said as he entered her workroom with Jean.

Verena shook her head. "We need a better solution." She noticed the half-empty bottle of cream in his hand. "How did your experiment go?"

"Pretty well. I need a cookie. You still have those stale ones?"

She grimaced. "Help yourself."

Eagerly, Hamish retrieved the cookies from a nearby cabinet. She wasn't sure how he had learned about that hiding place. It was the tenth one she'd used, but he always sniffed them out. She was starting to think he had developed a secret deep-sniffer mechanical.

Hamish poured a little cream over the first cookie and waited for it to soften. "Next time I'll have to see if I can freeze it."

"What would that accomplish?" Verena asked.

Hamish shrugged. "I won't know until I do it."

Verena asked Jean, "Has Hamish shown you any other parts of the compound yet?"

She shook her head. "Only his workroom."

"I've made sure some rooms are being prepared for you," Verena said.

"The girls' barracks are so much nicer than the boys," Hamish said. "We just get a bunk with a lot of other guys. The girls get their own rooms. You should see Verena's. She gets a whole suite. It's like a palace."

"So you visit Verena in her rooms a lot, do you?" Jean asked, one eyebrow raised.

Hamish suddenly looked panicked. "No, not really. I mean I do, but it's just because we're working on projects together."

Jean smiled. "Calm down, Hamish. I'm not worried about you, and I doubt Verena would take any grout from you anyway."

"She does like to punch people in the face," he said with a grin.

"Only when it's necessary," Verena said.

"Have you heard how production is going yet?" Hamish asked before taking an enormous bite of the cookie, which definitely still looked hard and stale.

"Not yet. Dierk said production is behind. I bet the quarries are still short on their quotas."

"I understand that," Hamish said, sharing a knowing look with Connor. "It's easy for people who don't have to do the work to promise more will get done."

"That worries me," Verena said. "We need a lot of power stone to create the mechanicals they're demanding for the war."

"They're going to have to find a way to get us some," Hamish said.

"And we need to look for ways to consume less. We used a lot on that trip to Obrion."

"We had a lot to do."

"I know, but we easily could have run out, especially quartzite."

"Well we flew a lot," Hamish said with a shrug.

"I don't think we're going to have enough quartzite to maintain that kind of burn rate."

"If we use less, we won't be able to fly."

"Maybe not. I've been thinking of the last time I toured the healthbed warehouse with Dierk. They were using a quartzite-assisted pulley lift to move some of the healthbeds down from a high shelf. The pulley lift was powered by a tiny piece of quartzite that looked way too small to move such a huge lift."

"How were they doing it?" Jean asked.

"The pulleys. The block and tackle system reduced the end weight."

"I don't think we can use pulleys to fly," Hamish said with a frown.

"Have you thought about asking for help?" Jean asked.

"What kind of help?" Verena asked.

"I would think for non-magical ideas like pulleys, and like the springs for that yanksnatcher, we need non-magical people, like carpenters or blacksmiths or other craftsmen. Have you talked with them?"

"We use craftsmen to help build pieces of the mechanicals once we come up with the initial ideas, but they're not usually involved in research," Verena admitted.

"Maybe they should be."

"I like it. There are a couple people I'll talk with and invite to brainstorm ideas." Verena liked having a bright mind like Jean's around. They should have thought of that. She wondered what other oversights Jean could help identify.

"Makes sense to me," Connor said, leaning against the bench beside Verena.

"If we use non-magical components, can we still call them Builded mechanicals?" Hamish asked.

"You might," Jean said, then frowned. "And can you explain why you call mechanicals Builded? You do realize that's not really a word?"

Hamish looked to Verena. "That's what they've been called since I've been here."

Verena nodded, "That term was coined by the first Builders as a way to differentiate what we do from the work of other craftsmen."

Jean said, "The idea makes sense, but the word doesn't. Can't we come up with something that doesn't suggest Builders are really led by a four-year-old, hidden away here in the compound somewhere?"

Hamish looked offended, but Connor laughed. Verena said, "The right word is important. I've never really thought about that one, though."

"You're good at coming up with new names. Let's make up a new Builded term," Hamish suggested.

Verena frowned. "I'm good at coming up with names for new things, not re-naming existing things."

Jean asked, "Could we say mechanicals are Touched?"

Hamish laughed. "Doesn't touched mean like when people are crazy?"

"I'm liking it more and more," Jean said with a grin. "Unless you can suggest a better one."

"How about buildering or buildered?" He grimaced. "Those are awful."

"Yes, they are," Verena laughed.

Jean said, "We'll have to think about it. I'm sure we'll come up with the right word eventually."

Verena said, "Right now, I want to examine this piece of slate."

The others trailed after her as she took the slate to an empty workbench. There she touched it with a finger and reached into it with her Builder senses.

"By the Tallan's blessed memory," she breathed, amazed by what she felt. Someone had indeed unlocked the stone's power, but in a way she had never felt before. It was revolutionary.

"What is it?" Hamish laughed, drawing closer. "You look like the king just ordered you never to punch anyone again."

"This stone," Verena said, staring at it with wonder. "It's unique. I picked it up at the Carraig. It was part of that sunken city."

"That place was amazing," Jean said. "I only got to see a little bit. It was such a tragedy that the elfonnel wrecked so much of it."

Hamish placed his hand on the slate. His smile faded to a look of wonder mirroring her own. "What is this thing?"

Before Verena could stop him, he licked it.

"Do you mind?" she asked.

He could have at least let her taste it first. Tasting a power stone was definitely an important part of the Builder process, but Hamish's habit of licking the stones was a little gross.

84

Jean drew closer. "For the first time in my life, I'm wishing that licking rocks made sense to me."

Neither Verena nor Hamish spoke again for a moment as they both concentrated over the slate. Subtle currents of power flowed through the stone, moving in a delicate, complex pattern unlike anything she had ever tried to craft within a mechanical before. The feeling was like a revelation from the Tallan himself, and her mind whirled as she considered how it worked.

"This is absolutely amazing," Verena breathed. "I think we stumbled upon one of the ancient secrets from before the Tallan Wars."

Jean said, "That sunken city was the ruin of the original capital of Obrion. I discovered that fact in my research with Evander."

Hamish frowned. "The release rate is pretty low, but I don't see how this stone could have survived since the Tallan Wars."

"Good point, but I still think it has." Verena closed her eyes and focused on the subtle currents again, trying to understand how the unknown Builder from days of old had harnessed that power.

"What do you feel?" Jean asked, opening her ever-present notebook and pulling a pencil out of her pocket. "Maybe we can figure it out."

Verena said, "Usually slate's pretty straight-forward. The stone's power pours into the earth when it makes contact. That's what raises a wallstone."

Hamish nodded. "This is different though. If we drop this piece of stone, I don't think it'll make anything."

She couldn't help herself. Verena turned it over then pressed the unlicked side to her lips. Slate usually tasted a bit like a garden, a garden rolled up and baked into a little cake. This stone tasted more like a handshake.

"It's kind of friendly," Hamish said, his brow furrowed in concentration.

"How can the stone be friendly?" Jean asked.

"He's right," Verena said. "And I'm thinking. . ." She got a crazy idea.

Rushing across the workroom, she picked up a piece of slate she had been preparing to use in testing a new form of moving wallstone. Now she brought that piece back to the table and placed it against the one they were studying.

"What's that for?" Hamish asked.

"Just exploring possibilities. Like you said, the stone feels friendly. This was just one of many stones in that plain. What if it was part of a larger construct?"

"I've never thought of linking multiple stones at the same time," Hamish said.

"It's sort of similar to what we do with the windriders. From the control levers, we extend our senses down to the thrusters."

"It's not really the same, though. We're not releasing the power of the quartzite in the control levers. We just use them as a vehicle to reach the other thrusters."

"Maybe what we've been doing is a more basic form of a similar concept."

Verena and Hamish both touched the new piece of slate at the same time. Verena opened her Builder senses to it, and was amazed to feel the same currents of power unlocked in this new stone as she felt in the original one.

"Wow!" Hamish exclaimed. "It activated the power of this stone too, and we didn't do anything." He glanced at Verena. "You didn't, did you?"

"No." She loved the feeling of pure discovery.

"How's that possible?" Jean asked.

Verena shrugged. "I have no idea. I wouldn't have thought it was."

Hamish grinned. "I think we're going to learn a lot from this thing."

Verena nodded, exulting in that feeling of excitement she always felt when working on developing new mechanicals. It rivaled those wondrous first days when she had first discovered her Builder gift. A sudden idea struck Verena like one of those rare punches from Hamish that landed solidly when they trained together.

"This is it! This is the key that I've been needing."

"For what?" Jean asked.

Verena laughed. "The key to making non-Builder flight possible."

CHAPTER SIXTEEN

"The full measure of the wind is tested only when the mountain tempts the heights, but the treasure of a whisper is most precious over the scent of a fresh-baked cookie."

~Connor

Say that again," Connor asked.

"I've been trying to figure out if it's possible to modify a windrider for a non-Builder to fly it," Verena said, looking ready to burst with excitement.

"Is that possible?" Jean asked, pencil poised over her notebook.

"I don't think it is," Hamish said.

"It might be now." Verena gestured at the piece of slate from the Carraig. "I had no idea how to attempt it before. Now I do."

The inner door of the workroom opened and Kilian entered. "You all look very studious today."

Verena presented the piece of slate with a flourish. "We made an incredible discovery."

"So you finally figured out how to make that exploding wallstone?" Kilian asked, looking like he wasn't sure that would be a good thing.

Jean grimaced. "Oh, that sounds terrible."

"This war is going to be terrible, unless we find a way to stop it," Hamish said.

"Forget about the exploding wallstone," Verena said, making a dismissive gesture. "I picked this up at the Carraig."

Kilian leaned closer. "What's special about it?"

Hamish said, "It uses a higher form of Builder powers we don't think anyone has seen since the Age of Discovery."

Jean glanced at her notes. "The stone is prepared in such a way that other pieces of slate placed beside this one are linked to it, like when people join arms in the challenge pull during the Sogail."

Connor added, "It was part of the false ground protecting that hidden city. The entire plain was shielded, making the Sentry students think it was built on solid bedrock so they didn't try to pry into what was concealed underneath."

Hamish snapped his fingers. "Brilliant. I felt that subtle shielding, but wasn't sure why it was present. It makes sense now."

"I always wondered how the plain was shielded all the time," Connor said. "Not even Evander could maintain a shield that big all day, every day."

Verena's eyes widened and she said, "So that's why the stone is still active. Like you said, this stone couldn't possibly have been activated all those years ago. Its power would be spent by now."

"Of course," Hamish said. "All Evander needed to do was replace exhausted stones."

Verena was nodding as he spoke, and Connor loved to see how her eyes sparkled when she was so excited about her work. "With how the power in these stones are builded, the replacement blocks would be linked in and maintain the shield without the need of a Builder."

"My sister was a clever one," Kilian muttered with a wistful smile. "I never understood a tenth of what she told me she was doing."

With that far-off look in his eye, he didn't seem to notice everyone staring.

"Now might be a good time to tell us about your sister," Connor suggested, trying to make the request sound casual, despite how eager he was to learn more.

Kilian blinked, as if just realizing what he had said. He gave them a wry smile. "With so much happening now that echoes all the way back to those dark days, perhaps it is time to share a few things with you."

Connor dropped into a nearby chair, and Verena leaned against him, one arm draped over his shoulders. Sitting together like that, he hoped Kilian took his time.

"My sister was Kirstin, the first Builder."

Verena look thunderstruck. "But she was the daughter of the original King Triath and Queen Dreokt."

Kilian nodded. "She was wonderful. And you are more like her than you imagine."

"You're the original prince of Obrion?" Jean asked, her expression awestruck.

Kilian chuckled. "It's been a very long time since I've answered to that title."

Connor tried to work his open jaw back to the closed position as his thoughts raced. Kilian had lived for over three hundred years. He had seen the Obrion empire at its height of glory, had lived through the Tallan Wars, which had ripped the empire apart. And Connor had been thinking his own life was hard.

"Why did your mother kill all the Builders and order the Great Purge if your sister was the first Builder?" Verena asked.

Kilian's eyes reflected an ancient sorrow. "Like you, my sister often got caught up in Builder invention frenzies. She invented the speedcaravan and most of the original builded mechanicals."

Jean frowned and muttered to herself, "Need a new word."

Kilian didn't seem to hear. "But she pushed the limits too far, too fast, without understanding the dangers of what she did."

"What happened?" Hamish asked, with a rather squashed muffin seemingly forgotten halfway to his mouth.

"I don't know exactly. She gifted to our father a new kind of builded stone, her latest invention. She was so excited for him to test it, she wouldn't tell me what it was beforehand. Whatever it was, it did something . . . bad to him. It drove him past sanity, and he raised an elfonnel. He was the one who destroyed much of our original home. You saw part of it in those ruins under the plain of the Carraig."

Connor grimaced. Having an elfonnel attack the school when the entire army was ready had resulted in tremendous damage. He shuddered to think of the horrors of that day with such a powerful elfonnel unleashed with nobody prepared to fight it.

Kilian continued. "His humanity was completely consumed by the elements he had unleashed. We couldn't stop him without killing him."

"That's why she did it," Verena breathed.

Kilian nodded. "Mother was terrified that whatever had happened to my father could happen to her. She executed my sister before even learning what it was that she had done. She always had a fearful temper, magnified when she embraced her elemental powers, especially marble.

"In order to destroy the monster my father had become, she raised a fire-bound elfonnel. I think the experience broke something in her mind, but I didn't understand that until it was too late. She ordered the Great Purge, and then she turned against me and my nephew, Tallan."

"So Tallan really lived," Connor said. It still amazed him to think the legend of Tallan started with an actual person.

Kilian nodded. "Tallan had been the favorite prince of the realm. He was the only one who matched the full power of my parents' affinities."

"They were the original Blood of the Tallan," Jean said.

Kilian nodded again. "My mother believed Tallan knew the secret of what his mother Kirstin had done, and she could not take the risk of leaving anyone alive who might know a way to destroy her."

Connor said, "You had to fight. The Tallan Wars."

Kilian sighed. "There was no alternative. After the Great Purge and the other atrocities that she began to commit, more and more of the noble houses revolted and joined us. I didn't want to see my kingdom torn by civil war, but I could not allow my mother to murder my nephew like she had my sister."

Verena looked close to tears and whispered, "So much tragedy."

Connor held her a little closer, but was not sure what to say.

"That's enough history for now," Kilian said, shifting to a more businesslike tone. "Let's focus on today's problems." He pointed at the slate on the table. "I'm assuming now that you have this, it will help accelerate our work?"

Verena nodded. "I think this offers the solution I've been looking for to make those non-Builder wagons fly."

"I think it holds the key to finishing that new speedcaravan route too," Hamish said.

Kilian said, "Good. Make this research your top priority. I doubt we'll have more than a couple of days before we have to head to the front. I want every available mechanical ready to go with us."

"A couple days isn't much time," Verena said.

"I don't even have that much," Hamish said with a grimace. "We've got a new Last Word bomb ready to deliver, and I plan to take it to the front personally."

"I thought Ingrid just left with the bomb," Verena said.

"She took one, but I've been enhancing a second bomb," Hamish explained. "I've been testing the effects of including activated tertiary-affinity stones within a bomb. They might help interrupt the connections of tertiary Petralists with their elements for a critical second or two."

Verena grimaced. "The precise time they would need those elements to help protect them from the blast."

Jean looked a little sick. "I can't believe you're researching that."

"What choice do I have?" Hamish asked. The same conflict Connor felt about the upcoming war reflected clearly on his face.

"You're going to cause the death of more people," Jean accused.

"If I don't, how many more people might die in the invasion?"

"Oh, Hamish, I'm sorry." Jean hugged him, tears in her eyes. "I'm a healer, and I hate to think our efforts might hurt or kill anyone."

"I don't like it either," Hamish admitted. "But what choice do we have?"

"None," Kilian said, his voice firm, but kind. "War is always ugly, my young friends, and I wish I could spare you these hard choices, but I cannot. If we fail to put forth our best effort, we could see this nation overrun and the deaths of many thousands. No doubt we would be among the first to be executed if Obrion wins."

Connor hugged Verena tighter. She and Hamish were Builders, and Obrion maintained a strict law, in place since the Great Purge, ordering death to all Builders. As for Connor, he would either be enslaved as breeding stock, executed again, or used by Dougal to wreak even greater destruction upon enemies of the realm.

"But do not abandon hope," Kilian offered. "By the time the rest of us join Hamish at the front, I hope to receive word from Obrion. We sent an embassy to petition a conference to discuss terms for peace."

"And if they're not willing to consider peace?" Connor asked. All that talk about the Tallan Wars and the tragedy of Kilian's first family made him hate the idea of the upcoming war even more than he had before.

Kilian said, "We'll have to deal with Dougal. This is personal for him, and he's the main voice pushing for war. His thirst for vengeance against me may drive him past the point of rationality."

"Because you killed his wife?" Connor asked.

Kilian held Connor's gaze, his expression grave. "I have done many difficult things in an effort to save the peoples of both Granadure and Obrion from the foolishness of their own leaders."

"I need to understand," Connor told him. He wanted to trust Kilian, but he could no longer follow anyone on blind faith. "Please. How did killing Dougal's wife help protect the nation?"

Verena looked like she wanted to punch him, especially after Kilian had shared so much of his painful history with them.

"His wife was a very powerful Petralist," Kilian said.

"I heard she was exploring deeper Petralist powers."

"By the way you're speaking, I suspect you've spoken with Camonica," Kilian said.

"She told me that you killed her husband too."

"Why?" Verena asked, glancing from Connor to Kilian.

"Because they were experimenting with raising elfonnel."

Hamish shuddered. "I'm glad you stopped them. Elfonnel are not something to mess with."

Kilian nodded. "You've all seen what they can do. Most Petralists who raise elfonnel must sacrifice all of their humanity. It's irreversible."

"So you had no choice but to stop them." Connor felt immensely relieved to understand, and to agree that Kilian had done the right thing.

Kilian continued. "Even for me, it is the ultimate test of my humanity to pull back from that elemental brink. I think the fact that I saw what happened to my mother motivates me to not succumb as she did. Most Petralists don't understand the dangers. Dougal's first wife did not. They had learned just enough of the ancient secrets to destroy themselves and take many others with them."

Jean was nodding as Kilian spoke. "That's what the stories of the elfonnel attacks in the last three centuries came from. Those were Petralists learning to embrace the elements, but who lost control."

Kilian said, "Exactly. Those of us who have walked as one with the elements can feel ripple effects all the way across the continent when elfonnel rise. When I feel that, I try to help."

"How can you help?" Connor asked.

"When I reach them in time, I try to warn them of the danger. However, few men or women can withstand the lure of such unrivaled power. In the case of Dougal's wife and Camonica's husband, there was no other choice but to stop them before they destroyed hundreds."

"I doubt that Dougal sees it that way," Connor said.

"Indeed not. We fought, and I made the mistake of leaving him alive. I had hoped he would learn wisdom."

"Why didn't you kill him when he started whipping Obrion into a war frenzy?" Verena asked.

Kilian considered the question. "Killing a high lord is not done lightly. I didn't want to give the other houses a common enemy."

"You won't be able spare him the next time you meet," Connor said. "He won't stop until he avenges his wife's death, and he had hoped to use me to do it."

"As I suspected," Kilian said, his expression grim. "No doubt he'll try again. It's clear that he has learned the secret of wresting the mind of another Petralist to his control, especially one weakened right after ascending."

Connor asked, "How does he do it, and how do I stop him? I don't have any more porphyry."

"Don't use obsidian around him."

Dougal's hold over his mind had seemed to solidify when he'd tapped obsidian.

"There's more to it than that, isn't there?" Verena asked.

"Yes. There is another secret that I thought had been lost since the Tallan Wars, but somehow Dougal discovered it."

"How do you keep all those secrets straight?" Hamish asked.

"Practice."

"But you'll tell us, won't you?" Jean asked. She looked ready to burst with questions. She loved new learning as much she loved healing.

"I think it's necessary. We must deal with Dougal eventually, and you must understand the danger. Dougal has somehow discovered that obsidian, of all of the igneous stones, offers a threshold."

"Wait, I thought thresholds were linked to the elements," Connor said.

"Obsidian is the only exception. To ascend with obsidian is a grueling task, one that only a handful of Petralists have ever accomplished. Dougal must have done so, and that unlocks the ability for him to link to the minds of others tapping obsidian."

"I wonder if that's how he defeated Aifric," Hamish said. "She had the advantage, but she was a Blade too. He challenged her to a duel, even though he was badly wounded."

"No doubt that's why he did so. She would not have understood the danger."

"It's a miracle he left her alive," Hamish said.

"Mercy is not a trait that Dougal has in abundance. I suspect he expected to return and to use her as leverage against her people," Kilian said.

"I'm really starting to hate that man," Jean muttered.

Connor agreed. The more he learned about Dougal, the more he wished Kilian had not spared him. So many lives had been damaged or destroyed by that man's ambition and thirst for vengeance. The thought of Dougal using Aifric against her people infuriated him.

Aifric was a secret Assassin, but in her persona as a Healer, she was one of the nicest people he knew. That time she had tried to kill him hadn't been personal, and they had gotten over it.

Friends didn't hold grudges.

The inner door opened and Dierk rushed into the room, looking upset. "Kilian, sir. We just received word of a raid against the Schmitten quarry in the south. Obrioner Petralists, hunting chisels."

"The raids have begun," Kilian said, not sounding surprised. "General Wolfram will no doubt dispatch raiders against Obrioner quarries in response. Did the invaders obtain any of the tools?"

"Negative."

"Was the strike team defeated?"

"No. They escaped."

"So more raids will be imminent. Has Obrion launched the full assault?"

"Not that I've heard," Dierk said, but he looked nervous. "Ingrid will arrive at the front tomorrow."

"Let's hope the situation remains stable until we arrive," Kilian said.

"I'll plan to leave within the hour," Hamish said. "I can take my enhanced bomb and as many other mechanicals as we can pile onto the windrider."

"If you need to do more development on it, remember we've got a secondary Builder research station at Harz Fortress," Verena said.

"I forgot about that. I'll have to stop by there after visiting the front."

Jean said, "I should go with you. When we get to that research site, we can begin fine-tuning your suit."

Hamish took her hand. "Sounds good to me."

"Perhaps I should join you," Dierk said. "I could take a spare windrider."

Verena asked, "Are you sure that's a good idea? You have a habit of trying to fall out of windriders."

"I'm not that bad," Dierk insisted, but neither Verena nor Hamish looked convinced. "Besides, I've added safety harnesses to all the wagons."

Hamish said, "Good idea. The new catch-fall mechanicals should be ready soon too."

Kilian said, "Dierk, wait until tomorrow. I need you to oversee loading the highest priority mechanicals and ensuring that manufacturing will continue while we're gone."

When Dierk saluted and left, Kilian said, "Quarry raids are usually launched when invasion is imminent. I suspect the attempt to establish last-minute peace talks has failed."

"What are we going to do now?" Jean asked.

"Study hard," Kilian said, gesturing at the slate. "Figure out how we can use this. We leave in two days."

"What can I do?" Connor asked.

Kilian turned to him and said, "You are an ascended Petralist, Connor. It's time you learn what that means."

CHAPTER SEVENTEEN

~Ilse

When they stepped into the bright sunlight outside of the research facility, Verena kissed Connor's cheek. "Study hard. I'll see you soon."

Connor loved the fact that he could kiss Verena any time, without worrying that Shona or Rory might appear and chastise him for socializing with the enemy.

He turned to Kilian. "What would you like to start with?"

"Basalt. Let's see if you can keep up."

"Let me purge, then."

He still had a bit of granite in his system, and he knew better than attempting to use two igneous stones at the same time. Double-tap sickness had nearly killed him the one time he'd tried.

Connor closed his eyes and focused all of his granite strength into the center of his chest, then drove it out through the skin. The itchy-crawly feel of granite change to an intense heat as he forced the power away. A fine, white powder formed on his shirt. Lamacal was the waste product produced when Petralists purged.

He brushed it away and was surprised when Verena lifted a hand a second too late, as if to stop him. "I want to collect some of that one of these days and study it," she said.

"Why?" Connor asked. "It's just waste, isn't it?"

"It is," Kilian said.

"But has anyone ever studied it?" she asked.

"Do you study other waste you produce?" Connor asked with a grin.

She punched him lightly on the shoulder. "You're gross sometimes."

"I'll save you some lamacal next time I purge."

He then opened his small bag of powdered basalt, thrust his hand inside and, with a bit of focus, absorbed some powder through his skin. The boundless energy of basalt rippled up his arm and spread through his body.

As usual, he found it hard to stand still, and motioned Kilian ahead. "Lead on."

Kilian dashed off, accelerating until he ran faster than a galloping horse. Connor leaped after him, drawing deep from basalt, and laughing with the thrill of pure speed. Kilian still pulled ahead, so Connor tapped more, to the point where his legs could not move any faster.

Not without breaking.

Fracking shouldn't still hurt, not with how often he had done it, but it did. He was ready for the sharp pain as a new joint formed halfway down his thigh, allowing his upper legs to shift outward and rotate in full circles.

That reduced the amount of motion his lower legs had to move and increased his speed tenfold. Once the fracking finished, Connor laughed again as he accelerated and caught up with Kilian. They sped up the valley, moving so fast they skimmed over the top of the long grasses.

Kilian nodded approval. "Not bad, but now that you've ascended, there is new speed to explore."

He accelerated even more, drawing ahead and racing toward the low eastern hills and the picturesque little town of Faulenrost.

Connor drew even deeper from basalt, max-tapping the stone and accelerating so fast it took his breath away. Literally. He was running so fast now that it was hard to breathe. He was going to have to get a mask and a pair of goggles. The wind carried a hint of winter ice, and it dragged tears from his eyes, making it hard to see.

He loved it.

That run was the closest thing to absolute freedom he'd ever experienced. He wondered if that was how Verena felt in the air.

Despite his incredible speed, Kilian somehow still kept just ahead. The two of them flashed across the valley and into the hills, veering around the town of Faulenrost, cresting hills so fast they caught air and soared like birds. They sped into the mountains, finally slowing near the base of a steep cliff that was cleft by a narrow opening near the top.

Kilian stopped near a large boulder, and Connor's legs snapped back into shape as he slowed nearby. It didn't hurt nearly as much going the other way. He didn't even feel winded.

He grinned at Kilian. "I could do this all day, but is there something different about running in Granadure? I only burned through a fraction of the powder I should have."

"The difference is you. One of the first benefits of ascension is a tighter integration with your affinities. You can now access greater power, but still consume less fuel."

"I didn't notice it with granite."

"You weren't tapping granite very deep. If you hadn't been so distracted by a pair of bright blue eyes, you might have noticed you had a lot of powder left when you purged."

Connor felt relieved that Kilian did not seem to mind his deepening romance with Verena.

Kilian continued, "Speaking of granite, go ahead and switch to that."

Connor wished he hadn't absorbed quite so much basalt. He no longer resided at the Sculpture House with Aunt Ailsa, who managed all the vast power stone resources of the Carraig. There he had access to all he needed. Now, as a fugitive from Obrion and a guest in Granadure, he felt it prudent to be cautious.

Kilian seemed ready to share his knowledge and his resources generously, but Connor didn't like being so completely beholden to the man. Maybe the next time they trained together, he could get some replacement stores from Verena so he didn't consume all of his small reserve.

He didn't expect to need to break away from Kilian, but he had learned to be careful. He trusted Verena, but her family was still an unknown. He felt a deep respect for Kilian, but there was always a chance, however slim, their paths might diverge. Kilian was the undisputed master of the arcane, and Connor wasn't foolish enough to think he understood Kilian's agenda.

More Petralists established their primary affinity with granite than any other stone. Maybe half as many Petralists established affinity with basalt instead, and only a few connected with obsidian. Connor loved the fact that he could use all three. The strength of granite rolled up his arm, itching just beneath his skin like a thousand little insects.

"Is there ever a time I'll be able to use both granite and basalt together without suffering double-tap sickness?" Connor asked.

"Not yet. Even though you've ascended, it will still disable you, so make sure you purge every time."

"So it will be possible eventually, like if I ascend through other thresholds."

"Don't jump to conclusions," Kilian cautioned. "You don't even understand the effects of your first threshold. It's far too early to teach you about others."

Connor felt an intense curiosity to learn more. Every scrap of knowledge helped. Like the gaffers liked to say, "Many a mickle makes a muckle." The little things eventually added up to big things.

Patches of dirty snow clung to the shadows and Kilian nodded in that direction. "Usually this entire area is covered by at least a foot of snow this time of year, but winter has delayed coming."

"I wish it would arrive," Connor said. "Verena suggested a heavy snow could delay the invasion until spring."

"Indeed. It's more than a little insane for Dougal to be rushing toward war at this time of year. A good storm would probably remind even him that next year is early enough to invade."

Connor would love a few quiet months with Verena to explore Granadure. No doubt Hamish knew the best sledding places too. It would be so nice to simply relax for a while.

Relaxing would have to wait. Kilian gestured toward the large boulder nearby, at least ten feet tall, roughly oval in shape. "Lift that."

Connor eyed the rock critically. That would challenge even his max-tapped muscles.

He stripped off his shirt. He didn't have any extras, and he didn't want to rip this one his first day in Granadure.

Tapping granite, Connor applied it throughout his body. His muscles hardened but he didn't max tap yet. If he had known they were going to use granite, he would have asked for a set of battle leathers, like the Boulders and Rumblers used. Those armored jackets possessed sliding plates that could accommodate the shifting bulk of Petralists.

As he felt for good handholds on the rock, he wondered at the purpose of the test. His granite curse was one of the strongest of anyone he knew. He had first begun training with Tomas and Cameron by ripping trees out of the ground, so he could lift a lot.

Connor found good grips and increased his tap rate. His muscles swelled with strength as his skin hardened and faded to gray. It was the signature color of pure Alasdair White.

When his muscles reached their maximum size, it still felt somehow like there were depths to his granite powers that he hadn't yet tapped. Like basalt, they seemed more profound than they ever had been.

This was going to be fun. Grinning, he gripped the rock and heaved.

It didn't move. His fingers dug into it, breaking off tiny chips around the handholds as he pitted his strength against the enormous, unmoving weight of the stone. His back strained and his legs swelled with granite power as his feet sank several inches into the hard soil.

Connor max-tapped.

He wasn't sure he could grow any more without turning into a big, solid chunk of muscle, but maybe his skin would turn black like that time he'd used the triple-strength enhanced granite that Aunt Ailsa had prepared for him.

That didn't happen. In fact, his muscles actually shrank. He still felt stronger though, so he poured all his strength, all his will into lifting. With every muscle quivering with the strain, he shouted with the effort and heaved.

This time he lifted it!

His rock-hard feet sank even deeper into the ground as he hefted the mighty stone, which actually extended another three feet under the ground. He was lifting several tons. Not exactly easily, but he was doing it.

"This is amazing," Connor shouted as he pivoted and heaved the stone.

Few things were as simply satisfying as throwing rocks. Throwing a really big rock was even better. The huge stone soared twenty feet before crashing to the ground and tumbling down the slope.

"Not bad," Kilian said, a little smile on his lips. "But, I told you to lift it, not throw it. Now you've got to go retrieve it and put it back where you found it."

"Seriously?" Connor complained.

"We can't destroy the area every time we want to train."

It took several minutes to fetch the stone and hoist it back into place. By the time he finished, Connor was panting from the effort, despite his new super strength. The fresh mountain air smelled of pine and clover, with the smell of stone coating everything.

"Why is it that now when I max tap, my muscles actually get smaller?"

"If they got any bigger you wouldn't be able to move," Kilian said, poking Connor's enormous bicep. "There is a physical limit to how big you can get before the sheer mass of your muscles impedes your mobility."

He wondered if anyone had ever managed it.

"So how can I be stronger and smaller at the same time?"

"It has to do with the way the tiny fibers of your muscles are connected to the bones. Normal muscle fibers run parallel to the bones, and they have to swell in size to produce a corresponding increase in power.

"Now that you've ascended, max-tapping granite triggers a physiological change, similar to fracking with basalt. Those little muscle fibers twine together into braided twists, making them far denser and more powerful. So it actually takes less mass to achieve greater strength."

"Wow. What do we call this effect? Braiding?"

"Plaiting actually, but we don't talk about it with non-ascended Petralists."

"Why plaiting? Sounds like the same thing."

"The term conveys the sense of plate armor. You may not have noticed, but your skin is also harder with granite now, offering better protection."

"I like it," Connor decided.

"Few people who have not ascended learn these secrets. As you probably have guessed by now, all of your affinities have strengthened as a result of your ascension. You have deeper reserves, and your fuel stones last longer."

"This is amazing. "Connor grinned.

Kilian continued. "But the most important aspect of ascension relates to your tertiary affinities."

As Blood of the Tallan, Connor could establish affinity with every power stone. Despite Kilian's age, experience, and that roguish air of mystery he wore with such flair, he couldn't. He was a Dawnus, with two tertiary affinities, elemental opposites of each other.

All tertiary affinity stones were metamorphic, providing a gateway for Petralists to connect with one of the elemental powers. All Petralists established their primary affinity with an igneous stone. Perhaps half of them established even a basic secondary affinity with a sedimentary stone. Only a small fraction of all Petralists could establish that critical tertiary affinity with a metamorphic stone.

Those tertiary-affinity Petralists could walk with the elements. Those few were the ones who decided the outcomes of battles. Managing their tertiary Petralists was perhaps the most important responsibility that generals faced.

"I've already noticed that I'm stronger with soapstone," said Connor. "Without that enhancement, I don't think I could've connected with it while I was a Rampager."

He thought back to that terrifying day battling the elfonnel. The memory of those moments of glorious, terrifying power still sent shivers down his spine. It also kindled a renewed craving for more porphyry. Maybe he could get Verena to share some of what they had captured from that rampager camp.

"No one who hadn't ascended could have managed it, and very few who had would have succeeded." Kilian's expression turned grave. "But I warn you, Connor. Porphyry seems to be extremely addictive. The rampagers we captured were desperate for that powder. It twisted their souls, and if you aren't careful, it could do the same to you."

"I can handle it," Connor assured him. "Do you want me to prove it?"

That would be the perfect excuse to get more powder.

Kilian shook his head. "No, Connor. I don't want you to touch it again. In fact, I have ordered the destruction of the little porphyry we captured."

"No!" Connor cried before he could stop himself, taking half a step closer to Kilian, one hand raised into a fist.

Kilian didn't look surprised. "As I suspected, you feel the grip of porphyry in your heart. Connor, you must never give in to that craving, or you could destroy yourself."

"I'll be careful, I promise." He wished he hadn't slipped and revealed so much. "I don't want to turn rampager again. It was nearly impossible to maintain control. But what if Dougal attacks me again? Shouldn't I have a little porphyry to defend myself?"

Kilian shook his head. "I don't think it's wise, especially since we know so little about it."

"But losing control to Dougal would be worse."

"Perhaps. I'll consider it."

So maybe he hadn't destroyed all the porphyry after all.

Kilian said, "For now, we will turn our attention to slate."

"Why not soapstone or marble?"

Water was his strongest element and he wanted to learn how to shield underwater.

"We'll get to soapstone," Kilian promised.

As Connor tucked a small wafer of slate into his boot, Kilian gestured at the rock he'd just lifted. "Go ahead and move that boulder again, but this time, no granite."

Connor released granite and sighed as his muscles deflated back to normal. A person could get addicted to the feeling of incomparable strength. Hector had, and that addiction had twisted him. Connor had grown up trying to hide his curse. He no longer saw it as a bad thing, but it wasn't how he defined himself.

Enough with deep thoughts. Time to throw another rock.

Connor formed the image of a sunken pit in his mind, lined with slate stones inscribed with the confusing riddles of Sentry speak. He imagined a stone door set in the ground of the pit slowly opening, creaking on ancient hinges, releasing the slightly stale scent of secret treasure troves.

Slate allowed him to connect with the vast powers of earth, but earth moved at its own pace and was sometimes reluctant to establish connections. It seemed to like the effort he spent preparing that image, though. In his mind, he stepped into the pit and jumped into the dark hole gaping below the open door.

Connor's senses extended into the earth like long, ethereal fingers that allowed him to see, touch, and even taste the earth. The area had good soil that tasted a bit like home-baked bread.

He focused on the boulder and reached out with his earth senses, grasping it underneath. He easily lifted it off the ground on a pillar of earth, popped it into the air, rolled it over a few times, then settled it back into place. Moving rocks with earth was as easy as thinking.

"I could have done that before I ascended."

"Except that's not what I asked you to do."

"What, then?"

"I asked you to pick up the stone."

Connor frowned. "But you told me not to tap granite."

Kilian nodded.

Connor figured old people had a right to be eccentric, so he crouched in front of the boulder and heaved. He didn't strain with all his might because he didn't want to pull a muscle.

Of course it didn't move.

He glanced at Kilian, who looked ready to wait a while, so maybe there was an actual point to the lesson. Kilian had specifically asked him to connect with slate. Why do that, if not to use it?

Walking with the earth did fill him with strength and vitality. Sentries generally lived exceptionally long lives, although he suspected other tertiary-affinity Petralists might as well.

Sentries were generally large in stature and mighty in strength. He had just assumed that kind of person would naturally tend toward earth, but maybe there was more to it than that. Just like a Boulder who maxed granite too often became permanently larger and stronger, perhaps a Sentry who used slate often was affected too.

Could that sense of strength he received from the earth make such a difference? Only one way to find out. As Uncle Martys liked to say, time to give it laldy.

Connor's earth senses mapped out exactly how huge the rock was, but he tried not to think about that. Instead he reached for the strength of the earth, and for the first time consciously sought to draw deeper from it, as if it was a dark well just under his feet.

He imagined leaping into that well, like when he used to jump from the cliffs above Loch Sholto. He plunged into that secret well of strength, and the power of earth flooded into him like an avalanche.

It didn't hurt, it didn't swell his muscles like granite, but it filled him with the rushing power of an earthquake.

Laughing with the wonder of it, Connor heaved again on the boulder. He felt connected to the earth, as if his legs had set down roots, linking him to the mountain. The rock might be heavy, but it was nothing in comparison.

Using the power of the mountain, Connor lifted the stone into the air. It was as if the mountain was doing the lifting, passing through him and using his limbs. As Gregor had once said, 'The bucket does not command the river to flow. It is filled only when placed in the waters'.

He was the bucket. He had stepped into the waters, and he was filled to overflowing. Only in that act of surrender could he unlock the incredible power of the earth. The feeling was profound and a bit disconcerting. Did Sentry speak result from those kind of deep thoughts the earth seemed to trigger?

He only held the rock for a few seconds. He might now wield the strength of the mountain, but his grip was awkward, so he dropped it back with a heavy thump.

"That's amazing," Connor breathed as his tight bond with the surrounding earth faded. "It was like I was part of the mountain."

"I've heard it feels like that. Consider what you've learned today. We'll make time to train with the other elements soon."

Chapter Eighteen

"The beauty of the weed is the thorn, but the tares may choke the golden wheat."

~Connor

Ilse awaited their return, resting in a soft earthen chair in the warm afternoon sunshine outside of Verena's workroom. Martys was snoring loudly in a hammock, attached to two earthen pillars Ilse must have raised for him. The rest of Ilse's team were nowhere to be seen.

"You made good time, Captain," Kilian said when he and Connor skidded to a halt nearby.

Connor combed fingers through his hair, which stuck out in wild disarray from the wind. He spat out several bugs that he'd caught in his teeth. He knew better than to laugh while running so fast, but he couldn't help it. Basalt was just so much fun.

He'd managed to swallow four bugs, including one big, juicy one that had nearly choked him. He wished he knew what kind it was. It was so big, it might have broken Hamish's record from the previous summer.

Captain Ilse rose and saluted, even though she looked exhausted. "Thank you, sir. We pushed hard."

"I thought you might have diverted to Harz," Kilian said.

"I probably would have, if not for him." Ilse gestured at Martys. "He insisted on rendezvousing with Connor. Besides, I figured it might not be wise to take a Guardian sworn to Dougal into Harz right now."

"Good point. The next day or two will be busy, then we're heading to the front. You can share your full report after you eat."

"Thank you, sir." She looked relieved.

Her earthen chair melted into the ground, as did the pillars supporting Martys. He awoke with a start when he landed on the ground.

"Oy, lassie, hold yer head! I'm pure done in here. Give a man a rest."

He scrambled to his feet, noticed Connor and Kilian, and laughed. "Speak 'o the Tallan, and in walks this pair, with me a pure nick." He brushed at his clothing, which helped as little as Connor's attempts to straighten his hair.

"We'll find you a bunk after you eat," Kilian offered.

"Aye, a full meal would be a grand thing," Martys agreed. He glanced at Ilse and added, "Ye did most of the work, lass. Ye're lookin' a bit peely-wally fer the hard miles."

Ilse rolled her eyes at his odd phrases, saluted to Kilian again, and headed inside. For his part, Connor loved to listen to his uncle talk, even though he didn't entirely understand him either.

Kilian said, "I'll show you two to the dining hall. Then I have some work to catch up on."

Martys made a shooing gesture. "Off with ye then. We'll find the food anon. But I think afore that, what I need the most is a bit of real exercise. What do ye say, nephew? Up fer crackin' them knuckles against a real blockhead?"

"Absolutely." Connor missed his daily bash fighting practice with Tomas and Cameron, and was eager to get a feel for his uncle's fighting ability. Besides, there was nothing like punching a man in the face to help develop a stronger friendship.

Kilian pointed toward a nearby field. "Enjoy yourselves."

He headed into the building, and Connor fell into step beside Martys. "How was the trip north?"

"Twas a fright," Martys admitted. "That Ilse moves over the land like an avalanche with a grudge. Barely stopped to rest. Fifteen hours of sliding over hill and vale nearly gave me the boke. That one's not got the quits in her."

Ilse was as determined as she was crafty. She might not be the most powerful Sapper in Granadure, but anyone who underestimated her would regret it.

"Do you have granite?" Connor asked.

Martys nodded, patting his belt pouch. "One ration. Enough for a couple fights."

"We can replenish it," he promised.

"Thank ye, lad. Wouldn't want to run out in enemy territory."

"Do you consider them enemies?" Connor asked. Martys looked relaxed, but he'd been a Guardian his whole life, and the fact that he now stood deep in Grandurian territory must make him feel nervous.

Martys shrugged. "They haven't attacked yet. I gave me word, lad, and I mean to swallow judgment until I know the truth. But I cannae speak fer how they will react to me."

"Just walk carefully, and I'm sure we'll be fine," Connor said, although he reminded himself to exercise caution when away from Verena, Kilian, or Ilse. Other Grandurians didn't know him.

They walked for a couple hundred yards to where the grasses were trampled flat. It looked like a favorite training spot, although it was empty at the moment.

"This will do." Martys stripped off his shirt, and his muscles swelled with granite power as his skin faded to gray.

Connor purged basalt, absorbed some granite, and did the same. He loved that thrill of anticipation just before a bash fight.

"Ready?" he asked.

In answer, Martys lunged, throwing a punch that, had it landed, would have tumbled Connor into tomorrow. The move might have caught him by surprise just a few months prior, but Connor's honed reflexes kicked in. He leaned, allowing his uncle's fist to slide by, missing by inches.

Connor's fists weren't in the right position for a solid punch, so he increased the tap rate and head-butted his uncle with his rock-hard noggin. His forehead cracked into Martys's nose, and Martys stumbled back. If he hadn't been protected by granite, that blow would have splattered his nose and probably cracked his skull.

"Good reflexes," Martys said approvingly. "Ye've had some training, have ye?"

Connor nodded as the two circled. "With the Fast Rollers."

"Start with the best, and the world's yer pie, ready to eat. Let's see how much ye learned."

He lunged again, raining a series of blows on Connor, striking with fists, elbows, knees, and feet. Connor parried, shifting, and dodging, while returning with fast punches of his own.

The two shifted around the field, the cadence of their fight rising as they took the measure of each other, confirmed each was up to the challenge, and pushed the fight harder. Uncle Martys was skilled, and he fought with a savage intensity that would've been scary if they were fighting for real.

"Don't hold back, laddie," Martys urged, his gaze intense, a wild light in his eyes as they pounded on each other as hard as any bash fight Connor had ever felt. "Release the monster raging inside of ye."

Connor was already fully committed to the fight, and he felt the stirrings of rage building in his heart, a shadow of the fury he'd felt while transformed into a rampager. Could Martys somehow know about that? The thought distracted him for a critical fraction of a second.

That was all the time Martys needed.

Slipping inside Connor's fist, he curse-punched Connor in the chest. The blow slammed into him like a charging torc and catapulted him off his feet. Connor landed hard, but rolled with it, using the momentum to tumble right over backward and roll to his feet again.

"Good recovery, laddie," Martys grinned. "But ye cannae let yerself get distracted when yer in the current so deep. A bash fight is like plunging into a river of fury, me boy, and ye've got to dive deep and let it carry ye to victory."

That wasn't exactly how Rory and the Fast Rollers had trained him. Rory had always drilled the importance of discipline and control. So Connor eased his tap rate and held up a hand to pause the match. "What did you mean about releasing the monster?"

"Just that," Martys said with a shrug. "Ye cannae win if ye no be willing to do what must be done. Fighting is nae like serving tea. Tis a monstrous thing most of the time, and ye must be willing to embrace the heart of the warrior."

"Have you done a lot of fighting?"

Martys nodded, his muscles deflating and his skin returning to normal. "I've traveled a lot, and fer a while was stationed down in the deep south. Lots of skirmishes with Sehrazad raiders. Even tussled with a Mhortair from out of the endless plains of Ravinder."

"You fought an Assassin?"

"Ye be full of surprises," Martys said, eyeing Connor with interest. "Not many know of the Mhortair, even among the Guardians."

Connor wished he'd held his tongue. He was enjoying getting to know his uncle, but he couldn't share everything yet. "I learned to keep my ears open at the Carraig."

"Good on ye." Martys clapped him on the shoulder, then scooped up his shirt. "Let's go find that dining hall. I'm hungry enough to strip an eoin to the bone."

"Me too," Connor admitted.

As they walked together back toward the Builder compound Martys said, "We'll have to train again, laddie. Ye've got a good foundation already, but I sense ye lack the instinct to take the fight where we'll have to go to win a war."

"I've done a lot of fighting," Connor assured him. "Although I'd rather capture people than kill them."

"Ye cannae capture everyone, and ye cannae hesitate on the battlefield, or someone willing to release the beast will get the best of ye. How many people ye love will die if ye let that happen?"

Connor considered that as they trudged through the field. Then Martys asked, "So tell me why ye think patronage is a lie? That be the mother of all lies if'n it be true."

"It's true," Connor assured him. "You're not going to turn unclaimed."

"I hope yer right, laddie. I really do." Martys sighed, his expression turning troubled. "I left me whole unit behind. They're a wild bunch, and they're preparing to go to war. It feels like I betrayed them somehow."

"I know what you mean," Connor admitted. "I had to leave the Carraig, but I was their commander. Some of them died fighting under my command. Now there's no one to help them understand the truth. If we don't find a way to stop this war, some of them are probably going to die, and I might have to fight them."

Martys gripped Connor's shoulder. "Ye cannae blame yerself for the bad choices of other commanders, lad. All ye can do is give it laldy every day."

"I'm trying." It was comforting to hear support from family, even from family he'd only just met.

"Ye mentioned ye train with the Fast Rollers," Martys said. "How is it ye know them?"

"I met them during the battles of Alasdair, and they were stationed at the Carraig this season. They're inspiring fighters, and good friends."

"How does that work with you being a traitor and all?" Martys asked, his tone light, but his gaze serious.

"It's a bit complicated," Connor admitted.

Martys grunted. "Me mates would tear me to pieces if they catch up to me."

Connor grimaced. "Execution wasn't fun."

"The stories ye tell," Martys laughed. "A lot of men I know who've been Guardians for years don't have half so many."

"The price for being famous, I guess."

They entered the Builder compound through the huge sliding outer door to Verena's workshop. She wasn't there, so they headed deeper into the building through the inner door. As they walked, Martys asked, "Did ye know any of Dougal's other special forces?"

"I know Captain Aonghus and Spitnail Camonica."

"I've heard of those two. Ye never met Dougal's trio of Bladed Pathfinders then?"

Connor shook his head.

"Few do. Over the years, they've mastered using small bursts of external air. They can fly short distances most days, generate dust devils to blind and distract, and use focused gusts of wind to accelerate throwing darts. They probably have other tricks up their sleeve, but I suspect the only people who've seen those are dead."

Connor didn't like the sound of that. Skilled Blades scared even Boulders. They were notoriously difficult to take down, and having a trio working together with such finely-tuned tertiary powers would indeed prove deadly. "Is there anything else I should know about?"

Martys nodded. "If ye don't know about those three, ye probably huv nae heard about the Striding-Solas who can make himself nearly invisible."

"Now I know you're joking," Connor said.

"I'm feart it be no joke, laddie. Ye know that Solas can bend light, aye?"

"How does that allow someone to go invisible?"

"From the talk I harvested, Dougal chored some highly custom prism glass from Sehrazad. He's got one Solas who worked it 'til he figured out how to bend the light through it and around himself. Makes him nigh impossible to see."

"Why haven't I heard about this before?" Connor asked.

Martys shrugged. "Secrets like that get held close to the chest lad."

"Then how is it that you know about it?" Verena asked as they rounded an intersecting hallway and found her and Kilian standing there. Connor moved to her side and gave her a quick kiss, but she didn't take her eyes off of Martys.

"Like I told Connor," Martys said, not seeming concerned by her distrustful tone. "I've traveled a lot. We clashed with the Sehrazad raiders in many a rammy in the south. One of me mates was on the raiding party that chored that prism glass.

"That Solas was stationed there too. It's a wee sort of town, hard to hide, and I caught a keek of him training once. 'Twas a Tallan-cursed nightmare, it was. Gave me the fleg. One minute he's a walkin' across the courtyard, then a burst o light, and then barely a shadow left in view walkin' away."

"How did you manage to catch even that much of a glimpse?" Verena asked, her tone definitely distrustful.

"It was me duty to guard the courtyard." Martys's smile had faded under Verena's continued questioning. "A couple kids was spied climbing the vines of the tower wall. Not uncommon fer the area, but not allowed that day, so I had to chase them youngins away. Seems to me, instead of accusing me of telling whoppers, ye should be thanking me fer bringing ye the new know."

"Could it be possible?" Verena asked Kilian.

"It's unlikely, but possible. I've only ever known one person who could make invisibility work, but I don't believe anyone has used that particular threshold since the Tallan Wars. I would need to understand the properties of that prism glass to know for sure."

"Ye may get the chance sooner than ye think," Martys said. "Not long afore I returned to Merkland, that Solas was sent on a mission. I dinnae ken the specifics, just that he was headed fer Granadure."

"How would you have learned even that much about a secret mission?" Verena asked, her tone mollified, but not quite trusting.

"I like the fact that ye dinnae take anything at face value," Martys said with a wink.

Connor was grateful that he wasn't riled by Verena's continued questioning. It was starting to bother him. How would she feel if he interrogated her family the same way when they met?

"Soldiers gossip, and when there be war looming, gossip about turning the tide in our favor is harder to contain than a belch after a good feed," Martys said.

"Something about that mission made people think it was going to help. Could be anything, but I wager that Solas was sent to assassinate someone important."

He looked from Connor, to Kilian, to Verena, and his voice turned grave. "Could be any one of ye, I suppose."

Merkland
Mt Osterwald
Abwehr Mts
Inner Gate
Outer Gates
The Cliffs
Army Camp
Watchtower
Badurach Pass
Blando

Chapter Nineteen

"Storm clouds gather over lofty peaks, ah, and drench the plain."
~Declan

Dressed in the gold and royal-blue commander's uniform of his newly-adopted house, Ivor approached the spacious command tent in the center of the Obrion army. The vast military force was camped on the plateau high up the slope of Mount Macduib.

The ultimate peak soared at least two thousand feet higher still, and Ivor swore that he felt its looming shadow even in the dark of night. The twin towers of sheer, snowcapped stone were split down the middle by Drumwhindle Pass, as if a giant ax stroke had sundered the center of the mountain. The peak was impassable on either side, and there were no other good passes anywhere through the range.

The early morning sun hung on the eastern horizon, back-lighting the long line of impassable peaks of the Maclachlan Mountains. Drumwhindle Pass glittered in the bright morning light, as if taunting the might of Obrion to dare the narrow gap and break themselves against the Grandurian defenses.

They really had no other choice, but no one was looking forward to the command to attack. There hadn't been such a gathering of military might in at least a generation, and Ivor did not doubt that a breach could be made. The cost would be high though, and it was both thrilling and terrifying to know he would play a part in the conflict.

The guard at the door was expecting him and motioned him through. A large, round table occupied the center of the command tent, ringed by the senior commanders and members of the war council, dressed in the uniforms and colors of their various houses.

Ivor had not expected to see High Lord Dougal and Shona seated near General Carbrey. Carbrey sat stiff and straight, every inch the commanding general of the most important military campaign in living memory. He proudly wore the blue and dark green of House Dougal.

For his part, High Lord Dougal wore a dark blue jacket that was not quite a uniform. He looked exhausted. His shoulders slumped where he sat, his face was lined, and dark circles lurked under his eyes. A cane leaned against the table beside his chair. Ivor had heard that he'd been seen limping at the Carraig the day after Connor had disappeared. With the Healers ready to serve him, he should have been long recovered.

Shona had changed out of the tight-fitting battle leathers she'd worn on the recent raid that he had led into Granadure against the Schmitten quarry. Her blond hair hung loose, nearly long enough to touch her shoulders. She wore a fine, green silk blouse and blue skirt. She didn't smile, but neither did she frown at him, and she looked even more serious than she had so often of late.

He wondered if she was still fuming over their failed raid, and if she knew anything else about their missing Strider. The man Oskar had abandoned their small raiding party and headed north on some kind of secret mission.

Ivor saluted and came to attention. "Reporting as requested, my lord."

"Come in, Ivor," High Lord Dougal said, waving him toward a seat near Carbrey.

As Ivor sat, he glanced around the table. He recognized flame-haired Captain Aonghus and the willowy Spitnail Camonica with her thick, tawny hair tinged blue at the tips. He knew most of the others by reputation. He felt a thrill of pride that he was welcomed into this elite group of military professionals.

"I hear good things about you, Ivor," Dougal said, his tired gaze direct and penetrating. Ivor was good at sizing people up, and Dougal was a man to tread very carefully around. "Your pending marriage to Lady Alyth isn't distracting you too much, is it?"

"I am ready for duty, sir," Ivor assured him.

He was actually pleased to have an excuse for a little extra time before marrying Alyth. There was nothing wrong with High Lady Islay's daughter. In fact, the life she offered was probably the best option Ivor could ever hope for. She was attractive, and she already ran most of her mother's small, but wealthy, realm. He'd been pleased to discover she possessed a sharp wit, a quick mind, and a ready smile.

Before he embraced that life though, he needed to speak with Connor.

Alyth seemed eager for the marriage, but not as eager as her mother. The marriage offered the house, which had been fading in influence in recent years, a chance to regain its previous glory.

He was already wildly popular with the house army, and no one had been surprised when he'd been given command. He hadn't expected to also be appointed commander of the forces from both House Lenox and House Pilib, although he immediately grasped their reasoning.

High Lord Dougal was simply growing too powerful.

One of Ivor's greatest skills was gauging the strengths and weaknesses of others. Dougal's list of strengths was unmatched, while his weaknesses were few. If what Connor had said about him was true, Dougal might be even more dangerous than most people knew.

The problem for the other houses was that he was the supreme commander and architect of the war effort, so they could not deny him their Petralists, auxiliary troops, supplies, or stores of power stone. Ivor's sources suggested that even King Turriff was growing nervous about how much power Dougal was amassing.

Assigning their armies to Ivor allowed House Lenox and House Pilib the chance to fulfill all of their wartime duties, while still insulating themselves from Dougal a little. Depending on how Dougal deployed his forces, it could bode very well or very ill for Ivor.

The tent flap parted for Redmund to enter. The broad-shouldered Dawnus looked impressive in his house colors of crimson and steel. He came to attention a bit slowly, and his salute lacked the crisp snap usually expected. His father, High Lord Feichin, was one of Dougal's most vocal opponents. Redmund did not look happy about serving under Dougal.

"The whisper of a Pathfinder can cross the plateau, but a single rain cloud may trigger the flash flood," Redmund said.

"We will need that indomitable strength of yours, fear not," Dougal said.

Ivor wondered if the man actually understood the several possible meanings of Redmund's Sentry speak. The high lord was renowned for his brilliant mind, but it always paid to keep an open mind when interpreting Sentry speak.

"Come," General Carbrey ordered, gesturing Redmund to the chair beside Ivor. "You two are our best new commanders. You've been invited to join us as we finalize plans for the long-awaited invasion. One of you will be chosen to take a critical role in that effort, which will win you and your houses unprecedented honor."

High Lord Dougal placed on the table two small sculptures, about the size of one of Shona's fists. One was made of polished slate, in the shape of an elegant Sentry tower, complete with crenelations.

The other was a piece of fine, pink marble, shaped like an elegant woman, hands on hips, a proud tilt to her chin, and her entire body wreathed in flames. They were both exquisite pieces, and Ivor felt his pulse quicken as he looked on the precious treasures.

"These are sculpted stones," Dougal confirmed. "And I will give one of these to one of you."

A low murmur rippled around the room. Even though those soldiers were professionals, not even they could look with silent discipline at such treasure placed within reach. Captain Aonghus's eyes began to glow with tiny flames, and Camonica placed a subtle restraining hand on his arm as he gazed with undisguised hunger at the marble statue.

Ivor couldn't blame him, but he'd beat Aonghus to a pulp if he tried snatching for the sculpture. Redmund leaned over the table, eyes locked on that slate statue. Even though Connor had been named Tir-raon champion, his disappearance had left a gap that House Islay and House Feichin were both petitioning to fill.

If Ivor or Redmund could be named Tir-raon champion in Connor's absence, one of them would win the coveted sculpted stone prize. This new opportunity was an unexpected and unprecedented chance to acquire another one.

Why would Dougal offer such a treasure? Why not gift it to one of his experienced commanders?

"I need a volunteer," Dougal said, watching them carefully. "These are from my personal stores, and I am committing one of them to the effort of breaking through the Grandurian defenses."

"One of us will lead the charge," Ivor guessed.

"Indeed," General Carbrey said. "You two possess the strength to wield such mighty power, but only one of you will be chosen."

With the power of a sculpted stone, Ivor was confident he could unleash a firestorm upon the Grandurian lines that their Flameweavers could never counter. Such a victory would win his new house much honor and secure his place in Obrion history.

He was surprised Dougal would offer such a potential honor to Redmund, whose house was so openly critical. Unless he was just making the offer to both of them so he could then choose Ivor. The snub would infuriate Redmund and his father.

Ivor desperately wanted that sculpted stone, although he felt he concealed his eagerness better than Aonghus. His desire for it nearly drowned out the quiet voice of caution that reminded him to tread carefully around Dougal, to understand his full purpose before locking himself into Dougal's service.

"The storms of opposition break down the weak of heart, but the tempest most fierce only fills the sails of the skilled hand."

Ivor glanced at Redmund in surprise. He had spoken in an almost reverent tone, and he gave Dougal a sincere bow. It seemed the tantalizing sculpted stone might be enough to challenge his prejudices. Nothing like unprecedented bribery to win over the most ardent critic.

"You're right," Ivor said, making his choice. "And I believe you were never given the opportunity to show your full potential in the Tir-raon. I think you should have this chance to be the hero of the invasion."

Redmund grinned. "The flowers of spring, though oft cast into the oven, yet may win the honor of adorning the brow of royalty."

"You'll be great," Ivor said, even though he had no idea what Redmund was trying to communicate with that one.

"Are you turning down the opportunity for this honor?" Carbrey asked, clearly disapproving.

"Not at all, General," Ivor said. "I would gladly accept the honor of bearing a sculpted stone during the assault. With that power, I could devastate the enemy and save the lives of many of my men. But since you said only one of us can be chosen to spearhead the invasion, I believe Redmund is that man."

"Take the fire, man," Aonghus urged, a single, flaming tear leaking out of his left eye.

Dougal raised a hand to silence further comment. He regarded Ivor thoughtfully. "It is rare for a young commander to possess the will to lead, tempered by the wisdom to know when to cede to another." He glanced at Aonghus, who settled back in his chair, the fires fading from his eyes.

"The choice seems simple enough today," Ivor said, trying to keep his expression calm under Dougal's penetrating gaze. "With that mountain of earth sitting just outside of camp, a Sentry is the better choice for the first strike."

Dougal nodded. "I concur."

He slid the sculpted Sentry tower across the table to Redmund, who accepted it with another bow. As one, everyone else began to clap. The sound echoed through the tent, and Ivor joined in, hoping he had made the right choice.

When Redmund touched the stone, his eyes widened with wonder. "Though the moon be not set, the dawning of a new day sheds light upon the face of the world."

Ivor glanced at Shona, and she gave him the barest nod of approval. Her gaze slid to Redmund, and her worried frown returned. Even with the power of a sculpted stone, Redmund faced a terrible risk. Even if he managed to break through the Grandurian lines, chances were extremely high that he wouldn't survive the day.

He didn't seem to care.

Redmund rose and saluted, his expression exultant. "I will break open this mountain for you, my lord."

"I believe you will," Dougal said with a smile.

In that moment, his exhaustion bled away. The lines of his face faded, his shoulders straightened, and he took a long, slow breath, as if to savor his restored health. Ivor had never seen such a healing, and he wondered how it was done, and why it had taken so long.

"General Carbrey," Dougal said, his tone crisp and full of authority. "The day we've worked toward for so long has arrived."

Carbrey saluted, grinning, and addressed the assembled commanders, who were equally brimming with eagerness to join in battle. "Commander Redmund will spearhead the assault. Commander Glynsk will lead the vanguard to secure the breach."

Commander Glynsk was a grizzled veteran Ivor had not yet met. He wore the crimson and steel of House Feichin, with insignia indicating he was a Bladed-Boulder Agor. Ivor wondered if he would choose granite or obsidian for the initial assault.

He looked surprised by the additional honor afforded his house and saluted smartly. "Thank you, my lord. We will not fail."

"I expect nothing less than your best effort," Dougal said, sweeping his eyes around the table. "We are embarking upon the great purpose of our generation, and we will see Obrion restored to its former glory. You are the finest commanders this nation has to offer, and I am proud to stand with you.

"Commander Ivor," Dougal added. "You will lead the second wave of the assault, under the direct command of General Carbrey."

"Thank you, sir," Ivor said, trying to hide his surprise. He was a junior commander, and he had expected a senior officer to be given that important command. "I had assumed General Carbrey would participate in the first wave."

"Not today," Dougal said.

General Carbrey added, "This attack will be a multi-wave assault, commander. When the first wave breaks through, they'll be tasked with clearing the initial defenses between the pass and the Grandurian plateau. We will be leading the bulk of the Petralist forces, and it will be our duty to drive into the main Grandurian army and break them. Our secondary objective will be to secure the Grandurian command center. Upon our success will hinge the outcome of the day."

Ivor saluted. "I will prepare my forces. Thank you, sir."

Dougal again glanced around the table. "Assemble your captains. Carbrey will issue final battle orders."

As one, they saluted, then exited the tent, eager to get their forces organized. Redmund slowly followed, engrossed in the treasure he had just won, and no doubt preparing for the battle that would define his legacy.

Ivor hesitated. He felt relieved he hadn't suffered any immediate consequence for allowing Redmund the honor to spearhead the assault, and he glanced at the marble statue still in Dougal's hand. If Dougal was willing to commit one sculpted stone to the invasion, would he donate another? With that much power, their victory would be assured.

Dougal noted his glance. "The day may well come that you must take up this stone, Commander, but it is not this day."

"As you will," Ivor said, saluting again and heading toward his army.

The camp was already transformed from the half-slumbering mass of waiting men into a whirlwind of activity as eager soldiers prepared for the long-awaited battle.

Ivor felt the same thrill of excitement, tempered by caution. The mock battles of the Carraig had lacked the element of deadly peril, but the battle with the elfonnel had taught him the ugly realities of war.

People were going to die today.

He did not plan to be one of them.

CHAPTER TWENTY

"When will the potential become the choice? That is the question that toppled kingdoms of old and holds in thrall the balance of lives even now."

~Evander

An hour later, Ivor stood at the head of his forces. They were formed in disciplined ranks on the eastern side of the high mountain plateau that faced Drumwhindle Pass.

The impassable peaks of the Maclachlan Mountains marched in an unbroken line to the east and west, with the mighty summit of Mount Macduib rising directly to the north, split by Drumwhindle, the only significant pass anywhere for hundreds of miles.

The plateau where Ivor stood was the only large flat expanse anywhere nearby, positioned just under the pass. A single, narrow causeway crossed a deep canyon that cut the mountain between the plateau and the entrance to the pass. That narrow causeway was secured at either end by thick, defensive walls.

That was the only route into Granadure, the dangerous road Ivor must traverse at the head of his forces.

Ivor felt confident the men and women of his command would win the day. His captains from all three houses had argued to keep their individual forces separate, but Ivor had insisted they work together as a single, cohesive unit. He only wished for a little more time to train them together to better leverage their combined might.

The three houses together fielded nearly a hundred Boulders and three dozen Striders. A corps of five Blades made up Ivor's personal guard.

House Islay was responsible for quartzite. Although most Pathfinders sent to the front were assigned to the general communications corps, three had been assigned to his personal command. He kept them active, gathering the information he so desperately needed to understand his new position.

House Pilib, which was really two houses merged together, oversaw both limestone and soapstone. They were so desperate to consummate Padraigin's marriage into their house that they had refused to send her to the front. No one had complained, although Ivor wished they had.

Padraigin was one of the finest Dawnus he had ever known, and the lingering bias against her was unfortunate. As the first Althin to participate as a commander in the Tir-raon, she had demonstrated true leadership and grace under almost universal hostility.

He didn't know anyone from Obrion who would willingly renounce their heritage and swear allegiance to a foreign power. He didn't pretend to understand why she chose the road she had, but he respected her for it.

Six Solas reported to Ivor, and he kept them close. Even though this would be a daylight assault, he did not forget the lesson he'd learned from Connor when his Solas had blinded three armies and tipped the tide of the first group battle in his favor.

The greatest strength to Ivor's force, and what made his little army a force to be respected, were his tertiary affinity Petralists. In addition to the soapstone of House Pilib, House Lenox oversaw marble. As a result, Ivor enjoyed an extremely competent corps of five Spitters and a wild bunch of three Firetongues, who made Captain Aonghus appear downright tame.

Only one Sentry served Ivor directly, but that would be enough. General Carbrey had three Sentries, so they would complement each other well.

"Commander, Redmund is moving toward the Sentry mountain," Papil reported.

The gangly girl, who had served as one of Connor's captains during the Tir-raon, was from House Islay, and her service with Connor had given her an air of quiet confidence that Ivor liked. She met his gaze, her huge blue eyes glowing with her active quartzite, and gestured toward the southwestern edge of the plateau. That was where the Sentries had gathered a mountain of earth to use in the assault of the pass.

"I want to see this," Ivor decided. "Keep an eye on me, and relay my commands to the captains."

She saluted, and Ivor tapped marble. Flames exploded under his feet, catapulting him into the air. Borrowing a trick he had learned from Connor, he formed wide wings of fire, secured at his back. Unlike Connor's simple construct, Ivor formed a double set of wings, with tiny fire devils rising between them. The tiny, fast-spinning vortexes of flame super-heated the air and generated many times more lift.

As he glided over the huge camp, he made sure to hold much of the heat along the underside of the wings. That way, it didn't escape and heat the air above him, which would have reduced his lift.

Firetongues often launched into the air, but he'd only ever seen Connor use wings. Fire didn't grip the air like feathers would, but the magical properties of marble allowed it some tangible properties. Ivor had advanced far enough in his mastery of fire that he could manipulate heat better than most Firetongues.

For being so new to his powers, Connor had a reckless flair that resulted in some impressive victories and some spectacular failures. It was a little annoying to think Connor probably hadn't really understood the complex construct he had created.

Ivor waved as he flew over the center of camp, but it was mostly empty. He glanced at the vanguard, assembled near the northern edge of the plateau, close to the causeway, but split into companies to either side. That left a wide conduit for Redmund to push through with all that dirt to deliver the initial overwhelming blow to crack the Grandurian defenses.

The Petralists of the vanguard would plunge into the gap that Redmund created, and Ivor and Carbrey would hopefully deliver the fatal stroke against the Grandurian defenses. Ivor appreciated the bold attack strategy and hoped it worked. If anything went wrong, a lot of good men and women would die in Drumwhindle Pass.

From a hundred feet in the air, he could easily make out the ranks of the vanguard, and they did look impressive. For the first time, he noticed that the bulk of the force was made up of soldiers from House Feichin, House Berach, and the King's own guard.

Interesting. If the initial strike went well, Dougal was positioning his most powerful rivals to win dangerous amounts of prestige. Then again, if something went wrong, those same critics risked suffering the majority of the casualties.

Ivor could not afford to remain ignorant of what game Dougal was playing. He could easily be sacrificed as a pawn in the game of high politics if he didn't figure it out quickly.

As Ivor neared the mountain of massed earth, he spotted Redmund ascending it, flowing over the earth without walking. About a hundred yards from the base of the mound, Shona and Gregor, along with a small group of other officers, had gathered.

Ivor angled his glide to land near them, flaring his wings at the last moment to land. His wings erupted into varicolored lights that spiraled away before exploding outward in a glittering shower.

"Oh, Ivor," Shona said sarcastically. "I didn't notice you there." She again wore her battle leathers, and she managed to look deadly, elegant, and alluring all at the same time.

"Do you know what he's planning?" Ivor asked. "Is he just going to plow all this dirt through the pass and smother them?"

"As if I could understand anything he said. In the last hour, his Sentry speak has gone from confusing to incomprehensible."

The huge Sentry, Gregor, whose intimidating presence always made Ivor a bit nervous, said, "The dam that holds the mighty river in check can be overwhelmed by the rains of spring."

"Well, I think his brains have sprung a leak," Shona muttered.

Up on the mound, Redmund raised the sculpted stone high and shouted, "The tempest may rage, the flood burst all bounds, and the tornado howl with fury, but the earth is moved only by the mighty shaking of its roots!"

Shona shook her head in disgust. "Told you."

Redmund rose upon a tall Sentry tower, and Ivor felt a bit disappointed. Was that all the show they'd get from him touching a sculpted stone?

The entire mound shuddered, masses of earth sliding in a rumbling hiss that Ivor felt through his boots. The earth flowed upward, forming walls and turrets. Redmund's Sentry tower grew and thickened, and the entire mound transformed into a massive, looming fortress. Redmund's laughter echoed across the plateau.

"You have to admit, that's pretty impressive," Ivor said to Shona.

"Let's hope he can cram that thing through the gap."

"Want to get a better look at it?" he offered, extending his hand.

She hesitated for only a second before nodding. "I suppose it's the only way."

"Best ride you'll find anywhere on this plateau," Ivor assured her.

Shona rolled her eyes, but still stepped close and wrapped an arm around his shoulder. She smelled faintly of roses, and her close proximity affected him more than he expected. Shona might be a lot of things, many of them deadly dangerous, but standing so close, he'd have to be dead and buried not to feel some attraction.

He liked the thrill of danger he felt in her presence and gave her a confident smile as he slipped an arm around her trim waist and pulled her to him. Then he tapped marble again, flames blasted out his feet, and he lifted them straight into the air.

They rose beside the mighty fortress of earth, and Ivor whistled softly in appreciation. The outer wall formed an octagonal shell, with the inside of the fortress rising into a series of huge palaces, ringed with nine lofty towers.

Ivor whistled again, accidentally spitting a little fire into Shona's face.

"Watch the hair!" she yelped, slapping his mouth away.

"Sorry," he muttered through a grin. She had a pretty good arm.

Then the entire earthen structure collapsed.

In an instant, it imploded from a majestic fortress back into a formless mound. Redmund's central tower crumbled and he plummeted down with the loose earth, his body limp and unmoving.

"Just like Connor," Ivor breathed, and his eager anticipation became tinged with worry.

In that momentary weakness at the Carraig, Connor had nearly died. He'd said that Dougal had invaded his mind and tried to control him.

Ivor glanced toward the center of camp, where Dougal's enormous palace tent stood near the central command tent. Dougal had not emerged, but Ivor didn't know enough to know if that should worry or encourage him.

Billowing dust rose in an obscuring cloud around the fortress. He and Shona both started coughing, so he wrapped them in a shell of delicate, blue flames to burn away the worst of it.

The ground rumbled with the falling earth, but instead of fading away to echoes, the rumbling grew stronger.

"I don't like the sound of that," Shona said, her expression turning worried and mirroring his growing concern.

"I don't think we want to be so close. Hold on."

With a stomach-wrenching heave, his fiery column threw them higher, and he sucked the flames along with them, forming another set of wings, larger than before. They snapped open, and the little fire devils caught the unsettled air with a roar, generating an enormous amount of lift and heat, which he used to bank them away from the potential danger.

Shona clung to him, and her muscles hardened with granite. "Don't tap too much," Ivor warned as he aimed for a gentle landing about a quarter mile away. "The extra weight could drag us right out of the air."

"You do know it's a bad idea to insult a girl's weight, right?"

Shona's lovely face was barely inches from his, so he couldn't miss the look of fear in her eyes. That surprised him. He hadn't thought Shona was afraid of anything.

"I'm sorry, does flying make you nervous?"

"Not nervous, angry. Makes me think of that Grandurian Builder wench." Hatred burned in her eyes, but another emotion was buried there too.

In the turbulent air, he struggled to maintain lift, but managed to glide almost all the way to Dougal's tent. The distance might not be huge when they were near earth movers, but he still felt a little safer.

"What's happening?" Shona asked as the rumbling intensified, shaking the ground so hard that they both staggered.

A giant monster leaped through the billowing dust.

It looked strikingly similar to the elfonnel they had faced at the Carraig. It resembled a gigantic scorpion made of earth and stone, but with the enormous, flat head of some kind of angry fish.

This one was a bit shorter, its sinuous, rectangular torso about seventy feet long, propelled by eight thick legs. The deadly claws on its three-toed feet cut deep into the soft ground. Spikes ringed its rounded torso and stuck out from its knees and head. It flicked its forward-arcing tail over its back, cracking the air all the way above its head.

"Tallan's fury," Ivor breathed, wondering if he had fallen suddenly asleep, the way Aifric had started doing at random times over the past days.

This was no dream. It was an elfonnel.

Shona's skin faded to gray as her body shifted into the perfect lines of max-tapped granite. It wouldn't help. The giant elemental monster was like a nightmare come to life, just as terrifying as when it had crashed through the Carraig outer wall.

"How?" she breathed.

"It's Redmund."

It had to be, but part of him refused to believe Redmund could become such a monster. "Connor was right. The elfonnel really are Petralists."

But there was no way Redmund knew how to raise the elements and give them living form. He was a powerful Sentry, but not nearly as clever as he pretended. If Ivor didn't know how elfonnel were raised, Redmund couldn't have learned the secret.

Ivor glanced again toward High Lord Dougal's nearby tent. Had Connor been right? Was this Dougal's doing?

The giant monster trumpeted, the noise like ten thousand lions roaring in unison. It echoed across the plateau, and the entire massed army drew back.

Gregor rose on a heavy tower near the elfonnel's head, and it turned to consider him. Ivor remembered how little Declan had tried challenging an earth elfonnel, but his bravery had only won him the honor of becoming the first to die.

"I don't like this," Shona said, taking a fearful step back.

"If you did, I'd worry you were cracked."

He definitely didn't like it. Didn't like the nightmarish memories the sight of the monster triggered, or the taste of fear that clung to his throat like bile.

"Clear the path," Gregor's voice boomed, enhanced by a Pathfinder. The mighty Sentry, who looked puny next to the enormous elfonnel, slid away from the monster on his tower.

The monster swiveled its head after him, tracking him with the two huge, silver eyes on the right side of its head. It opened its huge maw, revealing several rows of stalactite-like teeth, and roared again. The sound shook the plateau, its breath like a gusting, foul wind.

Shona shared a worried look with Ivor. "This shouldn't be possible."

"You go tell him," Ivor suggested.

For a moment, he feared the monster would pounce on Gregor, but it slowly turned its huge head to face the Drumwhindle Pass. With another bellowing roar, it charged the pass, with the entire remaining mass of earth flowing behind it.

Even though the gathered companies were assembled well clear of the monster's path, everyone pressed back farther. The monster was charging the pass, but Ivor had no idea if Redmund was controlling it, if Dougal was somehow directing it, or if it would suddenly change its mind and decide to eat them all first.

His heart raced with dark memories of that terrifying day at the Carraig. He shuddered at the terrifying memory of fleeing across the broken plain, carrying Verena, with the enraged elfonnel close on his heels.

Most of the soldiers didn't seem to understand the full extent of the danger. How could they? No one had seen an elfonnel in a generation. They were legends, stories whispered around campfires.

Some soldiers raised fists and cheered as the elfonnel raced for the pass, shaking the valley with the force of its passage. Ivor was suddenly very glad that he would not be leading the vanguard, trailing in the wake of the monster.

"I have to get back to my post." Shona looked shaken, but determined, and turned toward the central command tent.

The huge, double doors set in the outer wall of Dougal's palace tent opened and High Lord Dougal hobbled out, leaning heavily on his cane, with Healers at both elbows. His temporary health was gone, replaced by a look of weary concentration. He didn't seem to notice Ivor or Shona, but focused on the distant monster thundering toward the gap.

He bared his teeth in a fierce grin and whispered, "I have you now."

Ivor hoped Connor wasn't on the north side of the mountain.

Chapter Twenty-One

"One cannot force the young pedra to fly and to hunt. It alone must choose to take wing and leap off the cliff."

~Padraigin

Ingrid stepped into the Word Hub at the heart of the Grandurian army camp on the plateau beneath mighty Mount Osterwald and the narrow Badurach Pass. It still amazed her to think the Obrioners standing on the southern side of the same mountain called it by a different name.

She scanned the packed rows of tiny desks, each manned by a busy ear-scout. The women each managed several speakstones, cradled in little boxes along the upper edge of their slightly tilted desks. Each box was labeled with the name of the officer assigned to the little stone's twin. The huge tent was always a flurry of activity, and Ingrid loved the energy and the constant low hum of a hundred conversations melding together.

The duty captain, a pudgy ear-scout with a ready smile, approached. Ingrid had often seen her transcribe messages from half a dozen speakstones simultaneously. All the ear-scouts were women. Men seemed to struggle with tracking multiple conversations as well, and none had won places in the new, but already prestigious company.

"Builder Ingrid, welcome back to the Hub. We've got a lot going on today. The forward Longseer hovering over the pass has caught glimpses across the Obrioner side that suggest unusual troop movements. We've already got three pairings that need attention, and we're expecting a shipment of replacements today that will need to be activated immediately."

"I'll get right on it," Ingrid promised.

She headed to the back corner of the tent where her narrow desk was squeezed between two rows. It was cramped, but she was pretty small herself, and she loved it.

The news of troop movements made her nervous, and she hoped the dreaded first assault didn't begin before Uncle Dierk arrived. She felt far too alone without him. Even better, maybe Hamish would come with him.

Dozens of the ladies waved as she passed. She might be the youngest Builder, just turned fourteen, but the ear-scouts treated her with respect she had never experienced before. They depended on her, and she worked as hard as possible to not let them down.

She found the troublesome speakstones on her desk and picked up the first pair. With a flicker of her Builder senses, she explored the stones. As was usually the case with pairs that stopped talking together, one of the two contained a vortex of power that had altered the release rate, throwing the pair out of balance. It took her only a moment to correct the issue and get the stones speaking again.

"The right words can save lives," was a popular mantra of the ear-scouts, and Ingrid believed it with all her heart.

Ingrid wasn't much of a Builder yet. She had only discovered her Builder sense a couple months prior, but every Builder was needed to help the war effort. She couldn't build the complex mechanicals that were in such demand, but speakstones just made sense. Her innate talent with them had landed her in the Hub, and she was thrilled to be back.

Uncle Dierk had promised to continue her training soon, and Builder Verena had even promised to teach her. The thought of creating mechanicals with Verena was a favorite dream.

"Good morning, ladies." The deep voice of General Wolfram sounded in the tent, and every ear-scout not actively transcribing communications rose to salute.

Ingrid wove through the tight-packed rows of desks toward the general. He always asked her opinion about the status of the speakstone stores, and she took the responsibility very seriously.

Wolfram was a tall man with broad shoulders and large hands. His gray hair and long, drooping mustaches lent him an air of authority that was magnified by the penetrating gaze from those deep, blue eyes.

"Ah, Builder Ingrid," General Wolfram said, giving her a warm smile. He always treated her with more respect than she felt she deserved, and she loved him for it. With him in charge, how could the army ever lose? "I'm glad you're back. We'll need you to ensure everything works at top form today."

"I've already fixed the problematic pairings," Ingrid told him. "Everything else seems to be working fine."

"Very good."

She glowed with pride, reveling in the fact that her tiny gift was helping the huge, complex army communicate in ways it never had before. In moments like that, she felt almost confident enough to actually speak with the handsome Hamish the next time she saw him.

"General!" a nearby senior ear-scout cried, gesturing wildly. "Major alert. Urgent word from the Longseer stationed in the forward windrider."

Several other women started calling major alerts from officers stationed along the fortified wall that blocked the Grandurian side of the pass. Ingrid felt a thrill of fear as she followed Wolfram over.

The duty captain's face paled and she snatched the paper away from the ear-scout as soon as she finished writing the first line. "Sir, we have a report of some kind of giant monster closing on the pass from the Obrioner side."

"Reports of a mass advance from the Obrioner lines," another ear-scout shouted from the next row.

Wolfram took the speakstone and spoke into it. "This is General Wolfram. Describe what you're seeing."

"Oh, General. I'm so glad you're there." The woman sounded frantic. "It's enormous. I've never seen anything like it. Far too big to be summoned."

"Elfonnel," Wolfram said, his tone grave. "Has Dougal no sense? No respect for international law?" He handed the stone back to the ear-scout. "Record everything she describes, and bring it to me at once."

Ingrid didn't know what an elfonnel was, but the duty captain looked ready to faint. It had to be bad.

The general's voice boomed through the tent. "Ladies, listen up. We have a confirmed major alert. The attack is underway. Code Avalanche. Repeat, code Avalanche."

A gasp rippled across the assembled ladies, and Ingrid found it hard to breathe. She hadn't memorized all the pre-arranged code words the ear-scouts used, but she had seen Avalanche at the very bottom of the list. It meant that things were going very badly.

"Issue warnings to all units," Wolfram ordered, his voice loud, his tone serious, but his expression calm. "All auxiliary units commence full retreat. Evacuate the camp. Healers prepare all mobile treatment platforms at the lower end of the plateau and be advised of possible mass casualties."

As ear-scouts scrambled to get the word out, Wolfram turned to the duty captain. "Get me Anton at once. All tertiaries assemble at the southern picket. I want Solas ready for distraction bursts."

"Yes, sir."

She rushed off, shouting orders to the already-busy ear-scouts. Ingrid wasn't sure what to do, and she wrung her hands together nervously. Stress and fear radiated from the ear-scouts in nearly palpable waves.

"Which element?" Wolfram asked the ear-scout still transcribing from the Longseer. He leaned over her paper, scanning what she had already written, and his eyebrows drew together a bit, the only outward indication of concern.

"It's dragging a mountain of earth behind it," the voice came through the speakstone. "It has already leaped the Obrion causeway walls."

"Earth bound," Wolfram said. "We lack the water to stop it."

Several ear-scouts rushed up. "We're ready for additional orders, General."

"Good. Notify all tertiaries the elfonnel is earth bound. The Water Moccasin company is to prepare all reserves. Sappers must focus efforts on reducing its ability to seize the plateau. Flameweavers, prepare incineration initiative."

He turned to Ingrid. "I am afraid we may need that bomb of your uncle's, Builder Ingrid."

"It's ready to go, but I don't think there are any Builders available."

His brows crept closer together. Turning to the hovering ear-scouts he asked, "What are the current locations of our Builder corps?"

It took only a moment to gather the information, and the news drew his brows closer together until he was nearly frowning. "Are you telling me we have no Builders anywhere nearby?"

"No, sir," the lead ear-scout responded. "They've all been deployed. We never have enough Builders as it is, but we usually have at least one here at command."

Another ear-scout rushed up. "Sir, I just reached Builder Hamish. He's got Builder Dierk's speakstone. He's within earspeak range, and he said he's barely ten minutes out."

"Tell him to hurry," Wolfram ordered.

The news that Hamish was coming bolstered Ingrid's confidence and she spoke up. "Sir, there is one Builder available."

"Who?" All eyes turned toward her.

"Me." She spoke softly, a lump of nervousness nearly choking off the word. She cleared her throat and continued, forcing more confidence into her voice. "I'll take the windrider up and drop the bomb."

"Are you a flying Builder?" an ear-scout asked.

"I'm a flyer in training. Almost approved for solo flight."

Wolfram considered her, one hand stroking his majestic mustaches. Most of the ear-scouts had already returned to their duties, hastening to relay all his orders.

"Are you sure you can do this?"

The fact that he treated her with such respect, despite her youth and inexperience strengthened her resolve. She was a Builder. She would make her uncle proud, and if she did a good job, maybe Hamish would stop treating her like a little sister.

"I've flown with Uncle Dierk, and I did pretty well. Once I pass my last test, I'll be approved."

She didn't mention that she had failed that test miserably when she first tried it. She could handle lifting off and hovering just fine, but even though the controls for banking and turning were simple enough, the complexities of reading the wind and the air, and becoming one with it like Builder Verena taught were so confusing.

Still, she felt confident that if she could point it in the right direction, she could get the windrider to the gap. Then all she had to do was hover, activate the components of the bomb, and push it out the back. It couldn't be that complicated.

The nearest speakstone, the one from the Longseer in the scout windrider, spoke again. "Tallan preserve us! The elfonnel changed size and ran right into Badurach Pass. The entire opening is filling with earth."

The ear-scout tried to ask a question, but the Longseer cried, "Oh, no! It just consumed the barricade wall. Just buried it and everyone there. Wait. Look out! Go! Go!"

The voice cut off abruptly, and the ashen-faced ear-scout looked up at Wolfram. "I think they're gone, sir. But I don't see how. They were so high."

Looking grave, Wolfram turned back to Ingrid. "Builder Ingrid, you are perhaps our best hope. Take the windrider. Drop that bomb on that monster. Go with the Tallan's blessing."

"I won't let you down!" Ingrid cried.

One of the ear-scouts pressed a speakstone into her hand and gave her a little hug. "Keep us posted, and good luck."

Clutching the little stone to her chest, she rushed from the room. A cheer went up from the ear-scouts she had grown to love, and she vowed to destroy the monster that threatened their lives. She was a Builder, and it was her duty to protect.

The idea terrified her, and filled her with quivering excitement at the same time. Running helped, so she sprinted for the windrider. It waited in a little, walled courtyard, guarded by a pair of Allcarvers. When she burst through the door, they had already learned of her mission.

One of them saluted as the other hoisted her up onto the high wagon seat. "Good luck, Builder. Strike it down for all of us."

"I will!"

The wagon felt so much bigger when she was the only person riding in it, but surely the weight of that huge bomb in the bed would help settle her flight.

She glanced back at the Last Word bomb and wondered if it was really powerful enough to destroy a giant monster. It looked simple enough, just an enormous ceramic pot, over two feet in diameter, resting on fat, stubby legs, sealed with a plug of granite, surrounding a tiny core of diorite.

It was filled with a special blend of chemicals and materials that produced intense, explosive fire. Ingrid didn't know exactly how it worked, but did understand that she needed to open wide the release rate on the diorite core before pushing it out of the windrider. Then fly away as fast as possible.

First, get there.

Grasping the control handles, she felt for the thrusters and threw wide the release rate on all of them. Wind howled through the little courtyard, driving the Allcarvers back as the thrusters activated. The heavy wagon lurched off the ground, but twisted in the air and crashed into one of the walls.

Ingrid yelped as the impact nearly unseated her. She wished Uncle Dierk had installed those safety harnesses in this windrider too. Maybe she shouldn't have activated the directional thrusters yet.

The wagon pitched and spun, and for a second she feared it might tip over. The heavy bomb rocked up on two of its stubby feet, pulling against the restraining straps. If those straps gave, she doubted the gate across the back of the open-topped wagon bed would prevent the bomb from tumbling right out.

Terror helped Ingrid gain control, and she eased back the front thrusters while throwing wide the back. The wagon pitched forward so far, only her braced legs and grip on the control handles kept her from toppling right over the front. That was enough to orient the windrider better toward the open sky though, and it shot into the air, barely clearing the top of the wall.

"Good luck, Builder!" the Blades called again, a new edge of concern in their voices.

"I will not fail," Ingrid promised as she worked to even out the various thrusters and level the wagon. As she rose higher over the plateau, it seemed everyone was running. The entire camp was in commotion as soldiers rushed to form defensive lines and the thousands of non-Petralist forces helped evacuate the camp.

The early morning air was cool, but sweat dripped into her eyes as she worked the controls. After what seemed an eternity, she oriented the windrider toward the distant gap. She had never flown very high, so she tried leveling at a hundred feet, then threw wide the release rate on the rear push thrusters. With a satisfying roar, the windrider accelerated toward the gap at the top of the plateau, just over a mile distant.

When she focused on it, wishing she had a pair of long-vision goggles, she noticed waves of earth pouring through the gap and soldiers fleeing back from the barricades.

With a sinking feeling of dread, she realized she wasn't flying nearly high enough.

CHAPTER TWENTY-TWO

"Does the river choose to flow when the dam bursts?"

~Evander

Snapping his long-vision goggles into place, Hamish focused on the distant elfonnel, about four miles away. Even though it was slightly smaller than the one that had savaged the Carraig, it seemed just as deadly and destructive.

"How is it possible?" Jean asked, her voice trembling with fear as she stared through her own goggles.

"I don't know, but it's bad. Connor's not here to destroy it."

"Surely all of the Petralists in the army can stop it," Jean said hopefully.

"With our help, maybe they can."

The army at the Carraig had been so overpowered by that elfonnel, but there were ten times as many Petralists on the plateau. With his enhanced bomb to tip the tide in their favor, maybe they did stand a chance.

Earth was still exploding out of the pass, a hundred-foot horizontal avalanche. The elfonnel was already charging through the steep-walled canyon that led down from the pass. It leaped right over the barricade walls, ignoring the Petralists trying to flee, or the few tertiaries attempting to strike at it with elemental power. The wave of earth smashed through those barricades, sweeping away the defenders and burying them in an unstoppable flood.

"Oh, Hamish," Jean breathed. "They can't get away fast enough."

The sight sickened him. They had to destroy that monster.

The Sappers had formed a barricade line facing the southern canyon, and when Hamish focused on them, the mighty tower in the center drew his gaze. Anton stood upon the forty-foot turret, facing the charging monster, flanked by the other Sappers.

Water Moccasins held the left side, already prepared with a series of inverted waterfalls that tumbled back upon themselves in constant motion. The impressive display still looked minuscule compared to the avalanche the elfonnel brought with it. Flameweavers held the right side, and those men and women were already wreathed in white-hot flames.

As soon as the elfonnel charged out of the canyon, the ground between it and the Sappers buckled as the Petralists attempted to block its path. At the same time, the water moccasins flung vast sheets of glittering liquid at the monster.

Earth sprayed past the elfonnel, intercepting the waters and burying them in a muddy landslide. The Flameweavers struck next, but the elfonnel seemed to ignore the fire raging around his head. It charged into that broken, fractured land between it and the Sappers.

And stopped.

Its whole body quivered, leaning forward, as if pushing against a mighty, invisible weight, but somehow the Sappers managed to hold it back. If they could hold for just a few minutes, Hamish could get there and drop the most powerful bomb ever built.

He was not the first flyer to advance on the monster.

Hamish noticed a tiny shape flying past its head, seeming to wobble in midair. He focused on the windrider, and suddenly felt only terror.

Ingrid.

What was she doing flying a windrider alone, and so close to that monster? Then he noticed the heavy object in the bed of her wagon, straining against the restraining straps during the wild pitching of her nearly out-of-control flight.

She had the other bomb.

He snatched up his speakstone and shouted, "This is Builder Hamish. What is Ingrid doing up there?"

"Oh, Builder," cried the ear-scout immediately. "Can you help her? She promised she could fly that wagon, but she's having so much trouble."

"I'm just reaching the northern end of the plateau now. I've got another bomb with me. Tell her to retreat, and I'll take care of the elfonnel."

"Hold on," the ear-scout said. "I'm bringing you to her speakstone so you can communicate directly."

Hamish glanced at Jean, who pushed her goggles back and said, "She's so brave, but she's far too close."

"I'm glad we got here when we did."

Hamish pivoted the wagon a little so he could add some secondary directional thrusters and gain another half-raptor bit of speed. All the push thrusters were wide open already. Focusing on the distant elfonnel, he was encouraged to see new waves of fire and water tearing at the monster. Then a blinding light erupted right in front of it.

"Cursed Solas," he muttered, blinking for several seconds to restore his sight.

When he looked back, it took a moment to locate Ingrid. She had set her windrider into a hover not far from the monster, had left her seat, and clambered into the back of the wagon.

"No," Hamish groaned. Ingrid was so tiny, so young. She reminded him of his sisters, and seeing her in such danger terrified him.

He watched as she stiffened and pulled a speakstone from her belt pouch. "Builder Hamish, is that you?"

"Yes! I'm nearly there. I can see you."

She looked up, but of course he was still too far away to see with unaided sight.

"Get out of there," Hamish cried. "You're too close."

"I'm going to drop the bomb," she said, and the pride in her voice made him want to slap her.

"You can't drop it from there." Hamish kept his voice as calm as possible. "The blast would kill you too."

The monster seemed enraged that its forward progress was being hindered. Movement behind it drew his gaze, and his hopes sank.

Obrioner forces had followed it through the gap and were moving to flank the beast. Somehow they must be controlling the elfonnel, and that boded very badly for Granadure.

"Oh." Ingrid's voice took on an unmistakable note of fear. "I don't think I can go much higher."

"You don't have to. Just retreat. I'll take care of it."

Before she could respond, the elfonnel tipped its head up toward her. She was hovering barely higher than its back, so it was a miracle it hadn't noticed her sooner.

"Go!" Hamish and Jean shouted together.

Her scream echoed from the speakstone as the monster lunged, its terrifying maw opening wide, a dozen snake-like tongues snapping toward her. They yanked her and the bomb from the wagon just as those huge jaws snapped shut over it.

Another blinding light erupted around the wagon, blocking his view. Through the speakstone, he heard shattering timber and a final scream, which abruptly cut off.

Hamish stared at the stone in his hand, his heart suddenly cold, grief blinding him more than the Solas ever could. The Last Word never detonated. He had hoped the force of those jaws clamping shut over it would have triggered the explosion, but something had gone wrong.

"She can't be gone," Jean whispered, her face pale, her expression horrified.

Hamish would take care of it.

Blinking back tears, he scoured every thruster for any reserves of untapped power. The windrider thundered across the plain toward the monster. He was still two miles away, flying at over two thousand feet. He'd never drawn so much power from the thrusters before, but he didn't care that he might exhaust them before reaching the monster.

They'd hold. They had to.

If they didn't, he'd use his suit to carry the bomb the rest of the way. Nothing could prevent him from destroying that thing.

Obrioner forces attacked the Grandurian lines. New waves of earth smashed into the broken, contested land between the armies, while sheets of flame and tendrils of water rippled back and forth through the air above. The combined might of the Grandurian Petralists had held the elfonnel at bay, but they could never hope to do so and fight off the Obrioner Petralists too.

"Order the retreat." Hamish barely recognized the harsh, angry voice as his own. His initial grief had morphed into rage hotter than any Flameweaver fire. "Get everyone out of there, or they will die."

"On your word, Builder," the ear-scout replied, her voice quivering with grief. "Kill that thing. I'll warn the general that detonation is imminent."

"Can't you go faster?" Jean asked, her eyes blazing with fury as hot as his.

"Make sure your harness is tight. The ride will get rough when I blow this thing."

As Hamish covered the last two miles up the plateau, passing above thousands of men and women fleeing the plain, the rear guard began to retreat.

They had waited too long.

As Hamish had feared, the additional attack from the Obrioner forces tipped the balance, and the Grandurian resistance cracked. The elfonnel suddenly lunged forward against the right flank. Flameweavers rocketed off the ground to escape its path, like a flock of bright sparrows.

As the Grandurian forces scrambled to react, the elfonnel charged north, around the Sapper picket, which was retreating under a concentrated barrage from the Obrioner Petralists.

Unchallenged, the monster tore into the main camp and began smashing everything. It did not bury the entire camp in a wave of earth as Hamish feared it might, so perhaps the Sappers were still doing some good.

Hamish reached the monster and slowed to a hover high above.

"What are you waiting for?" Jean demanded, gesturing toward the huge bomb. "Aren't you going to drop that?"

"I don't know how many people are still down there. The blast will kill anyone not yet clear."

"Can they drive it south again?" Jean asked, glancing over the side at the fierce elemental battle raging along the southern edge of the plateau. The Grandurian lines were holding as they retreated, but they seemed barely able to withstand the concentrated Obrioner attack. More Obrioner soldiers were swarming into the camp, following the path of destruction the monster had left.

"Is anyone still in the Hub?" Hamish called into the speakstone.

"I'm one of the last," said the ear-scout who he had been speaking with. "Everyone else has evacuated."

"Can you get me in touch with Anton?"

"Hold on." A moment later her voice came back "Anton I have Builder Hamish for you."

"The voice of a friend, like the streaming sunlight after a storm, gladdens the heart."

"I think I can help stop this thing," Hamish said. "But my bomb is going to destroy everything on the southern half of the plateau. Can you shield everyone?"

"At the first sign of danger, the chicken spreads her wings over her young ones, but the fox may yet rend and tear."

"It's the best option we have," Hamish said, resisting the urge to fly down to Anton and punch him in the nose.

The bulk of the army had already evacuated the camp, but the elfonnel could easily run them down. A rear guard of Rumblers and Wingrunners was forming at the northern end of the camp, a desperate line of defense against the Obrioner forces that were streaming into camp.

The plateau would be overrun. There was no salvaging it now, and if Hamish did not act soon, he would miss his chance, or one of the Firetongues would notice him and burn him out of the sky. "You have ten seconds. Initiating the drop now."

The elfonnel was busy smashing through the camp, closing on the command tent. Hamish set the windrider to hover in that direction on an intercept course. Then he leaped into the back and used his belt knife to slash through the restraining ropes holding the bomb in place.

"Do you need help?" Jean asked.

"No. Stay there and make sure you're buckled tight. This will only take a second."

He gripped the stone plug sealing the mouth of the bomb and opened his Builder senses to it. The granite tasted like crackers in his mind, and the core of diorite that extended down into the heart of the bomb felt like licking lightning.

The bomb was the most powerful one he and Dierk had ever designed. In addition to the core of diorite, the bomb already contained a second piece of precious diorite, the size of a chisel, carefully ground to single grains of powder, with the release rate thrown wide. It was packed into the huge, spherical pottery jar with a deadly mixture of highly reactive chemicals.

Unlike previous bombs, this one contained one other unique component. Hamish reached through the diorite core with Builder senses and activated the slate. Maybe it would help counter some of the monster's connection with the earth in the critical second the bomb detonated. Then he did the same with the diorite, and recoiled with a gasp from the stone. It felt like he'd unleashed a lightning storm within the bomb. It seemed impossible that it hadn't already exploded. All it needed now was an impact to trigger the massive blast.

A bomb with but a fraction of that power had leveled half of Carbrey's camp near Alasdair. A small handful of diorite had ripped open the elfonnel at the Carraig. Now Hamish silently prayed this monster bomb would be enough to destroy the monster that had just eaten Ingrid and killed so many people.

As Hamish clambered back to his seat on the high pilot bench and strapped in, Jean touched his arm. "Hamish, there are a lot of Obrioner soldiers down there too."

He read the same conflict in her eyes that he felt. He loved his country, even though he'd been driven out of it by a stupid law. Now he was about to unleash unrivaled destruction upon the plateau and probably kill more of his own countrymen than any Grandurian ever had.

"I don't have any other choice," he said softly. "They chose to attack."

"I know," she said, tears in her eyes. "I hate that you're forced to do this." Her expression hardened and she added, "But you have to."

"Hold on then," he told her, preparing to flip the wagon and send the bomb tumbling out.

A groan echoed through the speakstone. "Ha. . .Hamish?"

"Ingrid!" he shouted, barely believing it. Jean clutched his arm, grinning with joy.

"Oh, Hamish." Ingrid's voice quivered with agony. "It feels like everything is broken."

"Where are you?" He glanced again at the monster as it shattered the command tent, directly below him, perfectly situated for the bomb drop.

"I'm in its belly," Ingrid said in a terrified voice. "It's like a big room, filled with black acid. It dissolved the wood and stone from the wagon, and the thrusters just cracked. I used part of the speakstone power to form a shieldstone to protect me and the bomb, but the shield is so small, and it's fading fast. I'm scared."

"I know what to do," Hamish told her, trying to sound calm and confident. "I'm going to drop my bomb. It'll break that thing open. When it does, you use that quartzite to launch yourself out. Do you understand?"

"Oh, Hamish, I knew you'd know," Ingrid said, her voice filled with hope and relief. "Hurry. I can't hold this shield for long."

"Dropping it now," Hamish assured her. Then he glanced at Jean and said, "Hold on."

The elfonnel was still rooting around over the wreckage of the command tent, as if celebrating. Even more than a mile below him, the monster seemed to fill the plateau.

Hamish gripped the control rods and abruptly changed the release rate on the thrusters. The wagon pitched forward, flipping an entire spin in the air. Only the safety straps prevented them from getting thrown clear.

Jean screamed, and the Last Word fell free and plummeted toward the monster.

"Tallan eat your soul," Hamish growled as he righted the windrider, added more lift, then sidled sideways to watch the bomb fall. He wanted to see it split wide open.

"It's away, Ingrid. Get ready."

"I am!"

As the bomb fell, Hamish refused to look at the Obrioner soldiers pushing into the camp. They would die with the monster, but he could not have made a different choice. The line of Sappers, led by Anton, had retreated to the north and, as the bomb fell, they sank into the ground, along with the last of the rear guard.

"I hope this works," Jean whispered, gripping Hamish's arm so tight, it felt like she was cutting off the circulation right through the armored sleeve of his flying suit.

The elfonnel seemed to sense danger, because it suddenly tipped its huge head back, and Hamish looked down into those enormous, silver eyes.

The bomb struck.

It hit the elfonnel at the tail end and blew the rear third of its torso clean off. Howling flames ripped the air. The concussion shattered earth and dislodged the heavy snow pack at the peak of Badurach Pass.

The explosion was even bigger than Hamish had feared, fire erupting across the entire upper half of the plateau. It engulfed the elfonnel, and snarling fire and tortured air boiled high into the air toward him.

The shock wave struck the windrider so hard timbers cracked and several thrusters snapped free. Again the safety straps saved Jean's life, but she screamed under the wrenching, spinning motion of the wagon. Hamish had buckled in too, and he instinctively fired some of his own suit thrusters to help stabilize them.

For a moment he knew nothing but terrifying pitching and tumbling as the turbulent air howled around them and tossed the heavy wagon like a leaf in a swollen spring river. His vision spun wildly, and his stomach couldn't take the brutal spinning. He vomited, spraying the contents of his last meal in an arc that could have beat his record if he could have found a way to measure the distance. Jean screamed again.

It took precious seconds to level out the crippled wagon. He had drifted far from the epicenter of the explosion and fallen a thousand feet toward the earth before stabilizing their hover. He gasped when he peered over the side to see the results of the explosion. The entire southern half of the plateau was a charred wasteland.

The rear third of the elfonnel was simply gone, two of its other legs were shattered, and its torso was cracked and blackened.

It wasn't moving.

Hamish focused his long-vision goggles on it. The monster was frozen in place, as if the fervent heat of the bomb had melted its armored hide and fused it into one huge brick.

"Did it work?" Jean asked. "Do you see Ingrid?"

"No." The blast hadn't split open the monster the way he had hoped.

Then one of its huge, silver eyes blinked.

"Tallan take you!" Hamish shouted. The elfonnel at the Carraig had repeatedly healed itself from seemingly fatal injuries. Could this one actually recover from such a blast?

Ingrid began to scream. Her cries echoing from the speakstone. "The acid! Oh, Hamish, it burns. I can't get out."

She was still alive! "We'll think of something," he assured her, but his voice sounded thin and unconvincing, even to him.

His mind had gone blank. He felt like he was living a nightmare. Several times since the battle at the Carraig he'd awakened in a cold sweat, heart pounding with fear. Always in the dream, he'd watched Verena, then Connor get swallowed by the elfonnel, but had lacked the diorite needed to blow open its belly. Now Ingrid was stuck inside, and he couldn't save her.

"Hamish?" Jean asked softly, renewed fear in her eyes. "What do we do?" The fact that she looked to him, that she believed in him, only heightened his sense of helpless fury.

"I'm a Builder," Ingrid moaned. "We protect. I can still help. I have the bomb."

"No," Hamish sobbed. "Ingrid, let me think, please."

Jean gripped his arm and they shared a horrified look. She knew the truth, and tears ran down her cheeks. She reached for the speakstone, as if she could somehow touch Ingrid and comfort her.

The bomb inside the elfonnel's stomach detonated.

For an eyeblink, the monster was outlined by white-hot brilliance, then its torso simply exploded, its vast bulk disintegrating under the second earth-shattering blast. Flames tore across the already-devastated area.

Then that blistering fire solidified into long streamers of boiling flame that flowed up the shattered plateau. It slithered over the avalanche-buried defensive walls, then formed a gigantic, burning archway at the end of Badurach Pass.

The tons of snow that had fallen from the peak had buried the pass in white, but now they melted into a river that flowed out over the plateau, pouring through that burning archway. The flood carried several figures, who stood upon the waters.

144

Chapter Twenty-Three

"The time of my choice is at hand and the world will bear witness if I chose folly or wisdom."

~Evander

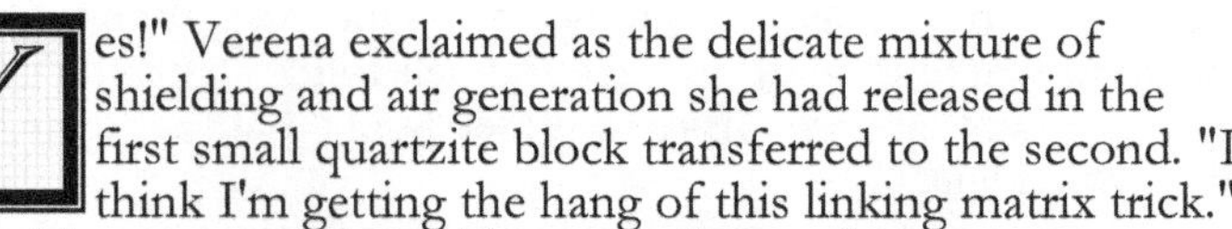

es!" Verena exclaimed as the delicate mixture of shielding and air generation she had released in the first small quartzite block transferred to the second. "I think I'm getting the hang of this linking matrix trick."

There was really nothing quite like exploring new concepts and teasing out new inventions. Kissing Connor came close, most of the time.

"Do you really think this will help you design a non-Builder flying wagon?" Connor asked.

The two stood at one of Verena's work tables in her huge workroom. Martys loitered nearby, eating some of the stale breadsticks Hamish had left behind.

"I think I'm getting close. I'm designing a keystone that will contain the thruster commands to allow a non-Builder to activate the various thrusters on their wagon."

"Is that enough?" Connor had waited patiently while she teased out the patterns of power within the quartzite, and the way he frowned in thought was simply adorable.

"What do you mean?"

He shrugged. "Flying is more than just riding a blast of air. I've tried it enough to know. How does a non-Builder make all the necessary adjustments they'll need?"

Verena sighed. "After the keystone, that's my biggest worry. How do we teach people to adjust for air hiccups or exhaustion pockets? We don't even know how they form or how to tell if we're going to hit one."

"I don't even know what those terms mean."

"Flying is so new, we've had to come up with a lot of new terms. There's slip-spin-drag, rollover rates, and wind-howl to name a few."

Connor grinned. "We've got to get Jean to write all this down."

"Good idea. I've named the flight principles we've identified, but we haven't done well at documenting everything."

"You'll need to if you're going to train new flyers." Connor found a sheet of parchment. "I can start taking notes and hand them off to Jean when we get to the pass."

Verena pushed her hair behind one ear and organized her thoughts. "Wind changes the faster you go. At low speeds, it's like a breeze. It's no big deal."

"As long as you don't spit straight ahead," Connor offered with a grin.

"Exactly what Hamish said," Verena smiled. "At higher speeds, or turning fast, it increases like a tempest. When it reaches the point where it's hard to hear yourself think, that's the wind-howl moment, and you have to understand what that does to flight balancing."

"Flight balancing is hard way before that point," Connor said. "At least when I try to use quartzite."

"Everyone has different tolerances. There's the stomach-lurch syndrome, for example. Some people lose their breakfast just spinning around fast a few times. They can't tolerate some of the stuff we do in the air."

The door of the workroom burst open and Kilian rushed in, followed by Ilse. "Pack your things," he ordered, his expression grave. "We're heading for Badurach Pass immediately."

"What happened?" Verena asked.

"The war has begun," Ilse said, her tone grave.

Verena exchanged a worried glance with Connor. It was too soon. They weren't ready.

"What do you know?" she asked.

Kilian said, "The Obrioner army attacked the pass, and Dougal used an elfonnel to lead the charge."

"How?" Connor asked. He looked as worried as Verena felt.

"I felt the stirrings through the elements," Kilian said. "Wolfram has contingencies in place for worst-case scenarios, but for elfonnel, those mostly involve delaying tactics until he can retreat."

"So there's an elfonnel rampaging through Granadure now?" Verena asked, horrified by the idea.

"That's bad, right?" Martys asked. Verena couldn't read his expression and wondered how he felt about his homeland invading.

"Just about the worst thing possible," Connor said.

Ilse said, "I think it may be gone already. When I connected with the earth, I felt something churning the ground from the direction of the pass, even from this distance. Then, all of a sudden, it disappeared."

"How is that possible?" Connor asked. "From everything we know about them, a rampaging elfonnel could rage for days, right?"

"We won't know until we get there," Kilian said, radiating impatience. "We've delayed here too long. Grab everything you can. We're leaving."

Verena said, "We'll take my windrider. We can't all fit on the Swift, and I'll need to fly."

"You can tether the Swift to the wagon," Kilian offered.

She nodded, already calculating how much they could cram into the available space. "It'll be tight, but I think we can all fit."

"We're not taking that many people," Connor pointed out. "Just us."

"Plus Erich and Anika," Ilse added.

Verena said, "I plan to bring along the materials to finish a new flying craft I've started working on." She gestured to the back of her workroom at the new construction project.

Connor chuckled. "I still say it looks like you dropped a windrider into a hurricane."

Wood and struts and quartzite blocks were strewn all around the skeletal framework of the new craft that stood not far from her windrider. It would be maybe a third of the size of one of the huge flying wagons when it was finished.

Kilian said, "I like the idea of getting a team transport platform in the air, but only if we can load it fast."

"We can be ready in less than half an hour," Verena promised. "We can finish assembly at Harz."

"Maybe sooner," Martys said. "I'll help ye make sure we've got all the tools and materials on board, and we'll have yer new flying craft done afore we reach the front."

"Really?" Connor asked, his voice echoing the same surprise Verena felt. "I thought you were a Guardian."

Martys grinned. "Dinnae mean a bloke can't learn other crafts in the long, cauld winters, do it?"

Kilian hesitated. "It may not be a great time for you to visit the front, but we'll worry about that when we get there. Let's move, people. Dougal's rash action threatens Obrion as much as it does Granadure. We don't have time to waste."

CHAPTER TWENTY-FOUR

"The bird may be caged to keep away the ravages of the hunter."
~Evander

In less than an hour, the heavily-loaded windrider lifted into the air above the Builder compound with a blast of huge lift thrusters. Wind howled around the group, and as always the air generated by quartzite smelled of fresh, high mountain meadows. It was a scent that always reminded Connor of Verena.

Most of the team wore heavy flying leathers to ward against the cold of the high elevations. Kilian didn't bother.

He sat beside Verena on the high front bench in a simple white, long-sleeved linen shirt, trimmed in black, with a standing collar. He'd also donned a light-weight, brown leather jacket, but had not fastened the silver buckles. He did not look cold, but lounged on the high bench with an ease that belied his haste.

Connor stood in the long bed of the wagon, directly behind Verena. Ilse sat on a pile of speedslings nearby. Erich and Anika reclined against the right wall of the wagon bed.

The bulk of the large wagon bed was taken up by the skeleton of the new flying craft, along with stacks of wood and other materials. Uncle Martys stood back there, talking to himself and planning the construction. Verena's Swift hovered behind the windrider, tethered to the big wagon by a secure line and piled high with mechanicals.

"How long do you think it'll take to reach the pass?" Connor asked.

Verena thought for a moment. "Depends on the winds. Windriders aren't fast, but I've got the push thrusters opened to three quarters. If we maintain this speed, we'll probably arrive some time after dark."

Kilian grimaced. "Can you increase speed?"

"I can, but they'll be nearly spent by the time we get there."

"Nearly spent is fine. Just make sure we don't have to land and refit replacements."

Verena touched one of the long, quartzite-lined levers in front of her that connected to the various thrusters. The roar of the big push thrusters at the rear of the windrider intensified.

"Do you think Hamish and Jean are there?" Connor asked, voicing his greatest fear.

Verena nodded, and when she glanced back at him, he read the same concern in her eyes. "Once we get closer, maybe I can reach him through the speakstone. This high up, we'll get pretty good range."

Martys joined Connor near the front. "Well laddie, 'twill be a right bonnie little wagon we mean to build."

Verena asked, "Are you sure you understand what I need?"

"Aye, lass," Martys assured her. "This here wee project be no great challenge. Come on, laddie. Work's a-lurkin'." He beckoned Ilse, then Erich and Anika over too.

Connor slid one hand along the main left-side beam. The plan called for a compact craft that could still hold nine people in three rows near the front, protected by wooden sides. It would be a tight fit sitting next to a big guy like Erich.

They lacked time and materials to add armored plating like the Swift, and the rear cargo bed would be open like the windrider. Martys had already updated the plan to include a series of clever storage boxes underneath to hold replacement thrusters and other critical supplies.

Martys lifted a wide wooden plank, already cut to the proper length by the dozen workmen Verena had summoned to help prepare for the trip. "Lend a hand, laddie."

He passed the other end to Erich, handed Ilse a hammer, and set her to securing the plank. Once he felt they understood what he wanted, he and Anika began working on the other side.

Like all kids in Alasdair, Connor had done some carpentry growing up, and it was obvious neither Ilse or Erich were much of a hand with hammer and nail. So by the third plank, Connor had commandeered the hammer. The windrider wagon bed usually felt huge, but packed with mechanicals and flying several thousand feet in the air, it wasn't the most comfortable workplace.

"Ye look like ye know how to use that," Martys commented after a few minutes.

Connor shrugged. "Hammers run in our family. As a kid, I used to practice all the time to be ready for the day I got to try the Ashlar's hammer."

Martys chuckled. "Ye planned to skip the years of training?"

"When you're a kid, all you focus on is the hammer."

Of course, when he finally had gotten a chance to try it, he'd broken his father's precious hammer. He had also shattered an entire block of granite in a single blow, and had gotten his first glimmer at the power concealed within deadly diorite.

Over the next hours as they worked, the new flying craft began to take real shape. Martys was truly a master craftsman, and he ensured the planks fit together snugly. Somehow his handiwork made the rough carpentry seem far more impressive.

They quickly boxed in the outer shell. While Connor and the others added planking for the floor, Martys assembled all of the storage compartments, including tight-fitting doors. He worked efficiently, as if he'd assembled similar projects a hundred times.

"How did you get so good at this?" Connor asked as Martys oversaw the installation of the three rows of chairs facing the front.

"I told ye. In times of long peace, when me mates would be getting all scunnered with the boredom, I learned I prefer to keep me hands busy. It helps keep the beast docile."

Connor regarded him thoughtfully. He hadn't really thought about how difficult it might be for soldiers conditioned to unleash the monster within to deal with extended peace.

"This beast," Ilse said, leaning against the far side of the craft. "You speak of the lust for battle?"

Martys nodded. "Ye be a warrior. I cannae believe ye huv nae felt the beast within when ye fight."

"I've felt it," Ilse admitted. "But you speak as if it's a good thing to embrace animal fury."

Martys shrugged. "I dinnae ken how ye fight in Granadure, but if'n ye won't do what ye must to win, ye've already lost."

"When land, we train," Erich said, sounding eager.

He added something in Granadure and Ilse translated for him. "He wants to see if your inner beast's head is thick enough to take a real bash fight."

Martys returned Erich's grin with a predatory look. "I like the way ye think, mate."

The turn in the conversation began to worry Connor. Erich was one of the best bash fighters he'd ever met. He sensed that both Erich and Martys might not hold back once they began fighting, and they couldn't afford for either of them getting hurt.

Martys seemed to have an unquenchable curiosity about their family and Alasdair. Despite all the questions he'd asked while they worked, he spoke little of his own childhood.

So to change the subject, Connor asked, "When you were growing up, did you get to swim much, Uncle?"

"Not enough, laddie. In the youth barracks we kept a strict schedule most days. I reckon ye swam a lot more."

"We did. Although Jean didn't like jumping off the rocks so much. We liked to try impressing her by how high we jumped."

He glanced toward the front where Verena and Kilian had turned to listen. Maybe he shouldn't mention how badly he'd wanted to win the first kiss from Jean.

"Sounds like heaven," Martys said. "But ye cannae tell me ye boys were all saintly little weans all the time. What did ye do to make yer mothers yearn to skelp yer behinds?"

When he hesitated, Verena teased, "We know you've got stories to tell, Connor."

"There's a reason you haven't heard them yet."

She laughed, but then raised an eyebrow expectantly. So Connor sighed and said, "Fine. I'll think of one."

"While ye talk, let's finish workin'," Martys suggested.

He directed Erich and Anika in extracting large blocks of stone from wooden crates stacked at the very back of the windrider. First came several pieces of marble, which Verena called Puking Dooms.

"Hamish's name," she explained. "They're defensive weapons that fire intense jets of flame. They work best underneath because of how much lift they generate."

While they installed the puking dooms, Connor told them about the time he and Hamish snuck into the tannery south of town the night before the Sogail. They were going to turn seven years old that year and hoped to find scrap pieces of leather to make armor for their mock battles. Instead, they had stumbled upon a slowly boiling vat of hide glue.

The large pail of hot glue they took hardened before they could decide how to use it. The only logical thing to do was hide it in the chimney of the temporary oven used for Sogail cooking in the town square. Stuart's shrew of a mother had arrived to begin work on her famous overnight stew and they'd fled before she spotted them.

"You didn't leave the glue there, did you?" Verena chuckled.

Connor shrugged as Martys finished securing the last block of marble. "We didn't have any choice. We thought it was safe up there, but she must have adjusted the damper and tipped the bucket. By the next morning, the glue had softened and leaked into her stew."

Connor laughed at the memory. "When she took the stew off the fire, the glue congealed and turned the entire pot into a solid block."

Martys roared with laughter, and the others joined in. It felt good to talk about times when such silly misadventures had seemed so earth shattering.

"Thanks for the story," Verena said, still chuckling. "I don't think I would've heard that any other way." She actually gave Martys a warm smile. "You've got a gift for getting people to talk."

"I cannae think of a better way to pass the time while working."

While they installed a pair of extra-long speedslings full of deadly hornets along the base on both sides of the craft, Connor asked, "What are you going to call it?"

While Verena considered the question, Ilse suggested, "How about the Raptor?"

"It may not be that nimble," Verena said. "Although it will be extremely fast."

"You give name," Anika prodded as she fastened the last of the control rods to the front panel.

"It'll come to me," Verena promised

"Maybe after you take it up for the first time," Kilian suggested.

"Well, we're nearly finished," Connor told Verena. "We just need to attach the main thrusters. Are you sure you brought the right ones? The only quartzite I see back here are replacements for the windrider."

"Those are the ones. Like I said, I designed it to be fast."

Connor whistled softly. Fitted with thrusters designed to move the enormous windriders, the smaller craft might fly right out from under them.

It took only a few minutes to install the thrusters, then Connor clambered up onto the high front seat beside Verena. "It's ready for you to inspect."

Verena kissed his cheek. "I'm amazed you got so much done."

"Thank Martys. He did most of the work."

Martys perched on a crate of supplies behind the bench, looking at ease in the sky. "Ye have talent for design, lass. Made me job easier."

"I can't wait to test it," Verena said.

"Go check it out," Connor suggested. "This wagon will keep flying, right?"

152

She gestured south toward a line of hills they were quickly approaching. "We're almost to Harz Fortress."

A moment later they got their first view of the walled fortress. The sun was already low on the western horizon, and late afternoon shadows made it hard to see a lot of details from so far out.

The fortress was gray walled and grim, with an outer curtain wall, a thick inner wall, and a compact, solid-looking keep, surrounded by several tall towers. A large lake just north of the fortress reflected crimson-tinged clouds, and a sizable town spread from the fortress and along the northeastern side of the lake.

They had to be getting close to the pass because the mighty Maclachlan Mountains blocked the southern horizon, and they could clearly make out the snowy peak of Mount Macduib. Connor reminded himself to learn the Grandurian names for the mountains, but it was a bit confusing sometimes to think of places having multiple names. Seemed a waste of time somehow.

Kilian pointed toward the fort. "Let's land at Harz. Hopefully they'll know what happened."

Verena pointed. "From the number of troops I see, we're looking at the army."

Kilian frowned. "That would mean the pass is lost."

"Not surprising if'n what ye said about elfonnel be true." Martys said.

"Perhaps," Kilian said, still frowning.

"If that's the army, I'll try Hamish," Verena said. After a brief pause she asked, "Hamish, can you hear me?"

Hamish's voice echoed from her helmet almost immediately. "Verena! It's so good to hear your voice. Where are you?"

"We're en route to Harz. We know there was an elfonnel."

"We killed it." Hamish sounded close to tears, not exultant with victory like he should.

"Then did you hold the pass?" Verena asked. Connor and Kilian both leaned closer to hear.

"No. I'm here at Harz with Jean. We're with Wolfram. Get down here, and we'll explain."

"Can you tell me more?" Verena prodded.

"Just come down." Hamish sounded exhausted. "I don't want to tell it twice."

"We'll be there soon."

The push thrusters roared louder and the wagon shuddered as it accelerated. As they drew within a mile of the fortress with its massed army, they passed a hovering windrider with a Pathfinder in the back, flown by a hugely overweight Builder. Verena waved, but Kilian urged her to keep going.

Connor spotted two other windriders hovering high over the valley in the distance. He wondered how many were stationed up there. A Pathfinder could see for miles from that vantage, even in the gathering gloom of early evening.

They flew low over the open lands around the fortress, slowing as they passed over the massed troops. There were so many that they camped all around the fortress and up around the western side of the lake, across from the town. Their hundreds of campfires twinkled like the first stars of the evening.

"That's a lot of soldiers," Jean said.

"But not as many as there should be," Kilian replied, his expression grim. "There were nearly thirty thousand stationed at the pass. Unless Wolfram's got more hidden away somewhere, what I see there doesn't look like nearly enough."

They landed in a small courtyard behind the central fort, beside a couple parked windriders. A sergeant was already waiting for them, and he whisked them into one of the towers overlooking the fortress.

They found General Wolfram in a large conference room filled with worried-looking officials and packed with tables covered in maps and charts. Connor did not miss the fact that a pair of Boulders remained stationed by the door, watching him and Martys with the intensity of men eager to find any excuse for violence.

The broad-shouldered general looked the same as Connor remembered, although a frown creased his brows. During all the battles of Alasdair, Connor had never seen the man look so ruffled.

Wolfram greeted Kilian warmly. "My old friend, I've never been happier to see you. I wish you'd been with us this morning."

"Me too. What happened?"

"The worst-case scenario." Wolfram puffed out his long mustaches. He turned to Verena and grasped her hands. "As always, it is a pleasure to see you, my dear."

Verena gave him a hug. "We were so worried. Did you lose a lot of people?"

"More than we can afford."

Wolfram turned to Connor next, and his gaze seemed to bore deep, just like the last time they met in Alasdair. The general extended a hand. "And Connor. You have experienced much since I saw you last."

Connor took the hand. "Seems the entire world has changed."

154

"Let us hope we can set it right again. Thank you for coming."

Connor had respected Wolfram even during those trying days of conflict around his home. He knew now that Dougal was his enemy, but wasn't quite ready to believe Wolfram was a friend. The man was a general, and he would leverage every resource to his advantage, including Connor.

Martys saluted. "Evenin', General. I've heard much about ye, but dinnae think to meet ye without beating past all yer guards first."

Wolfram sized up Martys in an instant. "What brings a Grandurian Boulder here? You're either a man of uncommon bravery or a wondrous lack of sanity."

Martys shrugged. "Cannae say I'm worth getting up to high doh over, General." He gestured at Connor with a thumb. "I be here lookin' after me nephew."

"See that you keep out of trouble," Wolfram warned. "And don't wander far or I cannot guarantee your safety. My men are rather keyed up right now."

"We'll keep an eye on him," Ilse promised. Erich and Anika nodded enthusiastically.

Wolfram turned back to Kilian. "What do you know?"

"Not enough. I know there was an elfonnel."

"Did you know the heroic actions of a pair of Builders saved us from catastrophic defeat?"

Chapter Twenty-Five

"The fool celebrates ascending the foothills when the ultimate peak is still in sight."

~Evander

olfram sent for Hamish, Jean, and Anton. While they were waiting, Wolfram described the battle at the pass and their retreat.

"You said two Builders stopped it?" Connor asked.

Hamish and Jean entered the room, followed by Dierk, and it was clear they had been grieving. Jean's eyes were bloodshot, Hamish looked pale, his eyes a little wild. Dierk had a hollow, numb look in his eyes.

Wolfram said, "Hamish was one of the heroes of the day."

Hamish shook his head. "Ingrid was the hero."

"Where is she?" Verena asked, looking toward the door.

Hamish's shoulders slumped, and fresh tears glinted in Jean's eyes. Dierk spoke through a sob. "She tried to take the bomb to drop on the monster."

"Oh, no, she wasn't ready to fly alone!" Verena gasped.

"She did it, though." Jean said.

"And that monster ate her," Hamish growled. "She managed to activate a shieldstone, but it wasn't strong enough to protect her in the monster's belly."

"I'm so sorry." Connor saw the same remembered terror in Verena's eyes that he felt.

"I tried to save her," Hamish said, his voice anguished. "But my bomb didn't break open its belly like we hoped."

Jean said, "When it didn't, Ingrid realized she was trapped, but her shieldstone was running out. She had the bomb in there with her, and somehow she triggered it."

"Oh, Ingrid," Verena whispered, tears in her eyes. "She was too young to face a choice like that." Dierk began to sob, and she moved to his side and hugged him.

"I couldn't save her," Hamish said, looking at Connor with overwhelming sorrow.

"I should have been here," Dierk lamented. "If I had come earlier, she wouldn't have died."

Connor had only barely met Ingrid, but he had liked the girl. It was clear that the others who knew her had loved her.

"She killed it," Hamish said. "The second bomb destroyed that monster." He pulled a mangled-looking breadstick out of his pocket and started raising it to his mouth, but sighed, and extended it to Connor. "I can't eat anything right now, but it feels wrong if no one does."

Connor took it, deeply moved by his friend's grief. That tiny gesture told him more about how much Ingrid's death had affected Hamish than any number of words he might have used.

The breadstick looked worn, as if Hamish had pulled it out of his pocket only to return it again more than once. Connor usually avoided food from Hamish's pockets, but this time he took a big bite. Sometimes friends had to make sacrifices for each other.

Kilian gripped Dierk's shoulder. "We will honor her once we drive out the invaders. She helped prevent an unthinkable catastrophe."

Wolfram huffed into his long mustaches. "The unthinkable part is that Dougal would dare raise an elfonnel at all."

"He did it at the Carraig," Connor pointed out. "And he targeted his own people. It shouldn't surprise you he'd do the same thing against you."

"I underestimated him," Kilian said with a frown.

"How could you have guessed?" Wolfram asked. "No one has broken that treaty since the founding of Granadure."

"What treaty?" Connor asked.

Kilian said, "The Baltray Treaty. Every nation on the continent swore to never use elfonnel in battle again."

"Why would they agree to that?" Verena asked, sharing a puzzled look with Connor. "Elfonnel are the strongest weapons."

"The cost is too high," Kilian said. "Remember, after the Tallan Wars, the majority of the most powerful Petralists were dead. The nations were reeling, on the brink of losing all access to the elements. The empire had sundered, and every powerful Petralist was desperately needed."

He continued, "Worse, raising too many elfonnel can destabilize the elements and trigger catastrophes. During one pivotal battle of the Tallan Wars, just below what is now Althing, no less than five elfonnel clashed.

"It was too many. An entire corner of the continent broke free and sank into what are still known today as the Broken Waters on the eastern side of the Sea of Olcan."

Connor grimaced as he tried to imagine such a disaster.

"To protect the integrity of the continent, all nations agreed to the Treaty of Baltray, and it has remained inviolate until now."

"Dougal broke the treaty for a reason," Wolfram said, his voice thick with disgust. "In his very first assault, he has declared his intent to wage unrestricted warfare upon us."

Kilian said, "It appears the attack at the Carraig was Dougal's trial run. He has learned more about the deepest secrets than I had feared."

"If he knows so much," Hamish said with a frown. "Why was the elfonnel at the pass smaller?"

"At the Carraig, the elfonnel seemed to recover faster too," Jean added.

"Well, we didn't hit it with bombs nearly as big," Hamish pointed out.

Kilian had turned thoughtful. "Perhaps Dougal doesn't understand all the dangers. By raising a second earth-bound so soon after the Carraig, he risked destabilizing the mountains all along the border. Additionally, the elements need time to regenerate. The elfonnel at the Carraig consumed vast energies."

"Are you saying that elements can run out?" Connor asked.

"No. There is always earth and water and air, and fuel to burn in fires. But when too much elemental power is consumed, as would happen by raising too many elfonnel, the elements revolt. The nations would be shattered before anyone could exhaust them."

"Let's not upset them then," Connor urged, and Verena nodded.

The door opened and Anton entered. He looked unchanged from when Connor had met him briefly during the battles of Alasdair. His dark hair still held a hint of gray, and his black-eyed gaze held the same heavy weight.

He saluted Dierk. "The young sapling extended over the torrent may save a desperate soul, but the scent of the candle extinguished early lingers in the air."

"How did you manage to hold the monster back?" Kilian asked.

"Necessity is an unyielding mother, and desperation a teacher without rival."

"Could you do it again?" Kilian asked.

After only a brief hesitation Anton said, "The jackals united may bring down the mighty lion, but the wolf scatters the flock unprepared."

"We may never have so many Sappers together and ready to fight as a single unit again," Kilian said.

"Don't count on the fact that we could stop another one," Anton said. "We would not have held it long, even without the additional assault of the Obrioner vanguard."

Connor shared an incredulous look with Verena, and Hamish exclaimed, "Wait a minute! You just spoke clearly. I didn't think Sappers did that."

Anton smiled. "Do you suppose that we forget the simpler forms of speech when we choose to speak the language of deeper contemplation?"

"Why do you do it then?" Connor asked.

"Out of respect for the father of all Sentries. You have met Evander at the Carraig, yes?"

"But he's Obrioner," Hamish protested. "You're Grandurian."

Anton shrugged. "The earth knows his name, as do all who walk with it. He is the eldest, so we adopt the speech he has chosen."

Kilian grunted. "That boy has always spent too much time alone. I think he started talking in those irritating rhymes just to annoy me."

"Sentry speech started as a practical joke?" Connor asked. He couldn't quite bring himself to believe it.

Anton looked offended and Kilian made a dismissive gesture. "Never mind. Just a long-standing pet peeve of mine."

"I'm glad you shielded that rear guard below ground before the bomb struck," Hamish said. "Too many people died as it is."

"The wolves slaughter even when hunger is sated, but the raging storm spends itself against the mountain."

Connor felt a little better that Anton had used Sentry speak. It didn't feel right to speak with those who walked the earth without feeling frustrated afterward.

Wolfram said, "I wish we had managed to save the power stores, especially the weakening powder."

"They have the secret?" Verena exclaimed. "That's terrible."

"And they could turn it against us," Kilian said with a frown.

"I buried the cache and left it shielded," Anton explained, again speaking in unsettlingly clear words. "But I suspect the

Obrioners have unearthed it by now. The Dawnus who commanded the second wave appeared far too competent to miss it."

"It was Ivor," Hamish said. "Made an impressive entry using the waters from the avalanche and the flames from Ingrid's bomb."

"Sounds like Ivor," Connor said.

"You know him?" Wolfram asked.

"I consider him a friend." He hoped Ivor was all right.

"Ye may not get the luxury of treating him such if ye meet on the battlefield," Martys said with a grimace from where he lounged against one wall. He'd been content to listen to the conversation, and Connor had forgotten he was there. "Same as me, yer old mates might be rippin' to kill ye."

"If I get a chance to speak with him, he'll talk," Connor assured them. He had mentioned the truth about patronage, and he was sure Ivor would be eager to discuss it more.

"The listening hub was overrun," Wolfram said. "Most of the ear-scouts escaped, but some remained too long, trying to coordinate the rear guard. I fear our supply of speakstones is compromised."

Verena said, "We can shutter the power of the ones here, which will break the link with their twins. Then we can re-link them to new partners."

"Perhaps soon," Wolfram said. "All of our remaining stones were gathered into a secure location, and the intelligence corps is enacting a complex charade to pass misinformation in case the Obrioners are listening."

"Good idea," Kilian said. "How are defenses here?"

"Solid, but not as strong as I fear they need to be. Even if the Obrioners do not raise another elfonnel, they will hold the advantage."

"You trounced Carbrey at Alasdair," Connor pointed out.

"And we will bring to bear every stratagem we can invent," Wolfram assured him. "But Carbrey fields more Petralists. He will be hard to beat."

Connor decided to voice something he'd been mulling over for a while. "Have you considered combining your various affinity forces to magnify their effectiveness?"

Wolfram looked thoughtful. "We do tend to keep the various affinities isolated. Specialization of each group is a mighty weapon."

"But is it the strongest?" Connor asked. "I started exploring the idea during the Tir-raon, combining different affinities in our mock battles. It surprised everyone and gave us a big advantage. There have to be other ways to do that."

Kilian nodded, looking pleased by the idea. "In the past, that type of cooperation was more common. Through the last few centuries, as the number of Petralists has declined, so has that inter-affinity cooperation."

"What do you suggest?" Wolfram asked.

Verena spoke first and said enthusiastically, "Mud!"

"That would be a challenge," Connor agreed. He was thrilled but not surprised that she caught on to the idea so quickly.

Wolfram nodded thoughtfully. "Indeed. The heavy water content would make it hard for Sappers to manipulate, but such dense impurities of earth also make it onerous for the Water Moccasins."

"But what if a Sapper and a Water Moccasin worked together over the same mud pit?" Connor asked. "They could reinforce each other's control. With a little practice, they'd gain a huge advantage."

Verena grinned. "Enemy Sentries or Spitters would try intercepting it individually, which would dilute their control."

"I like it," Wolfram said, then glanced at Anton, who did not look thrilled. "Although it will take some convincing to get our Petralists to implement it."

Verena faced Anton, who stood nearly twice her height, and gave him a sweet smile. "You'll try it for me though, won't you?"

He sighed and she grinned. "I knew I could count on you."

"A beam of sunlight may penetrate the darkest abyss, yet lack the force of the radiant smile of jubilant youth."

"You say the sweetest things."

"I hope your team will remain to help," Wolfram said to Kilian. "Your presence will bolster morale and I have no doubt it would tip the balance in our favor."

Kilian hesitated for a second. "We'll be here, but not in the main force."

"Why not?" Wolfram asked.

"This war is personal for Dougal. The most likely reason he would dare break the Baltray so early in the war is to draw me out in anger to counterattack."

Wolfram nodded slowly. "I am definitely tempted to place you and Connor at the front. Together, we could shatter the Obrioner advance and send them back through the pass."

Kilian said, "But Dougal possesses the greatest collection of sculpted stones of any Obrioner high lord. Once he confirms my presence, there is nothing stopping him from sacrificing other Petralists to raise elfonnel to fight me."

Connor hadn't believed anything could scare him more than the thought of fighting another elfonnel. Fighting several did the job handily.

"So I propose we prepare to defend Harz and take the fight to the Obrioners, utilizing the tactics Connor was just discussing, as well as all the mechanicals our Builders can prepare. Let us see if Dougal will dare raise another elfonnel, or if he'll allow the battle to run its natural course."

"And if he chooses to raise one?" Wolfram asked.

"Then we have no choice. I'll intercept it."

"I don't like it," Verena said before Connor could voice his concern. "That would still leave the threat of Dougal then committing other elfonnel to the field. You can't defeat several at once."

"Probably not," Kilian admitted, but a flicker of flame in his eyes made Connor wonder. Could Kilian really think he might?

"Even if you could," Verena continued. "We'd risk breaking Granadure apart, wouldn't we?"

"Letting elfonnel run amok and destroy Granadure wouldn't be much better," Wolfram pointed out.

"Then our plan is not complete," Verena said. "When the battle begins, Hamish, Connor, and I will position ourselves in the sky. If Dougal raises an elfonnel, everyone will be focused on it."

"It's almost impossible not to," Hamish agreed.

"What do you have in mind?" Connor asked.

Verena gave him a predatory smile. "They won't be ready for us to strike. We drop down from the sky and attack the commanders. We might even be able to intercept or capture the other sculpted stones before they're put into play."

Hamish nodded, his expression grim. "I like it. Take the fight to them."

"You'd be taking an awful risk," Kilian said.

"Too much," Martys agreed. "Ye're talking suicide, lass."

"I'm not. I know it's a risk, but all battle is a risk. It's better than letting Dougal unleash multiple elfonnel against us, and they won't be expecting it."

"Perhaps," Kilian said. "How long before the Obrioners advance this far?"

"At least a couple of days," Wolfram said. "Moving nearly forty thousand troops this far and preparing to fight will take time, even without the harrying strikes we've already launched."

"Good. That gives us time to prepare a more detailed battle plan."

Verena said, "And time to get our new craft tested. I think we're going to need it."

"New craft?" Hamish perked up at that. "Sounds fun."

"Inform me if you learn any intelligence about Dougal's sculpted stones," Kilian told Wolfram.

"Everything our spy assets discover," Wolfram promised. "But at the moment, all of our communication channels are in shambles."

As the group began to disperse to their various duties, Kilian pulled Connor aside. "I will likely be very busy over the next few days, but I think it's important we continue your training."

"You mean now?" Connor asked, surprised and excited at the same time.

"Do you have anything more pressing?"

He'd love to get some quiet time alone with Verena, but he didn't dare say that aloud. So he said, "No."

Martys said, "When ye're done, find me, laddie. After that long ride, I be needin' some real exercise too."

Connor grinned. "Of course."

Erich clapped Connor on the shoulder, smiling. "Is good. Fight for better sleeping."

Anika joined them and winked at Connor. "We wrestle, Connor boy. Is good show strong hands for Verena."

Martys gave her an appreciative look. "I'll take that offer, lass."

Connor shook his head as the siblings focused on Martys, a gleam of eager anticipation in their eyes. "Oh, that was a really bad idea."

Chapter Twenty-Six

"The pastry eaten fresh out of the oven is always better than the one found in a sock under the bed."

~Hamish

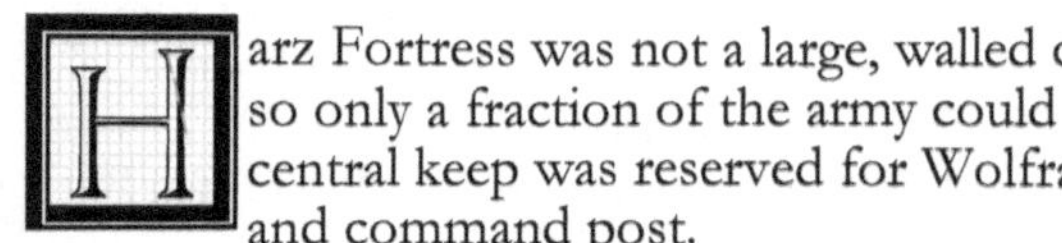

arz Fortress was not a large, walled city like Merkland, so only a fraction of the army could fit inside. The central keep was reserved for Wolfram's senior officers and command post.

Five round towers rose around the keep, with smaller buildings and courtyards between them. The thick wall surrounding that inner sanctuary was twenty feet tall, while the outer curtain wall that circled several hundred yards farther out, was almost thirty. They looked impressive, but would do little to block Sentries, or even Boulders in the grip of battle rage.

The main gate was closed for the evening so Connor followed Kilian out through a small postern gate. Together they absorbed basalt and raced through the township, past the thousands of soldiers camped in the fields flanking the fortress, and out into the long valley to the south. There they accelerated into a fracked sprint for three miles to a ridge at the southern end of the valley.

"This should do," Kilian said as he slowed to a stop.

The land south rose into a series of hills that faded into the early evening darkness. In that direction lay the border and the invading Obrioner army, but at the moment all was calm. The air was pleasantly cool, the sky clear, and the first of the stars already beginning to emerge.

Connor felt inside his battle jacket for the reassuring bulk of the precious sandstone pendant his Aunt Ailsa had sculpted for him. Touching it always comforted him, as if Aunt Ailsa stood nearby, ready to share her wisdom. He hoped she was doing well at the Carraig.

Kilian said, "We'll start with marble, but prepare soapstone too."

Eagerly, Connor extracted a small leather flask from his belt pouch. It contained a mixture of soapstone powder and water. Giving the flask a practiced swirl to make sure the powder hadn't all settled to the bottom, Connor downed a long gulp. Then he took a tiny piece of marble, slipped it under his tongue, and sucked on it.

He loved the initial spicy burst of flavor from marble. It reminded him of all of his mother's favorite spices, wrapped together and set to simmer for an hour.

He stopped sucking on it after just a moment, before the taste intensified to painful heat. Walking for long with marble must be something like walking on live coals, as Gisela had told him some of the Sehrazad raiders did as a show of bravery. Only he was walking with his tongue.

"What do you want to burn?" Connor asked, filled with the reckless confidence of fire. Not quite as savage as porphyry, it could still easily escalate into a firestorm.

"Burning things is easy," Kilian said as his own eyes filled with pulsing white flames. "I'm going to teach you a deeper truth."

That sounded fun, although maybe they should burn something while they talked. It seemed wrong to not incinerate things after fire had responded to his call.

Kilian lifted his left hand to chest height, and it ignited with crimson flames. "Most of the time, those of us who dare the dangers of fire focus on wielding the mighty flame. What many Petralists don't understand is that the flame is but one aspect of what we can do with marble."

"What else is there?"

"Heat. Fire is the outward manifestation of the reaction of burning fuel, but the heart of the flame is heat. We can manipulate that too."

Connor hadn't ever considered heat as separate from the flame. "How does that work?"

"Now that you've ascended, you've unlocked deeper sensitivities to the elements so it'll be easier for you to learn this truth now."

The flames winked out around Kilian's hand, and he extended it toward Connor. Connor reached out to grasp it, but recoiled when he plunged his hand into an invisible bubble of intense heat.

"Don't retreat," Kilian said. "You're walking with fire. You wouldn't fear clasping hands with me while flames burned around my skin."

"True." His connected to marble protected him from the flames. The heat hadn't harmed, but only startled him.

So he tried again. This time when he felt the heat, he focused on it, imagining invisible flames wrapping Kilian's hand. His marble senses grasped that heat, and he felt it respond to his touch, but not in the same way flames would.

When he walked with fire, it felt like a wild, hungry dog on a leash, tugging and urging him to let it lunge and feed. Pure heat, on the other hand, felt more like a sleeping nuall might, a soft coat wrapping a coiled, deadly power that only needed to be roused to fury.

"Amazing," Connor grinned.

Kilian relinquished the heat, and the invisible bubble of heat flowed across to him, wrapping his hand in a soft cocoon.

Kilian nodded approval. "Good. Now, shape it. Cool it, then intensify it."

Connor attempted to do so, but heat didn't leap to do his bidding like raw flames did. It really did seem half asleep, sluggish and reluctant to move. When he poked it hard with ethereal fire senses, it erupted into crimson flames that shot twenty feet into the air.

Kilian's will slipped around it and neatly plucked it away. The flames winked out, and a hot wind whispered around Connor, tickling the back of his neck, as if teasing him for failing.

"You can't whip heat around like you do fire. Manipulating heat is a more subtle aspect of your marble affinity, and thus requires a more subtle approach. When you find some quiet time, practice working small amounts of heat. Get used to how it feels, and remember pure heat is more like an oven baking sweetbreads, steady and even-tempered."

The thought of sweetbreads made Connor's mouth water. He decided he'd practice until he could take a bit of raw dough and cook it into a perfect sweetbread in front of Hamish. He doubted Hamish could accomplish the same with his Builder powers.

"On to soapstone," Kilian said.

"There's not a lot of water here."

Maybe they should have headed north instead, toward the lake. Or maybe Kilian knew of a concealed source underground.

"There's enough for our purposes."

Marble might allow Connor to generate heat and flames where none had existed before, but soapstone only allowed him to manipulate existing water. The purer the water, the better.

"You have experience working with soapstone and marble together, correct?" Kilian asked.

Connor grinned. "As the Masked Dawnus in the Tir-raon, they were my tertiary powers. Ivor taught me one of the techniques for making them work together a little better."

"What did he teach you?"

"It's a mental game. I imagine the gateways to the elements like actual doorways, facing away from each other. It was as if the elements needed to pretend their opposite was not in the room so they could avoid instantly launching into a fight."

Kilian nodded. "The mind of a Petralist is always their greatest asset. Their muscles and their affinities serve the mind."

"Do you use the same technique?"

"Not exactly, but you're off to a good start. Now, I want you to imagine those two doorways close together, back to back."

Connor wasn't sure how slate would react to that. He usually imagined the gateways for marble and soapstone standing to either side of the sunken, stone-lined pit of slate. But slate didn't get to play at the moment, so he'd deal with that later.

He released marble and banished his previous image of the gateway. The power of fire lingered in him, like a spicy meal recently consumed.

"Okay," he said once he was ready.

"Imagine the gateway to marble first."

"But I'm better with soapstone."

"Exactly. Get fire sorted first, and soapstone will still answer your call."

It made sense, although Connor wondered if water would feel betrayed. It took only a moment to form the image of the fiery doorway, then imagine the pulsing liquid gateway close behind it.

"You're creating doorways made of the elements?" Kilian asked.

"One step ahead of you," Connor confirmed, starting to feel a bit more confident. He knew he could make these elements work.

"For soapstone, imagine it as a smooth expanse of water but with a tempest ranging within."

Oh, he liked that. He might not understand the full, poetic implications of the image, but he did the best he could.

Imagining the tempest within the door turned the whole construct a bit chaotic.

"The tempest will come in time," Kilian assured him.

With the two images firmly fixed in his mind, Connor plunged a mental fist through the fiery gateway to marble. It opened without hesitation and flames burst around his right hand. The burn in his mouth grew hotter.

He next thrust fingers of thought through the gateway to water. It too opened at his touch, and he grinned at the familiar bubbling sensation of soapstone. But when he scanned the surrounding area for water to draw upon, he found nothing.

"Good," Kilian said, and water condensed around his left hand.

"Where'd you get that?"

"You have all you need."

That whole mystery approach to teaching was a little annoying.

The only liquid Connor could find nearby was his own blood, but manipulating blood in a living body was nearly impossible. The more a liquid deviated from pure water, the harder it was to use. Plus, the flesh that housed blood also seemed to offer some sort of shielding.

At the Carraig, the Spitter students were under a strict rule to never attempt it. The idea of ripping someone else's blood out of their body was fairly disgusting, so Connor had avoided thinking about it much.

He glanced up into the clear, evening sky and sensed no handy rain clouds. "Can I get a hint?"

"Look deeper."

Connor let the fire peter out around his right hand and focused entirely on soapstone. He was eager to figure out the mystery. Soapstone was his favorite tertiary affinity, but he felt no water nearby in the earth.

So how was Kilian doing it?

He cast his soapstone senses out in every direction, and only then did he notice the air around him glowed ever so faintly. Large or pure sources of water glowed brighter, and that's what he'd been scanning for. As soon as he noticed it though, he wondered that he hadn't seen it before.

Air was not water, so why would it glow? Intrigued, he grasped at the surrounding air and actually felt something. Not the direct, solid contact like a stream or even a cup on a table. This connection seemed wispy and fragile, but it was definitely there.

It was like holding fluffy dandelion seeds right before blowing them into the wind.

Connor cupped the air with his soapstone senses and squeezed. Four drops of water formed on his outstretched hand.

"How is this possible?" he laughed, peering down at the water, which appeared pure and clear. He had pulled it out of thin air!

"There's water all around almost all the time. Haven't you ever noticed that some days there's so much water in the air it feels heavy and hard to breathe?"

"Sure. Summer in Alasdair gets so humid, sometimes I could taste the water in the air."

"Water is water. Your sensitivity to it is enhanced now, allowing you to draw it forth even from the air, drop by drop. You can also extract water from solid ground, but that's even harder."

"Could I use slate with soapstone to make that work better?" Connor wondered.

"That would be an interesting experiment," Kilian said with a nod.

Connor decided he'd try it as soon as possible. Lack of ready water was one of the greatest limitations of Spitters in battle. Armies generally transported large water wagons as their fuel supply, but loss of that water could cripple Spitters. That was why Sentries were often considered the most effective battle Petralists.

Focusing again with renewed enthusiasm, Connor cast a wider net with his soapstone senses and pulled. The air around him grew absolutely dry as he drained all the water out of it into a tiny sphere floating over his hand.

"Very good," Kilian said. "The air here is dry enough that we won't get much, but we don't need to flood an entire battlefield in order to win. It's not so much how much force one brings to bear, but in how one leverages that force."

He'd first explained that term at Alasdair when he'd used a bucket of water to turn back Carbrey's army by nearly drowning Carbrey with it.

"You have the power to manage vast quantities of water," Kilian said, "but you must also learn to manage tiny portions. In time, you'll be able to accomplish more with that handful than most Spitters could with a flood."

"I hope you're right. I think we're going to need that advantage."

Chapter Twenty-Seven

"Thus light reaches even the dimmest corners of the darkened canyon at the rising of the noonday sun."

~Sentry class teacher

Verena poked Connor awake with her foot, and he rolled out from under the wagon, but kept his blanket wrapped around his shoulders. It looked far too early to be rising, and it was chilly. He glanced around and asked, "What's wrong?"

He and Kilian had returned so late from their practice that the others had already been sleeping. He'd missed his bash practice. He was tempted to punch Martys in the face to help warm up. He doubted his uncle would mind.

Verena grinned at him with far too much enthusiasm. "It's a beautiful morning. Perfect time to test our new flyer."

"Can't it wait until after breakfast?" Hamish asked as he too crawled out from under the wagon. Even though his bright red hair was cut short, he still managed to look disheveled and grumpy.

Verena said, "There's some fruit in the windrider, and probably some of yesterday's bread."

"That's a good start." Hamish dropped his blanket and leaped into the wagon. "Good thing I have some smashpacked omelets too."

"How do you smash-pack an omelet?" Connor asked.

"I don't think you want to ask too many questions," Verena suggested.

"What are you complaining about?" Hamish asked with a hurt expression. "You've eaten tons of them."

"Like I said, they're great, as long as I don't know specifics."

"Keep talking like that, and you'll get boiled tripe instead of omelets," Hamish grumbled.

"Stop moaning," Verena said with another bright smile. "We're flying today."

"And a day flying is a good day," Hamish agreed.

Jean entered the courtyard carrying a tray of mugs of steaming cider. Her blue dress was smooth, her hair already combed and shining in the early morning light, and her cheeks were flushed from an early morning scrubbing.

The cider chased away the chill, and they ate quickly. Connor had to admit the dense little smash-packed cube that Hamish tossed to him really did taste like a cold omelet. He popped a piece of marble into his mouth and drew upon a bit of fire to heat it. That made the tasty little cube absolutely delicious.

"That's a good idea," Verena said when he told her. She extracted a small piece of marble from her pocket and pressed it to her lips.

"I could heat up your lips easier than that," Connor offered. He was thrilled when Verena laughed and gave him a quick kiss.

She didn't linger, but put the marble back in her mouth, along with the smashpacked breakfast cube. She said around the mouthful, "Eating and kissing don't exactly work well together, Connor."

"Depends on how motivated you are."

Hamish jumped from the windrider, landing near Jean, but when he stepped close to her, she put up a hand to hold him back. "Don't think I'll kiss you while you've got something in your mouth either."

Hamish protested. "That'd be combining two of the best things ever."

Jean shook her head. "Not going to happen."

Connor grinned, "I guess that means you two have only actually kissed maybe once or twice?"

Verena laughed and raised a hand for him to clap. "Too true, Connor."

Hamish shrugged. "I just swallow whatever I'm eating. Hasn't stopped us yet."

"But you suck on rocks all the time," Connor pointed out with a grimace.

"I think we should change the subject," Jean said, extracting her notebook from a pocket and opening it. "If we're going to fly this morning, we need to focus."

While Verena and Hamish inspected the new craft one last time to make sure everything was ready, Connor glanced around. "Where's Martys?"

"He left early," Jean said. She had already settled into the middle seat in the second row. "Said something about finding breakfast."

Connor didn't like the idea of Uncle Martys wandering around Harz Fortress alone. Chances were pretty good he'd start a brawl.

Verena told him, "Relax. I sent a runner to find Erich and ask him to act as Martys's guide this morning."

"That's supposed to make me relax? Erich could easily be convinced that starting a general brawl would be good for morale."

"Do you really want to stay behind?" Verena asked.

"No, but if we come back and find the fortress demolished, it's not my fault."

"All ready," Hamish declared. He had donned his flying suit as they ate breakfast, and now pulled his helmet on. "Let's go."

The rest of them pulled on heavy flying leathers, then Hamish and Verena took two of the front seats, with Verena behind the control rods in the center. Connor climbed into the middle row beside Jean, and they both donned goggles and warm, woolen hats.

"Here we go," Verena said, a note of excitement in her voice.

The thrusters along the bottom of the craft roared to life with a blast of wind that whooshed through the courtyard, flinging dirt in every direction. It caught Hamish's blanket, which he hadn't stowed properly and sent it soaring through the air.

The craft lifted off the ground. As it rose above the walls of the courtyard, Verena tipped it back to about thirty degrees and added the push thrusters at the back. The craft accelerated smoothly and rose far quicker than the ponderous windriders would have.

Connor glanced at the fortress falling away beneath them. In the crisp, early morning light, it looked tranquil. People were already moving about, preparing breakfast, but the fortress lacked the grim feel it had the day before. The nearby town already bustled with activity, and the wide fields flanking the fortress were full of soldiers eating, tending to equipment, or assembling for morning drills. The lake to the north was smooth as glass and reflected the clear sky like a mirror.

Verena piloted them half a mile into the air, then began working the craft through a series of turns to test the various thrusters. Connor leaned forward and asked, "How does it feel?"

"It responds beautifully," Verena said with a grin. "It's so much more nimble than the windriders."

"Let's test the speed," Hamish said. "See if you can keep up."

He rolled over the port-side railing and momentarily fell out of sight, then reappeared a moment later with thrusters roaring. He pointed toward the row of hills marking the eastern boundary of Harz Valley, nearly three miles away. "First one to the hills."

Without waiting for a reply, he rolled away and ignited his boot thrusters, accelerating rapidly toward the target.

Verena pivoted the craft and shouted, "Hold on!"

She ignited the push thrusters, and they roared like lions. The craft vibrated, as if eager to race, and accelerated so fast the force drove Connor back into his chair and strained his neck. He wished he'd absorbed a little granite before taking off so he could reinforce his muscles. Beside him, Jean clutched her head and whooped, urging Verena to go faster. She really had spent far too much time around Hamish recently.

The craft continued to accelerate, driven through the air by those huge thrusters. They caught up with Hamish within a quarter mile, and Connor waved as they passed. Hamish was close enough that Connor easily read his shock, and Hamish's thrusters roared louder. When he continued to fall behind, he added the force of his hand thrusters, usually used only for balance and turning.

It wasn't enough. Verena laughed as they tore through the early morning sky, increasing their lead. The cold air that high numbed Connor's cheeks, but he didn't care. He loved the feeling of unrivaled speed. By the time they shot over the eastern hills, they had pulled half a minute ahead of Hamish.

Verena activated directional thrusters to turn the craft sharply back around, and the craft pivoted abruptly, slewing sideways in the air. The abrupt change wrenched at Connor's back as the huge push thrusters now threw them sideways to their original course.

Verena cut power and they slowed. She asked, "Are you all right?"

"What happened?" Jean groaned, rubbing her back.

"I forgot I wasn't in the Swift. In that, I can pivot even at full speed. This thing is much bigger, and it's even faster, but I can't use the same techniques."

Hamish caught up with them as Verena slowed to a hover. "That thing's incredible. I wouldn't have thought anything could outrun me at full power."

"It's the weight-to-power ratio," Jean said, glancing at notes she'd started scribbling in her notebook while they flew. "I've been making some calculations. You'd need thrusters twice as big as the ones you've got installed now in your suit to keep up."

Hamish shook his head. "Too big. That would mess up my air flow and would be too heavy for walking."

Verena patted the front rail of the new craft. "I think we should call this the Storm."

Connor nodded. "I like it."

Jean said, "Me too. It's faster than any thunderstorm."

"And we can rain destruction on Dougal's army," Hamish added.

"I need to test the turning, though," Verena said. "It's fast but not as nimble as I'd hoped. Still, it'll get the team where we need to go in a hurry. I might have to adjust the placement of the directional thrusters so we'll bank farther over when turning at speed."

Hamish nodded. "That should help. You might have to increase lift thrust along the front half to help pull it around through the air."

As they discussed ideal placement of the various directional thrusters, Jean tapped the corner of her mouth with her pencil, looking up into a nearby wispy cloud, her expression thoughtful. "You know, we may be able to improve the physical design of the next craft we build. If we're going to move this fast and need to bank and turn, we can probably improve performance by changing the boxy, wagon shape."

Verena said, "Good idea. I'll add that to the list of things we need to consider as we prepare to test the non-Builder flyer I want to design."

"I don't think we'll have time to build an entirely new kind of flying craft before we return to the Builder compound," Hamish pointed out.

"I know," Verena admitted. "I'm planning to do the first tests with one of the windriders. It'll be a bit crude, but we should be able to prove the concepts at least."

"And figure out how to explain flying to someone who's never done it," Hamish said.

Verena nodded. "Even most of the other Builders struggle with flying. Everything's so new, we barely understand half of it, let alone know how to teach it."

"Well that settles it," Jean said, with that confident tone she always used when diagnosing patients. "If we're going to do a proper series of tests and document the principles and hazards of flying, I need to be the first non-Builder test pilot."

Hamish shook his head and drifted right up to the rail of the Storm, closest to Jean. "You don't know what you're signing up for."

"I won't know until I experience it, will I?"

"I could test it," Connor said.

Verena grimaced. "No offense, Connor, but I've seen you try to fly. I think Jean's a better choice."

"I'm not that bad," Connor said, but he really was.

Flying the heatstone oven had been an accident. Flying with a block of quartzite had proven pretty disastrous too. He had managed to fly a bit tapping elemental air, but that was very inconsistent, not like the Builders could with their thrusters.

Verena said, "Hamish, you brag all the time about how smart Jean is. We need someone with an analytical mind to ask difficult questions and document her experiences. It's the only way we'll ever make this work and make it something we can teach others."

Hamish gave her a disgusted look. "If Jean gets hurt, I'll never let you punch me again."

"I don't think you really understand what the word 'threat' means," Jean laughed. "But I appreciate the sentiment. When do we start?"

"Not on the Storm," Verena chuckled. "I need to finish work on the keystone. Then we'll start in one of the windriders, hopefully tomorrow."

"I guess we could head down for breakfast then," Hamish suggested.

"You just ate," Jean said.

"That was a pre-breakfast, anti-starvation snack. I wouldn't call that an official breakfast. Flying always makes me hungry."

Connor smiled to see Hamish acting more himself. His lack of appetite the day before while they discussed Ingrid's tragic death had worried him. It was definitely not like Hamish to stop eating.

"It's a beautiful morning," Jean said, glancing around at the countryside spread out beneath them. "Shouldn't we test the Storm a little more?"

"We could scout farther south," Verena offered. "I think Dierk was scheduled to fly one of the scout windriders during the first shift after dawn. They're stationed ten miles south of Harz. We could see if they've seen any sign of the Obrioner advance."

Connor said. "Good idea. Let's do it."

Hamish settled into the seat on the opposite side of Jean, so Connor hopped to the front row with Verena. As she banked the Storm around and accelerated south, he draped an arm around her shoulder. Once they reached a fast cruising speed, she leaned against him.

He loved holding her like that, although it would have been nicer if she hadn't been wearing that helmet. It prevented him from touching her hair, or feeling the warmth of her cheek pressed against his neck.

"This is a good way to travel," she said over the wind.

It would be nicer if they weren't moving so fast. The air was warming now that the sun had crested the eastern mountains, and they could have enjoyed the view and the quiet togetherness a lot longer.

A few minutes later, they slowed and angled toward a windrider hovering over a very wide, green valley. Dierk was indeed flying it. A Longseer woman with her blond hair styled in an intricate braid sat beside him on the high pilot bench, huddled under thick furs and two blankets.

With a blast of thrusters, Hamish soared across the narrow gap between the wagons and landed in the long, empty bed of Dierk's windrider. The Longseer yelped and gripped her safety harness.

"Careful," she snapped, the sonorous quality of her quartzite-enhanced voice not masking her note of fear.

"Sorry," Hamish said as he trotted over to pump Dierk's hand. "I forgot you're afraid of flying."

"I am not afraid," she lied.

Verena waved as they hovered close. "Any sign of the Obrioners?"

Dierk shook his head. "Nothing this far north. We've got two other scouts flanking us, and one scout farther south watching the Obrioner camp."

The Longseer said, "They reported a small party of Obrioners moving north under a white flag."

"We should check that out," Connor said, and Verena nodded agreement.

"Be careful," Dierk cautioned. "They know to watch for flyers now, and a Firetongue could burn you right out of the sky."

"Not with me aboard," Connor assured him.

He pulled a small piece of marble from his belt pouch and tucked it under his tongue. He'd hate to need it and not have it ready.

"Besides," Verena said. "If they're moving under a white flag, they're probably messengers."

"Don't make assumptions," Dierk cautioned.

Verena waved, banked the Storm away, and accelerated south again. Hamish caught up, then she added some lift thrust to climb. "We can see farther from higher up, but that'll make it harder for them to interfere with us."

"Head for those." Hamish pointed toward a bank of wispy-looking clouds moving in from the south.

Verena slipped into the clouds, slowed a bit, then powered south. They could see for miles in every direction, but the clouds would help conceal them.

Connor said, "You should paint the Storm like the Swift. That pattern really helps conceal it."

"If we can find some paint at Harz. I forgot to bring any along."

They flew for another ten minutes in silence, studying the ground below. Hamish set Jean's long-vision goggles to a constant five times magnification. Connor just tapped quartzite. The landscape looked even more breathtaking through Pathfinder eyes. Every color seemed more brilliant and sharp, and he could swoop his gaze down over the land like a diving hawk.

Half an hour later, they spotted the Obrioner party marching north along the main road to Harz. Connor focused on the ten people and he recognized some of them.

"That's Ivor and Captain Rory," he exclaimed with a surge of excitement. Those were two of the people he most wanted to speak with.

"Rory," Verena growled, her hands tightening on the control levers. The Storm tipped forward into a steep dive, and the speedslings along both sides began to whirl.

CHAPTER TWENTY-EIGHT

"A small fire is soon quenched, but a little wind can transform a single spark into an inferno."

~Source Unkown

As the Storm plunged out of the clouds, Connor shouted above the rushing wind, "Verena, what are you doing?"

"I'm considering hitting them with a few hundred hornets," she said, her expression fierce.

Rory and his Fast Rollers had held Verena prisoner while Shona had used her to force Connor to submit to her. He hated the memory of Verena disheveled, her face bloody, standing in chains before Shona, who wore a gloating expression of triumph.

Since Shona had eventually let him go instead of sharing him with women from every high house, he hadn't thought much about that moment again. Apparently Verena had.

Connor placed a hand on her shoulder and squeezed gently. "I hate what they did to you, and I know a bit of how you must feel."

"Do you?" Verena asked sharply, glancing at him, her blue eyes flashing with anger.

"Actually, I do. Remember, Shona helped execute me once."

Some of Verena's anger faded and she sighed. "Those were crazy days."

"So are these." Connor hoped they could avoid execution again. It hadn't been pleasant. He leaned closer and placed one hand over hers on the nearest control lever. "I need to speak with them, Verena, not kill them. Please?"

She sighed again, and the Storm slowed and eased into a more gradual descent. The speedslings stopped spinning, and he breathed a little easier.

"If I see Shona again, I can't promise I won't kill her on the spot," Verena growled.

"Let's discuss Shona later," Connor suggested. He wasn't entirely sure how he felt about Shona, and that irritated him, but he didn't want to kill her.

"Pray none of them make any aggressive moves," she added.

"I'll cover you from the rear," Hamish said, rolling out of the Storm, igniting his own thrusters, and banking away to the left.

Connor sincerely hoped Rory didn't do anything foolish. He'd seen what speedslings could do at the battle of Alasdair, and even max-tapping Boulders had struggled under the deadly hornets. Verena and Hamish had enhanced the hornets and added exploding projectiles since then. If the Builders decided to go to war against Rory, there was a very good chance none of his company would survive.

"Circle in gradually," Connor suggested. "I want to give them plenty of time to see us and realize we aren't coming to attack."

"I see Aifric!" Jean exclaimed.

She was leaning forward over Verena's other shoulder to peer at the small force. The Obrioners had spotted them and had formed into a defensive circle.

Ivor stood at the rear of the group, his posture relaxed, but one hand wrapped in writhing flames, while the other held a globe of rippling water. Captain Rory, flanked by Tomas and Cameron, stood in the center of their tiny force of Boulders, while a Sentry Connor did not know knelt at the rear of the group, one hand thrust into the earth.

Aifric stood to one side of Ivor in her Healer robes, although as Connor watched, her face shuddered and her expression turned harder. Her smile faded to a grim frown, and one hand slipped into the pocket of her robes. He'd seen the transformation before, when she had assumed her alternate personality as a Mhortair Assassin.

He hoped she'd revert back to Aifric. She'd sworn to help him as an Assassin, but he'd rather not risk dealing with that aspect of her at the moment.

Connor then spotted another familiar face. Papil, his Pathfinder captain from his student army at the Carraig. Blonde and freckled, the gangly girl looked more mature than she had even a week ago when he had last seen her.

He stood at the front of the Storm and waved. She recognized him and the expression of joy on her face warmed his heart. He felt relieved to know at least one of his soldiers didn't hate him yet.

Connor swallowed a gulp of soapstone and water and made sure the marble was secure under his tongue. Tapping a bit of marble, he sent a jet of multi-colored flame shooting into the air. Then he switched to soapstone and pulled some water out of the air around them and sent a burst of snow crystals erupting around the Storm.

"They know who we are," he told Verena as he sat again. She had descended to just over five hundred feet. "Bank around one more time, then settle into a hover in front of them."

"Aye, General," she said with a mock salute.

"Sorry. Sometimes I forget I'm no longer a commander."

"It suits you. Just don't get carried away."

He knew better than that. Verena could easily punch him right out of the Storm if he irritated her enough. She hadn't hit him since their reunion, so he was cautiously optimistic that phase of their relationship was over, but it always paid to be careful.

"If this doesn't go well, don't use the puking dooms unless I tell you, or Ivor might seize the flames."

Verena slowed further and came around to the front of the group. She hovered at a hundred feet and slowly settled straight down toward the ground, aiming for a landing spot about fifty feet away from Captain Rory and his soldiers.

Connor definitely didn't plan to fight with fire. Ivor wielded fire with a degree of mastery Connor couldn't yet duplicate. Since Connor had ascended with soapstone he should have a solid advantage, even though he wasn't carrying a ready supply. The morning air was humid enough to provide what he needed.

He still felt convinced they wouldn't need to fight. They had too much to talk about first. Ivor and Rory moved to the front of the small group. The unknown Sentry worried Connor the most. The man hadn't moved, so Connor slipped a piece of slate into his boot. He wouldn't be able to connect with the earth until he landed, so if the Sentry decided to attack, now would be the best time.

Rory took a step forward and spoke, his voice magnified by Papil. "Connor, it's good to see you, lad."

Connor nearly saluted. Since Rory was leading an official Obrioner envoy and he was allied at the moment with Granadure, that wouldn't work so well. So he applied quartzite to his voice and replied, "We've come to talk, Captain."

Rory relaxed, just a slight shifting of his shoulders, but Connor knew him well enough to read the gesture. "Good."

Behind him, Tomas handed something to Cameron with a scowl, and Connor smiled to see it. The two loved to bet, and one of their favorite subjects to bet on was him.

Verena settled the Storm to the ground, but glanced at Connor. "Do you trust them?"

"With my life. Come on."

"I'm not sure that's a good idea," Verena said, frowning at Rory, who was approaching with Ivor, Tomas, Cameron, and Aifric. Papil remained with the rest of the tiny force, but she waved enthusiastically when Connor met her gaze. He waved back, and she grinned even wider.

"Please," he said and climbed out of the Storm, then offered his hand to help her and Jean. Neither of them really needed help, but he figured the gallant gesture was a good idea in the current, formal-ish meeting.

Connor glanced at Ivor, who trailed Rory by half a step, and Ivor gave him a friendly smile. Connor was eager to talk with his friend, and happy that Ivor had survived the explosive assault at the pass.

He extended a hand, which Rory shook with a solid grip. "I'm not surprised you showed up near the fighting, lad."

"The pass is already broken though," Tomas told Connor.

"You're too late," Cameron added. "I think Redmund was taking notes at the Carraig."

"Redmund?" That was a surprise.

"Aye," Rory said, his deep, rough voice graver than usual. "It was Redmund who somehow raised that elfonnel and led the charge through the gap."

"Poor fool," Connor muttered. He hadn't exactly like Redmund, but he still felt bad knowing that Redmund had been sacrificed.

Tomas said, "To many Obrioners, what he did makes him a hero."

"And what do you think?" Connor asked.

"Don't need to," Tomas said with a quick grin.

"We're just here for the fighting," Cameron agreed. "Captain's the one who has to think."

"He has to try, anyway," Tomas corrected.

Connor smiled. Their easy banter actually helped him relax, but he didn't let their self-deprecating words fool him.

Those two were shrewd battlefield tacticians, and they absorbed more intelligence than most people realized.

Captain Rory turned to Verena then and said softly, "Builder, I'm glad to see you safe."

"Are you?" Verena asked, her voice hard.

Rory nodded. "I had to obey orders, but I can tell you now that I hated to do it."

Tomas and Cameron stepped up to flank their captain, and in unison they raised hands in the crispest salute Connor had ever seen. Their normal air of joking disrespect was replaced by unusual sincerity.

Tomas said, "Captain's right, Builder. It was worse than insulting to treat you like that after your inspiring bravery during the fighting."

Cameron added, "You've got the heart of a Fast Roller."

"She's got Connor's heart now too," Tomas muttered, his serious expression cracking to a frown. "How many heart's she's collected, you think?"

Rory sighed and glanced at them. "You know, I was almost ready to feel proud of you two."

Cameron sighed loudly. "Whew! Glad we dodged that blow, Captain. Would've ruined a perfect record."

Not even Verena could maintain her anger in the face of those two, and she smiled and shook her head. She stepped closer and kissed Tomas on the cheek. "Thank you."

He looked thunderstruck, and for perhaps the first time ever that Connor had seen, he didn't seem to know what to say.

When Verena turned to Cameron, he was already grinning. After she kissed his cheek, he chortled, "Kissed by a pretty girl! Only thing better would be if you brought Erich along for a little bash practice."

"Sorry. Maybe another time," Connor said.

He hoped the next time they met, they'd get to practice fighting, but he feared the battle would be far too real. He hated to think of fighting these men who he respected so much.

"Has Carbrey started advancing north?" Connor asked Rory.

Rory hesitated. "My message is officially for Wolfram, lad. I also have a message for you too."

"From who?"

"From High Lord Dougal."

That shocked him. Bad enough that Shona got that letter to him in Alasdair.

"What message?"

Rory grimaced. "I have to deliver it in the presence of General Wolfram."

"Why?" Verena asked suspiciously.

"You'll understand once you hear it."

"You're not doing a great job of restoring my faith in you," Verena said.

"I know, lass, and I apologize."

"Then we'd better get you to Harz," Connor decided. "First, do you mind if I speak with Ivor and Aifric for a minute?"

"Be my guest."

Rory looked surprised. He had probably expected Connor to try questioning him further. In fact, Connor wanted to, but they'd speak at Harz, and he really needed to talk with Ivor.

As soon as Connor turned, Aifric rushed up and gave him a fierce hug. "Connor, it's so good to see you." She wore the open, friendly expression of Aifric the Healer, and he felt relieved that she had shifted back.

He returned her hug warmly. "I'm glad you came."

"Ivor invited me." She gestured to the big Dawnus, who joined them and extended a hand for Connor to shake.

"I've been hoping to find you," Ivor said.

Connor studied his friend. "I heard you're already a commander."

"Most of the senior students were recruited too."

"Are they. . ." Connor couldn't quite make himself ask if they had died in the explosion at the pass.

Ivor shook his head. "Most of the students were held in reserve. Everyone you knew is safe. Well, except for Redmund."

"I heard."

Ivor turned to Verena and extended a hand to her, "It's good to see you again, Builder."

"And you, Ivor." Verena ignored his hand and gave him a hug. "You saved my life, Ivor. I hug friends."

"Maybe when all this unpleasantness is over, you'll take me up in one of those flying wagons," Ivor said, glancing at the Storm.

"It would be my pleasure."

Ivor glanced up at Hamish, who still hovered in the air nearby, and waved. Hamish waved back and Ivor grinned, "That suit is a marvel."

"He's a marvel," Jean said with a smile.

Ivor bowed over her hand. "I'm surprised to see you here. You were Shona's servant, right?"

That was a perfect opening for Connor to ask about Shona, but Jean spoke first. "I've been Connor's friend a lot longer."

"You wouldn't have wanted to stay at the Carraig anyway," Ivor said. "With the older students all recruited, the younger students were sent home during repairs. I doubt the Carraig will be ready to resume classes on time next year."

"It was a mess," Connor agreed.

"Will you be joining Rory at Harz to speak with Wolfram?" Verena asked.

He shook his head. "Most of us will remain outside of the fortress, but I have so many questions. Everyone will want to know why you're in Granadure, Connor."

"Just tell them I'm trying to stop this war, and I've discovered some important truths I need to share."

Ivor glanced at Rory, then said softly, "Those are things I need to know."

"We'll find time to talk in private," Connor assured him. "I wish I had a chance to meet with the rest of my army."

Ivor chuckled. "My army now. Most of them report to me."

"Do you think it's possible?" Jean asked.

"I'll think of something." And Connor decided he really needed to. They deserved to know the truth. If he could convince them, together they could begin to change the evil system.

"Is Dougal in the camp?" Connor asked.

Ivor hesitated, but Aifric nodded. "He is."

Connor said, "Be wary of him, Ivor. If he ever offers you a sculpted stone, don't take it."

Ivor's expression turned troubled. "He's got one for me, Connor. He's already shown it to me."

"Don't use it," Verena urged, gripping Ivor's arm.

Connor added, "You'll be tempted to ascend through the threshold with it, and that's when Dougal will take your mind and sacrifice you the way he did Redmund."

"How does he do it?" Ivor asked.

"That's one of the things we're figuring out. We don't have time to go into it now. Just don't use one of those sculpted stones, or you're dead."

"If you have to die, that's a pretty remarkable way to go," Ivor said. Then he chuckled and made a calming gesture. "Relax, Connor. I'm joking. I'm not ready to die yet. I haven't even gotten married. My new house was furious there wouldn't be time for the wedding before I had to report for duty at the front."

"Who?" Jean asked eagerly.

Ivor smiled. "Alyth. High Lady Islay's daughter."

"You like her," Jean noted.

Ivor nodded. "It's probably the best match I could have hoped for."

Maybe not once the truth of patronage was known.

"I can't wait to hear more about her," Connor said.

Rory joined them. "I hate to break up the happy reunion, but we've got a long way to go yet to reach Harz."

"I could call in a windrider to carry you the rest of the way," Connor suggested.

"That's not a bad idea," Rory said. Ivor eagerly agreed.

Verena gripped Connor's arm a little harder than necessary, her expression guarded. "Can I speak with you?"

"Of course. Give us a moment, Captain."

While Connor and Verena retreated, Jean informed Captain Rory that Anika received his message. While the small group discussed that, Verena drew Connor a dozen paces away.

"Connor, the windriders are a huge advantage for us. I don't want the Obrioners knowing any more about them than absolutely necessary."

That was a valid point. "They already know they fly and that Builders fly them, but let's ask Dierk to make sure not to push the wagon too hard, so they won't get a feel for how much it can do."

She considered that. "I still think they should walk."

"That'll just make it take longer. In wartime, is it better to take as much time as possible, or to hear the official messages quickly?"

"Depends on whether or not the delay would actually cause Dougal to wait before advancing," Verena admitted.

"Do you think it will?"

"Probably not." Then she punched him lightly on the arm. "Sometimes it's annoying when you're right so often in one morning."

"I promise it won't happen again."

"Don't you dare," she grinned.

"Can you call Dierk on that speakstone?"

She shook her head. "Not directly, but Hamish can go fetch him." She turned away and added, "Hamish, we're going to give this company a ride to Harz in a windrider so Rory can deliver his messages. Can you go bring Dierk here to pick them up?"

"Pastry," Hamish said, then pivoted in the air and accelerated away with a roaring of activated thrusters.

Verena sighed. "He really needs a better code word."

Chapter Twenty-Nine

"Crabs pull down any who seek to rise, but eagles soar only when spreading their wings."

~Gregor

Hamish returned with Dierk twenty minutes later. It was clear the spectacled Builder hated the idea of giving rides to a bunch of Obrioners. Connor wished Hamish could have found a different Builder for the job. Dierk was still grieving the loss of his niece, and Connor didn't blame him for his anger.

The wagon had benches built around the perimeter of the long bed, and as the company took their seats, most of them looked nervously excited. Tomas and Cameron began loudly discussing the probability of surviving a fall from various heights. Their conversation made the Longseer in the front look progressively more terrified.

Aifric leaned out of the wagon and spoke softly to Connor. "I'm going to need some more obsidian. I can't requisition any from the army when they think I'm just a Healer."

"Good point," he said as he fastened the rear gate and motioned the all clear sign to Dierk. "I'll get some for you when we land at Harz."

Dierk triggered the thrusters, and Connor retreated from the whirlwind of air to join Verena and Jean in the Storm.

Hamish pointed at the windrider sluggishly climbing into the air, with Ivor leaning over the side, a boyish grin on his face. "I'll flank them on the left."

Verena said, "We'll take the right."

The ride back to Harz went smoothly, if slowly. Dierk flew the windrider at four hundred feet, barely faster than a galloping horse, a fraction of its possible speed. From what Connor saw of Ivor, it didn't matter. Ivor grinned the entire time, and even tried to get the nervous Longseer to speak with him. The idea of actually talking with an Obrioner seemed to terrify her more.

When Verena informed the hub of their approach with Obrioner messengers, she created quite a stir. A courtyard was emptied and prepared for their arrival. As they descended toward the fortress, Connor spotted an entire company of Rumblers, led by Erich, along with Anton and a full complement of tertiary affinity Petralists. Kilian and Wolfram joined the group as the windrider touched down. Connor was surprised not to see Anika.

Verena settled the Storm nearby, and Connor hopped out and joined Rory to help ease any possible tensions. The Grandurian soldiers looked eager for an excuse to fight.

Captain Rory saluted General Wolfram smartly as his little company formed up around him, with Papil carrying the flag of truce.

"I am Captain Rory, embassy of High Lord Dougal, high commander of the Obrioner army, bearing messages for you, General Wolfram."

Wolfram returned the salute. "I've heard you're a man of honor, but you still owe me a camp chest, Captain."

Rory's formal expression cracked into a smile. "You still own it, sir?"

"Of course. I keep it as a reminder to always remain on guard."

"What's he talking about?" Verena whispered to Connor as she slipped her hand into his.

Connor shrugged. "I have no idea, but I'm glad they're not trying to kill each other."

"I must ask you to surrender all of your power stones," Wolfram said.

Rory looked surprised, and Verena whispered, "That's unusual."

Wolfram's gaze shifted to Ivor. "I have also heard of you, Commander Ivor, and I will not willingly endanger my soldiers with you two in this fortress bearing power stones. They will be returned to you at the conclusion of our discussion."

"Very well," Rory said.

A pair of Rumblers collected the stones and small bags of powder.

Wolfram said, "I will not force you to purge, but I must have your word that none of you will tap your affinities while in the walls of this fortress."

"You have my word," Rory said, then glanced at Tomas and Cameron and gave them a hard look.

"You will join me in my study, Captain. The rest of your company will remain here."

He led Rory from the courtyard. Kilian waited for Verena, Hamish, and Jean. Connor paused long enough to motion Aifric to join them. One of the Grandurian officers began to protest, but Kilian motioned the man back.

"I am assuming you have a reason for inviting this Healer to join us."

"I do," Connor assured him.

"Explain when we get there," Kilian said. As the group left the courtyard, Erich followed at their heels.

Before they reached Wolfram's office, Anika rushed past. Her face gleamed, and her long, blond hair was freshly braided. She had incorporated brightly colored late-season wildflowers into the braid, and the intricate pattern made her look radiant. Even her battle leathers looked polished.

She was grinning so wide, it was a marvel her face fit through the door to Wolfram's office. Connor reached the doorway just as she swept Rory off his feet in an exuberant hug.

Rory's smile changed to a grimace of pain and he exclaimed, "Tallan's mercy, woman. You're going to crush me to jelly."

Anika dropped him and gave him a quick but passionate kiss on the lips. Her expression turned questioning. "Why no many strong hands, mine capitain?"

Rory rubbed one shoulder and glanced at Wolfram, who was watching them with open amusement. "I promised the general that I wouldn't tap granite in the fortress."

Anika turned to Wolfram and exclaimed, "How we wrestle?"

"I am afraid you'll have to content yourself with holding hands."

Verena took Connor's hand in hers, a wistful little smile on her lips, and said softly, "I don't imagine that relationship has any chance of success, but I can't help but think it was an unusual stroke of good luck that Dougal sent Rory."

Kilian looked thoughtful. "Dougal does not make such mistakes. I expect he must know of Rory's interest in our Anika, which begs the question, why did he send him?"

Connor led the way into the office. "Hopefully we're going to find out."

Anika looked ready to argue further, but Wolfram spotted Aifric as they all crowded into the study. "What are you doing here, young lady?"

The brown-haired, open-faced Aifric gave the general a happy smile, then stepped to Rory and touched one hand to his shoulder. His grimace faded under her touch and she said, "For the moment, it appears I am trying to preserve our good captain from the dangers of a broken heart."

Rory grunted. "A broken body anyway."

"I take it you know this girl?" Wolfram asked.

Connor said, "She is a trusted friend. One of perhaps nineteen I can think of at the moment."

He hoped he'd get to meet Aifric's other undercover personalities. She seemed to completely embody each identity she assumed, becoming a different person. If her other identities were as different, he couldn't wait to meet them all.

Aifric said, "The only one of the nineteen who matters right now."

Kilian approached Rory and extended a hand, which he shook. "Well met, Captain. I find it interesting that Dougal would risk such a valuable member of his staff as an envoy."

"I am not overly concerned about treachery."

Rory seemed at ease in the company, and Connor doubted that the simple, enthusiastic presence of Anika close beside him was enough to justify it. She usually made anyone else with a shred of self-preservation decidedly nervous.

Kilian said, "I, on the other hand, do worry. Especially after what happened at the pass."

Rory said, "I assume by our success at the border that neither you nor Connor were present during the assault."

"If we had been, it would've gone very differently," Connor promised. He leaned his back against a nearby bookshelf. He didn't want to face another elfonnel, but if he'd been there, maybe Ingrid would have survived.

Rory said, "I expect it would have, although I think the day would have gone badly for Redmund, either way."

Connor frowned as he thought of Redmund. "He must have ascended. I wonder if Dougal could have seized his mind and forced him to raise that elfonnel if he hadn't?"

"You think that was Dougal's doing?" Rory asked.

Kilian said, "Without a doubt. Dougal used him as a pawn, just as he was planning to do with Connor."

Hamish leaned forward with that surprised look that suggested he just had a thought. "If Dougal seizes Connor's mind and forces him to raise an elfonnel—"

"Don't even suggest it," Verena interrupted.

Hamish made a calming gesture. "I know, but if he did, would Connor appear as a monster that looked like Redmund did? His elfonnel looked just like the one at the Carraig."

"That's a good point, Jean said. "But Evander's looked more human-shaped."

Kilian gave Hamish an approving nod. "I'm impressed. That mind of yours works pretty well sometimes."

"I had twenty-three smashpacked cakes on the flight back to the fortress," Hamish said with a shrug. "Fuels the mind."

Connor shared a stunned look with Verena, while Jean just laughed.

Through his own chuckle, Kilian said, "The stronger the Petralist, the greater their control over the form they take. However, Dougal's influence might well affect the ultimate form chosen."

"How does he seize other people's minds?" Aifric asked.

"We'll discuss that question in more detail later," Kilian said with a glance at Rory. "I believe we are already taxing the captain's honor to the uttermost. There is only so much he can withhold from his high lord."

Rory gave him a wry smile. "It sure would be easier if I hated you people."

Hamish, who had been lounging near the door eating a sugared pastry, suddenly said, "Aifric, Dougal doesn't know you're here, does he?"

She shook her head. "I doubt he's aware that I was in the army at all. I was keeping a pretty low profile after what happened at the Carraig."

Hamish said, "You're insane to join that army at all. If he discovers you, he'll execute you."

"Worse, probably." Aifric said with an enthusiastic grin.

"I suspect there is history here that I should know about," Wolfram said.

"When High Lord Dougal was attacking Connor's mind at the Carraig, Aifric had me fly her up the mountain and find Dougal's secret hideout. She attacked him alone and nearly killed him." Hamish shook his head. "I can't believe you wasted time gloating."

Aifric grimaced. "I should have killed him instantly. Gregor must have figured out that I had tricked him and clobbered me from behind."

"Perhaps," Kilian said, his expression unreadable.

She shrugged. "All I can figure is that Dougal planned to return for me after he secured his hold on Connor." She gave Connor a happy smile. "You saved my life without even realizing it."

"It's the least I could do after how many times you saved mine."

Connor wanted to ask her more about that day to see if they could confirm that Dougal had flipped the trap on her using obsidian. She might not even understand what happened, but maybe together they could figure it out.

Rory interrupted. "Who are you?"

"Oh, Captain, I imagine that's another one of those things that would push your loyalty past the breaking point," Aifric said warmly.

Kilian said, "Don't get distracted, Captain. You came to deliver an official message."

"I did, but first General Carbrey ordered me to laugh in Wolfram's face." Rory regarded Wolfram, who now wore a wry smile. With his craggy face impassive, Rory said in a deadpan voice, "Consider yourself laughed at."

Wolfram shook his head slowly. "I suppose it's too much to hope that Carbrey will ever grow up."

"What's that all about?" Connor asked.

"Over the years, our ongoing clashes have become a personal vendetta for Carbrey. Every time he can claim the least bit of advantage from a skirmish, he is renowned for bragging about it and bemoaning the fact that he's never gotten the chance to face me man to man in single combat."

"I'd like to see that," Verena said, and it was clear which of the generals she expected would win.

Connor was not sure. He had never seen Wolfram fight, but knew the man had affinity with obsidian. As a Boulder, Carbrey would seem to hold the advantage, but a skilled Allcarver could still win.

Rory continued, "My Lord Dougal proposes an exchange. He will return the powdered primary affinity stone captured at the border in exchange for the diorite chisels recently captured in Grandurian raids across the border."

"It must gall him that his own identical raids failed," Wolfram said.

Kilian added, "What about the other power stones you captured?"

"He suspected you would ask about that. He wanted me to inform you that we discovered the entire cache, as well as the weakening powder. That powder, along with the tertiary stones, will not be returned."

Kilian kept his expression neutral, but Wolfram's brows drew together just a fraction.

Connor asked, "Captain, why don't you stay with us? It's clear you understand the kind of man that High Lord Dougal is. Come help us stop him."

Wolfram looked stunned by the audacity of the offer, and even Kilian looked surprised. Hamish and Jean were both nodding eagerly, and Anika looked like she was preparing to tackle him again to celebrate, but Rory shook his head.

He glanced at Anika and said, "I'll admit I'm conflicted, but my duty is to my men as much as it is to my lord. I could not live with myself if I abandoned them."

"Bring your men along," Connor offered.

He would love to have Tomas and Cameron join him in exile. Their irreverent outlook would fit the life of rebellion perfectly, and no doubt they could offer tremendous insights about how to best start a patronage revolution.

Rory actually hesitated before shaking his head again. "They wouldn't come, lad. You know that."

"One day they may."

He hoped that when that day came, Rory made the right choice. Now he knew the offer was open. Connor was beginning to understand that they would not defeat Dougal and restore peace without help from more of the honorable men and women of Obrion.

Besides, once they shared the truth about unclaimed, there would be even less holding Rory and the other Guardians back. He wanted to reveal the truth to Rory, but couldn't risk Dougal learning that he knew the secret.

"Now is probably the best time for me to deliver the message I have for you too, Connor. He suspected I might find you here, or find a way to get a message to you."

Connor wasn't sure he wanted to hear it. Even though he was safely away from Dougal, the man still scared him. Connor loved his country, and it still bothered him to think that he had been forced to fight his own countrymen.

"Shona did not have the authority to let you go. Her conditional patronage was respected, but only your high lord can choose to release you from service."

She hadn't mentioned that in her letter.

"He still clings to the lie," Verena growled.

"High Lord Dougal orders you to return and submit to him," Rory continued. He looked like he could barely believe the words he spoke.

Connor said, "He knows that's impossible. Why would he even suggest such a thing?"

"Because your refusal grants him justification for the rest of the message. If you refuse, he swears to punish you and those who have twisted your loyalty away from the cause of justice."

"He is such a legendary liar," Verena exclaimed. She looked ready to go hunt down Dougal and punch him in the throat. Twice.

Rory continued, his expression grim. "He promises to not only conquer Granadure, but to lay waste to the nation. His sworn intention is to stomp out rebellion. He will initiate a second great purge and destroy every last Builder and every last mechanical."

"Now he's made it personal," Hamish growled, his fists clenching.

"This war was always personal to him," Kilian said, looking unaffected by the threats.

Rory said, "He ordered me to suggest another alternative. If you agree to stay out of this war, he will show mercy and petition the king to allow the Builders to continue their work after Granadure is brought back under Obrioner control.

"Leave for the Arishat League, if you like. Or he is willing to grant you a palace in the southern part of his realm to live in. All you need to do swear an oath of neutrality."

Connor was not sure how to respond. He should laugh it off, but he hated to admit even to himself that he found the offer tempting.

He respected the people of Granadure, but the Arishat League did hold potential advantages. If Verena and his other friends came with him, he could guarantee their safety.

If they instead pursued the war to its uttermost end, they'd face constant peril for weeks or months or years. If any of them died when he could have offered them a safe alternative, he wasn't sure he could live with himself.

Wolfram said, "You have to admit that man is brilliant."

Kilian said, "No doubt he plans to remove you, even should you accept that offer. It is his way to divide and distract before striking."

Aifric nodded. "I guarantee he has contingency plans already in play. I swore an oath to protect you, Connor. While embedded in the army, I did not find an opportunity to take another stab at Dougal. However, I learned that Dougal has already sent at least one secret assassin across the border."

Connor exchanged glances with Kilian. That's exactly what Martys had suggested. "Do you know their mission?"

She shook her head. "All I found out was that they had a high level target." She glanced around the room. "Could be any of you."

Wolfram shrugged. "It would not be the first time I've been targeted, and it will not be the last."

Connor gripped Verena's warm hand tighter. The thought of a secret assassin possibly hunting her terrified him. It also filled him with rage. "If he did strike one of us, that would only guarantee that we'd fight that much harder."

"Like I said, contingencies," Aifric said.

"Will you excuse us, Captain?" Wolfram said to Rory. "We need to confer in private about your message." He gestured toward the door. "Anika, why don't you show the captain to the library? He can wait in comfort until we call for him."

She eagerly took Rory's hand and led him from the room. Erich looked furious that he was not ordered to follow.

After they left, Wolfram faced Aifric. "You're not just a Healer."

Connor answered for her. "She's Mhortair. I suppose I should introduce you to my personal Assassin."

Wolfram looked shocked, showing more emotion than Connor had ever seen. His stance shifted a little, and he suddenly radiated the deadly grace of an Allcarver tapping obsidian. Fire began to flicker around Kilian's fingers, and even Verena took half a step back, her free hand dipping into her ever-present satchel.

Aifric noted their responses and grinned. Her expression turned more predatory, her features shifting subtly as she slipped into her alternate Assassin persona. She curtsied, her movements as graceful as Wolfram's. "Pleasure to meet you all. I am here to join you."

Kilian chuckled. "What makes you think we would accept the Mhortair into our company?"

"Who better to stop an assassin than an Assassin? Connor, I swore an oath to protect you and remove any who sought to do you harm. I failed last time, so I'm asking for a chance to redeem myself and regain my honor."

"Of course you can join us."

Connor felt no reservation about accepting her. Sure, she had tried to kill him once, but they had cleared up that little misunderstanding.

Real friends didn't hold grudges.

CHAPTER THIRTY

"The fortified stronghold falls not to a single assault, but relents under the combined might of attacks on all sides."

~Evander

The next day passed quickly. Harz was a constant buzz of activity as the army prepared to meet the expected Obrioner advance. Connor saw little of Verena and Hamish. They disappeared with the other Builders into a laboratory set up in a huge barn at the outskirts of town. Jean joined them to study flying and to help Hamish fine-tune his suit.

Connor wanted to help, but had to admit he was pretty useless when it came to Builder work. Besides, he was needed elsewhere.

Captain Ilse introduced him to most of the high command of the Grandurian army. Their initial distrust usually faded to enthusiastic support once they learned he was Blood of the Tallan. The constant glares from soldiers who knew only that he was Obrioner got old real fast.

"What do you expect?" Ilse asked when he confided in her. "It takes time to build trust, especially now. Did you think that just because you've got a special gift that everyone would drop to their knees and start worshipping you?"

"Of course not." If anyone tried, Verena would probably punch him unconscious to remind him that he was still just Connor. "So let's build some trust and start developing those inter-affinity battle plans."

"Good idea."

They went to meet the battle marshal, responsible for overall coordination of the various affinity groups. He was a grizzled Sapper named Gunter, whose long fur coat made him look like a bear. When Ilse explained their plan to use mud, his Sentry-speak grew so convoluted that Connor gave up trying to understand.

Attempting to force the man to listen would probably just get him buried under half a mile of earth. So he decided to try using reason. "The courageous may tempt the rocky peaks, but all flee the fury of the mudslide unleashed by the raging tempest."

The old Sapper grunted and said, "Whispers in a cavern may echo to the uttermost corners, but the sleeping mind hears naught but the clamor of dreams."

That was a good one. Connor hoped it meant Gunter was realizing he needed to wake up and try something new. Or maybe he thought Connor was dreaming. Or was he suggesting Connor lock himself in a cave for a few weeks?

Ilse stepped in to help. "The snows of winter quench the budding flame, but waters of springtime nourish the seedling."

Connor had no idea what that was supposed to mean, but Gunter slowly nodded and sighed, the sound like a bellows deflating in a blacksmith shop. That was the turning point in the discussion. It still took a lot of fast talking to get the other leaders to consider the idea, but they all finally agreed to meet and try testing the concepts.

In the meantime, Connor saw Martys only once. His uncle had formed an unexpected friendship with Erich, and the two of them spent a great deal of time sparring and swapping stories. Connor wondered how much of what they both said was actually understood. Erich seemed to struggle with the simplest Obrioner, and Martys's highland sayings surely splattered against Erich's rock-hard cranium without making a dent.

Then again, the fact that they didn't really understand each other might make it easier to get along. They couldn't argue politics or discuss deep, emotional topics. Theirs was a friendship built on mutual respect from punching each other a couple hundred times. Connor decided there were worse foundations to build upon.

He saw next to nothing of Aifric after he got her a large supply of obsidian. She'd told Rory that she needed to stay to treat Connor for a lingering ailment.

The fact that she hadn't specified the exact malady had given Tomas and Cameron ample room to begin betting on what illnesses Connor must be suffering from. As the tiny Obrioner force had marched away from Harz, Connor had overheard Tomas insisting it must be mind-rot, while Cameron argued for severe bunions from blasting fire out his feet so often.

Aifric appeared at his side unexpectedly an hour after lunch the next day while he and Ilse were headed for the small lake north of the fortress. He started in surprise and laughed. "Aifric! Where did you come from?"

"Here and there," she said with a shrug and a smile. "Harz is fascinating, but I don't think Dougal's assassins have arrived yet. But Gisela just did."

"Gisela? Why would she be here?"

Aifric shrugged. "I suspect you should ask her. She's been sent to Wolfram's study." She regarded him more closely. "Do you have any idea why Ailsa would send one of her students into Granadure during a time of war?"

"I think we need to go find out."

Aifric didn't know Gisela's secret, but since she was now part of his team, it was time she learned. Gisela was an agent for the Arishat League, assigned as a contact to Ailsa, who ran an intricate intelligence-gathering organization.

She was also one of the few at the Carraig who had known Connor's secrets and helped him plot ways to escape Shona's control. If Gisela was at Harz, she'd know how Ailsa was doing, and probably a lot more.

"We're due to meet with the Flameweavers," Ilse pointed out.

"You'll have to take care of it. This is important."

Ilse didn't look happy about having to meet the Flameweavers alone, but he bolted. Aifric ran easily beside him as they made for the central keep.

"Do you know if Jean and the others have been informed?" Connor asked.

"I sent word."

Jean, Hamish, and Verena caught up in the hallway leading to Wolfram's office, their hair a bit wild after the fast flight over from the Builder laboratory. The guard was expecting them, and he opened the door immediately. Inside the office, a slender woman with white-blonde hair was seated at a chair in front of Wolfram's cluttered desk, facing the general.

"Gisela!" Jean rushed in and the two embraced, laughing.

Connor gave Gisela a hug in turn. "What are you doing here?"

"I have representing the Arishat League," she said in her lightly accented voice.

Aifric nodded. "I knew there was more to you. Should have looked into it."

"Why is a Healer having interest in me?" Gisela asked with a frown.

"It's kind of a long story," Connor explained.

"You can telling me later. I have bringing a message from your Aunt Ailsa."

That was great news. Ailsa had been his mentor, his primary confidant, and a treasured friend during the difficult times at the Carraig. "Is she well?"

Gisela nodded. "Very busy with sculpting many orders."

He felt relieved that Ailsa hadn't been punished for her association with him.

Kilian walked into the room, with Martys trailing behind. Kilian said, "I was afraid of that. Now that the war has started, it only makes sense for them to build up their arsenal of sculpted stones."

"She is finding many flaws in the stone," Gisela said with a wink. "A sculpted stone is always taking much time, but she may being very late in delivery."

Connor grinned. "Glad to hear she hasn't changed."

Kilian said, "That should buy some time, but she's not the only sculptor in Obrion."

"Ha!" Martys grunted. "Little Ailsa proves that good gear comes in small bulk."

Connor asked, "How do you know Ailsa? You never lived in Alasdair."

"She's famous, lad."

Gisela extracted a small rolled parchment from a pocket of her skirt and handed it to Connor. As he unrolled it she said, "Is lists of sculpted stones by house. I am thinking this list is very complete."

"No doubt you left a copy with your mother too," Kilian said.

Connor was not surprised that Kilian knew who Gisela was, or that he knew her mother. What did surprise him was that the list was so short. High Lord Dougal possessed twelve sculpted stones, three times as many as any other house.

Verena slipped under his arm to get a look at the paper. "He has so many!"

"I wouldn't usually think twelve is a big number," Hamish said.

"It is being many for sculpted stones," Gisela explained. "There are being no more than two sculpted in most years, and they have dividing among all the high houses."

"It took only one to destroy Redmund and raise an elfonnel through him," Jean pointed out.

Connor nodded. "So he's still got eleven, and we know he's targeting one for Ivor."

"I hope he doesn't take it," Jean whispered, and Connor heartily agreed.

"That leaves ten more," Kilian said grimly. "We need to locate and capture them if Granadure is to have any hope of surviving this war."

"That's assuming none of the other houses use any of theirs," Connor said.

Jean asked, "Do you think the other houses will commit their sculpted stones so early in the war?"

Kilian said, "It's possible, but unlikely."

"Why not?" Connor asked.

"Think about it. They'll know Dougal's got more. He can afford to spend them," Jean said. She pointed at the parchment. "House Islay's only got two. I bet they'll hoard that treasure until the moment that using it would guarantee a major victory. Otherwise, the loss would outweigh the benefit."

Kilian gave her an approving nod. "You studied hard at the Carraig."

She blushed. "Thank you."

Wolfram said, "Our primary focus remains the successful defense of Harz."

Kilian nodded. "After that, this group's primary focus must be to capture Dougal's other sculpted stones. We can worry about the other houses after that."

"I will helping you," Gisela said.

"As a friend and a student of Ailsa? Or as a representative of the Arishat League?" Kilian asked.

"Both. I am interesting to help you myself, and I can informing you that the Arishat armies will ready to invading Obrion if the invasion continues having success."

"I didn't think the Arishat League had many Petralists. How could you possibly invade?" Hamish asked.

Gisela said, "We are having few Petralists, mostly defending the generals. But for three hundred years, our nations are knowing that Obrion will someday attacking. We have focusing learning powers of the world not magic."

"What non-magical powers?" Verena asked, looking very interested.

When Gisela hesitated Kilian said, "We're sharing much with you, and if you stay, you'll see even more. The chances of the Arishat League needing to attack Granadure are minimal, and you know it. Trust goes both ways."

She nodded. "I think you will being correct. Each nation of the Arishat are many different. Althing has developing clever scientists with deeply knowledge of the chemicals and elements of the world. They have developing weapons of these that can disable even mighty Petralists."

"How is that possible?" Connor asked.

Gisela shrugged. "I am not scientist or warrior, so I am knowing little exactly how these are working."

"And the other Arishat countries?" Verena asked.

Gisela glanced toward the north. "Varvakis has making marvelous discovery just in last decade. They have learning to harnessing the Beautiful Dancers and stones that grab steel."

Connor said, "You told me the Beautiful Dancers are the lights along the far northern horizon, right?"

Gisela nodded. "I have not seeing how they harnessing the dancers, or what rocks grab steel, but my mother traveling there recently. She told me they have building lanterns that glowing with no fire. They have planning lights for the entire city."

"They create lights without fire and without limestone?" Jean asked.

"And how do lights represent a weapon?" Hamish asked.

Connor had used his Solas and the marvelous prism lanterns from the Rhidorroch to disable three entire armies for a critical moment in one of the mock battles, so it was possible.

Gisela shrugged. "I am knowing little more. Sehrazad is different focusing. They having too much sand, and developing kinds of glass that cannot be shattering."

Hamish barked a laugh. "Now you're making things up."

Gisela shook her head. "More bizarre than even unbreaking glass is rumors I have hearing from Tabnit, across the sea. They have discovering a black sand that can exploding with incredible anger."

"Diorite?" Connor asked.

"I am thinking no. They are using black angry sand in the mouths of long serpent weapons. The fire is so angry that it throws huge arrows and rocks hard enough to destroying a ship."

"Thank you for sharing what you've heard," Kilian said thoughtfully as he paced to one wall where a large map of the entire continent hung.

"Even this much information gives us hope that help could come if we need it. Please request more details from your mother. We need to begin developing joint counterattack strategies. In turn, we will share with you what we know. Together we can stop this invasion and restore peace."

"Gisela, I'd like to talk with you some more about how Aunt Ailsa is doing," Connor said.

"Of course. I am hope to speaking with you more too. My mother has asking many questions about what happening at the Carraig."

Connor wasn't sure he was ready to share everything with her mother and the rest of the Arishat League, but she already knew about porphyry and the secret of the unclaimed.

Verena gave Gisela a hug. "Welcome to the team. I'm looking forward to getting to know you more. Right now, I've got to get back to that keystone."

Jean nodded eagerly. "I think we should test non-Builder flight today, if possible."

"Oh no you don't," Hamish exclaimed. "You can't start a dangerous experiment just like that. Certain precautions have to be taken. Like eating a big lunch."

"We ate lunch an hour ago," Verena pointed out.

"But we didn't give it the right focus. Any meal could be your last, especially if you're about to fly for the first time."

Chapter Thirty-One

"A hunter may enter the den of a bear if his strength is sufficient to take the prize, but he risks much that would be avoided had he chosen a safer path."

~Evander

ean felt a thrill of nervous excitement as the windrider rose into the warm afternoon sky, with Verena at the controls. She and Hamish sat on either side on the high front bench. Jean would soon get her turn to try piloting the huge wagon.

They'd spent the past hour reviewing the controls and the plan while still safely on the ground. It had all seemed so clear and simple there, but now her heart raced as her turn loomed.

"I still think this is a really bad idea," Hamish said as they rose fifty feet above the field behind the Builder lab at the outskirts of Harz township.

"Relax," Jean told him and reminded herself the same thing. "We've taken abundant precautions."

"She's not even flying yet, and you're acting like a scared old maid," Verena laughed.

"You won't be laughing when she crashes this thing and gets hurt." Of course he didn't suggest that he or Verena would get hurt. He was wearing his battle suit, and Verena was more bird than human in the air.

Jean was determined to identify the underlying principles that made flight possible. If Verena could do it, Jean would find a way to figure out how to train others.

If she didn't die today.

To keep her fears at bay, she watched Verena carefully, but there was not a whole lot to see. Verena lightly grasped the controls, shifting her grip at random-seeming times.

Five long, quartzite-lined levers extended up in front of the high pilot bench seat where they sat. Each lever linked to different thrusters. The first lever controlled tip-over balance, followed by lean-over balance, slip-spin left and right, main lift thrusters, and finally the main push thrusters.

"Why did you just make that shift?" Jean asked as Verena moved a hand to the first lever, and a small thruster set into the front, left corner of the wagon fired for a second.

"Didn't you feel that shift in the tip-over balance?" Verena asked.

Jean shook her head. She was too new to flying to have a feel for the wagon, even though it was far more stable than the Storm or the Swift, and clearly the best choice for initial testing.

"Are you really ready for this?" Hamish asked.

"Nearly. Let's review the levers one more time." She took a deep breath to settle her thoughts, then touched the first lever. "Tip-over balance is the forward or backward leaning of the wagon, the vertical angle away from the ideal midpoint."

There were so many new terms and principles to learn before she could start quantifying flight, she wanted to squeal with excitement.

She glanced down at her notebook in her lap and frowned. "One question has been bugging me. Why don't we use nautical terms for some of these principles?"

"We're not sailing," Hamish said.

"I know, but some of the movements are similar. For example, the tip-over balance is the same principle as 'pitch'. The lean-over balance is similar to 'roll', and the slip-spin-drag is a fair approximation of 'yaw'."

"I always thought yaw was a stupid word," Hamish said.

Verena said, "Some of the principles are similar, but flying isn't the same as sailing. I decided not to use nautical terms when we first started flying because re-using terms that are similar, but not exactly the same, can be even more confusing."

Jean said, "Makes sense, but to me it's harder this way."

"I thought you loved to learn new things," Hamish said.

"I do, but I don't like spending effort learning new words when old ones might do. Better to spend the time studying truly new things."

"Flying is about as new as it gets," Verena said with a smile. "Trust me, once you start feeling the air and begin to control the movement, you'll realize it's really not the same."

Hamish nodded. "If a boat rolls entirely over, it sinks, but it's not a big deal for us in the air."

"It is if you're riding in the back," Verena said. "Passengers can't exceed the lean-over tip-out point."

"All right," Jean said, seeing she wouldn't convince them yet, but still jotting down the equivalent nautical terms in her notebook. "Back to the controls."

She touched the second lever. "This controls lean-over thrusters that manage the sideways roll of the wagon, or the horizontal angle."

Verena nodded. "Both of these first two levers are subject to the slip-spin-drag properties." She moved her hands rapidly across the control levers and sent the Windrider into a slow, flat spin.

Hamish said, "Gotta watch the slip-spin or it'll get you every time."

"You think about all of this while you're flying?" Jean asked, amazed and a little daunted. They spoke as if it was so simple and obvious.

Hamish grinned. "If we didn't, we wouldn't be flying for long."

"It's not as hard as it sounds," Verena reassured her. "After a while, you just feel the air and the craft and respond without really having to think about it."

"Well, I need to think about it, or we'll never figure out how to explain and teach it." Once she took control of the levers, maybe it would make more sense. "How do I start?"

"I think we're too high," Hamish said.

Verena shook her head. "If anything, we should go higher. It would take longer to fall and more time for you to save Jean if something goes badly."

While he thought about that, Jean said, "Besides, if I have to unbuckle from this safety harness and jump free, I might need a little space for this catch-fall mechanical to save me."

"We don't even know it'll work," Hamish protested.

Jean loved him so much her heart ached sometimes. Other times, it ached with annoyance.

She understood that his over-protective attitude was a response to his inability to save Ingrid at the plateau. That didn't mean she needed to accept his reaction to that loss as the best one. She accepted the dangerous things he was now called upon to do, but he needed to learn to accept that she could be brave too.

"It passed the initial test on the ground," Verena reminded him.

Jean didn't want their flight test to fail, but she was actually looking forward to testing the catch-fall in an actual jump. The simple harness secured to her back held a quartzite thruster, just big enough to arrest her fall and bring her to a hover. To activate the stone, she'd use the same keystone that Verena had developed for controlling the windrider.

Jean touched the second, tiny quartzite block set into the center of the chest strap that linked to the catch-fall thruster. "How does this work again?"

"I created a power matrix in that stone." Verena didn't seem to mind the question, even though she had already explained it three times. "When you twist that stone so the top end makes contact with that vein of quartzite in the strap, it'll activate."

Hamish said, "Simply brilliant. Would've taken me a lot longer to figure out."

Verena grinned. "If I'd let you continue working on your original plan, activating this thing would accelerate her fall."

"Everyone gets things backwards sometimes," Hamish said defensively.

"Except you had it backward, upside-down, and inside out."

Jean smiled along with Verena but said, "So turning this stone links the currents of power you activated inside of it to the thruster, right?" She traced the crystalline quartzite vein worked into her strap.

"More or less. It's a multi-faceted, layered build, far more complex than any mechanical we've used before."

If they could prove it worked reliably, both with the catch-fall harness, as well as with the levers controlling the windrider, the concept could open up nearly endless possibilities for what they could do with their mechanicals, and who could run them.

Jean felt deeply grateful for the opportunity to participate in proving these advanced principles Verena and Hamish were rediscovering. They possessed the gift for pure creation, but she could help bring their ideas to mature fruition.

"I know your builded stones work," Hamish assured Verena. "Just let me worry a little, all right?"

"While you're worrying, come up with some new ideas for 'builded'," Jean offered. "We still need a new word."

He grumbled, "I like builded. Our mechanicals are special. They're Builder-built."

Jean giggled. "I don't think that's an improvement. How about Builder-powered?"

"We don't power the stones, we unlock their power," Verena said.

Jean sighed. "We'll figure it out. Maybe we need to take the Builder out of the name."

Verena grinned, "First, let's take the Builder out of the flight."

Jean touched the cool quartzite worked into the wooden shafts. "I'm ready."

Verena pointed to the recessed tops of each lever. They still bore some chisel marks from the quick, recent work done to prepare them for the test.

"This set-up is still a bit crude, but it should work to prove the concept." She extracted from her satchel a small piece of quartzite and handed it to Jean.

Jean had studied the stone closely while they were planning for the flight. It was the keystone, similar to the one in her harness. All she had to do was place the rounded, bottom edge of it into the recessed top of each lever that she wanted to control, with the side containing the engraved quartzite symbol facing her. That would link the keystone to the control levers in a neutral release position.

The tiny symbol engraved onto the stone looked like the eye of a storm, with streamers of wind rippling away on one side. "I saw this symbol in my research, but there was no explanation."

"I doubt even many Petralists recognize the ancient symbols any more," Verena said. "I found them in one of the few tomes of notes from the original Builders that were preserved." Her eyes widened. "I bet Kilian himself rescued those from the Great Purge."

Hamish said, "Probably belonged to his sister. I wish he'd gotten all of them."

Jean nodded. The thought of destroying books filled her with seething fury.

"Let's start with some more lift," Verena said, gesturing toward the fourth lever. Jean decided she needed to add labels to each of them until she developed the intuitive understanding of which lever controlled which function.

Verena jumped into the back of the wagon, then took Jean's place when she slid to the pilot position in the center. Jean settled the little stone into place over the correct lever.

Verena leaned a little closer, eyes fixed on the lever in Jean's eager hands. Hamish was leaning in from the other side, eyes wide, a breadstick hanging from the corner of his mouth.

Verena said, "Twist the keystone to the right to increase release. The power currents augment the thrusters by degrees, depending on how far you turn it. Turning the stone the other way will have the opposite effect."

"Have I told you today that you're brilliant?" Hamish asked.

Jean couldn't understand how the magic worked, but she was impressed by Verena. "How did you determine the amount of extra thrust to release as I turn the stone?"

"It's still guesswork. Right now, it's split from neutral to full power across about a hundred degrees of arc. To reduce power, return the stone to the starting position, then rotate back the other way."

"We should have a keystone for every lever," Jean said. She should have thought of that sooner.

Verena nodded. "We'll probably settle on an entirely different configuration, but we have to start somewhere."

"So let's test," Hamish urged, his excitement overwhelming his worries.

Jean twisted the keystone. She planned just a little change, but it turned in the socket easier than she expected. She ended up turning it almost all the way. The roar of the powerful lift thrusters doubled and the wagon ascended sharply. The force pressed against her shoulders like a heavy weight.

"Too much," Hamish said, one hand reaching for the lever.

"Let her figure it out," Verena cautioned.

Jean turned the stone back to center, then twisted it the other way. She figured half a negative turn would bring them back to the previous hover, but the turn cut too much, and at the abrupt decrease of power, she slammed up against the restraining straps that held her to the seat and prevented her from soaring right off the seat.

Hamish whooped as he soared into the air, then ignited his suit's thrusters to return. Verena used a small quartzite stone as a personal thruster to settle back to the seat.

She explained, "You have to slow gradually, especially with such a big wagon."

"I had no idea it was so complicated," Jean said, her heart pumping with the thrill of the experience. It wasn't going great, but she was really flying the windrider! "I'll need to document the amount of change at each degree."

"Try the other levers," Verena suggested.

Jean shook her head. "I should test the lift a few dozen more times and document the results thoroughly. We might need to add gradient lines to the quartzite to mark major units of change of lift rate. Maybe every twenty percent. What units do we use, anyway?"

Verena shrugged. "We don't have a name for it yet."

"Just try the other levers," Hamish pleaded. "We need to make sure they all work the same way. I don't think I can handle a few dozen more tests of the lift alone."

"Why not? Feeling sick?" Jean teased.

"You can't make me sick," Hamish laughed.

So Jean moved the keystone to the top of the third lever and gave it a savage turn. The corner thrusters ignited with a roar. The windrider began a slow, flat spin.

Hamish chuckled, leaning back against the seat. "I think I'll take a nap."

Jean glanced to Verena, who shrugged. "It's a big wagon. It takes time for it to build up momentum for changes, especially from the smaller directional thrusters."

Jean moved the keystone to the first lever, intending to lean the wagon a bit and give him a start, but she turned too far and the lift thrusters under the front of the wagon dropped to a low whine. The front of the wagon pitched down, throwing them all forward.

"What are you doing?" Hamish exclaimed as Jean lurched against her safety straps and the two Builders tumbled right out the front.

"Oops," Jean breathed. "Definitely need labels." That had been the tip-over lever, not the lean-over one.

She twisted the keystone back the other way, but the wagon was nearly vertical by the time she did. So she twisted the keystone all the way to the right to max the front lift thrusters and tip them back the other way.

That's when she realized that the wagon was still spinning. The abrupt tip-forward motion seemed to have accelerated that spin, and she had left the slip-spin thrusters still activated. Verena had said the wagon took a while to pick up momentum, but the change seemed to accelerate with time.

The front thrusters roared and began to tip the wagon back the other way, but the spinning was accelerating so much that Jean started to feel sick. She moved the keystone to the third lever, but it took precious seconds to get it settled into place.

By that time the wagon was spinning like a top, and the front lift thrusters had fired too long, too hard. The wagon tumbled right over backward, somersaulting through the air in a back, rolling twist that overwhelmed Jean's ability to figure out how to respond.

The entire world was spinning around her, and Jean cried out with fear. Her initial exhilaration was already gone, and three seconds later, her lunch joined it as she reached the stomach-lurch point.

Jean clutched at her head as she vomited. Closing her eyes helped a little, but not knowing what was happening, not being able to see panicked her. The wagon was going to crash for sure, and she was going to die. Where was Hamish?

She'd killed him and Verena!

Filled with overwhelming fear, Jean pawed at the restraining straps, finally hitting the release latch. Instantly, she tumbled off the bench. The rear of the spinning wagon struck her as she rolled past, and she cried out as pain lanced through her ribs.

Then she was flying free, spinning wildly as she tumbled toward the ground. She clutched at her chest, her hands shaking with panic as she tried to twist the little keystone on the catch-fall.

With a welcome whoosh of air, it activated.

She was aimed headfirst at the ground.

The little mechanical only accelerated her fall. Jean screamed and flailed at the air, trying to right herself, but unable to manage it. How did Hamish soar like an eagle? All she could do was fall to her death.

Then Hamish swooped in and snatched her out of the air, pulling her close and twisting them both upright. The catch-fall on her back faded to silence, and the two of them hovered, blessedly motionless.

Jean clung to him, sobbing with relief.

"Are you all right?" Hamish asked.

"What do you think? I nearly killed us all."

"Stop exaggerating," Hamish chuckled, pointing to the right. Jean followed his gaze. Verena had somehow returned to the windrider, leveled out its flight, and was banking the big wagon around in a lazy turn toward them.

"I don't think I've ever seen anyone make a windrider do tricks like that," Hamish laughed.

"It's not funny," Jean said, not easing her hold on him. She couldn't if she had wanted to. Terror had locked her arms around him in a death-grip.

Hamish waved Verena to land the windrider and he settled the two of them to the ground nearby. Jean stepped away, her knees weak, barely restraining the urge to kiss the ground.

Verena hurried over and asked, "Are you all right?"

"I think so," Jean said as she vainly attempted to fix her windblown hair. "I'd say our first test can be classified a failure."

"I would've thought Assassins would sleep lighter," Hamish said.

"Right now I'm Aifric, and she doesn't worry about people sneaking up behind her."

"How do you keep it all straight?" Verena asked in a fascinated tone.

Aifric shrugged. "It's not that hard. When I'm Aifric, all I have to worry about is being me."

A subtle shudder passed through her frame and her features altered slightly. Her smile faded and her expression turned more predatory. When she spoke, her voice had lost its warm timbre. The words were sharper, her tone more coldly confident.

"When I'm Student Seventeen, all I have to worry about is my next mission."

"Student Seventeen?" Connor asked.

"That's me."

"Pleasure to meet you," Verena said formally.

"I never knew that was your name," Connor said.

"You never asked."

"That's an odd name," Hamish said.

"Not when you know my people," Student Seventeen explained. "All Mhortair children join the kill academy to see which have potential to become fully credited Assassins."

"What happens to the ones who don't make it?" Jean asked, shuffling her chair closer.

"Their lives are spent in supporting roles to our work." Her tone carried a hint of disdainful pride. It was fascinating to Connor to see the startling differences in Aifric's different personalities.

"We still need carpenters, cooks, blacksmith, and all the other regular crafts and trades, but for students who show promise, they are all named Student."

"So Student Seventeen means you were the seventeenth student in your class?" Connor guessed.

She shook her head. "Every time a student does something that could potentially get them expelled or executed, but they are given another chance to remain in the academy, a number is added to their name."

"You could have been killed seventeen times in school?" Jean exclaimed. "That's horrible."

"It is the way. Most students do not survive past four or five."

"Then how did you get all the way to seventeen?" Verena asked.

She allowed a wolfish smile. "I pushed the limits of my training, but I also held the top spot in my class. Instead of discarding me, my death trainers began assigning challenge missions as punishment. That's how I ended up at the Carraig."

"That's amazing," Verena said, sharing an astonished look with Connor. "Did you learn other subjects besides killing?"

"Of course, but details are not discussed. If my masters knew I had shared this much, I might reach number eighteen."

Another shudder passed through her frame, and her features relaxed. She blinked a couple of times, then sighed and rolled her shoulders. "Seventeen can be so uptight sometimes." She grinned and leaned over to grip Jean's hand. "How did your flying go? I'm so excited to hear all about it!"

Jean hesitated for only a second, and Connor wasn't surprised. The abrupt shift was startling. Connor wanted to ask Aifric about that process of shedding one personality and slipping into another, but Jean was already launching into her tale. Her near-disastrous first flight was fascinating.

Connor marveled that none of them had gotten badly hurt. "Wow. I thought research was usually pretty safe."

Jean chuckled. "Not today."

"We definitely need to attach one keystone to each lever," Hamish said.

Jean nodded. "Fumbling with that keystone compounded the problems."

The library door opened and Kilian entered, looking grim. "The outer windrider scout perimeter just confirmed that Dougal's army is on the march. We're expecting the main attack at dawn in two days."

Verena grimaced. "I hate that so many Obrioners are marching into Granadure."

"Rory made good time," Aifric said.

Kilian shook his head. "Dougal started the march before Rory returned."

Jean asked, "So he didn't bother to hear Wolfram's response?"

"He might not care," Kilian admitted. "He can't expect we'd surrender, and he's not about to withdraw just because we tell Rory we demand it. It's interesting that he even tried."

"What did he gain by it?" Verena asked with a frown. "Other than taunting Wolfram, and sending that ridiculous offer to Connor?"

Connor hated that the offer still tempted him. Even if Dougal actually planned to honor his word and not kill Connor and the others once they were safely away from the main fighting, Verena would never abandon her homeland. That meant he couldn't either.

Kilian shrugged. "It's a moot point. The army is coming. We'll integrate into Wolfram's battle plan as we discussed."

Jean asked, "What if you see other officers, or even Shona, when you're hovering and waiting for a chance to strike at those stones? Should you attack and try to kill them?"

"I'd prefer we capture, if possible," Verena said to Connor's relief. "Killing would be effective, but we could use more intelligence."

Kilian said, "I agree, but don't take unnecessary risks. If Dougal does not unleash another elfonnel, Wolfram should be able to drive them back. That will be the main focus of this engagement."

"I still think he's probably hoping to draw you or Connor out," Verena said.

"I can help from a distance, while yet concealed," Kilian said. "He may well be trying to draw you out, Connor. Another reason to not take unnecessary risks, although I doubt he could secure a hold on your mind unless you tap obsidian."

Aifric said, "No obsidian for you. In fact, just give me whatever you've got. Seventeen needs more."

"How could you need more? That portion I gave you was a two-week supply," Connor said.

"You might have asked for two weeks, but I barely got enough for a single sparring practice."

He could have sworn the pouch had held more, but shrugged. "Sorry. I should have checked it more carefully. I'll get you some more, but what if Dougal has another way? Maybe I should get some of that burned porphyry powder you told me about."

He tried to keep his tone casual, but his voice shook as he thought about porphyry. Verena had suggested the burned powder was less potent, but he felt a sudden overpowering urge to try it out anyway. If the battle went poorly, he might need it.

Kilian regarded Connor closely and shook his head. "That powder is not pure, which adds another layer of risk to an already dangerous situation. I don't think it wise for you to tempt porphyry again."

Gisela, who had sat quietly listening shuddered, "I am thinking porphyry is a bad idea too, Connor. The monster doesn't sleep easily after it is being released."

"I can control it," Connor assured her.

He knew when to let the beast out, as Martys liked to say, but he could rein it in when he needed to. Kilian's refusal infuriated him, and he was startled by a sudden urge to leap out of his chair and beat Kilian until he relented.

Rattled by the intensity of the violent impulse, Connor forced it down and took a deep, steadying breath. He focused on Verena's face, and that helped him relax.

"Then we need another way to block him," Connor said as calmly as he could. He glanced at Aifric, and a memory sparked an idea. "That night you tried to kill me, you hit me with something that blocked my primary affinities. What was that?"

"Wait, you tried to kill Connor?" Verena exclaimed.

Connor shrugged. "Half the people I know have promised to kill me. Even you and Hamish were probably planning to kill me if I lost control."

"How did you know that?" Verena asked, her cheeks flushing with embarrassment.

"It makes sense. Nothing personal, right?" He squeezed her hand. "Friends do what it takes to keep each other safe. Sometimes for us that gets a bit weird, but it's the intention that counts. Aifric, you told me I wouldn't be able to establish primary affinities for a while. That would work against Dougal too, wouldn't it?"

When she hesitated he said, "Come on, Aifric. You're one of us now. We guard each other's secrets. We'll keep yours too. This is important."

She sighed. "Loyalties sure get twisted around you, Connor."

"Helps you know what's really important," he said with a grin.

She smiled. "I suppose. The powdered stone I hit you with would affect Dougal too, but it's not quite as simple as it sounds. He attacked your mind from a distance, but that powder has to be inhaled to take effect. And it tends to impact obsidian less than granite and basalt."

"It's worth a shot at least. Do you have any?" Connor asked.

"Seventeen has a very little. Perhaps enough to disable one person." She spread her hands in apology. "It's a very closely guarded secret of her people."

"Don't you mean your people?" Hamish asked.

"Haven't you listened to anything we've told you? Seventeen is Mhortair. Aifric is Obrioner. Those crazy Assassins aren't my people."

"Does your head leak sometimes?" Hamish asked softly, staring at her with a bewildered look on his face.

"Hold on," Jean said, her brows furrowed in thought, even as she idly combed at her wild hair with her fingers. "You have a powdered stone that reacts negatively to primary affinities. We already know about another powdered stone that counters granite. Kilian, is there a stone that counters basalt?"

"Actually, there is. You're a quick study, Jean. We just discovered the existence of the anti-basalt stone this year. It's a metamorphic stone known as amphibolite gneiss, but we've only ever found one tiny deposit, barely enough to test."

"And what is the secret weakening powder?" Jean asked.

Kilian shrugged. "Obrion has acquired it, so it's not such a secret any more. It is also a metamorphic stone, known as granite gneiss."

Jean paced away, head bowed in thought.

"You're seeing something we've missed again, aren't you?" Connor was glad that Jean was on their side.

She turned to face them. "Metamorphic stones are formed out of other stones."

Kilian nodded. "That's right. Through heat and pressure."

"Is it safe to suppose granite gneiss was formed out of granite?"

"Power-grade granite?" Connor added, catching on.

"I'll have to check with the stone masters. I'm not sure we've ever asked that question, but it may be a safe assumption."

Jean said, "Have them check on amphibolite gneiss too. See if they can determine if it was formed originally from basalt."

"So if a power-grade igneous stone is transformed into a metamorphic stone. . ." Connor said, working through the logic.

"Then it stands to reason there might be a metamorphic stone somewhere formed from power-grade obsidian," Jean finished for him, her blue eyes bright.

"And it might nullify obsidian," Hamish said.

Kilian laughed. "Hamish, kiss that girl of yours." While Hamish eagerly obeyed, he added, "I'll send a message out to our obsidian quarries to begin a search of nearby areas for metamorphic stones. It's a long shot, but we might get lucky. Especially at the Emmerich quarry. They've had some unusual, localized earthquake activity recently. It's possible new veins of stone have been unearthed."

"Alasdair's had earthquakes too," Connor said.

"Do you think quarrying power stone sometimes has a negative impact?" Jean asked, looking worried.

"I've never thought it might, but now I wonder." Connor hated having something else to worry about.

"We can study that when we have more leisure," Kilian said. "We are soon heading into battle. We cannot allow Harz to fall, but we must coordinate efforts carefully. Do not face Dougal alone."

"But get those sculpted stones if we can," Hamish interrupted.

Kilian cautioned, "If the moment is right. Wolfram's challenge will be to drive them back, but not savage them so badly that Dougal feels forced to use another sculpted stone."

"I still can't see him accepting defeat without taking that option," Jean said with a worried frown.

Gisela said, "I am fearing the same thing. All intelligence I am seeing suggests this."

Kilian said, "If he does, I will deal with it. That will be your time to strike. You must locate Dougal while he's distracted." He glanced at Aifric. "Are you up for another attempt?"

"I don't think so."

Surprised, Connor looked closer at her and noticed for the first time that she looked pale. "Are you sick, Aifric?"

"I didn't want to say anything, but I've had a lingering weakness from when Gregor struck me down outside of the Carraig. I don't think I can go into battle again yet."

"Why didn't you say anything?" Jean moved to Aifric's side to place a hand on her forehead. "We could have found you a Healer."

"I am a Healer, remember? This isn't a wound that just heals, but an exhaustion that will recover with time."

"I've never heard of anything like that," Jean said.

"It might have to do with how he beat you," Hamish suggested.

"Perhaps."

"I'll arrange for you to sleep on one of the healthbeds. It might help," Verena offered.

Connor hoped so. He was glad Aifric shared her problem with them. That kind of hesitation was so unlike her, it worried him.

Aifric gave them all a warm smile. "Thank you. I really just need rest. I can still help with the injured, and watch for any Obrioner assassins."

"There is much for all of us to do," Kilian agreed.

"Not for Jean," Hamish said.

"What are you talking about?" she asked.

"I want you to go back to the Builder compound." Hamish took her hands, his expression earnest.

"I can help," she insisted, her expression hurt.

He said quickly. "I know. It's just, I don't think I can focus on what I have to do if I'm worrying about your safety."

"I won't be in the fighting. Why would you worry?"

Hamish hesitated, glanced at the rest of them, and flushed. He said softly, "Ever since I couldn't save Ingrid. . ." His voice trailed off into a gruff cough.

Jean cupped his face with her hands, her expression tender. "I know it's been hard for you, Hamish, but I'll be fine."

"Maybe Hamish is right," Verena said.

Jean looked hurt, and Verena added, "I'm not questioning your skills or your bravery. Just the opposite. I need someone who understands our work who can meet with the craft masters of Faulenrost to discuss developing advanced mechanicals. I think you're the best person to chair those meetings."

As Jean considered that, Hamish added, "We can send Dierk back to pick up another supply of mechanicals, and the newest Last Word bomb. It should be finished by now. He can give you a ride, and you can come back with him in a few days."

"I don't like leaving you." Jean gave Hamish another of those lovesick looks, and Connor was glad he and Verena didn't act all mushy like that.

"I think it's a good idea," Connor said before Hamish could waver. "I think you can accomplish most with your research."

Jean looked from him, to Hamish, to Verena, and frowned. "I still don't like it, but I can see I don't have any choice." Then she brightened, "I assume I have authority to start making plans with them?"

"Within reason," Kilian cautioned.

She gave him a dazzling smile. "Trust me."

"I will going with you," Gisela announced. "I have wanting to see the Builder home for some time. I can doing very little during the battle, but can helping Jean think of better mechanicals."

"Thanks, I'd love your company."

Kilian said, "I'll send a pigeon to Altkalen to get an update on their readiness. If things go badly, we might need them sooner."

"A pigeon?" Hamish asked, looking disgusted. "Doesn't that seem a bit old-fashioned now that we've got listening posts, speakstones, and flying machines?"

"Except that we have no listening post here at Harz, I have no windriders to spare, and speakstones don't communicate over such distances," Kilian said.

"We need to work on that. There has to be a Builded solution," Hamish said.

"Craft-made," Jean suggested.

He grimaced.

"Or Inventor-built?" Connor suggested.

Hamish's grimace deepened. "We're getting worse, not better."

"We'll find the right word," Verena promised. "But right now, we need to get back to the lab."

"I need more diorite darts," Hamish agreed.

"And we can begin calibrating the thrusters of your suit before I leave. Verena, I'd like to take that keystone with me back to the Builder compound."

"You can't fly without us," Verena cautioned.

"Really bad idea," Hamish agreed.

"I won't fly, but I'm sure I can learn more from it, or at least feel how it reacts when placed against the other stones on the Windrider." When the two Builders hesitated, Jean added, "I won't even climb aboard. I'll just circle the outside to do some testing. It'll give me a chance to establish a base level of responsiveness."

"Just be careful," Hamish urged her, taking her hands in his. "I can't bear the thought of anything happening to you."

She gave him a tender kiss. "Stay safe, Hamish. I'll be fine." Then she added with a grin, "In fact, I'll have all that extra food to eat for you."

CHAPTER THIRTY-THREE

"The mightiest ship is turned by a tiny tiller, but a single leak can invite the floodwaters to enter."

~Ilse

With the Obrioner army advancing, tension grew and preparations intensified. Connor spent half the next day on the banks of the lake with Marshal Gunter and the commanders of the tertiary-affinity companies.

They started with mud. As they gained proficiency working together with the mud, their enthusiasm increased. Soon they began practicing with combining air and fire, forming towering fire whirls. Connor shuddered to think about the damage such flaming tornadoes could inflict.

By the time he left them, they were eagerly discussing other potential combined attacks. He almost felt sorry for Carbrey's soldiers.

As he passed through the long fields west of town, he marveled at the number of auxiliary troops. Companies of swordsmen, spearmen, slingers, and even archers were crammed into the huge field, each hundred-man company led by a captain and ten sergeants.

Connor counted eighty companies, plus another dozen of heavy cavalry to the north. Even more soldiers camped closer to the fortress or around the far side of the town. He estimated that Wolfram commanded close to twenty thousand auxiliary troops, plus the Petralists, which numbered nearly two thousand. The thought awed him. It seemed impossible that the Obrioner army was nearly twice as big.

He had felt challenged managing about a hundred Petralist students in the mock battles of the Carraig. He'd commanded almost five hundred against the elfonnel, but Wolfram needed to organize and effectively utilize closer to fifty times that number. Connor didn't envy him.

He found Jean in the Builder laboratory with Verena and Hamish. The large, converted barn was literally buzzing with intense activity. Connor wasn't sure what was making that sound, and he hoped whatever it was worked properly. They didn't have time for new mechanicals to fail.

The Builders, led by Verena's quick mind and Hamish's boundless energy, had completed another dozen speedslings and several thousand hornets, including a few hundred with embedded diorite. Those were handled with immense care as they were loaded into the weapons, which were then sent out to the companies that would wield them against the Obrioners.

Verena only had a small supply of blind coal, but she produced three dozen gauntlets. They would each only work a couple times, but the aggressive slipperiness of blind coal would virtually guarantee the soldiers wearing them could avoid nearly any attack. They were delivered to captains and commanders who would be engaged in the direct fighting, and might prove a critical advantage.

Jean waved to Connor and pulled Hamish from under a windrider he was helping to repair. "I have to go, unless you prefer I stay until you're done."

"No, I'm coming," Hamish told her quickly.

Connor pulled Verena from behind a stack of recently-activated healthbeds, awaiting shipment to the auxiliary hospital on the north end of town. She looked tired, but enthusiastic.

"I'm glad you stopped by," she grinned and hugged him.

He savored the feel of her. She smelled of stone dust, wood polish, and quartzite air, and he enjoyed the soft, warm caress of her breath against his neck.

"Do you think you'll have everything ready?" he asked.

She gave a slightly exasperated sigh and ran fingers through her sandy brown hair. "The biggest challenge is lack of power stone. We've got a stockpile back at the Builder compound, but it's too far to fetch in time. This forward laboratory is new, and our supplies are severely limited."

"It doesn't look limited to me."

"Well, we're nearly finished with everything we have available. Wolfram refused to allocate more. He needs the rest to fuel the Petralists."

"It takes more stone than most people realize," Connor said, thinking back to the daily rounds he used to deliver at the Carraig for Ailsa. Wolfram probably needed an entire vault's worth for a single battle.

Verena sighed. "I know. Quarries are beyond maximum production limits, but stone stockpiles are not nearly high enough. Managing supply chains will be a major challenge if the war drags on."

"Hopefully it won't."

"If it does, we need to find ways to use our stones more efficiently. Jean's work might become critical to the war."

"Then we probably should go see her off."

Together they left the lab and returned to the windrider courtyard behind the main keep. Dierk was already strapped into place on the high pilot bench of one of the windriders. Jean was donning her flying leathers.

"Time to go," Dierk said, sounding a bit impatient.

"Just take off," Hamish told him. "I'll bring her up to you in a minute."

"Say your good-byes then, but don't take too long." With a wave to Connor and Verena, Dierk ignited the thrusters and the huge wagon lifted slowly off the ground, then accelerated north.

Verena gave Jean a warm hug. "Good luck with your meetings."

"I'm really looking forward to it," Jean admitted.

Connor hugged her too, and her expression turned serious. "Be careful, Connor."

"I'll be fine," he assured her. "Dougal can't get my mind. I gave Aifric all my obsidian yesterday, so I can't use it, even if I wanted to."

Verena looked surprised. "I got Aifric another double portion of obsidian too."

Hamish said, "She should have plenty then. Come on, Jean."

"See you soon," Jean said to Connor and Verena, then jumped onto Hamish's back and said enthusiastically, "Let's fly!"

Hamish erupted off the ground, and the two soared up into the clouds.

After they disappeared in the distance, Verena said, "Come find me after dinner. I want to go out scouting later."

"Sounds good to me."

CHAPTER THIRTY-FOUR

"The window does not importune the light, but accepts it every day with willing gratitude."

~Evander

Connor returned to the lake just as the practice session ended and the senior Petralists disbanded back to their companies. Many of them waved or called greetings, and he felt a little less like an outsider.

He approached the huge Marshal Gunter. "Where did Ilse end up?"

Gunter gestured south, toward the hills separating Harz Valley from the invading Obrioners. "The skirmishing soldier has passed the time for practice."

Ilse was a brilliant, crafty leader and he wasn't surprised to learn she was at the forefront of the fight, but he suddenly worried for her safety. "Already?"

Gunter grunted. "Did you assume no fighting would start until tomorrow?"

A straight question from a Sapper lent it extra weight. He had noticed the earth movers had been speaking more and more plainly as the time for battle drew near. Sentry speak was great for many things, but clear communication was not one of them.

"What's she doing?"

"Her team harries the Obrioner lines, intercepting scouts and Pathfinders, and shielding this valley from incursion before the allotted time."

"Sounds dangerous." It sounded perfect for Ilse.

Gunter nodded. "All prey flees the hunting pedra, but the fox can catch even the burrowing rodent."

That actually made a lot of sense. "She's clever, but pedras eat foxes when they catch them."

Gunter grinned and tapped the side of his nose with one thick finger. "If they catch them."

When he returned to the fortress, Connor found Uncle Martys sleeping in the back of a windrider. He'd been hoping for some bash practice, but decided not to wake him.

After dinner, as impending twilight turned the air purple and soft shadows began creeping out of their daytime hiding places, he returned to the Builder lab. He found Verena alone there, double-checking the Swift's armaments. Connor was surprised to see blades protruding from nearly every plane of the little craft. The glittering, double-edged steel reflected her green limestone light as she carefully inspected them.

"When did you add those?" Connor asked.

The rest of the huge barn was empty, bare of mechanicals. The shadowy silence seemed all the more intense compared to how busy it had been just hours before.

Verena began snapping the blades back into their concealed compartments. They were virtually invisible when stowed, but ready to snap out and lock into position.

"I only finished these today. Just in case we have to engage in close fighting."

He hoped she never had to get so close to danger. She tossed him a set of flying leathers.

As they donned the flying gear he said, "Looks like you were right. You finished everything."

Verena settled into the Swift and strapped herself in. "Let's go see the Obrioners for ourselves."

They exited the barn and accelerated into the sky above the town. The rush of cool air was invigorating.

Instead of soaring into the clouds, Verena slowed to a hover at about five hundred feet and pivoted back to face the fortress. Torches lined the solid stone walls, and a Solas had ignited a bright light above the central keep, illuminating the grounds so preparations could continue into the night.

"Do you have any quartzite?" Verena asked.

"Of course."

"Listen".

Not sure what she meant, Connor wedged a tiny piece of quartzite into his cheek and applied it to his ears. The lobes elongated, and as his hearing improved tenfold, a barrage of sounds thundered into his head.

The clink of armor and weapons from fields full of auxiliary troops was like a clashing flood. Tens of thousands of voices created a mind-boggling cacophony that overwhelmed his ability to process it. Using the trick he'd learned at the Carraig, he forced himself to ignore it all, letting the sounds wash by, like a powerful current in a river.

Once he felt centered, he scanned the chorus, flicking his thoughts across the torrent of sound for anything interesting. It was like casting a net, letting his thoughts touch the sounds as light as gossamer spider webs.

By holding in his mind certain words or concepts he was interested in, any sounds associated with those sought-after words would snag in his mind and attract his attention.

A rushing wind surprised him. It wasn't natural, and it remained centered over the fortress. It fluctuated in intensity, but did not fade away, and it was filled with random-seeming, discordant sounds. It was as if the wind had swallowed a hundred cats trying to play musical instruments.

"They're shielding, aren't they?"

Verena said, "Standard practice prior to a major engagement. It's possible that Pathfinders might have crept close enough to eavesdrop."

"Gunter said that Ilse's out trying to intercept spies."

Verena resumed their ascent toward the clouds now painted pink with the fading light of day. She slowed again after slipping into the concealing mists and pointed down at the land huddling in deepening shadow.

"It looks quiet, but there's a complex, subtle game played in the hours leading up to a major clash. Tertiary Petralists either try winning control over important pieces of land, or try slipping close enough to spy on each other, protected by complex shielding.

"Minor skirmishes are common, and both armies activate defensive measures against quartzite information gathering. Sometimes they even attempt to pass misinformation."

"We didn't get into much of that at the Carraig," Connor admitted.

"We studied it some at the academy. Ilse is one of the best skirmishers. She and her team will be in the thick of it for sure."

"Academy? Like the Assassin death school?"

"More like the Carraig. I'll tell you about it some time. I made some good memories there."

She accelerated again, making further discussion difficult. In moments they soared over the southern boundary of Harz Valley. The next valley to the south was filled with the enormous Obrioner army.

"They're definitely ready to attack tomorrow," Verena said when she slowed again and dipped to the very bottom of the clouds for the best view. Hovering there, they should still remain concealed from Pathfinders below. "They're already camped in battle array."

Connor swept his enhanced gaze over the army. There had to be at least thirty thousand troops, and he felt a chill of dread. Thousands of cook fires dotted the valley, outlining the battle companies.

There had to be close to three thousand Petralists and Guardians in the center. Like the Grandurian forces, a full half of them were Boulders. Half of the remainder were Striders. He even counted an entire hundred-man company of Blades.

"That's a lot of Petralists." His wonder at the sight was tinged with cold fear. That many affinity-powered soldiers represented a staggering amount of force. They made the thirty thousand auxiliary troops seem completely unnecessary.

Verena said, "That's the largest army since the height of the Tallan Wars. Even with our mechanicals and the work you've been doing with Gunter to integrate the tertiaries, tomorrow could easily go against us."

"Especially if Dougal uses more of those sculpted stones."

Verena nodded, her expression grim. "I worry about that, Connor. We've got a good plan if he raises one elfonnel. It'll get ugly, but I think we can deal with it. But what do we do if Dougal hands out three or four sculpted stones and orders his officers to use them to magnify their affinity without ascending?"

When Connor had used the soapstone sculpted stone, it had granted him an unrivaled connection to elemental water. If he had just used it to augment his normal affinity instead of ascending, he probably could have beaten ten other Spitters.

"I have the other sculpted stones Ailsa gave me, and I could use one to help counter something like that."

"Would Dougal spend such a vast treasure in that way, or is he saving them for elfonnel? Wolfram does have his own sculpted stone reserves."

"I figured he must, but why hasn't he mentioned it?"

"The fewer who know, the better. Wolfram's men won't raise elfonnel with them. They know better, and Kilian would never allow it."

"Why doesn't Kilian lead the army?" Connor wondered.

Verena shook her head. "Wolfram is a gifted general, and that leaves Kilian the flexibility to deal with elfonnel and threats of the deepest magic."

"Better if no one uses sculpted stones at all."

Unleashing any sculpted stones, even without raising an elfonnel, could rip Harz Valley asunder and probably kill thousands.

As they hovered there, studying the camp, Connor spotted several windriders monitoring the enemy from three miles out. The Obrioner central command tent was a huge, circular construct very similar, if larger, than the one Carbrey had used at Alasdair. Beside it stood an enormous tent that looked like a portable palace.

"Whose do you think that is?" Connor asked.

Verena said, "I was just wondering if my hornets could cover that much distance. I could send Dougal a little house warming present."

"It's pretty far." Connor liked the idea of raking Dougal's tent with explosive hornets, but only if he was sure Dougal was alone in there. He didn't feel like killing a bunch of servants.

"I'm still tempted to try, or climb over the clouds and dive to attack. I could probably close before they could stop me."

"Escaping might be trickier. It's too early for suicide attacks."

Actually, suicide attacks were a really dumb idea. Hopefully she wouldn't ever consider one seriously.

Just then, a series of high cloth screens rose around the central command area. The white fabric was suspended on wooden frames and covered the entire center of the camp. They blocked view of the command tent, the palace tent, and the surrounding area.

"They're starting their own defensive screening," Verena said.

When Connor tapped quartzite to his ears again, he heard another rushing, noisy wind from the direction of the Obrioner camp.

"You said it's standard practice."

"I know, but it's still annoying," she grumbled.

A grim mood settled over Connor as he surveyed the army preparing to attack tomorrow. Tens of thousands of men and women would try to kill each other.

The battle would be no student contest where everyone would live to celebrate or complain about the final scores. It would be like the desperate fight against the elfonnel, where death would walk the battlefield among them.

Suddenly he didn't want to look any more. "I've seen enough."

228

"Me too." Verena banked the Swift away, but instead of heading back toward Harz, she rose into the darkening clouds, then turned east.

"Where are we going?" Connor asked, leaning closer to her.

"I'm not ready to go back yet."

Eventually she descended out of the clouds above a row of low mountains flanking the eastern side of the valley, about five miles away from the Obrioner camp. They landed on one flat peak, shed their thick flying leathers, and used them as cushions on the solid stone.

With their backs against the side of the Swift, they gazed out over the valley. The distant campfires sparkled like crimson reflections of the stars now emerging in the clear, darkening sky.

Verena shivered next to him, and he wrapped an arm around her. She snuggled closer, but shivered again.

Connor wedged a tiny piece of marble under his tongue and savored the spicy burst of flavor. When Verena shivered again, Connor kissed her. As their lips touched, he released a trickle of heat through his lips to hers.

"I like those hot lips of yours, Connor," she grinned.

"I'm getting better at heating things up."

He focused on the heat. It was hard, since thoughts of impending battle fit perfectly with the wild ferocity of elemental fire, but he managed it after a few seconds.

Connor blew out a long, slow breath. Pure heat flowed out his mouth and he used it to gently wrap the two of them in layers of warm air.

Verena smiled. "When did you learn how to do that?"

"Kilian taught me."

She leaned her head against his shoulder and sighed. "This is nice. I could stay here all night."

If only they could. He glanced across the valley at the twinkling fires of the invading force. "I wish things were that simple."

She nodded, and after a moment she sighed. "I can't help thinking about all the people I know who will be in the thick of the fighting tomorrow."

Connor had been thinking about how he hated sending soldiers into battle while he hung back in a place of safety. "Captain Ilse is already out there. She and Erich and Anika could be in the middle of a fight right now."

Verena snuggled a bit closer, but her voice turned fierce. "If anything happens to them, I won't just fly up in the clouds tomorrow."

Connor's relationship with Ilse and her little band had transformed from initial hostility, to cautious animosity at the Carraig, to grudging alliance as the gealls and political maneuvering grew more complicated and dangerous. Now he agreed with Verena. Ilse and the deadly siblings were friends, and he would avenge them with severe prejudice.

He tipped Verena's chin up so he could look into her blue eyes. "Every person who gets hurt tomorrow while we wait for the chance to hit Dougal or those sculpted stones is a person I might have saved by leading the charge."

She touched his cheek. "We can't be everywhere. If we succeed, we can end up saving many more in the long run."

They sat together for several more minutes, warm and comfortable, and Connor simply enjoyed Verena's closeness. His dark mood faded away under the gentle influence of that peaceful moment.

She was so quiet that he assumed she fell asleep leaning against him, but a few minutes later she whispered, "No matter what happens tomorrow, Connor, I'm glad we have this time together."

He nodded into her hair, but didn't need to speak.

Far too soon, Verena pushed away and brushed her hair from her face. "It's getting late, Connor. Tomorrow is going to be a long day."

As they soared back toward Harz through the darkness, Connor hoped everyone they cared about would survive to enjoy another quiet evening.

CHAPTER THIRTY-FIVE

"Children play with glass and cast aside the words of wisdom that lead to treasures of knowledge."

~Evander

hile dawn was barely staining the eastern hills in brilliant shades of orange and purple, Connor hurried into the windrider courtyard behind the keep. Hamish was already there, dressed in his battle suit, along with Martys, who was dressed in Rumbler battle leathers like Connor.

He opened his mouth to speak, but Verena came around the back of the Storm, checking the thrusters. When he saw her all he could do was stare.

She wore a custom set of armor. Form-fitting steel plates covered her torso, shoulders, arms, and thighs, with burgundy leather peeking out from underneath. Small stones were affixed all over the armor with silver clasps. A wide leather belt dyed a deep burgundy encircled her waist, with at least a dozen small pouches attached by more silver clasps.

The armor was beautifully crafted, and she looked amazing in it. She carried her helmet under one arm, a pair of studded leather-and-steel gauntlets tucked inside. Her sandy brown hair was pulled back from her face and tied with a wide, burgundy leather strap, with the symbol of the Grandurian royal house worked in silver over her brow. Her regular, travel-worn satchel hung over one shoulder, a belt with five daggers hung over the other, and a short sword swung at her left hip.

Hamish laughed, "Connor, you look like you left your brain still sleeping under your blanket."

Verena giggled at the sight of him still staring. "He's got a point, Connor." She trotted over and gave him a quick kiss on the cheek. Her normal scent of high-mountain passes was overlaid by the scent of oiled leather and steel.

"You look amazing. Where did you get that?"

She glanced down at herself and her cheeks flushed slightly, making her look like an adorable, but very deadly, warrior maiden. "We are going to war today, Connor. My father had this made for me last year, and Kilian requested it from our estate near Edderitz. It just arrived yesterday."

Connor didn't usually like to think about her noble heritage, but in that moment he was happy she had such wealthy connections. He reached out to touch the leather-wrapped hilt of one of her five throwing daggers. "Do you know how to use these?"

"They wouldn't do much good if I didn't, would they?" she smiled and drew one of them. The double-edged, slender dagger looked well balanced and razor sharp. Verena bounced it in her palm a couple of times, then spun and threw in a single, fluid motion.

The dagger flipped once in the air and struck the wooden post of the door Connor had just entered through. Half a second later, a second dagger thudded into the wood, so close that it scraped the first. The rest of the daggers followed just as quickly, and all found their marks, slamming into the post right next to each other.

"Wow." What couldn't this amazing woman do?

He glanced back at Martys, who was nodding appreciation at Verena's skill. Hamish started to speak, but choked on a smashpacked cube and started coughing instead. Martys smacked him on the back hard enough to send him staggering. "I knew she's brilliant with a sword, but I've never seen her throw."

"Every girl needs a few secrets," Verena said with a prim little smile as she retrieved her daggers.

Connor was really looking forward to learning the rest of them.

A deep drum boomed three times over the keep.

"We need to get airborne," Verena said, leading the way to the Storm. "That's the signal that the Obrioner army has crested the southern edge of the valley and is marshaling for attack."

She jumped into the Storm and settled behind the controls. The Swift was already tethered to the back, its thrusters humming and keeping it aloft for easier towing. Several open-topped, wooden crates had been loaded into the small bed of the Storm, behind the three rows of seats. Most of them were filled with power stones, although one held a single large ceramic jar.

Hamish nodded toward it. "Not as powerful as the Last word, but might come in handy today."

As Connor and Hamish took seats to either side of Verena she said, "We couldn't use the Last Word anyway. It'd wipe out both armies and the fortress."

Martys climbed into the second row behind Verena and glanced nervously at the bomb. "I cannae say I like sitting next to that Tallan-spawned mechanical."

"Relax," Hamish said as Verena ignited the thrusters and lifted them into the air. "Connor's breath could kill us all even faster."

"Don't make me fill your suit with warm water," Connor retorted with a grin.

His smile faded as they ascended into the early morning sky. The Grandurian army was already assembled in battle formation a mile south of the fortress, facing the Obrioner army. A mile of empty valley separated them.

The Obrioner army filled the southern end of the valley. In the shadows that still held sway there, they looked like a swarm of insects as they marched into position. Company after armed company assembled, preparing to unleash death and destruction upon everyone standing in their way.

Verena soared above the Grandurian army, giving them a perfect view of the massed defensive forces. General Wolfram and his commanders were already assembled atop a high earthen tower at the rear of the main force. Wolfram was flanked by a pair of Longseers and several assistants to manage the speakstones linking the general with the ear-scout hub.

Connor had visited the hub the day before. He was impressed by how they had developed the basic idea of the speakstones into a battlefield-level strategy. The bustling hub gave Wolfram unprecedented communications.

Connor had no idea where Kilian was concealed, but he didn't doubt the man was ready. He'd seen Aifric earlier, and she had assured him that she would be on the move, watching for Obrioner assassins.

The many companies of the Grandurian army stretched east to west across much of the valley, with most of the Petralists in the front. Grandurian Sappers stood upon earthen towers, with Anton in the center. Marshal Gunter and several senior officers joined him on his wide tower.

As Connor watched, the Flameweaver there summoned crimson flames which flowed into grooves set in the outer face of the tower, forming several ancient symbols of power. A moment later, streamers of silvery water rose from a barrel behind the

Water Moccasin, a woman with long, blue-tinged hair, who wore blue plate armor. The water formed more beautiful symbols.

"Impressive to look at," Martys grunted as they soared past at three hundred feet. "But that won't win a battle."

"No, I think they will," Hamish said, pointing at the thousand Rumblers assembled in formation in the very center of the front lines. Many wore shifting leather battle armor like Connor and Martys, but some were encased in solid steel plate armor. They hefted gigantic shields, and wielded hammers so huge it seemed impossible that even their superhuman strength could manage them.

More Rumblers on both flanks were already carrying the deadly speedslings. Connor had expected to see more of the mechanicals. Maybe they were keeping some in reserve.

Wingrunners flanked the Rumblers on either side, ready to leap into a ground-eating running battle. The much smaller tertiary-affinity companies were assembled fifty yards behind the Rumblers, with a screen of deadly Allcarvers positioned immediately in front of them.

Huge pits had been opened in the earth directly behind the tertiary Petralists, filled with blazing bonfires. Water Moccasins were already pulling water from Harz Lake through gaps between the assembled companies.

Auxiliaries had assembled by the thousands, with swordsmen and spearmen flanking the tertiary-affinity Petralists. Archers and slingers were assembled behind. Heavy, armored cavalry stood at the ready farther back, long lances set at exact angles, armored mounts pawing the earth.

Several Builder catapults, like the Thump Driver that Dierk had used at Alasdair, were arrayed at the rear of the army. Connor studied them.

The siege weapons were built atop thick-timbered wagons, and looked like giant crossbows equipped with wire mesh slings instead of bolts. Eight foot tubes of basalt extended out the fronts, angled into the sky. They would help accelerate the payloads. A dozen traditional catapults flanked the thump drivers, but they looked pitiful compared to the complex Builder siege weapons.

The sun lifted free of the eastern hills a moment later and flooded the valley with bright, morning light. Verena climbed a mile into the sparse cloud cover and Connor surveyed the huge Obrioner army.

If the elemental Petralists fought to a standstill, the next wave would be the beloved bash fighting and the intricate running battles of basalt. With so many auxiliary forces poised to join the fray, they could potentially tip the final tide of battle too. They might lack Petralist powers, but there were an awful lot of them.

Verena settled the Storm into a hover, then climbed into the back to draw the Swift in closer. The Obrioner lines settled into position and advanced to within half a mile of the waiting Grandurians. There they stopped and an expectant hush settled over both armies.

Connor spotted Carbrey and his high command positioned atop an earthen tower, almost identical to Wolfram's, at the rear of his army. He did not see High Lord Dougal, but he did spot Ivor on the right flank, commanding a company of reserves, including many of the students from the Carraig.

That placement seemed odd. Why would Carbrey sideline a powerful Dawnus like Ivor? Did Dougal not trust him for some reason? Was he worried that if Connor appeared in open opposition to Obrion that some of those students might side with him?

Or was Dougal holding Ivor back to make it easier to give him a sculpted stone? Connor hoped Ivor was wise enough not to take it. The temptation to ascend would be hard to resist once he tasted that power.

Without preamble, a barrage of round, earthen missiles erupted out of the ground behind the front lines of Obrioner Boulders. About a foot in diameter, the missiles sailed over the empty middle ground before arcing down toward the lines of granite-hardened Rumblers.

"That seems like a weak opening volley. What's he playing at?" Hamish asked.

"Maybe he's probing the defenses," Verena suggested.

Earthen barriers rose to intercept the rain of earthen missiles in front of the ranks of Rumblers, and most of them simply thudded into the barriers and seemed to melt into them. Several of the missiles erupted on impact, though, and clouds of gray powder billowed across the lines of Rumblers.

"What be that?" Martys asked, peering through a pair of long-vision goggles. They were already activated at a five times magnification, so he could enjoy a better view of the battlefield than either of the generals down below.

"I hope that's not the weakening powder," Connor said, suddenly worried. He'd seen what it could do. Those clouds of billowing powder could disable half the Grandurian Rumblers, and it took hours for Petralists to recover.

He was surprised when Hamish grinned and said, "Excellent. Look!"

Instead of collapsing to the ground as soon as they inhaled the debilitating powder, Rumblers were donning masks that fitted over their mouths and noses. Water was already spraying across their ranks, washing the powder out of the air and off their skin.

"What are those?" Connor asked.

"They're breath masks," Verena said. "They're so new, we don't even have a good name for them yet. The concept is simple. Each has a tiny piece of quartzite attached that emits a steady stream of air, just enough to breathe. It protects them from the weakening powder until the Water Moccasins can wash it all off."

"That's brilliant," Connor said.

"We figured General Carbrey couldn't resist trying it after fearing it for so long. He had to be eager to throw it back in our faces," Verena explained with a proud smile. "We don't have an antidote for it either, but those breathing masks were one of the new mechanicals we came up with over the past couple of days."

Hamish said, "Verena thought of it, so I had to make most of them. Got so much glue on my hands attaching the cotton to the leather, I nearly starved."

Verena chuckled. "You shouldn't have tried eating those smashpacked cubes while you were working."

"Glue is supposed to dissolve," Hamish muttered.

Verena laughed. "He tried cramming half a dozen of those cubes into his mouth, but they all stuck together. Nearly choked himself. I had to beat him on the back to knock that goop out of his mouth."

"Nearly broke my ribs," Hamish complained. "I think you need to punch Connor more often to work out your aggression."

"Why didn't you tell me about them? I could have helped," Connor said.

Verena said, "We didn't tell anyone. There's no way we've found all the Obrioner spies at Harz. Wolfram's got spies in their camp too. We couldn't risk him knowing what we planned."

"I'm glad you thought of it."

Only a handful of soldiers had collapsed inside the cloud of weakening powder, and Wingrunners were rushing to drag them back to the Healers set up at edge of town. Even as mists of water scrubbed the air and the Rumblers clean of powder, five of the thump driver catapults fired a return barrage back at the Obrioner lines. Large ceramic jars shot high into the air.

Verena's smile turned predatory. "One of the opportunities that present themselves with the presence of spies is misdirection."

Connor watched with even more interest as fingers of earth rose in front of the Boulder lines to intercept the incoming missiles. The ceramic jars exploded in mid-air before impact.

Verena grinned. "Perfect. The timing for those was tricky."

Flames erupted from the exploding missiles, but the Obrioner Firetongues seized them immediately, and the fire sped harmlessly above the Boulder lines. Soldiers raised their fists and jeered the feeble Grandurian attempt.

"That can't be all," Connor said.

Verena shook her head, not looking away from the distant lines of Boulders. Without warning, dozens of tiny earthen walls erupted out of the ground. Barely two feet tall, and ten feet long, the stout little walls slid across the ground with remarkable speed.

They smashed through the surprised Boulder lines, toppling the granite-hardened soldiers and creating chaos in the few seconds before the Obrioner Sentries could seize control over the walls and sink them back into the earth.

"Midget-pounders. My idea," Hamish said proudly.

"They didn't accomplish much," Connor pointed out.

"They did what we needed," Hamish assured him.

The other five thump drivers were already firing. As their ceramic missiles arced toward the confused Boulder lines, Obrioner Firetongues cast whip-like lengths of fire to intercept them.

The missiles burst even earlier than the previous wave had, but instead of erupting into flames and a rain of annoying little earthen walls, they burst into silvery clouds that settled over the Obrioner lines.

"Wolfram made the Obrioners think we didn't have any more weakening powder," Verena said, her tone satisfied. "Those midget pounders were designed to make sure all those Boulders were actively tapping granite."

Sure enough, soldiers were already toppling unmoving to the ground as they breathed in the cloud of weakening powder and it interacted with their active granite affinity.

Martys whistled softly and glanced at Verena with new respect. "Ye skelped ol' Carbrey with that, lass. I dinnae ken how the daft fool cannae know ye've got more of that powder."

"People hear what they want to hear," Verena said. Down below, Obrioner Spitters were spraying the air above the Boulders to scrub away the disabling powder, but over a hundred Boulders had already collapsed. Auxiliary soldiers were rushing forward to carry them from the field.

Martys grunted, "A wink's as good as a nod to a blind horse, that's the truth."

"What is that supposed to mean?" Verena asked, and Connor was glad she did.

"Doesn't matter what ye say to a proud fool, if'n they dinnae listen," Martys said with a shrug. "Carbrey shoulda known better."

"You sound upset that it worked," Verena said.

"I dinnae agree with this war, an I cannae say I want to see me ol' mates get killed, but I hate to see men suffer from a fool of a leader."

Connor said, "I wish they'd all been affected. Maybe without any of his Boulders, Carbrey would retreat."

"I doubt it," Verena said.

With the weakening powder washed away, a burst of blue lights shot into the sky above General Carbrey's position.

"Here it comes," Martys said softly, leaning over Connor's seat for a better view.

Instantly, crimson flames erupted from the mass of Firetongues and tore across the middle ground, setting the dried, autumn grasses alight. The tops of enormous tanks of water that the Obrioner army had carried with them burst off, and battering-ram-sized pillars of water hurtled after the fire. The earth in front of Gregor and the other Sentries heaved, casting ripples into the middle ground between the armies.

The Grandurian lines were ready.

Flameweavers met the Firetongues with their own flames, pulled in white-hot sheets from the glowing pits of live coals. Water Moccasins cast their streams of waiting water into the air to join in battle against the Spitters.

The ground between the armies bubbled and boiled as the Sentries and Sappers fought for control. Occasional eruptions of dirt sprayed several hundred feet, driven by the immense pressures smashing in that invisible battle below ground.

The other elements clashed in violent, beautiful splendor overhead. Fire and water collided, twining and rippling back and forth, casting a multi-hued mist over the contested battleground.

Fire changed hues from crimson to white to super-heated blue. Droplets exploded from whipping, darting ropes of water, glittering like diamonds in the explosions of colliding flames.

With his eyes riveted on the contest, Martys said, "Once the elements be subdued, time for bash fighting."

For several long minutes, the contest appeared to be an even match. Fire whipped back and forth in tortured sheets and sudden bursts, covering the battlefield in shifting hues of crimson and white. Water sparkled and hissed into steam as deadly ropes smashed into glowing orbs. They were all then swept aside by long, horizontal sheets that burst into sprays of foamy mist when they struck opposing wills. Droplets condensed again before they could fall to the earth, and struck once more.

Then the Obrioner Firetongues, led by Captain Aonghus, who was wreathed entirely in blue flames, unleashed a new barrage of fire. It was so intense that it covered the entire contested middle ground in blinding brilliance and flashed all the water to steamy mist.

The Grandurian defenses were momentarily overwhelmed and the dueling flames began to writhe closer and closer to the Grandurian lines. The Firetongues pressed their advantage with wild rage and seemed to sense victory.

Connor worried about what was coming next. Aonghus must have burned through a full day's ration already.

"There's just too many of them," Hamish muttered, gripping the front rail of the Swift so hard with his armored hands that the wood creaked under the pressure.

Verena rapped him on the side of the helmet. "Breaking the Storm won't help."

"Sorry," he mumbled, but did not tear his gaze from the fight that was now clearly going against Granadure.

"I thought Kilian was going to help," Connor said as the Obrioner Spitters seized one of the streams of water away from the Grandurians and used it to knock several Water Moccasins flying.

His blood was pumping, as if he was in the fight himself, and he felt a powerful urge to leap out of the Storm and plunge his will and body into the fray. He had already swallowed a large dose of soapstone and water, and now he connected with that gateway.

All the water below glowed softly in his soapstone vision. Despite the distance, he felt the dozens of Water Moccasins and Spitters battling for control. Their wills whipped the elements into a wild frenzy.

If something didn't happen soon, the Obrioners would win the critical middle ground and open the way for a Boulder charge. With so many troops, they'd overwhelm Wolfram's army. Maybe Kilian was in trouble? If he didn't intervene, Connor would have to.

Then his worst fears were realized. The ground under Anton's command tower erupted in a spray of black earth, shredding the brilliant symbols of ancient power. Anton's officers and assistants tumbled away.

Somehow Anton himself managed to withstand the barrage on a slender pillar, even though spears of earth pierced the air all around him. His pillar slid back toward the main Grandurian lines, while he caught his companions with fingers of earth and pulled them to safety with him.

"No!" Hamish shouted, pounding the rail. "He's lost the center."

The Obrioner lines cheered so loud that Connor could hear the roar without tapping quartzite. He felt a sinking sense of dread as the Boulder lines broke into a charge, followed by the first wave of several thousand auxiliaries.

Strider companies leaped from their flanking positions and raced with fracked speed far out around the eastern side of the dangerous middle ground. Grandurian Wingrunners leaped away from their positions to intercept.

Connor had seen the intricate maneuvering of running battles before, but never with so many basalt Petralists involved. The land wasn't big enough for them to bank and turn properly. He feared they'd smash into each others' lines and half would die in the initial impact. The thought sickened him.

As the Obrioner army rushed forward into the breach, he realized the clever attack with the weakening powder hadn't done nearly enough. The Obrioner army was still far too big.

"We have to help," Connor cried.

Hamish reached for the controls of the Storm, but Verena slapped his hands away and said sharply, "No. You know our orders. We remain in position."

Hamish cried, "But they're going to lose. Then it'll be too late to help."

Connor was surprised when Verena shook her head and gave Hamish a reassuring smile. She gestured back toward the battlefield and said with calm confidence. "This battle isn't over, Hamish. It has barely begun."

CHAPTER THIRTY-SIX

"Even the ship that glides upon the waves is battered by the tempest."
~Evander

Connor, Hamish, and Martys leaned forward again as one. Water and fire still exploded above the middle ground several thousand feet below where they hovered. The earth appeared solid enough for the Boulder-led charge though, and the Obrioner main force appeared totally committed.

The Grandurians were not charging to meet them, but remained formed in tight companies, heavy shields raised, hammers and swords at the ready. As the Obrioners closed to within fifty yards, the front ranks of the Grandurian lines suddenly retreated five quick steps.

The movement exposed the next ranks. Every Rumbler in that line was holding a speedsling. As one, they lifted the weapons, the long tubes already spinning. With the speedsling companies Connor had spotted earlier flanking them, the entire front line of the Grandurian army unleashed in unison a storm of hornets.

The deadly little hardened-granite projectiles ripped the air between the two armies, and the front lines of the Grandurian advance seemed to melt under the onslaught.

A percentage of the hornets were embedded with diorite. They exploded with horrific effect among the tightly-packed soldiers. They tore through armor and stone-hardened flesh, ripping gaps in the Obrioner lines, and sending soldiers tumbling.

Verena had told Connor that they had improved the hornets, but he hadn't expected to see such devastation. Even heavily armored Boulders carrying thick shields crumpled under the onslaught. Some writhed and screamed, clutching at ghastly injuries, but many lay unmoving. The entire assault stumbled to a halt.

Some of the speedslings tilted higher, and the hornets soared completely over the faltering Boulders and tore into the thousands of auxiliary troops behind. Those men fell in waves, and the screams echoing across the battlefield clearly reached Connor, even when he released quartzite.

Hamish, his face pale whispered, "That's sickening."

Verena nodded with unshed tears in her eyes. "And we created those weapons."

In grim silence, they watched as the charge faltered under the withering onslaught, then reversed direction. As the desperate troops fled into the middle ground between the armies, walls of protective earth rose up behind them and the hornet onslaught ceased.

If the speedslings weren't out of ammunition yet, they soon would be. There were enough projectiles for at least a couple of rearmings, but Connor hoped they wouldn't be needed again.

Movement on the flanks of the battlefield drew Connor's attention. The long lines of fast-moving Striders and Wingrunners were closing on each other, and in his enhanced vision he could see the fury on the faces of the Striders. They had seen what happened to the Boulders, and it was clear they were eager for a taste of blood. They ran with short swords raised or daggers poised to throw.

Seconds before the lines of fast movers smashed into each other, the Grandurian Wingrunners suddenly all braced their legs and skidded to a halt. A dozen of them cast small stones to the ground.

Connor cringed. That could not be good.

Walls of earth erupted out of the ground. A little bigger than the midget-pounders, the low walls shot across the ground with tremendous speed and smashed through the Strider lines like balls into Tumble-Tosser pins.

"I forgot you distributed the speed-crack walls!" Hamish exclaimed.

"Good thing the Wingrunners didn't," Verena said.

A few of the Striders along the fringes managed to bank away from impact, but most of the tightly-packed Striders lacked the time to avoid the collision. Many tried to skid to a halt, but it was simply too late.

Moving faster than galloping horses, the Strider company smashed into the walls, which were sliding almost as fast in the opposite direction. The brutal impact sent some Striders tumbling in every direction, although most of them were simply plowed under. They were left half-sunken into the soft ground, broken limbs twisted into unnatural angles.

The Wingrunner corps descended upon the groaning, fallen ranks with clubs and chains, quickly capturing most of the Striders and dragging them back toward the Grandurian lines as helpless prisoners. The few Striders who escaped the initial impact raced away, with Wingrunners in close pursuit, meteor hammers raised to deliver crippling blows.

"I can't believe it," Connor whispered, stunned by the brutal encounter. "I've never seen Striders disabled so fast."

"I'd say more than three quarters of Carbrey's fast movers are out of commission," Verena said, trying to sound calm, but Connor saw the anguish in her eyes.

He took her hand in his, and her fingers trembled against his. He wasn't sure how to comfort her.

Bash fighting was so much fun, but this was war, not a friendly contest of superhuman warriors. Even the battles of Alasdair hadn't prepared him for such violence.

"I dinnae understand," Martys said with wide-eyed shock as he watched the unexpected changes of the battle. "Why dinnae the tertiaries strike down those Tallan-cursed Builder mechanicals with the elements?"

Verena pointed. "They couldn't. They weren't winning as easily as they believed."

As she spoke, the elemental battle above the contested middle ground, which had drawn perilously close to the Grandurian lines, shifted abruptly back to the center. A firestorm of blue-white flames, intermingled with ropes of glittering water, erupted from the Grandurian side and smashed into the Obrioner elements. The intertwined elemental barrage swept all the way across the battlefield to the retreating Boulders.

The earthen barriers shifted to arced, defensive mounds protecting the Boulders as they fled toward the dubious safety of the main Obrioner lines. Fire scorched those earthen barriers, leaving black streaks like whip marks.

"They dinnae need to harry them like that," Martys growled. He was gripping the rails in white-knuckled hands, his face a mask of fury.

"At least they didn't try flooding them out," Verena pointed out.

"Don't ye speak to it," Martys snarled, rounding on her, his skin fading to granite gray, but his face purpling with rage. His eyes blazed and actually seemed to glow red. Connor wondered if maybe Martys was a secret Solas.

Verena recoiled from his rage, while Hamish pivoted in his seat, hands coming up into fists. "She's not the one doing it, so back off."

"Just because ye spring from the same town, dinnae think I won't skelp yer wee behind if'n ye look for a square go with me, laddie."

"Calm down," Connor urged, shaken by his uncle's fury. "I might know some of the people caught in that speedsling trap too, but tearing the Storm apart won't help any of them."

Martys turned his angry glare on Connor, and he looked on the verge of losing control. If he did, Connor would have to knock him out of the Storm before he wrecked it. He prepared to tap granite, and verified his marble was already in place under his tongue.

"Me mates ain't in that mess," Martys growled.

"And neither are you," Connor reminded him. "You're the one who volunteered to come with us."

"I know, laddie," Martys said with a heavy sigh. His skin returned to normal color, and his expression softened. "I may be no longer with them, but I be no traitor, and no friend to Grandurian tricks."

"What do you expect?" Verena demanded, turning angry. "Your high lord started this fight. We're going to do everything in our power to kick him and his army back out of our lands. All that suffering you see down there is on his shoulders, not ours."

Martys shook his head. "Whether ye speak truth will come clear when ye try sleeping, lassie. Then we'll see if ye can justify yer wicked ways."

"Stop it," Connor snapped. He understood Martys's anger at one level, but his own anger was rising in response to Martys's insult.

Martys surprised him by grinning. "Good on ye, lad. The beast is awake in yer heart, and I see ye're prepared to unleash it to protect yer bonnie lass."

"No one should have to protect anyone up here," Verena said angrily.

Martys made a placating gesture. "Easy, lass. Ye made yer point an' I am no gaun to fight ye."

"Look," Hamish exclaimed, pointing down and drawing their attention back to the battlefield.

A huge, cresting wave of water had burst the banks of Harz Lake and now thundered between the Grandurian companies, pouring into the middle ground in a flood. Many of the Obrioners probably couldn't even see it coming, with their view blocked by those heavy, protective earthen walls and the dazzling display of fire and water colliding over them. The Spitters must have felt it, though.

The aerial display of battling elements faded as the waters tore into the middle ground and churned toward the retreating earthen walls and the Boulders protected underneath. Connor felt sorry for the Obrioners fleeing the new assault.

Then the waters abruptly plunged into the ground a hundred yards short of the Obrioner earthen defenses. The battered soldiers raised their hands in triumph. They interpreted the defeat of that deadly wave as a sign that the battle was again turning in their favor.

The truth always hurt the optimistic ones the most.

Those long, curved, protective earthen walls shattered, and a cresting wave of bubbling mud erupted out of the ground where they had stood.

"Tallan's fury!" Martys exclaimed in horror as the wall of mud struck the Obrioner lines.

The muddy waters swept the entire Obrioner center from their feet. It tumbled them back toward the central command position on the high ground near the southern end of the valley.

For a moment Connor worried that the army would suffocate in the muddy earth. Wolfram's forces needed to break the Obrioner attack, but he did not want to see hundreds of people slaughtered using an idea he had come up with.

The churning mudslide finally slowed just short of the Obrioner central command position and mud exploded in every direction. The heavy mud tumbled thousands of auxiliary troops off their feet, but deflected away from an invisible barrier protecting General Carbrey and his senior officers.

As the Obrioner Petralists wrested control of the earth, their soldiers began popping out of the soupy mess and sliding across the surface toward higher ground. The water began draining at the same time as the Spitters sucked it away.

"That won't work so well a second time," Hamish said.

"It worked this time, though," Connor said, pointing.

On the Grandurian side of the battlefield, Anton's central earth tower had re-formed, complete with ancient symbols of power outlined in fire and water. The Grandurian army appeared unaffected by the first attack, while the Obrioner lines were in disarray. Connor couldn't imagine how many soldiers had died or been wounded in the initial clash.

"The whole thing was a feint?" Hamish exclaimed.

Connor opened his mouth to respond, but a voice caught his quartzite-enhanced hearing and drew his attention.

It was Shona.

"Connor, I need you. Please hurry."

Chapter Thirty-Seven

"A sweeping rain that leaves no flood is anger without substance, but love will sacrifice to lift another from the deep."

~Gregor

They left Martys in the Storm, hovering in the clouds. They circled around the battle and the Obrioner army to the west, following the sound of Shona's voice. Connor rode on the back of the Swift, while Hamish flew beside them.

They spotted Shona behind a couple low hills that screened her from the rest of the Obrioner camp. She stood in the middle of a circle of small tents, already staring up at them.

"Keep watch from up here," Connor said.

"Wait," Verena called, but Connor let himself fall off the back of the Swift.

He laughed as he plunged toward the ground, spreading his arms to let the wind tear at his leathers while he lay back and looked up at Verena and Hamish. Verena had pivoted the Swift, and for a second he thought she planned to race after him.

Or was she planning to shoot him out of the sky?

Thankfully the speedslings didn't begin to spin up. She did descend, but at a much slower pace. Hopefully she would be wise enough to realize he was right and remain high and out of danger of whatever trap Shona was surely plotting.

Hamish waved.

Connor waved back, then spun in midair and faced downward. Shona's eyes were already locked on him, a little smile on her full lips.

He looked away from her lips. They carried too many confusing memories.

Shona looked pleased, but not surprised to see him dropping out of the sky toward her. It rankled that she knew him so well.

Her message had better be good.

The sight of her triggered so many memories that for a moment Connor just stared. Shona wore Boulder battle leathers with the same unique flair as always. Her shapely figure, confident stance, and proud, beautiful features set her apart from every other noble lady. Her thick, blond hair was drawn back from her face.

The many experiences he'd shared with Shona, both good and bad, flooded his mind. Their relationship had spanned so much, he still wasn't sure what he felt for her. Execution had definitely been a low point in their relationship, but it wasn't the only one. They'd had some good times too, but always her conniving ways had undermined her efforts.

He blamed her father.

Connor considered the best way to make his landing. He could simply tap granite and slate, and plunge into the earth, although he'd probably sink fifty feet before rising again.

That wouldn't convey the right impression. Slowing his fall with marble would be the easiest solution. He could even change the colors of the flames to add some flair, and he could probably torch all those tents too. If there were soldiers hiding in there, he'd know.

But Connor wanted to demonstrate to Shona that he had changed since he'd left her. So he focused on the gateway to quartzite and applied the stone externally. He had a few seconds, so he envisioned the gateway like a cloud-filled doorway above the other elements, then thrust his will through. The gateway opened without resistance, and his thoughts slipped into the air.

It was wild.

Air rushed about in mad confusion. Gusts collided in every direction, stronger currents twisted around themselves, and strange, unexpected eddies suddenly whipped into invisible whirlwinds. Air was always unstable, but he'd never felt it so wild. The massive elemental battle had churned it into a fury.

That made the challenge harder, but success would be all the sweeter. So Connor drove fingers of thought into the air, testing the turbulent, unruly winds, and tugging at them, seeking for purchase to help arrest his fall.

The wind seemed eager for an excuse to vent its frustration, and it roared in around Connor, buffeting him from every side. It tossed him to and fro and rolled him over in a complete somersault.

"Stop it!" Connor shouted, but the wind only tore down his throat and nearly choked him.

He spat it out and yanked savagely against the wind with the full might of his elemental connection. If it wouldn't come willingly, maybe he needed to show it who was boss.

For a second he owned it, felt it respond. He righted in the air and in that second felt united with it and glimpsed the marvelous possibilities that air mastery might offer.

Then the air rebelled and rushed in from every side, blasting every inch of his body. It packed in tighter and tighter, compressing so much that he had to tap granite to keep from imploding.

For three long seconds he hung motionless in the air, trapped by more pressure than he'd felt at the bottom of Loch Sholto. He couldn't breathe, and the air refused to obey his call.

Then it fled.

Air whooshed away, leaving him in a vacuum of calm, two hundred feet above Shona, whose expression had turned concerned. Air was always unruly, but it had never done that before. He wasn't sure what it meant, but hoped he hadn't ruined his chances for future flight.

So Connor sucked deep from marble, building a painful burn in his mouth, and calling forth mighty flames. White-hot fire erupted from his feet, and he laughed, filled with the exuberance of fire. It hadn't fled at his call, but seemed eager for a chance to burn.

The crazy tumbling had shifted him so he would now land on Shona's head. At the sight of a hundred-foot tongue of flame exploding under his feet, Shona yelped, grabbed protectively at her hair, and retreated behind the nearest tent.

Connor landed in the center of the circle of tents, on the very spot she'd been standing a moment before, and let the flames rise around him, circling him like hissing serpents.

He turned to Shona and gave her a friendly wave. "Hello, Shona. You called?"

Shona approached and gave him a long-suffering frown. "Connor, will you turn off that fire before you burn down my tent?"

"Don't you trust me?" Connor asked, directing the snakelike ropes of fire across the ground to circle Shona's feet.

She walked right through them, and Connor had to pull them aside to keep from burning her. She approached, joy infusing her lovely features. "I trust you above all others, my Guardian."

"That's close enough," Connor told her when she drew to within a couple of feet and seemed intent on stepping right to him.

He wasn't sure if she planned to embrace him, try kissing him again, or punching him unconscious. She'd greeted him in all those ways more than once, so he couldn't guess what she intended.

Shona gave him a warm smile. "That's all the greeting I get, beloved?"

For a moment, her eyes glowed with emotion so deep, it tugged at his heartstrings, even though he'd thought himself fully insulated from her.

"Even if I wanted to hug you, Shona," he told her, hating the flood of distracting memories, "I think Verena would probably kill you the moment I tried."

Shona glanced up, and her adoring look fell away to one of hate. Then she shrugged and her expression turned calm again. "She and I will meet to settle our differences sooner or later, but that's not the reason I called you to me today."

Connor hated how both girls kept promising final retribution against each other. They had lots of reasons to hate each other, but he didn't want either of them dead. He loved Verena, and although he wasn't entirely sure what he felt for Shona, he didn't hate her like he had once thought. It would be nice if she'd stop with the whole conquest-by-destruction-or-seduction approach to life, though.

"You can tell me your reasons after you toss me the granite you've got on your belt," he said.

"I showed trust in you by calling you here, despite what my father would do to me if he found out," Shona said as she pulled the leather pouch of powder from her belt and tossed it to him.

"And I didn't flatten those tents to make sure you don't have a dozen Petralists waiting to tackle me when I landed," Connor retorted.

She made a slight nod to acknowledge the point. Then her expression turned amused and she gave him a slow smile that set his heart racing.

"You know, Connor, I've got extra granite already applied to my battle plates, but if you're going to start ripping off my clothes to make sure I'm completely disarmed, I suggest we retire to one of those tents."

Connor flushed, and hated himself for it.

Shona laughed affectionately. "I love your shy, honest soul, my Connor. Don't forget, in the eyes of Obrion you and I are still engaged. A little dalliance is not unheard of."

A stream of hornets tore into the ground between them, missing both Connor and Shona by inches. One of the hornets carried a grain of diorite, and it exploded three feet past them, showering them both with dirt.

"She really is annoying," Shona muttered, glaring up at Verena, who had descended lower while they talked. "I didn't summon you here, wench. I summoned Connor."

"Stop wasting time," Verena shouted to Connor as Hamish settled to the ground a few feet away. "Shackle her and take her. We don't have much time."

Shona raised an eyebrow at Connor. "So you mean to do violence to me, do you, Connor?"

"Before you do violence to us," Hamish growled.

"This war will do all the violence to you that is required," Shona told him with a dismissive sniff. "People will die today, and the next day. That is war."

"Then what is your purpose?" Connor asked, although he was starting to wonder if she had any purpose other than to distract them.

"Honest battles have a purpose," Shona said, gesturing toward the hill and the battle raging behind.

Her proud bearing faded and she took a half step closer to Connor, her expression falling to one of open worry. "But the slaughter of non-combatants, no matter how complicit they may be, is not something I am yet willing to condone."

"What are you talking about?" Connor asked.

"This battle is a farce," Shona said, taking another step and gripping Connor's arm, even though Verena dropped lower and the speedslings began to spin again. If she fired on them, she'd hit them both, and neither of them were tapping granite.

"It seems pretty real to me," Connor said.

She made a dismissive wave. "The fighting is, but it serves only to distract you and Kilian from my father's real target."

"Who?" Connor and Hamish asked together.

"Your home," Shona said to Hamish. She looked up at Verena and added, "I know you can hear me, strumpet. Your home is the target."

"The Builder compound?" Connor asked.

Shona nodded. "The evil of Builders is well documented and must be stamped out, but in her wrath, Camonica will destroy everyone and everything in her path."

"Camonica?" Connor's heart sank. She hated Kilian with a fanatical fury, and she'd relish a mission to lay waste to a place dear to him.

"Why do you think my father delayed as long as he did, wasting time with that sham of an embassy? It was to give Camonica time to get into position."

252

"Jean's there," Hamish whispered, his face ashen with fear.

"You left her there?" Shona rounded on Hamish in a rage.

"It was supposed to be safer there," Hamish stammered.

"You've killed her, not saved her. That is, unless you can cover the leagues north by mid-morning."

"Why would you tell us your father's plans?" Connor demanded. The thought of Jean in danger terrified him, but could he believe it?

"I just learned of them this morning. My father sacrificed Redmund to raise that elfonnel, Connor. Did you know that?"

Connor nodded, studying her. He knew Shona as well as anyone could, and he read no deceit in her, just a heavy weight of sadness, and perhaps a hint of fear. "He tried to do the same thing to me."

She nodded in turn. "That's one of the reasons I had to send you away, Connor." She reached toward his face, but then let her hand drop, not bothering to hide her sadness. "I love my father, but I couldn't let him hurt you."

Verena drifted closer. "What are you waiting for? We don't have time to interrogate her now."

Shona shook her head. "There may be a time for kidnapping and torture, my dear Connor, but it is not yet. I won't shed any tears over the destruction of the Builder center, but Camonica will spare no one." She hesitated and added in a soft, fearful whisper. "Connor, my father gave her a sculpted stone."

Terror chilled Connor. He could no longer afford to doubt Shona. She might be lying, but could they take the risk? Camonica would gladly surrender herself to Dougal to gain such a glorious moment to wreak her long-sought vengeance.

"We have to go," Hamish cried, igniting his thrusters and rising into the air.

Shona said, "Jean was my servant, and I hold no rancor against her. Go. Save her."

When Connor hesitated, Shona smiled sadly. "I miss you. Thank you for answering my call. We'll speak again soon."

Then she turned and walked away.

"Stop!" Verena shouted, and the speedslings began to spin up.

Shona paused and glanced up at her. "I gave Connor to you, witch, and I'm giving you the chance to save another friend. If you choose to fight instead, the consequences lie upon you and you alone."

She raised her hand, and the tents all around were thrown aside, revealing a dozen Boulders, who moved to flank Shona. Daly, the Firetongue from the Carraig, was also there, along with Mactail, the captain of the Sentries.

Daly's eyes were already burning and he grinned, with flames dripping between his teeth. "Go on, Connor. Give me an excuse to burn that little bug right out of the sky."

The ground underfoot rolled slightly, like a gentle ripple on a still pond, and Mactail watched Connor with guarded interest. Connor didn't think of Mactail as an enemy, but he didn't doubt he'd fight for Shona. Daly had crisped his brain long enough that he seemed eager for a pitched elemental fight.

"Stay and fight," Shona said softly. "You might win, but you might not. Either way, your chance of saving your Builder home and your precious Jean will be gone. Think wisely, Connor. You can do that when you put your mind to it."

"Next time," Connor growled. Then he saluted Mactail, waved to Daly, tapped marble, and erupted off the ground.

"Can I go after him?" Daly cried.

"Hold," Shona commanded.

Verena intercepted Connor in mid-air and he stepped into the stirrups. As they shot into the sky, with Hamish trailing close behind, Connor pressed his face close to hers.

"You should have captured her," Verena said.

"It wasn't worth fighting through all of them, not with what Camonica's planning."

"Do you believe her?" Verena asked as they reached the concealing clouds and banked toward the still-hovering Storm. Martys lay reclined on the back seat, snoring loudly.

Connor considered the question. Shona never did anything that did not profit her somehow. The question was, how did revealing that surprise attack benefit her?

If the attack proved true, Connor would be forced to admit she had spoken the truth. He would owe her yet another debt. That tenuous hold was all that remained between them, and no doubt she already had a plan to leverage it and draw him ever closer to her again. Her undying optimism could be a truly inspiring trait if she ever applied it to a better cause.

After a moment he said, "I believe her."

Verena growled, "I should have shot her. She's the most dangerous woman I've ever met."

"Tell me about it." That meeting had not gone at all as he had expected.

254

Hamish dropped into the pilot seat of the Storm, rocking the craft and shaking Martys from his slumber.

"Back so soon? I haven't even had lunch."

"Forget the food!" Hamish shouted as he fired the directional thrusters, pivoting the Storm back toward the Grandurian camp. "Hold on! We need to find Kilian now!"

The huge push thrusters roared like demons and the craft leaped away through the clouds, with Martys shouting and clinging to his seat in the second row.

Verena gave chase, and Connor added a burst of fire to give the Swift a little more speed, but the Storm drew farther ahead, then dove toward Harz. Connor only hoped it was fast enough to get them all the way back to the Builder compound in time.

If they didn't, Jean and everyone there would die.

Chapter Thirty-Eight

"The farmer does not command the seed to grow, but plants it in good soil and allows it to fulfill the measure of its creation."

~Ilse

Jean slowly paced around a windrider with a group of a dozen of the master craftsman and craftswomen from the nearby town of Faulenrost. "I think wings are a wonderful idea. They would provide better stability and turning efficiency."

The master carpenter, a middle-aged fellow named Artur, had a lined, weathered face and twinkling, blue eyes. He had suggested the wings and now nodded. "Many good wing. No fat brick."

"I'm sorry." Jean tried puzzling out his meaning. Most of the gathered locals spoke at least a little Obrioner, although the carpenter's was nearly as bad as her non-existent Grandurian.

A tall, elegant woman named Carolin, who ran a training academy of the arts for local girls, and who had a beautiful accent asked him a question in Grandurian then said, "He suggests with wings this craft would look more like a bird than a flying brick. I concur. We should design a new craft that is both pleasant to the eye and performs better in the air."

Jean felt a growing sense of excitement as she discussed the possibilities with this eager group of locals. They were all skilled at creating things without the aid of magic. She felt convinced that applying all of their creativity and experience to mechanicals could produce amazing results.

These folks were already very familiar with Builder mechanicals. Some of them had even helped test some prototypes. Despite a few remarkable failures of some mechanicals, they seemed eager to participate in the development process.

Bruno, the burly master blacksmith, nearly as massive as a max-tapped Rumbler, had been crawling under the wagon. His blond hair was so light, it looked almost white. He had been examining how the thrusters were connected to the control levers and now scooted out from under the front of the wagon.

"Is much clever. Builder heavy smart. Verena is glorious famous. But can make better and less stone to work."

"That's wonderful. Any way we can streamline things and reduce the amount of power stone, the better." Jean ran her fingers across the outside of the control levers. "What do you think about modifying the keystone configuration so that instead of turning the stone we push the lever forward or pull it back? That would be more intuitive, and easier to understand."

"You beautiful good mind, girl. Easy change." Bruno smiled, his bright white teeth contrasting sharply with his deeply tanned skin.

A loud gong began insistently ringing through the compound, interrupting Jean's next comment. The locals exchanged nervous glances.

"What's going on?" Jean asked.

Artur said, "Bell mean bad."

Carolin added. "It usually rings when a Builder mechanical has gone badly wrong and there is some kind of danger." Looking concerned, she headed for the outside door, next to the huge outer door of the workroom, which stood closed.

"Last time I heard it, they had just started testing the hop-walkers. Lots of broken bones."

Jean followed her toward the door and a growing commotion outside. The rest of the group trailed after. Outside, she was surprised to see people running away from the buildings, heading for the distant hills.

That could not be a good sign.

"By the Tallan's blessed memory, what is that thing?" Carolin gasped and pointed.

On the far northern side of the fertile valley, almost three miles away, the Nister River appeared to be flooding its banks and spreading south at an exceptionally fast rate. A gigantic . . . something was moving through the center of that flood, heading in their direction.

The huge being looked like a tall woman in flowing blue robes. Jean extracted from a pocket a small crystal from one of the long-vision goggles that Verena had loaned her. Holding it up to her eye and squinting through it, her vision leaped across the valley and everything magnified five-fold.

"It's enormous," she breathed.

The tall woman appeared to be made out of pure water. Her blue dress rippled with currents, and her long hair blew in an unseen wind, like a frothing, crashing wave. Her beautiful face seemed to be looking directly at Jean. Although she appeared to be walking slowly, she covered a lot of ground.

Jean did not want to be there when she arrived. The form might be beautiful, but Jean recognized what she was looking at.

"That's a water elemental! An elfonnel. We're all in grave danger."

The watery woman's path brought her near one of the farmhouses dotting the valley. Jean's fear intensified she realized the elfonnel towered over the two-story farmhouse.

The elemental did not slow, but long streamers of water shot out of her dress and tore through the farmhouse and surrounding outbuildings. The water ripped everything to splinters in an explosion of destructive foam. Jean gasped in horror as she watched those churning waters swallow up the people trying vainly to flee.

"This is bad," Jean muttered.

Bruno grunted and pointed to her left. "Is worse."

Jean had been so busy looking into the far distance that she had not noticed the floodwaters flowing rapidly up both sides of the valley. Like long, encircling arms, they had nearly drawn even with her position. They seemed intent on cutting off the Builder compound.

"What are we going to do?" Carolin wailed, ringing her elegant hands. "I don't think it wise to try wading those waters."

Jean rushed across the length of the building until she could peer around the western corner, with a view to the south and the bulk of the Builder compound. Sure enough, the water continued south. As she watched, it passed the far southern end of the compound and began to circle inward.

She expected the waters would meet at the far side, completely encircling them, but then the waters rebounded from an invisible barrier. As more water poured in, it too rebounded and boiled backward, frothing and erupting skyward. Within seconds, the water had built into a ten-foot standing wave, continually crashing and rebounding from the invisible barrier.

"What's happening?" Jean asked.

Carolin exchanged rapid Grandurian with Bruno and Artur for several seconds then said, "We don't know, but perhaps the Builders have created defensive mechanicals."

That thought offered a little hope that they weren't about to die in the next few seconds. The Builder compound was full of deadly mechanicals, but she was no Builder and could not activate them.

"I've seen an elfonnel before, and I doubt anything will stop it for long. We need to find Dierk. He may know a way to fight it."

"Good idea," Carolin said, and together they ran back to the rest of the local craft masters, who had remained gawking by the workroom doors.

Jean muttered a curse as she ran. She needed Connor, Hamish, and Verena to fight this monster. She doubted anything she and the locals could throw at an elfonnel would do more than enrage it.

"Look!" Bruno cried, pointing into the air.

A windrider was rising above the many roofs of the Builder compound. It was one of the extra-long troop transport wagons, and Dierk was at the controls.

That wagon was designed to carry at least forty passengers, but it looked like he had packed in more than twice as many. It was a wonder he was able to lift off at all with so many people. The huge wagon turned sluggishly and headed northeast toward the higher ground near Faulenrost.

Bruno said, "Him return, but many people. Find weapon, yes?"

Artur replied in Grandurian, and the two men started arguing. Carolin explained, "Bruno wishes to raid Builder mechanicals and die fighting if we must die today, but Artur points out we cannot hope to fight the elements."

Jean tried to think, reminding herself to look deep and see clear, the way Gran always instructed. The fear that set her hands shaking and elevated her heart rate made it difficult. She looked back at the elfonnel that had continued its deceptively casual stroll up the valley.

It was closing on them with terrifying speed, but it would still need a few minutes to reach them. Bruno was right, though. Even if Dierk made record time, he might not have time for enough trips to save everyone.

The surrounding arms of water began sweeping inward, and Jean's fear spiked. The waters were barely a couple hundred yards away, and they'd reach them in seconds.

Then those onrushing waters rebounded from the same kind of invisible barrier they had hit on the far side. Churning and boiling, the waters grew into dark, standing waves that beat against the protective barrier.

Jean said, "We don't have much time, and I can't think of a weapon that will help against water."

Crowds of people were now visible, scrambling from the many exits of the Builder compound, milling about and looking for a path to safety. Many wailed with terror at the growing wall of angry water surrounding the compound, and some began running toward the last remaining gap. Jean was tempted to follow them, but what if the barrier failed? The thought of getting caught between those arms of churning waters terrified her.

She glanced again to where Dierk was setting down his first load of passengers safely on the first hills at the edge of the valley. Weighed down by so many people, Dierk could not fly as fast as normal. There was just no way he'd have time to save everyone.

She hated to feel helpless, and refused to admit that so many people were going to die because she could do nothing to help. Then with a surge of renewed hope, Jean realized there was something she could do.

"Come on! I have an idea."

Chapter Thirty-Nine

"The path to victory is fraught with danger not yet imagined. Hold fast to truth most cherished and soon to be discovered, and the fires of your tribulation may yet purify instead of destroy."

~Evander

Jean rushed into the workroom, and the fearful villagers followed. She gestured toward the huge sliding door.

"Bruno, Artur, get that thing open. The rest of you come help me with this wagon."

As the blacksmith and the carpenter started hauling mightily on the chains that hoisted the giant door overhead, Jean raced to the workbench where she had left the keystone. Snatching it up, she scrambled into the high pilot bench at the front of the windrider.

"I thought you told us you weren't successful flying that thing," Carolin said.

"I wasn't. But this time I'm not trying to do anything complicated. All I have to do is climb high enough to clear that water blocking our way. I can do that."

Hopefully.

"How?" Asked a portly fellow who oversaw the weaver's guild.

"When I get this thing to hover, push the front around so I'm pointing at those doors."

Jean refused to acknowledge the fear clawing at her innards. Her first attempt at flying had been a disaster, and this time all of their lives would depend upon her non-existent flying skill.

Hamish and Verena couldn't save them if she failed. The alternative was worse though, and she decided that dying while trying to save people was better than waiting to die as a helpless spectator.

Placing the keystone against the top of the fourth lever, she made sure the power symbol faced her in the neutral position. That should be the lever that controlled the main lift thrusters under the wagon, and she reminded herself they really needed labels.

In tense moments, it was too easy to forget. Holding her breath, she very gently turned the keystone to the right. She had learned enough in her first attempt to know the importance of small movements.

The huge lift-force thrusters under the wagon growled and came to life, spewing a stream of air through the giant workroom and tearing at the clothes of the milling locals. The wagon shuddered, but did not lift off the floor.

She risked another fraction of a turn, and the roaring wind intensified. The wagon began to shudder more heavily, and to bounce against the floor.

She did not dare turn the keystone any farther while they were still inside, lest she accidentally drive herself into the ceiling and end the flight before it started. She forced confidence into her voice.

"That should be enough. Push the front around."

Most of the weight was being held by the thrusters, so the villagers easily turned it. The scraping and bouncing of the runners against the floor grated in Jean's ears. It was as if the wagon was screeching in fear, begging her not to try the insane plan.

"Hush," she muttered to it. "And behave yourself this time."

Talking to it helped her rein in her terror. Outside the open doors, the still-building waters surrounding the compound had grown to over twenty feet, and the barrier seemed to be bowing inward under the weight. She looked away. Watching would only freeze her with terror.

"That's great. Right there."

Jean moved the keystone to the next lever, then turned it a fraction. The huge rear push-force thrusters came to life and blasting wind scattered papers and any small items not secured in the cabinets. The huge wagon began to slide across the smooth floor, so she risked turning the keystone another fraction.

The wagon picked up speed, the metal runners shrieking against the smooth stone floor. The villagers cheered and gave chase. As soon as Jean cleared the doors to the courtyard, she turned the keystone back the other way to cut the push-force.

Her feeling of jubilant victory at getting that far alive faded when she realized that in the moment it had taken to get the wagon out of the workroom, the elfonnel had crossed half the valley. Dierk was already returning for a second load, driving the huge transport wagon through the air with remarkable speed.

When he saw her emerge in the other Windrider, he banked down to land nearby.

While Jean had been inside, the crowd of terrified residents had grown to over two hundred. They cheered at the sight of Dierk descending and rushed to meet him, clamoring for a spot on the wagon.

"Climb on board, as many as can fit," he shouted.

Within seconds, the enormous wagon was overflowing with desperate people, and Jean wondered that it didn't collapse under all that weight. The villagers who had helped get her wagon outside had already climbed on board her windrider, and people who could not fit on Dierk's wagon rushed to join her.

Dierk shouted, "Are you sure that's a good idea?"

Jean pointed at the fast-approaching elfonnel. "Unless you have a mechanical that can stop that thing."

"There's one Last Word bomb," Dierk said, pointing toward the next workroom. "But I can't drop that until everyone's out, or it'll kill us all."

"Then let's get everyone out," Jean shouted.

She pointed at the encircling, angry water still churning and building, beating on the invisible barrier. "Do you have any more of those barriers?"

"I have no idea what that is. Sometimes Verena doesn't tell me everything. When you lift off, don't try anything fancy. These wagons are pretty stable, but watch the balance, and focus on lift and push thrusters."

"Thanks!"

She was grateful for the advice. Hamish loved to tease Dierk about not being a very good flyer, but he was an expert compared to her.

All the extra weight drove the wagon down solidly against the smooth stone of the courtyard. Jean felt a growing concern as more and more people piled on board. If she messed up, their deaths would be her fault. She had dedicated her life to healing, and the thought of killing so many horrified her.

With an almighty roar that sent the remaining crowds scrambling away, Dierk's wagon lifted slowly into the air, already pivoting toward Faulenrost. It sounded like he had maxed the lift thrusters, but it barely climbed. He had to wait precious seconds to ascend well above the raging, circling waves that sometimes erupted more than forty feet into the air.

"Is many good time leave now," Bruno said.

The burly blacksmith was squeezed onto the pilot bench with Jean and Artur. The two of them protected her from the crush of people behind.

Artur gave her a reassuring smile. "Luck of plenty."

Carolin, barely visible under a pile of women all trying to share the same seat with her said, "May the Tallan bless us."

Jean decided not to point out that Tallan had only been a man. She'd take help from either faith or fact at the moment.

She moved the keystone to the lift-force lever and turned it farther. The thrusters roared louder, the wagon shook harder, and many people shouted encouragement. With another quarter turn, the wagon slowly started to lift.

It immediately tipped to the right.

Trying to manage the lean-over thrusters in addition to the lift and push thrusters would guarantee disaster, so Jean shouted, "Everyone lean left."

Everyone obeyed, so of course they shifted too far, and the wagon started tipping the other way.

"Too much! Go back half way."

"You focus fly. I make balance," Bruno told her.

Standing on the bench, he started bellowing orders in Grandurian to individual people along the outer flanks of the wagon, getting them to lean either in or out. In a remarkably short time, he got the wagon onto an even keel. "Now no move, or all die!"

Someone started to sob, but Jean forced herself to ignore the fear that clung to the wagon like a palpable cloud. As soon as it seemed they weren't about to roll over, she increased lift, pushing the howling thrusters to the max. The wagon rose sluggishly into the air.

Jean shifted to the push-force thrusters, but forced herself to wait while she judged their height against the waves of blocking water. Dierk was just passing over those churning waters, with barely twenty feet separating him from one of the explosive geysers.

Then the waters seemed to coil and leap upward toward the huge windrider. Jean screamed a useless warning, even though he could never hear her.

Dierk must have seen the danger, because gouts of fire blasted out of the bottom of his windrider, driving it higher and flashing the top three feet of the water reaching toward him into hissing steam. Jean had no idea if her wagon was equipped with marble defenses, or how to activate them if it was.

"Go!" People started shouting, but she forced herself to wait precious seconds until the wagon clawed up to over fifty feet.

With a glance at the fast-approaching elfonnel that was shredding the ground and spraying trees and rocks hundreds of yards, Jean finally turned the keystone.

The huge push thrusters ignited, but the wagon hung motionless. With so much weight, partial thrust would never accomplish anything. So Jean twisted the keystone all the way. The thrusters roared, the wagon shook, and it began to accelerate slowly toward the deadly water barrier.

Jean wanted to whoop with exhilaration. It was working!

They had ascended to over sixty feet, and she felt no desire to reduce the lift thrusters. She didn't want to go too high, but would have gladly ascended to a mile before crossing those dangerous waters, if there had been time.

The wagon slowly picked up speed, aiming a little bit east of northeast. They would miss Faulenrost, but their direction was close enough, and she did not dare messing with the slip-spin thrusters. They passed over the boiling waters, and she tensed helplessly against the feared attack that would rip them out of the air.

In that second, the invisible barrier holding the waters back collapsed, and instead of erupting into the air to snatch them, the waters boiled forward toward the compound and the people still trapped there.

"No!" Jean shouted, twisting to look. Many others echoed her cries of horror, and the wagon tipped dangerously to the left as people turned to watch.

Bruno barked new commands in Grandurian and the wagon righted itself, but Jean barely heard. Her eyes were glued on those deadly waters racing toward the compound and the crowd still clustered outside of the buildings. It had continued to grow and looked as big as it had before she and Dierk filled their wagons. She didn't want to witness all those people die, but she couldn't look away.

Barely fifty yards from the screaming people, the water rebounded again off a second barrier, then erupted high into the air, as if infuriated at being denied its prize. The elfonnel screamed, and Jean twisted back around to look at it.

It had raised its arms into the air, and its face had darkened into an ugly scowl. Its scream was like the crashing of giant waves against rocks in a mighty tempest, and the air grew noticeably colder.

"We're going to make it," Jean told Bruno, who nodded grimly. Artur gave her an encouraging smile, then the two of them turned back to watch the tight-packed passengers.

No one moved. Several people seemed afraid to breathe. Dierk passed them with a third load of passengers. Jean hadn't even noticed him return from his last trip. He waved to her, and she raised one hand, but didn't dare wave back for fear of upsetting the delicate balance.

Dierk was already descending, although they'd barely soared a quarter mile past the deadly, encircling arms of water. The people he'd dropped off on his first trip were already fleeing toward distant Faulenrost and the dubious safety it offered.

At least they had a chance.

Gisela didn't.

Jean realized with a horrified sense of dread that she had forgotten all about her. She could be anywhere.

With tears of fear for her friend clouding her vision, Jean reduced lift and aimed the wagon for a flat section of hillside. She cut the power a little too soon and they crashed to the ground with a huge jolt, nearly tipping the wagon over entirely as it slid forward under the power of the still-howling push thrusters until Jean managed to turn them off.

People scrambled from the wagon, shouting their thanks as they sprinted for the hills. Carolin took her leave and rushed to check on her girls. Bruno and Artur alone lingered with her to inspect the damage.

Bruno reported, "Lift good live. Beat a second time kill for sure."

"Good enough for now," Jean said, twisting the keystone on the lever to activate lift force. "Push the wagon around for me, please."

The men followed her orders, but Artur said, "You good hero girl. But time no friend."

The elfonnel had drawn dangerously close to the Builder compound and was picking up speed. It seemed to be focused on the long warehouses along the outskirts of the main cluster of buildings. That might give her a little extra time.

The inner barrier was still holding the waters back, but she doubted it would withstand the arrival of the elfonnel. Dierk had already landed and begun taking on another horde of people, but there were still too many.

Jean pointed at the crowd of desperate people. "Point me in that direction. I have to try."

They pushed her around as she increased lift. Bruno jumped aboard beside her. "You fly girl. I make sure no wagon lean."

As she increased lift, then applied push-force, Jean gave him a warm smile. "You're insane, you realize that, right?"

"No do alone. You good girl. I have daughter too."

The return trip went significantly faster in the empty wagon, and they passed Dierk leaving with another enormous load of people.

Dierk saluted and shouted, "Make it fast! While we were loading this group, I activated the bomb. I'll drop it as soon as I get back, so make sure you're well away!"

"We will!" she shouted back.

As they approached the compound, flying high above the deadly waters, she almost couldn't make herself reduce lift thrust and descend toward the much smaller crowd. Her heart was racing and fear made it hard to breathe.

Jean wasn't sure they could take everyone, but they had no choice. Dierk's warning rang in her ears. Anyone still lingering when he returned would share the monster's fate.

Hopefully they had time to make this second trip. The waters beating on the inner barrier had grown far more quickly than they had against the first.

Jean wasn't sure if the elfonnel had committed more water to the assault, or if the smaller circumference of the inner defensive barrier allowed the waters to pile up more. It didn't matter. The barrier was already bending under the weight of the raging torrent.

Everyone needed to leave. Now.

It would be tight, but maybe if everyone held their breath to make themselves seem a little lighter, they might convince the wagon to give it a try. Bruno bellowed at the crowds in his mighty Grandurian voice, calling for space to land.

Jean glanced toward the elfonnel, visible around the corner of the last workroom. The elemental woman had nearly reached the long warehouses, barely fifty yards away.

In that moment, the elfonnel lunged, transforming into a tidal wave that smashed into the first warehouse and shattered it. Timber and stones exploded in every direction amid a frothing spray of foam. Without dispersing, the central wave tore into the second building. At this rate, it would destroy the entire Builder compound in minutes.

"Be many careful," the blacksmith warned. "No land hard or break lift."

He was right. She needed to focus. If she came in too hard, she'd destroy the lift thrusters and they'd all die.

Jean cut the push force and the wagon immediately began to slow. She hoped it would stop before they crashed into the building, but there was nothing she could do about it either way, so she decided not to look. Instead she focused on carefully reducing the lift thrust, descending slowly toward the ground.

The desperate people below shouted for her to hurry, but that was the last thing she could do. It seemed to take forever, and in those seconds, the elfonnel shifted directions and charged the dining hall. It struck the inner defensive barrier on the opposite side of the compound, and burst through in a spray of water and foam that erupted over a hundred feet into the air.

"Oh, no," Jean breathed as waters rushed through the gap and the elfonnel flowed over the ground toward the defenseless buildings. The rest of the barrier still held, but Jean doubted it would for long.

She lost sight of the elfonnel behind the building as she descended, but seconds later, it exploded through the distant roof of the dining hall, again formed into the shape of a beautiful woman. It gleefully lay waste to that central structure. Timbers howled as they shattered, and the air felt heavy with water. The humidity increased until it felt like Jean was breathing as much liquid as air.

As the elfonnel smashed through the dining hall, Jean caught a whiff of bacon. Had the cooks already started the midday meal? She hoped they had escaped and not chosen to die among their pots and pans.

Although Jean wished with all her heart for Hamish to show up and help her again, she was happy he didn't have to see the dining hall die. He would have had a hard time witnessing the senseless destruction of so much food. The thought of him helped ease some of her fear, and she brought the wagon to within a foot of the ground.

"Don't load them too fast. I'm going to have to adjust the lift force to keep us aloft while people get on board."

Bruno nodded understanding, and she was grateful he came along because his deep, commanding voice instilled a modicum of order. Jean forced herself to not pay attention as the elfonnel systematically destroyed the Builder compound, drawing dangerously close to where they were loading. If it decided to target them next, they were all dead.

Thankfully Gisela rushed out of a nearby doorway, waving and shouting. "Stop! Taking me with you!"

"Hurry!" Almost everyone was aboard, and the wagon was barely holding them all aloft, even though she had nearly maxed the lift force. Jean pulled Gisela up beside her.

"Where were you?" Jean asked, breathless with relief at seeing Gisela alive.

"I having gone to make sure all people are knowing to run."

"If they're not out now, it's too late." Jean hated deciding some people couldn't be saved, but as a healer, she knew that hard decisions were necessary.

"Bruno, push this wagon around or we're not going anywhere," she cried.

They had drifted to within five feet of the nearest wall. Maybe that's why the elfonnel hadn't noticed them yet, sheltered under that eave. Bruno leaped down from the bench and shouted for the last two men to help.

As the wagon sluggishly turned, Jean and Gisela pulled Bruno up beside them. "All on. Go two times!"

Jean moved the keystone to the rear thruster lever and twisted it hard. The thrusters released a whirlwind against the nearby building, cracking the wood, and driving the wagon slowly away. The tightly-packed mass of people cheered.

Gisela hugged her. "I not believing we all fit."

Jean switched the keystone to the lever controlling lift thrust and turned it all the way, pulling the last reserves from the huge thrusters. As the wagon began to climb, she looked for Dierk.

She'd gotten everyone, so it was the perfect time to get that bomb from the last workroom. The big door was already open. It was a miracle the elfonnel hadn't destroyed the long row of workrooms yet. It had just turned toward the southern end of the compound, ripping apart buildings and rampaging through the structures like a child smashing play blocks.

Her wagon clawed sluggishly into the air. It seemed to take forever to reach eight feet. She didn't dare apply more push thrust until they got higher.

She spotted Dierk rumbling back toward them in the empty windrider. He was flying lower than last time, aimed toward the last workroom and the huge bomb.

The elfonnel turned back toward the north and spotted him. It stood over fifty feet tall, and if it glanced farther to its left, it would spot Jean's helpless wagon.

It made a grabbing gesture. The waters that had been beating against the badly leaning inner barrier gathered together and formed a gigantic hand that snatched at Dierk's wagon.

Jean wanted to scream at him to look out, but she didn't dare draw the elfonnel's deadly gaze. Dierk rolled his wagon right onto its side, and the push thrusters, now aimed horizontal, threw the wagon off its previous course. The aggressive move saved his life, and the snatching waters missed by a terrifyingly small margin.

Even as the initial wave fell back, more water leaped after him. Dierk pivoted the wagon away and threw wide every thruster, again firing the puking dooms built into the wagon's bottom. Water struck from two sides, and for a second he was concealed in a billowing cloud of fire, water, and hissing steam.

Then the windrider erupted from the cloud, ascending at a steep angle away from the Builder compound. Grasping tendrils of water snatched after it, ripping away pieces of railing and the entire rear gate, but not gaining enough purchase to stop the powerful wagon from rising further.

"He has escaping," Gisela breathed, then cast a worried glance back at the elfonnel that was still focused on the retreating Dierk, its face twisted into an ugly expression of hate.

Jean risked applying some directional thrust for a moment to pivot their wagon farther to the left. Until they rose above the tall building housing the Builder workrooms, they would remain mostly concealed from the angry elfonnel's view.

She straightened out a moment later and risked adding more push thrust. They had to get more distance from that monster. She glanced to where Dierk had risen to over a thousand feet and begun to bank back toward the Builder compound. The elfonnel was still watching him, rippling watery arms raised in fury.

She realized with cold dread that Dierk would die if he tried to land again.

He could not get the bomb out.

Her wagon was rising very slowly, but maybe it would be enough. The waters no longer built into towering waves against the inner barrier. The elfonnel had breached the defenses around other parts of the compound, and waters were flooding in there. Her wagon was slowly accelerating, pointing more or less in the right direction.

They did not need her any more.

Jean adjusted the lift thrusters until the wagon leveled out at ten feet. Then she turned to Gisela. "Listen. When you reach those hills, the wagon should run aground, so make sure everyone jumps clear before it crashes. It'll probably start ascending as the weight decreases, so make sure no one stays aboard."

She shuddered to think of anyone getting trapped on the wagon. It'd ascend until the lift thrusters gave out and then plummet back down.

"What you talking about?" Gisela exclaimed, a renewed look of terror on her face.

Jean took a deep breath, not wanting to accept what she had just realized. "What do you think that thing's going to do once it finishes destroying the Builder compound? None of us are going to be safe unless we can find a way to slow it down until help arrives."

"What are saying?" Gisela asked.

"Dierk can't get that bomb, and it's the only chance we have."

Jean was out of time. They weren't going fast, but were still accelerating. She gripped Gisela's hands in farewell, then waved to Bruno. "Thanks for your help. Without you, none of us would have survived."

Then she jumped.

Chapter Forty

"A single petal of the rose, though ripped asunder by the torrent, hints at the beauty of the flower thus destroyed."

~Evander

The Storm tore through the air with Hamish at the controls, every push thruster roaring at max power. Connor sat behind Hamish, ducked low to shield himself from the brutal wind. Verena sat beside Hamish, their helmets protecting their faces from the beating. She had offered to take a turn piloting the Storm, but he had refused.

Kilian sat on Connor's right, behind Verena, and Martys sat to his left. Aifric, who had leaped aboard when they landed at Harz, had fallen asleep not long after they took off. She slumbered without moving, despite the roaring thrusters and the rushing wind that whipped her hair.

Connor worried about her lingering weakness. Once they verified Jean was all right, she really needed to take a closer look at Aifric. If that failed, he would try the power of his sculpted sandstone pendant. It unleashed such a torrent of healing power, he barely had to direct it to accomplish miraculous healings. Certainly with Aifric to guide him, he could figure out how to resolve her problem.

First they had to reach the Builder compound.

Kilian had met them at the keep. He hadn't wanted to leave while the battle still raged, but he'd agreed that the strategic value of the Builder compound couldn't be ignored either.

"I think Wolfram's lines will hold," he had said as they lifted off and soared away from the fortress. "I was helping only in subtle ways. Their training with mixing elements is really paying off."

They hadn't spoken much in the hour and a half that followed. Hamish pushed the Storm to its uttermost limits, his hands clutching the control rods, even though it didn't need constant attention once they reached cruising speed. Verena had expressed worry at one point that he might exhaust the thrusters before they reached the Builder compound if he continued pushing so hard.

Hamish had only said, "We have spares. We'll figure out how to replace them in the air."

Verena had shared a worried look with Connor, then placed a comforting hand on Hamish's shoulder.

His expression turned anguished and he said, "I couldn't do anything for Ingrid, but I will not allow Jean to die. We have to save her."

"We all want to save her," Connor assured him.

"Then look for ways to help, and don't suggest I slow down again."

So far the plan appeared to be working. The thrusters were holding. Hamish had found a good tailwind that gave them extra speed, and they had raced north over Granadure faster than birds or clouds.

Connor hoped it would be enough. He didn't think Shona had been lying, but he hoped she had been. Attacking the undefended Builder compound was a master stroke, so it made sense that Dougal had thought of it. Connor spent several minutes mentally kicking himself for not having suggested some kind of defense for that vital strategic target.

All of a sudden, Kilian sat bolt upright, his eyes blazing with living fire, and he grabbed Hamish's shoulder. "Stop!"

"Why?" Hamish asked, although he did ease the thrusters and slow so they could actually hear each other talking over the wind.

"We've been fooled," Kilian growled, looking south, back the way they had come. "An elfonnel has risen south of Harz. Fire bound."

"Oh, no," Verena gasped.

Connor tapped marble and flung out feelers of thought toward the south. He felt it too. Something vast and terrifying was moving far to the south, like a distant thundercloud in his marble senses.

"How can you tell where it is?" he asked.

"Practice." Kilian was frowning. "By why isn't it at Harz? It feels more distant, almost as if . . ."

His voice trailed off and he muttered something in Grandurian that had to be a swear word.

"What is it?" Verena asked. Everyone but Aifric was leaning closer to hear. She was still lost in that deep stupor.

"Emmerich Quarry is southeast of Harz. It was one of the locations I sent messengers to request they hunt for an obsidian weakening stone."

"How could Dougal know we were looking for that?" Verena asked.

"I have no idea, but it can't be coincidence. The sense I get is that it is moving north. It won't take long for an elfonnel to lay waste to the quarry and move against Harz. The battle will still be raging, and everyone will be distracted. It'll take them by surprise from the flanks."

"They'll be slaughtered," Hamish said, his face white with horror.

"Shona lied to us," Verena growled, glancing at Connor.

"It appears so," Kilian said,

Connor shook his head. "I still think she believed what she told me."

"Then maybe her da be more of a fiend than we thought," Martys said.

"Or maybe she thought she could win you back some other way," Verena told Connor. By her tone, it was clear she was thinking Connor was still susceptible to Shona's wiles. "If she thought the lie would distract us all long enough to win at Harz, she might have figured it was worth it."

Kilian said, "Whatever the reason, I have to go back. This is exactly what I feared might happen."

"I'm not turning around," Hamish said, gripping the control levers tighter, as if ready to fight over them.

Kilian opened his mouth to argue, but then he gasped, "Another elfonnel! Water bound."

"How is it possible?" Connor asked.

The thought of one new elfonnel terrified him. Kilian's stories of how multiple elfonnel had ripped the continent apart and cast it into the broken waters made him cringe. Not even Dougal could be that vengefully stupid, could he?

"Where?" Verena asked.

"North. The waters north of the Builder compound have risen."

Connor embraced soapstone, and as soon as he focused in that direction, he felt it too, like a tempest looming dark and ominous on the distant horizon.

"Shona wasn't lying." Life would have been so much simpler if she had.

"But it appears she wasn't telling us the whole truth either," Verena retorted.

"We have to go!" Hamish shouted.

"Yes, you must," Kilian said, his expression grim. "But I cannot allow the army to be overrun either."

"We can't stop an elfonnel alone," Verena protested.

"You must try. Connor, if you must use one of your aunt's stones, do not attempt to ascend. You're not ready, and the attempt would kill you. Do not give in to the elements, either. They'll tempt you to surrender to them, but that path leads to destruction."

"Don't you have any positive advice?"

They'd barely survived a fight with the elfonnel at the Carraig, and that was with Evander helping, and with an army at his back. "I might need some porphyry if things go badly."

He kept his expression calm as he spoke, but his fingers shook with an intense reawakened desire to get his hands on the dangerous, purplish powder. Porphyry had saved him at the Carraig, and if he needed to fight another elfonnel to get Kilian to share some with him, maybe it would be worth it.

"If the compound still stands, Verena knows how to find it," Kilian said after a brief pause. "But tempt it only in a moment of utmost desperation. Death by porphyry could be worse than death by elfonnel."

"I'll be careful," Connor promised, but his heart sang.

He glanced at Verena, and swallowed his excitement. She was frowning, her expression worried. He'd have to shield how badly he wanted it, or she'd never agree to show him where it was hidden.

For a second, he worried about that ravening hunger for porphyry. It didn't seem healthy, somehow. He didn't want Jean to die, but he didn't want to die either. He'd been forced to nearly die for a good cause enough times that the novelty had worn off.

He could survive porphyry. He'd done so before, and with every other affinity, it got easier to master with use. Could porphyry really be so different?

Kilian said urgently, "I left defensive wards in place around the Builder compound that should help delay even an elfonnel, although not for long. Connor, you must distract it until the rest of you can get the people out."

"We'll bring them to Faulenrost," Verena promised.

"That's a good start, but it may not be enough. I'll send aid, or come myself as soon as possible."

He gripped Connor's arm and his gaze grew freakishly intense, with one eye blazing with blue fire, and the other filled with frothing white water. "Take no unnecessary chances. Trust yourself, but don't get cocky. Water elementals hate fire, but your best chance might be to open a pit and swallow it in the earth."

"How big of a pit?" Connor asked while Hamish growled, "We have to go!"

"Big enough to stop an elfonnel."

Could he really make a hole that big? To move so much ground would weigh . . . well, more than he could calculate. He might not have a choice, because come Tallan or tombstones, he would not allow the monster Camonica had just unleashed to kill Jean.

"Good luck," Kilian said, then rolled over the side of the Storm. Flames blasted out from his feet and hands, and he shot away, angling down toward the silvery ribbon of a distant river.

"That man's got style," Aifric muttered, sitting up in the back row and rubbing her eyes.

Connor said, "He's been saving up. Hasn't needed it much in the past couple hundred years."

As soon as Kilian dropped away, Hamish threw wide the release rate on the push thrusters again, and the Storm accelerated again.

Connor got a sudden idea and clambered past Aifric to the cramped bed of the Storm. He picked up a couple spare thrusters out of one of the crates in the back, braced himself in the wagon bed, then gestured Martys to join him.

"What be ye thinking, laddie?" Marty asked as he squatted in the space beside Connor.

"Verena, can you activate these for us?" Connor asked.

She understood immediately. "We should have thought of that before."

"Didn't really need to," Connor said as she jumped nimbly to the back row of seats and leaned over him. "The Storm's crazy fast, and we hadn't felt the elfonnel yet."

Verena slid a caressing finger down his cheek, then touched the stone he held against his chest. Air erupted from the back of it, driving it against him so hard that he had to tap granite to keep it from crushing his ribs.

"Better tap granite, Uncle," he groaned as Verena shifted to Martys. His skin faded to gray half a second before air blasted out of his thruster too.

"The sacrifices we make for our friends," Martys growled.

"I can feel the difference," Hamish shouted from the front. "Verena, give them breathstones. I'm going to ascend higher to look for a faster tailwind. It might get hard to breathe."

Connor hoped he found one. Jean was running out of time.

Chapter Forty-One

~Evander

Jean rushed into Verena's workroom, sprinting faster than ever before. The ground shook, and water was starting to seep in through the far door. She tore through the room, barely slowing to snatch up a catch-fall harness before rushing back outside. Behind her, wood splintered as the inner wall of Verena's workroom collapsed.

The elfonnel had finally targeted that building.

Cursing herself for jumping out of her best chance of salvation, Jean sprinted to the last workroom. Timbers groaned and metal shrieked as the elfonnel laid waste to Verena's workroom behind her, but Jean refused to listen.

She raced inside, then nearly screamed in frustration. The doors were already open, and the windrider sat right there, with that giant bomb in the bed, but it was pointing the wrong way.

Jean scrambled aboard the high pilot bench. She placed the keystone over the third lever, the one that should control slip-spin-turning, pressed it into place, then slowly twisted it.

Nothing happened.

The sounds of destruction were growing closer, and Jean's heart beat so fast she could barely breathe. The clinical part of her mind recognized the onset of panic. It began documenting all of the issues that came with that, including the loss of rational thought and fine motor control, which she needed to handle the keystone.

She told herself to shut up.

Glancing at the keystone, she realized she'd been holding it upside down. Cursing herself for getting sloppy, she righted it and twisted it again. This time the directional thrusters ignited and the wagon moaned and slowly scraped sideways across the floor.

The struts shuddered, and Jean worried they if they snapped off, she might not be able to get the wagon out.

She hated moving to another lever with those directional thrusters still engaged, but she was out of time. Shifting the keystone to the next lever, she slowly twisted it from neutral. The lift thrusters ignited, and the wagon bounced against the floor.

The ride was rough, and she did not have time to fasten the safety straps, but the lift force helped the struts slide without buckling. She managed to turn off the directional thrusters before they pushed the wagon too far.

Facing the outer doors, she shifted to the push thrusters. She was sweating freely, and she yelped in fear when part of the roof ripped away and a torrent of water poured into the workroom.

Time to go.

Frothing waters tore into work benches. The room reverberated with the sounds of crashing destruction, and the air was so heavy with water, she could barely breathe. The waters formed into grasping hands and reached for the wagon.

The elfonnel had found her.

Jean twisted the keystone, forcing herself to keep in contact and not wrench it away in panic.

She'd never heard anything in her life as sweet as the roar of those rear thrusters activating. The wagon was already only half touching the ground, and it accelerated fast, skidding across the floor.

Water lunged after the wagon like a striking nuall.

Jean placed the keystone against the lift thrust lever and twisted. Even though she was still inside the workroom, she threw wide the release rate, and the thrusters seemed to approve.

The wagon lurched off the floor and Jean yelped and flattened herself onto the pilot bench to avoid getting decapitated by the top of the gigantic door as the wagon soared through. The very top of the huge bomb scraped the top beam. It rocked, despite the restraining straps, and for a heartbeat Jean feared it would tumble free.

Then the wagon cleared the door and shot into the air. Tendrils of water grasped after it, missing by a hair's breadth. Thankfully the bomb remained in place as the wagon shot into the sky.

Jean glanced back just as the entire workroom disintegrated under a wave of water. The elfonnel rose from the wreckage.

The majestic, beautiful elemental stared directly at Jean, its watery arms raised to pull her from the sky.

Jean screamed and twisted the keystone against the levers, trying to activate any remaining power, but both the lift and push thrusters were already fully engaged.

The wagon was accelerating, but so was the elfonnel. She could do nothing but watch in helpless horror as the elfonnel lunged into the sky after her, its watery arms extending with terrifying speed as it grasped toward the fleeing wagon.

"Come on," Jean cried, urging the wagon to greater speed.

She stood and faced the terrifying creature, chin high, terror swallowed up by a rising tide of defiant resolve.

"I saved them all from you, demon!"

A frown marred the perfect contours of those watery features, and it howled, the sound containing all the fury of a tempest unleashed. Its slender arms shot into the sky and grasped the rear half of the wagon.

Even though they looked delicate and fragile, the waters wrapped the rails and tugged, yanking the wagon to a stop. The abrupt change in motion tumbled Jean right off her perch at the front.

She managed to catch one of the levers and grab hold of the pilot bench before the lever snapped free. Screaming in fear, Jean hung for a moment from her fingertips before terror gave her the strength to grab hold with her other hand.

Her legs scraped uselessly against the smooth front of the wagon, then finally found purchase against the next control lever. With a heave, Jean pulled herself back into the pilot bench.

The lift thrusters were still working, but when she raised her head above the back of the pilot bench, she moaned in renewed fear. The elfonnel had ripped away the push thrusters and was drawing the wagon back toward its huge, beautiful face.

Jean looked into the eyes, like boiling whirlpools, fixed upon her, and she knew she was doomed.

Then the front of the elfonnel's face exploded.

A shockwave rippled through the creature, and its arms lost their hold for a precious second. The lift thrusters seem to have built up frustrated energy at being denied movement. The wagon shot into the air, accelerating so fast that Jean collapsed onto the pilot bench.

It took a moment to pull herself upright. The elfonnel stood directly below her, its terrifying face already re-formed and looking toward a second wagon.

Dierk had returned.

The huge transport wagon moved far faster empty, and Dierk had not descended very low to begin with. Good thinking because he was just barely keeping ahead of the elfonnel's snatching arms.

His wagon thundered into the air with Dierk shouting curses at the elemental. Jean heard the name Ingrid several times.

The elemental creature howled with rage. It threw its arms out wide and frothing tidal waves ripped out of its dress, smashing through the already shattered skeleton of the Builder compound.

Then it turned toward Faulenrost.

Jean's heart sank, and she felt a renewed flash of horror as she realized the creature's intention. Dierk had denied it the prize of her wagon, and it would take its frustration out on the entire village.

Unless Jean killed it first.

Her wagon was still rising fast, but the elfonnel was almost directly below her. So she scrambled into the back to the bomb. The plug at the top of the huge ceramic jar was made of granite. That must have been how Dierk had activated it.

She was grateful he had. She wasn't sure the keystone would work on it. Jean placed her hands on the cool ceramic, kissed the side of the deadly weapon and whispered, "Please. Please, for all the lives that depend upon this, let this work."

Then she unfastened the restraining straps and threw her weight against the huge bomb. It rocked, but did not roll, and she had to work it back and forth five more times until she managed enough force to roll it over.

With a scrape and a rumble, the huge bomb fell free.

Jean spat at the elfonnel. "Open wide and take your medicine!"

Although her wagon was still rising rapidly, Jean realized too late that she was still far too close.

The bomb crashed onto the monster's head.

It detonated!

The enormous, fiery explosion tore through the elfonnel, shredding the creature and spraying water in spectacular geysers. The waters of the creature's torso evaporated into shrieking clouds of steam.

Fire and steam boiled into the sky toward Jean. She felt a surge of satisfaction knowing she had done everything she could. Even if one bomb wasn't enough to kill the monster, at least she had given the people of Faulenrost a chance.

She threw herself to the bed of the wagon, just as the shockwave struck, smashing the wagon up against her.

She felt blinding pain.

Then nothing.

when the fireball had engulfed it. It continued to rise quickly, and as Hamish focused on it, he realized with a start that no one was controlling it.

Dierk was pivoting his huge wagon around to give chase, but Hamish could see he'd never catch it. The second wagon was rising under full lift thrusters and had a huge head start.

"Do you have a speakstone paired to Dierk?" he asked Verena as he returned to his seat at the front. She had slowed the Storm and sat staring at the devastation in wide-eyed horror.

"I think so," she said in a wooden, distracted tone, then shook herself angrily. When she spoke into her helmet, calling to Dierk, her voice was rough and filled with sorrow.

Dierk immediately banked the windrider around toward them and began gesturing toward the still-ascending one. He was shouting something, and Hamish leaned closer to Verena to listen. Dierk's voice was a bit distorted, but Hamish heard enough.

"Jean's in that windrider. She dropped the bomb!"

Jean was alive!

Hamish leaped out the Storm and activated every thruster, shooting after the pilot-less wagon. The Storm might be faster, but Verena seemed to be struggling to cope with the loss of her beloved home. Hamish couldn't bear to wait even the few seconds it would take to shoo her out of the pilot seat and fire up the thrusters.

Turbulent air rushed past, and he embraced it as he tore through it toward Jean like a living lightning bolt. He forgot about everything else, including the elfonnel as he raced to catch the rising windrider.

As he closed on it, his sense of dread increased. It looked battered, with sections of railing missing and all the push thrusters ripped right out.

What had Jean suffered from that elfonnel before he arrived? How had she managed to activate the bomb? Why was she alone in the windrider?

Hamish slowed as he ascended above it. He spotted Jean lying motionless in the back, her limbs sprawled, her hair lying in a wild tumble around her head.

There was blood on her face.

The sight of it enraged and terrified Hamish and he shouted her name as he swooped down toward her. He landed in the long bed of the wagon already running, cut power to his thrusters, and slid on his armored knees to Jean.

He ripped off his helmet and leaned over her, fingers trembling with fear as he touched her unmoving face. She was still warm, so maybe she'd be all right.

Hamish gently brushed her hair back and found the source of the blood. An ugly gash on her forehead was still bleeding, but he couldn't see any other visible injuries.

He pulled a cloth from the medical kit he carried clipped to one of his straps and pressed it gently to the wound. Jean stirred and groaned.

Hamish kissed her cheek. "Oh, Jean. You're all right."

She groaned again and blinked her eyes open. It took her a couple seconds to focus on him, then her face lit up with joy and she hugged him to her.

"Oh, Hamish, I was so afraid!"

"I'm here. We're here."

She kissed him and laughed, but then groaned and touched her injured forehead. "Ow."

Hamish eased her to a sitting position and handed her the cloth. "What happened?"

"Elfonnel!" Jean cried, fear returning to her gaze, and she looked toward the back of the wagon.

"What happened?"

Her expression turned grim. "That thing was destroying everything. Dierk couldn't land. I had to."

So Dierk hadn't been cracked when he said Jean dropped the bomb. "How?"

"I used the keystone," she said proudly.

"Wow." He kissed her again, eager to hear the entire story, but the wagon was still ascending under full power. "I'll bring the wagon back down while you tell me."

Jean followed him to the pilot bench, and he watched her carefully. He'd suffered enough head wounds to know sometimes they made a person groggy or dizzy for a while. He helped her to the seat, then touched the control levers, flicking his Builder senses through the wagon's thrusters.

It was a miracle the wagon still flew.

All the push thrusters were gone. Most of the directional thrusters were missing too, like little holes in his mind where flickers of eager wind should be.

The remaining lift thrusters had lost connection with the control lever. If they hadn't already been activated and driving into the underside of the wagon, Jean would have crashed into the explosion instead of rising above it.

He cut power to the thrusters he could reach, and the wagon slowed. "I'll be right back." It took only a moment to slip under the wagon and touch each of the remaining thrusters and reduce their release rate until the wagon started to descend.

"The landing might be rough, but we're going down at least," Hamish told Jean when he returned.

She touched the catch-fall harness she wore. "I had planned to maybe jump, but never got the chance."

"Good thing. You wouldn't want to land in that mess. Come on, I'll take you down to the others while this thing descends."

Jean wrapped her arms around his neck and gave him a lingering kiss that made his knees weak. "I am so glad you're here."

"Me too."

She was safe! His joy felt like a diorite dart had ignited in his chest.

The two lifted off the crippled wagon, and Hamish turned toward where Dierk now hovered beside the Storm, a quarter mile above the flooded eastern edge of the valley.

With Jean safe in his arms, Hamish studied the destruction of the valley while he flew. The spot where the Builder compound had stood was flooded with churning, debris-filled waters. The crazy, packed cluster of buildings were all gone. He flew back to the Storm and deposited Jean gently in the seat next to Verena.

Verena, who had been sobbing into Connor's shoulder, released him and gave Jean a fierce hug. "Oh, Jean. I'm so glad you're safe."

While Martys hovered close, Connor hugged Jean and asked, "You flew the wagon?"

"Sort of."

Dierk stood on the front bench of his nearby wagon, grinning wider than Hamish had ever seen. "Jean! That was amazing!"

"How did you do it?" Hamish was hovering just above the port side railing, close to Jean.

Dierk said, "She saved two loads of people in another wagon, and she saved the bomb. Dropped it on that monster when it wouldn't let me land."

Jean flushed under the attention. "You did so much more, Dierk."

He shook his head. "It's no big deal for me to fly a wagon. And even though you had so much trouble on the first load, you risked your life going back."

Hamish took her hand and gazed deep into her bright, blue eyes. "You're my hero."

"Well then, maybe you can finish off that monster before it goes after Faulenrost and kills everyone we worked so hard to save."

Only then did Hamish notice that the elemental had reformed.

Well, sort of.

Where before it had been the picture of elegant beauty, the elemental now look deformed, more like a crippled blob. It shambled through the valley, stumbling from one side to the other like a hunched-over drunkard.

Verena frowned down at it. "It looks broken."

"But it's not dead," Jean growled.

"It took two bombs to destroy the earth elemental, and one of those blew up inside of it," Dierk pointed out.

Verena nodded. "Kilian said water-bound elfonnel are susceptible to fire, so the impact was probably worse than for the earth bound."

"We don't have any more bombs," Hamish said as they all studied the monster that was moving in seemingly random directions back and forth across the rubble-strewn waters. "How do we finish it off?"

"Another explosion, probably," Connor suggested.

Hamish said, "We do have those chisels from Alasdair in one of the storage compartments under the Storm. I don't think anyone would object to sacrificing one to kill that monster, especially after it attacked Jean."

"And your home," Jean said softly.

Verena clung to Connor again, and fresh tears welled in her eyes. The Builder compound was a special place, but she seemed to be taking its loss unusually hard.

Connor said, "A full chisel will make a huge explosion, but will that be enough?"

"Weaken it first," Verena said, brushing tears from her face and glaring down at the elfonnel. Talking about killing it seemed to help her focus. "We've got soapstone in one of the crates."

Hamish nodded. "Good point. We can activate wellstones. Drawing water away from it might weaken it."

"Maybe ring it with them," Verena suggested.

Hamish nodded again. "We've got enough stone. You take some and drop them in a perimeter about a quarter mile out."

"My pleasure," Verena said.

"I'll drop some more closer around it, then hit it with diorite."

Jean gripped his hand with fierce strength. "Kill it, Hamish."

Hamish saluted, then descended to the side of the Storm to fetch a chisel. Connor handed him some pieces of soapstone from the back. Verena had already taken off in the Swift and made a quick circuit of the flooded valley, dropping activated soapstone every few seconds. As soon as the stones struck, geysers of water erupted.

"It's working," Jean cried, and it looked like it really was.

The wellstones drew the nearest water to them, and areas of dry ground were forming between each of them and the elfonnel in the middle, forming a barrier that blocked the elfonnel from its reserves.

"My turn." Hamish hefted the long chisel from his hometown and headed toward the monster.

It had slowly oriented toward the higher ground on the east side of the valley and the town of Faulenrost. It might be damaged, but it seemed to remember its destructive intent.

All of their mechanicals, all of their possessions, all their power stores, everything was gone. So much food wasted! It was one of the worst tragedies he could imagine.

"I suppose I'll never find that cookbook now," he muttered, but couldn't generate the sense of outrage the thought should trigger. Food had been his greatest passion until Jean usurped that spot, and knowing that she was safe eclipsed any culinary tragedy.

As he circled toward the slow-moving elfonnel, he decided he must be holding Stuart's chisel. Somehow that made him feel better about what he was about to do.

It took only a moment for Hamish to drop pieces of soapstone in a tight ring around the thirty-foot, pulsing blob of water that now made up the elfonnel. He dropped ten wellstones, barely fifty yards to either side of it.

Geysers of water erupted from every one, sucking water away from the elfonnel. That triggered a response, and it rolled forward with remarkable speed, engulfing the first wellstone. There it paused for a moment, and Hamish tossed the remaining wellstones around it. The monster seemed to shrink a bit, and he took that as a good sign.

Stopping to hover three hundred feet above the creature, Hamish licked the handle of the chisel, throwing wide the release rate. As it had the time he tasted the Ashlar's hammer, Hamish's entire body shook from a jolt of power from the chisel. It was as if he had just swallowed a sweetbread made of lightning.

The formless blob of the elfonnel contorted, and a woman's head formed along the top. It rotated up to stare at him, and undying hatred boiled in its eyes.

"Good night," Hamish growled, then threw the chisel with all his might.

The elfonnel opened its mouth wide, and sound like the crashing of a thousand waves boiled forth. The chisel plunged through its open mouth and disappeared inside.

Hamish imagined he saw an expression of surprise on the monster's face before an explosion ripped it asunder. The blast of white-hot fire was every bit as awesome as he had hoped.

More like a white-hot ball of living lightning than the normal, flame-filled explosions most of their bombs produced. The chisel erupted with a fury as if driven by all the vengeful indignation of an entire village that had nearly lost their favorite daughter.

The shock wave punched Hamish fifty feet higher, a brutal blow that cracked a couple of the protective granite leaves of his armor. It would have turned his innards to jelly if not for his suit. Hamish's breath erupted from his lungs and the world lurched as he spun seventeen back flips.

A keening wail rippled across the valley, like the final angry cry of the Petralist who had given her life so the elfonnel could walk the land. The screaming air pounded him from every side as it threw him higher, driving with so much force that he eclipsed the stomach-purge threshold almost instantly. He hadn't eaten nearly enough to fully take advantage of that moment, but he still achieved incredible distance.

By the time Hamish managed to level out and his head stopped spinning enough to look back at the elfonnel, the clouds of steam and fire were already dissipating. That second explosion was more than the elfonnel could handle.

Nothing but a charred crater remained of the elemental monster.

CHAPTER FORTY-THREE

*"At the rising of the sun, shadows retreat into darkness and brightness
of hope is rekindled."*

~Evander

erena cheered when the elfonnel disintegrated. She
jumped up and down, despite how that rocked the
Storm. The monster that had destroyed her home
was dead!

Martys clutched his seat and shouted, "Have a care!"

She ignored him and threw her arms around Connor and
kissed him joyfully. His comforting presence helped fill a bit of the
gaping hole in her heart left by the loss of her home. But when
she glanced out across the debris-filled, flooded lands that covered
her home, fresh tears threatened to spill free.

Connor placed an arm around her shoulders and she
leaned against him. The Builder compound had been her home
more than any of the grand palaces her family owned.

She'd abandoned everything to move there and explore her
Builder powers. Her family supported her decision, but she'd still
sacrificed so much. It had all been worth it, and she loved pushing
the limits of discovery and unlocking secrets lost for centuries.

Now all that hard work was gone.

Hamish landed in the cluttered bed of the Storm, looking
satisfied. Jean clambered over the seats toward him, but paused in
the third row and stared down in surprise. "Aifric?"

Verena had forgotten all about the Healer. How could
Aifric sleep through such a horrific experience? The thought made
her irrationally angry.

She joined Jean in the third row. Aifric was slumbering on
the floor, curled up on one side, one hand thrust into her coat.
She looked completely comatose. Jean crouched beside her,
shaking her lightly.

Verena shoved Aifric's shoulder roughly. "Hey, get up. This is no time for sleeping."

Aifric didn't move. She didn't snore or grunt or acknowledge the contact in any way. Verena frowned. Wasn't she supposed to be an Assassin?

"What's wrong with her?" Connor asked.

"Nothing," Martys said. He waved Verena back. "Leave off, lass. I've seen exhaustion wounds. She'll recover, but needs rest."

"I don't think so." Jean looked worried and leaned over Aifric to touch her forehead. "No fever. No visible marks of trauma, but lack of response to stimulus suggests traumatic brain injury."

She looked up at Connor. "This type of comatosis is not normal, and can easily degenerate to a life-threatening condition. It is beyond my ability to treat."

"Aifric be a Healer," Martys said, his tone impatient. "She said all she needs is rest."

"But what if she's wrong?" Verena asked.

Her anger had fled, replaced by concern. They had lost too much already. She couldn't bear the thought of losing someone even casually considered a friend.

"What should we do?" Hamish asked.

Connor said, "I'll see what I can find. Get her up on those seats."

Martys insisted, "Ye should leave her be. Ye dinnae want to anger a sleeping Assassin."

"I'll take my chances," Connor said.

Together they gently lifted Aifric and lay her across the last row of seats. The fact that she didn't rouse, even when Hamish banged her legs against the seat only intensified Verena's concern.

Connor crouched in front of her and pulled from under his leather jacket a sandstone pendant on a silver chain, shaped like a clenched fist. Verena had seen him use a similar pendant with marvelous healing power.

"Is that a gift from your Aunt Ailsa?" she asked.

Connor nodded. "It's sculpted sandstone, so it should have enough healing power to help."

Martys whistled softly, a look of wonder on his face. "Ye be full of surprises, laddie."

Connor was no Healer, but with his other pendant, he'd once healed Verena's broken leg. She had been captured trying to free the boy Nicklaus from the Obrioners. Of course, it was Connor who had caused the broken leg in the first place.

They watched in silent anticipation as Connor clutched the pendant in one hand and placed the other on Aifric's forehead. He bowed over her for a moment, and Verena wished that she could share what he felt.

After a moment, Connor looked up, his expression confused. "She seems healthy, but she's actively tapping obsidian."

"I thought Petralists weren't supposed to tap affinities while they sleep," Verena said.

"They're not, and she shouldn't be able to. Leaving primary affinity powder in one's system while sleeping usually triggers untapped reversal sickness. This doesn't make sense."

"Best to leave off and wait for her to wake," Martys suggested.

"I hope you don't take this wrong, but I don't think you know as much as you think you do about this." Jean told him, her tone frustrated.

Verena considered Aifric's hand thrust into her coat and got an idea. "Jean, help me."

Connor stepped aside so she and Jean could slip into the small space in front of Aifric and unbutton her jacket. Inside, her hand was clutching a leather pouch, with two fingers buried inside. Verena pried Aifric's hand open, and Jean pulled the bag free, then handed it to Connor.

He checked inside and nodded. "Obsidian, all right."

"She's been asking for a lot of obsidian ever since she arrived at Harz," Verena said.

Connor nodded. "I got her enough to last most Blades a month, but she kept saying it wasn't enough."

Verena said, "And I got her some twice. I'm thinking she's got a powder addiction."

"Professor Hector was addicted to granite. He had to use more to get the same kind of effect, but it never knocked him out like this." Connor glanced at Martys. "Have you ever seen obsidian addiction?"

"No, lad. 'Tis a mystery."

Jean said, "Let's get to Faulenrost. We'll have more room to treat her there, and we can check on the survivors from the elfonnel attack."

"I'll sit by her," Martys suggested.

"I will too," Jean said, and it was strange that Martys didn't look happy about that. Verena wondered why he took such an interest in Aifric's condition. Maybe it was because she was Mhortair.

Connor also lingered near them as Verena took the controls, explained to Dierk their plan, then banked away to the east. Hamish rolled off the Storm and led the way toward Faulenrost. Verena could have outraced him, but decided to take it slower with the strangely sick Aifric.

They left the floodwaters behind and soared over the hills marking the eastern boundary of the valley, heading toward the high ridge of Faulenrost township. Verena's mood brightened when she saw crowds of survivors from the Builder compound clustered on the outskirts of town. Dierk and Jean had rescued hundreds.

Jean's heroic actions made her love her like a sister. To think she'd managed two flights in a windrider full of refugees without tipping or crashing. It was astounding.

It was abundantly clear that they had stumbled upon something truly revolutionary with that keystone. She needed to study its full potential as soon as possible. That familiar rush of excitement that came with delving into deeper Builder truths helped ease the aching hurt from the loss of her home.

Hamish landed first, and was immediately surrounded by a huge throng, shouting happy greetings and asking if they were still in danger. Verena settled the Storm a little farther from the main crowds. She was happy to see that the people of Faulenrost had welcomed the refugees with their typical friendly enthusiasm, led by Lord Eberhard.

When Hamish informed them that the monster was dead, Lord Eberhard led a round of cheering. He then launched into a long, impromptu speech about the need for solidarity in the face of affliction. He promised to provide shelter and food until additional help arrived.

When he mentioned that he had already ordered a pigeon sent to the capital, informing them of the disaster, Verena noted Hamish's look of disgust. She agreed that there had to be a better way to communicate over large distances, but now was not the time to figure it out.

Bruno the blacksmith, who Verena knew from testing earlier mechanicals, rushed out of the crowd toward the Storm. He cheered when he saw Jean.

"You live!" Bruno laughed as he lifted Jean from the Storm. "You mighty brave girl!"

Jean flushed under the praise and explained, "Bruno helped manage all the people while I flew the windrider. Without him and his big voice, we would have flipped over for sure."

Bruno saluted Verena and said in Grandurian, "This young lady is the hero of Faulenrost! She saved us all from that monster. I thought she died when she jumped out of the wagon and rushed back to face that monster."

Verena told him, "It was a close thing, but she dropped a bomb on it. We helped her finish it off."

"Thank you, Builder," Bruno said with another salute. Then he took Jean's hand in his massive one and said, "Come, hero girl. Meet town. Meet Lord Eberhard."

Jean gestured back at the Storm. "In a minute. Our friend is sick. I need to find a place for her to rest."

Bruno nodded. "I find place. I bring."

Connor and Martys lifted Aifric, and Bruno cradled her like a child in his burly arms.

Gisela appeared through the crowd and rushed to Connor. "What is wrong?"

"Aifric is sick."

"You should bringing her to the inn. There is a man needing to speaking with us."

"Who?" Martys asked as he jumped from the Storm after Connor.

Her expression turned worried. "I do not knowing him, but I am thinking he is Assassin like Aifric."

CHAPTER FORTY-FOUR

"To remain unseen, one must embody what is not there."

~Ilse

As they followed the huge blacksmith into Faulenrost, Connor stayed close to Verena. She had seemed so devastated by the destruction of her home, but the happy reunion with so many friends seemed to help.

The loss of the Builder compound was a terrible thing, but Connor found he only dwelt on the loss of the porphyry. He was startled to feel a simmering anger at Verena. If she'd given him the powder when he'd first asked for it, it wouldn't be lost.

With effort, he forced the irrational anger aside.

Lord Eberhard intercepted them as they tried to push through the crowds. He and Verena spoke quickly for a moment in Grandurian. Bruno added his booming voice, which easily carried over the crowd. People cheered and pressed in closer around Jean, trying to hug her. Many wept as they tried to reach her.

Hamish shielded her from getting crushed in the press and shared a wondering look with Connor. "Who knew being a hero could be so dangerous? They're going to love her to death, if they're not careful."

Lord Eberhard spoke in a loud, commanding tone, and the crowds gave Jean a little room. She was flushing deeply, but waved to everyone. "I'm just glad I could help."

After another brief exchange, the cheering faded, replaced by a somber mood. Lord Eberhard began speaking rapidly, making grand gestures, his tone comforting and earnest. He had a good voice, and whatever he was saying seemed to help.

"He is again promising aid," Verena said, looking emotional herself. She took Lord Eberhard's hand and thanked him.

After that, the crowd parted for them and Bruno led the way into town, toward the village square. People called out to Hamish and Verena, many with tears in their eyes.

Connor was impressed that Hamish was able to converse with them. Although his Grandurian sounded rough, they clearly appreciated him speaking in their native tongue.

Connor decided he needed to begin learning Grandurian too. If this country was to be his home, perhaps for a long time, he should know the language. Besides, he loved listening to Verena speaking her native tongue. It would be even better if he understood what she was saying.

Faulenrost was a large town, and it appeared prosperous. The main street leading toward the central town square was eight blocks long, paved with slate cobblestones. Two-story, steep-roofed buildings crowded both sides.

The wooden buildings looked clean and recently painted. They were made in an interesting, half-timbered design, with the heavy framing timbers visible, the openings between them filled with bricks or plaster. Most were roofed with slate or ceramic tile.

In the narrow side streets, the second stories of the buildings extended out over the street a couple of feet. Twice, Connor spotted stone arches spanning the streets, with towers built atop them that rose even higher.

Shops occupied most of the ground floors, with living quarters above. Although the architecture was foreign, the town felt friendly. Connor decided he liked it.

The large main square, with streets emptying into it at every corner, was paved with an alternating pattern of brick and cobblestones that converged at a three-tiered, circular fountain in the center. No water was flowing at the moment, so of course a dozen boys had climbed the fountain for a better view over the crowds. The square would normally have seemed spacious, but at the moment it was cramped from the press of people.

A blend of clashing smells assaulted Connor's nostrils. A distinct, ugly reek of fear hung in the air over the massed crowds, although it was dissipating as news of the death of the elfonnel spread. The smell of fresh-baked bread and grilled meat wafted from shops set up along two sides of the square. Perfumes from many of the local ladies, the warm scent of horses, and the pungent smell of their droppings mingled under it all.

Lord Eberhard's palace and administration building on the opposite side of the square rose four stories. An enormous red stone building with two tall towers took up the left side. A huge well in its courtyard was capped with a miniature house that sheltered the buckets and pulleys. A three-story inn filled the entire right side of the square.

Bruno headed in that direction and led them inside. The main room of the inn was long and low, with massive exposed beams, darkened from age and lamp smoke. Tables and chairs packed much of the room, and most of them were occupied with patrons eating their midday meal.

Serving girls in azure dresses and crisp white aprons rushed to keep up, carrying platters of food and large, wooden tankards from the huge kitchen at the back. A long bar of shiny, black wood ran along the back wall to the left of the kitchen doors.

An immense fireplace was inset into the right-hand wall, with two dozen wooden rocking chairs facing it. Even though only a small fire was burning at the moment, most of the chairs were occupied by gray-haired old men sipping tankards and talking. A steady rumble of conversation made it hard to communicate.

A plump, elderly couple greeted them just inside the door. Their blue eyes twinkled with good humor and reflected the deep blue of their aprons. They greeted Bruno warmly, then hugged Verena joyfully, as if she was a long-lost daughter.

Hamish leaned close so Connor could hear him. "Evert and Liesa. They own the inn. Good people. I think they're somehow related to Neasa because they make the best sweetbreads anywhere in Granadure."

Jean said, "I would have thought Grandurian bread would be different."

"A lot of it is, but some is similar. They've got one little pastry called a bethmannchen." He sighed, with the same expression of ecstasy he usually reserved for Neasa's best confections. "You've got to try it."

Liesa was already gesturing them to follow, and she led them down a side hallway, then upstairs to a long hall with doors spaced regularly down both sides. She opened one. It was a sleeping chamber.

The small room was neat and tidy, with a soft mattress on the bed. Liesa turned down the quilt, and Bruno settled the still-unconscious Aifric on the mattress.

Jean shooed them out. "I'll watch her. Go meet that man Gisela was talking about. If he's really Mhortair, maybe he knows what's wrong with Aifric."

"Good point," Connor said and they all trooped back downstairs.

Gisela led them to a private dining room at the back of the first floor. It was empty but for one man sitting at the far side of a long table that could easily seat twenty.

The man was not large, but even seated he exuded a certain calm confidence as his gray eyes swept the group. To Connor, it looked like he was sizing them up as potential targets. His clothing was rich but plain, and he could have blended in with people almost anywhere without drawing attention to himself.

The man rose and made a short bow. "It is a rare treat to meet such a company." His low voice was not threatening, but not quite warm either. He spoke Obrioner with no accent whatsoever.

"You know us?" Connor asked as the man moved around the table toward them.

"By reputation."

Connor wondered what reputation that might be. Did he really know Connor as Blood of the Tallan, Hamish as the first Obrioner Builder in three hundred years, and Verena as nobility and one of the most brilliant Builders ever? Could he know Martys, or Gisela? If they were building an international reputation already, they had to think about what kind of image they wanted to portray.

The man studied Connor with unsettling intensity. He made no threatening move, but approached with a hand extended to shake. Still, Connor got the distinct impression that the man was considering whether or not to kill him.

That would make introductions a bit trickier.

He prepared to tap granite, but if the man was an Assassin, he probably had some of that weakening powder to combat primary affinities. Unlike when Aifric had attacked him, Connor was prepared to tap his tertiary affinities. He already had a piece of marble under his tongue. If the newcomer made a threatening move, he would introduce himself with fire.

"You are Blood of the Tallan?" the man asked.

"I like to introduce myself as Connor." The others seemed to sense the potential threat from the man and spread out a little.

The barest frown turned down the corners of the man's mouth. "Aifric's report was at best considered vague, and at worst treasonous. Why do you think I traveled halfway across the continent to meet you for myself?"

"Well I'm out of parchment for autographs. We kind of had a water problem today."

The man looked annoyed, then his gaze sharpened and he demanded, "Where is Aifric?"

"Why don't you tell me your name first? I make it a point not to hand over friends to creepy middle-aged guys who don't introduce themselves properly," Connor said, starting to feel a bit annoyed by the fellow.

"Then you consider her friend?"

"We haven't had to kill each other yet, so yeah, I think we're off to a good start."

"You may call me Sir."

Hamish barked a laugh. "That's funny. Why don't you call me Master?"

The man glared, and he had a really good glare. It had no impact whatsoever on Hamish, who popped one of his smashpacked cubes into his mouth.

Sir took a slow breath, and his demeanor relaxed. "I am not used to being questioned, boy. I will forgive your lack of civility this time, but I must see Aifric at once."

"Why?" Verena asked.

"I sense that she is in grave danger."

Connor asked, "How can you do that? She's not here."

"I know her."

Hamish said, "You'll have to do better than that. We know her too."

Sir took a deep breath and spoke slowly, as if measuring each word before releasing it. "A special connection is established between members of the Mhortair. I sense danger around her."

"Then would it concern you to learn she's fallen into a trance-like sleep, but is actively burning obsidian at the same time?"

Sir's expression turned alarmed. "Take me to her at once."

He moved toward the door, and Connor found himself and the others moving with him. He didn't remember deciding to trust Sir, but something in the man's commanding tone seemed impossible to disobey.

Martys didn't seem affected by it. He blocked the doorway, frowning. "Aifric dinnae seem well, and this bloke no has explained who he is. How do we know he's not the assassin Dougal sent?"

That was a valid point, although Connor suspected that Dougal's assassin would have tried to kill him or Verena already.

Sir smiled at Martys. "I like loyal friends, so I choose not to take offense. If I was here to do you harm, I would not have announced myself and waited in the open to greet you. You'd already be dead."

"That's comforting," Hamish mumbled.

Sir continued. "Obrion's invasion endangers the entire continent. I must see to Aifric and receive her report before I can offer any assistance."

Connor looked to Verena, who nodded slightly. He glanced at Hamish, who shook his head. That didn't help much.

So Connor said, "All right. We'll show you to Aifric, but that doesn't mean we trust you yet."

"I'd be terribly disappointed if you did."

When they returned to where they'd left Aifric, Sir entered the room, with Connor and the others crowding in after. If Sir did anything threatening to Aifric, Connor would blast him out the window.

Jean started to protest when they all began cramming into the room, but Sir made a calming motion. "I believe I can help."

He crouched over Aifric and studied her. Muttering to himself in a language that Connor did not understand, Sir touched her forehead.

Three seconds later, he gasped. "It is worse than I feared. She is in thrall to another mind."

"How is that possible?" Connor demanded.

"I cannot answer that until I free her."

"Can you do that?" Verena asked.

He nodded. "To do so, I need your promises that you will not interfere."

"What do you plan to do?" Connor asked suspiciously.

"I can save her, but the process is painful. I may need to make whoever is controlling her think I am killing her."

"I don't like the sound of that," Hamish said.

Sir looked annoyed, "They must believe. It may be best if you all wait outside."

"We're not going anywhere," Verena said, and Connor and the others nodded agreement.

Sir looked to each of them, holding them in his piercing, gray-eyed stare. "You cannot interfere, no matter what you think may be happening. If you interrupt the process, she will die, or at the least languish with a broken mind. Do you understand?"

Connor exchanged a worried look with Verena, who looked unsure. Hamish and Martys both looked like they preferred the idea of beating Sir senseless before letting him even pretend to hurt Aifric. Jean looked nervous too, but spoke with the decisive tone she used when treating patients.

"No one will interfere. You have our words."

"Hey," Hamish objected.

Jean raised an eyebrow and said, "Treatments can be hard, Hamish. If this is the only way to save Aifric, it must be done."

"There's no other way?" Verena asked.

Sir shook his head. "We cannot delay. If I am to save her, it must be now."

"Do it," Jean told him, but as he reached for Aifric's head she added in a cold, hard tone that Connor barely recognized as hers. "If you harm her, I swear to cut out your heart myself."

Hamish looked like he wanted to kiss her, and even Martys looked impressed. Connor decided he'd barbecue Sir's heart once Jean removed it.

Sir took her hand and looked deep into her eyes for several seconds. Then he smiled warmly. "Your heart is honest and brave, Jean. I agree to your terms."

He turned to Aifric and gripped her head, placing his middle fingers over her temples, index fingers over her eyes, and thumbs against her lips.

Connor suddenly realized Sir had called Jean by name, but they'd never actually been introduced. How had he known?

Aifric started awake, eyes wide, a look of fearful recognition on her face.

Sir's expression turned cruel and he growled, "Die knowing you've failed to protect the Blood of the Tallan from me."

Aifric's eyes rolled back and her body stiffened.

Connor and Hamish both tensed to strike at Sir, but Jean pointed at them, her expression hard. She shook her head, and he remembered Sir's warning.

Aifric began to scream.

"Jean--" Connor started to protest, but she shot him such a withering look, his protest died on his lips.

After making sure the others wouldn't interfere either, Jean turned back to Sir, who was bowed over Aifric, hands trembling with strain as he leaned close over her screaming form.

"This ain't right," Martys growled, one hand on his dagger.

Verena waved him back. "We watch for now. Tell everyone to keep back. This situation is under control."

Only then did Connor notice the sound of many feet thundering over the wooden floor as villagers came running to see what was wrong. With a final glower, Martys stepped into the hall and started shouting for everyone to get back.

Jean took Aifric's hand. "Pulse is dangerously high, and her temperature appears to be spiking."

Sir said nothing, and he and Aifric remained motionless, with her endless scream pouring from her lungs.

That sound tore at Connor's heart and drove him to act, to strike out against Sir. If Jean didn't decide soon that it needed to stop, he'd tap marble and act on his own.

Beside him, Hamish was growling, his expression fierce, hands clenched into white-knuckled fists. Verena's face had drained of color, and one hand had dipped into her satchel.

Aifric's scream abruptly stopped, and she sagged against the bed, mouth open, breathing dangerously fast. Sir slowly removed his hands and she blinked up at him. She tried to sit up but he pressed her back down.

She spoke words Connor did not understand. Whatever language she spoke was like whispers cast into an open sky. It wasn't that she spoke softly, but the words seemed to fade away too quickly. They were beautiful, flowing sounds, like a gentle wind through tall grasses, and she stopped far too soon for his liking.

"What did she say?" Connor asked.

Sir said, "Few speak Havaen, the language of breezes. She asked what I'm doing here." Then he asked Aifric gently, "What do you remember, Student Seventeen?"

Aifric's brows furrowed in thought. Then she gasped and her eyes widened. "Sir, I failed!"

Hamish threw up his hands in disbelief. "I can't believe it. His name really is Sir."

Sir sat back and smiled a genuine, warm smile at Aifric. "Now that you understand that, I must decide if it is time to change your name to eighteen, or execute you immediately."

Chapter Forty-Five

"History relinquishes its memories with a begrudging hand."

~Evander

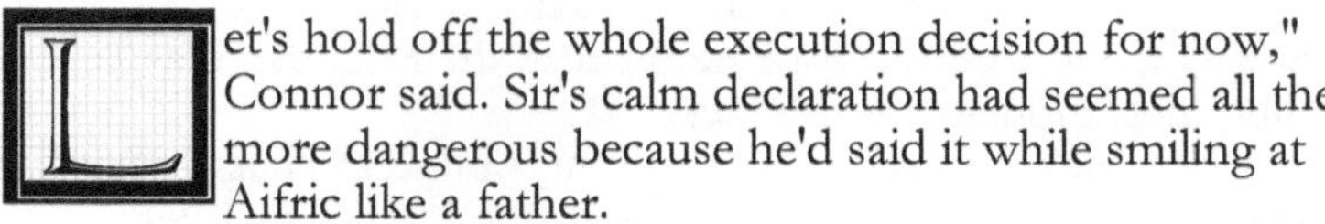

et's hold off the whole execution decision for now," Connor said. Sir's calm declaration had seemed all the more dangerous because he'd said it while smiling at Aifric like a father.

Aifric seemed to notice the rest of them for the first time. She scrambled to her feet, her cheeks flushing. "I made such a mess of everything, Connor. I swore to help you, but all I've done is put you in danger."

Sir glanced from her to Connor. "Swearing to help your target instead of removing him is usually considered a major mistake."

Aifric faced Sir with chin raised. "I had reasons for my choices, and I'm willing to submit to the inquisition to prove it."

That didn't sound good. She should have promised to discuss it over bacon.

"What happened to you?" Verena asked.

Sir stood and waved them to silence. "We have much to discuss, but not here with half the inn trying to see what's going on. I suggest we return to that private dining room."

"It is time for lunch," Hamish said hopefully.

As they descended past knots of villagers still clustered at the foot of the stairs, Verena assured Liesa that all was well. Hamish took the opportunity to ask her to send in a meal. Her nervous response confirmed that she had seen Hamish eat before.

They settled into seats around the table, with Sir at the foot and Connor at the head. He snagged a handful of smashpacked cubes from Hamish while they waited for lunch, and watched Aifric with lingering worry. Every few seconds she started, looking like a nervous rabbit, and sometimes exclaiming with soft cries of dismay.

Sir said, "Recovering from long-term external control can be a traumatic experience. Less disciplined minds have cracked under the strain, although I am confident that Student Seventeen will survive."

"What external control are we talking about?" Connor asked.

"Dougal, of course. He is the only person I know outside of our enclave who even knows how such a thing could be done. He may be the only person alive who can actually accomplish it."

Verena asked, "So Mhortair mind powers are different?"

"The influence we wield is a temporary thing, best for gathering information from others, not forcing them to do our will."

"You read people's minds?" Hamish asked, his expression mirroring Connors concern. Had Sir read their minds? Was he stealing their thoughts even now?

Connor formed an image of Sir, bound in chains, slowly descending into a giant vat of boiling water. He watched Sir carefully, but saw no reaction. So he changed it to an image of Sir, dressed in pink tights, playing a harp.

Still no reaction. Either Sir wasn't actively reading his mind, or the man had amazing facial control.

"Our creed does not allow us to siphon the thoughts of our allies," Sir told Hamish calmly.

Martys grunted, not hiding his doubt. "So we be allies?"

"I haven't killed any of you yet."

"And we haven't killed you," Connor said, trying to match Sir's calm. He created an image in his mind of Sir dressed in smallclothes and armed only with a chocolate pudding facing Kilian, who was encased in a blurring mixture of fire and water.

The briefest of frowns flitted across Sir's features. Had that been a reaction to the image, or something else?

Sir only said, "Then we're off to a good start, aren't we?"

"I don't consider threatening Aifric a good start," Verena said.

"The best way to root out an enemy so deeply embedded in another's mind is to make them think that person is about to die. They withdraw to avoid the pain and terror of death from radiating back through the conduit that links them to their prey."

"And that conduit is obsidian?" Connor asked.

Sir didn't look happy by the question. "Few know even that much."

"That's why you kept asking for more. You needed it to maintain the connection," Verena said.

Aifric nodded. "I kept secretly hoping you'd refuse, but I was prevented from voicing any warning."

Jean looked fascinated by the discussion. "How does that work? When you weren't in one of those deep trances, you seemed to be acting like yourself."

"Dougal's control was not heavy-handed. He blocked me from interfering with his access or warning you, but he was mostly interested in gathering information."

"He's been watching us this whole time." The thought sickened Connor. No wonder Dougal had manipulated them so effectively. So many people had suffered and died because of what Dougal had done to Aifric.

Verena exclaimed, "I hate cheaters!"

Tears stood in Aifric's eyes and she looked miserable.

What Dougal did to her enraged Connor. Dougal had tried to take control of him too. If only he'd realized the full danger she faced.

"I should have realized what happened," Hamish said, looking as angry as Connor felt.

"I should have killed him when I had the chance," Aifric said sadly.

Hamish nodded. "I was thinking the same thing at the time."

"How could you have?"

"I planted a speakstone on you when I dropped you off. I listened to the whole conversation. I'm no Assassin, but even I could tell you were wasting time."

Aifric glanced at Sir and flushed.

"Against any other target, her actions would not have been entirely inappropriate," Sir said.

"How could you send an Assassin to the Carraig without explaining the risks beforehand?" Verena asked.

"High Lord Dougal was not supposed to be there. She was supposed to identify the Blood of the Tallan and remove him. Nothing more."

"How do we know that's not your mission too?" Connor asked.

"Neither of us are dead yet, remember?"

"Well maybe we aren't interested in allowing you to linger until you change your mind," Verena said, her tone turning unfriendly.

Sir said, "Don't rush decisions about killing. Trust me, you want to be absolutely sure. Once you've killed someone it's hard to change your mind."

An Assassin speaking philosophy was so weird.

Aifric said, "Sir, I think I'm stable. Connor is not the monster we feared. It's Dougal we need to stop, and Connor is our best chance of doing it."

"Unless High Lord Dougal manages to gain control over his mind like he did yours. Then he would become the worst monster since Tallan himself."

Verena's hand slipped into her satchel and her expression turned even darker. "Be careful how you talk about Tallan in this country, Sir. I've heard rumors that it was the Mhortair who killed him. If that's true, I guarantee we won't get along after all."

Sir made a slight bow. "I appreciate your strength, Builder, and thank you for the cultural reminder. Connor, my mission today is not to remove you."

Aifric looked relieved. "Jean, I was terrified you were going to die. I could sense that Dougal was expecting that elfonnel to kill you. Your death would have demoralized the group."

Connor's anger at Dougal grew hotter, but Hamish surprised him by laughing.

"I guess she blew his calculating, plotting, devious, evil wickedness right out of the water!"

He was right. Connor added, "That's what he gets for underestimating our Jean."

Jean flushed. "Aifric, what I don't understand is why Dougal didn't force you to murder all of us in our sleep."

"He probably figured he couldn't get us all," Connor suggested.

Aifric shook her head. "He invaded my mind, but bits and pieces of his own thoughts flowed the other way. He wanted me only as a spy. He wants to destroy Kilian through an elfonnel that he controls. Slitting your throats in the night wasn't spectacular enough."

"I'm glad his sense of the theatrical overruled his practicality," Verena said with a shudder.

"It's scary to think he could strike through people we trust," Connor said.

Aifric stared at the table, frowning at her hands. "There was more, I think, but it's all hazy, like a dream. All I get is something vague about restless elements."

"What does that mean?" Connor asked.

"I have no idea."

"It will come," Sir told her, and his tone was almost comforting.

"Dougal's hold is broken, right?" Connor asked, just to be sure.

Aifric nodded. "He's gone."

Sir said, "I made sure of it. Aifric, I will teach you how to keep him out."

Connor perked up at that. "Can you teach me too? If there's a way to block him, I need to know it."

Sir hesitated. "I agreed not to target you today, Connor, but that does not mean I'm ready to share Mhortair secrets with you."

Jean said, "You're the one who pointed out how dangerous it would be if Dougal seized Connor's mind. Surely it's in your own best interest to teach him to shield and prevent that eventuality."

"You're a clever girl. I will consider it."

Connor wanted to push him, but too much pressure might make Sir deny the request out of pure stubbornness.

Aifric looked up sharply and snapped her fingers. "One thing at least is clear. Dougal has left the army and returned to Obrion."

That didn't make any sense.

Verena asked, "Why would he do that? He's got the advantage."

"That's precisely why." Aifric pressed one hand to her temple. "He forced me into that coma sleep when we started to fly north because his attention was split elsewhere."

"He was trying to manage two elfonnel," Connor said.

Aifric nodded. "Just before my mind succumbed to sleep, his shielding faltered while he was distracted. He expected Camonica to destroy the Builder compound, lay waste to Faulenrost, then cross the mountains and move against Edderitz itself."

Verena gasped. "That's horrible."

Martys looked impressed. "Bold plan, that. Woulda caused plenty of distraction."

Verena said, "Worse than the people who might have died, such an attack would have diverted critical reinforcements away from Altkalen. The delay could have been disastrous."

"Altkalen?" Connor asked.

"It's the biggest city in southern Granadure. It's a major trading center, and after Harz, it'll be the next target."

"I'm not sure if Dougal knows how much Camonica accomplished." Aifric glanced at Connor, then Verena. "I think you two were targeted by. . ." She started and looked to Sir. "By you! That's what you meant when you said I had failed."

"Indeed."

Connor prepared to tap marble. If Sir had been sent by Dougal, had he waited for this moment to strike after all?

Sir read his renewed tension. "Relax. Eighteen is a gifted student, but who do you think taught her to infiltrate Obrion?"

"Eighteen?" Aifric asked, looking relieved and excited at the same time.

"You have survived yet another potentially fatal blunder, Student."

"No one's ever made it to eighteen before," Aifric said with a proud smile.

Sir gave her a cold look and her smile faded. "And I doubt even you will make it to nineteen, so have a care before you make another rash decision."

She nodded quickly. Verena said, "You still haven't explained about your mission to kill us."

"I infiltrated Dougal's spy network. He gave me the mission to remove you, Verena, although I was to wait before striking Connor."

He made it sound so simple.

"So I'd have time to suffer?" Connor asked bitterly.

Sir shook his head. "No doubt that was part of his plan, but my orders were to ensure your grief sent you back to Shona."

"That. . ." Verena's words faded to an angry whisper in Grandurian, and Connor suspected he'd just heard another choice curse word.

The coldness of the plan infuriated him. Would Dougal have allowed Shona to comfort him, accept him again as her Guardian, marry him, and together serve Dougal's purposes? Or would he have seized Connor and turned him back against Granadure immediately?

Aifric said, "When Dougal saw you and felt my pain, I believe he assumed your mission was successful and that you were removing me too. I don't know what happened at Harz after we left, but he seemed confident enough to return to Obrion. I believe he plans to leverage the early successes for more political advantage and to gather additional reinforcements."

Connor frowned. "Is there another army close enough to Merkland to be a threat any time soon?"

Verena said, "Not that we know about, but it's possible. We need to return to Harz and share this news with Kilian."

"If there's still a Harz left," Connor said.

Verena's expression turned grim. "If Harz fell, then we go to Altkalen. That city cannot fall, no matter the cost."

Just then, Liesa entered the room, followed by a long line of serving girls carrying platters, trays, and bowls. Connor had expected a simple lunch, but Liesa seemed eager to honor Jean for her valiant defense of the valley.

Savory smells filled the room, and Connor realized he was ravenous. He eagerly piled his plate with spicy sausages and a large meat pie, covered in cinnamon sauce. A bowl of greens and vegetables and a huge tankard of fresh-squeezed apple cider rounded out the meal.

Most of the others dug in with as much enthusiasm, but Verena only picked at her plate. When Hamish piled his for a third helping of roast pork, she snapped, "How can you eat like that, Hamish? Our home was just destroyed!"

The magnitude of their loss had faded from Connor's mind during the discussion with Aifric. He felt terrible that he could forget something so momentous so soon.

Hamish lowered his fork and shrugged, looking surprised. "Verena, the Builder compound was our home. Seeing it destroyed was a terrible thing, but starving ourselves isn't going to help."

"Celebrating doesn't feel right," Verena said with a sigh.

"I'm not celebrating the loss of our home. I'm celebrating the fact that we're all alive."

Verena looked amazed, as if that different focus was completely foreign to her. Connor realized that with her privileged upbringing, she might not have ever suffered such a devastating loss before.

He said, "In Obrion, we were used to losing the little we had. Lord Gavin could even take away the right of families to stay together, and could enslave us at a whim."

"I hadn't realized that," Verena said.

"It be the ugly truth," Martys said between mouthfuls of baked potato.

"My mom always said to look for the good in every day, so I will." Hamish saluted with a sausage.

Verena lifted a fork full of meat pie and saluted in return. "Thanks, Hamish. That helps."

"The sausage helps more."

Verena smiled, and her dark mood seemed to fade. Connor hoped she could maintain the new perspective. He doubted they'd seen their last trial.

Sir insisted on coming with them when they left Faulenrost, and Connor was happy to leave the question of what to do with Sir to Kilian.

Jean said, "I'm thinking maybe I should stay here to help organize relief efforts."

Hamish shook his head. "Oh, no. You come with us. I sent you away once, and you nearly died."

"But I can't do any good in a big battle."

"You destroyed that elfonnel today," he pointed out.

Verena said, "I think you should come. We can plan the rebuilding while we travel. Besides, I'm thinking we're going to need to fine-tune the Swift and Hamish's suit as much as possible before the next fight."

"I do want to help with that."

Connor was happy to hear it. He didn't want to leave Jean behind. Their team felt incomplete without her.

Hamish's sighed. "I'm glad you're coming, but I'll still worry about you."

Jean took his hand. "Bad things happen, Hamish, especially in war." Her voice fell to a soft, tender whisper. "Like what happened to Ingrid."

Hamish nodded, and didn't look like he could speak.

Jean looked around the table. "We'll all do the best we can. That's all we can do. We can't let fear rule us, or we've already lost."

Connor felt moved by her simple, heartfelt declaration. She was right, and he wanted to go hug her.

Martys raised his mug of ale. "Aye, lass! Well said. Spit in the eye of evil an' fight to the last."

Connor raised his glass and said, "Fight to the last."

The others joined him, and they drank together.

CHAPTER FORTY-SIX

"But the sweetbread that falls off the tray and gets kicked under the oven is eaten only after the rest are consumed."

~Connor

You're going to like Altkalen," Verena shouted over the wind as they flew high over southern Granadure.

Connor sat right beside her in the front row, but barely heard over the wind. Gisela, who sat on her other side, staring at the view, didn't appear to have heard anything.

They were flying fast, pushed along by a helpful tailwind. Since they weren't sure if Harz fortress had fallen, Verena had suggested a slightly westerly course to check in at the trading center of Altkalen. The flight had gone smoothly, and they now approached a range of hills with pointy peaks that made them look like they were stretching upward, eager to be called mountains.

He tried to ask a question, but the wind whisked his words away. Verena frowned, then her face lit up and she plunged her hand into her satchel.

A shimmering shield of pulsing air formed into a half dome over their seats, blocking the screaming wind. Verena pushed up her visor and said, "I should have thought of that a long time ago."

"Does it affect speed?" Connor asked.

"I don't think so, and it makes travel so much easier. We'll see Altkalen soon. It's the biggest market in all of Granadure."

Sir seemed very interested in the air shield. He sat in the second row, flanked by Hamish and Martys. "Dougal must take Altkalen in order to survive the coming winter."

Verena nodded. "It's got plenty of supplies."

"Enough for fifty thousand troops, plus all the residents?" Hamish asked.

Connor wondered if the army would just kill everyone. He hoped Dougal intended conquest and not annihilation.

Verena said, "Altkalen's market center is bigger than the markets in all the other cities combined. I hope we find time to visit. It's amazing."

When Hamish didn't look impressed she added, "The culinary quarter, which is centered around the bakery district, is bigger than all of Alasdair. There are six hundred bakers and pastry chefs alone."

Hamish gaped. "How long did you say before we arrive?"

Aifric, who lounged between Jean and Dierk in the third row, leaned forward and smacked Hamish lightly on the back of the head. "You always think with your stomach?"

Jean laughed. Her braid had gotten tangled by the wind, and she was trying to straighten it. "That's Hamish."

Hamish shrugged. "When your stomach's full, most of life's problems seem a little less severe."

Connor couldn't argue with that, and he was happy to see Aifric looking herself again. She hadn't even dozed once. Jean was watching for any signs of lingering problems.

Verena said, "Every year, Altkalen holds an annual Eat Till You Pop competition in honor of old Schwinkendorf, the guy who wrote that cookbook."

"Even if it still existed, it's gone now," Hamish said with a sigh.

Verena's smile faded. "The contest will probably be canceled due to the war."

Hamish looked crestfallen. "We should visit the bakeries at least, in honor of old man Schwinkendorf."

"All six hundred?" Gisela teased.

Hamish nodded, looking completely serious.

Jean draped an arm over Hamish's shoulder. "We should."

They flew over the hills and a panoramic vista opened to the south. An enormous city sprawled across the northern half of a vast plain. Connor blinked, barely believing that one city could be so huge. It stretched for miles under a brilliant azure sky that had just enough puffy, white clouds to make the blue look even more intense.

Hamish whistled softly. "You said it was a market center, you didn't say it was the biggest city in Granadure."

Verena shook her head. "Altkalen is big, but only half as many people live here as in the capital."

Connor wasn't sure he wanted to visit the capital. That many people in one place could not be healthy. When he glanced back, he noticed Aifric staring in mute astonishment at the sprawling metropolis.

"Don't tell me a big city is enough to impress a deadly Assassin," Connor teased.

Aifric shrugged and smiled. "My home in the mountains of Ravinder is a tiny fortress. I thought the Carraig was impressive."

It was. Connor had gaped like a country fool at the majestic, many-towered castle city. Sir didn't look happy that Aifric was talking about their home, but even he looked impressed by Altkalen.

As Connor scanned the huge city again, its layout began to make sense. They were flying in from the north. That side of the city was covered in towering spires and huge palaces, all clustered around a mighty citadel.

The citadel walls were made of layered stones in different shades of gray, darker at the base and growing increasingly lighter. The breathtaking effect made it seem like the upper reaches were preparing to merge with the sky.

Granadure might be a different country, but Connor wondered if the rulers of Altkalen were different from other nobles he'd met. Most high born would be served well to live in poorer neighborhoods for a few months. He smiled to think how a slippered lady might handle stepping in a fresh, steaming pile of manure as she crossed a livestock paddock.

That grand, prosperous northern part of the city was separated from the rest by a river running through a deep channel cut into the rocky ground. In places the water reflected the light like a ribbon of silver, but in others it looked blue, yellow, red, and even orange. The effect was remarkable. The winding course of the river was spanned by five majestic, arcing bridges that looked wide enough for several wagons to pass each other without crowding.

"Why does the river have so many colors?" Connor asked.

Verena said, "This area's very volcanic. The top layer of earth is thin, and underneath it's extremely rocky. The river has cut deep enough to expose minerals that give it those colors. Every time I look at it, the river seems a little different."

"It is being very beautiful," Gisela said.

Beyond the river, the central sections of the city were laid out in grid-like patterns. Connor focused on groups of gigantic, low structures clustered around wide, tree-lined thoroughfares. They had to cover two square miles.

"What are those huge buildings?" Hamish asked.

"Those are the trading floors. That's where the merchant houses buy and sell goods that get shipped all across Granadure, the Arishat League, and even Obrion during times of peace."

The buildings were big enough to swallow entire caravans. It was hard to comprehend so much merchandise for sale. One of those houses could hold enough goods to supply Alasdair for a year. Well, maybe not with Hamish and Martys along.

South of the orderly trading houses, a warren of narrow, winding streets split off of the wide, straight main thorough-fares. Two and three story buildings clustered close around those little streets, packed in tight. No doubt that's where the poorer classes lived.

And the distant southern reaches of the city gave way to vast, sprawling tent communities, interspersed with enormous padd-ocks for livestock. Connor's eyes were drawn even farther south, to the enormous army camped a mile south of the city's outskirts.

Connor focused his quartzite-enhanced vision in that direction, but for a moment simply marveled at the vista. The plain sparkled in the sunshine, the enormous city reflecting hues uniquely visible to Pathfinders, transforming it into a breathtaking wonder. He wished Verena could see it the way he did.

About a mile southwest of the city, a modest lake was nestled between rocky hills with steep banks. From their height, it looked like a giant mouth, gaping wide, filled with water. The army was camped near the lake, spreading across the plain to the east. As his gaze swooped over the army, he recognized Wolfram's standards.

"That's Wolfram's army," Hamish said, rising to stand and point.

Verena was already banking the Storm to fly around the eastern fringe of the city. Her expression turned grim. "Harz must have fallen. There's no other reason Wolfram would have retreated all the way to here."

"We have needing information," Gisela said.

Verena cocked her head to one side and touched the side of her helmet. "Kilian? Ear Hub? Can you hear me?"

She must have activated the speakstones in her helmet. Almost immediately she smiled and said, "It's good to hear your voice, Kilian."

Connor hadn't expected Kilian to get hurt in the fighting, but knowing the ancient Dawnus was on hand helped him relax. Connor might be Blood of the Tallan, but Kilian's experience could not be replaced.

Verena said, "It's quite a tale. We defeated the elfonnel, but Jean did most of the work." She paused, nodding again, even though Kilian couldn't see her. "Yes. She's with us, so you can get the story directly from her when we land."

After another pause she said, "The whole group, plus another Mhortair named Sir." She paused to listen and glanced back toward Sir, who was staring calmly out over the vista. "Of course. We'll land in just a few minutes."

"Did he tell you what happened with that other elfonnel?" Connor asked.

"He said he'll explain when we land."

"Well, what did he say?" Hamish asked.

"He's saving dinner for you."

"Kilian's a good man, never doubt it," Hamish said with a happy smile.

As they swept around the city, Connor studied the huge plain, that ran for miles to the south and had to be almost five miles wide. It looked like the bottom of a giant box. The eastern boundary was formed by a long line of very regular hills. They looked like they were made of huge stockpiles of earth.

"That's a lot of dirt."

Verena said, "Those weren't here the last time I visited."

"When was that?" Connor asked.

As Verena began to descend she said, "A couple years ago. I'll tell you about it later."

That was odd. She didn't usually need to focus that hard while flying. A couple minutes later they slowed and dropped toward part of the field where half a dozen long windriders were parked. Connor spotted Kilian waiting for them with Wolfram and a large company of soldiers. They looked grim.

The reception was not what Connor expected. Kilian all but ignored the rest of them, his focus entirely on Sir. He did not look happy to have a Mhortair in Granadure, let alone at Altkalen, and he forced Sir to surrender all of his power stones.

Sir did not seem surprised by the cold reception and submitted to Kilian's demands. Before leaving to wait in a lone tent, set up in an empty field, surrounded by Petralists, including a Flameweaver and a Sapper, Sir said, "I came knowing the risks, with the intent to join forces against a greater enemy."

Kilian said, "Perhaps. We will speak again soon, Assassin."

"Kilian, he freed Aifric from Dougal's control." Connor understood the need for caution around the Mhortair, but Kilian's greeting seemed harsher than necessary.

"We will do nothing in haste," Kilian said, and Sir left under heavy guard.

Only then did Kilian relax, hug Verena and Jean, and give the rest of them a welcoming smile. "I am so glad you're all right. You have no idea how much danger you were in."

"I wouldn't have let him harm them," Aifric said.

"I know you believe that. Come. We have much to talk about."

Chapter Forty-Seven

"Can a road taken in haste be thoroughly enjoyed?"

~Evander

The group headed to Wolfram's command tent. As soon as they entered, a pair of Pathfinders stationed outside began active blocking measures around the tent. The inside was organized in almost exactly the same way as every other command tent Connor had ever seen.

A large, round table covered with maps, papers, and parchments dominated the main room. A huge map of southern Granadure was fastened to a board standing near the far end of the table, with brass pins representing allied and enemy forces.

Wolfram gestured them to sit. "I'm glad you're all safe. We cannot afford to lose any of you."

Verena said, "It was bad, but could have been so much worse."

"Tell us, Jean," Kilian said as they all sat around the table.

Jean flushed under the attention, but related what happened at the Builder compound. Dierk made sure she didn't downplay her contributions, and Connor was impressed anew by Jean's heroic actions. She was not the helpless girl they had assumed.

Wolfram and Kilian looked amazed by the story, and Kilian said, "Jean, I believe when this is all over, Granadure owes you a medal."

"Or five," Wolfram said.

"Any of you would have done more," Jean said.

Kilian said, "The abilities of others don't diminish your heroism. Without that keystone, we might have lost Faulenrost too. I wonder what else it might do?"

"Would it have activated the bomb?" Jean asked.

Verena said, "I'm glad you didn't have to find out, but it's possible. The keystone has a lot of potential. Exploring it is a top priority."

Wolfram cautioned, "We must not lose sight of the fact that we must repel the invasion here at Altkalen, or there may be no stopping it."

"What happened at Harz?" Verena asked.

"Dougal outplayed us," Kilian said bitterly.

Aifric spoke for the first time. "From the bits I gleaned from his mind, I believe he planned every aspect of these initial battles with exacting precision."

Kilian said, "I should have suspected the truth about what happened to you. I'm sorry, Aifric. I had assumed Dougal had been so focused on Connor that you escaped."

"Perhaps we can leverage my failure now," Aifric said.

"Did you sense what he plans next?" Kilian asked.

She shook her head. "Only that he was frustrated. His plan is working, but not as well as he needs it to."

Kilian nodded slowly. "That's true. Camonica achieved only a partial success, and the fire-bound elfonnel that destroyed the Emmerich quarry and drove Wolfram from Harz was in turn destroyed."

"You have to tell us more about what happened than that," Connor urged.

Wolfram asked, "Why raise that elemental so far away? If they'd raised it right there in Harz Valley, we might have suffered a full rout."

"Dougal couldn't ignore the quarry, not with the risk that we might perhaps discover a new stone to counter obsidian," Kilian said.

"What new stone?" Wolfram's usual unflappable calm cracked for once. He was an Allcarver, so an obsidian nullifying stone would be a direct threat.

Kilian said, "At this point, the existence of such a stone is only conjecture."

"This must be kept secret," Wolfram insisted.

"Dougal overheard our discussion through me," Aifric said.

"So what happened at Harz?" Connor asked again.

"The fire-bound drove Wolfram's forces back and could have wreaked terrible damage before I arrived."

"Could have?" Hamish asked.

Wolfram said, "We deployed two of our own sculpted stones to buttress defensive efforts, but even that wasn't enough. The Obrioners timed a renewed advance to the elfonnel assault. They also used slate and marble sculpted stones to augment their powers. Your friend Ivor was the one wielding the marble stone. We were very nearly overwhelmed."

At least it sounded like Ivor hadn't been sacrificed to raise the fire-bound elfonnel. "I'm not surprised. Ivor walks with fire better than anyone I know."

Kilian raised an eyebrow and Connor added quickly, "Except for you, of course."

"And you?" Verena asked.

"I probably match him for raw intensity now, but he's a lot more experienced. I think I've got the advantage with water, though."

Wolfram said, "He was very effective. We were forced to retreat north, with the elfonnel tearing at our rearguard. But the entire top half of a nearby mountain broke off and smashed down over the monster. The blow severely damaged it."

Kilian said, "I arrived shortly after that, and we finished it off. Evander's intervention was most timely."

"Evander?" Hamish and Jean asked in unison before Connor could.

Wolfram said, "Anton felt Evander's presence just before the mountain broke."

"Where is he now?" Connor asked, imagining the giant Sentry rising silently out of the ground right there under the tent and saying something incomprehensible.

Kilian shrugged. "I suspect he returned to Obrion. He rarely ventures this far north, but he shares my duty to defend the continent from elfonnel."

"Then why doesn't he join us?" Connor asked excitedly.

"With his help, we could sweep them all right back to Obrion!" Verena said excitedly.

Kilian shook his head. "It's not that simple with Evander. He and I do not agree on several important points, including the existence of Granadure."

Verena looked as confused as Connor felt. "He supports Dougal's invasion?"

"He's rather a traditionalist. He never liked breaking the original empire and would support the reunification of the continent."

"So he's lived since the Tallan Wars, too?" Hamish asked.

Kilian nodded. "Evander was Tallan's younger brother."

Connor tried to look calm as he absorbed the incredible news, but he felt that Kilian had wasted an important moment. Things that amazing needed to be shared with a little more fanfare, not dropped as an afterthought.

Gisela seemed less shocked than the rest of them. "I was knowing he was very older."

"If he helped you and Tallan fight your mother, why did he decide to live in Obrion?" Connor asked.

Kilian shook his head slowly. "Evander did not support our rebellion."

"He helped her kill the Builders?" Verena gasped.

Kilian shook his head again. "He abhorred that slaughter."

"Does he support anything?" Hamish demanded.

"Like I said, things get complicated with that boy."

"I think all that Sentry speak makes it hard to think simple thoughts," Connor said.

Maybe the next time he saw Evander he'd ask him what his favorite food was. He'd probably say something like, 'The fish do not seek the hook, but savor every morsel discovered in the eternal hunt through the weeds.'

Actually, that wasn't bad, although Connor wasn't sure what it meant. That would make it perfect to try on Evander, or maybe Anton.

"It is consistent with his perspective to both support the invasion yet intervene against an elfonnel to protect the integrity of the continent," Kilian said.

Wolfram stroked one of his long mustaches. "It's a good thing he did. Even with his help, the lands north of Harz are dangerously unstable. The rise of the elfonnel, combined with the use of all those sculpted stones destabilized the area. After we destroyed the elfonnel, we were forced to retreat north to Altkalen because the land north of Harz became unsafe."

Kilian said, "I've only ever seen the elements destabilize to that extent one other time."

"The Broken Waters," Gisela said softly.

Kilian nodded. "The land north of Harz is broken. The ground ripples and shakes, rent with fiery geysers and bubbling lakes of poisonous mud. The air is vicious, and fires seem to spring randomly out of the ground."

Verena looked close to tears. "They're destroying our country! They can't occupy Granadure either if it's not habitable."

Kilian patted her hand. "I doubt Dougal expected that result, but neither can I believe he was ignorant of the risk. I am hopeful the elements will settle in time. When we have time, we might even try coaxing them to do so. If Dougal had raised any more elfonnel, much of southern Granadure might have been destroyed, along with both armies."

Wolfram grimaced. "And with the lands spitting fire like that, it seems to have only delayed the onset of winter further."

"Oh, how I wish for a five day blizzard," Verena whispered.

"Don't count on it," Kilian said. "I don't sense any major weather movement coming."

Connor wondered, "Is it possible to manipulate the weather?"

"Not substantially," Kilian said. "The only person I've known with enough control to make any noticeable difference was my mother, but even she couldn't hope to turn a major blizzard."

Connor wondered what it would feel like to try.

"What if Dougal raises another elfonnel here at Altkalen?" Verena asked softly, returning to their greatest fear.

Kilian's expression darkened. "That could tip the balance over the edge. This area has a history of volcanic activity and would be even easier to destabilize than Harz. At the least we'd probably lose both armies and the city."

"That's over half a million people!" Verena exclaimed.

For a moment no one spoke. Connor struggled to grasp such an enormous number of people in one area. He just couldn't make himself consider so many dying together.

"Dougal must take Altkalen. He cannae afford not to," Martys said into the silence.

"And we cannot allow him to, no matter the cost," Wolfram declared solemnly.

While they digested that hard truth, Kilian said, "Dougal's original plan has brought him this far, but victory here is anything but certain."

"Then we have to assume he's ready to risk using those sculpted stones again," Connor said.

Verena banged a fist to the table. "We need to take them!"

Kilian nodded. "I believe you're right. We've got perhaps three days to figure out how to do it before they arrive."

Wolfram rose. "I am preparing to meet with the ruling council of Altkalen. We must coordinate defensive measures with them."

Verena shook her head. "We really need to speak with the lord marshal. He's the one responsible for the military."

Kilian said, "Actually, these days it's the lady marshal. The lord marshal suffered a stroke and his daughter has stepped up to assume most of his duties."

Verena's somber mode disappeared and her face lit up in a happy smile. "Saskia is lady marshal? Let's go see her!"

Chapter Forty-Eight

*"The avalanche may block a pass, but the waters flow ever
downward."*

~Ilse

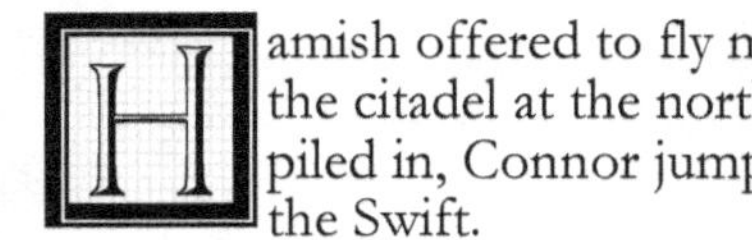amish offered to fly most of the group in the Storm to
the citadel at the north end of Altkalen. As the others
piled in, Connor jumped onto the stirrups at the back of
the Swift.

"Who's Saskia?" he asked as Verena ignited the thrusters
and the Swift lifted a foot into the air.

The little craft felt light on the air, as if it matched
Verena's eagerness to fly. The Storm's huge thrusters roared like
eager lions as it lifted off in a swirling blast of dust. Verena
ascended fast, with Hamish following close behind.

"Saskia was my best friend at the academy," Verena said
as Connor leaned close to hear over the wind.

"You've mentioned the academy before," Connor said as
they rose to five hundred feet and got a spectacular view of the enormous city sprawling away toward the horizon. "Tell me about it."

A soft smile played across her lips. "It's roughly
equivalent to the Carraig. The academy is where all the
Grandurian noble children earn their advanced educations, study
leadership, and of course develop any Petralist powers."

"Is that where you first learned to be a Builder?"

She shook her head. "Builders are so new, there's no
established curriculum. We really should include a better school in
our plan for a new Builder center. I discovered my Builder powers
at the academy and chose to leave to study with Dierk and the
newly-formed Builder corps. Before that, I was just another student.
I loved the academy and had a lot of fun with Saskia and her--"

Verena snapped her mouth shut on the last word, and
Connor was surprised to see a flush creep into her cheeks.

"Her what?" he prodded.

"Nothing," she said quickly. "The academy days are over. We should probably focus on today's problems, don't you think?"

"Sure." Now Connor was more eager than ever to meet Saskia. Maybe she'd tell him more.

They swept over the city that seemed to sparkle in the mid-afternoon sunlight. Connor wished they could stop to explore the huge market.

The fact that it was laid out in such a strictly ordered way seemed wrong, though. Most markets were chaotic, with vendors pressed close together, shouting over each other to steal the attention of prospective customers. A thousand scents would clash in the air, while shoppers struggled to find what they needed without getting cheated.

Actually, he hated most markets.

In minutes, they reached the citadel and landed in a courtyard beside two troop transport windriders. Hamish landed nearby in a rush of wind.

As everyone clambered out, Kilian said, "Martys, you and Aifric should probably wait here."

Martys shrugged and settled back into the third row seats. "Fine by me. I sleep better when there no be a mile of empty sky betwixt me and the ground."

Aifric looked like she wanted to argue, but then sighed. "I understand."

Connor was relieved that neither of them took offense at being left out. "We'll fill you in when we get back."

Wolfram took the lead into the citadel and led them up long hallways with arched, tiled ceilings and beautiful paintings on the walls. Servants hurried past, mingled with courtiers and soldiers. They climbed so many flights of steps that Connor began to wish they'd just flown up to whatever tower he was leading them to.

Finally they arrived at a wide corridor with a gilded ceiling, trimmed in silver. The hall ended at a wide set of dark wooden double doors, with a pair of Rumblers standing guard. They recognized Wolfram and opened the doors immediately, ushering the group into an opulent sitting room.

It was nearly as big as Connor's Dawnus quarters at the Carraig. He was a little surprised to realize rich surroundings no longer intimidated him.

Thick rugs covered much of the white marble-tiled floor. Warm wood paneling sheathed the walls, covered in several places by huge tapestries depicting panoramic vistas, including two separate views of Altkalen. The arced ceiling rose to nearly twenty feet, and a cheery fire crackled in a wide hearth on the opposite side of the room.

Several empty couches and chairs were arranged to face the fire. A small writing table stood on the left side near a clear window, framed by bright-colored stained glass. A tall, slender woman stood beside it and turned to face the doors when they opened.

She didn't look pleased by the interruption, with hands on hips, chin high, thick blond hair hanging in loose curls halfway down her back. Her dazzling blue eyes sparkled with an unmistakable inner light. She started to speak, but then her eyes drifted past Wolfram and she squealed with delight, leaping into a fully fracked sprint toward the group.

"Verena!" she cried as she braced her legs on a blue and gold rug, and the entire thing slid the last twenty feet. She stepped off and threw her arms around Verena's neck.

"It's so good to see you, Saskia," Verena laughed, returning the embrace.

Saskia released Verena and said,

> *"One day the princess went missing.*
> *Her boyfriend was sad from no kissing.*
> *She had lots of fun, building mechanical suns,*
> *and the rumors they never stop hissing."*

Verena grimaced. "I can't believe you're still limericking. Sentry speak is supposed to be more somber."

Saskia shrugged. "Then they shouldn't call it Sentry speak. We're Sappers on this side of the border." She turned to face Connor and her pale skin began to softly glow. The effect was quite alluring.

Connor hadn't known Solas could ignite lights under their skin. He'd have to try it some time.

She said,

> *"So this is the Blood of the Tallan?*
> *He's prob'ly got girls by the gallon.*
> *He is sort of cute, but to my brother that's moot.*
> *I can't believe that for him you've been fallin'."*

She had to twist the pronunciation of that last word to make it fit the rhyme. Connor wasn't sure what to make of the lady marshal. She was enthusiastic and pretty, and under the beautiful gown and perfectly styled hair, she looked about Verena's age.

He had gotten accustomed to dealing with Sentry speak around Evander, but couldn't imagine the giant Sentry ever using that fast, lilting limerick. It seemed to fit Saskia, though.

He made a bow like Aunt Ailsa had taught him. "Pleased to meet you, Lady Saskia."

She gripped his hand. "I can't wait to hear everything about you." She turned back to Verena with a little frown.

> *"But 'Rena, your heart's fickle as the weather.*
> *You broke poor Mattias's heart like a feather.*
> *You just had to fly, not even a good-bye.*
> *Now he pines for the days you spent together."*

Verena grimaced and actually blushed, casting a glance at Connor. "I can't hold a serious conversation with you rhyming."

Saskia grinned. "Good. It gets so boorish having to pretend I can't speak normal."

She added something in rapid Grandurian, glancing at Connor again. Verena's blush deepened and she responded quickly in turn. Hamish coughed into his hand in that way he did when trying to cover a laugh.

It was super annoying that Connor couldn't understand, especially since they seemed to be talking about him. So he asked, "Who's Mattias?"

"You haven't even told your new love about the passionate courtship you enjoyed with my brother?" Saskia exclaimed in Obrioner.

Verena was flushing bright red, and Saskia seemed to enjoy her discomfort perhaps a little too much.

Connor suppressed a flash of jealousy that began burning in his stomach like a bit of activated marble and asked casually, "How many times did she punch him in the face?"

Saskia laughed. "My brother is too fine a gentleman for Verena to need violence against him."

Connor shrugged. "Couldn't have been that passionate then."

Verena giggled, and Saskia glanced from her to Connor, her smile returning in a flash. She grabbed Verena's hand. "There's history here I just have to know!"

With a half smile on his own lips Kilian said, "Later. Right now we have more pressing matters." He bowed over Saskia's hand, and she curtsied in return.

"You can be such an old boor sometimes, Uncle Kilian," Saskia said with a sigh.

"What's on the agenda for the council meeting?" he asked.

"What do you expect?" Saskia's smile vanished. "Total warfare. Potential annihilation. The critical battle of our age." She sighed and touched his arm, her expression serious. "I'm so glad you're all here. It'll be easier to intimidate Dougal's emissary with your help."

"Who did he send?" Connor asked.

"A simple captain," Saskia said, contempt in her voice. "Some fellow named Rory."

Connor assured her, "Rory is far from simple, and I promise you'll never intimidate him."

"Aren't you full of surprises?" Saskia exclaimed, sounding delighted.

Hamish chuckled. "Surprises are pretty standard around this group."

Saskia glanced at him and one perfect eyebrow rose as she studied his unique battle suit. "You must be the Obrioner Builder I've heard about."

"In the flesh," Hamish said and actually made a pretty good bow.

"Excellent. You've spent a lot of time with 'Rena, so we must find some time to chat." She glanced to Gisela, who had hung back and said, "And if you're not Althin, I'll eat my hat."

It was a good thing Gisela nodded and curtsied because Saskia wasn't wearing a hat. Either that, or she'd made that bet already and lost. Connor had enough experience with girls and their hair to know she'd never eat those long, flowing tresses.

"Very pleasing to meet you, Lady Marshal," Gisela said formally.

Saskia grinned. "Verena, you bring such fun company. I hate that we don't have time to talk for an hour before the council meeting."

Connor said, "You haven't even met our Obrioner Guardian or our Mhortair Assassin Healer yet."

For the first time, Saskia looked flummoxed enough that she wasn't able to come up with a new limmerick.

"We've got another Mhortair in chains," Connor added helpfully.

"You're kidding, right?"

Kilian shook his head. "That one's a full Assassin, and might even be the ally he claims to be."

"But Assassins can steal information even sitting in a cell," Saskia said, looking worried.

Kilian said, "I took his chert and his serpentinite. At the moment, I believe him to be contained."

"What are those stones?" Connor asked eagerly.

Everyone else looked interested, although they couldn't potentially establish affinity with the Mhortair's secret stones.

Kilian said, "That's a good question, and you all should understand the danger. The Mhortair possess unique power stones. Chert and serpentinite are two of them."

"Plus the primary affinity weakening powder," Hamish added.

Kilian nodded, but Verena frowned. "Why don't we have access to those stones too?"

"They're the only ones who know where to quarry them," Saskia said, looking pleased that she could answer a question for Verena. "They guard the secret jealously."

Kilian added, "And my understanding is the only known deposits are very small to begin with."

"So what do those stones do?" Connor asked.

Kilian motioned them to take seats near the fire. "Chert is a sedimentary stone. It creates empathy."

"So people feel good about them?" Hamish asked with a frown.

"No, it allows them to sense the feelings of others, and at times to manipulate or influence those feelings."

"But Sir suggested they could actually read minds," Connor said.

"He may have been trying to impress all of you, unless he's ascended, in which case chert would allow him to do exactly that."

"If he's ascended, then he's even more dangerous than we thought," Verena said.

Kilian nodded. "He also had serpentinite, which Aifric too has established affinity with."

"Aifric?" Saskia asked.

"My Mhortair Healer, sworn to help us," Connor said in a casual tone.

Saskia's eyes widened. "I have to hear that story."

Connor would gladly swap that tale for more information about her brother, Mattias.

"Serpentinite has something to do with sound, right?" Hamish asked.

Kilian looked surprised. "How did you know that?"

"Dougal mentioned something about it when Aifric nearly killed him. I didn't understand what they were talking about at the time, but she had spoken in Dougal's voice to confuse Gregor, so it makes sense."

Saskia was looking between Kilian and Hamish, her expression astounded. "You have to stop dropping all these casual hints about your adventures. You make these incredible things sound common."

Hamish shrugged, his tone almost bored. "All in a day's work for this group of heroes."

Saskia gaped, but Verena started to giggle. That made Connor grin, which set Hamish to laughing in turn, and Saskia joined in. "I am so glad you're all here. We need a bit of levity."

Kilian said, "Back to your question. Yes, serpentinite does allow the manipulation of sound. Mhortair can block or mimic sounds and voices, and after ascension can use sound more aggressively."

"Like how?" Connor asked.

"I've heard they can emit a frequency that can immobilize their intended targets."

Connor shared a worried look with Verena, who said, "So Sir could have killed us all in Faulenrost?"

"Possibly. I've studied the concept, but have not experienced it personally. It is my understanding that the sound somehow locks up muscles and makes them non-responsive."

He added, "I suspect it may still be possible to tap elemental powers even in that state, but the danger is very real. They don't employ it often, but the potential for its use was one of the reasons I had to take those stones from Sir."

"Can I try some?" Connor was more eager than ever to establish affinity with those secret stones. Once he understood how they worked, he could figure out how to defend himself against them.

Saskia looked startled, then her eyes widened and she stared at him with a look bordering on worship. "You really are Blood of the Tallan?"

Verena chuckled. "Saskia, you should see your face. I haven't seen you so thunderstruck since Christoph asked you to the royal ball."

Saskia's cheeks flushed, but she did not look away from Connor. The intensity of her gaze was a bit unnerving. She spoke softly.

"Your interest is understandable,
The lure of such power is palpable,
But are you sure you know what you're doing, this Obrioner is such a risk to
try wooing,
Your heart after all is so flammable."

"My interest in Connor has nothing to do with his Petralist powers," Verena said firmly, her expression disapproving.

When she met Connor's gaze, he read the depth of emotion in her eyes, and his heart sang. She really did care for him, not just for his abilities. The difference between her Shona was so enormous.

Saskia looked startled by Verena's sharper tone. "I didn't mean any insult, 'Rena. It's just difficult to accept that the long-awaited descendant of the mighty Tallan has come to us from Obrion."

"He is a little disappointing," Hamish drawled.

"Eat rocks," Connor said with a grin.

"Actually, for Builders we say spit rocks," Verena said with a smile.

"Why?"

Hamish shrugged. "We like rocks. We lick them all the time. Telling us to eat rocks is no big deal. To spit rocks though, we lose connection and can't use them anymore."

"You are having many strange customs I do not yet knowing," Gisela mumbled.

"And I want to hear them all," Saskia said, again enthusiastic. "But first we have to join the council meeting with Rory."

Chapter Forty-Nine

"Fire can purify or destroy. Winds may cool or tear asunder. Truth that enlightens the understanding may overwhelm even the stoutest heart."

~Evander

Saskia led them to the central palace at the heart of the citadel. Connor and Verena flanked her, with the rest of the group trailing behind. Verena and Saskia carried on a constant, excited chatter in Grandurian and looked to be having so much fun reuniting. Connor dearly wished he could understand.

He glanced back at Hamish to see if he was listening, but Hamish was too busy gawking at the opulent furnishings, sweeping arches, and beautiful paintings. He hadn't lived at the Carraig, surrounded by wealth and soaring palaces. Jean and Gisela looked far more comfortable walking the grand hallways and chatting about the beautiful sights.

Connor drifted back to walk beside Hamish as they reached a vaulted intersection of three hallways. Between thick, gilded columns, the entire ceiling was painted, and each section seemed more breathtaking than the last.

Lords and ladies stood in dramatic poses, some wielding elements, represented by fantastic beasts or angels who bowed to their will. Connor could have paused for several minutes to stare. Hamish just tipped over backward, igniting tiny thrusters in the back of his suit to remain in a hover that made staring easier.

Connor poked him in the ribs. "I finally understand why you're always eating something. It's to keep your mouth from dropping open all the time."

Hamish snapped his mouth shut. "I haven't lived in places like this, Connor. Some of us have to work for a living."

Gisela laughed softly and Connor ceded the point with a nod. "My Dawnus suite was pretty amazing, although my little room in the Sculpture House always felt more like home."

As they continued on, Connor watched Verena. It was fun to see her acting like a normal girl. Usually she was too involved in creating Builder mechanicals or leaping into battle against men and monsters, often to save his life.

They eventually followed a wide, granite-tiled hallway on the fourth floor to where it terminated at a set of tall, wooden doors carved with intricate symbols, inlaid in silver. Eighteen armored Rumblers stood at attention flanking the doors.

Saskia pointed at the symbols. "These are crests of the great trading houses, as well as the insignia of the most influential guilds. Between the two groups, they own the bulk of the merchandise or do the bulk of the work. They make up two-thirds of the ruling council and ensure the city trading floors function effectively. The nobles make up the other third."

"What do the lion-headed door handles mean?" Connor asked, moving up to stand beside Verena.

"That's the symbol of the lord marshal, my father," Saskia said proudly. Then her expression fell. "He's so sick."

Verena touched her arm and said, "You'll do fine."

Kilian added, "Saskia commands the military and acts as ultimate executive and judicial authority over the city."

That sounded like a lot of power. Connor wondered how she balanced those very heavy duties with her natural cheery temperament.

Inside, the council chamber was enormous, stretching away at least a hundred yards, with a high, vaulted ceiling. Towering, arched windows occupied most of the left wall, offering a panoramic view south over the river and the wide expanse of Altkalen. The floor was clad with warm, golden oak.

Fluted pillars of white marble marched along the other walls, outlining a dozen alcoves hung with the colors and symbols of the city nobles, the trading houses, and the guilds. Vases of multi-colored flowers hung from every pillar, filling the room with their soft, pleasant aroma.

A long mahogany table occupied the center of the gigantic room. Ten council members sat in throne-like chairs spaced evenly around its gleaming length.

Papers and maps were scattered along the table, and Connor wondered if that much flat wooden surface held some kind of innate attraction for paper. He'd never seen a big table that hadn't acquired ridiculous amounts of clutter.

Captain Rory stood at the far end of the table. Erich and Anika stood guard nearby, and for once she wasn't grinning at the captain. All three of them looked a bit battered, and Erich was openly glowering. Nothing like a deadly battle to rock even such a strong impossible relationship.

Saskia's demeanor changed as soon as she entered the room. She dropped the excited, chattering girl persona as quickly as if she'd discarded a hat. She swept into the room, head held high, the picture of poised confidence.

"You weren't planning on doing something foolish before I arrived, like actually thinking Dougal's offer of peace was genuine?" she asked.

An elderly gentleman in a rich blue and gold surcoat said, "Lady Marshal, we discuss all offers before making decisions. You know that."

She sniffed, as if at a foul smell, and stepped to the empty chair at the head of the table. "Ladies and Gentlemen, you all know Kilian and General Wolfram."

She swept an arm around to indicate the entire table. "The ruling council of Altkalen, led by our four senior counselors." The four rose, and Saskia introduced them.

"Lord Pankraz, voice of the nobles and commander of the city watch."

A middle-aged nobleman in a gray velvet jacket bowed, exuding an air of solid dependability.

"Ulrich, the head of house Schulze and voice for the trading houses."

The old gentleman who had spoken earlier bowed his head slightly.

"Liane, matron of the seamstress guild and one of the joint voices of the guild councilors."

A mature and elegantly dressed woman made a graceful curtsy. Her long brown hair was stylishly swept back from her face to highlight her subtle streaks of gray.

"And Hette, who runs the culinary guilds with a wooden spoon," Saskia finished with the hint of a smile.

A plump, jolly woman waved. She wore a bright red dress, covered by an immense, pristine white baker's apron. Her black hair was rather short, and her blue eyes twinkled with mirth.

"We must honor your arrival," Hette gushed in a surprisingly high-pitched, girlish voice. She swept an entire tray of raspberry-cream cookies out from under her apron and began passing them around the table.

Old Ulrich grumbled loudly. "Here we go again. How many trays can one dress conceal, Hette?"

"Keep talking like that and you won't get any," she chided as she rushed around the table with more enthusiasm than speed, handing out cookies to the eager councilors. She even gave one to Rory, who ate it in two bites. Ulrich might grumble, but he did not refuse a cookie.

Hette gave Kilian a double-sized cookie that she pulled from a deep pocket of her dress. Connor marveled that his cookie was still warm, and the aroma of fresh-baked goodness settled around the group like a gentle hug.

He decided he liked Hette.

Hamish took two cookies and made a gallant bow to Hette, taking her hand and kissing it. "Baking magic is the best kind."

She flushed and fanned her face, a huge smile growing across her chubby lips. "I sense another food lover has joined us."

He nodded and tried speaking, although he had shoved one entire cookie into his mouth. "Mmm. If bery goob." After swallowing he added, "Care to try one of my own inventions?" He pulled a smashpacked cube out of his belt pouch.

Hette accepted the cube and considered it carefully. She sniffed it, then licked it. Hamish grinned in approval. She popped the little cube into her mouth, and her bright blue eyes widened.

She gushed, "Such intense flavor for such a tiny confection."

"That's because you're eating an entire smashpacked chocolate cake," Hamish said with obvious pride. "Builders don't just make weapons, you know."

"Kilian, this young man is a treasure," Hette beamed, handing Hamish the rest of the tray of cookies. She pulled a sack full of warm cinnamon rolls from another huge pocket of her voluminous red dress and began passing them out to the gathered council to celebrate.

Connor began to wonder if Hette might not be as fat as she appeared. Maybe she was a midget who just used that huge dress to cover the racks of pastries and desserts she seemed to carry around with her all the time.

Kilian shook his head slowly as he watched Hamish devour the rest of the cookies. "You may have to reinforce that suit before it bursts at the seams."

"Deal with the invasion first," Ulrich growled, although he did not reject the warm roll that Hette pressed into his hands. "Do you have any idea how much gold we're losing every day with that Obrioner army blocking the southern trade route?"

Rory spoke for the first time. "You don't have to lose any money. Surrender the city and trading can continue without interruption."

Saskia barked a laugh and pointed at Rory with her half-eaten cookie.

"Captain, you are a man of war.
But the truth is so clear we can't ignore.
Trading will die. Freedom will fly.
Under your rule, Altkalen would be gone forever more."

Old man Ulrich glowered at her. "Stop your incessant rhyming, girl. This is serious business."

"I am deadly serious," Saskia responded, her tone soft, but intense, and her eyes glowed with inner light. "My limericks highlight the absurdity of seriously considering Captain Rory's proposal.

"Of course we cannot surrender the city. Obrion is invading, people. You think you're losing money now? Wait until Obrion secures its hold on the entire southern half of Granadure. How long do you think it'll take for them to decide your treasure coffers are needed to fund the war effort?"

"Oh, it can't be as bad as all that," Hette said, gesturing at Captain Rory with the last cinnamon roll. "Even Obrioner armies need to eat. And you would pay for every meal, right?"

"Of course." Rory sounded earnest, but Connor could barely believe what he was hearing.

"Captain, it's good to see you again," he said loudly, stepping up to the table near Saskia's chair and drawing every eye. "You are a man of honor, but General Carbrey is not, and Dougal definitely can't be trusted. We both know that Altkalen would be sacked, pillaged, and its people enslaved."

"You really need to work on your tact," Rory muttered with a frown.

As an angry murmur rippled around the table, Ulrich demanded, "And who are you, boy?"

"I'm Connor." He waved.

"An Obrioner who should know better than to interrupt his superiors," Ulrich muttered, giving Connor a dismissive glare.

Saskia said, "I'm sorry. I forgot to introduce the rest of our guests. You all know Lady Verena."

Verena curtsied with courtly grace, and a murmur of greetings echoed around the chamber.

"And Hamish, a champion Builder."

"And rising cooking legend," Hamish added.

"And you all just met Connor, Blood of the Tallan," Saskia finished in a casual tone.

That got their attention.

Connor waved again. "I'd give a speech or something, but I wouldn't want to interrupt my betters."

Liane, the seamstress matron, smiled at Ulrich. "Once again you put that enormous foot of yours squarely into your mouth."

Ulrich growled, "Doesn't matter who he is. We need to respond to General Carbrey. This is a trading city, not a fortress. Look what happened to Harz when they chose to fight."

The man was a coward.

Verena spoke before Connor could. "And look what happened to Obrion. Builders are executed. Commoners are enslaved. Do you really want to surrender without a fight, Ulrich?"

Saskia declared, "Never going to happen. As marshal of Altkalen, military decisions are mine."

"If you break with the council, who is going to feed your troops?" Ulrich asked.

"Don't push me," Saskia warned, her tone turning icy cold.

Captain Rory interrupted. "There is another option. Surrender Connor and the Builders, and I am authorized to promise that Altkalen will be left in peace."

He paused, and Connor knew him well enough to recognize that his discipline was pushed to the breaking point as he tried to speak those lies. "The army will pass by without a fight, and we'll even purchase supplies."

Ulrich's eyes lit up at the idea, and several of the other councilors seemed to seriously consider it.

Kilian laughed, although his voice was devoid of humor and his eyes were filled with rippling water. "In Granadure, we do not sacrifice our friends to win false safety."

"Connor is Obrioner already. Why shouldn't we return him?" Ulrich argued.

Verena stared at him, expression incredulous. "He's Blood of the Tallan. Dougal could use him to lay waste to Granadure."

"You are such an unapologetic coward," Saskia said, her tone dripping with disgust. "Would you also surrender Verena to be executed? She's a member of the Grandurian royal house and a personal friend."

"Would the girl not willingly sacrifice to save so many?" Ulrich demanded.

Connor very nearly tapped quartzite to fly across the room and punch the man to Merkland.

Kilian's tone turned hard. "She wouldn't save anyone. Dougal's offer of peace is a lie."

Ulrich looked around the table, his scowl growing deeper. "So we're going to fight? You'd all prefer to see our city burn?"

"I'd rather see it destroyed fighting for freedom than preserved by sacrificing the blood of our friends," Saskia said.

"You're a good trader, but you're a terrible patriot," Liane told Ulrich, her tone disgusted.

"Patriotism never made any profit," Ulrich retorted.

"But it maintains a free nation." Saskia faced Rory and declared, "Inform your general that his army is officially denied permission to approach Altkalen. If he chooses to do so, we will take all necessary steps to defend ourselves."

"And we'll send him the bill," Ulrich added loudly.

Rory did not looked surprised. "I'll convey your response to him." He turned and marched for the door. Anika took a step after him, but Erich caught her arm, and for once she did not fight to get free.

Connor intercepted Rory before he passed the head of the table.

"We seem to meet at increasingly bad times," Rory said.

"War does that, I guess. Captain, you can't attack Altkalen."

He shrugged. "I do as ordered, lad. You know that."

Connor gripped his arm. "Captain, please listen to me. That attack at Harz has changed things. Dougal pushed the elements to the breaking point. If any other elfonnel are raised, they could destroy both armies and the entire city all together."

That triggered a round of nervous muttering from the counselors.

"I don't command Dougal, but I can tell you that he understands the risk."

"That doesn't mean he'll agree to change course."

Rory held out his hands in a helpless gesture.

"These people are angry. They won't hold back. They can't afford to. Neither can I."

Rory sighed. "I know, lad."

Connor told him, "I'm going to kill Dougal, and I can't guarantee the safety of anyone who gets in my way."

For a moment Rory looked torn and Connor wanted to again ask him to abandon his post and join them, but he knew the man would never agree to leave his men. Connor hated that some of his friends had to serve as opponents on the battlefield.

Captain Rory extended a hand. "Good luck, Connor." He glanced back at Anika and added, "I wish we could reach an accord."

"Me too."

Rory started to turn toward the door again, but Connor suddenly got an idea and pulled him to a stop. "Maybe there is something we can agree to."

"What are you suggesting?" Verena asked. She had approached while they talked.

"There's going to be a fight. I was thinking this would be the perfect time to exchange prisoners so both sides had as many soldiers as possible to join in."

"We'll have more after we trounce Carbrey's soldiers," Saskia said.

"Regardless, what do you say, Captain?"

Wolfram spoke before Rory could. "We took more prisoners than Obrion did. If we're going to exchange, you must also return the primary affinity powders you captured from our stores at Badurach."

"The idea has merit," Rory said, his expression thoughtful as he studied Connor, as if trying to read his real purposes.

"Both sides get their full strength, and you have something to offer your general when you return," Connor said.

Rory nodded. "I will deliver the proposal."

"Thanks, Captain."

Rory leaned closer and asked in a whisper that only Connor could hear, "What are you playing at, lad?"

"I'm just using the skills you taught me in the Tir-raon, Captain."

"That's what I'm afraid of."

Connor watched him go, thankful that he could call the man friend.

After Rory left, Saskia said, "You can't only be thinking about recovering a few soldiers."

"Of course not. The prisoner exchange is just a distraction."

"From what?" Verena asked.

The more he thought about his crazy idea, the more he grew excited about it. He gave them a confident smile.

"We're going to take Dougal's sculpted stones."

CHAPTER FIFTY

*"A snare traps the witless hare like fear in the heart of a brave soul,
but a child always looks for the light of morning."*

~Gregor

The council meeting broke up a short time later and most of the councilors left, anxious to return to their guilds and houses to plan for the upcoming defensive effort. As soon as the doors opened, Ilse entered the room.

"What's wrong?" Kilian asked when she joined them.

"Nothing, sir. The Mhortair is still well contained. I received word that I was needed here."

Kilian looked to Saskia, who shrugged. "Wasn't me."

When no one else seemed to know about the summons, Kilian said, "You're sure Sir is contained?"

She nodded. "I assigned three other senior tertiaries to replace me, just in case the message was a ruse."

Connor couldn't imagine how or why Sir might have arranged a fake message.

Kilian said. "We'll figure it out later. Right now we're about to discuss the city's defenses."

Connor was starting to worry about those defenses. If Ulrich's attitude reflected the state of the city, they were in trouble. Only Saskia and the four lead counselors remained in the room with Connor's group.

Hamish leaned close to Connor and whispered, "I know it's rude to beat up old people, but for that Ulrich fellow, I might make an exception."

"Unless I do it first."

Ulrich rose and stretched. His angry scowl, which had seemed a permanent fixture on his face, relaxed into a smile. "Saskia, that was an excellent performance. Do you think we fooled the famous captain?"

She rounded the table and gave the old grump a hug.

"How could anyone doubt such an artful coward?
Your grumpiness is an epic most flowered.
The captain was fooled, the council was schooled,
and now our defenses are newly empowered."

Liane kissed the old man's cheek. "Brilliant performance, Ulrich. Even I wanted to climb across the table and strangle you."

Connor raised a hand. "Me too."

Hette produced a three-layered chocolate cake, topped with sliced strawberries from under the table and began passing out huge pieces. "Captain Rory is no fool, but that deception turned out better than I expected."

"The prisoner exchange added a brilliant twist," Ulrich said, raising a fork-full of cake in salute to Connor. "I'm interested in hearing how you propose to use it."

"Eat. You'll all need your strength." Hette finished passing out cake, then kissed Verena on the cheek. "So good to see you again, my dear. You timed your arrival perfectly."

"It was all an act?" Hamish exclaimed between bites.

Ulrich snorted, "Of course it was. Do you think anyone could be as stupid as I was pretending to be?"

Connor admitted, "You made a convincing case."

"Exactly the effect I wanted to convey." Ulrich smiled and pumped Connor's hand. "An absolute pleasure to meet you, young man." He then turned to Hamish and took his hand too. "And the first Obrioner Builder. Magnificent."

Saskia spoke around a mouthful of cake. "Sorry I couldn't warn you of the planned deception. 'Rena's a brilliant actress, but I wasn't sure about the rest of you."

Kilian had already finished his cake. "We're happy to be here. Now that you've sent Rory off, hopefully believing Altkalen is reluctantly planning to mount a last-minute, disorganized defense, what do you really have in mind?"

Ulrich made a shushing gesture, and Saskia cringed. "We have shielding measures in place against eavesdropping, but we need to be extremely careful. Verena, do you have a mechanical that can help?"

"Of course." Verena dipped a hand into her satchel and produced a couple of quartzite stones. She placed one on the far end of the table, and the sound of loud snoring soon echoed through the chamber.

"What is that?" Connor asked as Verena rejoined them and activated a shieldstone, creating a pulsing shield around the group, sealing them off from the rest of the chamber.

"I left a speakstone under Martys's chair. Knew I could count on him."

With their conversation so well protected, the Altkalen group seemed to relax and Liane said, "First are the earthen mountains to the east. No doubt Rory has already spotted those."

"You sound happy about that," Connor said.

Ulrich said, "General Carbrey will assume that stockpiled earth will play a major part in our defensive plan. He'll focus his efforts on countering it, or even attempting to wrest control to use it against us."

That made sense. Flip the geall right back on them.

"But that's not really your plan," Kilian guessed.

"Of course not," Ulrich said. "We can't fool Dougal that easily. I met him a long time ago, just after he lost his first wife. Even then it was clear he would not rest until he won vengeance. It's been obvious for years that war was inevitable."

"So you positioned Altkalen so everyone assumes you've got no defensive plan, and that you only focus on trading profits?" Connor guessed.

"That's the first phase, but Dougal buys spies by the bushel, so we needed something more to draw their attention. We set up a secret defensive plan, centered on that accumulated earth. He'll know about that for sure."

"And since he's confident he knows your secret, you figure he won't look deeper?" Kilian asked.

Hette said, "Hopefully not. We've made a rather serious effort to conceal our battle plans. Since his spies had to work so hard to acquire the fake ones, they'll think they have to be legitimate. A dessert too easily won is not fully appreciated."

Hamish said, "Exactly. Sometimes you have to slide down the chimney to get the freshest sweetbreads."

"But you only managed to burn your hands," Connor reminded him with a laugh.

Saskia grinned. "So much history I need to know when this is over."

"When the Obrioners attack, it is our hope they will not recognize the danger that the southern reaches of the plain represent," Ulrich said.

"I thought there was a lot of solid rock on the Altkalen plain," Kilian said with a frown.

Liane said, "Exactly. They'll barely pay it any attention, and they certainly won't look deeper."

"What's deeper?" Connor asked.

Hette grinned. "Lots of very hot water. Altkalen has thousands of hot springs. Enough to supply all our heating and baking needs."

"We're preparing some surprises." Ulrich seemed reluctant to speak openly about their secret plans even to the small group. "The plain will be the main battlefield."

"So that's probably where we'll need to set up the prisoner exchange," Connor said.

"You will allowing the army to reach the plain so easily?" Gisela asked.

Ulrich considered that. "It might be a good idea. We can't stop them on the southern slope, although we were planning delaying tactics."

Wolfram said, "Usually I would recommend exactly that. We could inflict significant losses on them by fighting to hold that slope, although such an effort in itself would never stop them for long."

"If we allow them to ascend to the southern end of the plain, it would reinforce the image that we're rather clueless about defensive measures," Liane said.

Kilian nodded slowly. "We arrange the exchange on the plain. They're overconfident and no doubt plan to launch the full assault as soon as the exchange is complete."

"Only we strike first," Connor said.

Ulrich said, "That could prove extremely helpful. If you can distract them enough, that would be the perfect time to hit them hard."

Verena said, "The prisoner exchange will focus their attention, but that alone won't be sufficient distraction to hit their central command and steal Dougal's stones."

Connor's confidence faded and he admitted, "I hadn't gotten that far, but we have time to figure it out."

Gisela grinned. "I think I can helping with that."

"How?" Connor asked.

The outer wooden doors opened, interrupting Gisela's answer. A muscular man with a huge mustache, wearing custom Rumbler battle leathers marched into the room beside a tall, broad-shouldered man in a nobleman's jacket. His carefully-groomed, blond hair was a little longer than military standard, and his rugged face was perfectly tanned. When he smiled, his even, white teeth seemed to glow.

Verena gasped. "Mattias!"

Chapter Fifty-One

"The nuall that wanders far afield rarely finds success that could have been obtained closer to home."

~Evander

You've got to be kidding," Connor muttered to himself as Verena released the protective shield around the group. She moved toward the two newcomers, smiling so widely that it was a wonder her lips didn't crack. Connor really didn't want to meet Verena's old boyfriend.

Ilse wanted to meet someone.

She rushed across the room and leaped into the muscular, mustached man's arms, laughing with pure joy. Connor was astonished to see her kiss him passionately as he swung her around in his arms.

"Is that Mattias?" Hamish asked, looking confused.

"Of course not." Saskia gave him a disgusted look. "That's Lukas, Ilse's husband."

"Husband?" Connor didn't know she was married.

It seemed wrong for Ilse to act like a woman instead of commander of a clandestine special-forces group. He had grown so used to the hint of danger surrounding her that he felt unsettled seeing her kissing that man. Didn't she understand how that was wrecking the image she'd worked so hard to create?

"I think I know where that message for Ilse came from," Kilian said with a smile.

Verena moved to greet Mattias and although she walked eagerly, she didn't rush at him like Ilse had at Lukas. For his part, Mattias seemed to see only Verena. His pace quickened and his smile widened. His perfect teeth glowed brighter.

His movements slipped into the graceful dance of an Allcarver. He extended his arms toward Verena, and Connor feared for a moment he'd sweep her right off her feet. Seeing her punch him in the face for doing that would be really satisfying, though.

Verena stopped a pace away and gripped his hands in hers, although she still leaned forward a bit, as if fighting an urge to hug him. "What are you doing here?"

For a second he seemed startled that she spoke Obrioner, but he recovered quickly. "I'm happy to see you too."

He leaned forward to kiss her, but she turned so that he planted the kiss on her cheek instead of her lips. He definitely looked disappointed.

Connor felt relieved that Verena kept a little distance.

As the rest of the company approached, Mattias said softly, "We have so much to talk about. I missed you so much." His arms twitched, as if only Verena's grip kept him from embracing her.

Saskia took Verena's place and gave her brother a warm hug. "You're late. With father sick, your place is here."

"You're doing great, little sister. My place is serving the king." He glanced at Verena again, and Connor clearly read his expression. With Verena here, maybe he should re-think that statement.

"Did you get lost?" Connor asked as he and the others approached the newcomers.

Mattias chuckled, but his smile faded when Verena released his hands and stepped back a pace to stand beside Connor. Connor wanted to kiss her for that. Of course, that might anger Mattias, then maybe they could skip all the posturing and jump right into the fighting.

Before he could put the plan in action, Mattias extended a hand, which Connor felt obligated to grip. Mattias's grip was strong, perhaps a bit tighter than absolutely necessary, so Connor tapped a bit of granite and returned the grip even stronger.

If Mattias wanted to get physical, he welcomed the chance to show him what an ascended Petralist could do. Mattias's hair would look so much better after Connor burned most of it off. He had plenty of experience.

"You're the fellow that Verena was ordered to recruit," Mattias said, his tone completely neutral.

"Blood of the Tallan at your service. Happy to help Verena save her homeland."

"We'll need everyone for that," Kilian said, stepping between them and shaking Mattias's hand. "Last I heard, you were assigned commander of the prince's own guard."

"And I brought a company with me to reinforce the city, as well as Ilse's entire command."

"The Crushers are here?" Ilse exclaimed.

She stood close beside Lukas, gripping his hand in a very un-scary-commander-like way. She looked tiny next to the hulking soldier, who rivaled Erich for size.

Lukas grinned. "Brought 'em all, love. Prince Theodor sent orders for you to resume command." His voice was a deep baritone, and he spoke Obrioner almost as well as Ilse.

When she glanced at Wolfram, he shrugged. "I am not surprised. Now that the war is under way, your place is with your troops."

Kilian said, "This is good news. The Crushers can lead the charge."

"Who are the Crushers?" Connor asked.

Ulrich held up a hand. "Let's please return to the table. Builder Verena, will you restore that shieldstone?"

As soon as the pulsing shield of air again surrounded the group, Ilse gave another sickeningly happy smile to Lukas and said, "We developed the Crushers as a special response force against Obrioner aggression. We're a self-sufficient strike force, specially trained to target enemy tertiary Petralists."

"You kill the tertiaries?" Hamish exclaimed.

"With great risk, and through careful planning," Lukas said.

Verena said, "Hopefully with a little less risk now. I've been discussing with Ilse some mechanicals we can add to your arsenal that should help."

"I look forward to discussing those with you, Lady Builder," Lukas said with a bow.

"She's something, isn't she?" Mattias said, giving another glowing grin, the pride in his voice suggesting that he somehow deserved some of the merit for Verena's abilities.

"I never could have accomplished what I have if I'd gone to the capital with you," Verena said, actually sounding a bit sad about that.

Saskia said, "I heard the entire Builder compound was destroyed. Since you have to rebuild anyway, why not build closer to Edderitz?"

For a second, Connor feared what Verena might say. If they rebuilt close to the capital, she'd get to see Mattias more often. She clearly still liked him, and it seemed evident Mattias would welcome a chance to try winning her back.

"Schwinkendorf Valley is our home," Hamish said with a note of finality in his voice.

"The planning for rebuilding is already underway," Jean added.

Mattias did not hide his disappointment, and Ulrich interrupted. "If we fail to hold, we'll be discussing how to rebuild Altkalen too. There's still the problem of how to get the Crushers close enough to the Obrioner lines. The plain will be the main elemental battleground, and any incursion through that area will result in many casualties, no matter how well trained you are."

"They could attack from the western hills," Liane suggested.

Ilse shook her head. "The Obrioner flank will block our access from the sides. Our greatest chance of success lies in surprise attacks, not in cutting through half the army."

"I have an idea," Verena said with that smile she reserved for new mechanicals.

Connor didn't even feel jealous that her Builder work earned its own special smile. Even though she often pressed her lips to those power stones, she never kissed them the way she kissed him.

Had she ever kissed Mattias like that, though? Of course, he'd kissed Shona many times too. He hadn't been free to deny her, but he had to admit Shona was an amazing kisser, and he'd enjoyed many of those moments. It rankled that maybe he couldn't hate Mattias for having kissed Verena, but felt confident he could easily come up with other reasons.

Hamish said, "And I have an idea how we can take the fight to the Obrioners even before we settle the question of the middle ground. Especially if that prisoner exchange works well."

"What prisoner exchange?" Mattias asked.

Kilian explained, "We're trying to arrange an exchange on the plain prior to the main battle. We're hoping to use it as a diversion to strike the Obrioner command and steal Dougal's sculpted stones."

Saskia said, "We still need to figure out that diversion. Gisela, you offered help?"

Gisela withdrew from a pocket of her dress an ornate wooden box, banded with iron, no bigger than Connor's hand. She placed it on the table and opened it with exquisite care. She then withdrew from the heavily-padded interior a tiny vial, barely as long as Connor's pinky finger.

"I have receiving in my latest communication from Althing, a mighty weapon."

Hamish asked, "That's a weapon? It looks more like my mom's secret seasoning."

She lifted the vial for all to see, but slapped Hamish's hand away when he reached to touch it. "This will striking fear through the hearts of thousands, and wreaking havoc through Carbrey's army."

"How is it possible?" Saskia asked, voicing Connor's thoughts. Such a tiny vial did not look dangerous.

"Althin scientists have studying many years the worst chemicals they can finding. The liquid in here is stinking enough to driving people insane with horror."

Hamish grinned. "You brought a mega-stench? Can I sniff it?"

Gisela recoiled and clutched the vial protectively to her. "Have you not listening? One drop would making everyone in the citadel violently ill."

"What chemical is it?" Connor asked, happy that she hadn't let Hamish test it, but still not quite believing anything could smell that bad.

She shook her head. "I do not knowing name, but I know the stinking has true."

"Can you get a gallon of it? With that much, we might be able to drive them right out of Granadure," Verena said.

Gisela shook her head. "There is being not so very much in all of Althing. This vial is most of the stock piling. Making more take much time."

Kilian looked pleased. "This might be the key we need to make this plan work."

Gisela said, "With help from Aifric, I have another item that can helping spread more confusion."

Kilian said, "She's a good choice. She might be able to discover for sure where the stones are kept."

"Who is this Aifric?" Mattias asked.

"My Mhortair Healer," Connor said.

Mattias blinked, and Connor loved the look of confusion on his face.

Verena added, "If Sir really is willing to help, we should send him into the Obrioner camp too. Even if he decides to go on a killing rampage, he'd do it there instead of here."

"Who is Sir?" Mattias asked, and this time he looked ready to be impressed.

"He's the senior Mhortair Assassin who's pledged to help us fight Dougal's invasion," Verena said, and Mattias whistled softly.

They began working on specific plans, and Connor agreed that was important. However, he did not believe there wouldn't be surprises. No battle plan he'd ever seen survived the actual start of a battle, but the more he'd planned before a fight, the better he was positioned to respond quickly to the unexpected.

"What sort of power stores do we have available to work with?" Hamish asked.

Wolfram grimaced. "Too many of our reserves were lost at Harz."

"And we've exhausted most of our ready supplies replenishing Wolfram's forces and preparing our own," Saskia added.

Mattias said, "We brought a large cache from Edderitz. Most will be allocated to the Crushers and my own guard, but we can always find stone to support our Builders."

He looked at Verena as he spoke, and Connor cringed inside to see how much the words clearly pleased her. Would Mattias really stoop to trying to buy back her affections with wagonloads of power stone?

As they turned again to working out details, Hamish said, "Hette, I think we're going to need lots of cookies."

"I'll send for a dozen dozen."

Connor was a bit disappointed when she didn't produce them already baked from under her dress.

CHAPTER FIFTY-TWO

"Dross is cast off of the gleaming silver only through the touch of the refiner's fire."

~Evander

Assuming Carbrey accepted the prisoner exchange, he would most likely send Rory to oversee the meeting. That meant they should send Anika to distract him. Saskia expressed worry that Carbrey might send Gregor as well, which would threaten the plan.

Ilse suggested, "I'll go with Anika. I would like to challenge Gregor on his involvement at the Carraig."

"But we need you with the Crushers," Lukas objected.

Kilian said, "It might be necessary."

As the discussion continued, Connor felt eager to leave and get Verena away from Mattias. That softly glowing smile seemed to increasingly distract her.

Ulrich and Saskia still held back some of what they planned for the main assault, but Connor didn't mind. He understood their need for protecting some of their secret plan. The rest of them had enough work to finalize the planned distraction and attempt against the sculpted stones.

At first he assumed he would participate in that strike at the heart of the Obrioner camp, but came to realize Verena and Hamish wouldn't really need him there. So he said, "I plan to join the Crushers."

"Are you sure that's wise?" Ulrich asked.

Verena looked concerned. "Connor, I was thinking we'd hold you in reserve like we did at Harz. If something goes wrong, you could turn the tide for us."

Connor shook his head. "Kilian will be our reserve."

Kilian said, "At least until we know the sculpted stones are secured. Then I guarantee I'll join the fighting."

Connor hoped no one he cared about got in Kilian's way. "Let's surprise Carbrey. If the Crushers and I can remove a large number of his tertiary Petralists quickly, it could be a critical element to winning."

"We'll be in the thickest of the fighting," Lukas warned.

"That's right where Connor does his best work," Ilse said with a little smile. "He has a knack for breaking things."

Connor shrugged. "It's kind of my thing."

Lukas grinned. "I'd be a fool not to welcome the Blood of the Tallan. We can use your elemental powers. If you do not object, my lord Mattias."

Mattias hesitated. "Are you sure it's wise? He is an Obrioner."

Ilse did not seem concerned. "I am sure."

"Then he is your responsibility. We're all taking risks, but if we work together, we will prevail."

"We'll win," Verena said with her usual fierce confidence. "If the mega-stench works as well as we hope, the command structure should be interrupted too."

Connor liked the fact that she still looked worried for him.

"Plus, if we get the sculpted stones, that might wreck Carbrey's entire battle plan," Hamish grinned.

"I like it," Saskia said.

Kilian said, "It is a good plan, but let's assume something goes wrong. What else can we add to tip the scales in our favor?"

They thought about that for a moment, and it was Lukas who spoke first. "One of the biggest challenges is when the tertiaries recognize the threat and target us aggressively."

Saskia suggested, "What if we send a wave of Rumblers in first? They'd create a chaotic battlefield that you could strike through."

Ilse grinned. "That is a good idea."

Ulrich frowned. "We still haven't answered the question of how we will deliver your forces to the battle. You cannot cross the middle ground."

"We drop them from above," Hamish said.

Verena banged a hand on the tabletop. "Of course. We've got windrider troop transports."

"I am unfamiliar with those," Lukas said. Mattias was also frowning.

"Flying wagons." Verena gave Mattias a triumphant smile.

He laughed. "You really made them?"

"Yes!"

The two seemed to be sharing a moment far too special for Connor's taste, so he said, "Verena's a natural flyer."

Mattias barely acknowledged the comment, his attention fixed on Verena. "You've dreamed of reaching the sky for years."

"I did it. I'll have to give you a ride on my Swift. It's amazing."

"I'd like that," Mattias said.

Connor would prefer if she practiced shooting apples off Mattias's glowing face with diorite hornets.

They turned to calculating how many Rumblers they could spare for that first wave drop and how many wagons they'd need to carry them and the eighty Crushers. Verena and Hamish decided they'd need to build a few more wagons.

Hamish said, "The biggest challenge will be finding enough Builders to fly them. I guess we can leave some of the scout windriders hovering and borrow their pilots for the air drop."

"I'll fly one," Jean said.

"Are you a Builder?" Lukas asked.

Jean shook her head. "No, but I can fly a windrider."

"She's our first non-Builder test pilot," Verena explained.

"She pretty much killed an elfonnel single-handedly too," Hamish added, and Jean flushed under all the attention.

The meeting ended a short time later and Mattias immediately said, "Verena, I'd like a word with you."

Ilse interjected. "If you don't mind, my lord, can it wait? We have a lot to do to prepare the command for these unique battle orders. I would appreciate your help."

"I'll find you later," Verena promised.

Mattias didn't look pleased, but he agreed. Connor caught Ilse's eye, and she winked at him. He decided Lukas's presence was good for her.

As they descended toward the courtyard where they left the flying vehicles, Connor walked beside Verena, but she did not take his hand. She seemed lost in thought, and he wasn't sure what to say. Could Mattias's presence really confuse her so much? Was she doubting her interest in Connor?

That thought terrified him. They'd been through so much together. Part of him wanted to make her see how much he cared, but that was too much like what Shona had tried to do to him. The more she'd tried to force his heart, the more she'd driven him away. He couldn't make the same mistake with Verena.

Martys was still snoring in the Storm, and Aifric looked on the verge of shoving a blanket down his throat. She seemed relieved when Kilian said loudly, "Nap time is over."

Martys sat up with a grunt and a final snort. "What be the word?"

Connor summarized the basic outline of the battle plan and said, "I'm just worried about making sure we find all of the sculpted stones."

Aifric said, "He started with a dozen, and three have been used to raise elfonnel."

"Plus a couple were used at Harz to enhance the elemental attack," Kilian said. "I doubt those were fully consumed, so they may play a part in the next battle."

"We can't allow them to stir up the elements again," Hamish said.

"Anton will be prepared to face Gregor, even if he taps that stone again. I will deal with Ivor as soon as you secure the other stones."

Connor didn't like the sound of that. "Let me try first."

"Don't get distracted. You've already committed to the Crushers."

"Ivor will be in the thick of it. I'll stop him," Connor insisted.

Kilian leveled a serious look at him. "I know he's your friend, Connor, so you'll be motivated to show mercy. You must be prepared to kill him if he refuses to surrender that stone."

"I said I'll take care of it," Connor promised, his voice a bit sharper than he intended.

Kilian held his gaze for another second before nodding slowly. "See that you do. If I must intervene, I will."

Verena said, "That leaves seven sculpted stones, as far as we know. Do you think Carbrey will distribute them before the battle?"

Kilian considered that for a moment, but Martys spoke first. "I dinnae think so, lass. Those be the great treasure, an' from what Aifric told us, Dougal prefers to wield the elfonnel himself."

Kilian said, "I think you're right. Carbrey may have the stones as an emergency option, but I doubt he'll dare deploy them until we force him to."

"I hope you're right," Connor said.

Kilian said, "Carbrey is no fool. He's proud and eager to conquer, but he won't risk destroying his own army too. Distributing those other sculpted stones risks exactly that."

"We've got at least a couple days to prepare," Aifric said.

"And we'll need your help." Kilian explained the plan to send Aifric into the Obrioner camp to plant Gisela's chemical weapons. "Do you think Sir would be willing to assist?"

Aifric nodded. "He promised to help, and infiltration is his specialty. Together, we can gather any last-minute intelligence too."

"That would help a lot." Kilian admitted.

"I'd like to know if they've really been fooled by Ulrich's elaborate deception," Verena said.

"And if there are any other sculpted stones we don't know about," Connor added.

Hamish laughed. "Why not ask for a list of all their power stores while you're at it?" He gave Aifric an apologetic look. "Do you really think you can get all that?"

She stepped away from the Storm and a shudder passed through her, shaking her from head to toe. She shoved a hand into a pocket.

"Aifric?" Connor asked, suddenly worried Dougal might have somehow reestablished control over her mind.

Her faltering footsteps recovered before he could reach her, and she danced forward with the quick step of a Strider. Her expression changed, the muscles of her face somehow altering slightly, making her look leaner. Her stance became more energetic, and she bounced on her toes when she stopped moving, like Lorcc often did.

"You're a Strider, Aifric?" Hamish exclaimed.

She huffed. "Aifric couldn't infiltrate a sick bay full of unconscious patients, but I'll get into the camp, no worries."

"Who are you now?" Connor asked.

Aifric made a deep curtsy. "I'm the one and only Rith."

"Pleased to meet you, Rith," Jean said with a smile.

"So we're meeting another of your nineteen fake identities?" Connor asked.

"Fake?" Aifric-Rith asked, dancing closer, her expression turning belligerent. "Is Aifric fake? Is Student Eighteen fake?"

"You really become a different person, don't you?" Verena asked in a tone of wonder.

"Finally, someone who thinks a bit. I haven't let many people meet Rith in a while, and I was thinking it was a mistake."

"I think it'll be a pleasure to get to know you, Rith," Verena said.

"Of course it is. Only a fool wouldn't agree, and you're brilliant."

Rith seemed at least as confident as Dietmar, Ilse's cocky Wingrunner.

"You're still taking an awful risk slipping into the Obrioner camp," Connor pointed out.

Rith sighed. "You're like an old mother, Connor. I've done this before. I'll darken my hair and plait it into Strider tails. And I've got one of the King's Own Strider Corps uniforms, and this."

She pulled from a deep pocket of her Healer coat a piece of shaped, black leather and slipped it over her face. Connor recognized it as a Strider half-mask. The form-fitting mask covered the top half of her face, hooded slits shielding the eyes and nose from wind and bugs.

"It does help," Hamish admitted.

"But those half masks aren't exactly common," Connor objected. He had only seen Strider students at the Carraig wear them a handful of times. If anything, wearing the mask drew more attention.

"They are in Turriff's realm. I wear them all the time," Rith said.

"Where did you get that?" Hamish asked. He was openly grinning at Rith. Her confident good humor was infectious.

She shrugged. "Ask Student Eighteen. I just wear it."

"What do you think of Student Eighteen's new name?" Jean asked.

Rith shrugged. "Student Eighteen's got issues. I'm from a little town outside of Casur, right on the Macantacht. Our bloodlines run deep, just like our crops."

Kilian held up a hand to forestall Connor's next question. "Let's not get too distracted. We have a lot of work to do. Rith, you and Sir can leave after dark."

"Sounds good to me. Eighteen will take care of fishing for intelligence once we get there. She's crafty that way."

"Don't attempt tapping obsidian in the camp," Kilian warned.

"I'm not an idiot. Aifric can be a bit scatterbrained sometimes, but she doesn't use obsidian anyway. Eighteen's aware of the risk, though."

Connor marveled at Aifric's ability to keep her various personas separate. Aifric had downplayed the fractured state of her mind, but it seemed her different identities were actually different personalities, all living in the same head. Rith's comments were providing fascinating insights into how the various segments of Aifric's head kept their stories straight.

"So Aifric uses sandstone," Jean said, a thoughtful look on her face. "Eighteen uses obsidian and chert. Does she also use serpentinite?"

"Wouldn't be much of a Mhortair if she couldn't use that, now would she?"

"That's what I thought. So you really are Agor in both primary and secondary affinities. Are you also Dawnus, or is serpentinite your only tertiary?"

"I'm not Agor," Rith said. "Weren't you listening? I'm a Strider."

"But you're all the same person."

Rith held up a hand, and stopped bouncing. "You can't lump us together like that, Jean."

"But you are, aren't you?" Hamish asked.

"That would be mental."

The mental games she played made Connor's head spin, but were her different personalities really that different?

"How does that work?" Jean asked with a frown.

Rith shrugged. "We each use what we use. It's all separate. I can't use Aifric's stones or Eighteen's, and they can't use mine."

Connor exchanged an amazed look with Verena, who said, "We need to sit down and talk for a month when this is over."

Rith rolled her eyes. "Talk with one of the others. I can't sit still that long."

Kilian said, "I think we've settled your part of the plan. Why don't you go prepare for your incursion, then meet me back at Wolfram's command tent. I'll bring Sir."

"Good idea. I'll see you all after we trounce old Carbrey."

After Rith trotted from the windrider courtyard, Hamish let out a low whistle. "For a Healer, she's cracked."

"I'm glad she's on our side," Connor said.

Verena nodded. "She's far more complex than I imagined. I wonder how they do it?"

"We definitely need to dig into that and try to meet all of her," Jean agreed.

Kilian said, "She'll find out what there is to find. It falls to the rest of us to win this battle and flip this war back on Dougal."

Chapter Fifty-Three

"Can the blind lead those who cannot see, or the maimed guard against dangers unknown to them?"

~Sentry class teacher

Martys caught up with Connor as he left the windrider courtyard. "All this plannin' and talkin' gives me the boke. Come on, laddie, let's find a place for some simple, honest bash fighting."

Connor shook his head. "I'd love to, Uncle Martys, but we have so much to do."

"It can wait. Ye be headin' into battle the likes o' which ye no have tasted, me lad. Ye must be ready."

"I've done a lot of fighting," Connor assured him.

"Fighting aye, but killin'? Ne'er so much, I reckon." When Connor hesitated, he added, "Aye, laddie. Killin' be on the docket now. Ye cannae afford to hold back. This no be a fight fer points at yer school. This be the battle to decide the war, if'n what they all be sayin' is to be believed. So ye cannae show mercy, ye cannae hesitate, and ye cannea think that anyone ye fight is still yer friend."

There might be truth to what Martys was saying, but Connor didn't like it. "I can't just abandon friendship and kill people I care about."

"War is an ugly thing, but if'n ye will nay do that which must be done, those ye truly love may suffer. Come, lad. Ye need a taste of real battle."

He led Connor down several stone corridors, taking each turn as if he knew exactly where he was going. A few minutes later, they stepped into a small, stone-walled courtyard, open to the early evening sky. It was empty and smelled of sweat and leather, as if it was often used for sparring.

"You didn't just sleep while we were in those meetings, did you?" Connor asked as they walked into the middle of the empty courtyard and Martys turned to face him.

That was not the way most people would describe meeting an unclaimed. When Connor had turned rampager at the Carraig, most people had been simply terrified by his monstrous form, just as he had been when Professor Hector had transformed and nearly killed him.

"When did you see one?" Connor asked.

"Away to the south, on the borders of Sehrazad. One of me mates lost patronage for abandoning his post on the eve of an attack by the desert raiders. Luck be praised, when he turned unclaimed he attacked them instead of us."

Martys whistled softly. "Twas a terrifying an' inspiring sight, laddie. He savaged those raiders. They no had Petralists, but they no be cowards, an' they fought bravely. Died by the score, they did. He killed nearly two hundred afore he escaped into the night."

Connor grimaced to think of such slaughter. He knew better than anyone the unmatched savagery of porphyry, driven by that overwhelming rage and thirst for blood.

"I told you in Alasdair, and I meant it. Patronage is a lie, Uncle Martys. That friend of yours who turned unclaimed had another affinity with a stone called porphyry."

Martys looked shocked. "Can it be true?"

"I've seen it. I've proved it."

Martys drew closer and gripped Connor's arm. "Are ye sayin' that ye have turned unclaimed yerself?"

Connor nodded. "It's porphyry, Uncle. It can change us into those monsters."

"What does it feel like?" Martys asked in a tone of wonder.

"It's terrifying. And amazing."

"Go on," Martys urged.

Thinking back on that experience triggered another intense yearning for the powder. Connor's stomach cramped and his fingers clenched as he fought to control the renewed hunger. Porphyry had broken Dougal's hold on his mind, had transformed him into a monster savage enough to face the elfonnel, but it had pushed him to the brink of humanity. How could he put that into words?

"You feel stronger than life," Connor said softly, his voice shaking a little as he remembered the astonishing strength. He could have ripped Boulders apart and outrun the fastest Strider. "But it's savage and wild, and I only barely kept from killing everyone, even people I cared about."

"Ye mastered the beast," Martys breathed. "Connor, me lad, hold onto that memory when ye fight. Embrace the beast and ride the cusp of insanity, an I promise ye that no one will stand against ye an' live."

Then Martys clapped him on the shoulder and grinned. "Save the beast fer battle. Now it be time to fill the belly."

They found some food in one of the kitchens, then Connor left his uncle and looked for Verena, still haunted by Martys's words. They might be true, but could he accept so much blood on his hands? When the battle started, would he dare fight with such savagery?

Did he dare not to?

His dark thoughts were interrupted by Kilian, who entered the hallway from a connecting corridor, with Mattias trailing behind.

"Connor, I'm glad we found you. It's time for a little training with quartzite."

"Really?" The thought of training again with Kilian drove away Connor's worries. "Can you teach me quartzite?"

"He can't, but I can," Mattias said, and his smile did not glow at all.

"So there are other thresholds." That confirmation excited Connor, as did the idea of seeing heat. He could pick the best sweetbread every time.

Kilian nodded. "There are. We don't talk about them much. Few know about the first threshold, and fewer still can succeed in ascending. There are two additional thresholds, plus the obsidian threshold that Dougal used in order to gain the ability to seize the minds of others."

Mattias said eagerly, "I wasn't aware of that one."

Kilian warned, "Keep this information private. The second threshold can only be accessed by those with at least a Dawnus ability. It is only after that threshold that one can hope to raise an elfonnel and return to their humanity afterward. All others are lost."

That meant Kilian had ascended through that threshold. Connor wondered what else Kilian could do that they didn't know about.

Connor frowned as he realized something. "That means Evander is Dawnus too?"

Kilian chuckled. "He is, although he's pretty useless with quartzite."

Connor struggled to imagine the enormous, mysterious Evander as useless at anything. He wanted to ask for more details about that, but Mattias either didn't know Evander, or he didn't want to get sidetracked.

"And the third threshold?" Mattias pressed.

Kilian hesitated then said, "That one's a bit different, and is only accessible to the Blood of the Tallan."

"How is it different?" Connor asked.

"The day will come when you will need that information, but that day is not today."

It was a rotten thing to mention the third threshold, then not explain it. Connor opened his mouth to object, but Kilian raised a hand to silence him.

"You asked about risks and the price one pays for these new abilities. Each threshold has its own dangers. You ascended the first, and it has one of the most dramatic effects. The worst is that you can no longer father children."

"What?" Connor and Mattias exclaimed together and exchanged astonished looks.

Connor hadn't thought much about having children. He was still only sixteen, after all, but knowing he could never have a family of his own shocked him deeper than he would have imagined.

What would Verena think?

His face flushed at the thought. He loved Verena, and promising to each other was a definite possibility, but they hadn't actually talked about that potential future. If they did promise, if they did marry some day, would Verena accept the fact that they could not have children?

What would Shona think? He didn't actually want to think about Shona, but she'd played such a huge role in his life for the past months that he couldn't help it. She'd intended for them to wed, but would she have cared if they couldn't have children? Would her plans for conquest and power leave any room for children?

Then he thought of the edict from the king, granting breeding rights for all of the other high noble families. He wanted to spread the bloodline of the Blood of the Tallan. Did the king know Connor had ascended? Did he understand what that meant?

Kilian silently watched them. Connor's mind was still reeling, so it was Mattias who first recovered enough to ask, "Is that why so few Petralists are encouraged to attempt an ascension?"

"It is one of the reasons. Even though I despise the disgusting Obrioner breeding program, Granadure has also focused much effort on encouraging Petralist bloodlines to flourish. Both countries are working to rebuild the Petralist might we enjoyed before the Tallan Wars, but thresholds are a tricky thing.

"On the one hand, they offer unrivaled power that generals are hungry to obtain. On the other, they deny offspring to the very Petralists who possess the most powerful affinities."

"Aunt Ailsa mentioned there were dangers," Connor said softly. "But no one mentioned this."

"Don't lose hope, Connor. For any other Petralist, there would be no remedy that I know of. You alone might one day ascend through the third threshold. If you succeed and survive, that ultimate threshold restores the ability to sire children."

"So you can't?" Connor asked, then wished he hadn't.

Kilian shook his head, and an old sorrow reflected in his eyes. So many people called him Uncle Kilian, and that was the closest family he would ever have.

Connor felt a deep sadness to think of Kilian living for so long, but denied the joy of a family. He wondered if Kilian had ever married, but didn't dare ask.

"Enough of the deep lore," Kilian said, his expression neutral again. "It's a beautiful night for flying."

Chapter Fifty-Five

"All fountains of knowledge lie mapped and secure in the vault of memory thus guarded and cataloged?"

~Evander

It was a long way down to the cobbled streets. Even though Connor was ascended, he'd already proven that air still didn't like responding to his call.

"Any secrets you can share for controlling air better?" he asked.

Mattias grimaced. "Air is always a challenge. In legends, a few of the mightiest Petralists managed to walk with air extremely well, but most of us struggle."

Apparently Connor was not yet a mighty Petralist.

Mattias added, "Air is actually made up of many different currents. Most of us can't isolate them very well, but you should be able to feel them better, and even sense their history and purpose."

"How does air have history?"

"Think about it. Air doesn't dissolve. We breathe it, but somehow it's never exhausted."

Kilian's expression turned thoughtful. "As a boy, I learned something about how plants somehow help regenerate the air so it's always fresh."

"Plants don't have lungs," Connor said, chuckling.

"I don't know how it works, but there's some connection," Kilian insisted.

Mattias asked, "What about in deserts? The only plants are clustered around the oasis, but desert people don't die from lack of air out on the sands."

"Does sand breathe too?" Connor asked, shuddering to think about sand slowly breathing under his feet.

"I don't think so." Kilian was sounding a bit annoyed. "Just see what you can feel."

That wasn't very specific advice. It wasn't like Connor could communicate with it, listen to its stories like the old gaffers of Alasdair who liked to talk over their mugs of ale. That would be fun, though. Air currents must have seen a lot of amazing things over the years.

"Try it," Mattias urged.

"How about I connect with air and try to make it lift you off the roof?" Connor suggested.

Mattias's enthusiasm wilted. "Better to focus on yourself for tonight."

Connor appreciated the information Mattias was sharing, but he'd still summon a strong wind to throw Mattias over the city if he flashed another one of those glowing smiles at Verena.

He turned to face the night and imagined the gateway to air in his mind like a glittering crystal door above his head. He extended feelers of thought through it, and they drifted out into the air like wisps of invisible mist.

Now that he was focusing on it, he did notice distinct layers in the currents, all meshed together as they flowed past. Some were following the contours of the wall and seemed content to circle the citadel. Other currents coming off the river had collided with the wall and rose to cross and continue on a perpendicular course. For a moment, the different currents meshed together, like the merging of invisible streets, only to split apart and follow their different paths again.

Reaching farther, he sensed pockets of unmoving air, like pillows in the night, hovering over houses or in courtyards. Still other currents snaked around those pockets, fickle and unfocused, slipping around buildings and trees, as if playing an invisible game of Catch-the-Devil.

Higher above the city flowed more substantial currents, long-travelers that barely noticed the vast city sprawling below their path. He sensed that some had traveled immense distances. Others had spawned from storms far out at sea and driven across the land, slowly weakening until they combined with new currents to renew their energy.

Ignoring the smaller, unstable currents flitting around the roof, Connor grasped one of the stronger currents several hundred feet above his head and tugged it down. It actually responded, diving toward the roof in a rush of wind that set Kilian's hair dancing and blew dust into Mattias's perfect teeth.

Wrapping the air around himself, Connor threw his arms out wide and rose slowly off the roof. He laughed with the thrill of it. He was flying!

Then he hit a cross current and it threw him sideways, over the edge of the roof. That broke his contact with the air that had been lifting him. The current leaped away, and Connor began to fall.

He tried to grab the air that had disrupted his flight, but it was already gone, and another new current whipped past off the river. He managed to grab that one, and it lifted him again, but also threw him the other way, dragging him over the roof where Kilian and Mattias watched twenty feet below.

"Are you doing that on purpose?" Mattias shouted.

Kilian just laughed and waved.

"This isn't as easy as I make it look!"

Connor drifted over a row of trees marking the boundary of a nearby courtyard where a large cook fire was burning. The flames created a warm updraft that drove him higher, but then broke his connection with the current that had been carrying him along.

"Tallan take it all!" he growled as he tumbled back toward the ground, casting around for another current, but they fled his touch like minnows in the Wick.

Once again, flying really meant falling.

With a sigh, Connor tapped marble instead. As he fell toward the huge fire, he stole most of the flames away to blast himself back into the air. He arced back into the darkness and landed on the roof. There he bowed to Kilian and Mattias, as if he'd planned the move all along.

Angry cooks were shouting and shaking long, wooden spoons at him from the courtyard, so he threw the fire back. Most of it landed on the smoldering wood and reignited the cook fire. Some landed on one of the cook's aprons and it must have had a lot of grease on it, because it ignited like a torch.

Connor snatched those flames away and yanked them back to the roof where he stood. It wasn't the cook's fault that he was a bad flier, and setting the flames dancing back and forth across his shoulders was fun.

"I suppose you'll need more practice," Mattias said, clearly enjoying himself.

Kilian grinned. "Lots of practice."

They returned to Saskia's private study where she was chatting with Verena near the fire. Verena gave Connor a hug and a quick kiss. Connor didn't miss the quick glance she cast at Mattias. She might actually look a bit embarrassed.

"How did training go?" she asked.

"Pretty well, I think."

Kilian said, "With practice, I think Connor might make a decent Longseer."

"Thanks for teaching him," Verena told Mattias, and again her smile was too warm for Connor's liking.

"It was fun." Mattias grinned at her, although this time he didn't ignite that glowing smile. "I'm glad you all came."

It was clear he didn't really care about anyone but Verena. Before the moment got too personal, Connor clapped Mattias hard on the shoulder and said, "We're happy to help any way we can."

"We have much to plan," Kilian said, and they moved toward the couches and chairs facing the fire.

Saskia nodded. "We just received word that General Carbrey accepted the prisoner exchange."

Verena scowled and mumbled something angry in Grandurian under her breath. Mattias, who sat on the other side of her, looked shocked. Connor decided he really wanted to learn that word.

"That's good news, right?" Connor asked.

"Shona added a condition," Verena said with abundant disgust.

"That can't be good," Connor said. Shona was a champion meddler, but he hadn't expected her to mess with the prisoner exchange.

"While the exchange is happening, you must meet with her," Saskia said. She watched Verena with great interest. "What's the history with Shona?"

"It's complicated," Connor said as he considered the condition. He didn't like it, but he saw a chance to turn it to his advantage. "Send a reply that you accept the condition, but add the condition that she must bring Ivor and every student who participated in the Tir-raon this year as escorts."

Mattias frowned. "It is not usual protocol to add conditions upon conditions."

Connor grinned. "Good thing I don't know anything about usual protocol."

"Why do you want to meet with the other students?" Verena asked.

"They're my army after all. Lord Dail himself gave them to me. I think I'll inspect them and make sure discipline hasn't faded."

"You have to tell me that story," Saskia laughed.

"What's the real reason?" Verena asked.

"It's my chance to speak with Ivor. I need to warn him to not use that sculpted stone again."

Chapter Fifty-Six

"Many ants may devour an ox where a single lion alone would collapse, beyond sated."

~Connor

The next day passed in a whirlwind of activity. Scouts kept them updated on reports of the Obrioner advance into the next valley south of Altkalen. Over fifty thousand troops total, plus support personnel. Connor had to wonder if their plans to defeat such an enormous host with barely half the numbers could really work.

The next day, they would clash in the biggest battle since the Tallan Wars. Connor retired to the comfortable bed assigned him, but of course he didn't sleep much. A couple hours before dawn he finally gave up and went looking for Verena.

She was sitting with Saskia in her private study, high in her tower in the citadel. Together they scanned the distant troops through Verena's long-vision goggles.

Saskia wore a pink satin night dress under her royal blue velvet robe. When Connor arrived, she added another woven shawl. Verena was already dressed in her custom armor, and Connor could have looked at her for hours. Verena had sliced an apple with one of her throwing knives and still held one piece speared on the tip of the knife as she greeted Connor with a hug and a quick kiss.

"Neither of you could sleep either, I see," Connor said as he and Verena joined Saskia by the window.

Saskia said,

"No one this night will sleep,
while the enemy across the valley doth creep.
They've been marching all night, they're a terrible sight,
and I fear today many new widows will weep."

The Obrioner army had ascended to the southern edge of the valley and crept across the land like a slow stain. They were brightly lit by their Solas, and Connor easily marked their progress.

"No fighting yet?" he asked.

Verena shook her head. "Thank the Tallan, no. Reports suggest Carbrey is focused on securing his position. And of course we don't want to risk endangering the prisoner exchange."

"I hope Carbrey is convinced your council isn't very smart," Connor told Saskia.

"Me too."

Something odd about the shadowed landscape caught Connor's attention. "What is that black cut across the center of the valley?"

"Anton and a couple of my Sappers helped me strip away all the earth from that area just after dark," Saskia said proudly.

"Wow." The black area cut clear across the valley, from the eastern hills to the west. It was half a mile wide, spanned only by the hard-packed road. The road looked like a bridge, rising a full ten feet above the surrounding rock. That was a lot of land to strip to bedrock. He looked at Saskia with new respect.

"That'll block Sentries from sticking their noses into the middle ground," Verena said, leaning closer to the cold glass and peering through her goggles.

"Or Sappers, unless they bring earth along with them," Connor said.

Saskia nodded toward the distant eastern hills. They looked bigger now. "That's what all that earth will tempt them to do. While they're distracted with that, we hit them."

"How, exactly?" Connor asked.

"You know that part of the plan is our secret. Kilian and Anton know. Leave it at that."

"We have enough to worry about," Verena agreed.

She was right. For several minutes, they just studied the scene. Connor took Verena's hand, trying to enjoy the peaceful moment. It might be their last for a while.

"Do you think we're ready?" Saskia asked softly. Her usual confident bluster had faded in that quiet moment, hours before violence would be unleashed upon her beloved home.

"We're ready," Verena promised.

In that battle maiden outfit, she looked it, but Connor read worry in her eyes. Their plan was a good one, but nothing was certain.

"You're not, though," she told Connor.

"I'll find my battle jacket before breakfast," he promised.

"That's not good enough." She walked to one of the couches where some armor was piled. He hadn't paid it any attention before. She lifted the battle jacket and said, "This is for you."

Connor whistled softly as he hefted the armored jacket. The expandable leather plates were reinforced with steel, secured with silver-capped rivets. Each plate was engraved with one of the ancient symbols of the various affinities, with granite and basalt holding prominent positions on the chest plates.

Granite was represented as an intricate, eternal knot that exuded a sense of constant strength. Basalt looked more like a spiral of dark smoke, as if a Strider had raced through a fire. The faceted crystal symbol of obsidian was worked into the back.

The flaming fire of marble and the swirling currents of soapstone were engraved on the pauldrons over the shoulders. Solid, geometric slate and the rushing winds of quartzite were worked into the studded bracers over the forearms.

Verena showed him the armored leggings with the lantern-like symbol for limestone and the linked circles of sandstone engraved over the thighs. The entire suit of armor was crafted with meticulous care, with such fine artistry that it took Connor's breath away.

"Where did you get this?" he breathed.

"Jean helped design it," Verena said with a grin.

"And my best armorer built it," Saskia beamed. Literally. She'd activated limestone and her skin glowed as if she'd swallowed a lantern.

Connor wondered if she ever had problems with moths trying to fly into her mouth.

"I don't know what to say." Connor had missed his custom battle leathers from the Carraig, and hadn't ever expected to wear anything finer.

Verena held up a padded burgundy gambeson. The jacket was made of fine linen, lined with satin that made moving a breeze. He tried it on, and Verena then picked up the heavy, armored jacket, as if she planned to dress him right there. That would be fine, except Saskia picked up one of the armored greaves, and he realized she intended to help.

Connor flushed and held out a hand to stop her. "I can't have you doing that, Lady Marshal."

Saskia waved away his concern and crouched beside him. "Nonsense. I help Mattias dress for battle, just as I did my father. Your armor's not nearly so complicated, so you'll be easy."

374

Connor glanced at Verena for help, but she said, "Stop whining and let us help you."

He wasn't sure how to deny them, but it still felt weird as Saskia fastened the greaves into place and Verena helped him into the heavy, armored jacket. It settled over the gambeson with a comforting, solid weight. He'd worn Boulder battle leathers many times, but none had ever felt so right.

When they finished, Saskia brushed off her hands. "You look like the Blood of the Tallan, Connor. More importantly, you look fit to stand beside our Verena."

"Thank you." Connor reached out to take her hand, but she instead gave him a hug. Despite her slender build, she had the strength of a Sapper, and he felt the pressure right through his armor.

Verena hugged him in turn. He bet the two of them made a striking couple in their custom armor, but he still preferred holding her without so many layers between.

Saskia's smile turned a bit sad, and he wondered if she was thinking of her brother. Was she wishing Mattias was the one standing there with Verena? He wanted to ask her about that, but how could he broach such a personal subject?

By pretending to be clueless, that's how.

"Thanks for your help, Saskia. You don't think your brother will mind, do you?"

Verena looked shocked, and he tensed for a punch to the face. Saskia looked surprised too, but she only laughed.

"I like a direct question sometimes, Connor. I'm surrounded by Sappers and politicians most of the time."

Verena muttered, "Connor, that's a very personal question."

Saskia waved away her worry. "You and I have talked about it, 'Rena. Connor would have to be blind and stupid not to see that Mattias still loves you. You never would have chosen Connor if he was either of those, would you?"

"I don't want to talk about Mattias this morning," Verena said, and the slight flush that rose into her cheeks only made her look more beautiful.

It was probably for the best that the door opened and Hamish entered. His short, red hair looked wild, his pallor a bit green, and scorch marks criss-crossed his battle suit.

"What happened to you?" Verena exclaimed as he crossed the room toward them.

"I'm fine," he said, but he sounded a bit distracted. "Have you seen Jean yet this morning?"

Connor said, "No. I was hoping she actually managed to sleep."

"I doubt it." Hamish seemed to see them for the first time and his eyes widened. "Whoa! Connor, where did you get that armor?"

"Thanks to the girls here, and with Jean's help, of course."

"She's been busy. That armor looks great." Hamish patted his singed suit. "She's been helping me with a few last minute enhancements too."

"Is that why it looks like you fell asleep in a fire?" Verena asked.

"No. That was the only way to remove the stink after I figured out how to milk those skunks."

"What?" Verena exclaimed.

Saskia laughed, but her grin died when she realized he wasn't joking.

"Ah, skunks don't have milk," Connor said.

Hamish stretched, his suit creaking and the granite leaves clacking softly together. "I know, but that's the best term for the process of harvesting their stink."

"Is that even possible?" Saskia asked with a grimace.

"It is, but they don't like it. The most efficient method I've found is to really annoy them, then catch the spray in a pail when they try dousing me."

"Why?" Connor knew Hamish better than anyone, but milking a skunk surprised even him.

"Gisela's mega-stench inspired me."

"What do you plan to do with milked skunk stench?" Verena asked, although she looked like she wasn't sure she wanted to know.

Hamish shook his head. "That's a secret. You'll see once we get it to work."

"Good luck. I think," Saskia said hesitantly.

"Thanks." Hamish rubbed a hand through his hair and across his face, then waved. "I'm going to find Jean. See you all at breakfast."

Connor didn't plan to eat much. His stomach was already knotted as he thought about the looming battle and his meeting with Shona. "I'm going to have to leave soon too."

"I still don't like it," Verena said for the tenth time.

"I can't cancel the meeting without risking the prisoner exchange," Connor told her again.

"I know, but she still wants you." Verena gripped his hands in her warm ones. "I worry for you, Connor."

"I can handle Shona."

"The fact that you honestly think that's true makes me worry even more."

Saskia leaned forward. "You still haven't explained the history with Lady Shona and why she generates such emotion."

Connor shrugged. "I was Lady Shona's Guardian for a while."

Verena grunted. "If only that was everything. She was the one who discovered Connor is Blood of the Tallan. Ever since then she's been trying to manipulate him into marrying her so she can control his curse."

"Really?" Saskia looked thrilled by the news.

"That's all that matters," Connor said. She was cracked if she thought he'd give her details about his life that Mattias could possibly use as a wedge between him and Verena. As long as Connor didn't do anything stupid to give Shona any new leverage over him, he felt safe meeting her.

Verena handed him a leather and steel helmet, then pulled from her satchel something that looked like an arm bracer, with a quartzite stone set into the top, surrounded by four others. "Give me your arm, Connor."

"What is that?" Connor asked as she began fastening it to his left forearm.

"We call this the mini-hub." She pointed to the central stone, which was about as big as the end of his thumb. "This is a keystone, similar in design to the one we developed for Jean."

She pointed to the other four smaller stones. "These are paired to Hamish, Kilian, myself, and the ear hub. Just turn the keystone so the symbol lines up with whichever stone you want to activate and we'll be able to communicate."

"That's amazing," Connor grinned and tested turning the keystone. It was set in a clever base that clicked securely into position facing each of the stones.

Verena cautioned, "These stones are small. The range should be enough for communicating on the battlefield, but not much farther."

Saskia gave Verena an enthusiastic hug. "You're brilliant. All of the commanders will want one of these."

"Connecting through the ear hub will work for most of them, but we're likely to need direct communication. The advantage could be critical."

Saskia grinned. "You didn't sleep as much in class as I thought."

Connor bowed over Saskia's hand and thanked her again, then took Verena's hand and led her to the door. They stepped into the empty hall and there he wrapped his arms around her waist. They held each other for a long moment. He buried his face in her neck and breathed deep the warm scent of her, while trying to memorize the feel of her armored torso in his arms.

After a long moment, she gave him a tender kiss, then touched his cheek with one warm hand. "Be careful today."

"You're the one who's planning to assault the command center."

"I still feel you'll be in greater danger."

He gave her a reassuring smile, stole a final quick kiss, then left. They had a major battle to win. Compared with that, dealing with Shona should be easy.

CHAPTER FIFTY-SEVEN

"The slow drip of water from hanging stone will eventually fill even the deepest bucket."

~Evander

Connor slid southeast across Altkalen Valley on a Sentry tower, with water and fire rippling around its exterior. The multi-elemental display Kilian had used at Harz was too good not to borrow. Imitation was the best form of honoring a teacher, wasn't it?

Besides, he wanted to remind the students who he was. Managing three elements simultaneously consumed most of his attention, but he was the only one moving across the broken, rocky land between the massed armies anyway. He only wished he knew how to make those invisible trumpets and drums like Padraigin did. That would've been the perfect finishing touch.

Still, in his custom armor, he looked more like a general than he ever had. That thought gave him an idea, and he tapped granite. His armor barely creaked as the plates shifted and expanded with his muscles.

As the steel plates slid aside, brightly-colored designs became visible. On the right, it looked like flames rippling up his torso. The beautiful design included the ancient symbol of fire, worked in colors from crimson to white to blue. On the left, the symbol of water was worked into a flowing blue pattern that hinted at the ever-moving power of the seas.

Looking good wasn't everything, but it helped when meeting his army. They were noble-born, so they gave appearance a lot of weight. Then again, compared to the mighty Obrioner host massed across the valley, he'd have to be wearing a castle to feel anything but insubstantial.

Sliding his tower of earth across the stony ground was challenging. He'd borrowed a substantial amount of earth from one of the caches piled up behind the Grandurian army. It trailed behind him like a long umbilical to the road. He used it to cover the uneven ground for his tower to pass over.

The chill morning air smelled strongly of sulfur. Saskia had mentioned that the city imported most of its drinking water since the local ground water was so volcanic and always nearly boiling.

As he moved across the barren, shadowed landscape alone, he wondered how many people would die today? Would he be one of them? Would Verena, or Hamish, or their other friends?

Was it fair that he hoped only people he didn't know would fall? The grief of their loved ones would be no less intense because Connor didn't know them.

With an effort, he drove the dark thoughts aside and blew a breath into a cloud of mist. Their plan offered the best chance to save as many lives as possible.

The prisoner exchange would take place exactly halfway between the two armies, on a spot in the road that had been widened to accommodate the groups. They'd meet at the first light of day when the sun broke free of the eastern hills. That would happen in minutes.

Connor was tempted to scan the skies for Verena. She had promised not to interfere, but no doubt she was already watching. He double-checked the mini-hub mechanical on his arm to make sure it was set to the neutral position. He didn't want anyone, especially Verena, eavesdropping.

Hearing Shona's voice might drive her to do something rash. Since he'd probably be standing close to Shona, most likely he'd get hurt too, and starting the day by getting blown back to Harz probably wasn't a good idea.

He stopped his tower roughly parallel to where the prisoner exchange would take place, but almost half a mile to the east. Movement across the valley drew his gaze. Focusing his enhanced vision, Connor spotted Shona and Ivor leading a company of about a hundred and fifty soldiers out from the Obrioner lines and up the road.

He recognized every face. So far, so good. He bet Ivor had helped convince Carbrey that sending the students posed no risk.

When the company left the road, their two Sentries copied Connor, dragging earth from the Obrioner camp to form a smooth pathway to march across. Connor's captains marched near the front. Lorcc, Fearghas, and Princess Catriona looked eager to reach him. Papil, his Pathfinder captain, carried herself with a new air of confidence. She met his gaze and saluted. Her huge blue eyes glowed in the early morning light.

Connor returned the salute and said, "It's good to see you, Papil."

"You too, General!"

"Say hello to the others for me."

When she spread the word, Catriona waved so hard she nearly hit Shona. Shona glared, but then again focused on Connor. She winked, confident in the assumption that he was staring at her. She walked beside Ivor, poised and beautiful as ever in her battle leathers.

Connor decided those two would make a great couple. Ivor was conniving and intelligent enough that he might hold his own against her.

It would be a relationship forged in a cage match.

Watching his army coming to meet him was like coming home, and Connor savored the positive memories he'd built with them. His time at the Carraig had often been difficult and dangerous, but he'd enjoyed leading them in the mock battles.

When the group stopped about twenty paces away, Connor settled his tower to the ground and used the earth to create a flat meeting area. Then he threw the flames into the air in multicolored flashes. The waters he kept close, just in case things did not go as planned.

"You've gotten better at managing multiple affinities," Ivor said as he stepped out to greet Connor. His tone was casual, as if they were again meeting in his Dawnus suite.

"I'm not sure I'm using the Channeling-Grime technique or not, but I think there are a few things I could teach you now."

"Nice armor." Ivor's battle leathers were enhanced with armored pauldrons, trimmed in the gold and royal blue of House Islay, his new home.

"Thanks. One must look the part."

Ivor turned and raised his voice. "What do you think, troops? Are you happy to see General Connor?"

Most of the students cheered, and Catriona rushed up and gave Connor a fierce hug. While he was trying to detach himself, she whispered into his ear.

"I know you're on a secret mission, General, but we all still believe in you. I know it's only a matter of time before you keep your promise."

"Promise?"

"Second breeding rights of course." She actually blushed and tried looking up at him through her eyelashes. Jean and Shona both knew how to make the move look alluring. Catriona only managed to look like a stalker.

Shona elbowed Catriona aside, but then glanced up at the early morning sky. "I'm not going to get blown up for coming to say hello, am I?"

Connor shook his head, hoping he was right. He would probably feel bad if Verena struck Shona down with thousands of exploding hornets, but what was life without a little risk?

He took her hand, and she leaned forward and kissed his cheek. As always, she smelled faintly of roses, and the scent triggered a multitude of memories. Some were even pleasant.

"It's good to see you all," Connor said loudly, stepping away from Shona. She was at least as deadly in her way as Anika. Or Verena when she got really mad.

At his words, many of the students surged forward to grip his hands, led by his captains. He spent a moment catching up with them, and couldn't stop grinning.

"We don't have much time." Ivor gestured back toward the Obrioner lines.

Captain Rory, Gregor, and twenty Fast Rollers were leading a large group of Grandurian prisoners north along the road. Connor hadn't realized so many had been captured. There had to be nearly two hundred soldiers, mostly Rumblers and Wingrunners. The Fast Rollers were carrying large sacks. Probably contained that captured powder.

A similar company was already leaving the Grandurian lines. There were more than twice as many Obrioner prisoners, and nearly half of them were Striders, captured in that initial surprise attack at Harz. He spotted Ilse and Anton with Erich and Anika, who led the Grandurian soldiers escorting the prisoners.

He was surprised to also see Hamish soaring above the group. That hadn't been part of the plan. Had Hamish snorted one skunk too many?

There was nothing he could do about it, so he tried to look relaxed. "We have enough time."

He allowed himself another minute to mingle with the troops, chatting with them and listening to their worries. Many of them had been involved in the fighting at Harz, and he could tell. Some looked hardened, steeped in anger or hatred of the Grandurians. Others still looked shaken, and glanced at the Grandurian army nervously.

Many of them asked him what he was doing in Granadure and why he was helping their enemies? He managed to delay answering for a bit, but finally Fearghas demanded, "General, it doesn't make sense. We need you. With your help, we can route them and take Altkalen. All of southern Granadure would fall."

Many students added their voices in agreement, so Connor raised his hands for quiet.

"As Princess Catriona was clever enough to figure out, I'm here in Granadure on special assignment." Catriona blushed and took a step toward him, arms already extending.

Ivor intercepted her and pumped her hands. "Well done, Princess."

Shona shifted to block Catriona's progress too. Connor appreciated Ivor's quick intervention. Otherwise, Shona might have felt obliged to physically restrain Catriona, and they didn't need a fight yet.

"This war is not as straight-forward as you might assume," Connor said to the group. "I've been tracking down some important truths that could change the war completely."

"What truth?" Fearghas asked.

Shona said, "Connor's mission is not yet complete, so he can't share the details. His work is top secret. In fact, I need to debrief him regarding that mission now."

She moved away from the group and motioned him to follow. He was tempted to argue, but the students, who were used to house secrets and information safeguarding, looked like they believed her. He needed to speak with her anyway, so he decided to get that over with first. He'd shout her down later if he had to.

Shona led him about fifty feet from the others, and Papil raised a shielding wind around them.

"What is it, Shona?" he asked, speaking with a tone of impatience to remind her that he no longer served her.

"So testy this morning," she said in a teasing tone. "Is that new armor pinching somewhere?"

"I have a lot to do."

She sighed. "Oh, Connor. I bet you hate me now."

"You sound surprised."

She stepped closer and took his hands. He tensed. "You probably think I sent you away from Harz to give my father advantage."

"You did."

"No," she protested, her expression anguished, her lovely eyes wide and vulnerable. That look used to melt his heart, but he steeled himself against it. "I didn't know he planned to raise that fire-bound elemental. I took a huge risk to warn you."

Her performance really was masterful, but then so was everything she did.

"I swear on my honor," Shona said, standing straighter, chin high, giving him that imperious look that used to cow him.

"But we're talking about whether or not that honor is stained," Connor pointed out. "So swearing by it doesn't help."

"Listen to me," she said, her tone frustrated. "Camonica really did attack, didn't she?"

He nodded.

"And you saved Jean?"

He nodded again.

She actually looked relieved. "If I hadn't warned you, Camonica would have succeeded."

"Maybe." Connor decided not to tell her about Jean's heroic efforts or the work they were doing with that keystone.

Shona chided, "Stop trying to be stern, Connor. It's not like you."

He gestured toward the armies. "I have a lot on my mind today."

"Listen, Connor. I'll prove that I have your best interests at heart. My father's not here, but he left his other sculpted stones behind for Carbrey to use if needed."

"You can't let him. Raising another elfonnel would probably destroy this entire valley and both armies."

"I know, and I think I've convinced Carbrey, at least for now. But Connor, he's obsessed with beating Wolfram. If the battle goes poorly today, he might decide it's worth the risk to distribute some more of them."

"Carbrey's not that big a fool," Connor said, but he didn't believe himself. Carbrey's intense hatred for Wolfram had driven him to reject the peace accord Connor had negotiated at Alasdair.

Shona only raised one eyebrow, and he sighed. "We'll find a way to deal with those stones. Can you tell me where they are?"

She smiled. "Oh, Connor. A secret that big would require something equally valuable in return."

"Like what?" he asked, although he didn't want to know.

"Return to Carbrey's command tent with me. I'll force him to give them to you and submit to your command."

Only Shona could make such an audacious offer sound reasonable. "You don't have that authority."

"Actually, I do. When my father left, he commissioned me high marshal. Carbrey has day-to-day command, but I have authority to overrule him, and all of the senior leadership know it.

384

If you come and promise to return to Merkland with me, I can give you victory today and safety for Granadure."

It was such a tempting offer, and for a moment he seriously considered it. Then the truth reasserted itself. "I believe you might even mean every word you're saying, but we both know that when your father returns, he'll overrule you."

"What if we don't let him?" she asked softly, leaning closer, her gaze intense.

"I'm going to have to kill him. Are you saying you'd help me arrange that?"

"Killing him while you stand with the Grandurians won't stop the war, but together we could replace him."

"You're serious?"

She nodded, her gaze as intense as that night at the Carraig when she'd confessed her ambition of unseating the king of Obrion and rising to rule with Connor. It appeared her dreams hadn't gotten any less grand or disturbing.

"Connor, we both know this war is foolish. There's no profit in it, but together we could stop it. I love my father, Connor, but I can see that he's lost his reason. If you return and marry me, together we can rule House Dougal and stop this war."

"You really think they'd follow us?" He tried to sound calm, but her words shocked him.

How could she speak so calmly about helping arrange a coup against her own father? He knew she was ambitious, but would she really do it, or was she orchestrating a complex, subtle game to capture and control him again?

"You are Blood of the Tallan," she declared in that same tone of victory as the first time she'd said it. "United with me, no one would be able to deny your right to lead. Come back with me, Connor, and together we can do so much good."

Her definition of good was a little unusual. Conquest and oppression might seem good when you were the one enjoying the spoils, but it wouldn't be pleasant for anyone else.

Still, he felt torn.

What if she was even partially right? If they could turn back the army and remove Dougal, they might gain enough leverage to actually make changes from within the Obrioner ruling system. They could potentially save tens or even hundreds of thousands of lives.

All he had to do was sacrifice his future happiness.

Was it selfish to think of his own future more than that of so many others? What else would Shona demand of him? What else would Obrion demand? There had to be a better way.

He needed to speak with Verena, but when he scanned the sky, he saw no sign of her. He was tempted to try the mini-hub, but didn't want Shona seeing the revolutionary new mechanical. He glanced to the center of the valley where the two groups with their prisoners had nearly reached each other. The exchange was about to begin. He was nearly out of time.

Shona was watching him intently, her warm hand still on his arm.

It was a perfect time to test her resolve.

CHAPTER FIFTY-EIGHT

"The circle of history repeats, and yet there is time to prevent the full reckoning."

~Evander

Hamish soared over the Grandurian force marching south along the road toward the prisoner exchange, exulting in the absolute freedom of flight. In his suit, he was one with the air in a way that not even Verena completely matched. He was starting to suspect Jean might one day get it, though.

She was as brilliant as she was beautiful, and as Hamish swept his Builder senses across the many mechanicals built into his suit, his grin widened. Jean had helped him make some important improvements, and he was eager to test them.

With thrusters firing just enough to keep him hovering at about ten feet, he moved to the front where Erich and Anika led the party. Erich looked eager for a chance to bash fight.

Today he'd get his wish.

Martys, who flanked Erich on the right, looked just as eager, even though he'd be facing his own countrymen. Those two were building such a fascinating friendship, based on the pillars of daily pummeling and mutual lack of understanding.

A hand-picked company of twenty-five Rumblers herded the captured Obrioners toward the exchange point. Captain Rory and his similar company were already advancing up the valley to meet them.

On the right flank of the group, Ilse and Anton flowed across the land on miniature towers. They would deal with Gregor and any elemental threats, leaving the bash fighters to focus on pure, unrestrained violence. Hamish was there just to make Carbrey think the Builders were also focused on the exchange and not planning any other devilry.

Connor was already meeting with Shona and Ivor. That extra bit of complexity increased the chances of something going wrong.

Hamish descended closer to Erich, who was already humming to himself. The man loved to sing battle songs while he fought.

Anika just looked eager and commented in Grandurian, "I feel like a giddy little girl, getting so excited to see him again." A foolish grin momentarily broke her calm expression.

Erich gave her a worried frown. "You are acting pretty silly. Don't let him think he's already won your heart."

"How do I do that?" The honest question in her eyes startled Hamish.

Erich scowled. "Hit him harder."

Hamish actually felt sorry for Anika. He couldn't imagine dealing with the challenges Anika and Rory faced. Captain Rory was respected by people in both countries, and from what Hamish could see, he and Anika were perfectly suited for each other. He could also see the relationship had less than no chance of ever working out.

Anika insisted, "I do. He doesn't care. He's . . ."

"Don't say it," Erich urged.

"He is one I could surrender to." Anika spoke so softly, Hamish almost didn't hear.

"Don't ever say that again," Erich growled, and Hamish found himself nodding.

He'd learned a lot about the culture of the Rumblers in his time in Granadure. As far as he knew, no battle maiden had ever surrendered willingly to an Obrioner.

"What be buzzing up yer britches?" Martys asked, and Hamish chuckled to see the look of confusion on Erich's face.

Erich had told him once that he usually understood maybe two-thirds of what Connor said. He considered Obrioner a barbaric, difficult language. He had decided the language was weak, and he could not tolerate weak things. That's why he had so much trouble with it.

"You seem to figure it out," Hamish had told him.

Erich had shrugged. "When I can't understand, I usually just threaten to punch people. The system seems to work pretty well."

Now Erich turned to Martys and spoke in his broken Obrioner. "Will be good fight Rory."

"No doubt," Martys said with a grimace, for the first time looking nervous.

"You want no be here?" Anika asked.

Martys waved away the question. "Me boy Connor needs me, so I'll see the task through."

The two groups met exactly halfway between the two gathered armies. Even though it was the obvious meeting spot, a Sapper had marked the ground with a sunken "X". Hamish chuckled. He bet it was Saskia's handiwork.

Captain Rory managed to glance away from Anika a couple of times to scan the others. He always looked back quickly, though. Anika scared any man with a shred of interest in self-preservation, but that danger only seemed to attract Rory all the more.

It was too bad they hadn't been born in the same country. Then again, having those two teamed up permanently would be a terrifying force for whichever side commanded their loyalty.

The Grandurian captives looked healthy and eager to return to duty. They'd get their wish sooner than they expected.

Anika stepped forward with that strut she used only for Captain Rory. She utterly failed to conceal her adoring expression as she gazed at him. "Come, mine capitain. We wrestle, yes?"

He gave her a slow grin. "You have no idea how tempting that is."

"Then do," Erich said, cracking his knuckles.

Although he still seemed to hate the fact that Anika had fallen for an Obrioner, he'd explained that he'd proven Rory's strength in the brother-duty contest and couldn't deny Rory was worthy.

"Are you kidding? No threat to break my head?"

Erich shrugged. "Can head break every day."

"We've got time," Tomas said. He and Cameron were watching Erich with obvious eagerness.

Ilse and Anton had moved away from the main company and were meeting privately with Gregor. Seeing those two famous earth walkers standing side by side was an impressive sight, but Hamish was glad he was dealing with big granite Petralists instead.

Rory hesitated and Martys spoke. "It no be that complicated, Captain. If the prisoners exchanging from both sides just happened to get their hands on some of that powder ye were so kind to bring along, we'd have to fight over the spoils, wouldn't we?" He winked and added, "There would be none to notice the two of you wrestling in all the fun."

A look of expectant hope lit up in every face, be they Obrioner or Grandurian. Hamish wanted to laugh. Bash fighting for them was the purest form of contest, stone beating stone in the ultimate test of strength.

"You're a wise man," Cameron said, grinning. "Why do I feel like I know you?"

Martys said quickly, "We no have met, but I know you lot by reputation."

Rory considered him. "Few Guardians desert to the enemy, and you're not even turned unclaimed."

"I be the truest patriot ye'll ever meet," Martys said with a shrug. "Like I tell me nephew Connor, failing means yer playin', an' I mean to grant yer boys a public skelping today."

Erich frowned at Martys, clearly not understanding. So he grunted and pounded one fist into his other open palm. It seemed appropriate.

Tomas chortled. "Ha! Captain, you've got to approve a little bash fight now."

Cameron grinned in agreement. "We're so used to teaching, it'll be fun to inflict some learning on one of Connor's relatives for a change."

Martys grinned. "I dinnae mean a little bash fight, laddie. We no do things by halves here at Altkalen. How many times have ye gotten a bash fight to last as long as ye want?"

"Never." Everyone within earshot answered in unison.

"It's a very tempting offer," Rory said, rubbing his stubbled chin and looking at Anika, who blew him an inviting kiss.

"Fight many good," Erich urged.

Hamish decided to add a final push. "It's not like you have anything better to do, Captain. We are men of action. Leaving now is like choosing to dig new latrines instead of fighting."

Cameron grimaced. "I hate digging latrines."

"You have to stop using your teeth," Tomas replied.

Hamish said, "Once the main assault begins, the tertiaries will get all the fun. Could be hours before you get another chance."

Rory nodded and a grin spread over his face. "You're as clever with words as you are with those mechanicals, Builder. It's a sad day that Obrion lost you."

"That whole death sentence thing made it hard to stay."

"Let's get organized then, shall we?" Rory said, rubbing his hands together.

"Release the prisoners and prepare to fight!" Erich shouted in Grandurian.

They completed the exchange in record time and distributed powder to every warrior. Even though the Striders and Wingrunners were eager to participate, there wasn't room for a running battle. Reluctantly, they agreed to remain in reserve, but promised to lend a hand wherever possible.

Then with a simple raised fist, Rory signified they were ready.

"Charge!" Erich shouted and led the way, bellowing his favorite boisterous battle song. He swelled with granite power and pounded forward to meet Tomas and Cameron.

Rory and Anika came together with a crack of rock-hard bodies, beating on each other with a fury that most people would misinterpret as actual hatred. They laughed as they fought. After the first exchange, they paused for a deep, passionate kiss.

Although Rory had proven himself in the honor duel at the Carraig, the sight of his beloved sister kissing a barbarian still enraged Erich. Venting the anger in a roaring bellow, he leaped upon Cameron and pounded him to the ground with a single overwhelming blow. Tomas tackled him immediately, and the resulting fierce pounding between them was exactly what the men seemed to need.

Anika finally broke off the kiss and punched Rory off his feet. After that, they fought with such brutal ferocity that no one ventured near them. Rory was grinning even as he beat her face. She sang a hauntingly beautiful battle song that stirred Hamish's heart as he listened.

Hamish soared over the fighting at first, just watching the lines crash together. Boulders and Rumblers beat on each other with unrestrained fury. Few received major injuries, and they looked like they'd happily pummel each other all day, if given the chance.

Martys started singing a discordant highland chant as he plunged into the fight against his own countrymen. Hamish was impressed. If only they could settle the war with an enormous bash fight. The armies would have so much more fun, and they'd save countless lives.

Hamish decided he could watch Erich fighting Tomas and Cameron for hours. The two Fast Rollers worked together perfectly, even while they insulted each other and teased Erich relentlessly. They hit with fists like hammers, and no matter how many times Erich pounded them off their feet, they rebounded, grinning as widely as he was.

The two fought with brutal efficiency. Even though Erich was one of the best bash fighters among the Rumblers, their combined attacks thundered into him and tumbled him to the ground again and again. His skin cracked in half a dozen places from their brutal beating, but he didn't seem to care.

Shouted battle cries, grunts of pain, and the crack of mortal combat echoed around the melee. Hamish rose to twenty feet and surveyed the scene with satisfaction. Talk about an excellent diversion.

Cameron took a brutal hit from Erich, but only staggered back a step and laughed. "Your voice hurts more than those girly fists of yours ever will."

Then Martys shoved a fist into his mouth and the two tumbled to the ground, rolling and beating on each other with unrestrained glee.

"You face break eye," Erich laughed at Tomas as the two of them exchanged a rapid flurry of heavy punches.

"And you talk like a baby," Tomas retorted.

Erich grabbed him by the head and threw him into a knot of struggling warriors nearby. The entire group went down in a heap of pummeling brutes. Erich raised his fists in triumph and roared with battle fury.

"Big baby. Throw tantrum." Cameron laughed, landing a flying kick into Erich's ribs and sending him sprawling face-first into the dirt.

Hamish was tempted to intervene, to test his new battle suit enhancements, but he didn't want to interrupt their fun. Martys was fighting like a Rumbler who finally found his way home. Erich plunged into the thickest of the fighting, flinging soldiers from both armies out of the way to face Tomas again, singing louder than ever. They might be bitter enemies, but they shared the simple joy of brutal bash fighting.

Hamish felt a stirring of battle fury as he watched. He had to go meet Verena, but he needed to hit someone first. Even Ilse was participating. He caught sight of her punching Gregor, then the ground erupted between them.

If the tertiaries were entering the battle, that might wreck the whole bash fight. Hamish was out of time. He scanned the battlefield again and noticed a group of Boulders had formed into a tight knot on the right flank and were pushing the Rumblers back.

Perfect. Hamish soared over that way and tossed a midget pounder to the ground at the leading edge of those Boulders. The little wall rose only two feet, just high enough to plow into soldiers' knees.

It slid south for ten feet, sending Boulders tumbling in every direction and shattering their tight little unit. Rumblers swarmed the fallen Boulders, beating them back to the ground as they tried to rise.

In a tiny pocket of calm, one burly Obrioner Boulder looked up at Hamish and waved mightily. "Hey, coward! Come face a real man."

That was exactly what Hamish was looking for. So he settled to the ground several feet away from the man, ready to unleash everything at him when he charged.

Someone tackled him from behind.

It felt like he was run over by one of his own speedcrack walls. The impact blasted him off his feet and knocked the wind out of him. He crashed to the ground before he could think to activate his thrusters, and a heavy weight slammed on top of him.

Strong arms encircled him, and he was surprised to hear a woman's voice speak into his ear. "For someone who's supposed to be so dangerous, you're an idiot."

"Just trying to fit in," Hamish croaked, struggling in vain against her powerful grip. "You've mastered the whole hitting a guy while his back is turned perfectly."

The woman growled, "I'm going to squeeze you to jelly, and my boyfriend's going to rip your head off. We'll be heroes! The first to kill a Builder in three centuries."

Hamish had blind coal available, but that wasn't nearly sporting enough. "Murder isn't heroic."

He activated tiny jets set into the torso of his suit. They ejected a film of slime that he and Jean had developed just the night before. As it coated the leaves of his battle jacket, they became slick and he managed to twist in the woman's grasp to face her.

She grinned at him. "You can't escape, Builder. The last face you'll see before you die is mine."

Her boyfriend hovered close by, laughing and making sure no one interfered. "Rip him in half, love!"

Hamish shuddered. She wasn't exactly ugly, but she wasn't Jean. "And the last thing you'll see for a while is this."

Squeezing his eyes shut, he activated a couple pieces of limestone set into the outside of his helmet. Light blazed so bright, it turned his vision from black to white, even behind his eyelids. The woman shouted in surprise, but did not loosen her deadly grip.

Perfect.

Hamish ignited a tiny piece of quartzite at the base of one of three little vials set into protective sheaths along the sides of his helmet.

Extract of milked skunk.

The vial blasted into the woman's open mouth and splattered against the back of her throat.

She gagged, then her entire body stiffened. Half a second later, she screamed and threw Hamish away. He activated thrusters and caught himself four feet off the ground, then pivoted to look at the results of all his hard work.

The woman was howling and scrambling around on the ground, shoveling handfuls of dirt into her mouth. Her skin had shifted from granite-hardened gray to sickly green. She vomited explosively all over herself several times.

Each heave grew more powerful than the last, until it looked like she was trying to suck her feet up through her stomach and spit them into the nasty pile of chunky liquid splattering her and the ground all around. Even from several feet away, the strong stench of skunk was nearly overwhelming.

Her gaping boyfriend glared at Hamish. "What did you do to her, you demon?"

"I promised to kiss her. I think she's overreacting, don't you?"

The Boulder shouted with rage and charged. "I'll rip your arms off!"

He was a lot more optimistic than intelligent.

Hamish swooped at the man and twisted in the air to avoid the grasping hands. As he flew past, he shoved a diorite dart down the front of the man's leather pants.

The muted thump of the single grain of diorite exploding was followed by a remarkably high-pitched shriek. The man clutched his groin and toppled to the ground next to his still-shrieking girlfriend, who promptly threw up all over him.

As Hamish soared into the air, he lifted his hands in victory. He'd started developing the battle suit to prove he could face down Petralists and win.

Mission accomplished.

Feeling completely satisfied, Hamish threw wide the release rate of his thrusters and accelerated into the air. Time for his part in the morning's assault.

As he flew high over the barren valley, the entire might of the Obrioner army began advancing north to battle. He thought about Ingrid, and the pain and terror in her voice as she'd faced death alone, but with remarkable bravery. She was no bash fighter, but she'd saved countless lives. He vowed again to do whatever it took to get those sculpted stones and prevent another elfonnel from rising.

Both armies were advancing, and in the distance he spotted a tiny speck dive out of the concealing clouds a couple miles above the Obrioner command center.

He angled to intercept Verena, hoping they'd find General Carbrey when they struck. If the mega-stench didn't render him useless, Hamish had another vial of milked skunk extract with Carbrey's name on it.

Chapter Fifty-Nine

"But 'Rena, your heart's fickle as the weather.
You broke poor Mattias' heart like a feather.
You just had to fly, not even a good-bye.
Now he pines for the days you spent together."

~Saskia

I'll consider your offer," Connor told Shona, and she grinned like she'd already won his promise to return to Merkland with her.

She looked so relieved, so happy, it seemed she honestly believed her crazy proposal. That was so messed up on so many levels.

"You love your father?" he asked.

"Of course I do."

"But you're willing to help me kill him?"

"For the greater good, it's a sacrifice I'm willing to make," she told him, assuming a tragic but determined expression.

"You love me?"

She gave him such a tender look, he felt the stirrings of emotion that he'd thought long dead. "Oh, Connor, of course I do."

"So how long before you decide it's time to kill me for the greater good too?"

"That's not fair. Connor, I want to spend my life with you, share everything with you!" She squeezed his hands and actual tears threatened to spill from her eyes. She might be crazy, but she was passionate about it.

"Since you agree your father is evil, I think it's time I share with my troops some of the truths I've learned."

Shona blinked a couple of times as she shifted from vowing eternal adoration to defending the family name. "Connor, spreading lies about my father won't help, and it could end up damaging our position."

Meaning her position.

"What I have to say is important. They need to know the truth."

Would she really agree and accept the potential damage to her own high position? Was she ready to sacrifice a fraction of what she was asking from him?

"All right. I owe you something to prove I'm being forthright."

"Really?" he blurted out. That might be the first real concession she'd ever made.

"But I need something in return."

That was the Shona he knew. He got a mental image of a pedra promising a kiss only to fling open its disgusting, double-jawed mouth to rip his head off. "You're already asking me to give you a lot."

"But you haven't promised yet. I know you'll see reason eventually, but I need a token gesture today."

"What token?"

She gave him a slow, inviting smile. "In the eyes of our nation, we're still betrothed. I need everyone to recognize that you and I are still connected, despite your current mission." She leaned closer and said softly, "Go, speak with them, Connor. But afterward you have to kiss me in front of the entire company."

"Shona--" he began, but she raised a hand to cut him off.

"Kiss me like you mean it. That is my price for allowing you to defame the name of my father. When you recognize that my proposal is the best possible solution and return to me, it must seem inevitable to everyone."

Connor hesitated, and he decided maybe he did hate her. She still didn't seem to realize there were other ways to try swaying him to her side. On the other hand, he had survived many kisses with Shona. Could he really walk away from this chance to address all of these noble-born Petralists and begin to share the truth with them?

"I need your answer, Connor," Shona said. "We don't have much time.

She was right. The exchange was about to begin and the valley would erupt into battle shortly thereafter.

"All right, Shona," Connor said, although every word felt like lead in his mouth. He couldn't believe he was agreeing, but he didn't see any other way.

She gave him a warm smile that seemed to hold true affection. "I love how smart you are, dear Connor. I can always count on you to make wise choices."

As Connor led her back to the waiting company, he wracked his brain for a way to escape his promise. Maybe if he angered Shona enough, she might attack him and force him to beat her senseless. Then he could tell her that he kissed her while she was sleeping.

Shona was an incredibly talented kisser, but she wasn't Verena.

As the students all gathered close, Connor considered his words. "After speaking with Shona, we've agreed that you all deserve to understand some of what's really behind this war effort."

Catriona said, "We understand the need to bring Granadure back under our rule and stamp out their abominable Builders."

"That's not what this is all about. High Lord Dougal has orchestrated this war for personal vengeance against Kilian."

"The man who murdered his wife?" Ivor asked.

"His wife was tampering with elfonnel powers," Connor explained. "She would have lost control and killed hundreds."

"You can't know that," Shona said.

"Actually, I can. There are risks that they were purposefully ignoring that guaranteed she would have died, and would have killed many along with her, including him."

"How can you know that?" Fearghas asked.

They were listening, and that encouraged him. Soon they would understand the truth.

"That's what I've been studying. Dougal knows the risks now, but he's summoning elfonnel anyway. He killed Redmund."

Fearghas frowned. "Connor, we were there. Redmund somehow raised an elfonnel and smashed through the pass. The Grandurians killed him with some kind of Builder devilry. High Lord Dougal was in his tent the entire time."

Connor shook his head. "High Lord Dougal gave Redmund that sculpted stone, knowing that he would tap it to exhaustion. By doing so, Redmund placed himself in Dougal's power. He has a way of seizing the mind of a Petralist in that state, and he was the one who raised an elfonnel through Redmund's sacrifice."

He paused to let the truth sink in, and was astonished to see many of the students glance at each other and shrug, as if it didn't matter.

Shona was frowning. "Even if what you're saying is true, Redmund had agreed to lead the charge. The way he did it saved a lot of lives."

Many of the students nodded in agreement, although Ivor looked troubled. Connor tried again. "Dougal lied. He set Redmund up to sacrifice his life. Redmund never had a choice."

"You were a Guardian," Fearghas said. "So you should understand that the lives of soldiers under a high lord's command are his to use as he sees fit. Through Redmund he won a great victory. How he did it doesn't really matter to the houses. He won, and fewer people died as a result."

Fearghas did not look happy explaining that, but Connor could see that the other students, sons and daughters of the high lords and high ladies of the realm, believed it. That was so frustrating!

Shona gave him an apologetic smile. "I understand what you're trying to do, Connor. Trying to make my father look evil justifies what you've felt you need to do. However, you're just wrong. He is not evil."

"Was it not evil that he sent Spitnail Camonica to die, to raise an elfonnel farther north in Granadure to lay waste to the Builder compound?"

"The Builder compound is destroyed?" Lorcc exclaimed, and Connor was surprised to see him smiling.

Many of the students cheered. They actually considered it a great victory. They had been taught all their lives that Builders were living incarnations of the Tallan's own evil. Eradicating Builders was one of the duties they were strictly commanded to enforce.

Connor felt sick. He struggled to reconcile the reality of the world as he saw it with the reality that they lived. These were his friends, people he cared about and would fight and sacrifice for.

So were Verena and Hamish and Kilian and other friends he was making in Granadure. To know that some of his friends were content with the destruction of other friends seemed illogical and deeply wrong.

Before he could figure out how to formulate a new argument to help them see, Shona spoke loudly, "Thank you all for helping me remind Connor of the truth. Grandurians have a way of twisting reality until even the best of us can begin to believe our cause is not just."

"We believe in you, General," Catriona encouraged him, and many of his friends nodded agreement.

Their happy blindness sickened him and enraged him, and he blurted out, "None of you know the truth! Your own parents are lying to you. Patronage is a lie, and unclaimed are created by a secret power stone that Dougal has kept concealed from everyone!"

Stunned silence greeted his words.

None of them had known. Even Shona looked shocked, although her expression quickly changed to one of thoughtful consideration. She was clever enough to put the pieces together. Ivor looked nervous as he watched the other students' reactions.

Connor insisted, "It's true. That's how I turned unclaimed at the Carraig during the battle with the elfonnel, and how I changed back. You all saw it."

"We saw something," Fearghas admitted.

"And none of you had ever seen the unclaimed before," Connor said, pressing the point. "It's because they don't exist without that secret affinity. Our entire society is built upon that giant lie."

"You have to be wrong," Catriona said. She was white-faced and trembling.

Shona leaned close to Connor and said softly, "Connor, you are such a good-intentioned fool. You don't even realize that you've just turned all of these potential allies into enemies."

"Stop twisting the truth, Shona," Connor snapped. "I'm trying to fix things."

"That doesn't fix anything!" Catriona shouted, and many other voices began clamoring in agreement, shouting that he was lying.

Shona gave him a pitying look and spoke so only he could hear. "Oh, Connor. If what you say is true, you're threatening to destroy Obrion. Without patronage and Guardians under our control, our society will be ripped apart by rebellion, and maybe civil war.

"Our houses, our power, our very lives are threatened. Once everyone has time to think through the ramifications of what you're saying, what conclusion do you think they'll reach? It can only be that you cannot be allowed to live and spread such a vicious, dangerous claim."

Already some of the students were glaring, and Connor realized she was right. He wanted to beat himself with a stick for a month. He needed to share that truth with the Guardians enslaved to the high houses, not with the heirs of the very corrupt system he needed to change.

He had forgotten who they were for a moment, but they never could.

Shona touched his cheek, her expression pitying. "Connor, don't delay. Come to me soon, and we'll figure out how to undo the damage you did today."

She was cracked and scrambled.

But she turned and raised her arms, shouting, "Calm down. I'm sure Connor is confused. Forget about it, and wait until I get to the bottom of the lies these Grandurians have been using to twist his mind."

Connor started to protest, but Ivor caught his shoulder and forcibly pulled him away from the angry crowd. "Sometimes you're brilliant Connor, but today you're naïve bordering on suicidal. Shut up and let Shona talk. You can't do any good now, and you'll only make it worse."

"You believe me, don't you?" Connor asked as he let Ivor pull him a couple dozen paces away from the crowd of students. He still considered them friends, but would they really try to kill him if he dared spread the truth to the Guardians who served them?

"I do, but you can't start a revolution with the ruling class, Connor."

"I just. . ." He trailed off, not sure how to explain it.

"I know, but today's not the day. We're about out of time."

The prisoner exchange was already under way. Connor tapped quartzite to his eyes and spotted Ilse, flanked by Anton, speaking with Gregor.

She planned to accuse him in a fittingly roundabout Sentry speak way of colluding with Dougal to raise that elfonnel at the Carraig. There were things about that day that they still didn't understand, and she hoped to get some information out of him.

Connor doubted she'd succeed. Sentry speak was notoriously difficult to interpret, and he secretly suspected that even the Sentries and Sappers who spouted the confusing lines didn't understand themselves more than half the time. That would explain why they didn't talk too much.

Still, Ilse had shared the line she planned to use on him first. "The mightiest ship is turned by a tiny tiller, but a single leak can invite the floodwaters to enter."

That was a good one, and it suggested that she knew some of Gregor's involvement and that his actions were undermining his own cause. Connor hoped it worked, but even if it didn't, the morning was shaping up perfectly for the battle to begin any second.

"Ivor, I heard Dougal gave you a sculpted stone at Harz."

Ivor nodded, a look of wonder on his face. "He certainly did."

"It's too dangerous to use. Give me what's left. I can make sure it's safe."

"I can't do that, Connor," Ivor said with a chuckle.

"Didn't you see what happened at Harz? Using those stones could shatter the ground and destroy us all."

"Only if I use it to raise an elfonnel. I don't think there's enough power left to ascend and do that, even if I wanted to."

Connor started to protest again, but Ivor shook his head. "That naive streak of yours is running a mile wide today, Connor. I understand the danger, and I won't use it unless I have to."

"You can't use it at all," Connor insisted.

"Perhaps. I respect what you're doing, Connor. I really do. And if the time is ever right, I might even help you with the revolution you're trying to start, but today is not the right time. I have my own responsibilities and my own future to worry about."

Connor couldn't believe what he was hearing. "You're going to stay, even though you know your patronage is a lie?"

Ivor shrugged. "Knowing the truth might offer certain advantages at some point, but right now my position is better than most of those born to noble houses. I've got command of a mighty army, I'm engaged to a beautiful, clever woman who wants me to rule her house with her. Turning traitor now wouldn't help anyone, least of all me."

Shona joined them, interrupting Connor's reply. She gave him a hard look. "You made a mess of that, Connor. You'll have to think deeper if we're going to accomplish all that we agreed to."

"I haven't agreed to anything yet," Connor told her angrily.

She sighed. "You're going to be obstinate and foolish again for a while, are you?"

"I think we're just about finished here," he said.

"Not quite yet." Her annoyed look faded to one of determination. "You still owe me that kiss."

"You've got to be kidding," Ivor said, incredulously.

Shona said, "We are still engaged, and Connor agreed to show the world that he still cares."

"Make that naive two miles wide," Ivor muttered, shaking his head. "Carry on. I'll assemble the company to watch."

Connor was tempted to punch him back to Harz. "Thanks for watching my back."

Ivor gave him a serious look. "A good laugh at your expense is exactly what they need to get over that monumental idiocy of yours. Make sure to look terrified, Connor. I know I would."

"Oh, begone," Shona snapped, then stepped in front of Connor, hands on hips, one eyebrow raised, a smile on her full lips. "No terror today, Connor. Show the world you love me."

Connor's heart began to pound, and he felt his hands turn sweaty. How had the morning turned out so messed up? As Shona drew closer, students began to whistle and call encouragement. Ivor might be right, but the price still seemed too high.

Shona drew his gaze to her. No one else could see her face, and in that brief instant, she allowed him to see how uncertain she felt. She bit her lower lip, a surprisingly vulnerable gesture.

Connor's feelings for Shona were powerful and completely conflicted. He'd been convinced more than once that he was in love with her, and many times had hated her. Usually he settled somewhere in between, but always confused.

She had worked so hard to manipulate him, but she had also chosen to release him from the marriage he could no longer escape. That sacrifice might have actually cost her a great deal. Shona was many things, but in that moment she seemed to be a girl trying to figure out her place in the world just as he was.

No, Shona knew her place. She was just trying to figure out the best way to get there.

"I only ever wanted us to be happy together," Shona said with a sad little smile.

Connor took a deep breath and considered blasting himself away with marble. "I always wanted to be the best Guardian I could for you, Shona. I just wished we both had a choice in the matter."

She took the last step to him, draping her hands over his shoulders, and leaning against him. He placed his hands on her waist to hold her back, and steeled himself for what was to come. He only hoped Verena wasn't watching. She would probably drop a bomb on his head.

"I know," Shona said softly. Her gaze was intense, and he could see real emotion building in her eyes. "You just need to know that I always would've chosen to be with you, no matter what."

She leaned in and brushed his lips with hers, barely making contact before pulling back again. He should tell her no right now, and Tallan take the consequences. It was just a foolish promise after all.

"You gave me your word," she reminded him, as if reading his mind. "Give me just one good kiss, and make sure I know you mean it."

Connor decided to just get it over with. He could find a way to make it up to Verena, and he probably had enough healing power left in the sculpted sandstone pendant to survive until she finally forgave him.

Ivor interrupted before he could. "Bash fight! Form ranks and prepare to move out."

Shona glanced over her shoulder, breaking the moment and glaring. "Can't the world wait just a minute?"

"Not today, Shona," Ivor called, beckoning her to join him. "Get over here and take command of your company."

The prisoner exchange had erupted into an enthusiastic bash fight. Connor easily spotted Anika and Rory in the center, wrestling in a tiny calm space amid the other bashing soldiers. Rory was trying to look serious, but Anika didn't even pretend she wasn't enjoying herself. Her bright smile shone with a purity that Mattias could never match.

The others were fighting with furious intensity, as if understanding they probably wouldn't get enough time. Hamish began to rise above the crowd, then plunged back down, and Connor lost sight of him in the press. He hoped Hamish didn't get distracted. He had work to do.

The rocky ground on the north side of the fight began to buckle, with earth fountaining high into the air. The earth movers were committed too.

Shona broke away, growling, "I'll kill every last one of them."

Connor barely believed his luck. Shona whirled back to face him and pressed a finger to his chest. "You owe me, and everyone here stands as witness. I will collect that kiss, and you cannot deny me."

"Well you did actually kiss me," Connor pointed out.

"Oh no. That was just a tease. The deal was you kiss me so that I know it. When I collect that kiss you better leave me blushing and about to pass out from lack of air."

Then she spun away and raced after the company that was already retreating toward the Obrioner army, which was advancing north to engage. Connor looked after her, wishing now that he had gotten it over with when he had the chance.

She was so worked up about it now, he might have to spend half a month kissing her to make her feel like she got what she deserved.

Chapter Sixty

"A pebble cast upon the mountain may yet unleash the avalanche."
~Evander

Verena dove out of the high, puffy cloud she'd been concealed in since just before dawn and plummeted in a vertical dive, straight toward Carbrey's central command area. Roaring wind tore at her as she accelerated faster than she ever had before, driven by every thruster and a towering rage.

"You're diving too fast," Hamish cautioned, his voice issuing through one of the speakstones attached to the inside of her helmet. She caught sight of him soaring up to meet her. "We want to surprise attack them, not surprise splatter ourselves all over them."

"You're late," Verena growled. The rational part of her mind recognized that she was taking a foolish risk, but the rest of her told that part to shut up.

A moment ago, while scanning the valley, she'd again focused her long-vision goggles on Connor and his meeting with the students from the Carraig.

"You idiot," she cursed at the memory of Connor standing close to Shona, her arms around his neck, his hands on her waist, while she leaned in to kiss him.

She'd tried to warn him that Shona could not be trusted, but he'd gone anyway. Had he known she'd try to seduce him again? Had he honestly thought he could withstand her manipulations? Or had he secretly looked forward to another chance to kiss the beautiful Shona?

"What did I do now?" Hamish asked.

"I wasn't speaking to you," Verena snapped, trying to control her seething rage as she plunged toward the camp. Carbrey's Pathfinders had surely spotted Hamish's approach, but she doubted anyone was ready for her insane dive.

The first of the Altkalen secret defensive measures was about to be released. Even she didn't know exactly what they had planned, but at the moment she didn't care.

She hoped whatever it was killed Shona. Slowly.

Elements of the Obrioner army were already advancing, with Boulder companies in the center, Striders ranging along the flanks, and auxiliary troops marching east and west. It looked like they planned to circle the valley and attack Altkalen from the sides.

Hamish asked, "Did you give Connor the new speakstone mechanical? Did you hear how the meeting went? Did he get anything good from Shona?"

"He didn't have it turned on," Verena said. From what she'd seen, Shona was the one who got what she wanted, not Connor.

"By the way, you'd better pull up," Hamish said, worry growing in his voice.

Verena was plunging toward the cloth-protected central command area of the Obrioner camp fast enough to outrace a diving hawk. She'd fallen below a thousand feet, and at her rate of descent, she'd plow into the ground in a matter of seconds. She had planned to dive at a steep angle and swoop over the camp to launch her strike, but a new idea fit her mood better.

Snapping closed the rear thrusters, Verena threw wide the forward thrusters, and the Swift decelerated rapidly, her protective front panel driving into her chest as her weight dragged against her safety harnesses.

The Swift was nimble, with thrusters on every plane, but the biggest were in the rear. The much smaller thrusters on the front would never stop her before she crashed.

"Pull up!" Hamish shouted.

Verena was too focused on the fast-approaching ground to respond, calculating her timing, and trying to ignore a rush of fear that maybe this hadn't been such a good idea.

At one hundred feet, still dropping like a diving pedra, Verena snapped close the forward thrusters while triggering directional thrusters that pivoted the Swift back to an upright position. At the same time, she threw wide the release rate on all of the marble blocks lining the underside of the Swift.

The Puking Dooms erupted with white-hot flame that roared like lions and boiled down through the air, vaporizing the protective covering over most of the command area. The up-force of the flames drove against the downward momentum of the Swift, and the force change felt like someone had dropped a wagonload of stone on her shoulders.

Verena groaned from the strain, and her fear spiked higher as she realized that although the Swift was rapidly slowing, she had triggered the Puking Dooms a second too late. She was barely fifty feet above the tents, which were erupting into flames while officers were fleeing the sudden firestorm, and she was still falling far too fast.

So Verena tilted the Swift up just a bit and ignited the full force of the rear thrusters. The Swift leaped forward, its downward momentum shifting in two terrifying heartbeats to horizontal speed.

She remembered to toss over the side the tiny vial that Gisela had given to her, containing a dozen drops of the murky mega-stench. Then all she could do was hold on and scream with fear and defiance while the Swift roared away, barely clearing the tops of the tall tents. She flashed over them for more than a hundred yards before she managed to pull higher and bank back around.

Hamish had slowed to a hover about three hundred feet above the scorched central command area. The fires had already been seized by a Firetongue and were whipping into the air behind Verena. If she hadn't changed direction and fled so quickly, she might have been consumed before she could escape.

Then the fires, which had been compressed into well-formed spears, dissolved into a shower of flame. She didn't need Connor's enhanced hearing to tell that the mega-stench was already working.

As she rose and banked to join Hamish, she enjoyed a perfect view of the chaos she'd unleashed upon the camp. Gisela had described the mega-stench as the most horrific smell imaginable.

It looked like she'd underestimated it.

Men and women were screaming, clawing at their eyes and noses and vomiting with explosive force all over each other. They rushed blindly about, seeking escape from the unparalleled assault on their senses that seemed to make them wish they had simply died. People trampled over each other in their desperate attempt to escape the stench.

The high walls of cloth surrounding the center of camp billowed as they fell to the ground, cast aside as their bearers fled. Within seconds the area cleared, except for a few people lying prone and unmoving.

Verena couldn't tell if they'd only fainted. She feared they might be Pathfinders who had been using their enhanced sense of smell when the mega-stench struck. The shock might have killed them.

Hamish breathed, "That's amazing. And by the way, you're officially insane."

"Look what it's doing to them," Verena said, barely believing it. That tiny bit of liquid had excised the heart of Carbrey's army in seconds. The chaos was still expanding.

If only they had more. With a gallon of the stuff, they could send the entire army fleeing. Of course, if the wind blew the wrong way, it could depopulate Altkalen too.

Although the mega-stench had definitely disrupted the central command area, the bulk of the army was unaffected and probably didn't even realize what had happened. Thousands of soldiers were marching north to meet the Grandurians, led by the bulk of the Petralists. They would reach the stripped area of naked rock in seconds, and then the battle would really begin.

Many people had fled toward a row of cook tents a couple hundred yards away. They were splashing water on their faces, or rubbing spices across their skin to try masking the stench. At least one Firetongue had surrounded herself with flames, but she was vomiting so profusely, it didn't seem to be helping.

They should have run a different way.

Without warning, the central cook tent erupted from within. A strange, gray foamy mass exploded from under it. That foamy material grew with astonishing speed, like an inverted waterfall, smashing aside cook fires and tents and piles of food stores. It completely surprised the distracted soldiers, engulfing everything like a twelve-foot, sticky tidal wave.

It rolled over scores of soldiers, but slowed after about a hundred feet and quickly hardened into a lumpy, gray hill where once the cooking area had stood. Verena spotted several Boulders breaking free, but even with their enhanced strength, it would take them long seconds to escape the clingy mess. It looked like there was enough air in the foam that no one would suffocate, but it would take hours of heavy labor to free everyone.

They wouldn't get hours.

Within seconds, two other eruptions of the strange foam exploded through other cook areas. Then another amazing eruption of the same material rippled down through the long lines of latrines along the edge of camp. It flung debris and excrement into the air and no doubt added another layer of stench over the already unbearable smell.

The Assassins had done their work perfectly.

Hamish laughed and rolled completely over backward. "I really need to learn what that stuff is!"

Verena could think of little more dangerous than that stench in Hamish's hands. "Be happy with that skunk stink you milked."

"Hey, I got to try it out. It was spectacular."

She'd take his word for it. She hated skunks. She would like to study that sticky foam, though. Gisela had called it Pedra's Spittle. That soft-spoken Althin had shattered the center of the camp with her chemical weapons, and Verena wondered what else her countrymen had developed to deal with Petralist incursions.

Verena said, "Let's get down there while we can."

She descended in a more controlled dive this time and settled the Swift into a hover inches above the ground outside the charred remnants of General Carbrey's command tent. She kept the nozzles of her speedslings pointed at the ruined tent, but no one remained to challenge them. She hadn't seen Carbrey, but hoped he'd gotten a whiff of the mega-stench. It would serve him right.

Hamish landed nearby in a rush of thrusters, but almost immediately pitched forward onto his hands and knees, vomiting explosively into the inside of his helmet.

"What's wrong?" Verena exclaimed, pivoting the Swift, ready to unleash a storm of hornets, but saw no threat.

She flew to his side and landed, leaping out of the Swift and dropping to one knee beside him. It seemed the entire ground was covered in vomit from those caught in the mega-stench. The sight was disgusting, but she didn't smell any of it. She had activated enough quartzite inside of her helmet to force a positive pressure that prevented the stench from entering.

Hamish laughed, then vomited again. He peeled his helmet back and scraped the inside covering. His eyes were red and watering, and he looked absolutely green.

"I can't believe your helmet failed," Verena said.

Hamish shook his head and staggered to his feet. "The helmet's fine."

He gave her a lopsided grin, then clutched at his nose and twisted away to throw up one more time. Obviously holding his breath, he splashed water across the inside of his helmet to clean it off, then reattached it.

His voice came through the speakstone in her helmet a few seconds later. "I had to know. I've experienced some wonderful smells in my life, but I've never seen anything that could clear a camp. I couldn't live with myself without knowing how it felt."

"You've got to be kidding." Verena sighed, tempted to slap him on the side of the head. She should have known.

Instead, she took his arm and led him into the command tent to complete their mission. He wobbled, but managed to stay on his feet.

Hamish looked around and muttered, "No Carbrey. Wish he'd gotten a whiff of that stuff."

"You saw what it did to those men and women, and you exposed yourself to that on purpose?" Verena asked, still barely believing it.

"Of course. We're researchers. It's what we do. Can you honestly say you're not the least bit interested in understanding how it works?"

Verena explored the tent, a throwing dagger in one hand and a piece of marble in the other. She was tensed and ready to fight, but the tent was completely empty.

She gave Hamish an incredulous look. "It was abundantly clear how it works. A stench that vicious is worse than a skunk family reunion. Why would I want to experience that for myself?"

"You don't get it at all," Hamish said, then made a gagging sound and clutched at his face. He didn't throw up that time, but breathed fast and shallow for a moment. "It's more like a skunk family reunion, condensed a thousand times, then shoved directly into your brain. And even that's not bad enough. It's like the Tallan's own. . .I don't even know."

"Which is why you should've kept your helmet on."

Verena explored farther, passing the command table cluttered with blackened charts and maps. She stepping into the back room that held Carbrey's personal effects.

"It was a life-altering experience," Hamish said in a tone of wonder.

His voice still sounded unsteady, and he bumped into a few chairs as he followed her, but that wasn't exactly unusual for him.

Under Carbrey's own bunk she found what she was looking for and dragged out a heavy, wooden strongbox, banded with iron.

In his suit, Hamish easily ripped the lock off, and Verena had to admit he was a handy guy to have around when he wasn't puking on the floor. She eased open the lid and breathed a sigh of relief. Inside, nestled into padded individual slots, were eight beautifully sculpted stones, most smaller than her fist.

"Whoa!" Hamish exclaimed.

Verena reverently touched an exquisite pink marble carving, shaped like the head of a pedra. Its strange, overlapping outer jaws were gaping wide, with fire pouring out its inner jaws.

She touched it with her Builder senses and gasped at the vast power contained in that tiny stone. It felt like the heart of a raging forest fire, condensed and magnified almost beyond comprehension. She didn't dare try releasing even a fraction of its power. That would incinerate her, Hamish, and everything within fifty yards.

Hamish reached out to touch it, but Verena slapped his fingers away. "Don't. This thing is too dangerous. I wish I hadn't touched it."

"Really?" He eagerly reached out again.

She slapped his hand away again, harder. "Don't. Now's not the time."

"We were looking for seven, but there's eight."

"Maybe one of the ones that had been loaned out to Ivor or Gregor was returned," Verena suggested. "Whatever the reason, it looks like they're all here. Let's go."

Hamish hefted the crate and brought it with them. While he carried it to the Swift and placed it in the supply box in the back, Verena paused to gather up all the maps and documents she could. Many were singed, and some so badly burned they looked unreadable, but she stuffed them all together into a canvas sack she'd brought along for that purpose.

Before she left, she applied a thin layer of special adhesive to the underside of the table, then pressed a thinly cut piece of quartzite to it. Wedged in the junction of two of the supports, it would be very hard to notice.

She activated it. The stone was already paired with another she carried in her satchel, but not like a full speakstone. This was only a listening stone that would allow her to hear everything around the table without the risk of transmitting anything back the other way.

Feeling very satisfied, she tucked the sack of papers into the supply box on top of the crate of sculpted stones. It was amazing to think that so much treasure, so much vital intelligence, and such an unrivaled threat to her country could fit in that single, small space.

"No one'll wreck the continent today," Hamish said proudly.

Then the ground shook and they shared a worried look. The fighting was about to begin. The two of them rocketed into the air, not slowing until they returned to the clouds that would shield their flight back to the Grandurian lines.

That high up, they should be safe, but Verena didn't plan to take any chances. If Carbrey realized what they'd taken, he'd try everything to strike them down and retrieve those stones.

She glanced down at the battlefield as they flew north. Both armies had reached the edges of the stripped, rocky ground, and the Obrioners were pushing north, up the road. Their Sentries were expanding the road so a hundred soldiers could advance abreast.

The Grandurian army had stopped, although twin mountains of earth were growing on the flanks of the front lines. Verena couldn't tell where they were pulling all that earth from, but it was obvious they were preparing for a major strike.

No doubt that's what the Obrioners would believe too. They knew about the Altkalen supply of earth, so they'd focus on that.

Verena hoped whatever surprise Saskia and Ulrich had prepared was ready, because pitched battle was about to begin.

CHAPTER SIXTY-ONE

"The wind that one day will rise into the mighty tempest is but a gentle breeze until that fateful day."

~Evander

Connor landed beside Ilse and Lukas atop a long, mounded ridge of earth at the rear of the main Grandurian army. He'd soared over the valley with wings of fire and spotted the Crushers preparing to load into their windriders. The ridge was about a dozen feet tall and shielded them from Obrioner view. It also made a pretty good spot for watching the initial stages of the main battle.

The Grandurian army had stopped at the edge of the rocky middle ground, facing the advancing Obrioner forces. Rumblers made up the center, positioned where the road extended into the middle ground. Wingrunners and other troops flanked them or massed behind. The majority of the non-Petralist soldiers were marching east and west to intercept the wide Obrioner flanking maneuvers.

The Obrioner auxiliaries outnumbered the Grandurians by at least two-to-one, so Connor hoped they had a few Builder mechanicals to help even the odds. Otherwise they faced a desperate battle to protect the flanks, and he doubted many Petralists would be available to render aid.

"How did your meeting go?" Ilse asked.

"Not as well as I'd hoped. Shona is difficult," Connor admitted.

Ilse raised one eyebrow. "Did you expect anything else?"

"Not really. It's still frustrating, though."

Lukas said, "You'll have plenty of opportunity to take out your frustrations on other Obrioners soon enough."

"When do we go?" Connor asked, glancing back at the Crushers.

The men and women of the elite company looked tough. Most were Rumblers, although he spotted one Wingrunner in each ten-person squad. They wore leather and steel armor similar, if less fancy, than his own new suit.

They bristled with weapons, including war hammers, axes, and swords. They carried a lot of throwing weapons, from small axes, to knives, to javelins. At least one in every squad carried tightly-rolled nets in sheaths on their backs. Others had whips coiled at their hips. They looked grim and eager for their dangerous mission of attacking the tertiary Petralists.

Ilse maintained her usual calm. "Soon. For now, watch. Verena and Hamish took off from the enemy camp a moment ago, so hopefully their mission succeeded better than yours."

That reminded Connor of his mini-hub. He lifted his left arm and turned the keystone to line up with the speakstone that would link him to Verena.

"Verena, can you hear me?" he asked, speaking close to the stone.

No reply. He tried again, then switched to Hamish, but still no reply. He glanced at Ilse, who shrugged and showed him the mini-hub affixed to her left arm.

"She gave me one too, but warned me the range is short."

"I'll try again in a minute." He hoped nothing had gone wrong.

The advancing Obrioner army had already covered almost half of the middle ground up the road toward the waiting Grandurians. Heavily-armored Boulders led the way, carrying massive shields.

With the Sentries widening the road, he wondered if all the work to strip away the earth was really worth it. The labor didn't seem to be slowing them down.

Then the ground collapsed under their front ranks.

There was no warning. The ground under the roadway and for twenty yards to either side simply vanished, tumbling half a hundred Boulders out of sight into the earth.

"What happened?" Connor exclaimed.

He wondered if Captain Peadar was among those armored Boulders who had just fallen and probably died with no chance to defend themselves. He realized with a grim, sinking feeling that those were but the first of many casualties.

Ilse was frowning. "That area is supposed to be solid rock, but I felt Anton's presence briefly. It was just a hint, and it's already gone."

"He can't walk through solid rock, can he?" Lukas asked.

"I don't think so. That's simple volcanic rock, not power-grade stone. I don't understand how that hole was made."

Connor tapped marble and blasted himself into the air on a column of fire. Ilse and Lukas scurried back from the flames, shouting at him to be more careful. He'd apologize later.

He focused on the huge hole gaping across the roadway. With quartzite-enhanced vision and the vantage of two hundred feet of altitude, he saw deep into the vertical-sided pit plunging into the earth, but did not see the bottom.

The walls of the pit were scored with chisel marks. Connor had grown up in a quarry village, so he easily recognized the signs of stone work.

He reduced the tap rate of marble and settled back toward the earth. It seemed the Altkalen defenses had been under construction for a while. They'd mined under their own road.

Anton would only have needed to strike the spot to crack the thin covering that remained over the pit. Until that moment, it would have felt like solid rock to any Sentries who scanned it. It was a clever and chilling tactic.

As soon as he touched down, Connor tapped slate and quested in that direction with his earth senses. He felt nothing but a blank, unbroken wall of rock that he could not penetrate.

So he switched to soapstone and connected with the many water-filled fissures that criss-crossed the solid stone of the valley. He discovered a deep pool of scalding hot water two hundred feet below the roadway beneath that hole.

At the bottom of that pool he found the fallen soldiers. Burdened by all that armor and heavy weapons, they must have sunk like rocks.

It felt wrong to just leave them lying there, but he wasn't sure what to do. Then he felt the waters moving. He sensed Kilian and other presences also touching the waters and driving them up.

"Look," Connor pointed.

The Obrioner army had retreated from the gaping hole, but more earth was already beginning to flow over it. No doubt the Sentries were reinforcing their work to ensure the soldiers could march across without falling, even if the underlying ground fell away again.

Water erupted from the partially-closed hole like an upside-down waterfall. The ground rumbled, and water exploded from hundreds of other holes in the ground, spraying high into the air, then pivoting toward the Obrioner army.

The Water Moccasins had entered the fight.

Most of the water targeted the Boulders exposed on the roadway, although some of it leaped across the middle ground toward the bulk of the Obrioner Petralists. The first blast of water from the huge hole swept an entire hundred-man company of Boulders from the roadway, tumbling them across the rough, rocky middle ground like leaves in the Wick during the spring thaw.

As the other soldiers fled the danger, the churning waters slowed, then stopped. The wall of water boiling across the middle ground toward the Obrioner army halted before reaching the soldiers.

Ilse frowned. "What were they thinking, hitting with water? The Spitters can counter that too easily."

Boulders who had been scattered across the middle ground were struggling to stand. They looked battered, but otherwise unhurt. Connor had to agree with Ilse. The elemental attack seemed impressive, but they should have waited until the Obrioner Spitters were distracted.

Lukas said, "Now the tug-the-rope contest begins. Might be they're trying to distract the tertiaries. Would make a good time for us to prepare to jump."

"If that's what they intended, they should have warned us," Ilse growled, then waved a signal to the waiting soldiers below. The men and women of the Crushers scrambled for their windriders.

Connor turned the keystone on his mini-hub to point to the speakstone marked Kilian and raised it to his mouth. "Kilian, can you hear me?"

"Connor? How did your meeting go?"

"Just like old times."

"That bad?"

"Pretty much. I'm with the Crushers. Should they prepare to attack?"

"Not yet. The main event is about to begin."

The ground began to shake, and that shaking intensified until it was hard to stay upright. Connor had not expected an earthquake. For a moment he feared Verena's mission had failed and Dougal had raised another earth-bound elemental.

He twisted his mini-hub. "Verena, can you hear me?"

She responded immediately and sounded excited. "Connor, where are you?"

Then her voice turned cold. "We need to talk."

Connor's heart sank. Had she seen him and Shona? He'd wised for more time to think of a proper way to explain the situation to her.

"I'm with Ilse and the Crushers. Where are you? Did you get the sculpted stones?"

"Our mission was a complete success," she said happily, and he breathed a sigh of relief. "The mega-stench worked better than we'd hoped, and we got eight sculpted stones."

"Eight? That's even better than we'd hoped for."

So Dougal couldn't have raised an elfonnel. Connor didn't see the mountains of earth on the army flanks moving, so why was the ground shaking? "Where are you?"

"We're monitoring the battle from up in the clouds. We'll rendezvous with you and the Crushers as you begin your attack."

In that moment, an enormous fissure gaped open in the center of the middle ground. Another geyser of superheated water erupted forth, covering the land in a deadly, hot mist.

The air was growing foul with the smell of sulfur and the other minerals in the waters. Connor frowned. More water wasn't going to change the situation.

The lava, though, was a total surprise.

Connor gasped as a river of molten stone boiled out of the fissure, spewing a hundred feet into the air. The rotten-egg scent of sulfur grew sharp, and the temperature rose twenty degrees.

He tapped quartzite to his ears and clearly heard the cries of dismay from the Obrioner soldiers, particularly those Boulders stuck out on the rough, rocky middle ground.

Those cries turned into screams of fear as the lava spread rapidly across the middle ground, then started rolling south in a thirty foot wall of molten stone.

No doubt the Sentries tried to stop it, but lava was a brilliant tactic. It was rock, but it was also fire. Just as the mud during the battle at Harz had momentarily baffled the Sentries and Spitters, lava could only be manipulated by earth and fire working together. Worse, with the ground stripped of earth, Sentries lacked any ready material to raise barrier walls to block the lava.

The signature tower of mighty Anton the Sapper rose at the forward edge of the Grandurian army. Kilian stood beside Anton. Again water and fire flowed around the outside of the tower, forming ancient symbols of power.

Driven by the two mighty Petralists, the flood of lava rolled south, gaining speed as it went, leaving a thin layer of red-hot, molten stone behind. The Boulders stranded on the middle ground scrambled to retreat, but the jagged, uneven ground was treacherous, and most of them were too slow. The lava rolled right over them.

418

Connor suddenly wished he had released quartzite. The agonized screams from those soldiers were brief, but all the more intense for that brevity. He glanced at Ilse, whose expression had turned grim where she stood holding hands with Lukas.

Connor took a deep, steadying breath, but the sulfur-laden air made him cough. A strong breeze picked up from the north, blowing the worst of the smell toward the Obrioners. He wasn't sure if Longseers had pulled the breeze in, but he was grateful for it. As the lava rolled toward the Obrioner lines, he hoped his friends weren't in its path.

The Obrioner army began to retreat.

Lukas said, "Time to go. We'll drop while they're distracted by the lava."

Ilse raised her mini-hub to her lips and said, "This is Commander Ilse. Tell Wolfram that the Crushers are preparing to attack."

They clambered aboard the high pilot bench at the front of the first wagon. Forty troops were crammed into the long benches in the back. As soon as they were seated, their Builder pilot activated the huge thrusters. A howling wind blasted around them, filling the air with dust, but washing away some of the sulfur reek.

As the wagons rose ponderously into the air, a second group of wagons rose on the opposite flank of the army. Dierk flew the lead wagon, with three other windriders following close behind, carrying the first-wave strike teams. Jean flew the last wagon.

Despite all the time she'd spent helping the rest of them fine-tune their armor and prepare for battle, she had found a little time for herself too. Even though she was no soldier, she was flying troops over the battlefield, and she'd dressed for the occasion.

Today she wore a white silk shirt under a form-fitting leather vest, with leather bracers on her forearms. A wide leather belt encircled her narrow waist, loaded with vials and pouches of medicine. Brown leather boots peeked out from under her dark green skirt, and a larger medical kit hung from a strap on her back. She'd braided her long blond hair, and wore a leather headband.

Jean had proved many times she was far more than just the most brilliant person who had ever lived in Alasdair, and she was doing it again. She looked nervous but determined as she flew her enormous wagon filled with Rumblers and a truly nasty surprise.

Most of the Flameweavers in Altkalen had participated in summoning creatures that appeared roughly man-shaped. Dressed in spare bits of leather armor, they looked enough like soldiers that no one would think anything different until it was too late.

The summoned creatures would drop just before the first wave of Rumblers. When they landed, and once they were surrounded by enemy soldiers, they would detonate, spewing their flame-filled cores over the unsuspecting troops. Dierk had come up with the idea, and even suggested they add a tiny bit of diorite to each one to magnify the explosions.

Connor still shuddered at the cold brutality of those summonings. Hamish had dubbed them bomb-cases.

Dierk had looked disgusted with himself for suggesting the idea at all, but then had added, "They killed Ingrid. They brought this war, and by Tallan's blessed memory, they will regret it."

While the first wave accelerated toward the lava-covered middle ground, the second wave of windriders with their load of Crushers continued to ascend, awaiting their turn to strike. Down on the valley floor, the lava had nearly reached the Obrioner side of the middle ground. All the forward elements of the army had begun retreating from the onslaught, which their Sentries did not yet seem able to stop.

As the ranks of soldiers retreated from the danger, one small group was left facing the lava. Connor was shocked to see children with them. He focused his enhanced vision on the distant group, and gasped with horror.

"That's my family!"

Chapter Sixty-Two

"A fool uttereth all his mind, but wisdom is gained only through listening."

~Gregor

Connor blinked, but the view did not change.

His entire family, Hamish's family, and even Jean's grandmother all stood facing the approaching flood of lava. They looked terrified, the children crying, but held in place by soldiers with blades drawn and held against their throats. Even the children.

The sight filled him with horror and rage so intense, it was like another wave of lava had erupted in his heart. He found it hard to breathe, hard to think. His hands clenched in fury, and he unconsciously tapped granite. His expanding muscles quivered with the need to smash.

Lukas cautioned, "Take it easy, Connor."

He'd forgotten he wasn't alone on the windrider bench. Connor grabbed Lukas's shoulder. "My family. Hamish's too, and Jean's. They're hostages, right there in front of the lava. Tell Kilian to stop!"

Not waiting for a reply, incapable of waiting while his family stood in the path of imminent death, Connor leaped from the windrider and tapped marble. The intense burn of fire that erupted into his mouth fit his boiling rage, and he embraced it like never before.

White-hot flames erupted from his hands and feet and catapulted him through the air toward the middle ground. The searing heat only fueled his rage. As he roared south, over five hundred feet in the air, he tried to think, but only one thing was clear.

It was time to kill.

Verena's voice cried from the speakstone on his forearm, and he held it to his ear. "Connor, I'm coming to meet you."

He glanced up just as the Swift pulled out of a steep dive and flew past, close enough for him to grab the handles at the back. He hugged Verena and pressed his face close to her helmet.

"Thanks for coming. We have to save my family."

"I just spoke with Kilian. They're stopping the lava."

Sure enough, the advance of the molten stone stopped on the very southern edge of the middle ground, barely a hundred yards from his family. Four year-old Wallace was gaping at the lava and crying, one hand tugging at the soldier gripping his collar. Eight year-old Roderick looked white with fear, and held one hand in front of his face to ward against the heat, which had to be intense.

Connor's mother was holding Fiona, turning constantly to check on the children, even though a soldier was gesturing with his blade, warning her to stop moving. Hendry looked furious, his powerful hands clenched into fists, as if on the verge of leaping on the soldiers, even though he was unarmed.

Hamish's family was no better off, with children weeping, their mother scolding the soldiers angrily, and Amhain quivering with anger and suppressed violence. Mhairi was speaking to him, and appeared to be trying to calm him down.

Connor didn't dare apply quartzite to his ears to hear what they were saying. The sound of the children begging for help would drive him past rational thought.

Instead of banking south and spooling up the speedslings to rain destruction upon those soldiers, Verena angled the Swift back north, toward where Kilian stood on Anton's tower.

Connor demanded, "What are you doing? We have to go save them."

"We're going to save them. I promise we will, but flying down there won't help them. Not yet."

"Of course it will! Verena, I am going to save them, and I need your help."

"I'm helping you." She pushed up her visor and he clearly read the worry in her eyes. "Oh, Connor. I can't imagine how terrified you are right now."

"I'm not terrified," he lied. "I'm angry."

Hamish swooped over to join them, his expression furious. "You're going the wrong way."

"We can't go rushing in there," Verena said in a placating tone. "That's just what Carbrey will want."

Connor was trying to think, to understand how their families could be there in mortal danger. Only one idea seemed possible. "Dougal wasn't returning to Obrion for reinforcements. He was going to fetch our families."

"I hope you're right," Verena said.

"You're happy our families are in danger?" Hamish exclaimed.

"Of course not! We'll save them. I'm just hoping that Dougal isn't bringing back another thirty thousand troops for us to fight too."

"All we have to fight right now are the ones holding knives to their throats," Hamish growled.

Connor nodded. "I'll hit them with fire and water and knock them away. Then you two strike with diorite."

"Sounds good to me," Hamish said, fists clenching in anticipation.

"Kilian wants us to meet with him," Verena said.

Hamish snarled, "I don't care what Kilian wants. Those are our families!"

Connor agreed. He was already chafing at the delay and barely refrained from leaping off the Swift. He would call upon all the elements and unleash the beast in his heart in an overwhelming assault of vengeful destruction.

Verena spoke in a tone that seemed far too reasonable. "If you fly over there right now, not even you can kill all those soldiers before they start slitting throats."

"Don't say that!" Connor shouted, gripping the rail on the Swift so hard it crumbled in his hand.

The thought of his parents, his brothers, or his baby sister dying right in front of him was like a splash of cold water in the face, though. The red-hot anger clouding his mind faded enough for a little rational thought.

Hamish spoke, his tone mollified too. "We have to do something."

"We will," Verena assured him. "But we need a plan."

Connor said, "We don't have time for that."

"I think the battle's paused," Verena said, pointing down.

She was right. The Obrioner center had stopped retreating, and the windriders full of air-drop Rumblers had slowed to a hover over the middle ground. Only the auxiliary troops had continued their advances on the distant edges of the valley.

They would reach the outer limits of the middle ground and clash within minutes. Everyone else seemed to understand that the outcome of the hostage standoff had to be determined before they could continue.

Carbrey's voice, amplified by a Pathfinder, cracked like thunder over the battlefield. "Wolfram. Kilian. You have one minute to pull that lava back. Connor, Hamish, and Jean must surrender immediately, or their families will all be executed."

Connor growled, sounding like a rampager, and in that moment he yearned for porphyry so he could turn into one. He would rip apart Carbrey and every member of his army.

Verena said softly. "Breathe, Connor. Think. Going now and surrendering won't help save your family."

He snarled, "I'm not going to surrender. I'm going to kill Carbrey and every one of those soldiers!"

"The danger to your family is too great," she reminded him in that infuriatingly reasonable tone.

"I can't not go!" Connor shouted, trembling with fury and fear.

He had known something bad would happen if he didn't bring his family to safety when they'd stopped in Alasdair. He raged to think of their stubbornness for not heeding the warning, and for his foolishness in not forcing them to leave.

Hovering in the air nearby, Hamish's entire suit erupted into flames, but he didn't even seem to notice.

Kilian's voice boomed over the battlefield. "Don't be foolish, Carbrey. We need twenty minutes to respond."

Carbrey's booming voice laughed. "Do you think I'm a fool, Kilian?"

"Just a coward for hiding behind children."

"No!" Connor shouted. "He can't taunt him. He might kill them out of spite."

Verena shook her head. "He won't. He'd lose the very bargaining position he's trying to leverage. Trust Kilian."

Carbrey responded a few seconds later. "I will allow a little more time, but the price is that you must surrender too and bring with you the stones stolen from my tent this morning."

"He knows that's never going to happen," Verena said with a frown.

"So let's go kill him," Hamish urged.

Verena suggested, "Go get Jean. She needs to be part of this."

Hamish rocketed away, and Connor wished he had something useful to do too. He couldn't seem to focus on anything other than calculating how best to kill every one of those soldiers before they could hurt his family.

424

He hadn't found the right solution yet, but he would. When he did, they would die. Then he would find Carbrey, no matter where the man tried to hide, and he would kill him too.

Kilian was already responding. "I will confer with the generals and leaders of Altkalen."

Connor held his breath for the long seconds until Carbrey responded.

"Ten minutes."

He sighed, feeling a glimmer of hope. In ten minutes, surely they'd figure out what to do.

Verena pulled his head closer and kissed him. "We'll save them, Connor. I swear it."

"Thanks." He leaned his forehead against hers and savored the contact. "And I swear that Carbrey just made the worst mistake of his life."

Thirty seconds later, they met on Anton's tower, which he expanded to hold them all. Kilian was already there, and Wolfram arrived seconds later with Saskia, Mattias, and Ulrich. Hamish and Jean landed immediately after. Martys followed. His anger was better controlled than Connor's, like a simmering bonfire that would only need a gust of wind to whip into an inferno.

Ulrich frowned at the Obrioner army. "We never imagined they'd try something like this."

Saskia looked grim as she spoke. "I hope we can find a clever solution because we cannot surrender."

"We can't incinerate our families with lava either," Connor retorted.

Saskia placed a hand on his arm and gave him a compassionate smile. "My heart aches for you, but all our families are in danger today. We swore an oath never to surrender, no matter the cost, and we cannot rescind it at the first test of our resolve."

Ulrich grunted. "In all the history of warfare, I've never heard of an invading army using their own citizens as hostages."

"I will free my family," Connor promised them, and he barely recognized the cold, furious voice as his own. "And anyone who gets in my way will regret it."

Saskia warned, "Don't start threatening us. If Altkalen's best interests are served by striking now, we will."

"How many people are you willing to lose?"

Verena held up her hands in a calming gesture. "I agree with Connor. We cannot attack until their families are freed."

"Think about what you're saying," Mattias told her. "If Altkalen falls, we lose all of southern Granadure. The lives of a few Obrioners are not enough to justify such a sacrifice."

"They are to me," Connor growled, happy to focus his anger on Mattias, and hoping he'd try flashing that glowing smile. Connor would break all those shining teeth.

"And we can't afford to alienate Connor, Hamish, and Jean," Verena replied, holding Mattias's gaze. "They've already sacrificed so much to help us."

Wolfram spoke for the first time. "Everyone try breathing instead of threatening each other. We are not the enemy, and your positions are not mutually exclusive. It is clear we must defeat Carbrey today, using whatever means are at our disposal."

He held up a hand to forestall any argument. "It is also clear that we must deal with this unexpected threat before that first stated goal can be accomplished."

Martys said, "Dinnae think too long about it. We must go and kill them."

"But we have to be smart about it," Kilian cautioned.

Martys sidled close to Connor and whispered, "Lad, this be the time I was preparing ye for. In this ye must be willing to unleash the beast and fight to kill."

Connor nodded. "Don't worry about me, Uncle. I'll do what it takes."

"Good lad."

"We need ideas," Ulrich said.

Verena said, "He wants the stones. What if we filled the box with diorite and blew it up in his face?"

Connor and Hamish nodded. That sounded perfect, but Kilian shook his head. "The distraction would be excellent, but it wouldn't disable the soldiers. It is far too easy to slit a throat."

"What if you used a shieldstone?" Connor asked Verena.

She shook her head. "Those soldiers are standing close. They'd probably get included in the protective barrier with your families."

"We could slip everyone a piece of blind coal," Hamish suggested.

Jean said excitedly, "I could do it. They won't see me as a threat."

The idea had merit, but Connor immediately saw the flaw in it. "I doubt Carbrey would let even you start handing out stones to everyone."

Saskia said, "We're running out of time."

"I don't see how we can do it without compromising our security," Ulrich said sadly.

"Shona!" Connor cried, getting a crazy idea.

426

Verena turned on him. "What does she have to do with anything?"

"When I met with her, she told me that her father appointed her high marshal. She said that if I return to her and promise to. . ." He couldn't finish, couldn't say marry Shona in front of Verena.

"What?" Verena asked, her tone turning icy.

"She can overrule Carbrey and appoint me commander. I could save our families and order a retreat."

"Then why haven't you done it yet?" Ulrich demanded.

"Because he'd have to marry Shona," Verena said, seeing the truth instantly. Her expression turned angry. "And I guarantee that once she secured her hold over him, we'd have even less chance of surviving the next invasion."

Connor said, "I don't think she plans to invade, at least not any time soon. She wants to secure her power base in Obrion."

"This Shona sounds like quite the woman," Mattias said. He looked eager for Connor to accept the offer.

Ulrich growled, "Sounds like her father, and you can't trust anything people like that say."

"But it might work." Connor was desperate enough that he was seriously considering returning to Shona and accepting her offer.

"Is that why you were kissing her?" Verena asked in a deceptively calm tone. Her eyes glittered with anger.

"She was kissing me," Connor corrected, but that didn't seem to help.

"No one should have been kissing anyone!" Verena shouted, advancing on him. "I told you she was trying to manipulate you."

"It was the only way I could get a chance to speak with the others," Connor tried to explain.

"Think, Connor!" Verena shouted, while the others retreated a step, abandoning Connor to face her wrath alone. "Shona just happens to outline a plan for you to give her everything she wants just in time to miraculously offer the one solution you so desperately need today."

Connor frowned. "You think she planned this?"

"What else am I supposed to think?" Verena stormed. "That's actually better than thinking you arranged that stupid meeting with her just because you wanted an excuse to kiss her again!"

He opened his mouth to respond, but for the life of him, he couldn't imagine anything he could possibly say that wouldn't make her angrier.

He very nearly said, "You know I love you," but somehow it didn't seem like the right moment.

"You can't trust Shona," Kilian said, saving Connor from having to reply.

"Of course we can't," Verena snapped, pacing away and drawing one of her throwing knives. She twirled it in her hand, as if that helped calm her nerves, but Connor watched it closely. She could stick that thing between his eyes in a blink if she chose.

He really wanted to tell her how attractive she was with that sense of danger clinging to her like an exotic perfume.

"Then I think I need some porphyry," Connor said.

"That's a bad idea," Kilian said.

Verena turned and pointed the knife at Connor. "No, that's plain stupid."

"Well, do you have a better one?" he retorted. He hated speaking angrily to her, and he didn't want to encourage her to stab him, but he couldn't seem to control himself very well at the moment.

"I do." Aifric, dressed in her white Healer's robe, climbed to the top of the tower to join them. "Or more precisely, Student Eighteen does."

Chapter Sixty-Three

"The moth is consumed by the flame, no matter its intent to seek but the comfort of warmth or light."

~Ilse

Aifric gave Connor a hug and an understanding smile. "I'll go with you."

"I'm glad you're here," Connor said, hoping she had a great idea. If not, he'd be back to attacking with overwhelming elemental rage.

Jean drew closer and said, "Kilian suggested once that maybe you can immobilize people with serpentinite. Is that true?"

Aifric looked shocked and glanced around. Everyone was eagerly listening. "We don't talk about such things."

"Is that what you had in mind?" Connor pressed. He didn't have time for games.

She hesitated, then shook her head. "I do not yet have that ability."

"Then what's your plan?" Hamish asked.

"Serpentinite can still help. I can suppress Carbrey's voice, prevent him from issuing the order to strike. I can even speak in his voice. I could tell the soldiers to stand down, or something to distract them for a moment."

"Like you did with Gregor on the mountain above the Carraig," Hamish said.

Aifric nodded.

"We can work with that," Connor said.

It wasn't as good as immobilizing the soldiers, but it might be enough. He only needed a couple seconds to hit them. He'd only get one chance before the soldiers realized what was going on and murdered his family, but he felt confident he could do it.

"Is there anything else you can do with your secret affinities that we should know about?" Jean asked.

Aifric frowned. "I don't make a point of asking about your secrets in public."

Kilian said, "But her secrets are not likely to endanger our lives."

Aifric's frown deepened. "I swore an oath to Connor. Does that mean nothing?"

Connor placed a hand on Aifric's shoulder. "I trust you. All of you."

Aifric flashed her trademark smile. "I appreciate that, Connor. We've all agreed to support you." She paused and added. "Just remember when Rith is in charge to use her name. She gets cranky when she gets lumped in with the rest of us."

"I'll keep that in mind," Connor promised.

Saskia said, "Your families are your responsibility. I wish you luck, and we'll grant you time to strike, but we will resume the attack as soon as you move against Carbrey."

Verena said, "The Crushers are ready to drop. I'll ask Ilse to task a squad to drop nearby to assist."

"Thanks," Connor told her, grateful that she seemed to have controlled her anger.

She even sheathed that knife. Once they saved their families, they'd be standing directly in front of the entire Obrioner army. They'd need the Crushers' help.

"Well then, let's go complete negotiations with Carbrey," Kilian said in a grim tone, his eyes flickering with fire.

As the group dispersed to issue new orders to their commands, Verena drew Connor to one side, took his hands in hers and gave him a serious look. "Be careful, Connor."

"I'll save them," he promised her.

"I know, and I'll be watching from above." For a second, it looked like she wanted to say something else, but she instead turned toward the Swift.

Connor placed a hand on her shoulder, and she turned back to him. "I'm sorry I let things get so messed up with Shona again. You were right. I thought I was the one being clever, but all I did was play into her hands again."

Verena sighed. "Shona can read you even better than I can, Connor. Let's talk about it after we save your family."

He let her go, wishing there was a good way to explain that he still owed Shona a passionate kiss. He definitely needed to make sure he had the healing pendant with him for that conversation.

430

Connor joined Hamish, Jean, and Martys while they waited for Kilian to finish conferring with Wolfram, Saskia, and Ulrich. "Uncle Martys, I want you to lead our families back to the Grandurian lines when the fighting starts."

"I mean to strike a blow by yer side," Martys objected.

"I know, and I appreciate it, but I'd feel better if I knew you were watching over them."

"Very well, lad. I'll do yer bidding, but make sure ye do what is necessary."

"I will." He meant it.

They decided that Hamish would fly them in the Storm to meet with Carbrey. Verena took off in the Swift, flying north, away from the battlefield until she ascended into the clouds and out of sight. There she would bank around and observe from above until the fighting started.

General Carbrey's voice boomed across the valley with one minute to go before the deadline was up. "You're just about out of time. These people are going to die."

Connor was already seated between Kilian and Hamish in the front row of the Storm, with Jean, Aifric, and Martys in the second row. The box that had contained all the sculpted stones sat in the little bed at the back. The precious stones had been removed and sent to the citadel with Mattias. The empty box had been filled with knives.

Tapping quartzite, Connor applied it to Kilian's throat. His voice boomed out in response. "Very well, Carbrey. We submit to your demands. Don't harm anyone. We're coming over."

Hamish activated the thrusters, and the Storm rose in a whirlwind of stinging sand. He ascended to about three hundred feet before accelerating out over the middle ground. With the molten lava covering the area, the air was brutally hot, and the Storm pitched in the turbulent air.

The Obrioner army had left a clear buffer zone of more than a hundred yards from the lava. The massed ranks of several thousand soldiers, including many Petralists, forming that unbroken ring of men was a daunting sight.

The hostages stood alone in the open buffer zone, less than fifty yards from the line of lava. The road began less than a hundred yards to the east. Carbrey stood on the left end of the line of hostages, with Captain Aonghus and Gregor flanking him.

"We didn't plan on them," Hamish muttered.

"Leave them to me," Kilian said.

"Even Gregor?" Connor asked. Standing on open ground, Gregor would be a formidable opponent.

Kilian nodded. "Even Gregor. But dealing with those two will require my full attention. You all must see to rescuing your families."

"We're ready," Connor assured him.

Hamish growled, "More than ready. As long as Aifric can get us that distraction."

"I'll take care of it." Aifric still wore her Healer's robe, but her expression had turned more predatory and her voice carried a hard edge to it. She was again Student Eighteen. "Gregor might recognize me. Best I stay in the Storm. I can manipulate the voices from here."

"Good idea," Connor said, and Aifric slipped into the third row of seats and lay down on the floor to stay out of sight.

Hamish set the Storm down about twenty feet away from Carbrey, with the speedslings pointed straight at him. He whispered, "I could shred him in two seconds."

Connor said, "And I doubt he'll ever realize that you held his life in your hands and chose not to take it."

Dozens of grasping tendrils of earth snaked up out of the ground all around the Storm and wrapped around the craft, locking it down to the ground.

"Easy," Kilian breathed as they climbed out. "Stay focused on Carbrey."

Connor led the way to meet Carbrey, flanked by Hamish and Kilian. Jean followed with Martys, who carried the box of knives.

Carbrey grinned and held up a hand to stop them about ten feet away.

Hendry spoke before Carbrey could, "You shouldn't have come, son. Get away while you still can."

The soldier standing behind him cuffed him in the side of the head. Hendry flinched, and Connor was grateful his dad didn't challenge the man. Not yet.

Their siblings were looking at them with desperate hope. Lilias and Peigi both looked torn between wanting to urge them to flee and plead for help saving the children. Amhain looked angry enough to fight all the soldiers bare-handed.

Kilian spread empty hands to either side. "We're here, Carbrey. Let them go."

Carbrey chuckled. "All in good time. To think the mighty Kilian is defeated by a handful of useless commoners."

432

"Keep talking like that, and we'll change our minds," Connor said.

"Hush, boy," Carbrey told him in an annoyed tone. "You've played at being grown up long enough. Kilian will submit to being chained, and you will pledge your service to Shona again right here, right now.

"And you, Builder." He scowled at Hamish and spat the word with abundant disgust. "You will remove that abominable suit and surrender all mechanicals."

"You've been practicing making ridiculous demands," Connor told Carbrey.

"And you're about to see your families die," Carbrey growled, raising one hand. The soldiers tensed, weapons drawing closer to exposed throats, and the children began to cry.

Connor fought the urge to strike Carbrey down right there. After a couple of seconds managed to say, "We submit, you coward."

"You really don't understand the meaning of the word submit, do you?" Carbrey asked.

Connor closed the distance, walking slowly. Aonghus's hands ignited with fire, and Gregor's gaze was like a physical weight. Any aggressive move would be met by precipitous violence.

He looked at his feet, trying to adopt a more submissive pose, but really needing to conceal his fury. He felt the beast raging in his heart, eager for release, hungry for bloodshed. Once he embraced it, he wouldn't need porphyry to become a cold-blooded killer. He was surprised that the thought still disturbed him.

"Once Kilian is in chains, I will send for Shona. Any foolish heroics from any of you, and I will order the executions."

Barely three feet away, Connor looked up to meet his gaze and spoke so only he could hear.

"I have a better idea. I'll just kill you."

Chapter Sixty-Four

"A pedra in bloodlust will slaughter for sport, but even the doe will fight to defend its young,"

~Gregor

Carbrey's arrogant, gloating expression evaporated as he met Connor's angry glare. He opened his mouth to shout a warning, but the sounds that came out didn't match the movement of his lips.

"Captain, we have reached an agreement. Release the prisoners."

The officer in command of the guards, positioned at the end of the line of hostages, frowned at Carbrey's back. "Sir?"

Looking panicked, Carbrey started to turn, but Connor caught his arm. He tried to make it look like they were shaking hands to seal their agreement.

"I said release the prisoners!" Carbrey's voice shouted, and the soldiers guarding their families stepped back smartly. Some of them sheathed their blades. Aifric's ability to manipulate Carbrey's voice was flawless.

Carbrey glared and swelled with granite power. Connor matched him. Together their muscles expanded, their armor creaking. The sound stirred the beast in Connor's heart.

"You shouldn't have threatened my family," Connor growled. He wanted to beat Carbrey to a pulp, but he couldn't risk alerting the others that something was wrong.

"Sir, is there a problem?" Aonghus asked, taking a step closer, frowning at Carbrey's expanding bulk.

Connor dared to tap slate, and even more strength flowed up through his feet. As soon as he connected with earth, he felt Gregor's presence lurking there.

Carbrey began squeezing in a vain attempt to subdue Connor by strength of arm. Gregor must have sensed Connor too, because he sealed the earth beneath Connor's feet, blocking him out.

"Beware," Gregor cried, but before he could intervene, Connor max-tapped granite and with a single mighty squeeze, crushed Carbrey's hand.

Carbrey's stone-hardened fist shattered to dust.

He screamed, but Aifric denied him voice for the pain. He fell to his knees, his expression turning panicked. It looked like he finally understood that he'd pushed Connor too far.

The ground buckled under Connor's feet, but he threw every ounce of earth power into an enormous pulse to fight Gregor's influence. Their wills crashed together, and Connor sensed Gregor's surprise as his snatch at Connor rebounded away.

That gave him just enough time to throw Carbrey at the captain of the guards. Aifric didn't block the general's startled squawk as he bowled the surprised captain off his feet.

Captain Aonghus leaped at Connor, fire erupting from his hands in a blistering wave.

That wave rebounded away before Connor could tap marble. Kilian shot past like a living comet, completely wreathed in flames. He intercepted Aonghus, and the two of them tumbled away, wreathed in brightly colored flames.

A fist-full of water materialized in the air and plunged into Gregor's mouth.

Connor breathed a sigh of relief as Gregor staggered, clutching at his throat. Kilian had used a similar tactic against Carbrey at Alasdair.

He'd sensed Gregor massing for another strike that would have probably swept him right into the super-heated lava field. The Sentry's attention now wavered, and Connor erupted the earth under his feet, sending him tumbling.

Most of the soldiers were still gaping in surprise at the fiery clash when Connor tapped soapstone and tried to draw water from the air to hit them.

There was no water left.

Too late, he realized that the intense heat from the lava had parched the air. Kilian had sucked out what little there was left for that single fistful he'd used to distract Gregor.

The soldiers were professionals, though, and they recovered from their surprise quickly. Men snatched at daggers and reached for their prisoners.

Hamish leaped into the air in a blast of thrusters and shouted, "Run!"

With a soft whooshing sound, a tiny vial shot from Hamish's helmet. It smashed into Gregor's face as he stumbled back to his feet, still struggling to breathe through the choking water. The extract of milked skunk shattered on impact, and Gregor fell in a heap. Earth rolled over him like a concealing blanket. Connor hoped the water and that horrible stench would keep him distracted for a few precious seconds.

Most of their families responded instantly to Hamish's voice, running toward Connor and away from their captors. Mhairi moved too slow as she tried to shepherd Hamish's five year-old brother Grier. A burly soldier grabbed her by the hair. Hamish's mother, burdened by the two year-old, also moved too slowly. Another soldier grabbed her shoulder and spun her around.

Both Hendry and Amhain turned on the soldiers instead of running. Amhain tackled the man grabbing his wife, and the two went down in a tangle, with Amhain shouting curses and beating him savagely.

With a shout of fury, Hendry barreled into the men reaching for his family. Although unarmed, his fists were hardened from a lifetime of hard labor and he smashed men off their feet with every heavy blow.

The sight of those soldiers lunging after his family with blades drawn infuriated and terrified Connor. He switched to marble.

There was a nearly limitless supply of heat available, radiating from the lava. It took only a tiny effort to seize the heat and condense some of it into living fire. He whipped it across the row of soldiers, batting men aside, burning faces, and setting hair on fire. When they turned to run, he set their breeches on fire for good measure.

He drove a handful of flames into the mouth of the soldier striking at Mhairi. The man dropped his knife and screamed, clutching at his burned mouth. Mhairi kicked him in the sweets, doubling him over. The pitch of his scream raised several octaves.

Then Hamish reached the soldiers. He tore down their line, flying at chest height, arms crossed over his chest like a living battering ram. He toppled most of the men aside, then reversed course and lifted Hendry into the air by the belt and flew back toward Connor.

Jean had rushed forward, and most of the family had already reached her in a frightened mass. Blair gaped at her outfit, and Mhairi gave her a quick hug.

Martys dropped the box of knives and rushed forward shouting, "Release the beast, laddie. Now's yer chance!"

He was right. Connor stalked forward and embraced his rage. It swept through him with almost as much power as if he'd tapped porphyry. He raised his hands, and flames boiled through the air above the soldiers, who cowered in fear. The flames intensified from crimson to white to blue.

Martys shouted, "Yes! Let their deaths serve as a lesson and a warning to all who witness!"

"No!" Lilias ran past the others to Connor, her expression horrified. "Connor, don't. You're better than this. Son, let those poor souls go."

Her voice cut through his driving rage, and for the first time he really saw the stark terror on the soldiers' faces. They had planned to kill his family, but they'd been following orders. Carbrey was to blame, not them.

The beast raged in his heart, and Connor trembled with fury. White-hot tendrils of fire crackled along his fingers, and he yearned to destroy those men.

He couldn't do it, not in front of his mother. He lowered his hands and the flames flickered and vanished.

She hugged him, tears in her eyes. "Oh, Son, I'm so sorry you have to deal with this, but I'm proud of you."

Martys advanced on Connor, his face furious. "What are you doing, laddie? Ye cannae win a battle if ye no will do what needs doin'."

"Shame on you." Lilias faced Martys's rage with unflinching calm. "Connor will fight, but you're talking about senseless murder."

"I know what needs doin'. Ye no have seen battle, so dinnae try tellin' me."

"Murder is never the right choice."

Hamish dropped Hendry nearby, and Connor gripped his dad's hands. "I'm so glad you're all right."

"I've half a mind to go after those brutes again," Hendry growled. His knuckles were bloodied, but he didn't seem to notice.

"There are a couple of hammers in the Storm," Hamish suggested, and Hendry's eyes lit up.

"Go," Connor told them. "Take everyone. That's your ride out."

"What about you?" Lilias asked.

"I've got work to do."

Connor's voice turned grim. The nearest companies of Obrioner soldiers were distracted by the fiery duel between Kilian and Aonghus, but they wouldn't be for much longer.

He was barely controlling his rage. He needed his mother and siblings to leave. They couldn't witness what was about to happen.

Carbrey had brought the war. Connor would throw it back in his face.

"Come on, brother," Hendry said, clapping Martys on the shoulder, then raised his voice. "Everyone, get to that flying wagon!"

As the family headed for the Storm, Martys fixed Connor with a reproving look. "Ye cannae hesitate, laddie. Yer mother dinnae understand war. Ye must be strong."

"I'll deal with this. Keep them safe."

Martys ran to the Storm to help everyone cram in. It would be a tight fit, but they'd manage.

Jean was already sitting in the pilot seat. She looked nervous about flying the nimble craft with all of their families crammed aboard, but Connor needed Hamish.

He tapped slate and was relieved that Gregor still hadn't taken control over the ground. In fact, he couldn't locate Gregor at all.

With a thought, the earth that had been restraining the Storm melted away. Immediately the thrusters ignited, and the little craft ascended and banked away. Jean was getting very adept at using that keystone. Most of the family looked terrified, but Hendry and Amhain saluted with their hammers.

Connor saluted in return, relieved beyond measure to see them safely away. Then he turned and his smile vanished. It was time to demonstrate what the Blood of the Tallan could do when he got really angry.

The battered soldiers who had been guarding the hostages were all scrambling to return to the Obrioner lines. Student Eighteen stood over Carbrey with a dagger in her hand. A bloody bruise marred the side of his head, and he was groaning and clutching his shattered hand.

The lava resumed its forward progress with a grinding, hissing growl, and the molten stone crept onto the solid ground behind them. A fresh wave of sulfur-laden air washed past, and the heat intensified.

The lava ground to a halt almost immediately, though. Connor wasn't surprised. The Obrioners had plenty of time to prepare their counter. He felt the straining invisible forces battling overhead and underfoot.

Sentries and Sappers fought for dominance, while Firetongues and Flameweavers strove to drive the fire against each other. The opposing forces only served to lock the lava into place. It also kept most of the strongest Petralists distracted.

Not far away, Kilian abruptly encased Aonghus in a pillar of ice, imprisoning him to his neck. A final flicker of fire snatched the marble right out of Aonghus's mouth.

Kilian must have found an underground source to produce that much water. Aonghus was shouting curses, but Kilian leaned against the pillar of ice, looking relaxed. He spoke, and Aonghus calmed and looked surprised. Connor would pay a lot to be one of those fire devils dancing on Kilian's shoulders and hear what he said.

The fight had taken long enough that four Firetongues and five Spitters had gathered to help Aonghus. The Spitters had drawn water along with them, and the two teams attacked Kilian with a barrage of whipping flames and pounding water.

"We have to help him," Hamish said as the elemental barrage boiled over Kilian, obscuring him from view.

Connor had already tapped both marble and soapstone, and Kilian blazed in his elemental senses like a bonfire wrapped in a thundering, standing waterfall. Kilian stood at the center of the elemental onslaught, both hands raised, a roguish smile on his face.

He shouted, "Who taught you kids how to fight? You're not working together at all."

"I'm not sure it's a good idea to give the other side constructive criticism during a battle," Hamish commented.

"He's keeping them distracted."

Connor plunged his will into the wild contest raging around Kilian just long enough to snatch a hefty streamer of water away and wrap it around himself like a glittering, silver snake.

Windriders were already sweeping over the Obrioner army, and the first wave of Rumblers and fire-filled bomb-cases were jumping out. The Crushers would arrive in moments. If the battle over the lava and Kilian's dramatic performance could keep enough of the tertiaries distracted, their job would be all the easier.

"Let's deal with Carbrey," Hamish growled, and the two of them turned in unison toward the cowering general.

In that moment, Gregor's will returned in a rush, battering Connor's earth senses aside and sending him stumbling. The Sentry struck like an underground lightning bolt, straight for Carbrey.

Carbrey seemed to melt into the earth. Student Eighteen leaped at the spot and drove her dagger deep, but the ground buckled and tossed her back.

"No!" Hamish shouted, leaping into the air on a rush of thrusters, snatching for the mini speedsling holstered at his hip. As powerful as those hornets might be, they'd never penetrate deep enough.

Connor snatched for that area with his earth senses, but they deflected away, turned by a sturdy shield. He pounded at it and swept his earth senses around it, trying to find a way in. The shield was formed like a long conduit, leading back toward the Obrioner army.

"No way you escape!" Connor threw himself into the air with a burst of fire and soared over the invisible, shielded conduit. No doubt Gregor was spiriting Carbrey away through it.

He couldn't tell exactly where Carbrey was, but Gregor's shielding outlined the only possible places.

Connor embraced the raging beast, and his flames boiled to steel-melting intensity. With a blast of that fire, Connor flung himself out of the air and thundered into the ground above Gregor's shield. He struck with every ounce of earth power, smashing into the shield.

It rippled under the brutal impact. Connor released earth and again tapped both soapstone and marble together. He drew so heavily from both stones that the piece of marble in his mouth burned into his lip.

Venting all of his rage into a single massive strike, Connor plunged dozens of spikes of fire deep into the ground. The earth around each hole charred as the blue-white fire perforated Gregor's shield.

Connor slammed a fist into the rippling ground and unleashed the water he'd taken a moment ago, whipping it down the underground conduit Gregor had formed.

He found Carbrey twenty feet away.

One spike of fire had punched through Gregor's wall scant inches from Carbrey's head.

Gregor responded with remarkable speed, trying to wrap Carbrey in a protective blanket of earth. In three seconds, he could have broken Connor's attack.

That was two seconds too long.

Connor threw every ounce of water at Carbrey, hardening it into a thick spear of ice. It ripped through the general, and his entire body convulsed. He probably tried to scream, but Connor didn't give him time.

A porphyry-like rage swept through him, coloring his vision red, and Connor roared with battle fury. He drove a blistering inferno up the track the ice had just used. Riding the wave of fire-induced berserker fury, Connor threw his hands wide and howled, pouring every bit of fire power into the breach.

Carbrey disintegrated.

His leather armor melted under the fervent heat as Connor tore the life out of him, then cremated him on the spot.

Gregor sealed off the ground a second later, blocking Connor's connection, and he let the Sentry drag Carbrey's remains away.

He remained crouched, one hand pressed against the earth as super-heated fire circled him like a tempest. He hoped Gregor attacked him because he would eagerly do battle with even the mighty Sentry in that moment.

"Connor!" Hamish circled nearby, one hand raised to shield his face from the heat.

His fury was like a living thing, and for a second he saw Hamish only as a new potential outlet for his rage. He felt a terrifying urge to boil Hamish right out of the sky. The thought shocked him so much it snapped him back to reason.

He shuttered the fire and his surroundings seemed to rush back in. He stood in a scorched ring of earth, the air heavy with smoke. The scent was a mixture of the rotten-egg stench of sulfur and the harsh smell of charred earth. The air was stiflingly hot, and felt thin, as if he'd burned most of it away.

Connor felt a bit light-headed and staggered when he tried to walk.

Hamish landed beside him and offered a hand of support, his expression worried. "What happened?"

"Carbrey is dead." Connor's voice was harsh and cold. He pointed into the ground.

"Good," Hamish said, scowling at the area. "Serves him right."

Connor nodded, but saying the words somehow made what he'd just done more real, and a new emotion chilled him.

He'd just killed a man.

Carbrey deserved it, more than almost anyone Connor knew, but the abrupt, violent fight left him shaken. He was no stranger to death, but this was different.

He took a deep breath and thought about Martys and his mother. His uncle would laugh and congratulate him. Part of him wished he could savor the victory with as much relish, but what would that make him?

Would his mother accept that he'd needed to kill Carbrey, or would she feel ashamed of him?

He whispered, "He can't hurt you any more."

"What was that?" Hamish asked.

"Nothing. It is done."

He glanced around. Carbrey's death was so momentous for him. It felt wrong that no one else seemed to have noticed yet. The tertiary Petralists were still fighting Kilian in a spectacular display of elemental savagery. Other soldiers had circled the fighting and were again moving toward the road, about fifty yards to his right.

That one path across the dangerous middle ground was the critical link, and the Grandurian army was pressing south along it as well. Controlling the road would be critical.

Connor wanted to go find Verena and just breathe in the scent of her while they held each other, but the battle was far from over. "I'm going to slow them down and give the Grandurians time to break into this side."

"Then I'd better go get some bigger bombs. Be right back." Hamish took off with a rush of thrusters.

Connor again tapped marble and focused on the searing heat radiating off of the mass of stalled lava. The Flameweavers and Firetongues were fighting over the fire, but not the heat. They weren't ascended, so couldn't manipulate it well.

Seizing some of that heat, he cast it out over the roadway, forming a shimmering wall to block the advancing Obrioner soldiers. There was so much heat that he extended the wall, pressing it south into an enormous half-circle, three hundred yards long. It completely blocked the Obrioner advance.

The blistering heat reddened exposed skin and appeared as a shimmering, translucent wall. Connor allowed himself a satisfied smile. Maybe they could break the fighting before too many more people had to get hurt.

Then Aifric placed her dagger against his throat and spoke with the same icy tone she'd used the day she'd tried to kill him at the Carraig.

"I helped you save your family, Connor, but I have new orders now."

Chapter Sixty-Five

"Names are cloaks sometimes chosen for warmth and sometimes for concealment."

~Evander

Connor tensed at the feel of the cold steel of Student Eighteen's dagger touching his throat. She could slash his life away in the blink of an eye.

"Aifric, you swore an oath to me," he said softly and dared turn very slowly to face her.

Her eyes were cold, her face hard. He had thought they'd moved beyond that almost-murder awkwardness stage of their relationship.

If he tapped granite to try to harden his skin, she'd notice and slash through it before it offered nearly enough protection. He could knock her aside with earth or fire, but would that catch her by surprise, or would her blade snick that one inch deeper?

Besides, Aifric was his friend. At least she had been until two seconds ago.

"I have new orders," Aifric said again in that same cold tone.

"So Sir was lying when he said he wanted to help?"

"He does not lie."

"Well if this is what he thinks the word help means, will you tell him that I prefer he help Dougal?"

"Sir has new orders too. Mister Five arrived yesterday."

Connor frowned. "Can I be honest with you? Mhortair names are ridiculous."

Aifric's mouth twitched, but he couldn't tell if she'd almost smiled, or if that was just a sign that she was about to kill him.

"Mister Five is a member of the ruling council of Jagdish, a senior kill instructor, and his word is law."

"But you've broken laws before," Connor pointed out. Just being an Assassin had to break a ton of laws he didn't even know about.

"Not his."

"Why didn't you warn us about him then?"

"I didn't know he was coming." He dared to hope he caught a glimpse of doubt in her resolve. "He allowed us to complete the mission to deliver the pedra's spittle so he could witness its effectiveness, but issued new orders after that."

Connor hadn't really trusted Sir, but he decided Mister Five ranked on his need-to-kill list right after Dougal.

He still dared to trust Aifric, though. Was she about to prove that his trust was fatally misguided? That would be a rotten thing for a friend to do.

"Aifric--" he started, using the name that he trusted most. It also happened to be the least lethal of all the personalities he'd met so far.

"Don't make this any harder for me than it is already, Connor," Aifric warned.

"Um, do you really think it's my duty as a friend to make your experience of double-crossing and murdering me as easy on your conscience as possible?"

"Stop talking," Aifric growled, her brow furrowing.

She hadn't killed him yet, so he reminded her again, "You swore an oath. I'm one of those old-fashioned sort of guys who actually believes an oath means something."

She glared, and he prepared to seize that shimmering wall of heat still holding the Obrioner army back. She might kill him, but he'd take her with him. In the few seconds it would take him to bleed out, he'd melt her into the ground. He didn't want to. It was actually a really gross mental image. But he would.

"I know my duty," Aifric snapped, but she still looked like she was struggling to decide what to do. Usually he liked decisive women, but in the moment he was glad she hesitated.

"You will bleed out in three seconds when the carotid artery is cut." She spoke with clinical coolness, and in that moment her doubt faded and her eyes cleared.

With a graceful movement, Aifric lifted the blade away from his throat, twisted it, and pressed the flat of the steel back again. He felt the beating of his blood against the pressure. If she had used the edge, he'd already be dead.

He opened his mouth to ask what was going on, but her glare turned fierce. "Will you just shut up for a minute, Connor? Let me work through this."

"Take your time," he told her as calmly as he could, even though time was one thing they were about to run out of. Then again, if she slashed his throat, he'd run out of blood a lot faster.

444

The leading edges of the Grandurian army were nearing the Obrioner end of the middle ground. The Obrioners were desperate to get through his wall of heat. Firetongues were trying to pull against it, although he could hold them off for a time.

The real threat was from a couple of Sentries who had pulled away from the invisible wrestling match over the lava and raised a tunnel of earth, wide enough for fifty men to march through. They were extending it toward the heat wall to form a safe passage through.

If not for Aifric's dagger distracting him, he could redirect the heat to drive the soldiers back, or shove the heat into the tunnel and turn it into a giant oven.

Aifric pulled the blade away from his neck, and he sighed with relief. He'd known trusting her was the right choice. When he opened his mouth to thank her, she held up a hand. "I said be quiet, Connor."

He should back away, should tap granite and punch her over the middle ground, but that look of doubt and almost fear in her eyes made him wait. This was important to her, maybe as important as living was to him. He'd give her a few more seconds to figure it out.

Aifric moved the blade down to his bicep and placed the edge against his arm. "Eight seconds to bleed out when the brachial artery is cut."

Again she twisted the blade and pressed the flat against the critical point. Then she shifted the blade to his thigh. "Twenty seconds to bleed out from the femoral artery."

Teaching time with Aifric was kind of unnerving, but Connor held his tongue.

Once more she twisted the blade, pressing the flat against his leg. Then she reversed the blade and gently placed the pommel against his right eye before drawing the dagger back and saluting with it.

She sighed and gave him an exhausted smile, as if she'd just run all the way from Harz. She wiped her brow and blew out a breath. "Well, Connor, I've touched steel to flesh in every major kill location, but you're still alive. I don't see what else I could have done to obey orders. I guess it's just not that easy to kill the Blood of the Tallan."

Connor gave her a hug, which she enthusiastically returned. She trembled against him, and when he released her, he noticed her hand shaking as she returned her dagger to its concealed sheath.

Girls could be so complicated sometimes, and Aifric was in a league of her own.

"Thank you for making the right choice."

"Thank me later," Aifric said, her expression turning serious again.

"I know, we're sort of standing right in the middle of the battle zone," Connor said.

"Forget the battle. We have to save Verena from Mister Five!"

Chapter Sixty-Six

"The fledgling wanders often from the safety of the nest, but cannot learn to fly without leaping from the tall branches."

~Evander

Your kill instructor is targeting Verena?" The thought terrified Connor.

Aifric nodded. "She is considered one of the most dangerous people to the stability of the current world order."

"Don't worry. She's safe."

Verena was flying concealed up in the clouds. Not even a secret Mhortair assassin could reach her there.

Just then, the Obrioner Sentries plowed through his heat wall with their protected earthen corridor. Obrioner Boulders rushed through. They charged up the road toward the Grandurian Rumblers, who had almost reached the southern end of the middle ground. The two groups would clash barely fifty yards to Connor's right.

At the same time, Spitters flung sheets of water into the air against his heat wall, trying to weaken its intensity. Connor snatched the heat away to preserve it, and the shimmering wall collapsed. The Obrioners cheered and charged en masse toward the advancing Grandurians.

He wasn't finished.

With that much heat, he could strike down those soldiers like he had Carbrey, or suffocate them with superheated air. But Aifric had just made a hard choice, and she'd chosen loyalty and friendship when she could have chosen murder. For a second he hesitated, not sure what to do.

The hot, sulfur-laden air was making him feel queasy. The clanking of armor and weapons from thousands of soldiers created a constant din. The noise was punctuated by shouting officers, their voices enhanced by Pathfinders, urging the men to kill all Grandurians.

The thought sickened him. He didn't want to see hundreds or thousands more slain. He didn't want their blood on his hands.

They weren't giving him much choice.

Connor struck the advancing Obrioner lines with the vast pool of heat. He swept it across their lines, but targeted the metal of their helmets, armor, and weapons instead of their vulnerable skin and faces. Within seconds, the metal heated to painful levels.

The charge slowed as soldiers cringed and cried out as the hot metal singed them through their padded undergarments. Some dropped weapons or yanked helmets off their heads, and they all panted in the searingly hot air. The delay gave the Grandurians time to reach the middle ground and begin establishing fortified lines.

Spitters reacted quickly, casting a cooling mist over the Obrioner soldiers. Connor switched to soapstone and fought them for control. The Spitters didn't work together as a solid unit, but each concentrated over separate sections. Thankfully they hadn't yet taken Kilian's advice to heart. Connor was stronger than any one of them, and he wrested away individual sections of the mist.

Snatching that water, Connor condensed it into fist-sized balls that he used to trip soldiers or knock weapons out of their hands. Then he drained away the heat from the water, forming snowballs, which he shoved down the fronts of their armored trousers.

The charge faltered as soldiers staggered, many starting to hop and dance about, trying to shake out the snow. Even with that distraction, he still wasn't doing enough to stop the advance.

He needed more affinities.

Verena's voice came over his mini-hub. "Connor, I'm right behind you. Get on and we'll have a better vantage to fight from up here."

"Oh, no," Aifric gasped.

Verena swooped in over the still-glowing middle ground, the Swift bucking in the hot, unstable air.

"She has to get away!" Aifric lunged for Connor's mini-hub, but screamed and pitched sideways, clutching at her side.

A charred hole had appeared in her white Healer's robe, and blood was already beginning to spread in a crimson stain.

Connor helped settle her to the ground. She screamed again as he pried her trembling hands away from the wound and ripped the cloth back enough to see. Something had pierced her side, but he could not see the weapon. Maybe it was a projectile, something cast from a sling?

The wound was barely half an inch long, and the skin around the edges looked charred. As blood oozed out, it steamed, as if on the verge of boiling.

The sight sickened him, and Connor reached into the wound with soapstone senses to quench whatever fiery dart had stabbed her. He was startled to sense water in the wound, not fire.

The weapon that had struck Aifric was a small dart made of ice, but ice that somehow burned with unbelievable heat. As soon as he touched it, the ice transformed into water, and liquid geysered from the wound.

Aifric screamed again, writhing on the ground, but she grabbed his hand with desperate strength. Sweat beaded her skin, and her eyes were wide with agony, but she gasped, "It's Mister Five. He's here! Get Verena away!"

Then she sagged back, again clutching the wound with one hand. With her other she pulled a piece of sandstone from a pocket of her robe. Immediately the lines of pain marring her features eased as she applied her healing gift.

Connor rose and looked around for Mister Five. He'd struck down Aifric in a way Connor still didn't understand, but if he didn't find the Assassin quickly, Verena would be next.

"What happened?" Verena spoke again through the mini-hub. She was barely thirty feet away, slowing the Swift as she came in for a landing.

Connor ran toward her, waving mightily and shouted, "Go! You have to get away."

Verena looked surprised and confused. "I'm sorry I got mad at you earlier, Connor, but I can help."

"You don't understand." She was barely six feet off the ground, the thruster blast washing over him as he ran toward her. "You're in danger."

The little craft dropped suddenly in the turbulent air, nearly falling all the way to the ground, and Verena screamed. For a second he thought she was just worried about crashing, but then she clutched at her shoulder where a red stain had just blossomed.

Mister Five.

Connor wanted to jump to the Swift and help her deal with that wound. He could only imagine the searing agony of that strange burning ice, but if he delayed, the next dart might kill her.

He spun, and spotted Mister Five.

Most of the Obrioners were charging up the road toward the Grandurians spreading onto the solid ground, about fifty yards to Connor's right. One man had broken free of the others and was walking straight toward Connor. He was slender and rather short, dressed in Strider running leathers. He had no visible weapon.

His hands were raised though, and even as Connor locked gazes with him across the distance, Mister Five threw his hands out toward Connor. A flash of light erupted from him, shooting across the distance with unbelievable speed.

Connor was already tapping soapstone and he felt the dart approach, like a meteor in his mind. He threw himself to the side while swiping at the missile with his soapstone senses. He managed to deflect the dart high so it couldn't possibly strike Verena or Aifric.

When he rolled back to his feet, he felt the beast raging in his heart, and this time he did not hesitate to let it out.

Mister Five was Mhortair, a deadly Assassin who attacked in a unique way. He had struck Verena and Aifric in a matter of seconds.

Time for him to die.

Connor tapped granite to harden his skin against any other weapons Mister Five might employ, then he tapped slate. Earth opened to him immediately, and Connor slid across the ground faster than even his best fracked sprint. He raised one granite-hardened fist to shatter Mister Five's skull, just as he had the torc's the first time he'd used his curse.

Mister Five had apparently seen death enough times to recognize it coming. He turned and fled. Fracking instantly, he raced into the charging Obrioner lines, slipping through the huge Boulders and disappearing from view.

Connor planned to follow. He didn't care if he had to knock aside the entire army. He'd find that man and rip his head off. But a tortured cry behind him snapped him around.

Verena.

Kilian raced past, ringed by intertwining shrouds of fire and water, and shouted, "I'll get him."

He accelerated into a fracked sprint right at the Obrioner lines. As much as those soldiers might be focused on the Grandurians, they couldn't fail to see Kilian closing on them like a living comet. Their lines split apart, with soldiers diving aside to allow him to pass.

Connor left him to the chase and raced back to Verena. She still had that burning dart cooking her from the inside.

The Swift had settled to the ground, and Verena's entire body was locked in rigid lines of agony. Her face was pale, she breathed in quick, shallow gasps and wept with pain as she struggled with her one good hand to tug at her armor to get at the wound. Mister Five's strange dart had drilled right through the layers of steel and leather protecting her shoulder.

Connor placed his hands over Verena's wound and with his soapstone senses grabbed the dart embedded deep in her flesh. It again melted instantly, transforming from super-heated intensity to cool water, and geysered from the wound. It was as if the burning ice had been pressurized, but his touch released it.

Part of him wished he could study it more, but he needed to help Verena survive until he could check on Aifric again.

A wave of screaming made him glance up and look around for new threats. They were still standing close to the mountain of lava. It had started creeping forward again now that some of the Sentries had been forced to divert their focus. They were also far too close to where the next major clash of the battle was beginning.

The only indications he saw of Kilian were periodic bursts of flame and water that toppled entire companies to the ground. The disturbance was moving fast through the Obrioner army. He wondered if Kilian was still chasing Mister Five, or if he was just wreaking chaos on the army. Either way, it wasn't enough. The army was still pressing forward.

Well, they had been.

The front lines of Obrioner soldiers had closed to within thirty yards of the Grandurians. Instead of charging to meet them, the front four lines of the Grandurian advance had dropped to their bellies.

Every one of the soldiers behind them carried a speedsling.

These were larger versions of the deadly weapons, heavy contraptions of basalt-lined stone, supported by iron frameworks. The weapons easily weighed a hundred pounds. Builders had already activated them, setting the large drums of projectiles spinning. In unison, the Rumblers wielding them opened the release levers.

One hundred speedslings fired together, each one spitting five thousand hornets a minute, creating a solid wall of buzzing, hardened granite projectiles, traveling almost too fast to follow.

The front of the Obrioner charge disintegrated.

The heavily armored Boulders collapsed under the brutal onslaught as hornets tore through shields and armor alike and drove deep into stone-hardened skin. About one in a hundred hornets contained a grain of diorite, so a series of small but lethal explosions tore across the lines of screaming Boulders.

The sight of the slaughter sickened Connor and stoked his rage at Dougal. All of that death and pain was his fault. Carbrey had paid for his folly, but no doubt Dougal would keep throwing away lives until Connor stopped him too.

He vowed to make that happen soon.

First he had to heal Verena.

Focusing with that horrible battle raging so close was difficult, but Verena's obvious agony helped him concentrate. Connor drew deep from the sandstone pendant, pouring a river of healing energy into the wound.

The sandstone power carried his affinity senses into her shoulder, giving him a clear picture of the wound. The ice had driven deep, cracked the ball of her shoulder, and slashed through muscle and many of the little tendons that made up the complicated joint. Without healing magic to help, Verena would have lost the use of her arm forever. With the magic, she might have a chance, especially if Aifric could tend her soon.

Connor surrounded the wound with healing energy, binding the cuts and the broken bone, and drawing away the pain. Verena sighed and seemed to deflate as her tension relaxed.

He spent precious seconds working over her injuries, trying first to stem the damage from those internal third-degree burns. Then he eased the hurt and attempted to reverse it. He wasn't a Healer, but he knew enough to realize those burns were a serious problem.

The pendant provided such a flood of healing power that it did most of the work, but he tried to remember the little he had learned. His worry for Verena made it hard to think.

Then the ground lurched underfoot.

He glanced up and saw that the fighting had progressed while he was distracted. The Obrioner Sentries had come to the aid of their embattled Boulders, raising walls of earth to block the deadly hornets. The wounded were retreating, and the Obrioner lines were in disarray.

The speedsling wielders shuttered the weapons, and the front lines of Rumblers leaped to their feet and charged. Several Sapper towers rose along the flanks of the army as Anton led a team of earth movers into the fray. The earthen walls protecting the retreating Boulders tumbled to the ground, and the Rumblers charged through, crashing into the disorganized ranks of Obrioners.

Eager Obrioner reinforcements pressed in. As the fighting intensified, shouted battle cries, the clashing of steel on steel, and the sharp ringing of steel on stone-hardened skin rang across the valley.

Sheets of water began rippling back and forth, just over the heads of the fighting soldiers as Spitters and Water Moccasins battled for dominance. So far they seemed evenly matched. Both earth and fire remained locked in a stalemate over the glowing mounds of lava. For the moment the bash fighters got their dream battle.

Verena touched Connor's arm and drew his attention back to her. She looked pale, but better. She gave him a weak smile.

"Thank you, Connor. That hurt more than I can describe."

Connor felt an overwhelming sense of relief to see her stabilized. He smiled and kissed her forehead, but hated how cool and clammy her skin felt. She might be out of immediate pain, but it looked like she was going into shock. "Can you fly the Swift back to safety with Aifric?"

She nodded, and Connor ran to Aifric, who was still lying nearby, hands clutching her wound, eyes closed in concentration.

"Aifric, are you all right?" he asked as he dropped to his knees beside her.

"I'll live," she said, but tears shone in her eyes.

"Are you still in pain? What can I do to help?"

She shook her head. "Help me up."

Connor drew her arm over his shoulders and eased her to her feet. She grimaced, but said, "The wound is the least of my problems. Connor, I disobeyed Mister Five."

Connor tried to remember how she had said it. "You touched steel to every kill location, right?"

"That was justification for me alone," she told him as he half carried her to the Swift. "There will be no Student Nineteen. My life is forfeit and my own father will be tasked to lead the expedition to hunt me down and return my head to Jagdish."

"That's barbaric," Verena said, and Connor agreed.

Aifric settled onto the supply box at the rear of the Swift and shrugged. "It is our way, and from the perspective of my people, it makes sense."

"We'll talk about it later," Connor told her. "Go, Verena. You two get back to the healing centers. Maybe we can figure out what he hit you with."

"Mister Five has rediscovered a technique not seen since before the Tallan wars," Aifric said.

Connor definitely preferred it when they were the clever ones. "Tell me about it later. Go."

"Come with us," Verena said.

He shook his head and pointed up to where the two windriders full of Crushers were flying overhead. Soldiers were already jumping out.

"I have work to do."

CHAPTER SIXTY-SEVEN

"Understanding is a flower whose petal opens fully with time and contemplation."

~Evander

The bash fight intensified. It was a wonder they didn't all just shatter. Soldiers on both sides beat on each other with unrestrained violence, and the air rang with the sounds of battle. A smoky scent hung over the battlefield, smelling of broken stone and the metallic taste of blood, overlaid by the rank stench of death.

The initial Rumbler advantage was offset by the sheer number of Boulders attacking them. More Grandurians were rushing up the road to reinforce the two hundred soldiers who had gained the southern edge of the middle ground, but they faced the full might of the Obrioner shock troops.

The duel of water was still pretty evenly matched, and the air was heavy with liquid. Over a dozen rainbows glittered in the early morning sunshine. Five Sapper towers had risen among the Grandurian front ranks, but they seemed completely dedicated to holding off the Sentries and could offer no assistance.

Connor could.

Air-drop soldiers and humanoid bomb-cases were already falling into the Obrioner ranks, so it was the perfect time to disrupt the delicate balance of powers. Connor was surprised that he felt no anger toward the fighting men. He'd consumed most of his raging fury to kill Carbrey. The rest had fled with Verena, Aifric, and his family.

He had to fight, but that didn't mean he had to kill his countrymen. He was surprised to feel a spark of excitement as he marched toward the nearest fighting. All he had to do was disrupt the battle lines and give the Grandurian advance the chance they needed to finish the battle.

Breaking things was his specialty.

So Connor tapped marble and soapstone together. The paired elements answered his call without hesitation. The air was so hot and humid that he easily drained all the water he needed out of it, then seized the remaining dry heat and intensified it into open flame.

Connor rose twelve feet into the air on eight spider-like legs formed out of intertwined fire and water and accelerated toward the Boulder lines. They couldn't help but see him coming, and a dozen Boulders shifted to face him, a wall of massive shields held at the ready.

Their optimism was as inspiring as it was foolish.

Connor plowed into them, kicking out with each long elemental leg in turn. Boulders tumbled away and crashed into the tightly-packed ranks of soldiers pressing north to join the fight.

"Never enough time to bash fight," Connor apologized.

He set a course across the battle line, kicking and swatting Boulders on every side. He threw head-sized balls of mixed fire and water at soldiers farther away, knocking them off their feet and creating as much confusion as possible.

Then a war hammer whooshed past his head from behind, missing by a fraction of an inch. Other soldiers seemed to like the idea and started throwing weapons too.

Connor dropped, and drew his elemental legs in close to form a spinning, protective sphere instead. Then he added spikes of ice along the outer edge.

The nearest Boulder, a bearded fellow with a huge nose, grimaced and shouted, "Here comes the pain, boys!"

The spikes dug into the ground, and the sphere shot forward, plowing right over ranks of nearby soldiers. Most of them took the elemental beating stoically. They were used to tertiaries interrupting their fun, after all. Connor saluted down at the big-nosed fellow as he ran over the man and squashed him into the ground.

Connor set his sphere barreling back and forth through the enemy ranks, running soldiers over and extending dozens of arms of twined elements to swat at men farther out. His entire focus remained on simply disrupting their battle lines to reduce the pressure against the Grandurian advance.

He was really good at it, and he thoroughly enjoyed that moment, despite the deadly serious nature of the conflict.

Then the bomb-cases thundered into the Obrioners. Their fantastic eruptions threw Boulders violently in every direction and rent gaping holes in their ranks. Air-drop Rumblers landed behind the bomb-cases and plunged into the Boulders with wild abandon. They quickly formed into small companies and thew themselves into battle, creating a dozen little pockets of fighting.

That's when the Obrioner tertiaries decided Connor was a bigger threat than the Grandurians they'd been elemental wrestling with. A pair of Firetongues and a pair of Spitters attacked together, snatching for his elements.

They glowed in his elemental senses like torches in twilight. Boulders scrambled to escape the escalating elemental battle as fire and water arced all around Connor, crackling and snapping like angry nualls.

Connor wasn't about to make it easy for them. He whipped the sphere into a tight turn toward one pudgy Spitter who was sliding through the press toward him on a thin sheet of ice.

The fellow looked eager for a fight, but must have expected their combined assault would overwhelm Connor quickly. He wasn't prepared when Connor launched himself forward like an arrow from a bow, driving intertwined fire and water ahead of him. The pudgy Spitter made a valiant effort to deflect the waters away.

Connor appreciated his spirit, so he split his elemental assault to either side of the man. The fellow grinned, but then spotted Connor soaring through the elements, curse-laden fist poised to punch him back to Drumwhindle Pass.

The Spitter was a Strider in primary affinity and he tried to run. He was still standing on ice, and his fast-flying feet failed to find purchase.

Connor pulled his punch at the last second to avoid shattering the unlucky fellow's chest to pieces. He still collided with him hard enough to crack several ribs, and catapulted him off his feet. The fellow's plump shape really helped him roll, and he got almost fifty feet before careening into a trio of heavy Boulders.

That was one Spitter who'd be sipping his meals through a straw for a while.

Several of his friends were eager to take his place, though. Connor regained his footing in the middle of a growing open space in the heart of several thousand Obrioner soldiers.

The distraction initiative was working amazingly well.

Next step: don't die.

Wrapping the elements tighter around himself, he stalked toward the nearest tertiary. The precious seconds he'd spent knocking out the Spitter had given his opponents time to get organized, and more reinforcements had arrived.

Two Firetongues, encased in crimson flames, struck at him from the sides. A pair of female Spitters, half submerged in foamy pedestals of water, snapped tendrils of water at him. In unison, they attempted to seize his elements away.

Connor might be ascended, but those four worked well together, and he struggled to maintain control. Only the fact that he kept the elements mixing and whirling together prevented the Obrioner tertiaries from overwhelming him.

Time to introduce them to the Blood of the Tallan.

Connor tapped slate.

The strength of the earth rose through him, and for a second the entire battlefield spread clearly to his earth senses, like a map in his mind. The wide, flat plain vibrated under the tramping of tens of thousands of feet. Sentries and Sappers were still battling over the deadly lava and along the leading edges of the fighting. None were free yet to target or assist him directly.

Most of the ground was locked into that struggle for dominance, but Connor didn't need much. While he fought his attackers for control over his protective sphere of mixed fire and water, he tugged just a bit on the ground.

Fist-sized arms of earth erupted between the feet of each of the Firetongues, striking them solidly between the legs. He also opened holes under the Spitters' watery pedestals. Both of the men toppled, their flames flickering as they made high-pitched strangling sounds.

Ilse and Lukas charged out of the press of fighting behind one of the men. They were invisible to Connor's earth sight. Ilse's shielding was the best he'd ever seen.

Lukas threw a mace. It struck the Firetongue in the back of his helmeted head. The man actually looked more peaceful unconscious than he had while moaning and clutching at himself.

The Spitters reacted better to the abrupt holes, and flowed back out almost immediately. Connor charged the nearest one, hoping she'd remain distracted, but she slid away, her watery pedestal moving as fast as a Strider. Two other Spitters and another Firetongue joined the fight, and he couldn't fend them all off and seize her water too.

He glanced back at Ilse to see if they could intercept the woman, but Ilse was just finishing chaining the unconscious Firetongue.

That's when he felt the surging will of a Sentry strike. It was like an underground shooting star to his mind. The ground under Ilse and Lukas buckled, sending them soaring. Spears of earth erupted after to finish them off.

So much for her excellent shielding.

Connor snatched the two of them out of the air with whips of water and threw them after the escaping Spitter. He pulsed his own earth senses into the ground in every direction to help shield their landing.

That was a really clever way to draw the attention of the Sentry.

Connor threw himself into the air as the ground under him dropped into a spike-lined pit. Fighting with two elements had been difficult. He wasn't sure he was ready for three.

He should have thought of that before he tempted slate.

Connor blasted himself across the open battleground and crashed on top of a skinny Firetongue. The lad looked young enough that Connor should have known him at the Carraig. He was another Strider primary and he collapsed under Connor with a squawk of pain. Connor brained him with a gauntleted fist.

The other tertiaries were figuring out their attack plan, and Connor could feel their influence melding tighter together. They were like hunting nualls that had the scent of their quarry and were moving in for the kill.

Trying not to think about the growing danger, Connor mixed his three active elements together. It was tricky, but he'd walked with all three before, and failing meant dying. Getting martyred for a noble cause hadn't been much fun the last time, so he felt motivated to avoid it.

He threw out his hands and shouted, "Last chance to surrender!"

They didn't surrender.

They looked determined. He scanned the circle of enemy tertiaries and tried not to feel afraid. Men and women, professional soldiers, ready to kill or be killed.

If only he could distract them with a red flag.

Instead, he whipped the three mixed elements around himself into a protective sphere. It crackled and hissed and growled in a way that he loved, and it smelled like springtime bonfires after a light rain.

The Obrioners didn't appreciate it and attacked with combined fury. Great sheets of fire and water slammed into the outer edges of his sphere, while deadly spears of earth plunged up from below.

Connor severed them all. As every element drove into his sphere, it mixed with the others, giving him a chance to snatch control away.

He was actually doing it! He was fighting several experienced Petralists with three elements at once. It was amazing.

It was really hard too.

Sweat formed on his brow, and he started breathing hard. He lost track of time, completely immersed in the tricky balancing act of keeping the three elements mixed and fending off the ongoing attacks.

The Obrioners had dealt with mud and lava recently, but trying to untangle three was a lot harder. The fact that he was doing it drew even more attention and he felt three more Petralists join the offensive against him.

This was really getting unfair. Where were the Grandurian tertiaries? He didn't have time to scan the area and see if they had run into trouble.

The Obrioners seemed to have decided that they needed to remove him quickly. At least two Sentries were massing for a mighty attack that he'd never manage to deflect. Maybe he could escape into the air, but that would mean admitting defeat, and he really didn't want to do that.

Then Hamish swooped out of the sky and fired his last vial of skunk milk stench into one of the Sentry's faces. The grim-faced fellow looked competent and deadly. At first he ignored the little vial and turned after Hamish, sending grasping fingers of earth to grab for him.

Hamish flung himself into a wild spin and roared away in a thunder of air and fire.

Two seconds later, the Sentry gasped and pitched right off of his short tower. He screamed and clawed at his face, then started clobbering himself with shovel-sized clumps of loose dirt to try removing the stench.

Hamish circled over the Petralists attacking Connor, throwing something at each of them. A small bomb detonated at the base of one Spitter's watery pedestal, ripping it apart and sending him tumbling away. Connor spotted Ilse circling around toward him.

A wellstone landed beside another Sentry and immediately started gushing water, weakening the Sentry's connection with the earth. Connor felt the tug of the builded stone as it sucked at his water too. The Sentry started to slide away, but Connor yanked at the earth under him, slowing his retreat by a couple critical seconds.

The spreading mud weakened his connection just long enough for Hamish to drop a speedcrack wallstone. The little wall plowed through two Firetongues, breaking their knees and knocking them from the fight.

Furious Petralists threw fire and water into the air after Hamish, but he soared higher, just escaping the danger. He taunted them as he flitted out of range, keeping them distracted.

Connor wanted to turn his mini-hub to Hamish's speakstone, but he couldn't waste the precious distraction.

Walking with three elements was like juggling several Sogail balls while trying to snatch a sweetbread from Hamish's sisters.

Adding a fourth was like doing that while wearing mittens soaked in grease.

He had to try. He was Blood of the Tallan, and now was the moment to prove it. The Grandurian advance was picking up speed. He only needed to last a little longer and help would come. Probably.

Holding the images of the gateways fixed firmly in his mind, he called upon air.

His quartzite senses radiated into the air and he felt a fast-moving current high above the battlefield. He pulled on it. Hard.

Energized by the heat still boiling off of the lava, the air whistled down around him, plunging into the mixture of elements.

No sweetbread ever tasted so good.

Connor laughed at the thrill of riding all four elements. The air seemed to respond better to his call than ever. He wasn't sure if it was because he was melding all the elements together, or if the threat of impending destruction gave him better control.

He decided not to think about it too much. In his mind, it was like riding four powerful stallions that appeared content for once to run together. So as the enemy tertiaries returned their focus to him, he gave the elements a mental slap of the reins.

Connor rose out of his protective sphere, and it transformed beneath him into a huge tower made up of all four mixed elements. It looked like a boiling storm cloud, split by crackling flames. It smelled like a spring rain spraying over a cook fire.

Ten tertiaries ringed him now. A couple must have joined the party in the last minute, but now their connections to the elements seemed shaky and unsure. The masses of fighting soldiers battling all around them created a wild backdrop that drove home the desperation of the moment.

The enemy Petralists looked nervous.

They needed to feel terrified.

Connor threw his hands out wide and shouted, "Welcome to the new world!"

His tower exploded. Mixed elements erupted in every direction, covering the entire space between him and all the tertiaries in a concealing mist. Every one of his opponents recoiled. The unique blanket of elements had to be dampening their senses.

Connor struck through it.

He sent missiles of combined elements whipping through the mist at each of them. Some of his opponents either felt danger coming, or realized they were in trouble. One Sentry simply dropped down into the earth, wrapping herself in protective ground as she fled underground. Two of the Firetongues erupted out of the mist, feet blasting crimson flames.

The others hesitated a critical second too long.

The clinging, mixed mist acted like extensions of his hands, and Connor's missiles struck true. One after another, he knocked them off their feet and severed their elemental contact.

Connor caught each of them in bubbles of mixed elements, which he set spinning around him like mad tumble tosser balls that forgot how to stop. Rolling and tumbling like that, the disoriented tertiaries could not regain connection with their elements. Two of them reached the stomach-lurch point and vomited all over themselves.

He allowed the mist to fade out of the rest of clearing, except for those racing prison bubbles. That's when he spotted Ilse and Lukas, along with three other Crushers. The Grandurians had indeed capitalized on his distractions, and the front line of fighting had almost reached him.

"About time," Connor told Ilse. "I was thinking I'd have to chain all these myself."

"We've been busy."

Lukas threw Connor a sharp salute. "Not as busy as you, though."

The Crushers fanned out, and Connor ran each bubble to them in turn. He stopped their spinning abruptly and drained the mist away from the shaken Petralists. Before they could recover, a Crusher knocked them on the head and sent them into dreamland. It took less than half a minute to capture them all.

Connor expected another wave of tertiaries to rush in and attack in turn and try to save the prisoners, but none did. For a moment, he and the Crushers remained in a pool of calm in the center of the battleground as Grandurian Rumblers pushed south to their position.

Dougal's voice boomed over the battlefield. "Retreat! Battle order twenty-seven!"

Kilian appeared, arcing over the battlefield, trailing streamers of fire and water. He landed beside Connor, glowing in his mixed elemental sight like a multi-colored beacon. He looked completely unscathed from his intense, solo attack against the Obrioner army. He watched the retreating Obrioner lines like a pedra scanning a herd of fleeing goats.

"You're motivated today," Kilian said with an approving nod.

"I may be starting to get the hang of it."

"Don't pat yourself on the back yet. Don't you feel it? Dougal's trying to regroup and salvage the day. He's unleashed those two sculpted stones like he did at Harz."

Connor had been so focused on the near battle that he hadn't noticed. As soon as he extended his senses farther, he immediately pinpointed the danger.

Gregor was on the eastern side of the battlefield, his presence like a storm within the earth. He was moving northwest toward where the main road met the middle ground. If he could sever Grandurian access at that key point, Dougal's forces might surround and defeat the leading elements of the Grandurian forces after all.

On the west flank of the army, Ivor rode a twined pillar of fire and water. He looked lost to the elements, arms thrown wide, twined elements striking out in a constant barrage that drove the Grandurians back on that side.

"I feel them," Connor said.

"We cannot allow them to continue. This area is far too unstable on a good day. Using the lava was a bold choice, but it's left the ground on the verge of a major eruption. Anton and the Sappers are working to bottle it back up, but they can't fight Gregor at the same time. You and I have to stop those two before they trigger a catastrophic elemental disaster."

That would definitely wreck his moment of victory. "What do you have in mind?"

"Wolfram can't risk distributing any of his sculpted stones to counter them. We need less elemental fighting, not more. You and I need to do this, and fast. Best bet is for you to help Anton block Gregor while I kill Ivor."

"Ivor is my friend," Connor protested.

"I know, but he's at the point of losing control. I've seen it before. If he surrenders to the elements now, with this land already on the brink of destabilizing, I don't think we could stop the disaster."

"I can stop him," Connor promised. He couldn't bear to see a friend die without at least trying to save his life.

Kilian fixed him with a grim look. "Hundreds of thousands of lives depend on this."

"Just give me a chance." The magnitude of the looming disaster frightened him more than he wanted to admit, but he couldn't just throw Ivor's life away.

"Don't risk using slate. Anton is busy enough without anyone else crashing around down there."

Connor grimaced. Without earth to tip the balance in his favor, stopping Ivor would be a lot harder. He couldn't guarantee he could best his friend while in the grip of sculpted marble frenzy.

"I can do it," he said confidently.

Kilian nodded. "Very well. I'll help Anton against Gregor. Hamish should be back soon with a couple mechanicals that might help turn the tide. If you don't stop Ivor quickly, I will have no choice but to kill him."

Chapter Sixty-Eight

"The greatest tree may fall to lightning, and the sapling may weather a storm best by bending to the wind."

~Evander

onnor soared over the battlefield. The Obrioner lines were in full retreat, trying to regroup on the southern boundary of the valley. The Grandurians couldn't advance through Ivor and Gregor.

Connor landed about thirty feet away from Ivor and pulsed his earth senses one final time. Anton and the Sappers had formed a gigantic shield just north of his position. Gregor stood motionless on his tower a mile to Connor's east, unmoving and alone on the empty plain. Underground he was assaulting that barrier like an avalanche, and Connor quickly withdrew. He didn't want either side targeting him.

Ivor stood wreathed in flames, hovering eight feet off the ground in a billowing cloud of water and fire. As soon as Connor landed, he pivoted to face him. Ivor's eyes were filled with crimson flames, and snakelike tendrils of super-heated blue fire slithered all over him.

"Ivor, you've got to get out of here. The army's retreating and you can't take on all of Granadure alone."

He thought that was a very rational, well thought out argument.

Ivor wasn't feeling rational.

He laughed, spitting flames, and shouted, "Go away, Connor. Not even you can stop me now. I will see victory and honor for my house."

"You think that fiance of yours will be happy to learn she's engaged to the first Dawnus prisoner of war?"

Ivor settled to the ground and said in an almost sane voice, "Last chance, Connor. Today we can't be friends, and I don't want to hurt you."

Connor chuckled. "That was exactly what I was about to say."

In response, Ivor lifted his left hand, and Connor tensed to fight. He expected Ivor to unleash a firestorm.

The ground split open beneath his feet and a geyser of boiling water erupted. He felt it half a heartbeat before it struck.

After training with Ilse, that was plenty of time.

Ivor wasn't actively controlling the water. He'd just triggered the geyser. Connor easily split the geyser around himself, allowing water to shoot two hundred feet into the air. It all glowed in his tertiary sight.

He focused on the intense heat and snatched control of it, forming an invisible whip to strike at Ivor. He hoped spanking his friend with his own fire might unsettle him enough for Connor to seize those flames.

Ivor stopped the heat.

His control wasn't as good as Connor's, but the heat was far closer to him, and that proximity gave him an advantage. He wasn't ascended, but his influence over the heat was far stronger than anyone Connor had met besides Kilian.

"You're a novice," Ivor growled.

He threw out his hands, and the firestorm Connor had expected finally came. Flames rippled from crimson, to white, to blue as Ivor poured in more heat. The billowing wall of fire expanded, reaching out to consume Connor.

He met those flames with the waters of the still-erupting geyser. The elements crashed together with a hissing eruption of steam. Ivor was so deeply immersed in the sculpted-stone-driven flames that he ignored the water and attempted to drive the flames right through.

Connor threw his will into the firestorm and mixed the water into it as the two opposing forces met. For a second, he gained advantage and turned the tide back upon Ivor, sweeping the combined elemental attack right over his friend. For a moment, Ivor was concealed from view under a cloud of water, fire, and billowing steam.

Connor could feel him, though.

Ivor stood unmoved, unaffected by the crashing elements. He quickly leveraged his own will over the waters battering him, and sealed himself in a cocoon of defensive elements.

Connor could probably pierce that shield, but he didn't want to kill Ivor, so he hesitated.

Ivor didn't.

The mixed elements roared out again. Although he still focused more on the flames, Ivor did include water in the attack. Connor threw out his hands and his will and met him head on, battling for control.

Water and fire boiled around and between the two of them, hissing and crackling angrily. It smelled like burning, rotten eggs. A foul taste crept into Connor's mouth, unlike anything he'd tasted before. If the Lower Wick caught on fire, it might taste like that.

Connor held a distinct advantage with water, but Ivor overpowered him by a little with raw fury of fire. He had always been exceptionally strong with fire. With the aid of the sculpted stone, he might have been able to challenge even Kilian's control.

Connor couldn't stop him.

He dragged more water into the mix to give himself more advantage, but couldn't bottle Ivor's wild fury. Ivor began stalking toward him, arms out wide, completely encased by blue fire. The closer he drew, the stronger grew his influence.

The air between them became charged with power as the embattled elements whirled and struck. The nearest Grandurian soldiers were already over a hundred yards away, but they withdrew even farther.

Connor's senses merged with water, as he had done a couple of times in the past, but he also had to draw deeper from marble at the same time. He was wielding only two elements, but had to unite with them deeper than ever, and a feeling of wild exhilaration stormed through him.

If Ivor wanted to fight, he'd get a fight to rival the legends.

As Ivor continued to advance, the firestorm of flames mixed with a screaming tempest, forming a tornado-like funnel around the two of them.

So Connor filled it with water.

He hoped to block Ivor from the waters and distract him long enough to snuff out the flames, but Ivor deflected the waters away from himself and drove spears of white-hot fire at Connor's heart.

This fight was turning deadly!

Ivor was too swept up in the insanity of marble. Fury made him stronger, but less disciplined. Despite Connor's own close connection with the elements, he only barely severed those deadly spears and whipped them away into the mixed elemental storm.

For the first time, Connor felt fear. Fear that he might have to kill his friend to stop him.

No. He didn't want to kill again.

Connor started toward Ivor, slipping through a sheet of crackling flame, then an inverted waterfall of super-heated water. He was tempted to leap into a bash fight too, but which of them would that distract more?

Countering Ivor's influence over the flames taxed Connor's uttermost limits. Ivor was like a firestorm encased in flesh, and Connor had to draw ever deeper on marble. His union with water helped insulate him from the growing intensity of the burn in his mouth and the wild insanity now tempting him to unleash the beast raging in his heart.

He could do it. If he struck Ivor with the intent to kill, he could burn him to cinders.

He didn't want to. Did he?

It was hard to think. The crashing of the screaming elements around them and inside of his mind was drowning out thought, replacing them with raw emotion. The one that was rising on the tide of fire was fury. He needed to stop Ivor now, or he'd kill him.

Ivor's eyes were burning, his hair was burning, and his skin was glowing, as if fires were burning just beneath. Connor could feel it too. Ivor was on the cusp of complete union with fire. Connor had stepped across that line with water, and he knew how tempted Ivor must be to surrender everything to the flames.

"Ivor, beware, or the burn will incinerate you!"

"You feel it too. Don't pretend you don't." Ivor laughed in a tone of wonder. He grinned, and flames dripped from his mouth. "The fire can also purify, Connor. I know the deeper lore. Sometimes surrendering to the flames can refine Petralists like gold. There's only one way to find out. Are you willing to take the risk?"

Ivor's expression turned expectant and he gazed at Connor with burning eyes, as if hoping the two of them could take the ultimate dare together and see which of them could survive the purification.

"Are you cracked?" Connor asked, filling his voice with as much disgust as possible.

Ivor scowled. "Coward!"

He was burning too deep. Even his words echoed as he spoke, filled with hot air.

That was the answer.

Ivor struck again, more intensely than ever, and Connor had to throw everything he had into blocking him. Flames leapt all around him, and the heat blistered his face before he could drain it away. Ivor's will over the flames was more powerful than ever, and he threw his arms out, as if in ecstasy.

Ivor started to scream.

Connor stepped through a crackling wall of white-hot flames. As Ivor drew in a deep breath to scream again, Connor tapped quartzite.

He shoved a blast of wind down Ivor's throat.

Ivor's ecstatic trance snapped and he convulsed, trying unsuccessfully to cough. His eyes widened as his chest expanded, his lungs filled to bursting with the sudden rush of air. The flames dimmed noticeably as he tried to expel the choking air.

Connor shoved in a little more.

Ivor glanced at him, and Connor saw recognition in his eyes. He was pulling back from the brink. A wave of relief swept over Connor as he closed the last steps to Ivor, who began beating at his own chest to try forcing air out.

Connor gripped him by the shoulder and met his frightened gaze. "You had me worried there for a minute. You nearly burned yourself alive."

Ivor gestured at his mouth frantically, his eyes pleading.

"Release your tertiaries, and I think I can help."

Ivor's influence disappeared, and Connor controlled all the fire, all the water still whirling around them. It was a heady feeling, being absolute master of those elements.

"You know, we have a lot to talk about. As soon as you wake up."

He curse-punched Ivor in the stomach.

As Ivor doubled over from the blow, Connor allowed him to release all the air trapped in his chest. Ivor coughed several times, gasping. After a moment he finally stood up straight.

So Connor curse-punched him in the chin.

It was a good one too.

Riding the euphoria of that mingled, elemental storm, he punched perhaps an ounce or fifty too hard. Ivor was tapping granite a little, so the punch didn't rip his head off. It still knocked him off his feet.

Ivor crashed to the ground and lay still. Connor released the elements and beckoned to Ilse and Lukas, who had chased him across the plain and were circling nearby. They rushed in and chained Ivor.

Connor pried the worn fragment of sculpted stone from Ivor's still-closed fist. It radiated power, and Connor tucked it into his belt pouch.

"We should kill this one," Lukas said, gesturing at Ivor with his war hammer. "He's one of the most dangerous I've ever seen."

"He's a friend, and hopefully will become an ally," Connor said.

"You trust people too much," Ilse said.

"I trusted you, and that turned out all right."

"So far."

Ivor groaned, and Ilse helped him sit up.

"Drink this," she said in a gentle, motherly tone. She poured something into his mouth, forcing him to swallow.

Ivor coughed and swallowed. Then his eyes widened and he vomited explosively. He fell back to his knees, heaving again and again.

Lukas explained, "This purges soapstone. He won't have enough left in his system to spit."

Between heaving bouts of vomiting Ivor glanced at Connor, looking disgusted. "That was a rotten trick."

"What? Saving your life?"

"Is that what you call this?" Ivor turned away to heave again. Nothing came out, but he groaned and clutched his stomach.

Connor dropped to one knee beside him and placed a supporting hand on his shoulder. Ivor looked sickly gray, and very miserable, but he was alive.

"If I hadn't intervened, you would have destroyed yourself, or Kilian would have killed you. So yes, that's what I call it."

He helped Ivor to his feet and gestured south, where the Obrioner army was in full retreat, pursued by Kilian and elements of the Grandurian forces. In the distance, Gregor was sliding south fast on a short little tower that looked worn and beaten. Hopefully that meant that Anton had defeated him with Hamish's help.

"Looks like today's fight is pretty much over. Try to get some rest. I'll come find you after I check on Verena."

Ivor grimaced. "Do you really think Alyth will be embarrassed of me for failing today?"

"You didn't fail. You held off half the Grandurian army long enough for your company to retreat to safety. She'll probably think you're a hero."

"It does sound better when you put it that way," Ivor agreed.

Connor clapped him on the shoulder. "I might even pull some strings and have you transferred to my staff. I could use a valet."

Chapter Sixty-Nine

"The raft upon the waters can but steer within the torrent, but the dam athwart the chasm may subdue the raging flood."

~Anton

Connor found Verena in a comfortable, private room in the citadel, not far from Saskia's quarters. A maid in Saskia's colors ushered him into the bedchamber where Verena rested in an enormous four-poster bed.

She looked tiny, with the fluffy, white down comforter pulled up under her arms. She sat propped up by half a dozen pillows, and although she looked pale and tired, her smile seemed to light up the room.

The sight of her safe and recovering filled him with joy. The battle had gone well for Granadure, he hadn't died, and neither had his close friends. Just looking at her helped ease the ache of knowing he'd been forced to kill. He felt so happy, nothing could wreck the rest of the day.

"I'm glad someone's here who can tell me what's going on. I forgot to grab my mini hub," she said, eagerly gesturing him closer.

Connor moved to her side, and sat on the edge of the bed. He couldn't help but notice how she'd phrased that statement. The Shona situation was still clearly on her mind. That might just rain on his happy day.

He took her warm hand in his and asked, "Are you all right?"

"I'm fine, but the Healer insisted I needed rest. So Saskia ordered me closeted away in here like some invalid. What's happening out there?"

It was a good sign that forced bed rest irritated her so much. She had to be healing quickly. Unfortunately, that made reconciling with her over Shona that much harder.

"The Obrioners have been driven back. Anton staved off a general volcanic eruption. I killed General Carbrey."

Verena gasped and leaned closer, her warm hands gripping his. "That's wonderful news!"

He looked down and nodded. "I had to."

When he looked up again, her smile had disappeared, and she looked concerned. "Are you all right?"

He hesitated, then nodded again. "Like I said. I had to do it. He made it personal."

"I'm sorry you had to do that." She squeezed his hand again. "I'm glad you did, though. Did that turn the tide?"

He shook his head. "Hardly. Almost no one seemed to notice at first. I helped the Crushers capture enough of the tertiaries that they had to retreat. I even defeated Ivor and took him prisoner."

"I'm glad you didn't have to kill him too."

He wasn't sure he could have. "Kilian is chasing the Obrioners to make sure they keep retreating."

"Let me know when he returns. I'll check up on the listening stone I planted in Carbrey's tent. I've had an ear-scout assigned exclusively to that one."

"I doubt we'll learn more than we already know."

"Maybe we'll learn who Dougal appoints to replace him." She sighed then and gave him a serious look. "Connor, I'm glad Altkalen is safe and you survived, but I'm not sure I'm ready to spend more time with you right now."

He tried not to grimace. He needed to explain about Shona, and fast. Otherwise she might get her satchel full of stones back before he saw her again. Or her throwing knives. He hated the look of sorrow on her face, and hated more that he was the cause of it.

Verena meant everything to him, and he decided he really did hate Shona for causing this rift between them. His relationship with Verena was already unsettled from his worries about her royal connections. This latest episode with Shona threatened to derail it completely. How could Shona cause so much damage even now?

He wanted to hug Verena, but didn't want her to feel pressured, so he only wrapped her hand in both of his.

"Verena, I'll leave if you want me to, but I think now is the best time to explain what happened out there with Shona."

She did not pull away, but her frown deepened. "Connor, my home was destroyed on Dougal's order. Today a lot of people died. Their lives, and those of their families are destroyed because of him."

She didn't hide her anguish at the loss of her home. He'd thought she'd gotten over the worst of it while they were in Faulenrost, but clearly the tragedy was still very fresh. Although he was conditioned to deal with loss like that better than she was, he understood her grief. His home had been destroyed once too.

Verena's expression turned harder. "Shona is the daughter of the man who caused all that destruction. How could you have allowed her to kiss you again? After everything we've been through to get you away from her, don't you have any sense?"

"I'm sorry, Verena. I didn't want to, but. . ." How could he explain it so that it made sense to her like it had in the moment to him?

"You didn't exactly look like you were fighting her off. She is not your patron anymore, Connor. You don't have to do what she says. I thought you understood that."

"Things get crazy around Shona." He understood her anger. He shared it. He had been an idiot to let Shona position him like that. He appreciated the fact that Verena was giving him a chance to explain.

"Kissing her is not the way to clear your head," Verena snapped.

"I needed to explain to the others what was going on," Connor protested. "The only way I could do that was to agree to kiss her afterward. I felt it was worth the price if I could convince them that patronage was a lie. I thought it might be the best way to begin spreading the truth."

"Oh, Connor, even you can't be that dense!" Verena cried, pulling her hand from his grasp. "They'll inherit the very houses that keep Guardians enslaved. They'll never risk their position by changing things or even allowing the truth to be shared."

"I know that now, but at that point I still hoped they might."

She shook her head in amazement. "You lived at the Carraig, Connor. You know them. Why would you think that?"

"Because I know them," he snapped back, unable to rein in his frustration.

He wasn't sure how to explain that he felt they should be better. He wanted to trust them with the truth so they could rise above the lies they would soon inherit. He met her gaze and added, "I had to try. They're my friends too. That's why I accepted that condition."

"Shona understands you too well, Connor. She played you perfectly."

When he started protesting again, she raised a calming hand. "I can't believe it, but I can actually see your point. It was foolish of you Connor, but at least that's behind us now, and I don't think you'll make a mistake like that again."

"Well. . ."

"What?" she demanded, instantly suspicious again.

He wished he could just let it go, leave the conversation there in that good place, but she'd find out the truth eventually. "We didn't actually get a chance to kiss. The bash fighting started and Ivor ordered his entire command to form up. Shona had to leave."

"I saw her kissing you," Verena stated.

He shook his head. "That was just a tease."

Verena sighed and gave him a relieved sigh. "Why didn't you just say so, Connor? That's not nearly so bad. I'm glad the bash fighting interrupted. Now you can stay away from her."

When he looked down and didn't respond, she asked slowly, "What haven't you told me yet?"

He felt like an idiot, wanted to beat himself senseless, and was barely able to meet her unhappy gaze. "I still owe Shona that kiss. I swore an oath when we made the deal, and she expects me to keep my word."

Verena's expression turned fierce. "Not if I kill her first."

"Verena," he warned. The last thing he wanted was for her to hunt down Shona in a blood-oath rage. The two already seemed intent on fighting to the death, and the thought terrified him.

"Don't 'Verena' me," she snapped, and hit him with one of her pillows. "I can't believe you still plan to honor that twisted agreement."

"I gave her my word. . ."

"I don't care!" Verena shrieked. She threw another pillow and shouted, "Get out, Connor!"

He held up his hands in a placating gesture, not sure what he could possibly say that might make things better. He really should leave, but would she ever speak to him again? "Verena, please listen."

"No, you listen to me, Connor," she declared in a regal tone unlike anything he'd ever heard her use before.

She sat straight, her chin up, her eyes flashing with indignant anger, and in that moment she looked as regal as Shona had ever managed. "You made a choice to come with me, Connor. You chose to leave Obrion behind. I risked my life to save you! You cannot go back to her, or everything you've done, everything you've said to me is a lie. Can't you see that?"

By the time she finished, tears shone in her eyes. Connor wanted to tell her she'd never looked so beautiful. Even he realized that would be a colossal mistake. She was far too worked up, and such a gesture would probably send her scurrying to find a stone or a knife.

"I think we need to wait until you're better before we finish this conversation," he said.

"This conversation is over. And we're over if you ever go back to her. Connor, can't you see how stupid you're being?"

His sorrow and shame at allowing Shona to manipulate him was turning to anger. He'd done so much for Verena and for Granadure. He'd just beaten and captured a good friend to save her and Altkalen.

"I'm not the only one acting stupid. You're acting like Shona now more than ever."

"How dare you!" she shrieked.

"How dare you?" he shot back. "I was stupid, yes, but what makes you think you can dictate our relationship? We're supposed to be working things out together. You claim you're different, but listen to yourself. You're trying to control me and place conditions on my life to suit your pleasure."

"Get out," she hissed, her expression seething with fury.

Connor stormed from the room, wishing there was still an army close enough for him to fight. In that moment, he would have released the beast in his heart without hesitation.

Why did she have to be so unreasonable?

CHAPTER SEVENTY

"A mighty stone, marred by invisible cracks, crumbles under the force of a single, well-placed hammer."

~Connor

erena paced the plush bedroom, filled with boiling fury, hands clenched so hard her wounded shoulder ached. Her bare feet padded silently across the thick carpet, but she wished she had boots on so she could kick something.

She growled angrily as Connor's words seared her memory. She snatched up one of the pillows from the floor and threw it with all her might. It bounced harmlessly off the window, and she was tempted to find something harder to smash it with. She really could savor the sound of breaking glass right now.

She couldn't believe Connor actually planned to honor that agreement with Shona. How could he? She'd never gone back on her sworn word either, but then again, she'd never swear to such a ridiculous agreement in the first place.

She loved Connor, but at the moment she hated him too.

The worst was that he honestly seemed to believe that she and Shona could be at all similar. Getting compared to that vile woman infuriated Verena so much, she found it hard to think straight.

She had thought she knew Connor, that she understood him, but clearly she didn't. Was it a difference in their cultures, or just something in him that made him so block-headed?

She wasn't trying to control him, but she would defend her right to his exclusive attention with fierce and implacable determination. Connor had chosen her, and she had chosen him. How could he not understand that he owed her complete fidelity?

A knock on the door interrupted her angry pacing and she spun toward it, shouting, "Go away, Connor!"

The door swung open, but it wasn't Connor who peeked inside.

It was Mattias.

He smiled, and his handsome face still tugged at her heart strings. "I'm glad to see you're up and about."

"What are you doing here?" she exclaimed, her anger replaced by embarrassment. She wore only a linen robe over a simple cotton night dress.

Mattias, ever the gentleman, averted his gaze as she scurried back to the bed and pulled up the covers. Her cheeks felt warm, and she hoped she wasn't blushing.

He chuckled as he entered the room and scooped up a couple of pillows. "That ornate headboard can't be comfortable behind your back."

She scooted forward to allow him to place the pillows behind her. That did help. Mattias sat on the edge of the bed, exactly where Connor had a few minutes before. He took her hand.

"I was so worried when I heard you were wounded by a Mhortair Assassin."

"I'll be fine," she assured him, but then rubbed her aching shoulder.

The Healers had explained about the severe damage that Mister Five's unique attack had done. If not for the healing power that Connor had poured into her so quickly, she might have suffered permanent damage.

She was still mad at him, though.

"From the state of your room and your obvious anger, I think it safe to assume you've already received reports of Connor's dalliance with the lady Shona this morning," Mattias said, one eyebrow raised.

"I saw it myself," she snapped.

The thought that other Longseers had seen his stupid action only stoked her anger. How many people knew? Would rumors reach her family in Edderitz? She cringed inwardly at the thought of the unpleasant conversations she'd have to endure if that happened.

Mattias patted her hand. "Relax, 'Rena. I've already issued orders to those who witnessed it keep it strictly confidential. I told them he was performing a misinformation initiative on behalf of the council."

Verena gave him a relieved sigh and squeezed his hand. "Oh, Mattias. You're such a good man."

"Protecting your honor has always been a duty I take seriously."

She was surprised that she felt the need to explain Connor's actions. "I warned him that meeting Shona was a stupid idea, but he didn't listen, and she manipulated him like she always does."

"He comes from a humble background, yes?"

She nodded. "Very."

"Then he is unused to the intrigue and manipulations that nobility grow up with. You were right to suspect he would fail. It's a shame he's not wise enough to heed your counsel."

Mattias understood things so clearly. Why couldn't Connor?

"Tell me about the battle." She hadn't gotten any specifics from Connor, and not knowing was yet another irritant.

He told her, and as always, she loved the rich baritone timbre of his voice. As he spoke, he slowly stroked the back of her hand. She had always loved that when they were dating at the academy.

When he brought her up to date on the situation, she leaned back against the pillows and closed her eyes. She felt relieved that the fighting had gone so well and that the Grandurian casualty count was lower than it could have been. She really was tired, but she was still so worked up, she doubted she could sleep.

Mattias began to sing.

He sang softly, with that beautiful voice that she'd fallen in love with. It wasn't a victory song like those surely being sung loudly across the city by soldiers relieved to have survived the day. It was a simple melody, one he had sung to her on many occasions while they sat on the banks of a lovely little lake just south of the academy.

The simple verses celebrated peaceful days and good friendship. As he sang, dozens of happy memories flitted through her mind. She should tell him to stop, but the sounds eased her anger, and drained away her tension. She allowed herself a luxurious moment to do nothing but lean back on the pillows, eyes closed, a half smile on her lips, as she enjoyed the simple pleasure of his angelic voice.

When he finished she sighed, "Thank you, Mattias. I needed that."

"I'm glad I could help." He leaned a little closer and touched her cheek. "Verena, I know your spirit. You'll do whatever needs doing, no matter how hard it is. I love that about you."

"I appreciate that, Mattias, but what are you saying?"

"Life doesn't have to be so difficult. I know you feel drawn to Connor, but I can also see the relationship is difficult."

"All relationships are difficult." Her voice dropped to a whisper as she stared into his eyes and read the same emotion there that she remembered. "Even ours."

478

He leaned forward and kissed her cheek. "I regret only that I didn't find a way to bring you and the entire Builder compound to Edderitz sooner. Know that I'm here for you, 'Rena. No matter what you need, when you need it, and for as long as you'll allow me to."

She touched his face, moved by the depth of his emotion, and surprised by how strongly she still felt for him. If things had turned out differently, she didn't doubt they'd already be promised to each other.

When he leaned forward to kiss her lightly on the lips, she did not push him away.

For a second, it felt just like old times. Feelings that she'd thought bottled up and discarded long ago ignited in her heart anew.

But the kiss was a mistake.

Verena pushed Mattias back, felt his reluctance to move away, his desire to kiss her again. She looked deep into his eyes and saw his honest emotion, but shook her head.

"We can't do this, Mattias."

He frowned and his tone became bitter. "Why not? You still feel it, 'Rena. Don't pretend you don't. We could make it work."

"I was just furious at Connor for letting Shona kiss him again. He had his reasons, just as I had for allowing myself to kiss you just now. It's not right for him to do it, and it's not right for us, and you know it."

"Not if you leave him and come back to me."

She absolutely hated the fact that tears threatened and her heart ached with remembered pain. She thought back to the day he'd left for the capital and she'd gone the other way toward the Builder compound.

"We had our chance, Mattias, and we chose different worlds. Our worlds are still different, and our lives have moved on."

"You can't say you still want to choose that common Obrioner over me," Mattias said angrily.

"At the moment, I don't know what I want, but I know that I need time to figure things out." She gestured between the two of them. "This isn't helping."

Mattias rose and took a deep, steadying breath. "I love you, 'Rena. We separated because we had no choice, but now you do. I'll give you time, but you owe me an honest answer soon. Don't let your infatuation with the Blood of the Tallan cloud your better judgment."

After he left, Verena buried her head under the covers and let herself really cry for the first time in years.

Chapter Seventy-One

Connor paused outside of the ornate, wooden door to Saskia's private library, where his family was waiting. He took a long, calming breath, trying to let go of his still-simmering anger. He'd taken a long walk through the citadel, but completely failed to regain the happiness he'd felt prior to the argument.

Verena was right about some things, but she was so wrong about others. He'd never imagined she'd treat him like that, assuming the regal, authoritarian bearing so like Shona. He'd worried her family might be as problematic as the Obrioner nobility at the Carraig, but he'd never imagined Verena might be infected with that pride too.

He loved Verena, and the thought of losing her added a fluttering panic to his already riled-up emotions. He had absolutely no idea how to set things right. He could never again accept a one-sided relationship where his only role was to serve and do his partner's bidding, but how could he make her understand?

Women were always a mystery, and he hated that feeling of cluelessness. He'd never understood Shona, but he'd hoped he might get to that point with Verena.

With an effort, he forced his worries, his anger, and his fears aside, assumed a happy expression, and pushed open the door. The library was small by citadel standards, meaning it could have only held half the town of Alasdair.

Vaulted ceilings rose over twenty feet to domed panels, painted in brilliant mosaics, depicting Grandurian history. Most of the walls were covered in bookshelves made out of a delicate, creamy-looking wood. They rose almost to the ceiling, with three levels of narrow catwalks circling the room, accessed by tightly-spiraling staircases.

Two huge windows on the far side of the room flanked a fireplace with an ornately-carved walnut mantel. A cheery blaze was burning, and several couches and chairs were drawn up around the hearth.

Hamish and Jean stood near the fire, holding hands, surrounded by Hamish's family. Mhairi sat nearby in a chair so stuffed with padding it seemed to be trying to swallow her. Martys stood on the opposite side of the hearth, speaking with Hendry and Lilias, while Connor's brothers chased each other around the couches.

They spotted him first, let out a happy cheer, and raced across the room, nearly tackling him off his feet in their excitement.

Little Wallace gave Connor a serious look. "What took you so long, Connor? Were you making that squirrel for me?"

"I had a few things to take care of."

When he reached the hearth, his mother enveloped him in a long hug, which he was happy to return. He didn't know if all mothers had that amazing ability to make everything seem all right. His mother had perfected it.

"We were so worried for you," she said.

"If'n ye hadn't confused the lad with that rubbish about mercy in battle, ye widnae have had such fears," Martys said, giving her a disapproving look.

She stiffened and her eyes flashed with anger, but before she could make an angry retort Connor said, "It's all right, Uncle Martys. Everyone survived, so no harm done."

He grunted sourly. "Not this time, but ye must accept the fact that there be times when ye must fight to kill."

"You don't know everything I had to do out there," Connor said. He stepped away from his mother, whose expression turned concerned.

"Enough of killing talk for now," Hendry said, clapping his brother on the shoulder. "Let's celebrate the miracle that we're all alive and all together."

"For now," Amhain said. He looked uneasy in the beautiful library.

"Hush, love." Peigi gave him a disapproving look.

"Where's that lovely girl of yours, Connor?" his mother asked.

"She was hurt in the fighting, but she'll be all right," Connor assured her.

"Where is she? I should go visit," Lilias said.

Mhairi said, "I'll come along. Those Petralist Healers seem overly reliant on their magic to cure what tonics and herbs can do better."

"I think she needs to be left alone for a while," Connor cautioned.

Some of his lingering anger must have crept into his voice because his mother said, "Oh, Son, you two aren't fighting, are you?"

"I don't want to talk about it."

He still felt such a turmoil of shame and anger that he wasn't sure he could talk about it.

Hendry gave him an understanding look. "Son, every relationship has struggles. In a time of war, the stresses are even worse. Don't let momentary anger cloud the truth of how you two feel about each other."

"I said she's fine," Connor said more sharply than he had ever spoken to his parents before. His mother raised one eyebrow at his tone and he sighed, "Sorry. It's been a rough day."

She hugged him again. "I know. It's a miracle we're all here."

"More like a nightmare," Amhain said with another scowl.

"What's wrong, Dad?" Hamish asked.

Amhain barked a laugh. "Can you ask that? We're in Granadure. We're surrounded by the barbarians. They could do anything to us."

Connor was surprised to see Peigi nodding. He caught his parents exchanging a worried look too. Most of the kids seemed more interested in exploring the higher levels of the bookshelves, though.

He'd feared the Grandurians at first, but he'd learned long since that there were good people on both sides of the border, just as there were bad. He understood their fears, but they didn't have time for incorrect prejudices.

Time to break them of bad habits. So he laughed.

"Are you serious? These people helped save your lives. They've taken you in and treated you well, haven't they?"

Amhain said, "Aye, that they have, but High Lord Dougal himself showered us with gifts until he decided it was time to use us as hostages."

Hamish said, "I warned you about Dougal, Dad. These are good people."

"It's still not right to laugh off the danger," Peigi said nervously.

Jean said, "I know it breaks everything we've known our whole lives, but we can actually trust some of the Grandurians."

"You're forgetting that they invaded our home last year," Amhain pointed out.

Jean said, "Even so, Connor and Hamish are right. We have good friends here."

Amhain didn't look convinced, but Hendry wrapped an arm around Lilias and said, "We haven't seen anything to make us doubt your word. I'm just glad everyone is safe."

"Tell us what happened and how you ended up here," Connor said.

They took turns telling the tale. Dougal and a force of wild soldiers had appeared without warning in Alasdair. They had captured and subdued the lookout boys so no one got warning of their arrival. Dougal had informed the families that they were needed, that their service would help end the war sooner.

"He made it sound a grand thing," Hendry said with a scowl.

"The reality was the opposite," Lilias agreed.

Peigi shivered, rubbing her arms. "Those soldiers were the most terrifying part. The way they looked at us! It was like they were eager for any excuse to kill."

"I shouldn't have spared them," Connor growled.

Lilias shook her head. "The men holding us prisoner today knew nothing of who we were. They weren't the wild ones who dragged us north. Those men and women remained with Dougal."

"I think they're his bodyguards," Hendry said.

Hamish and Jean exchanged a worried look and he said, "Sounds like those rampagers we captured during that first raid."

Jean explained, "They're soldiers who can turn unclaimed at will and transform into horrible, deadly monsters."

"Why in Tallan's unholy name would Dougal surround himself with people like that?" Lilias exclaimed.

"Because they're his last line of defense against us," Hamish said.

Connor was barely listening. The thought of rampagers in the Obrioner camp meant that somewhere not far distant was someone with porphyry. If only he'd known, he could have hunted them down and taken the powder.

He was struck by such a powerful urge to do just that, he took a single step toward the nearest window before he checked himself. For just a second, he'd intended to leap right through the window, even though he didn't have marble or quartzite ready.

Could he have pulled a stone from his pouch and connected with the element before plunging to his death?

Part of him didn't care, and he fought to control the urge to jump anyway. It was the fastest way to get the powder, so it was worth any risk.

He shuddered as a dreadful chill crept slowly down his spine. Maybe Kilian was right about porphyry. Still, there had to be a way to use it safely. He wished Verena was nearby. The touch of her hand always helped center his mind, although at the moment thinking of her didn't calm him.

"Are you all right, lad?" Mhairi asked. Somehow she stood right beside him, looking up at him with concern in her gaze.

He hadn't even seen her move. He blinked and glanced around. The others hadn't seemed to notice, but were listening with rapt attention as Hamish described rampagers in terrifying detail.

"I'm fine."

She held his gaze for another second or two before slowly nodding. "I have only two medicines that can make a patient look like you did just now. Whatever is ailing you, Son, seek help from someone who understands the danger before you hurt yourself or someone near you."

Connor gave her a warm smile. "Thanks. I'll remember that."

There was no way she understood what he was going through. Dealing with porphyry was nothing like her medicines, but he wouldn't ever dare tell her to mind her own business.

"I'm so glad we got away from them," Peigi said as Hamish finished his account of his first encounter with rampagers and how they'd smashed his flying board.

Connor said, "We'll have to make sure Wolfram knows about them. Even a couple of rampagers could kill a lot of people."

Hendry drew closer to Connor and placed a hand on his shoulder. "Thanks again for saving us. You took a terrible risk. I know your places are here, dealing with these dangerous people, using powers that are more legend than reality. But what of us?"

"We need to go home," Lilias said.

The others all nodded in agreement, and Connor wanted to pull out his hair with frustration.

"You can't go home. Dougal kidnapped you once. If you return, he could do it again, or worse."

Peigi looked stricken. "We've got nowhere else to go. Alasdair is our home."

"And the village needs us," Hendry said.

The door to the library burst open and Aifric rushed inside. "Sorry for interrupting, but there's a meeting we need to attend. Right now."

"We'll figure things out," Connor promised his family as Jean and Hamish said good-bye and headed for the door with Aifric. "I promise."

The only thought that came to him as he jogged down the long corridors of the citadel after Aifric was that his family would never be safe as long as Dougal lived.

CHAPTER SEVENTY-TWO

"Fear is the darkest hour before dawn, but shadows flee the touch of the sun."

~Gregor

ifric led them to Saskia's private sitting room where they'd first met her. Saskia was there, along with Kilian and Wolfram. They all still wore their battle garb. Verena sat in an overstuffed chair, wearing a simple cream colored dress.

She looked soft and beautiful, and Connor longed to rush to her. He couldn't quite make himself do it, though.

"Good. Perfect timing," Wolfram said, gesturing them to join the group in comfortable seats near the fire.

Connor couldn't look away from Verena. If he dropped to his knees and begged her forgiveness, could he repair the damage their argument had caused?

She looked up and met his gaze. He was startled to see her flush and actually look embarrassed. Had she realized she'd gone too far?

While Hamish and Jean took a couch nearby, Connor dropped to one knee beside Verena and placed a hand on hers, where it rested on the arm of her chair. She met his gaze and he said, "Verena, I--"

She shook her head. "Not here, Connor."

"All right." He pulled another padded chair up to her left side and exulted in the feeling of relief he felt. They'd work things out. The argument had been stupid, after all.

Then Mattias hurried into the room and pulled up a chair on the other side of Verena. He cast Connor the least friendly look he ever had, and made a point of touching Verena's hand. "Are you feeling any better?"

"I'm fine, thank you," she said softly, and only barely looked at him.

So he glared at Connor again.

Connor winked.

He had no idea why Mattias was suddenly acting angry. He had seemed to be dealing pretty well with the fact that Verena was with Connor. Had something changed?

Maybe he felt frustrated because Connor had played a central role in the recent battle, while he'd lurked in the rear in an administrative command position. Connor would be happy to give him some first-hand experience in getting punched in the face, if that would make him feel better.

"Thank you all for coming so quickly," Wolfram said.

"What's going on?" Hamish asked.

"That listening stone you and 'Rena planted in Carbrey's tent, that's what," Saskia grinned.

"Never underestimate a crafty girl.

She'll give your heart a nasty whirl.

When 'Rena wants the truth, she digs better than a sleuth, and secrets open to her like shining pearls."

"You've grown positively poetic today, Saskia," Mattias said with a chuckle.

"I'm an optimist."

Kilian added, "And as you so eloquently suggested, the ear-scout monitoring that listening stone heard just moments ago that Dougal has called a war council. It should start shortly."

Saskia turned to Connor and saluted.

"I heard you killed old Carbrey.

Tonight we'll all raise glasses to thee.

Now Dougal's on the run, his invasion is no more fun, and his life is next we'll all agree."

"It had to be done," he said simply.

Wolfram saluted. Kilian nodded approval, but his expression suggested he understood how hard killing Carbrey had been. That fact helped ease Connor's lingering guilt at what he'd done. Mattias scowled, and that made Connor feel even better.

Kilian beckoned, and a young woman dressed in the tan uniform of an ear-scout settled a small piece of quartzite onto a cloth on a low table in front of the fire.

As they drew closer to it, Verena said, "This is a one-way speakstone. They can't hear us."

"Can we amplify the sound?" Saskia asked.

Verena shook her head. "I don't recommend it. This pairing is already fragile. We could drain the stone's power before they complete the meeting."

"Better to leave it," Kilian said.

So they all drew even closer, sitting knee to knee in a tight circle around the little table. Connor enjoyed sitting so close to Verena, although he hated the fact that Mattias got the perfect excuse to sit just as close on her other side. He could not read what Verena might be feeling. She stared fixedly at the stone.

A moment later, sounds of chairs scraping echoed from the little stone, followed by Dougal's voice welcoming people. Connor recognized the names of several high-ranking Obrioner officials, including Captain Rory.

Aifric said, "He just mentioned one of King Turriff's generals, and Flichity is High Lord Lenox's representative. Rith got a strong sense that he wasn't pleased with the war even before the rout this morning."

Lord Flichity barely waited for Dougal to complete his greeting before snapping, "Are you mad, Dougal? You can't seriously plan to retreat all the way back to the border!"

"Have a care how you speak to my father," Shona said. Connor hadn't heard her introduced, and the sound of her rich voice startled him. He glanced at Verena, who was glaring at the listening stone.

"Certain lapses of protocol can be forgiven during the stresses of war," Dougal said, his voice calm and confident, despite the bad day. "All is not lost, and this retreat is but the process of setting the board for the final trap that will lure Kilian and those cursed Builders to their doom."

Connor exchanged a surprised look with Verena. Could Dougal really have contingencies already in place to turn the day's brutal defeat into an ultimate victory?

Hamish muttered, "I really hate the fact that I used to respect that guy."

Jean shushed him as Lord Flichity said, "You've made grand promises before, Lord Dougal, but this invasion appears to be faltering."

"All plans face unforeseen setbacks, particularly when cast across such a vast arena of combat. Adversaries of this caliber do not fall easily."

"Forgive me if I express lingering reservations. We are in full retreat, Kilian and that Connor together ravaged our army, the Builders unleash new devilry at every encounter, and your promised assassin did little more than run away."

Shona spoke in icy tones. "Have a care with your tone, Lord Flichity. You're conveniently forgetting that we took the pass with almost no loss of life, razed Harz to the ground, and advanced farther than any other recorded incursion."

"And yet now we are ordered to retreat and surrender all that hard-fought advantage," Flichity retorted.

"I'm liking this," Verena said with a predatory smile as she leaned over the stone. "Maybe they'll start fighting."

Connor was just glad he wasn't the one she was eager to see get hurt any more. She was adorable with that air of danger that often surrounded her, but he preferred kissing her to getting punched in the face.

"I appreciate your candor," High Lord Dougal said, sounding unruffled by being openly doubted by one of his senior advisers. "But you lack the proper perspective. Ground may be retaken at our leisure once we remove the only true threats to our dominance."

"And you really expect to give us victory, even though they've stolen all of your sculpted stones?" Turriff's general asked.

"What better way to defeat them than by snatching victory away in the very moment they think to obtain it? I will raise an ancient elfonnel, more powerful than any seen in three centuries. I will destroy the hated Kilian and the troublesome Builders, and drive the fool Connor back to my daughter for proper management."

Connor glanced at Verena, whose glee at their infighting again turned to an angry glare. She'd produced a dagger from somewhere and was gripping it as if she wished to somehow drive it through the little stone.

"Lady Shona, do you think you can control the Blood of the Tallan this time?" Flichity asked.

"Blame the king for Connor's loss, not me," Shona retorted. "If not for his idiotic decree of second breeding rights, I would have secured Connor to me for all time."

"The order will be rescinded," Dougal promised. "You must be prepared to draw him gently back into the fold when the time comes."

"I want nothing more than such an opportunity," Shona said, and Connor cringed at the eagerness in her voice. She sounded so sincere. That would only stoke Verena's anger. "If only that assassin had struck true when he had the chance."

Connor glanced at Aifric, who cringed at the mention of Mister Five. She looked miserable. "Mister Five orchestrated that attack beautifully. If not for the turbulent air, Verena would have fallen today."

"I'll kill him," Connor growled.

"Unless I get to him first," Mattias said.

"I can take care of myself, thank you both very much," Verena said, her tone brusque, including both of them in her disapproving frown.

"And who will take Carbrey's place to lead this grand retreat trap of yours?" King Turriff's general asked. Even through the stone, Connor picked up on his eagerness for the position.

"Captain Rory, of course," Dougal said simply.

"What?" Hamish and Saskia exclaimed together. Verena and Jean both shushed them, and everyone leaned closer.

Connor exchanged a surprised glance with Verena. Rory was a good man, but he was only a captain.

A rumble of surprise from the other assembled officers echoed from the stone, and Rory spoke, sounding a bit shaken. "My lord, I am not the most senior officer."

Dougal spoke, and Connor could imagine him raising calming hands. "I recognize this appointment is a bit unorthodox, but I have worked hard to position you where I have, Rory. You know the enemy better than any of my other officers. The Grandurians respect you and will hesitate to strike at you like they would anyone else I might appoint."

He paused, then added. "Although, if anyone would like to volunteer to draw Kilian's and Connor's wrath, such a sacrifice could be useful in drawing them deeper into my trap."

"He is so wicked," Saskia murmured, her tone tinged with respect.

"He's right too," Connor said. "I don't think I could kill Rory."

Dougal let the silence stretch for a few seconds before saying, "General Rory, you will take command immediately."

After that, the conversation turned to mundane items of managing the withdrawal. They planned to continue south steadily all the way back to the border, despite ongoing objections from both Flichity and the king's general.

Finally Kilian gestured for the ear-scout to take the listening stone away, with orders to continue monitoring it. After she left he said, "Excellent work planting that stone, Verena. That was a spectacular intelligence coup."

"But how can he do it?" Jean demanded. "He admitted the sculpted stones are gone, but he's claiming that he can raise another elfonnel."

"What does he mean by an ancient elfonnel?" Hamish asked.

"It sounds like he's bragging," Connor said.

Kilian rose and paced to the large window. He stared out of it for a moment while the rest of them watched and waited. Finally he turned.

"The reference to an ancient elfonnel suggests Dougal has learned yet another secret I thought long buried. When a Petralist raises an elfonnel, there have been times when those elementals did not die or expire.

"Instead they simply leave. In those cases, they fade away and are lost to all elemental senses. The Petralists who raised them are never found."

Jean said, "So if an elfonnel disappeared like that, you're saying it's almost like they hibernate instead of dissipating? Could it be possible to wake them up again?"

"Not if you don't know where to find them," Connor said.

Verena's angry frown had turned worried. "It sounds like Dougal might have figured out how to find one. The way Dougal spoke of it, he seems to think an ancient elfonnel might be even more destructive than the ones raised so far."

Kilian said, "He might be right. Some of the most powerful Petralists of all time were lost in that way during the Tallan Wars, including my own mother."

"Really?" Jean and Verena asked at the same time.

"During the battle that resulted in breaking off part of the continent, she raised one of the elfonnel. When the elements revolted and the land split, her elfonnel was buried in a gigantic explosion of lava. We lost contact with her, and she never reappeared. Either she died or hibernated. No one has ever raised a hibernating elfonnel before."

"Maybe they have," Connor said.

His thoughts had turned to the strange pyramid with the stone cairn that formed where he'd killed that elfonnel at the Carraig.

"That elfonnel that attacked the Carraig was a lot harder to kill than the ones we've faced since. I know there are other factors that might play into that difference, but Evander seemed to know him. He called him old friend, or something. I didn't understand at the time, but maybe that was exactly what we're talking about here."

"So the Carraig might have been a trial run for more than just Dougal trying to control an elfonnel," Hamish said.

"If he found one and figured out how to raise it, then that settles it," Kilian said.

"What?" Connor asked.

"Some of you have to go visit Evander and find out what he knows."

"Do you think it's worth such a long trip to ask him that question?" Verena asked.

"No, but there's only one other possible interpretation of Dougal's words. He might have found a way to raise an elfonnel without using a sculpted stone, and without having access to an ascended Petralist who could do such a thing. Again, Evander might be the only person who might have an idea of how that might be done."

It took only a few minutes to plan their trip. Connor, Verena, Hamish, and Jean would fly back to the Carraig. Aifric insisted on coming, then Mattias did too.

"No way," Connor blurted out immediately.

"It's not your decision to make," Mattias snapped back, and he looked ready for Connor to finally punch him over the river.

"I don't think it's a good idea," Verena said, snatching the moment away. "Evander doesn't exactly like Grandurians."

"You're going," Mattias grumbled.

"She's been there before," Connor said.

"And she's a lot cuter than you," Hamish added.

"What does that have to do with anything?" Jean laughed.

Hamish shrugged. "More than you think."

Unfortunately, Kilian interceded before the argument could get heated. He ordered Mattias to stay with his troops and urged the others to hurry.

It would take a few days for the enormous Obrioner army to retreat back to the border, with Wolfram, Kilian, and the Grandurian host in careful pursuit to make sure they didn't change their mind. There would be enough time if they didn't dawdle.

"And we can drop off our families in Alasdair on the way south," Hamish said.

"They can't stay," Connor objected.

Jean said, "Of course not, but they'll have time to pack. We can pick them back up on the way north."

That was actually a really good idea. They could transition leadership of the women's circle and appoint a new Ashlar. With a proper good-bye to their homes, maybe they'd be ready to leave forever. Connor didn't even have a new home yet, but maybe they could find one together.

Besides, Dougal had no idea they were returning. In the short time they'd be in Alasdair, they'd be safe.

Chapter Seventy-Three

"Shades of the past walk shadows and whisper truths that few have ears to hear."

~Evander

Night had fallen hours ago. Connor shivered with cold as the Storm soared through a high pass in the Tairseach Mountains in central Obrion.

The Carraig came into view as they rounded a flank of the towering Mount Murdo. A partial moon and thousands of glittering stars shone through the clear, cold air, making it easy to scan the Carraig with his enhanced vision.

The sight of the recent destruction shocked him. He hadn't really internalized how much damage the Carraig had sustained from the elfonnel. The plain that had concealed the hidden ruins of the ancient city was all cleared away. Debris was piled along the western stretch of the broken outer wall. The three lakes nestled in the ruins that had been concealed for so long glittered in the moonlight.

That broken western plain, and the extensive damage within the inner city gave the Carraig a lonely, desolate feeling that made Connor shiver again. Repairs were clearly underway within the many palaces of the inner city, but it looked like the first steps had been to tear down several additional damaged palaces.

He counted eleven gaping holes in the Carraig skyline where familiar towers and spires should have stood. Mounds of rubble still clogged many of the once-beautiful streets.

Hamish let out a low whistle from his seat in the second row beside Jean. "What a mess."

Verena said softly, "It's a shame that Dougal has caused so much destruction even in his own homeland."

"It feels quiet," Aifric muttered with a frown from the third row.

"Because it's nearly midnight," Hamish said.

She shook her head. "Even at night, there's a feel to the Carraig, a sense of life. It's missing."

Connor felt it too and realized what it was. "The students are gone. Remember, Ivor mentioned the older students were all recruited, and the younger ones sent home during repairs?"

"I had forgotten about that," Verena asked.

She was piloting the Storm and hadn't protested Connor sitting beside her. She still hadn't spoken about their fight. He had tried to broach the subject, but she had only told him she needed more time.

Did girls just need a minimum amount of time to feel angry after an argument? Or was that troubled look that had often clouded her face mean there was something else he'd done wrong that he wasn't even aware of? He debated just apologizing for the unknown infraction in advance. It might save time later.

"So much for blending in," Aifric said with a wry smile.

"As if any of us know how to do that," Connor chuckled.

"I am quite talented at blending," Aifric objected.

Hamish said, "You do blend nineteen people all the time. Must be a simple thing to blend with people not already in your head."

"Usually."

"This should actually make it easier for us," Verena said as she slowly descended, the lift thrusters barely throwing enough air to keep them from falling from the sky.

The Swift on its long tether trailed after, like a shadowy bird gliding in their wake. As they drew closer to the soaring towers of the Carraig, Connor heard the distant chorus from the city's many musical gargoyles.

They caught and channeled the winds around the palaces. The sound seemed unusually discordant with so many gargoyles missing. Instead of the normal pleasant melodies, the sound was more like a lament from the battered palaces, mourning their fallen comrades.

"This place sure has gotten creepy," Hamish muttered.

"Wait till we get to the under city," Jean said. She shifted closer to him, and he wrapped an arm around her shoulders.

"Where do you think we're most likely to find Evander?" Connor asked.

Jean said, "I've been thinking about that. I usually met with him in the inner library or the secret inner library. But even though I spent a lot of time there, sometimes days passed when I didn't see him."

Verena grimaced. "We can't wait that long. We've got to head back toward the border by tomorrow morning at the latest. I want to report to Kilian before Dougal has time to spring his trap."

They had made excellent time. They'd flown a windrider, packed with their families for the trip to Alasdair. On the way south, they had circled wide around the retreating Obrioners and the broken lands north of Harz. Their circuitous path had taken them close to the Emmerich quarry, and they'd decided to fly over it.

The town had suffered heavy damage, with one entire section little more than a charred ruin. The nearby quarry was located in a patch of barren, rocky land that rose into a large hill that held the quarry pit. The northern edge of that pit was ruptured, as if a huge explosion had ripped through it, tossing debris for half a mile.

"That must be where the elfonnel struck," Hamish had said.

Verena frowned down at the devastation. "What a stupid waste."

Amhain had grumbled, "Can't even build a quarry right. Everyone knows quarries should be on a mountain."

Connor had laughed. "As if they decide where they'll find power stone."

Peigi had commented, "But what a strange life, quarrying that black, glassy stone."

Connor smiled at the memory as Verena circled the inner city at about a thousand feet. They had dropped their families just outside of Alasdair, concealed the windrider at the top of Alasdair Mountain, and picked up a strong tailwind south.

They had flown all the next day, remaining high above the clouds. Connor felt pretty sure that no one knew they were in Obrion. They had stopped only briefly in secluded areas to stretch their legs and relieve themselves. Hamish and Verena had taken turns flying, and they had all slept when they could.

All they had to do was find Evander and get him to share information quickly and clearly. No problem.

Connor said, "Head for the ruins. Every time I set foot in there, Evander showed up. I bet he'll feel us land."

"And he could bury us without anyone the wiser," Hamish pointed out.

Connor shook his head. "Evander might not care about the rest of us, but I don't think he'd hurt Jean."

Hamish hugged her little tighter. "Of course. Everyone loves our Jean."

Jean gave him a warm smile, then leaned forward for a better view as they soared lower and Verena dropped the protective air bubble that had blocked out the wind. Its faint shimmering tended to blur their view a bit.

Jean grinned excitedly. "It's strange. The entire time we were here, we were trying to figure out how to get away, but somehow I feel like we're coming home."

"That's because for you, home is where you have the most patients or the most books," Connor said.

"And for you, a place isn't home till you've destroyed it," Hamish joked.

Verena swooped once over the plain so they could study it. Connor hadn't gotten a chance to really look at the ruin that day they fought the elfonnel.

It was even more impressive than he'd sensed while exploring it. Seeing the ruin next to the wrecked modern Carraig helped him gauge the scope of it. The little that remained was like a shadow of the past, but it suggested a city of unrivaled glory.

Crumbling walls had once been palaces even bigger than the ones in the inner city. The rubble-strewn streets and the broken lines of once-magnificent fountains hinted at beautiful thoroughfares. The graceful, soaring palaces of the inner city had always seemed almost more than he could take in. Now he was starting to realize the modern Carraig was but a pale shadow of what the city had once been.

Verena swooped around for a landing and settled the Storm into the ruins. She chose the open arena. The plain had once reared over fifty feet above. The many broken stone bleachers were mute reminders of when the elfonnel had chased Connor down into the concealed under city.

They landed in a swirling cloud of fine dust thrown up by the Storm's thrusters and Connor spoke through a cough. "You're right, Jean. With all the memories of near-death struggles, this really does feel like home."

Verena cut power to all the thrusters, but just sat for a moment, staring at the stark, deeply-shadowed arena. "I thought I lost you here that day."

She had just barely arrived in the Swift in time to see the elfonnel corner Connor on the plain. From her vantage it must've looked like it had eaten him whole.

He had only barely managed to drill a hole through the concealing stone that had held up the false roof over the ruins. He was tempted to summon that same little squirrel with the big feet that he had formed to distract the elfonnel. It would make the homecoming feel more complete.

He placed a hand over hers. She did not draw away, but met his gaze. He was surprised to see her eyes brimming with unshed tears.

She whispered, "How has everything gotten so crazy?"

"We'll figure it out," he promised.

Her emotional reaction to returning to the Carraig made him nervous. He wasn't used to seeing her like that. She was the strong one, the girl who punched boys, who could stop entire armies with her mechanicals.

He hoped Evander arrived soon. Maybe that would help her shake off the strange mood. Connor climbed out of the Storm. As he offered a hand to assist Verena, he reached through the gateway of slate already wedged into his boot. He connected with the earth and the gateway opened almost immediately.

The ruin held a sense of vast age and layered history. As always, the earth carried with it a faint taste. That ruined ancient capital tasted like cider left too long in storage, right on the point of turning. He also caught the scent of quality work, like a whiff from his Aunt Ailsa's workshop.

As he carefully extended his senses farther, scanning that ancient ruin, he quested for Sentries. He expected to feel Evander moving toward them, or even snatching away his access to the earth altogether, but he felt nothing.

After a moment Hamish asked, "So, where is he?"

Connor exchanged a glance with Jean as Verena activated a small lightstone. The faintly greenish light from the limestone illuminated the area, but also made it feel somehow more lonely.

Connor shrugged. "Maybe he's sleeping."

"Maybe you should break something," Hamish suggested.

Jean snapped, "Don't you dare."

"This ruin is already pretty well destroyed," Hamish agreed. He led the way out one of the gaping exits of the crumbling arena and pointed down the nearest street. "I suppose we could knock over another one of those palaces."

Verena said, "We actually don't want anyone to know we're here. The students may be gone, but we don't want an open battle in the Carraig."

"That might not actually be a bad idea," Connor said with a grin. Breaking things at the Carraig was one of his best-proved talents, after all.

Hamish nodded eagerly. "Yeah. If we took over the Carraig, they would almost have to send an army to fight us."

Aifric grinned. "It would kinda be fun to rule the Carraig, at least for a while."

"Lord Hamish does have a pretty good ring to it." Hamish puffed out his chest and assumed an arrogant pose.

"Lady Aifric sounds better."

Their enthusiasm made Connor grin. "Wrestle over titles later."

Jean gave Hamish a playful punch in the shoulder, then turned to Aifric. "You've been hanging around us too long. Aren't Healers supposed to fix things?"

She shrugged. "When I need to break things I can be someone else."

"Do you have any good bash-fighters in that head of yours?" Hamish asked.

"Later," Jean said. She started marching up the lane with purpose. "Let's check the inner library."

"You said he often doesn't go there," Verena pointed out.

"True, but sometimes he leaves me notes or messages. If he's not there, we can try the inner secret library."

As the rest of them followed her, Verena hesitated. "I'm tempted to take the Swift, but I suppose flying it underground isn't the best choice. I hate not having it with me."

"I could pull off one of those speedslings and carry it along for you," Connor suggested.

She actually considered the idea before shaking her head. "It's not designed for easy disassembly, but I should add that as a future upgrade. I could see times when it would be helpful to have a portable speedsling along."

Walking through the ruins of the ancient city under the pale moonlight was a unique experience. Connor could almost imagine they were walking through time back to when that city was the center of the mighty Obrion Empire, spanning the entire continent. He tried to imagine what it must have been like, but glimpsed little more than shadows of that reality.

They reached the border of the ruin about a quarter of a mile from the inner city, where the ground again concealed the lower levels. A huge steel door had been installed across the corridor that led all the way to the undercity concealed under the Carraig palaces.

Connor pried it open using slate, hoping the movement of the earth would draw Evander from his hiding place, but still saw

498

no one. They walked the long, dusty corridors under the Carraig and reached the inner library without encountering anyone.

While they walked, Connor tapped quartzite, listening and sniffing. The air smelled of dust and broken stone and torn timbers and recent destruction, but he smelled nothing of living beings. There were fewer torches than he remembered, and their far distant hissing and sputtering only reinforced how empty the Carraig felt. Even the wind that sighed down the open corridors seemed to complain that it found nothing to brush against.

The library was cold and empty. None of the fireplaces looked like they had been used since Jean had last been there. A thick layer of dust covered all of the books and the many comfortable chairs scattered across the big room. Jean paced around the room, her fingers tracing the spines of the heavy tomes. A couple of times she paused to look at particular titles.

"You really don't have time to read any of it," Connor reminded her.

Jean gave him a wistful smile. "Despite all my research, I only read a fraction of them. These weren't the interesting ones anyway. Evander had taken all the best ones, and shared a few of them in the secret inner library."

"How many libraries does one guy need?" Hamish asked.

Aifric retorted, "How many meals does one man need?"

"Good point." He pulled a handful of smashpacked cubes from the pouch at his belt and passed them around.

Connor popped one into his mouth and was amazed by the rich flavor of roasted pork. Whatever sauce it had been cooked in was delicious, and the flavor was so intense that for a moment all he could do was just chew slowly and savor the dense meal.

While they ate, Jean led the way out of the library and through the warren of darkened corridors to the secret inner library. Verena called for more light from her activated lightstone.

Connor could have probably done the same thing, but limestone was one of the last stones that he had established affinity with. Sometimes it still seemed to begrudge that fact and resist working for him.

The secret inner library was much smaller, just a couple of padded chairs facing a fireplace, with a small bookshelf nearby. The bookshelf was empty. The fireplace looked like it had not been used in weeks, although less dust coated the room than in the other library.

Jean drummed her fingers on the bookshelf, clearly frustrated. "He even took the books away."

"Well, you weren't here to read them." Hamish said.

"What now?" Aifric asked. "Should we go kidnap Lord Dail to see if we can get Evander to react?"

Hamish nodded. "I vote kidnap and take over the Carraig."

"If Evander hasn't come to find us yet, I'm not sure he would react well to that," Connor said.

Jean frowned, "So where is he? The ruined city is exposed, the Carraig is partially destroyed, and a lot of his secrets must be coming out. Not many people knew about that ruin under the plain, and I bet they're asking him all sorts of questions."

"What if he's still traipsing around Granadure?" Connor asked.

Verena looked horrified by the idea. "How could we not have considered that?"

Connor shrugged. "Evander and Carraig pretty much go together." He didn't want to consider the fact that they might actually have no idea how to find the giant Sentry.

"Maybe I should say a limmerick," he suggested.

"Please don't."

The deep voice surprised them all. As one, they spun toward the door, hands reaching for weapons.

Evander stood just inside, and none of them had heard him enter.

Chapter Seventy-Four

"This battle we fight with water and fire.
To win is your only hope and earnest desire.
You'll try really hard, and stay on your guard,
But your troops will mourn like a pitiful choir."

~Connor

Jean recovered first and stepped toward the giant Sentry, whose head reached almost to the high ceiling.

"Evander, thank you for coming!"

He sank to one knee to greet her and she took his extended hand. "I'm so glad you're here. I heard you helped stop that disaster at Harz, but no one knew if you were all right."

The hint of a smile cracked the mahogany façade of his face. "Fires may ravage the sun-dried forest, but reunion gladdens the heart with a deeper flame."

"Oh, I'm glad." Jean stammered, actually blushing a little.

Hamish elbowed Connor as the rest of the group slowly approached. "Told you everybody loves Jean."

Connor envied him the absolute confidence he felt in his relationship with Jean. He could enjoy the fact that she received such universal love without even a hint of jealousy or worry.

Connor glanced at Verena, who still had one hand inside her satchel and was watching Evander with guarded concern. He hoped they'd get to that point eventually, but couldn't imagine how.

Aifric stood to one side, a slender dagger in each hand, her stance relaxed and poised in the deadly stillness of a Blade ready to strike. It was comforting to know she was ready to help if the situation turned violent.

It probably wouldn't help against Evander, but it was comforting anyway.

Evander scanned the rest of the group with his dark eyes. As usual, the weight of that gaze made Connor nervous. He was all too aware of Evander's physical might and his unmatched power with earth. Hopefully they could all get along.

Evander's expression darkened when he glanced at Aifric. "The Mhortair are not welcome here."

Connor had no idea how he knew. Even more terrifying than the low, growling tone he used was the fact that he spoke clearly. Aifric seemed to understand the danger and she paled.

"Then you should be welcoming her," Connor said before violence could erupt. "She's broken with her people and sworn her oath to me."

Evander terrified him and they needed the knowledge that the ancient Sentry alone might be able to share, but he would not allow the man to harm his friend.

Evander glanced from Aifric to Connor. "The strongest tree is one that grows against much opposition, but true friendship is a safe harbor that few find in the storm."

Connor hoped that meant that Evander approved. Better that than assume Evander was the storm about to shatter him before he could find safety.

So he said, "We need your help."

"The fool proclaims the time of the harvest when vines are laden and heavy, but the wise man sows and plans for the reaping."

"Do we look that desperate?" Hamish asked.

Connor decided he had probably interpreted that one correctly. Maybe it was time to share the height of fashion.

> *"There once was a man from Altkalen.*
> *Trading problems upon him had a-fallen.*
> *The Obrioners had come, beating war on their drum,*
> *but their invasion instead has stahlen."*

"Stahlen?" Hamish asked.

"It's art. Work with me," Connor whispered.

"Failed art maybe," Hamish said with a chuckle. "We came here to ask for help, not to confuse the guy."

"Just stop it you two." Jean sounded frustrated. "Evander, I bet you know exactly what has been happening."

"A murder of crows feasts only in times of blood, but the shaking of the earth cannot be restricted to a single mountain."

"Exactly," Jean said, giving the big man a warm smile. "The problem is, High Lord Dougal is retreating toward the border as a ruse. We know he plans to raise another elfonnel, one he claims is ancient and powerful. But we took his sculpted stones, and he has no ascended Petralists. We're hoping you can help us figure out if it's possible that he might have discovered how to track down one of the ancient, hibernating elfonnel."

Evander looked from her to the rest of the team, his expression unreadable as usual. His eyes settled upon Verena then glanced at Hamish. "Time steals the sound of laughter even from the mind, but the glimpse of new life rekindles the faint memories."

"Your uncle Kilian mentioned once that I remind him of your mother," Verena said softly, taking a step closer and pulling her hand from the satchel. "Please help us so we can avoid another great purge."

An old sadness deepened the lines of his face, and he glanced down at Jean, who patted his arm reassuringly. "I know the old memories can be painful, but we're trying to make better new ones."

Evander sighed, the sound like a blacksmith's bellows.

"Mountains of ice in the ocean float mostly underwater, and the fires of hatred burn hottest in the heart."

Connor exchanged confused looks with Hamish and Aifric. He wasn't sure where to go with that.

Jean tucked her hair behind her ear and looked up at Evander with a warm smile. "I usually love speaking with you. I enjoy having to think deep before figuring out what your words mean. Today we're kind of in a hurry, though. I'm sorry."

"Come." Evander pushed open the door and led them back into the corridor.

Without speaking more, he traversed nearly a quarter of a mile through the gridlike pattern of dim hallways before reaching a long stair that descended into pitch darkness.

"I've never been to the lower levels," Jean said in a hushed voice when they paused at the top. "They always felt wrong, somehow."

Evander nodded. "Truth, though an ugly beast, appears most tame when spoken by the simple beauty of youth."

"He's quite a charmer, isn't he?" Hamish muttered.

Hamish activated another limestone light to illuminate the long stair better, and Connor took another and willed it to life. It was one of the few power stones that worked in very similar ways for both Builders and Petralists, and he loved the fact that he and Verena could share a talent.

His stone sputtered and emitted a pulsing light that confused more than helped. Connor shook it and whispered, "Work with me here."

Hamish chuckled. "I guess Blood of the Tallan operates best in the shadows."

"Spit rocks," Connor said out of habit as he focused on the stone, abundantly aware that Verena and Evander were both watching him. After another moment, he finally managed a bright, even glow and grinned in victory.

"Good thing no one's life depended on you lighting that quickly," Aifric said with a smile.

He shrugged. "Some talents are too subtle for most people to appreciate."

As soon as they began their descent, Connor understood what Jean had been talking about. The air was cold and felt unsettled. When he tapped quartzite and tried to get a sense of it, the air seemed to scatter away, like insects fleeing unexpected light.

That mental image set his skin crawling.

Jean was right to sense that things were not safe. If Evander spent a lot of time down there, no wonder he seemed a bit odd.

The lower levels were a chaotic mass of corridors that made the undercity they had just left behind seem downright boring. They walked broken hallways shored with spare timbers. Others were twisted and pitching at odd angles, as if the ground under the buildings had shifted and fallen, dragging them into the depths.

Silently, they followed Evander through shattered halls, mostly filled with rubble and earth. Enough hints of the buildings' previous majesty remained to suggest they must have once rivaled the finest palaces in the Carraig. Bits of color from ancient murals clung to broken sections of fallen ceiling, while occasional limbs of alabaster statues poked from the rubble, as if still trying to pull free of the disaster that had claimed them.

Many times, the corridors they followed were blocked by barriers of solid rock that split the halls apart. The rock was in turn cut by rounded passageways that bored through to other battered corridors and collapsed palaces. It was as if a colony of ground squirrels snorting porphyry had gone wild underground for a thousand years.

After a few minutes, Verena shifted close to Connor and said, "We could get hopelessly lost down here if Evander chose to leave us."

He would have preferred she just punch him a few times. Now that she mentioned the scary thought, he couldn't help thinking about it. Even tapping slate, enough solid rock blocked his earth senses that he couldn't get a solid mental map of the area.

They spent another quarter hour creeping through ancient ruins, moving ever deeper into the earth. Eventually they stepped out of yet another passage carved out of solid rock and Connor paused to stare.

They had entered an opulent study, perfectly preserved, as if Evander had transported one from Lord Dail's palace and stuck it down in the ruin. Rich cherry wood sheathed the walls. Intricate paintings covered the ceiling, the colors as vibrant as the day they'd been mixed.

One in particular drew Connor's gaze. He recognized the towering peak of Mt. Murdo, but the spectacular city depicted at its base made the modern Carraig look like a hamlet. The shadows of grandeur that remained in the ruins had suggested a magnificent city, but if the towering spires and graceful castles were real, that city had been the jewel of the world.

Its destruction was that much more tragic.

"Was this your home?" Verena asked as the rest of the team clustered around Connor to stare.

Evander nodded, but did not speak.

"This place is amazing," Hamish breathed as he paced around the study, examining several mahogany chairs with complex carvings on the backs. They stood beside an enormous desk made of wood that looked remarkably similar to blue patterned marble.

In that room, they could almost forget they were standing deep under the surface, within a chaotic jumble of ruins. Connor hoped there was a point to the field trip.

He said, "Kilian suggested you've been searching for secrets down here ever since the Tallan Wars. Have you found anything that might help us figure out how to stop Dougal?"

"The hunter with a single arrow could loose it against the nuall savaging his flocks, or against the pedra swooping high overhead."

"What is that supposed to mean?" Hamish asked.

"Is the gravest danger the one present, or the one still waiting to strike?" Evander asked softly.

Hamish shrugged. "The pastry eaten fresh out of the oven is always better than the one found in a sock under the bed."

"Sometimes I wonder about you," Verena said with a slow shake of her head.

Jean touched Evander's arm again. "There's risk in any path we choose, but you wouldn't have brought us down here if you didn't plan to help."

Unless he planned to bury them alive. Or leave them to wander lost until they died of thirst and hunger. Or . . . Connor shook his head to dispel the litany of dark possibilities. They weren't helping.

"Truth is often but a reflection in murky waters. Come, fair one, and we shall see if the vision becomes clear."

He left the room, leading them into a wide hallway that looked perfectly normal, except for the steep slant to the floor leading even farther down. An odd, keening wind began blowing past, although Connor had no idea where it might be coming from.

Hamish shivered, his head cocked to one side as he listened to the soft, wailing cries contained in the wind. "It's like the lingering voices of people who got lost down here."

Jean grimaced. "How can you say such a thing?"

He shrugged. "It's what it sounds like."

"It sort of does," Connor agreed.

Verena sighed. "Leave it to you two to find a way to make it even creepier."

"We want you to enjoy the full experience," Connor said, sharing a grin with Hamish. That moment felt like old times.

Evander led them down the sloping corridor, his bulk seeming to fill the hallway. Connor still marveled that he could squeeze through all the tight spaces.

They clambered into an intersecting corridor that jutted into their hallway, its floor nearly four feet above theirs. That one twisted and turned, like a noodle bent at crazy angles across a plate.

Strangely, it didn't look broken. The domed ceiling, over twelve feet high, retained its gilded paint and complex crown molding. The wooden flooring shone, as if recently polished.

"This is beautiful," Jean breathed.

Evander nodded. "A single petal of the rose, though ripped asunder by the torrent, hints at the beauty of the flower thus destroyed."

"This area seems better preserved," Connor commented.

"The goose flies hundreds of miles for the winter migration, but it returns to the same nest it once abandoned."

"You lived here, in this part of the city?" Verena asked.

Evander did not reply, but led the way down the hallway to a thick wooden door, covered with carvings of trees and animals. It looked ancient, but Connor noted the lock looked new. The huge Sentry pushed the door open and led them through.

Another hallway. Growing up in that palace must have been really confusing.

The hallway ended in a wide set of double doors. Evander threw them open and led the way into a low-ceilinged room, barely twenty feet across, which extended beyond the bright glow of their lightstones. The entire room tilted down at a thirty degree angle and canted to the left. Both walls were lined with floor-to-ceiling bookshelves, and the floor was tiled in a rough, black ceramic that offered excellent traction.

Hamish threw out his hands and chuckled. "I should have known. An inner under double secret hidden library."

Chapter Seventy-Five

*"The studious mind grasps every moment of learning, when the fool
thinks of naught beyond terror."*

~Connor

As they followed Evander into the sloping library,
Connor wondered how many libraries the man had
secreted around and under the Carraig. If Hamish had
been the one hunting for secrets for centuries
underground, they probably would have run across a dozen
stashes of stale sweetbreads by now.

Evander approached a plain, wooden table bolted to the
sloping floor. Jean led the rest of the team after him, gazing
eagerly at the long rows of books.

She whispered, "We don't have nearly enough time."

Connor grimaced at the bookshelves. "I hope there's a
summary page somewhere. We need to understand the secrets
Dougal has uncovered, and fast. Controlling elfonnel is becoming
the key to this war."

"No," Evander boomed, swinging around to face him, his
expression furious. "Elfonnel destroyed my family and my nation.
My uncle and I have stood guard against the return of these
secrets for over three centuries."

It must be incredibly frustrating for him to realize that
Dougal had somehow penetrated the secrets anyway. Connor
chose his words carefully. If Evander was riled up enough to
speak plainly, he could easily entomb them all down there if they
pushed him too far.

"Then help us figure out what Dougal is planning. We'll
guard the information carefully, but we can't stop him if we
don't understand."

Evander paced away and made a flicking gesture with his
hand. Lanterns mounted on the wall every five paces suddenly lit
with bright limestone illumination. The library was longer than

Connor had thought. It extended down and down, almost beyond the limit of his unenhanced vision.

"So many books," Jean breathed, her hands clenching slowly as she viewed the treasure trove.

Evander gestured at the long, narrow room. "Thus the fruit of long toil is gathered in."

"Have you read them all?" Connor asked.

"Wisdom is gained like the drip from the tip of the stalagmite, but the earth reveals no secrets to one who has never touched a shovel."

Connor sighed.

"There once was a phrase so cloudy,
That Blood of the Tallan grew pouty.
He stood on one leg, and started to beg,
And said please don't treat me so foully."

"I didn't get that one either," Hamish whispered.

"Don't be daft, you two," Jean said, hands on her hips, sounding annoyed. "Of course he was saying that he's read all those books. They wouldn't be of any use if he hadn't."

Aifric whistled softly. "I can't imagine reading so many books. Eystri would love it though."

"Who is Eystri?" Connor asked.

Aifric tapped her head. "Another shadow of me. She's an Althin. Loves the archives in Dagmanson."

"I'm looking forward to meeting her," Jean said.

Evander did not look happy at the thought of another one of Aifric's personalities appearing, eager to read his treasures.

"Is this the information from your grandmother's secret stashes?" Connor asked.

"As many as I have found. Our home was severely damaged, caught in the turmoil of elements. It has been the toil of lifetimes to find as much as I have."

It was usually a toil of lifetimes to understand him, but he seemed more menacing when he spoke clearly.

"Do you know how Dougal plans to raise an ancient elfonnel?" Jean asked.

Evander hesitated, a frown again creasing his face. "The mosaic once broken and scattered yields but piles of suggestive fragments. The artist only with the vision and skill can reassemble the original to its former glory."

Verena frowned. "So you found a bunch of hints, but nothing concrete. Dougal somehow got his hands on those pieces, and he figured out how to put it all together."

"Why can't the evil mastermind of the war be an idiot?" Hamish grumbled.

"A servant can have but one true master. All other oaths are rendered meaningless beneath that highest loyalty. Betrayal of one is but service rendered to another."

Connor guessed, "Gregor. He was your student, wasn't he?"

Evander nodded.

"So he probably got his hands on the bits and pieces you learned, and Dougal, that crafty son of a pedra, figured it out," Aifric said.

Jean said, "Maybe if we see those bits and pieces too we can figure it out."

Evander headed deeper into the long, narrow library, passing hundreds of tomes, any of which could contain vital secrets. The rest of them followed silently, although Jean trailed a little behind, her eyes glued to all the books they didn't have time to crack open.

Hamish took her hand. "Just focus on the fact that you're going to read a better one. It's like skipping the salad so you can go straight to dessert."

Jean smiled. "I actually like salad."

Evander stopped in front of a bookshelf that looked no different than any other. Instead of reaching for one of the tomes, he pulled on the lantern attached to the wall. With a click, it slid out on a concealed arm, revealing a hidden nook that held a tiny notebook. He withdrew the little book, which looked ridiculous in his huge hand, and passed it to Jean.

She took it with reverent excitement. It creaked from disuse as she cracked open the cover. Connor leaned over her shoulder to see. The small pages were yellowed with age and cracked along the edges. They were covered in a clean, flowing script very similar to Jean's. She scanned it in an instant and flipped to the second page.

"What does it say?" Hamish asked.

He did not even bother trying to look, and Connor quickly gave up too. They could never hope to match Jean in a reading contest.

There were only about thirty pages in the notebook, and Jean scanned them in just a few minutes, then returned to the beginning. Only then did she look up with a frown.

"These notes discuss many of the elfonnel attacks over the last three centuries. I've read another account of those, but this one includes a reference to an elfonnel attack from prior to the Tallan Wars."

"Does it tell you how they were raised?" Connor asked.

Of course she shook her head. If the answer was that simple, Evander would have figured it out.

"It does have some details I haven't seen before. For example, it lists the names of the Petralists who raised the elfonnel. In almost every case, they were like Dougal's wife and Camonica's husband, recently ascended Petralists experimenting with powers they didn't understand."

Evander nodded, but Connor frowned. "Almost all?"

"There are two with no names."

She looked to Evander who said, "Steps in the darkness can find hidden treasures, but mighty ships may pass in the fog without ever knowing another soul is near."

Jean nodded, as if she understood that cryptic answer. She really had been spending too much time around Evander.

"What if you couldn't figure out who was responsible because those two weren't young Petralists who had won sculpted stones? What if those were ancient elfonnel somehow awakened after all these years?"

Evander's huge head tilted a bit as he considered the idea. "I hadn't thought of that. Uncle Kilian stopped one of them, but I faced the other. It was unusually potent, like the one we faced here at the Carraig. Feet walk the path best remembered unless the mind is focused."

Jean gave him a dazzling smile. "Sometimes you need a fresh perspective on a stubborn problem."

"So where did those two rise from? Is there anything similar?" Connor asked.

Jean thumbed back through the little book, and the others drew a little closer. Connor sensed maybe they'd made an important breakthrough, but could they really figure out something that Evander had missed for so long? He had recorded the information, but what if he hadn't studied his own notes closely? It was information he already knew, after all.

Jean looked up and tapped the book. "This is interesting. In both of those cases, the attacks came near quarry communities."

Hamish shrugged. "Maybe they were just avoiding the big cities where there would be more Petralists."

Connor said, "That fire-bound elfonnel was raised at Emmerich quarry."

She nodded. "Wolfram commented on how strange it was that Dougal raised it so far from the battlefield. Maybe our assumption that Dougal was trying to block discovery of an anti-obsidian stone was wrong."

Aifric snapped her fingers, her expression excited. "You know how I said I had sensed some of Dougal's thoughts when he was controlling my mind? Something about unsettled elements. There's some connection with quarry, but I can't quite remember it."

Verena paced up the sloping floor, then turned, her expression thoughtful. "So where does that leave us? We know Dougal might be trying to raise a hibernating elfonnel, but usually they're impossible to sense. We have two possible instances of ancient elfonnel arising from their sleep, and in both cases they appeared near quarries, but we don't know why."

"Maybe they need power stone to feed on like that one at the Carraig did," Hamish suggested.

"That would explain why they'd hit quarries once they formed," Jean said thoughtfully.

Verena said, "You know, we don't actually have con-firmation that Dougal used a sculpted stone to raise that fire-bound at Emmerich. What if he actually raised a hibernating elfonnel?"

"We did find one extra stone in that box," Hamish said.

Connor leaned against one of the bookshelves, but Evander frowned at him, so he quickly stood straight again. There had to be more to it than that.

"So why Emmerich? What would have tipped off Dougal that he could find an elfonnel there, if that's what happened?"

They all looked to Verena, who held out her hands apologetically. "I don't know much about that quarry."

Jean said, "Kilian mentioned something about it when we were first discussing the weakening powder, didn't he?"

Hamish nodded slowly, his brows furrowed as he thought back. "Something about unusual earthquakes."

Connor turned to Aifric. "What if that term restless elements meant earthquakes?"

Jean said excitedly, "Dougal overheard the discussion about the anti-obsidian stone through you, Aifric, so he knew about the earthquakes. What if they're actually caused by an ancient elfonnel stirring?"

A sudden fear struck Connor like a bolt of ice from Mister Five. "That would mean Alasdair's earthquakes might be caused by another one!"

"Oh, no," Hamish breathed.

Jean clutched his arm. "That's why Dougal wanted the army to go south again. He needs them closer to the border."

"Closer to Alasdair," Connor finished for her.

"I can't believe we left our families there! That's where Dougal plans to strike. Let's go!" Hamish exclaimed.

He led the way toward the exit at a run.

CHAPTER SEVENTY-SIX

"The tallest mountain avails little when the path leads through canyons."

~Connor

Connor carefully slid forward on his stomach, inching to the edge of the wide Lookout Rock above the path leading down to Quarry Road. The others flanked him, and together they peered down at Alasdair from that distant vantage. The others had all donned long-vision goggles, while he tapped quartzite.

High Lord Dougal had beaten them to the town.

He sat at the high table in the town square, with the entire village assembled around feasting tables. Most of the townsfolk looked nervous. High Lord Dougal couldn't possibly miss the signs that he wasn't as wildly popular as he had been the last time he visited.

Lord Gavin, Lady Isobel, and their daughter Moira sat nearby, dressed in their best finery. Gavin's brown surcoat only made him look older and more sickly than ever. Isobel's many-layered hoop skirts prevented her from drawing closer than five feet to anyone.

Connor fumed that they hadn't arrived sooner. They'd pushed the Storm to its max speed. Even with a powerful tail wind, they had activated extra thrusters and Connor had burned through two entire pieces of marble adding the force of flames. The wind and altitude would have made it impossible to breathe without the protective shieldstone protecting them.

They were still too late.

Connor glanced at Aifric, who lay on the stone to his left, just past Jean. She gestured an okay signal with her pinky finger, indicating that she was blocking any sounds they made.

"I'm glad we came in from the back side of the mountain," Verena said softly.

Hamish had landed the Storm in a copse of small alder trees, touching down as lightly as a butterfly. Connor had tapped slate and extended a careful shield under them as they crept to Lookout Rock.

He was glad he did because Dougal had brought Gregor with him. Despite the distance and the fact that Gregor stood on solid stone, Connor still worried he'd sense them or realize someone was shielding that area.

"We should have had time to get here first," Hamish grumbled.

"Now we have to figure out how to get everyone away without starting another pitched battle in the streets," Jean said, looking worried.

Dougal stood as a large party entered the square, led by Captain Aonghus, who walked sheathed in crimson flames. People cowed away from him, but Connor's eyes were drawn to the group that followed him into view.

Their families.

"Tallan take it and grout it for dinner," Connor growled. "They're supposed to be hiding in the bolt hole."

"Those are rampagers shepherding them in," Aifric said.

Connor had been so focused on their families that he hadn't noticed the other soldiers. Aifric was right.

Three men and two women flanked the small party, and even when not tapping porphyry, they moved with a predatory grace, conveying a sense of coiled danger. It was as if they only barely refrained from leaping upon the helpless villagers and tearing them to pieces.

"There are more rampagers prowling around the perimeter," Verena pointed out. "I count a full dozen."

Hamish whistled softly, his expression grave. "That's a lot of rampagers."

"What are they saying?" Verena asked as they all leaned forward and watched the group approaching Dougal's table.

Connor was already applying quartzite to his ears. The lobes elongated and he pivoted them to better focus on the distant Alasdair. As usual, a flood of sound assaulted his mind as his enhanced ears seemed to suck in every sound for miles around.

Birds called to each other, trees creaked in the late afternoon breeze, and the Wick gurgled softly as it poured from the loch and began its long journey down to Merkland. After filtering out all of that, plus the sounds of his companions breathing and his own fast heartbeat, he finally caught the distant sound of voices from far below.

Dougal was speaking. "So good of you to join us. Where is your son, Ashlar?"

"He's safely away from here so you can't hurt him," Lilias declared, standing unafraid before the high lord.

"It is not my intention to hurt your son," Dougal said calmly.

One of the rampagers, a burly fellow with a wild black beard, prowled closer to Lilias, as if eager for Dougal to take offense so he could kill her.

"Then why did you have your general threaten to kill us unless he surrendered?" she demanded.

"Easy, love," Hendry cautioned. He too looked far from properly submissive standing in front of the high lord, but he gave Lilias a nervous look. She met Dougal's gaze, her chin lifted slightly.

Connor had never felt so proud of her, or so terrified. Challenging the high lord usually guaranteed a swift execution.

Dougal only smiled. "I see where Connor acquired his strong, stubborn attitude."

"Thank you."

His smile faded and for the first time he looked annoyed. "Don't be daft, woman. That boy needs training and guidance. His foolish choices have cost this nation dearly, and his rash actions have placed him in league with some of the most dangerous people in the world. If I can't rescue him, I'll be forced to destroy him. Is that what you want?"

Her defiance faded and she said softly, "I only want to see him safe."

"Here in this beautiful valley, you are sheltered from the brutal reality of the world," Dougal declared, his voice rising, every person hanging on every word.

"Connor thinks he understands a complex situation that even many of the high lords don't fully grasp. I did use you and your family, and I recognize that the ordeal was terrifying for you. My intent was to force Connor to return to his senses and come home so I can teach and train him."

He smiled, a benevolent, understanding smile. "Connor is destined for great things. I can help him become the man who will in turn help bring peace to the continent for the first time in centuries."

"Connor is a fool," Stuart cried from his seat near the front.

"And a thief!" someone else shouted.

"Please give him another chance," shouted old Clifden.

Dougal raised a hand for quiet. "As your own venerable healer likes to say, think deep before making rash decisions. Consider my words while we enjoy this feast.

He gestured their families to take seats at an empty table at the front, and asked Hendry to sit at the high table with him.

Lady Isobel scowled at that breach in protocol. "My lord Dougal, that man is only a linn. Your generosity risks encouraging his lesser qualities, which we will be forced to deal with after you are gone."

Dougal said, "On the contrary, my sources have made it clear that you would have run this town into ruin and starved out your entire population if not for the talents of the Ashlar and his wife."

While Lady Isobel sputtered in indignant outrage that she couldn't vent upon the high lord, Dougal said, "The food looks delicious. Thank you all for making such a mighty effort on my behalf. Let the feast begin."

Hamish muttered, "Dougal could convince a drowning man that all he needs is a long drink of water."

"I wonder if he practices in the mirror," Connor said.

Jean said, "I believe he's convinced himself that his cause really is just."

"That's what makes him so dangerous," Verena said.

Connor said, "In a way that makes our job simpler. He's cracked. There is no way we could convince him to change his mind. All we can do is put him down like a rabid dog."

Verena rolled up onto one elbow, close enough that he easily caught her clean scent, even without applying quartzite to his nose. "We can't do it without help, though."

Jean scooted back from the edge, far from view from any Pathfinder Dougal might have in his company. She sat in the grass and said, "I counted nearly a score of Boulders, plus the rampagers, Aonghus, and Gregor. Dougal brought a powerful force."

"They could kill a lot of people if they decide to," Connor said.

"We need to fetch Kilian and reinforcements," Verena said. "If we hurry, we could probably return by morning."

Connor shook his head. "I'm not leaving. We don't know what he plans to do with our families, or when he plans to raise the elfonnel."

"We need Kilian," Verena repeated.

"I know, but we need to save our families too. What do you think Dougal will do when he sees us swooping in to attack?"

"Hopefully he'll be too busy running."

Jean said, "Connor is right. They could start killing, or they could take everyone hostage to force us to submit. He has to know we won't risk their lives."

Hamish nodded. "You have to fetch Kilian, Verena. You're the only one who can."

"Why don't you go?"

"This is our home," Hamish said, his expression as serious as Connor had ever seen. "When people threaten our families, we have to deal with it."

"I don't like it. You can't promise me you won't do something rash," Verena argued.

"No, I can't," Connor admitted. "But that doesn't change the situation."

"I could just fly close enough to get into speakstone range," she offered.

Connor said, "Might as well go pick him up. The range isn't far enough through the mountains."

Hamish cursed softly. "That's the problem with the speakstones. They revolutionize communication, but they don't have enough range. If only we had a way to boost. . ."

His eyes widened and he laughed, then grabbed Jean and kissed her enthusiastically.

"Did you have a special reason for that?" Jean asked in a breathless voice when he finished.

"I know how to boost the speakstones!"

Chapter Seventy-Seven

"Swine trample and tear without thought or care. Impetuous tongues are silenced by the stern mistress of dire need."

~Evander

"How?" Connor and Verena asked together.

Hamish led the way back to the Storm. "We need every spare thruster. In fact, let's just take them all."

Verena frowned. "You'd better have a good reason for disabling the Storm. Without it, we can't leave."

Hamish said, "Relax. I don't think we'll use up all their power, but I need all of them to make sure it works."

"Make sure what works?" Verena asked in an exasperated tone.

Hamish held up a small piece of quartzite and focused over it. Verena extended a hand to touch it, but Hamish licked it.

She dropped her hand with a frown. "Fine, be all mysterious."

After a moment he grinned and handed it to her. "See what you think."

She took it and held it for a moment. Her brows furrowed and she deliberately turned it over before pressing it to her lips. After another thoughtful moment, her eyes widened and she grinned.

"Brilliant! I should have thought of that."

"Yes, you should have. You're supposed to be the smart one."

"What are you talking about?" Aifric asked.

Verena pulled a small speakstone from a pocket of her flight jacket. "This stone is paired with one we left with Kilian. The problem is, it lacks the power to transmit our voices very far."

Hamish gestured at the Storm. "We're going to collect all of the quartzite we can get our hands on. We should be able to link them all together so they help boost the transmitting power of Verena's little speakstone. It's similar to the advanced Builder principles we've started using with that keystone. I think it'll help throw the sounds a lot farther, but still tuned into that single, activated pair."

Connor frowned. "Are you saying you're going to make the stone shout loud enough for Kilian to hear?"

Verena shook her head. "Not even Pathfinders can hear speakstones. If Hamish's plan works, we should be able to finally communicate via speakstones over greater distances."

"It'll work," Hamish insisted.

"Let's prove it works before celebrating," Verena said.

The Builders' excitement was contagious, and the group quickly pillaged every last quartzite block from the Storm. They piled them all on top of the storage box on the back of the Swift and strapped them securely in place.

"So do you just start speaking?" Connor asked.

Verena shook her head and pointed up. "I'm going into the clouds. That way the force of these stones will already be starting above the mountains before the speakstone starts casting the words north. It should increase the range even farther."

"If it works, it'll put all those pigeons out of business," Hamish said, rubbing his hands together. "And pigeon makes excellent pies."

Jean said, "If this works, I'll bake you the first one."

Verena handed the speakstone to Hamish, then slipped into the Swift and activated the thrusters. She took off gently, reducing the potential for echoes that might alert Dougal to their presence. Connor craned his head back to watch her and the nimble little craft zip around Wick Torr and up into the clouds.

A moment later, Verena's voice spoke through a second speakstone that Hamish held. "I'm way above Mount Ingram. I can see all the way into Obrion."

So Hamish held the speakstone paired with Kilian's to his mouth and said, "Kilian, can you hear me? Respond with Pastry if you can."

"You really have to stop using pastry as a code word. No one gets it," Verena said.

"You don't have to shout," Kilian's voice sounded abruptly from the speakstone, his voice sounding as clear as crystal.

"Ha!" Hamish cried, pumping his fist in the air, then saluting no one in particular with a breadstick.

Kilian asked, "Where are you? General Rory has massed his army in the pass for what looks like a determined last stand."

"Forget about that," Connor said, grabbing the stone from Hamish, who seemed more interested in his victory dance than in the actual conversation. "We're just outside of Alasdair."

"How is that possible?" Kilian asked, his tone surprised. "Speakstones don't have that kind of range."

"They do now," Hamish laughed.

"That's not important either," Connor said.

"Well, it is sort of important," Hamish objected.

Connor shushed him. "With Evander's help, we figured out what Dougal is planning. He's learned how to find hibernating elfonnel. He can raise them without sacrificing a Petralist or a sculpted stone."

Kilian's voice turned intense. "We've never been able to track them once they went to ground. Not even for the non-earth elementals."

"They seem to be drawn to quarries, possibly to replenish their strength from the power stones. We believe that the earthquakes at Emmerich Quarry were a sign of an elfonnel becoming restless. That's why Dougal raised it there."

"The earthquakes were unusual, but I never thought anything of it."

"Alasdair's been having earthquakes too," Connor continued. "Dougal is here with a company of Boulders and his rampagers. We think he plans to raise an elfonnel here."

"The fool!" Kilian exclaimed, such fury in his voice that Connor recoiled a little from the speakstone. "Has he no sense? There's no telling which one he might make contact with!"

"I think that's the point," Connor said, exchanging a surprised look with Hamish.

Kilian gained control over his anger and added, "His plan finally makes sense, but he is playing with risks he does not understand."

"I think he'd kiss a pedra if it helped him destroy you," Hamish said.

"There has to be more to the trap, though. Dougal must know that most likely I will succeed in defeating even an ancient elfonnel that he might raise there."

"He seemed convinced his trap will destroy you," Jean said.

Kilian said, "I fear he may be planning to raise a second elfonnel once I am committed to the fight."

Connor's heart sank. "If he raised the one at Emmerich the same way, then he might have that marble sculpted stone we thought he had used there."

"That must be why Captain Aonghus is with him," Aifric said.

"Two?" Jean breathed, looking horrified.

Kilian said, "Even with the rampagers, victory is not guaranteed with a single elfonnel. Facing two, I would have no choice but to raise my own elfonnel."

Jean said, "You couldn't fight two at once. They'd destroy you."

"Perhaps."

Even though it sounded like he was agreeing with Jean, his tone and inflection left no doubt that he was not terrified about potentially facing two raging elemental creatures. When he grew up, Connor wanted to be like Kilian. Or at least make people think he was.

"The greater danger is that the elements are already wild and unstable. Raising three elfonnel there so soon after Harz and Altkalen could destabilizing the entire region. If Dougal is so rash, your precious valley could get buried under half a mile of stone. The devastation could spread all the way downriver to Merkland and threaten his home too."

Hamish and Jean shared worried looks, and Connor struggled to accept such a horrible reality. "You really need to work on how you deliver bad news."

"We have to get everyone out," Hamish said.

Connor's fear turned into anger, and he felt the beast stirring in his heart. Dougal had pushed and pushed, and now he was threatening everyone Connor cared for. "I think we're overlooking the most simple answer. I need to kill Dougal first."

Kilian said, "No. Do nothing until I arrive. Dougal has planned this too well. Together we might be able to stop him without having to raise an elfonnel. That's the safest way."

That made sense, but Connor decided he would do whatever it took to protect Alasdair, sense or no sense. "Find Dierk. Get the biggest windrider you can. You're really not that far by air."

"It would be faster if you sent Verena or Hamish to come get me."

"I need them here. If Dougal and his soldiers start hurting people, we won't wait."

"I know it's hard, Connor, but you must. We'll have to plan carefully to deal with this. If elfonnel are raised, the area will be in deadly peril. Do you have your sculpted stones?"

"They're in the Swift. I thought using them was a bad idea," Connor said.

"Keep one handy, but make sure it's not marble."

"Because Dougal might raise a fire elfonnel?"

"No, because that's the only one that will tempt you with your second threshold, and you cannot risk ascending anywhere near Dougal."

"Another threshold?" Hamish asked, drawing closer.

Connor said, "I'll explain later. Kilian told me that trying to raise an elfonnel before ascending the second threshold guarantees a Petralist's destruction."

"These are the sorts of things we need to talk about sooner," Hamish grumbled.

Kilian said, "These are the sorts of things that kill people. We don't ever discuss them, and we never attempt to raise an elfonnel except in the most desperate of times."

"I'd say these times are pretty desperate," Jean said.

"Not enough to destroy Connor. A sculpted stone, either slate or quartzite, could tip the balance of the fighting in our favor, if it comes to that. But you cannot ascend again or raise an elfonnel. Either choice would destroy you."

"I won't," Connor promised. He had a reputation for dying for a good cause, but that didn't mean he wanted to kill himself. "But we are going to see if we can do something about the villagers."

"You can't attack until I get there," Kilian insisted.

"We won't pick a fight, but we might be able to do something," Connor said him.

"What?"

"We're still working on it. But make sure you get the biggest windrider you can."

"Why?"

"Because I think you should invite Ilse and the Crushers along for the ride."

CHAPTER SEVENTY-EIGHT

"The kite knows not whence the wind blows, nor wither it goes, but rises upon the currents, confident only in the string."

~Gregor

hen Verena landed, Connor swept her off her feet in an enthusiastic embrace. They laughed together with the success of boosting the speakstones, but when Connor leaned in to kiss her, she pushed him back.

With that same infuriating hesitation in her eyes she said, "Not yet."

He wanted to demand, "When?"

That wouldn't help, so he released her. At least she'd hugged him instead of punching him.

Together they helped the others restore the thrusters to the Storm. While they worked, Connor considered and discarded half a dozen ideas for freeing the villagers. Every idea ended in pitched battle against Gregor, Aonghus, and the rampagers.

They returned to Lookout Rock to watch the end of the feast. Most of the villagers seemed willing to believe Dougal, and the festivities seemed far more boisterous than before. The table where their families sat, with a pair of soldiers prowling nearby, was a notable exception. Connor was just happy no one had been hurt or shackled.

"Such a waste," Hamish muttered.

"What?" Jean asked.

"They shouldn't have used up so much of the bacon."

"You're really cracked, you know that?" Verena chuckled.

"Bacon is a precious commodity, and they're wasting it on High Lord Dougal. We should've taken it when we were here last time."

"We did take the chisels," Connor reminded him.

Verena added, "Taking the bacon would have been downright barbaric."

Hamish sighed, "I suppose, but it's such a huge sacrifice."

Jean kissed Hamish on the cheek. "When this is over, I'll cook you a whole side of bacon."

"You really do love me."

Aifric spoke softly. "This is a nice town. Must have been good growing up here."

"It was," Jean said.

"Why bring that up now, when it might be destroyed soon?" Connor asked.

"I'm going to remember this place. Might even settle down here for one of my future personalities."

"First Alasdair assassin?" Hamish asked with a grin. "Sounds good."

"Don't get distracted," Connor urged them.

The problem was, watching other people enjoy a huge feast was not all that much fun. He tried to use the time to come up with a better plan, but all he managed to do was calculate that at least one ton of the bacon probably remained, even after all the feasting.

"Rampagers are starting to leave," Verena said a few minutes later, sliding one finger past Connor's cheek to point them out in a gesture that transformed into a quick, reassuring hug.

As Connor scanned the square again, his gaze was drawn to Stuart, who seemed to have grown a couple more inches in the days since they last visited. He was returning to his table with a basket of fresh rolls when one of the rampager women intercepted him and took the basket right out of his hands. When he protested, she laughed, her eyes glowing purple.

Stuart quickly retreated, and he looked like she scared the grout right out of him.

"They're so wild, even in human form," Verena whispered.

Connor nodded. "It's the porphyry."

"How are you doing?" she asked softly, pushing up her long-vision goggles to study him.

He hadn't disabled quartzite from his vision, and for a moment he couldn't speak as he drank in the sight of her. His gaze slid along the soft contours of her face and he savored the waving of her hair in the soft breeze as it caressed her cheek and throat. Then his gaze drifted to her big blue eyes, and his mind went completely blank, filled with nothing but the minute details of those beautiful orbs.

She tapped his forehead, shaking him out of his reverie. "What is wrong with you?"

"Sorry," he stammered, releasing quartzite so his eyes could return to normal. "Sometimes when I look at you with quartzite, I worry I might never look away again."

"You sure have a smooth tongue," Verena said with a soft smile. She kissed his cheek, but her expression turned troubled again, and she looked away.

"What's wrong?" he asked, hating that he wasn't sure how to reassure her, how to close the distance that he felt growing between them.

"Don't get distracted," she said softly.

"Verena. . ." The others were too close for the kind of heart-to-heart talk they probably needed, but he had to say something.

She gave him a serious look. "You never answered my question. How are you managing that hunger for porphyry?"

He admitted, "Some days it's pretty bad, although kissing you seems to help."

"Nice try," she said, but her smile looked almost sad. He'd thought that was a good one. Girls were so hard to understand.

"Have you been listening to what they're saying?" Jean asked, and Connor was happy for the interruption.

"Nothing too important. Lady Isobel and Lord Gavin keep asking for more money and new cutter tools. Captain Aonghus seems distracted by Moira, and most of the village seems to be enjoying themselves."

"Eating all the bacon," Hamish muttered.

As Connor focused again on the feast, he savored the sights of so many people he'd known his entire life. They seemed happy in their ignorance, choosing to disbelieve the Ashlar. They should trust him more than anyone.

Connor couldn't entirely blame them, though. They were powerless to change their situation, and no one challenged the high lord. For them, ignorance really was better.

High Lord Dougal retired a short while later, accepting Lord Gavin's invitation to join him across the Wick in the manor house. That might be the break they needed. Connor was even happier when Gregor and Aonghus and all the rampagers left with Dougal.

The Boulders spread through town, guarding the town gates and the long river wall. The villagers were essentially trapped. They didn't need close guarding.

Hamish said, "We should go. They put the bacon in Neasa's shop."

"We do need to warn our families and plan a way to evacuate everyone," Jean said.

The beginning of a plan was forming in Connor's mind. "Soon. Let everyone settle in and let the guards get comfortable."

"We have to get in there," Hamish urged.

"But we can't alert the guards," Aifric said.

Jean added, "And we can't fly. Even if you block the sounds, Aifric, I can't believe Dougal hasn't warned his men to watch the skies."

Connor said, "Gregor is across the river. The Wick will block his ability to easily monitor this side, and Alasdair is built on solid granite."

"Really?" Verena asked.

"That's where the original quarry was located, until they discovered the better quality white granite up the mountain," Hamish explained.

"So once we get into town, Gregor won't be able to easily sense us," Jean said.

"Even if he can't sense us approach, with Boulders on the wall and at the gates, it'll be tough sneaking in on foot," Hamish pointed out.

"I think there's a better way," Connor said as his ideas firmed into a plan.

"What way?" Verena asked.

"We'll use the underwater Slide."

Verena glanced toward the river. "That'll get us close, but we still have to get past the guards."

"We could use the Flood-Under," Hamish said eagerly.

Connor nodded. "That's what I'm thinking."

Jean explained to Aifric and Verena, "It's a small, caved-in section that tunnels under the river wall. It's a squeeze, but it's well concealed."

"Sounds good," Aifric said.

It took only a few minutes for Verena and Hamish to ferry them to the Wick, downriver of the scoured rock of Lord Gavin's plateau. Concealed from the town by the curve of the river, Connor tapped soapstone.

The smoothly flowing waters of the Wick felt like an old friend, and at his thought, the hull of the Slide formed by the shore. Its sleek lines would be all but impossible to distinguish more than fifty yards away in the fading twilight.

They settled the Storm and the Swift to the aft deck, then sat in the comfortable chairs that Connor formed closer to the bow.

"This is amazing," Aifric laughed as she bounced in her partially-reclined chair, splashing droplets of water but not getting wet.

"It wasn't so much fun before Connor got the hang of it," Verena said.

"Hey, I only soaked everyone once," Connor protested.

"Let's not do it again," Jean said.

"I'm sure he'll do fine," Verena said, her tone light, but her hand drifted closer to her satchel and the shieldstone in there.

"Are you sure it's a good idea to bring the flyers?" Hamish asked. He was leaning back in his chair, chewing on a smashpacked cube.

"We can't have them a mile from town if we need them," Verena pointed out.

"But they won't fit in the Flood-Under."

Connor said, "I can leave them concealed in the Wick if I have to. No one will find them there."

Silently, and with barely a ripple, the Slide began moving upriver. As soon as they reached deeper water, Connor drew them under the surface, and he exulted in the wonder of that unique form of travel. He cut the current in front of them, allowing the waters to part around them while they slid through the temporary hole.

Night was falling over the valley, so no light drifted down to the depths where they passed unseen upriver. They couldn't risk activating limestone and maybe alerting the guards of their approach. So they rode in darkness, with the softly-hissing waters passing close by on either side. The air dripped with humidity and carried the faint scent of fish, mud, and wet wood.

Verena slipped her hand into his, and he gave it a single, soft squeeze. In the darkness, it was too easy for doubts to begin forming, fears that they wouldn't get everyone out before the fighting started. Her simple touch helped bolster his confidence.

It took only moments to reach the town, and Connor slowed the Slide parallel to the river wall. He extended a protective sphere over them to keep the waters out now that they were no longer moving.

"Any sign we've been noticed?" Verena asked softly, her voice echoing in the little open space.

"I haven't sensed any Spitters," Connor said.

"How are you going to make sure no guards notice when we surface?" Hamish asked.

Connor had been planning to send up a fine mist to help him get a feel for the wall and anything on it. But then he got a better idea, something wondrous enough that it might impress the villagers into believing him again.

So he tapped slate and granite together. His earth senses felt nothing, entombed as they were in the heart of the river. He kept slate active anyway, then extended his water senses and easily mapped the nearby steep bank.

It was made of slick mud, but Connor drove slender fingers of water through. In only a moment he dug under River Road to the bedrock under the wall. There he touched the solid granite foundation of the town.

His earth senses dove into it.

Connor grinned as he explored the precious power-grade granite below the town. The original quarry had not been completely exhausted before the town began quarrying the purer granite higher up the mountain. Tapping granite along with slate allowed Sentries to walk through power-grade stone as if it was earth.

"We're not going through the Flood-Under."

"What then?" Jean asked.

Connor shifted the Slide close to the bank, but still a dozen feet below the surface. Focusing the waters into churning little scoops, he dug through the bank and scraped the mud away from a large section of the rough stone under the town. Then he parted the waters beside the Slide, forming a tunnel to the granite.

"What are you doing?" Verena asked softly. It was too dark for them to see, but they could hear the gurgling sound of moving water.

"I'll show you in just a minute."

Connor seized the stone under the town, split it into blocks, and used them to form an archway wide enough for even Stuart to easily walk through. He tunneled under the town, pulling the excess stone out of the hole, using it to extend the tunnel out through the softer earth of the bank. He settled the extra displaced stones gently to the bottom of the Wick.

"Connor, are you going to explain those noises?" Jean asked, her voice a bit tense.

"Almost there," he reassured her.

In minutes, he excavated a tunnel deep beneath Alasdair. Then he slid their chairs off of the Slide and into the tunnel.

"Whoa, what are you doing?" Hamish hissed, and Connor could feel him gripping the arms of his chair.

Once they entered the tunnel, Connor drew some of the blocks into the opening behind them, sealing the exit so no light could escape.

"Verena, do you have any limestone handy?"

"I do, but they'll see."

"Not any more."

"You're enjoying this, aren't you?" Jean asked.

"Why do I feel stone?" Aifric asked.

A small piece of limestone began to glow very faintly. Verena held it shielded in her hands and looked up, as if to make sure no one noticed. Then her eyes widened and she looked around in surprise.

Connor threw out his hands and declared, "Welcome back to Alasdair!"

"Where are we?" Jean asked as they all stared in surprise at the smooth, granite-lined tunnel.

"We're nearly twenty feet below Alasdair."

"Ah, Connor, you missed," Hamish said with a frown.

"How did you do this?" Jean asked, sliding one hand along the stone wall.

"It's power-grade stone," Connor said.

Hamish whistled softly. "And to think we've been living on a treasure trove all these years."

Verena increased the light from her little stone, bathing the tunnel in green-tinted light. "I'm impressed."

"How do we reach the surface?" Aifric asked.

Connor led the way through the tunnel, toward his home. With his slate and granite senses able to walk the stone, he easily mapped the surface. He stopped at the base of a stair leading upward.

"We'll come up under my family's living room. We can get everyone out without anyone suspecting a thing."

Hamish clapped him on the shoulder. "And since the guards are only patrolling the outskirts of town, they won't care if people go visit the Ashlar."

Jean gripped his hand excitedly. "Brilliant, Connor. Everyone will be safely away by morning, even if we take just a few at a time."

Aifric frowned at the tunnel. "Where to, though? Are you going to excavate more ground under here and hide everyone under the town?"

Connor shook his head. "Once they discover folks are gone, Gregor will search. No way I can shield everyone from him."

"So we take everyone out in the Slide?" Hamish asked.

"Sort of." Connor started climbing the stair. It ended in solid granite, but that plug was only a few inches thick. Once he pushed that away, all they'd have to do was break a hole in the floor. Hopefully his mother wouldn't mind too much.

"I'm going to make a tunnel through the Wick. Everyone can just run down to the point where we started tonight. From there, they can sneak into the bolt hole. That's solid rock, so Gregor can't find them. They'll be safe until we deal with Dougal."

"I like it," Aifric said.

"I'll need you all to help lead the groups," Connor said.

Hamish rubbed his hands together eagerly. "I wish I could see Dougal's face when he returns in the morning and finds everyone's gone, and we've taken all the bacon."

Chapter Seventy-Nine

*"A murder of crows feasts only in times of blood, but the shaking of
the earth cannot be restricted to a single mountain."*

~Evander

Connor crouched at the top of the stairs, staring up at the
floor of his family's living room. They had extinguished
their light, but he felt the others through his slate
senses, crowded close behind him. He had planned to
just smash through the floor, but realized that was a bad idea.

How angry would that destruction make his parents?
How loud would it be? If his family started screaming or shouting,
would that draw the guards?

So he and Verena had arranged an alternate plan.

Connor drew a little water from the distant Wick, where
the Slide was still drawn up next to the tunnel and the waters
remained parted. If he released soapstone, the passage would
flood and block the escape route.

He directed the water up to the floor, forming the
perimeter of a square. He made it a bit bigger than the opening to
the stairs, the border about as wide as his outstretched hand. Then
he parted that border, forming a narrow, dry line down the middle
of it.

His father had laid that floor, and it took a moment to
find a crack big enough to slip water through. Connor formed a
similar double square outline on the top side of the floor,
positioned directly over the one underneath.

"All set," he said.

Verena joined him and lifted a piece of marble to the
exposed underside of the floor, aimed at that dry strip in the
middle of his square border. An intense but narrow jet of blue fire
erupted from the little stone as she pressed it to the flooring.

The flames burned through in seconds. Connor kept the
waters in place on either side, draining away the heat so the flames
did not spread.

Verena moved her stone along the open track, quickly cutting through the floor, using the flame as a saw. She grinned. "It's working."

He hoped the minimal damage would make it easier to repair, even though there would be a blackened streak marring the beautiful floor. They even had to cut through one of the heavy beams that supported the structure. It was still better than curse-punching their way through.

As Verena began cutting the third side, footsteps sounded above them and little Wallace's voice called out, "Dad, why is the floor leaking?"

"Wallace, back up. It's me, Connor, and I'm coming in."

Wallace shrieked, "Dad! Connor's turned into a puddle."

"What are you shouting about?" Hendry asked, and his footsteps echoed on the floor. "What is going on in here?"

Connor spoke louder. "Dad, it's me. Keep back. We're coming in."

"Connor! Why'd you come back? Dougal's here with soldiers."

Lilias entered from the kitchen. "Did you say Connor?"

"He's here. Under the floor."

"Connor's turned into a puddle," Wallace wailed.

"I did not. Just stay back and you'll see."

Verena finished and Connor heaved, pushing the severed section of flooring and following it up into the living room. His family was all gathered, and they stared in astonishment.

They gaped even more when he reached down to help the fully armored Verena, then Jean in her battle clothing, then Aifric in her Healer's coat into the room. Even though they'd seen everyone just days before, Connor had to admit they made a pretty impressive entrance.

Hamish bounded up last of all and grinned, "Did you save us any bacon?"

As Connor set the square section of flooring aside Blair said, "Connor, you know the door works, right?"

Connor laughed. That set off everyone else. His mother gave him a warm hug, and Connor felt like he had come home. He felt tears building, but quickly blinked them away. He needed to be strong and decisive, not emotional. It would be hard enough to convince the villagers to flee into the night.

He wanted to hug his mother for a month, but he was quickly surrounded by the rest of the family. They all hugged, while their father repeatedly warned them all to be more quiet.

His parents hugged Hamish and Jean, then Lilias gave Verena a tender hug. "It is so good to see you, dear. Are you all right?"

Connor was stunned to see tears in Verena's eyes as she stammered something he couldn't hear. His mother glanced at him with that reproving look she used when he'd done something particularly stupid. Usually he knew what he'd done and had excuses ready.

"There, there," Lilias said, patting Verena's shoulder. "We'll talk it through in a minute."

Little Wallace tugged at Connor's battle jacket. "Did you bring me that squirrel, Connor?"

"I'll make it for you as soon as I get a minute."

Wallace's eyes widened in wonder. "You can make squirrels? Live ones?"

"Sort of. It's got big feet, so you can't laugh at it."

Wallace nodded with absolute sincerity. "I won't. I promise."

Hendry extended a welcoming hand to Aifric. "Welcome to our home. We were never really introduced in Altkalen."

"I'm Aifric, a Healer and friend of Connor's," she said, making a graceful curtsy. Connor was glad she hadn't introduced herself as an Assassin. His family wasn't ready to know everything.

His father then glanced down into the dark staircase cut into solid stone. "Not a single chisel mark. I didn't know you could cut stone with your curse."

"Only when it's power-grade stone. We figured sneaking into town quietly would be best for everyone."

Lilias said, "I should think so. We don't want another pitched battle here. We've only just managed to rebuild."

Connor said, "We might not have a choice. The town's in danger. We believe that Dougal came here to set a trap. He wants to kill Kilian, Hamish, and Verena and enslave me to Shona again."

Hendry scowled. "The man's a smooth liar."

"We heard. We were listening from up on Lookout Rock. Everything he said was lies or half-truths. We have to get everyone out of town before he comes back."

"You mean to fight him, don't you?" his mother asked.

She still had one arm around Verena's shoulders. Blair handed her little Fiona, who stared at Connor cautiously. She seemed nervous by the many plates and straps of his battle jacket.

"We have to. If we're right, he could destroy the entire valley. The future of Alasdair is at risk. We have to stop him."

Hendry frowned. "Worse than we figured. We told everyone to act like they believed him. Had to for their sakes, although after his fancy speech, some of them might really believe his pack of lies. He's done a lot of good for the town in recent months, after all."

Lilias muttered, "What a waste. And he chastised Isobel for poor management."

"Even if people don't believe everything, they should be ready to hide in the bolt hole if they know there'll be fighting by morning," Connor said.

"Wish we had a couple more weeks for finishing touches, but it'll do, if we can get there," Hendry said.

"We'll get there," Connor assured him.

Lilias glanced down the stairs plunging into the dark tunnel. "Is that why you came in this way? You think we can escape out the same way?"

Aifric grinned. "I see where you get your cleverness. This is definitely a good location to craft another me."

At his parents' quizzical looks, Connor said, "You really don't want to know. And yes, we can get out this way."

When he explained his plan, their eyes widened with wonder. Of course Wallace wanted to go down immediately and see if he could catch a big fish from inside the river.

Hendry shushed him. "We put an evacuation plan in place even before we started rebuilding. Blair, you and Roderick can start spreading the word. We'll evacuate through the tunnel in the established run groups."

"We'll stop by Hamish's house and get his family to help," Blair said.

Hamish said, "Don't bother. I'll tell them."

"Better borrow one of Hendry's coats," Lilias said, glancing meaningfully at his suit.

"I'll go get Gran," Jean said, and accepted a wrap from Lilias to cover her very non-villager attire.

The group slipped out through the kitchen door, and Connor hoped they were careful. The boys wouldn't attract attention, and as long as Hamish and Jean were careful, they should be fine.

Hendry said, "The bolt hole is the first gathering place. If that's still too close, we'll move into the mountains."

"It may come to that," Connor said. "For now, let's focus on getting everyone to the bolt hole. Load up with all the provisions you can there, then move up the mountain. If we all make it that far, we can figure out what to do next."

"I agree." Hendry gripped Connor's shoulder and gave him an approving smile. "It's good to have you back."

"I need you and mom to lead everyone. Hamish's family and Mhairi will help."

"But how can you hope to fight Dougal and all his Petralists?" Lilias asked.

"You saw a little of what I can do at Altkalen. We have more help on the way, but I want you all safely away before the fighting starts. It could get ugly."

Lilias asked Verena. "And you'll fight beside him, dear?"

Verena nodded. "We're a team."

"Don't worry about Verena," Connor assured her.

Aifric added, "She's considered one of the most dangerous people in Granadure for a reason."

"I have to worry. I'm your mother. I worry about you and about your girl, and Hamish. And poor Jean. A battle's no place for her."

Verena said, "You'd be surprised. She single-handedly saved hundreds of people in my home when Dougal sent an elemental monster to destroy our valley."

Lilias's eyes widened. "How is it possible?"

Connor said, "The world is a dangerous place. More than we ever knew, and Dougal is at the heart of most of it."

Hendry sighed. "I hate that such a burden has fallen to you, Son."

"There's no one else who can stop him."

"Then you must." His father gripped his shoulder, his expression grave. "If you've got the strength to help others and to fight for what's right, you have the responsibility to do so."

"Oh, Hendry." Lilias passed Fiona to him, then drew Connor into another hug, holding both him and Verena close. She spoke in a soft but fierce whisper to them. "If you must do this, know our blessing and all our hopes are with you."

She stepped back a pace and her expression turned hard. "Kill that man if you must, but don't become a monster to destroy one."

Again her strength helped bolster his confidence. Without her confident conviction that he spare all who could be spared, he would have killed many more people at Altkalen. He was so grateful he didn't carry that additional burden.

"I'd rather not kill anyone, but he hasn't given us any alternative."

She placed a hand on each of their shoulders. "Stay true to each other. Let nothing come between you, and together you are so much stronger than either of you alone."

Connor glanced at Verena, moved by the strength of his mother's words. He did want to stay true, but Verena's gaze looked troubled. There was something holding her back.

Could she still be that hung up on his promised kiss to Shona? He had to find a way to reconcile with her, but he couldn't believe that the answer to any disagreement was to just surrender completely to her wishes. They needed an equal partnership, or it would never work.

Hendry said, "People will start arriving soon. Lilias can lead the first group, Peigi the second, and Mhairi the third. What else do you need from us?"

"Well, for starters, we need the rest of the bacon," Connor said.

"I don't see how that's important," Lilias said with a frown.

"It is to Connor and Hamish," Aifric said with a smile.

Connor nodded. "Psychological advantage."

"I'll make sure we have every other possible advantage," Aifric said. She removed her Healer coat and skirt, revealing dark slacks and blouse, with daggers belted at her waist. A little shudder rippled through her, and her expression turned harder as she assumed her persona as Student Eighteen.

"What do you have in mind?" Connor asked. A handful of Boulders were unlikely to pose much of a threat against a Mhortair, but he didn't want any fighting to start until the villagers escaped.

"For now, just scouting the opposition. Trust me." She gave him a reassuring, but predatory smile, then slipped out the kitchen door and disappeared into the night.

Lilias rubbed her arms as Connor closed the door. "Why do I suddenly feel nervous around that young woman?"

Connor said, "Aifric is complicated, and she can be very dangerous when she needs to be."

"Strange quality in a healer," Hendry said.

"But she fits right in with our group," Verena assured him.

"While we're waiting, I need to return something to you, Dad," Connor said.

Verena drew from her satchel the precious Ashlar hammer and handed it to Connor. He hefted it and presented it to his father.

"This village needs you, and you need this."

Hendry took it with reverence. "Thank you, Son."

With that hammer in his dad's hands, Connor suddenly felt a renewed sense of confidence. Everything was going to turn out alright.

Chapter Eighty

"Reason at times may be found in the depths of shocking distress."
~Anton

While they waited for townsfolk to arrive and begin the secret exodus of Alasdair, Lilias drew them all to the long couch on the far side of the room. They sat together, little Fiona on his mother's lap, and Wallace prowling around the room, pretending to be a stalking pedra.

Lilias patted Verena's knee. "I am sorry you have to deal with so many of our problems, dear."

Verena glanced at Connor, and he was relieved when she gave him a warm smile. "We're in this together to the end."

"Don't you worry that one of you will get hurt again?" his dad asked.

Connor said, "It's possible, but we've made it this far."

Verena added, "And we've saved each other's lives more than once."

Lilias gripped her hands. "You've been through such trials. I hate it."

"They've made you strong," Hendry said in an approving tone.

Connor shrugged. "We haven't had much choice, but together I think we can save a lot of lives. We have to try."

His father nodded. "Stay true to each other, and to what's right. I'm a firm believer that right will always win out eventually."

"I agree," Verena said, but a frown flickered across her face and Connor wondered if she was thinking about how wrong he was to keep his word to Shona.

Lilias rose and paced away, hands clenching. "I hate liars. To think, High Lord Dougal ate food with us, helped us rebuild, even complimented us on the job we were doing."

Connor said, "He's a complicated guy. He was probably acting genuine with you. That doesn't mean he won't sacrifice us all for what he considers a more important cause."

Wallace jumped onto Connor's lap and gripped a couple straps of his battle jacket. "Where's that squirrel, Connor?"

"Now's probably the best time to make it, actually."

"Can you really?" his mother asked.

"Captain Ilse taught me how it's done."

His father shook his head, a wry smile on his lips. "I still find it hard to believe that those people who invaded our home and threatened our lives turned out to be your best friends."

Connor wasn't sure he would call Ilse a best friend. Half the time he'd spent around her, he'd worried she was planning to assassinate or kidnap him. If circumstances required it, she would still kill him to protect her homeland.

True friends were like that, he supposed.

"Just one example of how crazy life has been this past year." He dropped to one knee on the floor beside Wallace, who regarded him with eager expectation. "Now, about that squirrel."

"With big feet," Wallace reminded him.

"Can't forget that."

Fiona spoke for the first time. "Feet!"

While his mother shushed her, Connor withdrew a little piece of marble from his belt pouch.

"Are you sure that's wise?" Verena asked.

Connor considered the little stone. "It should be fine. This isn't sculpted, and I'm not planning to ascend. Those were the things Kilian warned me about."

"What does it do?" Lilias asked.

"This allows me to control elemental fire."

Wallace's eyes widened and he reached for the stone. "Really?"

Lilias snatched his hand away, as if the stone could burn him.

When Connor slipped it into his mouth, under his tongue, Wallace said, "Hey, don't eat rocks. They're bad for you, right, Mom?"

"Right."

"I won't eat it, I promise. Only Hamish does that."

Tapping his granite and slate again, Connor drew some mud from the distant riverbank, drained the water out of it with soapstone, and pulled the resulting clay up the stairs to the living room, balling it at his feet.

It was possible to perform a summoning using only an element and granite, but that consumed far more of the precious power. Using clay to form the body, wrapping it in granite strength, and powering it with elemental innards made the process a lot easier.

Then he got a sudden thought and glanced at Verena. "I wonder if I could use sweetbreads. Or bacon!"

"You don't really want to give the rampagers more reason to find it and eat it, do you?"

"Probably not," he admitted, but decided he'd have to try it some time. He easily imagined Hamish chasing a tiny, summoned creation made of bacon.

Connor sucked on the marble and savored the spicy explosion of flavor before it intensified into a steady burn. A ball of flames appeared in front of him, growing until it was about the size of his cupped hands.

"Wow!" Wallace reached out to touch it again, but Hendry scooped him up.

"Just watch, Son. Don't touch."

His voice was soft, and they all stared at the flames in fascination. To them his curse was still mostly a mystery, an unexplained wonder.

Tapping granite, he focused on the image of the squirrel with the big feet that he had created at the Carraig. With the image firmly in mind, he willed it over the small pile of mud, then drove the ball of flames into it too. Concentrating the power of granite in the center of his chest, he pushed it out toward the burning, muddy mixture.

With a muted thunderclap and a spray of rainbow light, the flame-filled mud snapped into the correct shape. Its skin faded under an outer shell of granite. A second later, a perfect little squirrel stood on the floor, facing Wallace.

"I love it!" Wallace shrieked, squirming off their father's lap and reaching for it.

"Is it safe?" Lilias asked as she restrained Fiona from following.

"It only does what I make it do."

The squirrel occupied part of Connor's mind. He could look through its eyes, hear through its ears, and even smell through its nose. Again he was struck by how odd it was that the little creature had sharper senses than he did.

With a thought, he sent the little squirrel scampering up Wallace's arm to sit on his shoulder. Wallace shrieked with delight and snatched for it. Connor sent it scurrying across the room, with Wallace in hot pursuit. He grinned as he ran the squirrel just fast enough to keep ahead of the eager child.

"I'm a pedra, and I'm going to eat you!" Wallace shrieked, shifting to run on hands and feet, growling like a hunter.

"You realize he's going to cry for days when that thing is gone?" Lilias asked.

"It'll keep him busy for a few minutes. Then I plan to send it across the Wick to spy on the rampagers."

"Shouldn't you wait until we complete the evacuation?" Verena asked.

That would probably be the wisest course of action, but he felt a growing urge to scout the rampagers as soon as possible. "I doubt even they would pay much attention to a squirrel. I might even get a chance to steal some of their porphyry."

"But then you'd have it," Verena said, watching him carefully.

Exactly. He felt a thrill of excitement at the thought of finally getting his hands on more of the powder, but also felt annoyed that she clearly didn't trust him with it.

"I know how to control it."

"What are you talking about?" Hendry asked.

Verena said, "Porphyry is a power stone that Dougal has kept very secret. It turns people into deadly, unclaimed monsters."

Lilias gasped. "Tallan's cursed memory, no!"

Fearing porphyry was a wise choice for most people, but Connor had used it to save hundreds, if not thousands, of lives.

"It's a powder, Mom. Patronage is a lie. Porphyry is a tool, nothing more."

"It's horrifying is what it is," Verena said with a shudder. "Connor had to use it once and he controlled it, but porphyry is very addicting. From what we've learned, it doesn't let go once it gets a hold of someone's heart."

Hendry's expression turned thoughtful. "So attempting to take it might disarm those wild soldiers and make your job easier, but then you face a new risk, don't you?"

Connor nodded slowly.

"If you get it, cast it into the river," Verena urged.

"I'll be careful," he promised.

He gave Wallace a few minutes to chase the squirrel. Fiona slowly grew accustomed to his presence and even let him hold her for a bit. By the time Connor prepared to head out on his squirrel spying mission, Wallace had run himself to exhaustion and plopped down on the rug nearby with a sigh.

He patted the squirrel's head and said, "I think it's even better than a pedra."

"Let's hope so. While I'm focused on the squirrel, it'll seem like I'm sleeping, but I'll be back."

Verena kissed his cheek. "Be careful."

A kiss on the lips would have been a better send-off, but maybe she felt self-conscious kissing him in front of his parents. He closed his eyes and focused on the squirrel, allowing it to fill his mind and consume his entire focus.

Connor became the squirrel.

Getting petted by Wallace felt surprisingly good, but he slipped away and headed for the back door. Lilias let him out, and he scurried into the darkness. In moments, he scampered through town and out the flood-under hole under the wall. He sensed two guards patrolling the long wall, but they walked slowly and seemed bored. Perfect.

In the next five minutes, he raced around Loch Wick, scampered across the new bridge across the Upper Wick, and followed the new road leading to Gavin's manor.

He smelled the first rampager half a minute later.

The man was crouched beside the narrow road, silently watching. That slightly wild smell clung to him, and it sent a shiver through Connor's little squirrel body.

Night had settled fully over the valley, and stars and a partial moon had risen. Connor silently slipped into the sparse underbrush, scurried up a tree, and leaped from branch to branch above the unsuspecting man's head.

Other local wildlife had fled the predator scent of the rampagers, and he moved alone through the silent forest. Taking to the trees was a good idea. He doubted the soldiers had noticed the lack of small animals, and any watchers would ignore a little squirrel. Even better, he was invisible to Gregor, who was surely monitoring the area through the earth.

With growing confidence, he scampered through the forest, using the highway of branches to approach the wide clearing with the manor house. Not as grand as the previous one, it was still quite impressive, especially considering how quickly it had been built. Constructed of timbers upon a solid stone foundation, it rose three stories, with a tiny hint of a tower above the main entrance, facing the town and quarry.

Connor had planned to sneak inside, but the rampager soldiers had set up camp in the field, not far from the trees. No doubt Lady Isobel was thrilled when Dougal had left his wild soldiers outside. He saw no sign of Captain Aonghus, and he smelled no fire other than the campfire the rampagers had built and were now sleeping around.

It seemed like a wasted opportunity for Aonghus. The night was young, though, so maybe he'd sneeze a spark or two onto Lady Isobel. The solution she used to dye her hair burned like lamp oil.

As he expected, Gregor stood upon a Sentry tower near the main entryway. It looked like he had sacrificed one of Lady Isobel's flower gardens for his spot. Connor grinned, showing his little squirrel teeth. She loved her flowers, and no doubt she was angrily pacing, still fuming about the desecration that she didn't dare reprimand.

The other eleven rampagers had already rolled into their blankets around the fire, and three were snoring loudly. Connor wasn't surprised by their lax attitude.

Gregor would notice anyone approaching. Besides, even if someone attacked, they could absorb porphyry in a matter of seconds and transform into rampagers. Since they were sleeping, that meant they had purged their powers. If he did get the porphyry, they'd be unable to transform.

Connor slipped down the tree, but paused at the base. He took a moment to focus on the earth, connecting with the ground nearby.

Gregor was there, his presence like a beacon in Connor's earth senses, his influence like rays of sunlight through the ground. He would sense even the movement of a little squirrel.

He might not pay much attention at first, but he'd surely be drawn to a stealthy prowl around the rampagers. He would realize that something not natural was going on.

So Connor carefully pushed his influence into the ground by that tree. He formed the image of a blank space, like a hole in the earth, ever-so-gently deflecting Gregor's attention aside. The Sentry would certainly pick up on even that faint shielding if he was focusing on the area, but he had no reason to do so.

Even in a half doze, Gregor could trust to his earth sense to warn him of approaching danger, like the feel of an insect scuttling across his skin. If alert, he'd be focusing on the distant Alasdair. The loch and the river would make that difficult, drawing even more of his attention.

With deliberate care, Connor expanded his tiny shield until it was just big enough for him. Holding his little squirrel breath, he eased off the tree and onto the earth, glancing at Gregor for any hint that the Sentry had noticed.

544

When Gregor did not move and the earth did not swallow him up, he started breathing again and slowly crept into the grass behind the rampagers. He moved with all the stealth he could muster, crouching low over the ground, his bushy tail wrapped around his shoulders to keep it from dragging.

As he closed on the first sleeper, he realized that he had never tested using his powers through a summoned creature until he'd just used slate. He wasn't sure how it worked, but decided not to think about it too much. It would be far too easy to convince himself that what he was doing was impossible. Then he wouldn't be able to do it any more.

The nearest rampager was a beefy woman, whose long brown hair formed a thick mane around her head. He focused on the little pouch at her belt, and his heart rate increased with excitement. He could do it, could get the porphyry.

He should test it somewhere private to make sure it was good quality powder. Even though he knew better than to tempt porphyry again, the insidious thought clung to the back of his mind.

With the powder so close, the hunger for it grew to a distracting need. He felt tempted to rush the woman and simply claw his way through the bag to get at it.

Using the image of Verena in his mind like a shield against the foolish impulse, Connor crept forward. The woman was snoring and she smelled more animal than human. She hadn't washed recently, and he could easily smell the bacon she'd eaten during the feast.

That faint, wild scent clung to her and stood the hairs on his little head on end. His tiny heart beat even faster as he approached the danger that screamed at his animal instincts to flee instead of approach.

He leaned over her, sharp teeth poised to snap through the leather cord securing the pouch to her belt. The smell of porphyry was maddening, and he placed one paw on the bag as he leaned forward to bite.

The bag shifted under his weight.

A strong hand snatched him off the ground.

The woman sat up, staring sleepily at him. "What have we got here?"

Connor bit her thumb.

Instead of screaming and flinging him away like most women would, she growled and lifted him closer to her face. "You shouldn't have done that, beastie."

She bit his head off.

Connor fell right off the couch where he'd been seated while his mind ran with the squirrel. He scrambled to his hands and knees, eyes wide with the recent beheading. He leaned back and patted his neck even as the rational part of his mind tried to remind him that only his squirrel had died.

A wave of fury roiled through him. He clenched his fists and fought an urge to howl. He'd been so close! A few seconds more and he would have gotten the porphyry. Knowing the powder was so close, yet still so far out of reach set his entire body trembling with anger and the urge to rush over there in person and rip the porphyry away from that woman.

"What happened?" his mother asked, her voice worried.

Connor growled as he looked up, and she recoiled from his angry expression.

Verena dropped to one knee beside him and cupped his face in her warm hands. She held his angry gaze and asked softly, "It's the porphyry, isn't it?"

"I almost had it," he panted.

"Breathe," she urged, holding his gaze, her expression worried. "Center yourself, Connor. You can't give in to it."

"Are you all right?" His father asked, looking concerned.

"I will be. Give me a minute."

"What happened?" his mother asked.

She looked frightened, reached toward him as if to comfort, but then withdrew her hand. Then she frowned and dropped to her knees beside Connor. "We trust you, Connor. You're stronger than any foolish powder."

Connor took a deep breath and tried to shake the feeling of those teeth biting through his neck.

"I hope you're right, but it doesn't really matter now. I failed. They'll know a Petralist is here. It won't take them long to guess it's us."

CHAPTER EIGHTY-ONE

"The greatest threat of your condition is thus spoken by your own lips."

~Evander

The kitchen door opened and Hamish's family poured into the house. They moved with purpose, with far less jostling and teasing than normal, and even the children looked serious. They had seen battling in the streets of Alasdair before. They each carried a pack, and Connor didn't doubt most of the space was dedicated to food.

Hamish entered last and discarded the coat he'd borrowed from Hendry. As his siblings clustered around Connor and Verena, glancing nervously into the dark stairs leading underground, he looked around and asked, "Are we really the first ones back?"

"You are," Hendry said as he clasped wrists with Amhain.

"We have a problem," Verena said.

Peigi, who had just taken Fiona from Lilias glanced around, as if to make sure her children were all safe. "What happened? Was someone discovered?"

Connor nodded. "I was."

He told them briefly about his out-of-body reconnaissance across the river and failure to steal the porphyry powder.

"She bit your head off?" Peigi exclaimed, rubbing at her own neck and grimacing at the thought.

"Animals," Hamish muttered. "Didn't even try cooking you first."

"You should've waited until everyone was away," Verena said, giving Connor an exasperated look.

"We can cry about it, or get to work," Connor told them. It was easy to second-guess a bad decision, but he didn't regret trying to get the porphyry.

The door opened again and Jean and Mhairi slipped

inside. They were both burdened with large canvas packs with many pockets, filled to bursting with healing supplies. Hamish greeted Jean with a hug and a quick kiss. His nervous siblings didn't even tease him.

Mhairi scanned the group, and her initial smile faded. "Something's happened."

The door opened again and Aifric entered. She gave Connor a disgusted look. "What did you do? I hear the rampagers starting to howl across the loch."

"We have to start moving everyone down to the escape route," Verena said.

Connor shook his head. "There's no time now. I can't hold the tunnel open through the Wick while fighting rampagers."

"And probably Aonghus and Gregor," Hamish added.

"Thanks for the reminder," Connor said sarcastically.

He wasn't sure he could stop those two. They were his teachers, men he respected and honestly feared.

"Then we have to make a run for it," Jean said resolutely.

"But the guards," Lilias said nervously.

Connor said, "Jean is right. You need to run for East Gate, and gather everyone you can on the way. Hamish can take point. Jean, I'll pull the Storm out of the river for you to fly."

Jean didn't hesitate at the thought of flying the Storm again. "Blair, I'll need you, Roderick, Mysie, and Neilina with me. We've got some small bombs in the back."

The chosen children looked excited, but Peigi looked terrified by the idea. "Bombs? You can't be serious."

She was probably right to worry, but Connor said, "They'll be out of harm's way up in the sky. Hopefully they won't need to drop anything, but it might come to that."

Hamish looked thrilled by the idea. "I'll keep an eye on them too."

Peigi did not look comforted.

Aifric said, "Don't worry about the guards, Lilias. I'll run interference." Her hands dropped to her daggers, and the hint of an eager smile tugged at her lips. Connor almost felt sorry for any Boulders who got in her way.

Verena adjusted the strap of her satchel, then touched her short sword and faced Connor, her expression grave. "That leaves the two of us to deal with Dougal's forces."

Connor nodded, embracing the feeling of nervous excitement that fluttered in his stomach. Aonghus and Gregor represented a threat he wasn't sure he could overcome. Adding a dozen rampagers to the mix, and he wished he had half of Wolfram's army at his back.

He didn't have an army. He and Verena would be all that stood between his home, his family, and gruesome death.

He focused all of his simmering anger at Dougal into a fierce determination and growled, "Let them come. This is our home, and I swear none of them will make it across the Wick alive."

Verena nodded, her expression grave. "Then we go after Dougal."

Hamish frowned. "I don't like it."

"Me neither," Aifric said.

"Once you get everyone safely away from town, join us," Connor told them.

"Then let's go," Aifric said, gesturing toward the door. "Move, everyone! Those monsters will be here in minutes and they'll rip this town apart."

Their families ran for the doorway. Lilias and Hendry snatched up partially-filled packs, but lacked time for more preparations.

"Be careful, Son," Lilias told Connor when they all assembled outside. She gave him a fierce hug, then hugged Verena in turn.

"I can't promise I won't kill anyone," he told her.

She sighed and kissed his cheek. "I trust you to make the right choice. Don't forget who you are."

His father gripped his hand, then turned and led the way toward the square at a jog. His voice bellowed into the night. "Evacuate! Run groups assemble now! Danger is imminent. This is a scramble alert!"

The cry echoed down the street, and instantly doors flung open and other villagers took up the shout.

Connor and Verena headed the other way, down Wall Street toward the distant Wall Gate, with Jean and her band of excited young children in tow. Connor was impressed by how fast everyone responded. Within seconds, villagers began boiling out of their homes, still stomping feet into boots, throwing on jackets, and stuffing a few items into packs.

"Get me the Swift," Verena told him as they ran.

"On its way.

Connor tapped soapstone and connected with the nearby Wick. The river glowed in his water senses, even though the river-facing wall blocked it from view.

550

Three Boulders were rushing along the wall, drawn by the shouting and the mass movement of villagers. They clearly intended to circle along the wall and reinforce the Petralists guarding East Gate.

Connor drew a long tendril of water out of the Wick and snapped it along the top of the wall, like a broom whisking across a floor. It caught the surprised Boulders at waist height and knocked them tumbling off the wall and into the Wick.

They'd emerge in moments, but by then Hamish and Aifric should have disabled the guards at the gate. With a thought, Connor drew the Swift and the Storm out of the river, lifted them over the wall, and deposited them nearby. They were completely dry and ready to fly.

Jean climbed into the Storm with the children while Verena slipped into the Swift. Thrusters ignited almost before she snapped her harness into place. Connor kept running, urging the press of fearful villagers to hurry for the square.

He rounded the western corner of the street and pounded toward Wall Gate. Rampagers howled on the far side of the Wick, and the deep-throated voices sent a shiver of excitement down his spine.

He had howled like that, and the memory of his unmatched savage power drove him on. He'd find a way to conquer those monsters and take the powder from them. Then he'd unleash the ultimate beast against Dougal.

Running with granite wasn't fast enough, even though each lumbering stride covered a dozen feet. So he tapped soapstone and marble together, casting waters along the street and draining away the heat. In just a couple heartbeats, the entire street was covered with a sheet of black ice. Connor leaped onto it and planted his feet, driving himself forward with soapstone. He slid across the smooth surface, accelerating until he flashed up the street like a Strider.

Four Boulders stood blocking Wall Gate, swords and maces at the ready. They stared up Market Street toward the commotion of villagers pouring into the distant square from every side. They spotted the ice and turned to face him.

Too late.

Connor cast a sheet of ice across the entire gate. The Boulders max-tapped granite in a vain attempt to withstand the sudden elemental barrage, but the ice catapulted them off their feet. Connor kept them tumbling all the way to Loch Wick.

He followed them through the gate. Verena caught up to him there, swooping out of the night to take up position above and to his right, the speedslings on the Swift already spooling up. She was like a deadly guardian angel, ready to rain destruction upon the Boulders if they turned to fight.

They didn't. Showing more intelligence than Boulders were usually credited with, they took one look at Connor and Verena descending the road toward them. Then they bolted away toward the bridge over the Upper Wick.

Reinforcements were already on the way.

Rampagers, already transformed into deadly monsters, seemed to erupt out of the tree line. The terrifying sight of them awed Connor. The dozen monsters raced toward the bridge, their claws ripping the ground in their eager haste, glowing purple eyes already fastened on Connor.

They moved at least as fast as fracked Striders, their huge muscles rippling under their reddish hide. Their bald, leathery heads seemed to be made almost entirely of elongated, fanged maws and those burning eyes.

They were coming to destroy his home and his people.

They would regret that.

Connor again tapped soapstone. All the water he needed was right there in the loch and the fast-flowing Upper Wick.

As Boulders and rampagers all raced for the bridge from opposite sides, he heaved on that water, and it erupted, shattering the narrow bridge into thousands of pieces. The sharp crack of exploding timbers echoed from the steep cliffs of the Torr.

Boulders cringed back from the inverted waterfall, but Connor seized them with the waters and threw them over the lock. They tumbled into the trees on the far side like stones cast from a catapult. Lacking a bridge, they would find it difficult to return and cause any trouble.

The rampagers came on without slowing, howling with blood lust. Connor swept the waters at them, hardening the liquid into horizontal blades. It swept across them, blasting them out of the air in mid-leap and tumbling them back a hundred yards. They rebounded to their feet, not visibly hindered by the brutal strikes.

Verena unleashed thousands of hornets. The little projectiles buzzed as they ripped through the air in a deadly cloud, tearing into the monsters. Many staggered back. Some hornets were tipped with diorite and they exploded against armored rampager hide, snapping off bony protrusions and ripping open gashes with tiny sprays of fire and blood.

That only seemed to enrage the monsters further.

"They really are nasty, aren't they?"

The voice caught Connor by surprise and he looked up. Captain Ilse was slowly settling to the ground nearby, her catch-fall harness hissing loudly. Lukas and a dozen Crushers fell slowly through the sky behind her.

A huge windrider, over a hundred feet above his head, was banking around for another pass. Connor caught sight of Dierk at the controls, with Kilian standing on the high pilot bench beside him. Connor was startled to see Martys standing in the bed of the wagon, holding to the back of the pilot bench.

Mattias stood at the back too. He waved mightily, his teeth glowing in the dark sky and shouted, "Verena, catch!"

He jumped out of the wagon.

He was not wearing a catch-fall harness.

Mattias might have been hoping to prove he could command the air and slow his fall, but Verena responded to his call. She swooped around and caught him. He stepped into the stirrups at the back of the Swift, exactly the same way Connor usually did.

As Verena circled back around toward Connor, she pushed up her visor and glanced back at Mattias. Connor couldn't hear what she was saying.

Mattias leaned forward and kissed her on the lips.

The sight seared into Connor's mind like a diorite dart through the eyes, and he gasped in horror. His heart howled like the rampagers, who were charging toward the Wick again.

Connor shouted a wordless cry of heartbroken rage. Why would Mattias pick that time to dare kissing Verena? Could she have somehow encouraged him to do so? The thought tore at his mind, and the waters of the wick reacted to his anguish.

Water erupted high into the air, bursting the banks and flooding the western shores. It ripped trees and bushes up by the roots and tumbled the rampagers out of sight in a frothing, watery avalanche.

Connor barely noticed, his eyes glued on Verena and Mattias. She pushed him away, but Connor couldn't see her expression. She was strapped into the Swift, so it was hard to read her body language, but one thing was clear.

She hadn't punched Mattias in the face.

Verena landed nearby, amid the company of Crushers, and Mattias jumped lightly from the back. He was grinning and looked immensely pleased with himself.

Connor decided that smile would look best at the bottom of the loch. But before he could drown Mattias, Ilse gripped his shoulder.

"What's the situation, Connor?"

He wanted to shout, but he forced himself to bottle up the rage and try to speak calmly. "Hamish and Jean are evacuating the village with Aifric's help. They're taking East Gate and might need assistance."

"And the rampagers?"

Through his soapstone sense, he felt them scrambling out of the distant edges of the flood, running away into the hills to the northeast.

"They seem to be running."

"We should hunt them down and eradicate them right now," Lukas said.

The windrider descended nearby and Kilian shouted, "I thought I told you not to rile everyone up before we got here!"

"Things didn't go according to plan," Connor said, not feeling like elaborating.

"I'd say not. Mattias, you help the Crushers evacuate the village. We spotted Gregor and Aonghus ascending the mountain toward the quarry. Connor, you and Verena with me. We have to stop him."

That was why the mighty Petralists hadn't responded to the alarm and come to fight. Dougal was planning to raise the elfonnel. If they didn't stop him, all their efforts would be wasted.

Connor headed for the wagon, but Verena pivoted the Swift closer and gestured him to jump on. He met her gaze, and she gave him that same troubled look she'd had so often of late. He had thought she was still angry about his deal with Shona, but now he realized the truth.

"Were you going to tell me you were dating Mattias again?" he demanded as she lifted off after the windrider. Rage and devastating loss churned through him, and he wasn't sure which emotion would win out.

Verena glanced back, tears in her eyes. "Oh, Connor. I'm so sorry."

So it was true.

"Why didn't you tell me you loved him instead?" Connor hated to say those words, hated how his voice shook, hated that he hadn't punched the man to Sehrazad already.

She shook her head violently. "It's not like that. It was just one kiss."

554

"One kiss? You were furious with me because Shona forced me to agree to one kiss before I could share important information with my troops." His eyes narrowed and he continued in a softer, but angrier tone. "Did you agree to kiss him as the price to get him to help train me?"

"Of course not!"

"That would explain why he agreed to it."

"He taught you because he's a good man," Verena exclaimed.

"Good enough that you can't resist kissing him again, right after that long, self-righteous rant about how we need to commit to each other."

"I'm sorry!" Verena cried, her tone anguished. "I made a mistake. Will you forgive me?"

When she looked at him again, tears in those big, earnest eyes, the emotion and fear he saw there extinguished his anger like water flooding an open flame.

"Where are you two going?" Kilian's voice spoke over the speakstone in Verena's helmet, loud enough for Connor to hear.

They had drifted east, and now Verena banked back toward the windrider rising up the long cliff above town, and the quarry beyond.

Connor tried to control his anger, tried to focus on the hope that he hadn't lost Verena. And on how glorious it would feel to break every bone in Mattias's glowing body.

"When we finish this, we need to have a long, honest talk."

She nodded, for once looking subdued. "All right."

Connor took a deep, steadying breath as they rose above the edge of the cliff and caught sight of the quarry dug into the flank of the mountain beyond. The regular, stepped tiers of the quarry were clearly visible, the white stone glowing in the moonlight.

Dougal stood on the west rim, flanked by Gregor and Aonghus.

As they banked in that direction, Connor growled, "First, I really need to kill someone."

Chapter Eighty-Two

"Darkness veils the face of purpose, but many walk the shadows."
~Evander

Verena sidled through the air, keeping the speedslings aimed at Dougal. The windrider rumbled through the air nearby, eighty feet above the south rim of the quarry. Connor was about to ask Kilian how he intended to attack, but movement at the west rim, to Dougal's left, drew his attention.

The rampagers swarmed over the rim there, leaping up the steep western slope above the Upper Wick with remarkable ease. Instead of forming a protective screen around Dougal as Connor expected them to, they leaped down the stepped western side of the quarry and assembled on the lowest level. Aonghus's billowing flames provided ample illumination to see them.

The long sloping ramp that led up to the exit tunnel on the eastern side of the quarry ended near them. The position made sense if they were expecting an attack from Quarry Road, but they had to know the attack would come by air.

"That's odd," Verena said with a frown.

Then the rampagers transformed, returning to human form. "And that doesn't make any sense," Connor said.

Dougal had to be planning some kind of subtle trickery, but he couldn't imagine what it might be.

Dierk slowed the windrider to a hover. Kilian, who stood on the high pilot bench beside him, gestured down at the southern rim of the quarry, almost directly below them. Dierk descended.

Verena swooped in toward the rim after them and called, "Kilian, what's the plan? I can shoot Dougal from here."

Kilian shook his head, his expression grim. "Dougal is mine. Connor, you deal with Gregor."

"No problem," Connor said, and his voice didn't even tremble.

Of course Gregor would be a problem. Only Anton could face the mighty Sentry with confidence, and he was probably smart enough to feel nervous.

Hamish roared up over the rim of the quarry nearby and waved as he pivoted in mid-air and slowed. "Everyone's out of town."

Martys waved from the back of the windrider. "Where are they headed?"

Connor said, "Don't worry about them. They've got a bolt hole concealed in the plateau just outside of town. They'll be safe there until we finish this."

Verena said, "Good timing, Hamish. You and I will keep the rampagers off of Connor while he deals with Gregor."

Hamish said, "Especially if we hit them before they transform. Why haven't they started charging?"

"That's what bothers me," Verena said.

The windrider touched down. Martys leaped from the wagon before Kilian and rushed down the inside access ramp toward the lowest level. The rampagers formed into ranks and faced him.

"Wait!" Connor shouted. Martys was a great fighter, but a suicide charge wouldn't help anyone. "Those are the rampagers, Uncle. Get back, or they'll kill you!"

Captain Aonghus rose into the air on a pillar of fire. In his hand he held a sculpted marble statue of a beautiful, burning woman. His laugh echoed across the quarry, repeating and building upon itself into a crescendo.

He raised the statue high. "Kilian, this time I'm the one with something to teach!"

Kilian approached along the southern rim, walking with a casual stride that belied the impending violence about to erupt across the quarry. "Did Dougal tell you that if you ascend today, he'll raise an elfonnel through you?"

"Fire is a purifying agent," Aonghus laughed. "And the threshold is the ultimate burn."

"Did he also tell you that if you do this, there is no coming back? You will be consumed."

Aonghus's grin faltered and he glanced at the statue in his hand. "You've done it."

Kilian nodded, still advancing. "That's because I know what I'm doing. There are required steps that Dougal has withheld from you. Today is not your time, Aonghus. Don't throw away so much potential. There's so much more I can teach you."

When Aonghus hesitated, Dougal shouted, "Don't listen to his lies, Captain! Kilian has murdered and plotted and thwarted our nation for centuries. Your duty is to fight for me, and I command you to ascend!"

Connor was surprised Gregor hadn't moved to block Kilian. He looked more closely at the big Sentry, tapping a bit of quartzite to enhance his vision. Gregor was standing as if in a trance. The rim of the quarry was made of solid granite, but it was power grade stone. If he was tapping granite, he could walk his senses through it as easily as earth.

So Connor tapped granite and dropped from the Swift to the rim of the quarry. He reached for slate and his senses plunged through the gateway.

He immediately sensed Gregor's presence. The man didn't hold sway over the entire quarry, but his presence was concentrated into an intense pillar directly below his feet, stretching deep into the mountain. A low note, like the gong of an immense bell, pulsed straight into the ground beneath him. Several seconds later, another one sounded.

Connor didn't understand what he was doing, but it couldn't be good. He glanced at Kilian again, who had stopped about fifty yards away from the corner of the quarry where the southern and western rims met. Aonghus, on his pillar of fire, was blocking the corner, but Kilian could easily blast himself across the short distance to Dougal.

Connor called, "Gregor is doing something odd. Some kind of tone pulsing into the ground."

Kilian frowned. "He is seeking the slumbering elfonnel. Time to stop him."

"I don't think so!" Martys shouted.

While Kilian had been trying to talk sense into Aonghus, Martys had continued to the floor of the quarry. The rampagers had moved to meet him, and the entire group faced him, barely ten strides away. They stood right next to the strangely cracked section of quarry floor that Connor's dad had told him about. If they embraced porphyry, they could shred him to pieces in seconds.

"Get out of there, Uncle Martys!" Connor shouted again.

He couldn't stop Gregor and save Martys at the same time. The thought of having to sacrifice another person he cared about in order to block Dougal terrified and infuriated him.

Hamish and Verena, who had been focused on the confrontation with Aonghus, lifted off the rim to support Martys.

"Ye dinnae understand, me boy," Martys said, his voice strangely calm. "I told you me mates were a wild bunch."

Dougal shouted, "Martys, your timing is unexpected. He's not ready."

Martys shook his head. "Nay, my lord. The beast is awake in his heart, an' he willnae resist the call to join the pack."

The truth struck Connor like a blow from his father's hammer.

"You're a rampager?"

Martys saluted. "Aye laddie, and ye no should have told me where your family is hiding."

He was such an idiot!

Connor shook his head in disbelief as fear chilled him to the bone. He cursed himself for not putting the clues together sooner.

No wonder Martys knew about rampagers. No wonder he talked so much about unleashing the beast. And when his eyes glowed, it wasn't because he was a secret Solas, but because he was fighting the urge to transform and embrace rampager battle lust.

"Why would you do this?" Connor cried, horrified by the magnitude of Martys's betrayal.

They had accepted him, made him part of their team. Connor had trained with him, had felt like Martys sometimes understood him better than anyone.

Martys barked a laugh. "Because ye are a fool, boy. Ye've filled yer head with tripe. Ye think Grandurians be yer friends, but Kilian teaches ye to show restraint instead of striking with all yer fury. Ye think ye love a Grandurian." He spat in Verena's direction. "But her love is false."

Connor wondered how Martys knew. Had he seen Verena kissing Mattias? Had they spent more time together than she had suggested? Was she still lying to him?

Martys's voice turned hard. "It be past time fer ye to accept yer place in the world, serve yer high lord, an' take the only woman worthy of your potential."

"You're a traitor to your family," Hamish shouted from where he hovered twenty feet above Connor. His face was red with anger.

Martys shook his head and gestured at the other gathered rampagers. "These be my family, boy. I lead this pack, an' today Connor will join us."

"Today I'm going to kill you," Connor declared. The words were like ash in his mouth, and he hated Martys double for making him say them.

Martys grinned in a disturbing, predatory way. "I hope ye be finally ready to unleash the beast, laddie, or I'll rip out yer throat. Here be your choice. Me mates and I are going hunting. We're going to kill every last living soul on that plateau."

He raised a small pouch, then dropped it to the stone at his feet.

Porphyry.

Connor felt a wild hunger erupt in the pit of his stomach, and he took an involuntary step toward the pouch.

Martys grinned wider. "There be no other choice today, laddie. Unleash the beast an' give me something more interesting to hunt than your siblings and your dear, sweet mother."

"I swear I'll kill you," Connor snarled, so angry he could barely think.

"Only one way to do that boy," Martys grinned, pointing at the porphyry. "And you won't come back from that road. Not a second time."

Verena opened fire, raining a stream of deadly hornets across the quarry at Martys.

He was ready for it. He leaped aside, then began to howl as he transformed.

The sound dug into Connor's ears, reminding him of those terrifying, thrilling, unrivaled moments when he had changed into a rampager and become an unstoppable killer. He had faced the elfonnel unafraid. Ripping Martys and his mates apart would be simple in comparison.

The rest of the rampagers joined the chorus, convulsing where they stood as they changed from men and women into ravaging beasts. Their muscles bulged, stretching their skin to the cracking point as it thickened into tough leather, covered in a sparse carpet by coarse, burnt-orange hairs. Short spikes of bone protruded through a second later.

Their arms lengthened while their legs shortened, hands and feet shifting into deadly clawed paws. Their skulls expanded, forming heavy brow ridges and long, powerful muzzles. Their hair melted into their heads, and the resulting bald scalps were covered in maroon colored hide. Their eyes transformed into glowing purple orbs.

The transformations still horrified Connor. The monsters rose on all fours, looking roughly like giant wolves the size of bears. They possessed the speed and strength of Petralists, resistance to elemental damage, and the full force of their intellect twisted into rage and bloodlust.

560

They were simply the most perfect killing machines on the planet.

Verena and Hamish swept in, spraying hornets across the transforming creatures and gouging terrible wounds in their hides, but not seeming to have any effect.

Connor shouted, "Stop! The transformation heals them. You can't do any good until they're changed."

"Hornets won't stop them once they are," Hamish shouted back.

"Connor." He turned and met Kilian's gaze. "Go. Protect your family and kill that traitor. I'll deal with Dougal."

"But what about Gregor?"

"One problem at a time," Kilian said, his eyes igniting with white-hot flame.

Connor leaped off the rim to the next wide step ten feet below. He tapped granite to absorb the shock of landing, then sprinted with ponderous, leaping strides down the quarry tiers toward Martys.

His uncle rose, a massive beast with reddish-gold hide, an enormous maw, and eyes burning with purple light. Martys howled once, joined by the dozen other rampagers, and stared across the distance at Connor.

Challenge accepted.

Verena shot Martys in the face with a hundred hornets.

Some of them contained diorite, and the explosion knocked Martys backward. He rolled and came up running. With terrifying speed, he and the other rampagers bounded up the steep ramp toward the exit that would lead them out the tunnel to Quarry Road and past the empty lochs to the plateau beyond.

Connor stopped running and growled, "You shouldn't have threatened my family."

Then he tapped slate, and his mind plunged into the earth. For the first time in his life he was eager to kill.

CHAPTER EIGHTY-THREE

*"The tree knows not to fear the avalanche, but claims the
mountainside as its domain."*

~Evander

Tapping granite, Connor's earth senses walked as easily
through the quarry as they did clean earth, expanding to
touch every corner of the open pit. For a second, the
entire quarry glowed in his earth senses, perfectly
mapped and complete.

Growing up, the quarry had always been at the heart of
his family and the town. Despite the countless hours he'd spent
exploring its regular steps and watching the cutters work and
move the heavy stone, he had never comprehended it so well.

Movement along the surface drew his attention and he
focused on the thirteen rampagers galloping up the exit ramp.
Martys and the lead monsters had already passed onto the road
beyond the quarry, and the mixed grade there made it harder to
track them.

The others would not be so lucky.

Connor yanked at the stone, and the solid ground under
the remaining rampagers dropped away beneath them. Most of the
beasts leaped up in spectacular bounds to escape the trap. Connor
snatched at them with fingers of solid granite that moved to his
will as easily as the waters of the loch.

He grabbed hold of the two rampagers lagging behind the
rest and yanked them back down into the hole. They struggled
with inhuman fury, howling their rage and snapping the slender
bands. He wasted precious seconds reinforcing his hold upon
them, long enough for the other monsters to escape the trap. With
growing irritation, Connor slammed the walls of the hole closed.

Tons of solid granite shifted three feet, closing the deep
hole in half a heartbeat. The crack of stone smashing into stone

shook the quarry like a thunderbolt, drowning out the mushy splat of the hapless rampagers squashing into jelly.

Connor felt no remorse.

He yanked again on the earth, creating a minor explosion of stone under his own feet. It catapulted him across the quarry and down to the floor. He landed beside the little pouch Martys had dropped and reached for it. His eager anticipation mixed with terrified reluctance.

Hamish was already soaring over the shoulder of the mountain in pursuit of the rampagers, but Verena banked the Swift to a hover nearby and shouted, "Don't use it, Connor!"

"I can control it," Connor assured her, despite his own secret doubts.

"How can you be sure?"

"I can't be," he admitted.

They didn't have time to argue. The need to chase Martys was like a living thing raging through him.

She drifted closer, her expression anguished. "He wants you to use it, don't you see? If you do, you might never come back."

She was probably right. "There might not be any other way."

"There has to be. We'll stop him somehow," she insisted.

"I will do whatever it takes to save my family." Connor tapped slate, sealed his feet to the granite underfoot, then accelerated up the long exit ramp after the rampagers, sliding over the stone like ice.

Verena gave chase and Connor said, "If I lose control, do what you must to stop me from hurting anyone."

"Don't ask me to do that, Connor."

He gave her a reassuring grin. "You've been prepared to kill me before, Verena. You're stronger than you pretend sometimes."

"That was different," she insisted, sounding anguished.

"It's the same. Promise me, Verena, or I'm going to take that porphyry now."

Verena glared at him. "That's not fair, Connor."

"Neither is finding out that you still love Mattias," he snapped back.

She opened her mouth to reply, but no words came. He turned away from those bright eyes filled with emotion. He couldn't afford to let her distract him, not now.

Maybe she did love him. Maybe she loved Mattias more. They could figure it out if they survived.

The roar of the thrusters on the Swift tripled, and the nimble little craft accelerated away. Verena swooped right through the exit tunnel.

As Connor tapped quartzite to listen for the rampagers, he heard her whisper, "I hate you for asking that of me, Connor."

He nearly stumbled. The thought of Verena hating him was like a stone chained to his heart, but he couldn't afford the time to work things out with her. Any hesitation, and his family would die. Verena was many things, and he loved every aspect of her.

Except the part of her that still loved Mattias.

He would find a way to secure her love somehow. But first he had to kill his uncle.

His hands shook with the need to rip open the bag of porphyry and shove his hand inside, but he forced himself to tuck it into his belt. He'd use it, but maybe he could wait until after they defeated Martys and could do so in a more controlled test.

He wouldn't let Martys dictate the fight. It was time his uncle learned what Connor could do when he was really angry.

As he sped toward the exit tunnel after Verena, a flicker of movement drew his gaze and he turned his quartzite vision on the eastern flank of Wick Torr, high above the quarry.

Mister Five was crouched there, already bringing his hands together in that telltale sign he was about to unleash his deadly, long-range, compressed ice bolt. He looked to be aiming at either at Dougal or Kilian.

Connor tapped soapstone just as Mister Five released the bolt. It flashed down from the mountain and across the quarry, moving too fast for him to seize it, but he managed to yank at it, pulling it from its path.

It had been aimed at Kilian.

On its new trajectory, it instead drilled into Gregor's shoulder, nearly a hundred feet away, rocking the big Sentry out of his trance. He took a step back, and the solid rock of the quarry rim rippled like the waters of a pond.

Connor felt torn as he slid toward the exit faster than a fracked Strider. Mister Five was a deadly threat, but he had to focus on stopping the rampagers from slaughtering his family. Kilian must now recognize the danger and could take care of himself.

Another flash of movement drew his gaze.

Aifric.

She was sneaking up behind Mister Five, creeping along a ledge fifty feet above and behind him.

She glanced in Connor's direction and saluted.

He almost saluted back, but that might tip off Mister Five. He silently wished her luck, and was happy to know she was on the hunt. He glanced back a final time toward Kilian and Aonghus.

Upon his pillar of fire, Aonghus burst into white-hot flames. His laugh echoed across the quarry, driven to the brink of insanity by the deep burn he was embracing. "I don't need to ascend to defeat you, Kilian. Not even you can quench the sculpted fires." He launched into the air toward Kilian.

In the center of the quarry, at the deepest point of the pit, the stone began to shake and bubble, like soup beginning to boil. It was at the weakened spot that had appeared during the recent earthquake activity. Connor wasn't sure what the new activity meant, but he didn't have time to deal with it.

With renewed determination, he reached the top of the exit ramp and threw himself into the air with an eruption of stone. Then he tapped marble, and fire erupted out of his feet, hurling him higher still. As he soared above the hillside at the beginning of Quarry Road, he gained an unobstructed view of the road. His gaze swept past the empty holes that had been lochs until he blew the mountain.

The rampagers had already reached the edge of the steep cliff overlooking the plateau and were vaulting over the edge.

Connor applied quartzite to his throat and shouted as loud as he could, "Ilse, beware! Rampagers!"

In the distance, he heard the first scream.

As he fell back toward the earth, he purged granite and absorbed some basalt. Then he max-tapped and outran the landing.

His legs fracked immediately, but he didn't even notice the pain. Pouring on every ounce of speed, he flashed down the road to that cliff edge. Not slowing, he ignored the steep, switchback road and leaped off the edge, throwing his hands out wide and soaring like a nuall pretending to be a pedra.

He tapped marble, forming fiery wings as he scanned the plateau. The rampagers had nearly reached the bottom of the cliff, bounding down in fantastic leaps that would have shattered the strongest Boulder's legs.

In the center of the rocky expanse of the plateau, Ilse, Lukas, and the Crushers stood in formation, facing the onrushing danger. The men of Alasdair stood behind them, armed with spears and axes, led by Hendry and Amhain. The rest of the villagers were probably already concealed down in the bolt hole.

In front of everyone, Mattias stood alone, twin swords drawn, his entire face glowing like a miniature sun, illuminating the entire scene. Connor focused on him with quartzite vision, and the sight of the man who was trying to steal Verena away filled him with murderous anger.

Mattias opened his mouth, and a horrific sound erupted from his lips. It was brutally loud and it stabbed at Connor's mind like invisible daggers.

He wobbled in flight and dropped fifty feet before stabilizing. If he'd been tapping quartzite to his ears, the horrible noise might have knocked him out.

The sound rose to a teeth-jarring crescendo as Mattias sang with all his might the worst song Connor had ever heard. Verena had said he had the voice of an angel, but if that's how he sang love songs, maybe Connor shouldn't feel so threatened by him.

The monsters cringed under the vocal onslaught, rubbing their ears against the solid rock and howling in pain as the brutal sounds tore at their ears. Mattias kept singing, but the rampagers recovered from their initial hesitation and resumed their charge.

Mattias ran to meet them.

Connor spotted Hamish and Verena, both diving toward the plateau to help, but they'd arrive too late. The monsters would tear the fool Mattias apart.

Verena opened fire with her speedslings, but the rampagers barely seemed to notice the stinging hornets. Even the small but concentrated explosions of the diorite-tipped projectiles barely slowed them.

Martys led the charge, speeding toward Mattias with the speed of a Strider, howling with bloodlust.

"Mattias, look out!" Verena screamed.

Connor reached for the waters of the Wick, running past the far side of the plateau. Through his soapstone senses, he connected with the deep waters and pulled.

An inverted waterfall erupted with a roar that drowned out Mattias's horrible song, as the waters responded to Connor's need. It seemed half the river tore free of its bank and churned up and over the slope of the plateau, surging across the scoured stone surface toward the monsters.

With a sinking feeling of dread, Connor realized the waters would arrive several fatal seconds too late. He wanted to shout at Verena to look away, but knew she wouldn't.

Martys was in the lead, his rampager hide distinct by a splash of white on one shoulder. He leaped at Mattias, huge jaws snapping.

Mattias flowed around him, slashing him half a dozen times with swords that flashed like bolts of lightning. His movements were so fluid and graceful, his limbs seemed to blur.

Then he dove into a roll that took him right under the next leaping rampager, one sword trailing a long gash in the monster's snout. He rolled back to his feet as more rampagers leaped at him, dancing through their raking claws and snapping jaws with grace and speed that was inspiring, even for an Allcarver.

Ilse and the Crushers broke into a charge, with the shouting men of Alasdair on their heels. The sight of his father running to battle against the deadly monsters filled Connor with horror.

He tucked his marble wings in closer and banked into a steeper dive, while pulling even harder on the waters. It would be close, and he doubted Mattias would last even those few precious seconds. He just couldn't get there fast enough.

Hamish could.

He plunged into the mass of rampagers, taking them completely by surprised as they pressed in, eager to rip Mattias to shreds. His entire suit burst into flames, and he smashed into the beasts, tumbling monsters in every direction. He flung out his hands repeatedly, throwing small stones.

Several were diorite, much bigger than the single-grained darts and hornets. Explosions tore into the rampagers, gashing skin and shattering bone. One monster caught a piece of diorite in its maw, and its entire snout exploded in a gush of blood and bone.

Other stones sprayed fire, while two were speedcrack stones. They accomplished little on the solid stone surface of the plateau, however, forming little walls barely six inches high.

Martys, at the front of the pack, was the last one that Hamish passed. That brief extra instant was too much time.

He leaped at Hamish, deadly claws raking down Hamish's torso, ripping right through the layered, hardened granite plates and tearing into his flesh.

Hamish screamed, and Martys managed to rake one claw down Hamish's leg and rip through his left boot. The thruster burst free, and Hamish somersaulted away, out of control. He struck the stone of the plateau and bounced over and over, tumbling fifty yards after he cut off the last thruster. When he finally stopped rolling, he lay in a crumpled heap, motionless.

Martys lifted his muzzle and howled with victory.

Mattias slashed him across the throat with both swords, parting even his thick hide and leaving streaks of crimson. The blades didn't sink deep enough to pierce vital arteries, though.

Martys leaped upon Mattias, knocking him off his feet and into the middle of the pack.

Connor's waters were barely seconds away, but Mattias was doomed.

One rampager lifted him by the throat, its huge maw gaping wide enough to rip his head off in one bite.

Verena dove out of the night sky, her speedslings whirling. Hornets tore into the ranks of rampagers, distracting them for a precious second. Mattias slipped out of the monster's grasp.

Connor realized with horror that Verena wasn't banking away. Screaming with fury, she held her course, aimed at the monsters.

"Verena!" Connor shouted, his voice cracking with terror.

The monsters leaped toward her, despite hornets continuing to rake their faces and explode across their torsos. They'd snatch her out of the air and rip her apart.

Connor couldn't pull the waters faster, so he tried grasping air to knock her sideways, but the fickle air currents didn't respond quickly enough.

He couldn't save her.

A split second before she collided with the monsters and died a glorious, gruesome death, steel blades snapped into position along every side of the Swift. Flames erupted down their lengths, with more roaring from every surface as Verena activated every bit of marble on the Swift. The thrusters howled a different note, and the nimble little craft tumbled into a wild spin.

Every hate-filled pair of purple eyes widened in surprise.

Verena smashed into the tight pack of rampagers like a bladed meteor, slashing and burning and scattering the monsters in every direction. She hit them so hard and so fast that none of the monsters managed to bite or snag her out of the air.

She hit the stomach-lurch threshold and spewed her last meal as she spun, but she didn't slow. She continued on like a tornado of fiery steel, screaming defiance at the deadly rampagers.

"Verena!" Connor shouted her name again as his new war cry.

The waters of the river finally reached the rampagers, and he struck with all his anger, all his vengeance, sweeping the pack off their feet. He was forced to split the waters around Mattias and Verena as she began banking away.

As the rest of the howling pack tore uselessly at the waters of his fury, Martys leaped through that gap and sank his claws into the supply box at the back of the Swift. Verena was still

568

trying to settle her flight path, and the unexpected impact knocked the Swift into a backward spin.

Martys hung on for half a rotation before the twisting force ripped him free and sent him flying over the charging Crushers and bouncing toward the entrance to the secret bolt hole.

Verena tried correcting her flight path, but she was too low, and the Swift clipped a protruding rock. The impact tore free a section of thrusters, which broke the delicate balance even as Verena increased thrust. The Swift careened sideways, bouncing and smashing against the rocks as it skidded across the plateau in an out-of-control tumble.

Verena screamed once as more thrusters broke free and she lost control. The battered little Swift ground to a halt on the far side of the plateau. Verena lay unmoving and limp, still strapped in her seat.

Connor landed in the flood he'd summoned, raging with terror for Verena and anger at Martys. He had to kill his uncle, had to check on Verena.

First he had to kill the other twelve rampagers.

The monsters tore at the waters, struggling to pull themselves out of the flood and return to the slaughter.

Their days of slaughter were over.

Connor drove snakelike tendrils of water down each snapping maw. With brutal determination, he filled the monsters with water until they swelled to bursting, every cavity flooded. Rampagers writhed and slashed at the confining waters, but they were in his power now. Connor knew how to destroy them.

Professor Hector had taught him that one final lesson.

He turned all that water to ice.

The rampagers convulsed one final time, their joints snapping, skin rupturing as the water expanded inside of them. In a single painful heartbeat, they transformed into frozen, monstrous statues.

Connor drained the rest of the water away, revealing the gruesome, frozen beasts. So much for falling to the call of the pack.

"Connor!"

He turned at Ilse's shout. She stood nearby with the Crushers and men of Alasdair. Several were tending to Mattias, who looked battered, but remarkably whole. He hadn't even broken a single, glowing tooth in that incredible fight.

Ilse was pointing back toward the bolt hole.

Martys stood on his hind legs, holding Hendry two feet off the ground, one clawed hand around his throat.

Chapter Eighty-Four

"The leaf that falls in the storms of autumn cannot return to the tree, but is lost to rot, like fallen honor cankering the soul."

~Ilse

Aifric crept along a narrow ledge, about thirty feet above and behind Mister Five. She moved with all the skill of activated obsidian and every bit of hard-won craft she'd learned in the brutal kill academy. As always, a faint chorus seemed to beat in her heart as she tapped serpentinite.

She had missed embracing the unique tertiary stone owned by the Assassins. She hadn't dared touch it during her stay at the Carraig. Even though the happy Healer Aifric was her favorite alter personality, sometimes she needed to step into the shadows of her heritage and walk with serpentinite again.

Sounds hung in the air all around her, radiating from their sources like ripples of light. They changed color with their frequency, from the slower reds, through the hues of the rainbow, all the way up to the exciting, eager violets.

She could seize those bands of sound, capture them, redirect them, or change them. Walking with serpentinite, she owned sound.

The soft sounds of her cautious approach clung to her skin. She refused them the ability to leave and perhaps alert Mister Five of her approach. They would fade eventually, unless she replenished them or allowed them to spring away to spend their minute energy in the air.

She considered weaving them into a different sound altogether, perhaps casting them into the air as hints of approaching thrusters. That might distract Mister Five with the threat of Connor or his friends returning to rain death upon him from above. Then again, he would become alert, scanning the sky and the nearby area. She couldn't risk him noticing her before she struck.

Mister Five had to die, but she had never defeated him in a fair fight. Good thing she didn't plan to fight fair.

He was one of the deadliest of the Mhortair. Maybe her skills had developed to the point where she could defeat him in an honest duel, but why bother? He had always taught her to strike from a position of advantage in a moment of surprise.

So she crept forward, seeking her chance.

After Connor had deflected the bolt of fiery water, she had expected Kilian to attack Mister Five. She had hung back to stay out of the way, but Kilian was distracted by Aonghus's fiery attack.

Instead of striking at the two powerful Petralists while they dueled with fire across the quarry, Mister Five had settled into a patient, waiting stance. It appeared he would allow Kilian to dispatch Aonghus and Dougal and only then strike the man down in his moment of victory.

It was the Mhortair way.

Aifric settled into a crouch above him. She would in turn steal the victory from him as he rose to claim his ultimate prize.

So she turned her attention to the dueling Petralists. Aonghus had embraced the power of the sculpted marble and attacked with white-hot flames that had intensified to blue. Sheets of fire rippled back and forth over the stones as Aonghus and Kilian leaped and flew around the quarry. They were driven by the heat of their flames, protected in the midst of the firestorm by their elemental connection.

Kilian did not tap water to counter his opponent, but faced Aonghus flame to flame. Even though Aonghus was drawing upon the strength of the sculpted stone, Kilian withstood every assault.

Twisting spears of flame exploded against sheets of defensive fire. Each time Kilian managed to tumble Aonghus back with unexpected twists of the firestorm, or with horizontal tornadoes of fire.

While the hot-headed captain grew increasingly wild in his attacks and his mad-tinged laughter echoed from the heights, Kilian remained calm and unruffled. Of course that only served to enrage Aonghus further.

She was glad she hadn't crept any closer. The air was growing dangerously hot, even high on the flank of Wick Torr where she crouched. Anyone standing down in the quarry would be consumed.

Dougal had retreated to the lip of the northern rim of the quarry. After vainly shouting for Aonghus to ascend and finish Kilian, he had slipped over the side, hanging over the steep northern slope to escape the intense heat.

If only she had a good crossbow, she could pierce his hands and send him tumbling down the long slope. He wasn't a Boulder and she doubted he'd survive the wild slide.

Gregor had not joined the fighting and seemed impervious to the heat. After that one surprised step he'd taken when Mister Five's bolt struck, he had remained motionless on the northern rim, eyes closed, hands hanging loose by his side.

She wasn't sure what he was trying to do, but doubted it was working. The stones at the very center of the lowest level of the quarry pit had begun buckling upward and occasionally geysered like water instead of solid granite. The debris was piling at the floor of the quarry, not rising to snag Kilian out of the air.

"Why won't you die?" Aonghus screamed, erupting off the eastern rim.

Dierk had fled moments ago in the windrider. Now Aonghus shot through the air at Kilian, who was hovering over the quarry on streamers of fire. Aonghus clutched a burning dagger of intense blue flame in his hand as he closed on Kilian, and crimson fire bled out his eyes and wreathed his head.

With a burst of new flames, Kilian shot forward to meet him. Aifric expected him to seize Aonghus's flames or strike unexpectedly with water.

He did neither.

The two collided in midair and Aonghus drove the fiery dagger at Kilian's heart.

Kilian caught it.

The blade stopped inches from his chest. Aonghus heaved on it, but could not drive it forward.

Kilian spoke softly, and Aifric spotted the wisp of sound drifting around them. She was about to snatch it to her to hear his words, but Mister Five grabbed it first and pulled it to him.

Aifric dared touch it with her serpentinite senses. She didn't move it out of its course, but just let it slide past her thoughts.

"You're like a child given a club, Aonghus. You flail around breaking things, thinking that makes you a man, but you have no idea what you're doing."

In the air above the quarry, Kilian seized Aonghus by the throat and the flames ringing the angry captain's head winked out.

"How?" Aonghus cried, beating uselessly against Kilian's grip.

"Because I know."

Kilian threw Aonghus away. He struck the northern rim of the quarry hard and bounced against Gregor's feet. He stumbled to his feet as Kilian drifted closer, all the flames they'd thrown back and forth in their fight ringing him and keeping him aloft.

The flames split into bands of orange, crimson, and blue. They wove around each other, forming ever-changing, complex patterns. The ancient symbol of Petralist fire formed beneath his feet. Standing in the air atop the writhing flames, Kilian indeed looked like the master of the element.

An iron hand seized Aifric by the throat, while another grabbed her right wrist and wrenched it behind her back.

She snapped out of her reverie and realized Mister Five had snuck up behind her. She didn't struggle. She'd never broken out of that hold in all the years they'd trained together.

"You shouldn't allow yourself to get distracted, Student Eighteen," Mister Five said in that slightly disapproving voice he always used when she failed a lesson.

"What gave me away?" she asked, proud that her voice remained calm, despite the fact that death circled her now, waiting only for Mister Five to strike.

"When you touched that sound wave."

"I didn't move it," she protested.

"But you didn't account for the fact that I might have shrouded it in my will. By brushing it with yours, I sensed your presence."

"I didn't realize you could do that."

"Which is why you are but a student." His voice turned harder. "You do know better than to allow yourself to get distracted."

"You're right. Thank you for reminding me."

He chuckled. "It saddens me to have to deliver you to your father for execution. You once showed great promise."

Aifric's heart sank. If only he would simply gift her a quick death. She couldn't bear to kneel in shame before her father and the entire clan, forcing him to take her life to cleanse the family name.

"I made the right choice," she declared, refusing to accept Mister Five's judgment. "Connor is the best hope for the world and we should ally with him."

"The decision is not yours to make."

Icy waters snaked around her arms and legs, binding her and dragging her to the ground. Mister Five dropped to the ledge where he'd been standing a moment ago and the waters binding her dragged her down after him, like tentacles drawing her toward destruction.

She landed hard and grunted in pain, but he seized the sound and scattered it, preventing Kilian from hearing her distress. She could scream all day to no avail. Even if she propelled her voice with her own gift, Mister Five was far more experienced. While he was focused on her, she could never hope to break through his warding.

"Watch the destruction of the son of the matriarch of evil," Mister Five declared, and the waters binding her lifted her off the ground to kneel beside him, forcing her to watch as he prepared to strike Kilian down.

"At least wait until he removes Dougal," she urged.

He gave her a disgusted look. "Since when do I need your counsel?"

She shrugged. "Since you decided to make Connor our enemy."

On the northern rim of the quarry, Dougal was scrambling to his feet to face Kilian. He scowled at Aonghus. "You fool. I told you to ascend."

Kilian declared, "It's done. He fought bravely, but he's not the one who has to die today."

Aifric leaned forward, eager to see Kilian boil Dougal's blood from the inside.

Without warning, the solid stone of the rim under Gregor's feet erupted into grasping fingers that wrapped him in binding lengths. His eyes snapped open and he cried out with fear as his limbs were yanked outward. The rope-like fingers of stone lifted him spread-eagled off the stone rim, despite his struggles.

Aonghus and Dougal stumbled back from the spectacle, their expressions as amazed as Aifric felt. She couldn't imagine the mighty Sentry held powerless by earth. What had gone wrong? What had he done?

Mister Five frowned. "What devilry is this?"

The stone restraints flowed off the rim, carrying Gregor down into the quarry, stretching his limbs farther apart until he screamed.

As the imprisoned Sentry approached the center of the quarry, the turbulent ground there erupted in a giant geyser, flinging house-sized chunks of stone high into the air. Gregor was dragged into the geyser, and stone chips and debris slashed into him, leaving him bleeding and gasping with pain and terror.

"I fear an ancient evil has awakened," Mister Five whispered, not even bothering to block his voice from slipping away.

"Kilian!" Aifric shouted, hurling the sound toward him, hoping Mister Five's distraction would give her the chance to warn Kilian of the danger.

Mister Five crushed the sound just before it reached him. She breathed a curse. Half a heartbeat more, and she would have managed it.

The geyser ceased. A deep calm settled over the quarry, punctuated only by the hissing of Kilian's flames.

A slender woman rose from the depths, and when she stepped forward, the stone flowed into a smooth surface, like water. Her entire being glowed with light.

Her thick golden hair was streaked heavily with gray, like a cloudy sunset, and it blocked Aifric's view of the woman's face. She decided she really didn't want to see who had emerged from the heart of the quarry, and she cringed back against her bonds.

The woman considered Gregor with a disgusted expression. Then she slapped him across the face. The blow looked unhurried, almost casual, but it whipped his head around so hard, it was a wonder his neck didn't snap.

He rocked back in his constraints, and a coughing groan escaped his lips. The little sound flitted frantically about the quarry before fading away.

The woman said, "You remind me of my naughty grandson. Always meddling where he's not welcome."

She turned and surveyed the quarry with a frown. Her unlined face looked mature, and her eyes were a blue so penetrating that even though she wasn't looking at Aifric, it felt like those orbs were digging into her mind.

Atop the northern rim, Dougal exclaimed, "What are you doing? You're supposed to be a monster!"

"She is a monster," Kilian growled. He looked furious, and the flames encircling him intensified to glowing blue.

The woman looked up at Kilian hovering high above and frowned. "You're not dead yet?"

"Hello, mother."

Chapter Eighty-Five

"Where the mountain meets the wind, history itself is witness."

~Connor

Lukas and several of the Crushers moved toward Martys, but Connor called them back.

"You have to do something," Amhain cried as he and the other villagers rushed up to Connor.

"I will," Connor promised him, not looking away from Martys.

"Why hasn't he crushed Hendry's throat?" Ilse asked softly as she fell into step beside Connor.

"Because he's not the target."

Connor yearned to run to Verena and check on her, then go check on Hamish, but he forced himself to let go of all other worries, all concerns.

The monster who was Martys beckoned him on and growled, "Raw pagh."

"Is that thing trying to speak?" Amhain asked incredulously.

Connor nodded. "That thing is Martys, and yes, he said, 'Law of the pack'."

"Tallan's curse, can it be so?" Amhain asked.

"Go check on Hamish and Verena." Connor pointed in their direction, not needing to look to know exactly where the two had fallen. "I'll deal with Martys."

"What are you planning?" Ilse asked as the villagers scrambled away to do Connor's bidding.

"Hendry!" Lilias appeared at the secret entrance to the bolt hole, one hand to her mouth as she stumbled up onto the plateau, eyes glued to the monster that held her husband an inch away from death.

"Stay back, Mom," Connor shouted. "It's Martys. He's betrayed us. He's waiting to fight me. Dad will be all right."

Martys nodded his hideous maw and bared his fangs, his long tongue lolling out, dripping with saliva.

"I can't strike with slate," Ilse muttered. "There's no earth on this cursed plateau."

"I know, and if I attack with water, he'll rip out my father's throat before I can take him."

"What then?" She pulled him to a stop and forced him to meet her worried gaze. "Connor, even if you had porphyry, you can't risk it."

"I have it. He gave it to me. This is what he wanted all along."

"Which is why you can't do it." This from Mattias, who limped over with Lukas's help.

Mattias was the last person Connor was willing to take advice from. He glared at the Blade and reminded himself to breathe. "Get away from me before I do something stupid. Go check on Verena."

He really didn't want Mattias anywhere near Verena, but someone had to go. Even Mattias was better than no one. Sort of.

Lilias took a couple hesitant steps closer to Martys, but stopped still fifty yards away. "Martys?"

He turned to look at her and she rose to her full height and snapped, "You should be ashamed of yourself."

He made a huffing sound that Connor understood as laughter. Then he shook Hendry, as if to warn her that insulting him at that moment was a bad idea. Hendry was gripping the monstrous arm holding him and only allowing him to sip at the air he needed, but he was like a child in the rampager's claws.

"Martys, let them go. I know what you want, and I'll do it," Connor shouted as he marched toward Martys. He stopped forty feet from the monster as Martys turned back to him.

"We'll help you as soon as he releases the Ashlar," Ilse said softly.

Connor shook his head. Martys had threatened the town, had hurt Hamish and Jean both, and now threatened his father. Connor's anger and fear had solidified into a burning determination. He felt the beast stir in his heart, and this time he embraced it.

"Martys is mine."

He looked at Ilse and added, "But if I lose control, do what you have to."

She gripped his shoulder, her expression grave. "You're stronger than that, Connor. You'll return."

"Promise me," he urged.

She nodded. "I'll do what must be done."

Connor shed his battle jacket and drew forth the pouch of porphyry. He faced Martys and pried open the drawstring. "You owe me one final duel, Uncle."

Martys's maw opened, his purple eyes focused on the bag in Connor's hand.

Lilias cried, "Connor, if you have to kill him, just remember who you are and don't become a monster to destroy another."

He hated that she had to witness what was about to happen. "I love you, Mom. Sometimes there's no other way."

As Connor let the purplish, powdered stone slip through his fingers, his hand quivered with anticipation. The yearning to absorb it and embrace the dangerous power was like a living thing, tearing at his restraint. There were so many reasons to feel terrified of embracing porphyry again, but they all paled against the simple truth that he had no choice.

He might die if he embraced the monster in his heart.

His father would surely die if he didn't.

Connor looked to his mother, who stood facing him, hands clasped, looking terrified but resolute. Then he gripped the powder and opened himself to it.

Immediately the powdered stone began biting into his skin like a thousand little teeth. His hand locked around it, the muscles cramping with pain.

There was no going back now.

As those invisible teeth chewed up the inside of his arm, Connor groaned in pain and clutched at his forearm. Why had he been so eager to experience this again? How had he forgotten how much it hurt? With growing fear, Connor staggered.

His mother took a step forward. "Connor, we love you. No curse can destroy you unless you yield to it."

He groaned. "Get back. Get--"

The porphyry ripping up his arm reached his heart.

Connor convulsed as pain exploded through his body. He felt his arms snap out wide and his back arch, beyond his control.

"Help him!" his mother shouted.

"It will pass. You must stay back," Ilse said. She looked worried, and the Crushers retreated from Connor, weapons hefted, expressions guarded.

A scream of pain and terror ripped from Connor's lips. His thoughts seemed to fade to pure emotion. Rage and hatred swept through him. As he stumbled toward Martys, the sound shifted into ranges beyond what should be possible. It became a deep-throated howl of animal fury as the porphyry ripped him apart and remade him into a monster.

Martys tossed Hendry aside like a toy and lifted his own muzzle into the air, howling long and loud, the sound melding with Connor's cry of exultant horror.

Then the pain disappeared, replaced by the euphoria unique to porphyry. Connor howled again, relishing the power of his animal voice.

He leaped to his four feet, filled with more strength than even granite and slate combined had ever provided. The purple haze of fury intensified, and he raged to think how long he had denied himself this glory.

He smelled fear and heard the rapid beating of many hearts nearby. A half-circle of pitiful humans faced him, puny weapons held at the ready. He easily tracked the pulsing of their blood, visible to him through the thin shells of their soft hides. He yearned to feast, but another scent drew his attention the other way. A mighty beast faced him across the stony ground.

Their purple-eyed gazes locked and a growl rumbled through Connor's chest. Its stance, its challenging gaze, and the scent of blood and death that clung to it made its intention clear. It intended to invade his territory and kill the herds that were his to savage. He stalked toward the intruder and it mirrored his moves, its own growl echoing across the plateau.

A thought floated to the surface of his hate-filled mind. He needed to fight this, to maintain control over something, but what?

What was there but the hunt, the kill, and the blood feast?

Something . . . Something soft. But what soft thing was good for anything but food?

Verena's smiling face appeared in his mind, like a buoy line that helped him awaken from the purple haze of rage and lift his thoughts above the bloodlust. For a second Connor remembered who he was, recognized Martys and why they really had to fight.

Then he saw in his mind Verena lying broken and motionless in the shattered Swift at the base of a cliff, saw again Hamish bleeding on the stones of the plateau. Rage swept away his rational mind and ripped a howl of fury from his fanged maw. His thoughts tumbled into a maelstrom of rage and lust to kill.

Connor leaped, and Martys lunged to meet him. Connor threw himself against Martys with every ounce of fury he possessed, driven by the need to rip out the hated enemy's throat.

They collided in a fury of snapping jaws and ripping claws. Connor drove against the enemy with every ounce of strength, but Martys twisted him off balance, knocking him to the ground and raking his underbelly. The beast's maw gaped wide and snapped at Connor's throat.

He kicked it away and rolled free, trailing blood. The pain enraged him, but also instilled a hint of caution. He would rip out Martys's throat, but if he leaped in without control, he would be the one to die.

The two circled and Martys's tongue lolled out in a mocking laugh. He growled words incomprehensible to human ears, but Connor understood.

"You're young and untested, Connor. I could teach you much. Swear fealty to the pack and I'll spare your worthless family."

Connor risked a glance at his parents. Hendry was sitting, looking dazed, with Lilias kneeling beside him. Tears streaked her cheeks, and she was sobbing with fear. The sight helped ground him to who he was. They were the reason he was fighting.

Martys's pack was dead. They had been a gang of wild killers, with no honor, who killed without remorse or mercy. They represented everything his parents had taught him to oppose.

"My family is my pack."

Martys growled. "You killed my pack, pup. You and yours will die together."

Martys lunged and tried to slam a shoulder into Connor to knock him from his feet and expose his throat again. Connor slipped aside and raked Martys from ear to shoulder. Then they came together again, snapping and clawing, trying to gain advantage. The rage drove Connor to fight with unbridled fury, but he struggled to maintain enough clarity of mind to keep from making another stupid mistake.

The two of them fought and tore at each other across the rough stone plateau, smearing the rocks with their blood. The human cattle scattered, but he could hunt them later.

Connor exulted in the absolute power of porphyry. He shed brutal injuries without slowing, his hugely-muscled limbs quivered with inexhaustible strength, and he moved with unrivaled speed.

Martys spun and caught him with a kick of his hind legs, sending Connor tumbling. He rolled back to his feet before Martys could take advantage of the opening, and the two circled. Martys matched Connor for size and speed, but he was more experienced.

Connor could not defeat him.

Not if he limited himself to a beast.

He had managed to tap soapstone fighting the elfonnel. The thought of Verena had given him the strength to focus, the humanity to connect with his other affinities. He focused on her now as he and Martys circled, growling and probing.

Verena's face came into his mind, but it lacked the power to motivate him as it had last time. He loved Verena more than life, but she loved Mattias. The lingering doubt that she wasn't being honest with him dulled the effect he'd enjoyed in the past.

Martys lunged, jaws snapping at Connor's throat. Connor twisted and knocked Martys away with his shoulder and a fast-slashing claw that laid open Martys's right foreleg.

Connor glanced again at his parents. His father was standing, one arm draped around Lilias's shoulders, and they were watching him, terror and courage on their faces.

They were his pack. They were the reason he fought. That thought helped him focus, and the gateways to soapstone and marble glowed in his mind. He'd lost his piece of marble, but he'd sucked deep enough on it before transforming that the connection was still strong.

The Wick glowed in his soapstone senses. He could summon the waters and drown Martys the way he had the rest of the pack, but that didn't feel right. The wild ferocity of fire melded better with the savagery of his rampager form.

"Time to die, boy," Martys growled, crouching to spring.

Connor's fangs began to burn.

Martys paused, his stance radiating surprise and perhaps a hint of fear. So Connor leaped at him, snapping with those burning fangs.

His uncle responded with unabashed fury, and the two of them again swarmed around each other, ripping and tearing, fighting to reach a jugular vein, or to disembowel each other.

This time, Connor left scorch marks on his uncle's hide. As he embraced marble deeper, his claws also began to burn. When he raked them against his uncle's flanks, they left nasty, bubbling wounds.

Martys began to give way and Connor pressed his advantage, drooling flames as he attacked the hated betrayer. He dimly recognized that the human warriors were flanking them on both sides, shouting words he didn't bother to understand. He'd deal with them later.

With a snarl, Martys lunged up at him, trying to turn the momentum of the fight, but Connor seized his foreleg with his jaws and snapped it almost in half.

When Martys flinched, he slashed his muzzle with burning claws. Martys broke away and began circling again. He surprised Connor by laughing.

"I don't have to defeat you, boy. You've just killed everyone you love."

Connor involuntarily glanced toward his family, and Martys lunged. He slammed a shoulder into Connor's ribs, knocking him off his feet.

The two rolled over and Connor tore at his uncle with burning fangs and claws. Martys ignored the ghastly wounds and snapped his heavy muzzle across Connor's throat, tearing into the hide and muscle, fangs digging for the lifeblood of his main arteries.

Connor ripped at Martys's belly with his rear claws, opening it and spilling hot guts to the cold stone, but Martys did not relent. His jaws continued to close, a fraction of an inch at a time, slowly and inexorably crushing Connor's breath and shearing into his flesh.

Connor could not defeat him.

The cold truth helped his mind awaken. His rear legs were still slashing, ripping Martys's innards out. Martys would die within minutes, but he still had the strength to take Connor with him.

If he couldn't defeat Martys with his claws, he'd defeat him with his fire. Connor focused all his waning energy on that gateway to fire.

It too was fading as he burned through the last of his marble. With no way to replenish it, he only had enough for one final strike.

Connor threw all of the flames, all of his focus, all of his will to live into a white-hot spear of fire that he drove between Martys's hind legs.

Not even a rampager could ignore castration by incineration.

Martys's jaw released its deadly hold, opening wide in a high-pitched howl. Connor grabbed his jaw with both paws, sinking claws into his maw and ripping with all his strength in one convulsive heave.

Martys's bottom jaw ripped away in a spray of blood and flesh, and he fell to his side, shaking with agony.

Connor leaped upon his back, digging claws into his hide and chomping down onto the back of his neck with all his might. His flames winked out as he burned through the last of his marble, but he didn't care. He tasted blood and sensed victory, and his mind was swept away in blood lust.

Martys writhed under him, but his many devastating injuries were finally taking their toll, and his strength failed him.

"I can't die this way," he groaned, the growl barely distinguishable through his shattered snout.

Connor leaped off and slashed Martys, rolling him onto his back and exposing his throat. "You're right."

He snapped his jaws across Martys's throat and bit with all his strength. In the face of violent death, Martys found a last reserve of strength and tried fighting back, but managed to do little more than roll the two of them over a couple of times.

Connor ended up on top again and braced himself better, holding Martys down as he slowly plunged his jaws deeper and deeper into Martys's throat.

His uncle had nearly killed him that way, but the remembered terror of that near death only drove Connor to bite harder. With a final wrenching heave, Connor crushed Martys's windpipe and his teeth severed the main artery. Hot blood gushed across Connor's fangs and into his mouth.

He swallowed some of it.

The taste of the life blood of his hated enemy triggered a wave of bloodlust like Connor had never known. His aches and pains seemed to fade under a new rush of strength and he threw his muzzle back and howled long and loud, exulting in the victory of the kill.

The beast at his feet was dead, but Connor could kill again.

With renewed strength, he turned toward the herd of pitiful humans. He howled with anticipation and bounded toward them. Most of the flock scattered, as they should, but the warriors held their ground. A dim memory tugged at his mind, but he drove it away, refusing to be distracted from the hunt.

One large human stepped in front of the others. It looked injured, but faced him with a stone hammer in its hands, its stance and scent declaring its willingness to fight. A much smaller female joined it, and her scent was familiar somehow.

He padded toward them, growling his intent to kill, even as he tried to puzzle out those scents. They did not flee, and another human joined them, this one armored and wearing twin swords. He was helping a wounded human to stand, one with gashes on its chest, a shredded suit hanging from its limbs. That one touched the hammer, then licked it.

The strange move tugged at Connor's memory, and he paused in front of them, shaking his maw, trying to understand.

The confusion enraged him, and he decided he'd kill them first, then figure out the mystery.

He'd waited too long. As he crouched to spring, the man with the hammer leaped forward, swinging the ridiculous hammer in a useless gesture of defiance.

The hammer struck Connor in the face like a falling mountain, and lightning ripped through his skull, blinding him and scattering his thoughts. His entire body shook from an explosion that shattered his hearing and threw him away with unbelievable force.

Unable to breathe, unable to think, unable to move or howl or react in any way, he tumbled across the plateau, bouncing all the way to the steep slope above the river.

Tumbling down the slope, he splashed into the cold waters and sank like a stone.

CHAPTER EIGHTY-SIX

"The rope woven from many tiny strands holds fast against even the mightiest tempest."

~Evander

By all the oaths of the people, this cannot be," Mister Five hissed. He looked terrified.

Aifric didn't blame him. Stories of Dreokt, the queen mother of Obrion, were told not only to scare children, but to motivate all the Mhortair to pursue their mission with unwavering vigor. That's why they sought to remove Kilian and block the return of the Blood of the Tallan. They had sworn the oath of generations to rid the world of all traces of that most evil bloodline.

The Matron of Evil was back.

Aifric barely believed it, but how could she doubt it?

Even as she struggled to comprehend what had happened, Kilian leaned forward into a dive toward his mother. His fires condensed to a hundred spears of bright blue flame that shot ahead of him.

Dreokt made a shooing gesture, and the flames deflected away. "Is this any way to greet your mother after all these years?" she asked in a disgusted tone.

Kilian stopped twenty feet above her, but sent all the rest of his flames whipping around her in a deadly firestorm. Raging flames completely obscured her.

The crackling roar rose to a crescendo that reverberated back and forth across the steps of the quarry, building upon itself until the air shook. Aifric had to push some of the sound away to keep it from becoming painful.

Kilian would have overwhelmed Aonghus in a heartbeat with that attack. Aifric held her breath, hoping he could destroy the demon mother of Obrion.

A few seconds later, Dreokt erupted out of the flames. She soared across the quarry, batting aside whipping flames. Kilian pursued the attack with more intensity than anything Aifric had ever seen, but Dreokt snatched away the flames far too easily. She used them to blast herself into the air and away from him.

"Take her," Mister Five urged, leaning forward, intent on the battle.

"Good thing you didn't kill him already," Aifric said.

"This changes everything," he moaned, and when he glanced down at her, she read stark terror in his eyes.

She decided she should be a lot more scared than she already was. She hadn't known anything could terrify Mister Five. What else did he know about the queen mother that she hadn't been told yet?

Dreokt landed atop the northern rim of the quarry, looking annoyed by Kilian's relentless attack. Dougal cringed away from her, and crazy Captain Aonghus threw up a wall of fire and retreated when she looked at him.

Dreokt made a shooing motion, and Aonghus's flames winked out.

"Go!" Kilian shouted as he drifted closer, riding a tornado of flame. A fresh wave of fire erupted away from him and swarmed over his mother.

She leaped out of the flames, shooting across the northern rim toward Aonghus, one hand outstretched. He was already moving. He leaped off the rim and blasted himself away with an explosion of flames.

As he shot down and out of Aifric's sight, Dreokt turned to face Kilian, scowling. His attacking flames whisked away, as if caught in a sudden cross-breeze.

"Stop it, Son, or I'm going to become peeved."

"You're going to become dead, like you should have three centuries ago," Kilian growled.

"So long?" She looked surprised, and Aifric had to wonder what state she'd been in. Had she been trapped under the quarry somehow?

A twisted rope of water leaped up the north slope from the Upper Wick behind the queen mother and seized her by the waist. She actually yelped, looking worried for a moment before swatting the water aside.

"You're weak, mother," Kilian snarled. "You picked a bad day to arise."

"I hate getting up early," she growled.

She made a beckoning motion, and Gregor's stone bonds began dragging him across the floor of the quarry, then up the stepped levels toward her. At the same time, a giant grasping arm of stone erupted out of the quarry floor toward Kilian.

He somersaulted away, his fiery tornado pedestal sliding sideways to catch him again. Two more stone hands erupted from the western rim and swatted at him. He dodged and spun, easily avoiding the deadly elemental attacks.

Mister Five nodded, his expression hopeful. "I've heard that returning from the embrace of the elements is an arduous experience. Kilian is right. She is weak."

While Kilian was distracted dodging her stone hands, Dreokt drew Gregor to her. She cupped his terrified face with her hands and spoke softly.

Aifric snatched at the sounds as they drifted from her, but Mister Five caught them first. He drew them across the quarry, then surprised her by sharing them.

"You will ascend and fight my son."

Dougal looked shocked, and when he spoke, Mister Five drew his words to them as well. "How is it possible? My sculpted stone lacks enough power for an ascension."

"This is what the world has come to?" Dreokt asked, frowning over at Dougal. She pressed her hands harder against Gregor's face, and his terrified expression faded to one of rapt ecstasy.

"She has taken his mind," Mister Five growled.

Suddenly a wave of water erupted over the western rim of the quarry and formed into a giant octopus. Its many-tentacled legs seized the stone limbs still chasing Kilian around the quarry. They dug into the stone and snapped the limbs to pieces.

"I thought stone was stronger," Aifric said with a frown.

Mister Five shook his head. "Kilian is in his fury, while his mother is weak and distracted."

Dreokt tossed Gregor off the rim and into the quarry. Instead of bouncing off the hard stone when he struck, he sank into it, then rose on a pillar of stone. He looked into the sky and shouted, a cry of exultant joy as he threw his arms out wide.

"I should still be sleeping," Dreokt grumbled as she turned to face Kilian, who was again approaching on his fiery tornado.

"You'll get eternal rest in a minute," Kilian said, striking again, this time with intertwined fire and water.

His mother staggered back from the assault, slapping the elements away. Her annoyed expression turned to one of concern as he pressed the attack.

Aifric silently urged Kilian on. Everything she knew about Dreokt screamed at her to beg Mister Five to release her so she could flee. She applauded Kilian for daring to stand against his mother, but she wanted nothing more than to run.

With an angry shout, Dreokt threw her hands out wide and the elemental assault shattered, filling the air with glittering droplets of fire and water.

Even as Kilian seized them again, Mister Five rose and brought his hands together, his expression one of utmost concentration.

"He isn't strong enough."

"Don't you dare kill him," Aifric cried.

He shot her a disgusted look. "Have you forgotten all your training? Kilian doesn't matter. The Matron of Evil is our ultimate target and ever has been."

"Let me help you," she urged.

"You could do nothing but die." He made a shooing gesture, and the water binding her began dragging her back up the cliff. "At least one of us must bring word to the clan."

Aifric stared in mute astonishment. She had never imagined Mister Five might have a heroic streak. As her bonds dragged her back up to a higher shelf and out of sight from below, she grabbed the sound of his words and tucked them into a pocket to listen to again later.

Mister Five again turned to face the quarry and brought his hands together. When he threw his hands out and released the fiery ice bolt, Aifric willed it to strike true. The bolt flashed across the quarry, so fast she caught little more than a hint of movement.

It stopped a hair's breadth above the Matron of Evil's heart.

She turned and stared up the mountain, her expression furious. "You dare strike the one who created you and gave you purpose?"

Mister Five stood defiantly, already bringing his hands together again. His voice boomed across the quarry, magnified by the strength of serpentinite as he intoned the heart of the Mhortair creed.

"Tainted blood to purge, evil hearts to pierce!"

Dreokt waved away another attack from Kilian and scowled up at Mister Five. "You have fallen so far. I don't have time for this."

She made a flicking gesture, and the bolt of compressed, burning ice seemed to pierce the air as is sped back the other way.

Mister Five threw his hands out to stop it, but it drilled right through his palm and punched through one eye. His head exploded in a shower of gore and water.

Aifric's bonds dropped from her wrists and she stared in mute horror at Mister Five's corpse. She was no stranger to death, but she couldn't believe he could fall so easily, and from one of his own specialty bolts.

Her fear intensified and she shook and cringed against the stone. Had Dreokt seen her? She didn't dare look for fear of catching another of those bolts in the eye.

Mister Five's last words rang in her mind. She had to warn the people, had to rally them to fight the return of this greatest evil. Did Sir know that she had broken with Mister Five in Altkalen? If he did, she'd be branded an outcast and executed if she returned home.

She had no choice.

The mountain shook, the ground rolling underfoot, and an intense sound erupted from the quarry. It was as if an avalanche had swallowed a hurricane. Aifric dampened the sounds to protect her ears and had to see what was happening.

Gregor was gone. In his place, rising from the floor of the quarry, was a giant elemental made of precious Alasdair White. Unlike the monstrous elfonnel that had attacked the Carraig, this one was roughly man shaped, its face still carrying a shadow of Gregor's image. The four silver eyes, spaced across its wide forehead, were completely devoid of humanity.

On the opposite side of the quarry, a flood of water boiled over Kilian, obscuring him in clouds of churning spray. A heartbeat later, a giant man rose in his place, formed of rippling waters, with flames for eyes.

Aifric's heart sank. Two elfonnel, and they were about to fight directly below her.

As the earth-bound elemental roared a challenge, the queen mother nodded in satisfaction. "Nothing like elemental fury to brighten a woman's day."

The earth-bound elemental shot across the quarry, sliding across the smooth stones, and slammed into the watery giant. It split apart, allowing the earth-bound to crash right through, then formed behind it and slammed ice-covered arms onto its back.

Aifric focused on the queen mother, dragging the bits of sound waves to her as the woman spoke softly.

Dreokt snatched the quailing Dougal off the stones and stared into his eyes for a moment before nodding again. "Yes, you are a servant who may prove useful. Come, linn."

"But, I'm--" Dougal objected.

She slapped him, snapping his face to the side and bruising his cheek as blood sprayed from his mouth. "Hush in the presence of your betters."

She glanced at the titanic battle raging in the center of the quarry and smiled again. "This is more like a fitting homecoming." Then she tapped her foot once on the stone, which rippled at her touch. "No longer will lesser Petralists benefit from my slumber."

Humming a happy tune to herself, she leaped into the sky, still clutching Dougal by the throat, and soared away over the mountain on a whistling wind. The rippling of the northern rim intensified, then faded away.

Four seconds later, the ground started to shake in an unmistakable earthquake.

"Rith, I need you!" Aifric shouted, and started to run.

CHAPTER EIGHTY-SEVEN

"The student who reads only every fifth word knows less when they finish than when they began, but even the mindless bee finds nectar inside a flower."

~Ilse

Connor became aware that he was floating in the Wick. He wasn't drowning. Even in his semi-comatose state, and despite the trauma of getting blasted right off the plateau, he still had soapstone flowing through his blood.

He was one with water, and it would never kill him. His senses flickered through the river, and in an instant he recognized his position near the southwest corner of the plateau, floating downriver.

He was no longer a rampager. The truth startled him. He didn't remember transforming, but he was happy his thoughts were no longer clouded by the purple haze of fury that came with porphyry.

He was out of porphyry.

Connor only barely bit back an animal howl. His body trembled with a sudden fierce need to consume more and return to that glorious form.

He rose to stand upon the surface and slapped himself in the face. The sting helped center his thoughts again. What a grouted fool he was. He didn't want to ever touch porphyry again.

And yet, part of him did. A dark corner of his soul, hungry to taste hot blood and feel the thrill of the kill.

"You know, if your dad didn't hit you hard enough, I'd be happy to slap you some more." Mattias stood atop the steep, stony bank leading back to the plateau, about thirty feet away. He would have been nearly invisible in the darkness, despite the bright starlight, but of course he lit up his face like a Sogail lantern.

Connor rose on a pedestal of water, sorely tempted to drag Mattias into the river and drown him. Enough people had been hurt already though, so he fought the urge and instead lifted himself up to where he could step onto the stones beside Mattias.

Only then did he realize he was barely clothed. His pants were ripped to shreds, his boots were gone, and he'd removed his battle leathers before transforming, so his torso was bare.

"You're a mess," Mattias said. "Your mom's got your jacket and that pendant. Are you up for some healing?"

With a rush, Connor remembered. He grabbed Mattias's arm. "Is Verena all right? Hamish? The others?"

When Mattias hesitated, Connor's heart sank, and he flung himself north along the plateau on a boiling wave of water, dragging Mattias along with him. He felt more naked for lack of power stones than lack of clothing. He'd lost everything but the final vestiges of soapstone. He needed his battle jacket. His stores were attached to it.

"What's wrong with Verena?" he demanded as they flowed toward the knot of people about a hundred yards away. He lacked quartzite to enhance his vision and scan for her.

"She won't wake up. Jean's been tending to her and reported several broken bones." After a brief hesitation he added softly, "She might have cracked her skull."

Connor wanted to howl with rampager fury. That was the only sound that might do justice to his terror, but at the moment he'd just sound like a lunatic. So he just cursed under his breath and drove them on faster.

"Hamish will be fine," Mattias offered. "He'll have some impressive scars unless you tend to him soon. He seems more worried about his shredded battle suit."

Connor grunted, but his entire focus was on finding his mother and the sculpted sandstone pendant so he could treat Verena. He spotted his father first, leaning on a spear and waving. Lilias stood beside him, with the children clustered close by her. Most of the other villagers were milling nearby, and they all turned to watch him approach.

Most of them, including his younger siblings, backed away as he drew closer.

The sight of their fear tempered his impatience and he stepped from the waters with a heavy stride. "I am so sorry."

His mother rushed up and gave him a fierce hug. She kissed his cheek and draped his battle jacket around him. "I'm just glad you returned to us, Son."

His father approached and Connor couldn't meet his eyes, but stammered another apology. Hendry gripped his shoulder and forced him to look up.

"Connor, you did what had to be done. We're alive because of you."

"But, I nearly killed you all."

"But you didn't. The stroke that never fell can't be counted against you."

Hamish was sitting nearby, with Mhairi tying a bloodstained strip of someone's shirt over the last of his wounds. His battle suit was destroyed. All that remained were the leggings. He gave Connor an enthusiastic grin.

"You always said you wanted to feel your father's hammer. For a minute there, I was worried you felt a little too much."

Connor dropped to one knee beside his friend. "Thanks for doing that. I needed someone to knock some sense into me."

"He needs a tonic," Mhairi muttered.

Hamish grimaced. "What I need is about a dozen smashpacked pot roasts."

Connor's mother handed him the sandstone pendant. "I'm told you can heal with this, Son. There's lots who need it."

Connor took it eagerly and draped it around his neck. Gripping it with his left hand, he tapped the wondrous, concentrated healing power of sandstone. It thundered into him, a warm tide that eased his pains and filled him with peace that helped drive out the last lurking bits of rage left over from porphyry. He placed his other hand on Hamish's shoulder and let his senses flow into his friend along with a river of healing warmth.

Hamish's eyes widened and he sat straighter, his tension draining away. Mattias was right. Hamish was bruised, battered, torn, and burned, but all of his wounds were superficial. Connor bound healing power to each of them, then rose, leaving Hamish's body to get to work.

"Rest. You'll start feeling better. I'll finish the job when I can."

"You should leave me a couple scars. Maybe that one running over my shoulder. I think Jean would be really impressed."

Mhairi slapped him lightly on the side of the head. "She'd be more impressed with less of an idiot."

Hamish's good humor helped ease some of Connor's gnawing worry, but he couldn't delay any longer. "Where is Verena?"

"Jean's tending your girl," Mhairi said in that gentle voice she used to share bad news. She did not try to hide her concern.

Mattias led him down the line of injured. Each one looked to Connor with hope of relief. He hadn't realized so many people had gotten injured in the brief, intense fight. As he hurried past, he promised a quick return, but did not stop.

Verena lay on a blanket that someone had brought up from the bolt hole. Her skin was pale and clammy, her hair matted with blood and dirt, her clothing torn and battered.

Jean and Dierk knelt on either side of her. Jean had already set Verena's broken right arm and right leg, but the sight of her many wounds made Connor want to howl.

Jean looked up and smiled with relief. "Oh, Connor. I'm so glad you're back. She needs you."

She had cleaned Verena's face. Connor dropped to the ground on the opposite side of her and cupped Verena's bruised cheeks, leaning his forehead against hers as he poured his healing senses into her.

Verena was broken.

Connor silently wept tears that dripped onto her eyelids as he scanned her many injuries. In addition to the obvious breaks in her arm and leg, she'd broken six fingers, four ribs, and cracked her spine. Her internal organs were battered, but seemed whole. He didn't feel real fear until he scanned her head.

She had indeed cracked her skull and bruised her face and head badly in the wild tumble across the plain. Without the protection of her helmet, she might not have survived.

Connor lost track of time as he gently wrapped her hurts with sandstone healing, binding broken bones and mending torn tissue. He straightened her broken limbs and filled her with a flood of healing power. He didn't know what to do about her mind, had never tried healing a brain before. All he could do was hope that her body knew how to heal itself if he but gave it the tools to do so.

A gentle hand shook him some time later and he blinked, becoming aware of himself for the first time in a while. He mumbled, "I'm sorry. I know I took too long, but I had to be sure."

Jean kissed his cheek, tears in her eyes. "You've done so much, Connor. Her vitals are so much stronger, and her injuries are already healing. You're amazing."

His mother crouched nearby, her expression tender. "We understand your concern, my boy, but some of the others are pretty badly off too, particularly a couple of those fighters Ilse brought with her."

Connor rose, glancing one more time at Verena's unmoving form. "Jean, will you come with me? I have healing power, but you have the knowledge I don't. Together I think we can accomplish more."

Mattias, who stood nearby, as if on guard, frowned and held up a hand. "Do you hear that?"

Connor turned, feeling a rush of worry. He felt sure they'd destroyed all the rampagers, but was there something else Dougal had planned that they hadn't anticipated? He fumbled with the straps of his battle jacket and began securing them. His store of power stones were still attached to the waist.

A moment later, he felt more than heard the ground beginning to shake.

"Another tremor," his mother said with a frown.

"It'll pass," Hendry said, limping to join her.

It didn't.

The shaking of the ground intensified and Connor shared a worried look with Hamish, who had approached. Already he looked much stronger.

"Remember what Kilian said?" Hamish muttered.

"Gregor was summoning the elfonnel," Connor said. He'd forgotten during the fight to the death with Martys and the rush to heal Verena. "We weren't there to help him. What if. . ."

The rumbling of the earth intensified, and Connor caught sight of a fast-running form cresting the top of the steep, switchback road that led up to Quarry Road. He found a piece of quartzite in his belt pouch and wedged it into his cheek. Applying its power to his eyes, he easily recognized the girl racing down the slope at breakneck speed.

"It's Aifric!" Hopefully she knew what was happening up at the quarry on the other side of the mountain.

"Sounds like the fighting might not be going well," Dierk muttered. "I had to leave before that crazy Aonghus burned me out of the air. Might be time to head back up there and scout."

He pointed toward the windrider, which he had landed near the base of the switchbacks, about a hundred yards away. The shaking continued, and even though the plateau was basically one solid rock, it began to vibrate. With an ear-splitting crack, the face of the cliff above the plateau broke free and tons of rock thundered down.

"Go!" Connor urged Aifric uselessly.

She leaped the last fifty feet of slope, landed right beside the parked windrider, and outran the rocks, fracking and speeding away. The avalanche crashed down right behind her, shattering the windrider and burying in in tons of stone.

Dierk muttered a curse.

Connor said, "At least you weren't on it. I think we're past 'what if'. Everyone, get back from the cliff! Head for the river."

He thrust a finger into the pouch of stones at his belt and absorbed a hefty portion of granite. His lifelong curse skittered up his arm like a thousand insects, comforting him with its familiar maddening itch. Tapping a little to his tired muscles, he scooped Verena gently into his arms.

Aifric rushed up, looking terrified. When he started asking her to check on Verena, she waved away the question.

"We don't have time, Connor. There's a couple elfonnel dueling on the other side of the Torr! They've shattered the quarry and destabilized the entire mountain."

"What about Dougal? Did Kilian kill him?"

Aifric's expression turned grave. "Worse. The elfonnel he raised is a monster, Connor. She's Kilian's mother. She took Dougal and triggered that earthquake."

"What?" Connor and Hamish exclaimed together.

"I don't have time to explain, but she makes Dougal seem like an old friend." Aifric gripped Connor's hand. "Connor, you don't understand. She's shaken everything. I've never heard sounds like this, coming all the way up from the depths. This entire valley is going to shake itself apart. We have to get out of here."

"How? We can't fly," Hamish said, picking at the remnants of his suit.

"We do have the Storm," Jean said, pointing toward the south end of the plateau.

"Wish I'd parked on that side," Dierk muttered.

"Go get it, quick!" Connor said.

Jean and Hamish took off in that direction. The Storm could carry only a few to safety. Hamish or Dierk could take Verena and the other injured north. They could reach the army with all those Healers in a matter of hours.

What to do with everyone else, though?

"Come on. We need to get farther from the mountains," Connor said. "We need to get across the Wick and out into the valley."

As the villagers and soldiers gathered the wounded and followed him toward the river, the shaking of the ground grew worse and it became hard to stand.

Lilias suddenly gasped, one hand going to her mouth as she pointed northwest, toward Alasdair. "The torr's coming down!"

With a groan like the death-knell of the heart of the mountain, the face of the cliff of Wick Torr broke free. Almost in slow motion, it fell with ponderous majesty through the bright moonlight. It crushed the town and buried Lock Wick in a thundering avalanche of stone.

As one, the villagers cried out in anguish at the sight of their destroyed home. Connor shouted with them, his heart breaking at the sight. They'd fought so hard to stop this disaster, but they'd failed.

His parents clung to each other, tears in their eyes, expressions grief-stricken.

"Must move faster," Aifric urged, but running was impossible on the shaking ground.

"Where's Kilian?" Connor asked.

"Raised one of those elfonnel."

"He'll deal with the other one, and I'm sure he'll be fine, but we have to get out of here."

All of the mountain was shaking, with stones cascading in sheets down the slopes. Standing on the plateau, with Mount Alasdair and several smaller mountains flanking it, including the Torr, they were still far too close. Any second, they could get swallowed up in a major avalanche.

Most of the villagers weren't ready to move. They were pointing at the devastation, shouting with anguish. Connor wanted to take a minute to just hug everyone he knew, to try comforting them in that moment of ultimate disaster, but they didn't have time. At least the people were safe, but if they didn't move, they wouldn't be.

Connor tapped soapstone and seized the waters of the Wick, which were churning from the earthquake and responded to his call like a skittish horse. Connor tried shouting directions, but couldn't be heard above the grinding of stones and thunder of rocks.

Clouds of debris and dust were billowing into the air, obscuring the valley in a sinister, black cloud. The dim illumination of the stars and moon winked out, and Mattias's brightly glowing face became a blur in the thick dust.

A deep rumble of sound began building up on Alasdair peak. It sounded like the mountain was coming down.

It would sweep them all away.

Connor yanked on the waters, drawing them around and under his terrified, screaming people and lifted them off the rocks.

Many flailed with fear, but he didn't have time to explain or be as gentle as he wanted.

Trying not to hurt anyone, he massed everyone together and drove the entire group off the edge of the plateau. Instead of following the path of the Wick, which ran close to the danger of the mountains, he yanked waters from the river and drove the group out into the valley.

Seconds later, the plateau was buried in a landslide a hundred yards deep as the mountain collapsed. The shaking grew worse and the sound of snapping rock and thundering landslides threatened to overwhelm Connor. He caught only glimpses of the disaster through the billowing darkness, but felt it through the waters as the avalanche consumed the Wick.

He breathed a sigh of relief as the Storm emerged from the billowing cloud that obscured the stars and plunged the valley into pitch black night. Hamish had activated several pieces of limestone, and the craft blazed like a miniature sun. Mattias called forth another huge light in the air over their company, bright enough that it illuminated the clouds of dust.

Once they were out of immediate danger, Connor slowed their movement and solidified the waters under them. He shifted Ilse and Lukas closer to him so they could confer. Hamish settled the Storm to the waters nearby, and Connor placed Verena gently into the back. Aifric climbed in to check on her, and Jean oversaw the loading of the other wounded. Soon they packed the Storm.

Connor called the leaders of the group to him. The Crushers helped keep the press of frightened villagers at bay.

"We're not safe here," Ilse said. "The earth is reeling like a drunkard. I've never felt anything like it. Walking this earth right now is perilous."

"Where can we go?" Aifric asked. "There are mountains on both sides of the valley."

"North would be best, but I don't think we can cross Mount Ingram with everything shaking like this." Connor decided.

Ilse said, "I agree. We need slate to move fast enough to escape the disaster, but the mountains to the north are completely destabilized."

As if to punctuate her words, the night rang with the heart-stopping rumbling of falling stone. It sounded like Wick Torr, or even Mount Ingram itself had just collapsed. New clouds of dust billowed across the valley, growing so thick it became hard to breathe. Mattias's blazing light looked wan and weak twenty feet in the air.

598

Connor accelerated their watery ride deeper into the valley, but that wouldn't save them for long.

"The mountain came down," Ilse said, her expression more afraid than he'd ever seen. "But the shaking is still building. This entire valley will be buried soon. We have to tempt slate. There's no other way to get out of here fast enough."

"We can take groups in the Storm," Hamish said.

Jean nodded. "We can find Wolfram and return with some windriders."

"That'll take too long," Connor said. "I do need you two to get out of here in the Storm. Take Verena and the wounded to Wolfram. Dierk should go too. Get some windriders and try to find us. In the meantime, the rest of us will head over the lowest peak of the western rim of Alasdair Valley. We might make it to Drumwhindle plain."

"You mean to go through Badurach?" Ilse exclaimed. "Are you cracked? The entire Obrioner army is massed there."

"Do you have a better idea?"

Lukas blew out a breath. "When you put it that way, I vote for glorious death in battle against a force a thousand times larger than ours over getting buried alive here."

"I appreciate your optimism," Connor said.

Ilse asked, "How do you mean to get there? Even if the mountains weren't tearing themselves apart, carrying this many people over those peaks would strain the mightiest Sapper. Neither you nor I can do it."

Connor smiled and reached into the special pocket of his battle jacket where he kept the sculpted stones Ailsa had gifted to him. He extracted the exquisite slate tower. Just touching it connected him with earth, and he gasped as his senses radiated into the ground.

Ilse was right. The valley was shaking as if in death throes, and he could feel the very roots of the nearest mountains quivering as those peaks shook themselves apart.

He handed the sculpted stone to Ilse. "Actually, I think you can."

She reached for it with reverence, her hand actually shaking, but snatched her fingers back. "You're Blood of the Tallan, boy. This was gifted to you, so you should use it."

Connor shook his head and pressed the stone into her hand. "I'll support you and help in every way I can, but I need you to do this. I'm exhausted, and you're more experienced walking the earth. It has to be you."

She took it and grinned. "If you think I'm going to turn this treasure down twice, you're more cracked than that Builder friend of yours."

Connor pulled a little piece of slate out of his pouch. He lacked boots to slip it into, so he crouched and pressed a hand to the earth. "I'm going to see if there's anyone else in the valley we need to pick up on our way out."

"Lord Gavin and Lady Isobel," Hamish said, then frowned. "If their manor house isn't buried yet. It seems wrong to save them, though."

Jean said, "We should save Moira. So that means her parents too."

"If that shrew tries scolding me, I can't promise I won't leave her perched on top of a mountain somewhere," Ilse warned.

"Fair enough. Let's do it."

CHAPTER EIGHTY-EIGHT

"That which was sundered may yet be repaired, and those lost may return to the fold. Morning breaks only after the darkest of the night, and rejoicing may indeed replace mourning."

~Evander

Badurach Pass," Ilse said with a tired smile.

"On this side, it's called Drumwhindle," Connor reminded her.

She grimaced. "I can't say that word with a straight face."

"Fine, call it Badurach. You've earned the right."

They'd escaped Alasdair with nearly every living soul, including Lord Gavin, his family, and all of Dougal's Boulders Connor had knocked over the wick. It seemed weeks ago, not just a single, long night.

Connor had carried the group across the shaking valley on a sliding sheet of ice, with destruction chasing them the entire way. The ominous thunder of falling rocks as the mountains tore themselves apart was made worse by the darkness.

Ilse had taken over when they reached the western slopes, but even with the sculpted stone, moving several hundred people over that rugged terrain had been harrowing. When the western hills had begun to collapse, Ilse had nearly lost control.

With Connor's help, and by consuming nearly all of the sculpted stone's incredible power, she held on. They finally made it across one crumbling saddle between two peaks shortly before those mountains collapsed back into the valley they had just escaped.

Now they stood atop a wide shelf of stone near the summit of a mountain along the eastern edge of the high plain that ran north up to the jagged stump of the once-mighty Drumwhindle Pass. It had survived the battle, the assault by Redmund-turned-elfonnel, and even the enormous Last Word explosions. Some time in the previous night, it had succumbed to the widespread earthquake.

The cold air cut right through Connor's battle jacket and reminded him that his pants were still little better than rags. At least someone had found a pair of shoes that fit him in one of the farmhouses they paused at to pick up more refugees. Everyone else huddled far back from the edge, resting and sharing a meal of meager provisions some of the villagers had brought along from the bolt hole.

"Something's coming!" Stuart shouted from where he stood guard at the northern edge of their little safe haven.

That couldn't be good. The only people who could scale that mountain would be Petralists.

"What does it look like?" Connor asked as he and Ilse jogged over to Stuart. Lukas followed, and the Crushers rose and reached for weapons.

Stuart pointed northeast, up toward the ultimate peak of the mountain. A dim form, back-lit by the morning light, was flying over the peak, wreathed in flames.

"Is it an elfonnel?" Stuart asked nervously.

Connor already had a piece of quartzite in his cheek and focused on the distant figure. He breathed a sigh of relief.

"No. It's Kilian."

"Tallan be praised," Ilse said with a relieved sigh.

Stuart gave her an incredulous look. "Leave the Tallan and Kilian both well away from here."

"It'll be all right," Connor reassured him.

He shared Ilse's relief. He had told himself many times through the long, terrifying night that Kilian would be fine. He knew how to raise an elfonnel and how to return. He'd done it before.

But when the shaking continued hour after hour, and entire mountains fell behind them, he had started to worry. Even the mighty Kilian might be consumed by such a catastrophe.

Kilian landed nearby, his face haggard, dark circles under his eyes. His flames winked out immediately. He took one staggering step toward them and muttered, "I feel terrible."

Lukas caught him as he collapsed. He gently lowered Kilian to the cold stones as Connor and the others gathered around.

"Is he all right?" Ilse asked.

Connor tapped healing power from his sandstone pendant. It was looking decidedly worn from its recent heavy usage. He poured healing power into Kilian and scanned for injuries.

Kilian seemed whole, but every muscle quivered with exhaustion so deep, it was a marvel he hadn't collapsed hours ago. Connor eased his aches, and Kilian breathed easier.

After a moment, Connor sat back and said, "He'll be fine. He's just exhausted. Let him sleep."

Lukas went to fetch him a blanket and Ilse gestured toward the Obrioner army massed along the northern edge of the distant plateau, blocking the pass. "Do you have a plan for getting through that?"

Connor said, "Even though the pass is partially collapsed, it still looks like there's a path through. Unless you want to risk trying to bridge the chasm."

Ilse shook her head and considered the tiny remnant of the once-beautiful slate tower. "This stone is all but spent. It'll barely last long enough to get us down there. This far out, the ground's no longer shaking, but spanning that chasm will challenge my remaining strength."

"And as soon as we try, we'll have Petralists from both armies coming to stop us," Connor agreed.

He suppressed his frustration. They had made it through the mountains, but now had to escape Obrion. Connor had kept a constant eye toward the northern sky, but had not seen the hoped-for windriders coming to rescue them. Even if the windriders came, would they know to look for them so close to the Obrioner positions? Connor didn't want to fight through the army. Could he talk his way through?

Then he got an idea and checked Kilian's pockets.

He found a speakstone.

Connor hefted it triumphantly and held it close to his mouth. "Hamish? Dierk? Can anyone hear me?"

Nothing.

Ilse drew close, her gaze locked on the stone. "Tallan's blessed memory, we could use a spot of luck right now."

Connor tried every thirty seconds for the next several minutes, wishing Hamish was there with some extra quartzite blocks to strengthen the signal. They were high enough on the mountain that the signal should be reaching into Granadure, but he had no idea where Hamish or Dierk might be.

As much as he hoped to hear them respond, he really longed to hear Verena's voice. Worry for her had eaten at him ever since he'd watched the Storm disappear into the night sky hours ago. Would she be all right? Had she awakened?

Would she ever?

The thought of never seeing her bright blue eyes or hear her silvery laughter again made him want to curl up and cry. He'd sent Mattias along with Aifric in the Storm to watch over her.

Wolfram would surely see to Verena's safety, but Mattias would no doubt leverage all of his connections to help heal her. Connor hated having to rely on his cursed rival, but he'd do anything to save Verena.

If she had awakened, would Mattias's glowing smile be the first thing she saw? Would Connor's absence give Mattias the chance to solidify his hold on her heart?

A voice issued from the speakstone, snapping Connor out of his worried reverie. "Connor?"

"Hamish? Is that you?" Connor cried, holding the stone close and shouting into it.

"Me and Dierk both, with a whole squadron of windriders in support. Where are you?"

Ilse clapped Connor on the shoulder and raised her fist in victory. He mimicked the move, then shared their position with Hamish.

"We'll be there in a few minutes." Hamish's happy tone turned grave. "Connor, we just flew over Alasdair Valley. It's gone. Wick Torr, Mount Ingram, Mount Alasdair, they're all flattened. The river's gone, and the valley is filled with rubble. It's like Alasdair never existed."

Ilse said softly, "It is as I feared."

Connor glanced to where his family, Hamish's family, and the rest of the village were sitting huddled together against the cold. "Just get here as quick as you can. Alasdair still lives, as long as our families do."

"What do you mean to do with everyone?" Ilse asked.

"I'll drop Lord Gavin and his family and those Boulders at the base of this mountain."

If Lady Isobel didn't stop haranguing everyone, blaming Connor for the loss of her home, and threatening daor on everyone she saw, he might just throw her off the cliff.

"And the villagers?"

He took a long, slow breath. "I know what I want, but they need to choose it too. Come on."

Everyone stood when Connor approached, looking to him with the last slivers of hope that had survived the harrowing night.

"I have some good news. Hamish will be here soon with a fleet of windriders to carry us off of this mountain."

That elicited a cheer, but Lilias asked, "And what news of Alasdair?"

Connor hesitated, and silence settled over the group. "The mountains all collapsed. The valley is filled with rubble. There's no returning there. I'm sorry, but our home is gone."

"What are we to do?" Amhain asked. Peigi huddled close to him, and the children looked at Connor with wide, worried eyes.

"I know this disaster is almost the worst we could imagine," Connor said.

Peigi interrupted. "What could be worse? We've lost everything!"

As many other villagers grumbled their assent Connor said, "We still have our families. Look around. We're still together, and most of us are healthy. The wounded will be healed, and I know you're all stronger than any disaster. We can start over."

"Where?" Amhain asked.

"Come with me to Granadure."

A ripple of nervous murmurs ran through the crowd. Few looked surprised, but most looked worried.

Hendry gripped Connor's shoulder and gave him a nod of approval. "You're right, Son. Well said. We are Alasdair, and we'll take it with us wherever we go."

Lilias joined her husband, rocking sleeping Fiona in her arms. "Connor, we've just lost our homes. You're asking us to leave our nation too."

"I'm asking you to come find a new home."

"How would we live? What would we do?" Hendry asked, and several of the others echoed the question.

Connor grinned. "I just so happen to know of an obsidian quarry that needs mending, a village nearby that needs repairing, and stone that needs good cutters. Dad, Mom, you've seen it. I can promise equipment, supplies, and new chisels at no charge to any of you."

That elicited a round of interested murmurs.

"Would we have to eat Grandurian food?" Stuart asked.

Ilse grunted. "You might be surprised, boy."

Connor said, "There are locals there. I'm confident we can work things out so you can share the town and teach each other your favorite recipes."

"Grandurian neighbors?" Peigi asked, sounding nervous.

"They're not the monsters we've been led to believe," Connor assured them. "They're people, and more importantly, at that quarry, they're cutters. Just like us."

Hendry looked doubtful. "Obsidian is pretty fragile. We're used to striking granite. We'd break more than we'd quarry."

Connor shrugged. "Doesn't really matter, Dad. Most of it needs to get powdered anyway."

Hendry smiled. "Then maybe we can make it work."

"There will be challenges, but there you can rebuild in safety. Here, High Lord Dougal might seek vengeance."

Lady Isobel pushed through the crowd, followed by Lord Gavin and Moira. She looked haggard. Her fine gown was dirty and torn, her hair mussed, and her hands scratched from climbing over rough rocks.

She thrust a finger at Connor and shrieked, "Criminal! You will hang for your crimes! These are our linn, and after last night's disaster, they are all my slaves!"

To think he'd once felt cowed by her. Connor lifted his own finger and called forth a bit of crimson flame. "Do you remember that day the heatstone oven blew up in your house?"

She cringed back, one hand going to her black-dyed hair. It had regrown in the months since that disaster, but she still used the same dye, and no doubt it would burn just as hotly.

"Oh, shut up, Isobel," Lilias snapped, glaring at her lady with undisguised scorn. "You've robbed, cheated, and abused this village for too long."

Hendry added, "Thank you for helping make our decision for us." He raised his fist and declared, "I am going with my son to a new home. A free home."

Other villagers took up the cheer while Isobel sputtered with rage. She started to shout again, but Lord Gavin grabbed her arm and pulled her around to face him. For the first time ever that Connor had seen he spoke sternly to her.

"Stop your foolishness, Isobel. You're only making things worse."

"But we've lost everything!" she wailed.

"And if not for Connor and these Grandurians who you've been insulting all night, we would have died too. Moira would have died."

For once, Isobel opened her mouth, but seemed to not know what to say.

Lord Gavin faced Connor and extended his hand. "My boy, I don't agree with some of what you are doing, but I understand why. I thank you for thinking of us when we . . ." He paused and gave a rueful smile. "We thought of no one but ourselves."

Connor took the proffered hand, more surprised by that bit of honest humility than just about anything he'd seen all night. "Thank you, Lord Gavin. We'll see you safely down the mountain."

Then he raised his voice. "Anyone who does not wish to join us can join Lord Gavin and Lady Isobel."

They all voted to go to Granadure.

Three minutes later, five windriders banked around the peak of the mountain, thrusters roaring. Hamish piloted the lead wagon, with Jean sitting beside him. He had discarded his broken suit and wore warm flying leathers.

Dierk piloted the second. They flew long troop transport wagons, with many blankets piled on the back seats. As villagers clambered aboard, Jean passed out travel provisions.

Hamish stood with Connor and Ilse, overseeing the loading. Lilias approached and gave Hamish a warm hug. "Thank you for coming to get us. I'm proud of you."

Hamish looked startled by the praise and said with a shrug, "Just doing what any good Builder would do."

"It's still hard to believe that you share Verena's amazing ability to quicken these stones. It's like you bring them to life to power your mechanicals."

Hamish gaped at her. Then he laughed and gripped her hands. "That's it! That's the word we've been looking for. We quicken stones!"

"That's what I just said." Lilias frowned at him, just like she had all their lives. "Are you all right?"

Hamish laughed again and gave her a hug. "Better than you could imagine."

Connor grinned with him. They'd wracked their brains for the right word, and now Lilias had stumbled upon it by accident. He hoped Verena would awaken soon to hear it.

Dierk agreed to fly Lord Gavin's family and the Boulders down to the plateau. As Connor turned to survey the distant Obrioner army massed near the pass, he realized he couldn't leave yet, despite how much he yearned to go check on Verena.

"I'm coming down there with you," he said.

"Why?" Dierk asked.

"I need to pay a visit to General Rory."

Hamish tossed him some warm leathers. "Then you might want to put some pants on."

Chapter Eighty-Nine

"Braying of hounds deters not the lion, but often leads the hunter to the prey."

~Redmund

Connor's friends tried to dissuade him from risking a trip down to the Obrioner camp, but he remained resolute.

"We can't save you if you get stuck down there," Hamish said finally. "My suit is wrecked, Verena's unconscious, and Kilian's sleeping so heavy I could shave his head and he'd never twitch."

Connor smiled. "I love the image, but better not shave him."

"Only if I could convince him Mattias did it." Hamish's smile faded. "We're barely holding on, Connor. We've got our families and the entire village with us. We're not ready for another pitched battle."

"I know. That's why I have to do this."

"You're not making sense," Ilse said with a frown.

Jean regarded him closely. "Hendry did hit you awfully hard on the head with that hammer."

"I'm fine," Connor assured them. "Listen. Dougal's been captured by Kilian's insane mother. This entire section of border is completely destabilized. None of us can afford another full-scale battle, not now. It could destroy half the continent."

"They haven't listened to reason before," Lukas pointed out.

"But Dougal's not there, and they'll want to find him."

Hamish shook his head. "I still think it's foolish, and if even I think an idea is foolish, it's definitely time to think again."

Their points were valid, and Connor didn't fool himself into believing he could fight his way free of that entire army. The problem was, when they saw how battered and tired he was, they'd be more likely to attack, not less.

He trusted Rory, but Rory was new in command. Would he be able to keep the other officers in line?

Probably, but Connor needed something to impress them, to remind them that he was Blood of the Tallan and far too dangerous to meddle with. He couldn't use slate. Even without Gregor, he could never intimidate the Sentries. Besides, the sculpted slate stone was nearly spent.

That was it! He could use another sculpted stone. He only had marble and quartzite left. Marble would be great, but Kilian had warned him repeatedly not to risk using marble. Dougal might not be nearby, but it still might not be a good idea.

That left quartzite.

Connor drew the beautiful sculpted stone from his inner pocket, and his friends stared with the same wonder he felt. It was shaped like an exquisite bird, wings outstretched, and as soon as he touched it, he felt connected to the wind. The chill breeze seemed to whisper in his ear as it passed, and even without focusing on the air, he felt the currents whistling along the mountain.

Hamish, who was starting to look really worried said, "So entering a hostile army without any backup isn't crazy enough? You want to tempt the air?"

"It'll make them hesitate."

"It'll kill you. I flew here, Connor. The air is wild. I've never felt it like this, and you've always said quartzite is the hardest stone for Petralists to use."

He hefted the sculpted stone. "That's why I'm going to use this."

They continued to argue, but he waved them to silence. "I appreciate your concern, but I'm convinced I have to do this. I'll see you on the Badurach side of the pass soon."

With a final wave, he turned and ran for the edge of the shelf. Ignoring their cries for him to wait, he leaped out over the four thousand foot drop.

As he plummeted down, air whistling in his ears, he clutched the sculpted stone and envisioned the gateway to air like a glittering doorway in his mind, filled with a whirlwind.

It opened, and his senses burst through.

Connor became one with the air.

He'd always felt it as an external thing, but now it felt like a part of him. His breath became an extension of the winds curling around him, and his body like a leaf in the current. Air was not a single giant, invisible mass, but more a crowd of eager, independent personalities. The various currents were like a friendly mob, twining and rippling around each other. Some were mighty, some tiny. Some gusted with enough strength to snap trees and level buildings, while others huddled in place, lacking the energy to move.

Connor's mind slipped in among them, and for the first time the air currents greeted him as an equal and responded without hesitation to his call.

He barely felt it as a howling wind wrapped around his body and arrested his fall, leveling him into a fast glide. His mind soared across the land like a sparrow, skipping from one air current to another.

Hamish was right. The air was wild. The shaking of the earth all night and the collapse of millions of tons of mountains had whipped the regular currents into a frenzy.

The air currents grew older and stronger the higher he cast his senses. Some had spanned the entire continent and would rush out over the wide oceans without fear, seeking foreign lands and uncharted currents beyond. If he had the time to fly with them, he felt confident he could learn their secrets, truths that clung to them from the ages like bits of invisible mist.

Some of the air had been trapped in Alasdair valley for long periods of time, content to flit between the mountains, but unwilling to test the heights to escape. Now cast beyond the limits of those toppled mountains, the sudden freedom churned them into wild and uncertain winds, gusting in every direction.

Others were new, spawned last night during the earthquake. They flitted about with nervous energy, like foals galloping around mature horses. He sensed that some would fade to exhaustion, while others would meld into established currents and fly away to see the world.

Connor soared over those gusts, wrapped in a strong current that felt capable and sure. His laugh bubbled out of his mouth, and the nearest air current took up the vibration, laughing along and carrying him higher still.

He had never imagined the air could be so complex or so invigorating. It seemed fickle because Pathfinders touched it so rarely, and they usually only connected with the young, restless currents that didn't know where they were going or how to get there. His training with Mattias had given him the foundation to understand what he was sensing, and he exulted in the absolute freedom of flight.

If that was how Hamish felt all the time, no wonder he spent so much time in his suit. Verena must understand. She flew better than most birds.

Thoughts of Verena dampened his good mood, and he hoped his friends were wrong. He didn't want to die, didn't want any delays keeping him from Verena. He could not ignore the opportunity to possibly stopping the fighting.

As he soared high over the valley toward the long plateau where the Obrioner army massed, Connor decided he needed everyone looking at him so he could maximize the impact. So he tapped marble. He wouldn't dare the sculpted marble stone, but he also wouldn't dare enter that army without some marble in his mouth.

Flames burst from his outstretched hands, and he formed a tiny set of wings to help stabilize his flight. He was enjoying flying with air, but he wasn't foolish enough to trust it.

Of course the army sighted him long before he banked into a steep dive toward the camp. At first he had planned to land outside of camp and enter on foot to reduce the chances of their interpreting his approach as a threat.

As he dove, he decided a different approach better fit the image he was creating.

So he angled his dive and swooped over the camp, sending out bursts of multi-colored fire that blazed across the bright morning sky. He glanced back at the flames creating a gentle arc, marking his path, and got a great idea.

Banking around again, he swooped and turned, passing over the army several times. After a busy minute of aerial fun, he stopped directly over the central command tent, two hundred feet in the air.

As soon as he did, the air currents slipped away. So he settled into a hover on a pedestal of fire and spread his fiery wings farther to help catch the heated wind and hold him aloft.

He grinned as he surveyed his handiwork. Burning in the morning sky, marking his swooping path, was the ancient symbol for air. Connor hovered in what looked like the eye of a storm, with streamers rippling toward the west, suggesting strong winds.

It was an impressive sight, but was it impressive enough to give him a chance to talk before he was attacked?

Only one way to find out.

As Connor descended toward an open space outside of the command tent, he scanned the mass of soldiers gathered to greet him. He recognized a company of Fast Rollers, with Tomas and Cameron at the lead. His relief was short-lived, though. He also spotted several senior tertiaries.

General Rory stepped to the door of the command tent. More senior officers followed, along with Shona. Connor couldn't read her expression. He was just glad Rory was present.

With everyone staring up at him like that, he was suddenly grateful that Hamish had tossed him those pants. He only wished he'd asked Hamish if he had any more extract of milked skunk.

When he dropped below a hundred feet, Connor waved and called, "What's for breakfast?"

Tomas and Cameron put their heads together, talking excitedly. Coins changed hands. Connor dearly wished he knew what the day's bet covered.

Rory lifted a hand in greeting, and spoke to his men. Connor couldn't hear what he said, but the assembled soldiers appeared to relax a little.

As soon as Connor landed, he tapped slate. He felt the presence of several Sentries prowling the earth beneath his feet, and was careful not to probe any deeper. He didn't want to get buried alive before he got a chance to talk.

Connor had made a point of landing facing Rory instead of Shona, and he waved. "Good morning, Captain!"

He almost said 'General', but remembered just in time that he wasn't supposed to know Rory's promotion yet.

"Are you here to kill more generals?" Rory asked as the gathered soldiers drew closer, hands on weapons.

They must know what he'd done to help the Grandurians at Altkalen. He had captured many of their senior Petralists, killed their general, and defeated Ivor.

Maybe landing in the middle of that army hadn't been such a good idea.

He was there, so he decided trusting Rory was the right choice. He and the Fast Rollers were the only ones who showed any signs of welcome.

Shona wore a half smile and raised one eyebrow at him when she caught his eye. She was dressed as a high lady, wearing a red silk blouse and a long gray skirt. A wide leather belt with a pair of daggers circled her slender waist.

Connor said, "Alasdair valley is destroyed. We rescued everyone we could."

"After you destroyed it," a middle-aged man accused.

Connor recognized his voice as Lord Flichity. He was a bit overweight, with heavy jowls that made him look like a grumpy dog.

"Wasn't us. High Lord Dougal sacrificed Gregor to raise another elfonnel. He knew the danger, and he did it anyway. He destabilized the area and buried Alasdair under half a mile of rubble. You felt the shaking all the way out here, didn't you?"

"We did," Rory said.

"Does my father live?" Shona asked, and he couldn't tell if she was eager or worried.

"As far as I know."

"You're not telling us everything," Flichity said with a glare. "Aonghus arrived in the night, so terrified he can barely make a spark, and he's making no sense."

"He's lucky he survived." Aifric had described events in the quarry to Connor. "Kilian helped him escape certain death."

"Kilian is a murderer," Flichity declared.

Connor gave him a disgusted look. "Stop it. We all know where we all stand on all that. I don't have the patience to argue the point. We have bigger problems to deal with."

Rory took a step closer and gestured at Connor's still-burning emblem in the air. "What problems are bigger? You fly in here like the Tallan reborn, right after we receive reports of windriders massing to the east. Wolfram's army is poised to attack from the rear. And now you tell us Alasdair is gone and these lands are unstable. Those would be enough problems for most days."

"Don't worry about Wolfram. He will stand down."

"And how do you know that?" Flichity asked, his tone derisive.

"Because I'm going through the pass when we're finished here, and I'm going to tell him to."

"I bet you will," Shona said, giving him a tiny nod of approval.

"Assuming we don't incarcerate you first," Flichity said.

"Don't try my patience today, Lord Flichity," Connor growled. When the man looked surprised, Connor added, "I know who you are, and I know Rory is in charge."

"How?" Shona asked.

He waved away the question. "I'm tired. I'm hungry, and I've seen friends badly hurt trying to avert the catastrophe Dougal brought down upon his own realm. Gregor is dead, and this kingdom is in more danger than ever before."

The lord huffed, but for the moment looked cowed.

Connor dismissed him and turned back to Rory, who allowed perhaps a hint of an approving smile. It was hard to tell, but Connor decided he had.

"The bigger problem is that Dougal was trying to raise an ancient elfonnel that had been slumbering under Alasdair quarry."

"So that's what he was talking about," Shona said.

"He didn't understand the danger as well as he thought. Instead of raising a sleepy elfonnel that he might seize control over to send against Kilian, he raised Queen Dreokt herself, and she wasn't happy."

Shona suddenly looked worried. "I've heard a lot about Dreokt, but none of it was good."

"Based on what she did last night, she's worse than the rumors."

As a murmur ran through the gathered soldiers, Tomas asked, "How is it possible? She's been dead for centuries."

"Not dead. Hibernating. She was lost during the great battle that sundered away part of Althing and formed the Broken Waters. It seems she got trapped in the elfonnel she raised when it retreated into the earth."

Cameron shuddered. "She'd go stark raving mad stuck in the ground that long."

"From what I learned from Kilian, she was insane before the battle, so she's got to be well and truly cracked now. She's the one who triggered the earthquake that destroyed Alasdair. She's captured Dougal and flew away somewhere with him."

Rory grunted, his expression grave. "Seems to me our primary duty is to find him and render aid."

"I figured you'd see it that way," Connor said.

"Our primary mission is to repulse the Grandurian invaders, as ordered by Dougal himself," Flichity retorted.

"His orders were to hold until he could send aid," Rory said. "Clearly he intended those elfonnel to kill Kilian, then come scatter the Grandurians. The situation has changed and we now have an unknown, but potentially deadly enemy in our midst."

"She's the queen," Flichity retorted.

Rory turned the full weight of his stare on the man. "Are you saying you'd swear fealty to her over King Turriff?"

Tomas pursed his lips. "Good question, that one."

Cameron nodded. "Do we hang him for traitor if he does, or if he doesn't?"

"Might have to hang him either way, just to be safe."

"Insolent bash fighters," Flichity mumbled, but his glare didn't faze the two. He turned his gaze to Shona. "You are Marshal, Lady Shona. You have the authority to overrule Rory. I recommend we take this insolent fool into custody."

614

"This insolent fool is the one who brought us word of the danger my father faces," Shona said. She regarded Connor thoughtfully. "I can think of better uses for you than in prison, Connor." She extended her hand. "Join with me, my Guardian, and together we can end the fighting and save my father."

He shouldn't be surprised that she'd make a final play to win her back to him. His place was with Verena.

What if Verena no longer wanted him?

Without Verena, was there a good reason to deny Shona? United to her, he could wield the full might of an Obrioner lordship. What good might they do together?

She noted his hesitation and stepped closer, her big eyes full of hope, but he shook his head. "Again you show me much honor, my lady Shona, but I cannot accept your offer today."

She drew even closer and asked softly so only he could hear. "But perhaps some day?"

"I can't make any promises either way at the moment."

She nodded and touched his hand. Her skin was warm, and her soft scent of roses tickled his nose. "Then I will cling to the hope that you will see reason."

Connor raised his voice so all could hear. "Please don't underestimate the queen. Dreokt makes my curse look pitiful. She treated Kilian like he was an annoying child, and she flew away with your father, as if using air was a simple thing. She's nothing like anything we've ever seen, and getting lost inside an elfonnel that long, I doubt there's much, if any, humanity left in her."

"We'll find her," Shona promised.

"I'm worried you will. I can't say what she'll do, but it won't be good."

"Can you really keep Wolfram on his side of the mountain?" Shona asked, her gaze searching.

Connor nodded. "I can. And I can get a proposal for at least a temporary peace treaty, if you're willing to consider it."

"I am willing to consider it, and I would prefer if you delivered it in person."

"If I can," he promised.

"I support such a plan too," Rory said, eliciting another scowl from Lord Flichity.

Shona said, "Then General Rory, I suggest you issue commands to stand down. I want scouting parties to begin hunting for my father."

"Wise choice," Rory told her softly with an approving smile. Then he turned and began loudly issuing orders.

Shona took Connor's hands in hers. "I'm sorry your home was destroyed, Connor."

"So am I, but I got everyone out. I'm taking my family and everyone who's willing with me to Granadure."

Her eyes widened in surprise. Maybe he shouldn't have told her, but she'd learn about it from Lord Gavin. "I should object the fact that you're absconding with an entire village, Connor."

He shrugged. "Your father was targeting them, so I have no choice. You can keep Lord Gavin and his family, though."

She winced, then sighed. "I suppose there's no way I could convince you to take him too?"

"I might take him and Moira, but Isobel wouldn't last a day before someone put her out of her misery."

"Be safe, Connor," Shona told him.

He turned to leave, and Rory fell into step beside him. "I'll see you to the border, lad."

"Thank you. General?" he added.

Rory shrugged. "The world's a surprising place."

Connor gripped his hand. "I believe appointing you general might be the wisest decision Dougal ever made."

They walked together for a few minutes, and after they left the clustered group of soldiers, Rory glanced at Connor, blew out a breath, and rubbed his craggy face.

"Tallan take it and swallow it whole, Connor, but you've got the courage of a naked pedra hunter."

Connor smiled. "I had to warn you all of the real danger we now face."

Rory grimaced. "Speaking of danger, I've got a favor to ask, lad. Perhaps harder than catching the old queen mother."

"What?"

"I need you to tell Anika . . ." He sighed, his expression tortured. "I have no idea what to tell her. Just, I'm sorry, and I hope..."

Connor understood Rory's predicament better than he imagined, although Rory's new position might make it harder to find an excuse to wrestle with Anika. Connor too needed to figure out how to reconcile with the woman he loved.

"I'll ask Jean. She'll suggest something."

Rory looked relieved. "Thanks."

When he reached the northern picket line, he shook Rory's hand and headed alone into the pass. The narrow passage was nearly blocked with rubble, and he resorted to tapping marble and blasting himself into the air to fly through to the other side.

And of course, the Grandurian defenders nearly killed him.

Once he talked his way through that nearly-fatal encounter, he soared with fire and air over the deep canyon and its shattered defensive walls and finally reached the camp.

Ilse and Hamish were waiting for him.

"I can't believe you're not dead," Ilse laughed.

"Not before breakfast," Connor grinned, relieved to be back among friends.

Hamish nodded approvingly. "You understand life's priorities."

As they headed into camp, Ilse sighed. "It's good to be home."

Connor cringed. "I can't call it home yet."

"It's more home than anywhere else, isn't it?" she asked.

"That's the problem. Every home I've had recently gets destroyed."

Hamish handed them both smashpacked sweetbread loaves and said, "Why don't you claim Merkland as your home? Then Dougal's house can get wrecked for once."

"We'll figure out home soon enough. For now, I just want to see Verena."

Ilse said, "She's still sleeping. Aifric and Mattias are with her."

Connor sighed. Why did the situation feel almost normal? He was trying to broker a peace accord and resettle his entire village in a new country while the girl he loved was in a coma, attended by an Assassin-Healer and the man trying to steal her away from him.

His life really was twisted so far out of normal, he wondered if he'd ever managed to straighten it out.

He started to walk faster and asked, "Hamish, do you have any limestone?"

"No, but I can get some. Why?"

"I need to figure out how to make my teeth glow."

Thumbs Up?
Or Thumbs down?

How did you like the book?

Are you willing to take 5 seconds and share it with the world? Now, while it's still fresh?

Reviews help more than you imagine. How many times have you looked at reviews of books or products before buying?

If you've never posted a review before, it's super simple. Just two steps:

• Rate the book 1-5 stars. Be honest. Be generous.
• Write a short review. One or two sentences is plenty.

What goes in those sentences? Here are a few suggestions:
• Your feelings about the book.
• Something you loved about it. (no spoilers please!)
• The fact that you couldn't put the book down all night.
• Your favorite line of Sentry speak.
• Who is your favorite character?
• If you were a Petralist, what affinity would you most love to have?

Just pick one suggestion, or come up with your own. It's that simple.

And just like that, you really help me out, and help other readers considering buying this story.

To post a review on Amazon: http://smarturl.it/yv37jy

Thanks!

Frank

Do you want exclusive content?
First notification of new covers, new maps, and upcoming events?
Exclusive opportunities to submit your ideas and suggestions for future stories?

Join the Reader's Group!

To join: http://smarturl.it/4u6hmm

I send emails to the group on a regular (but not annoying) basis.

I hope you'll join the team. I look forward to your input.

Frank

Petralist Stones

Three for the masses
Two for the many
Four for the privileged few

Igneous

Basalt
Speed, agility
Tapped: Powder
through the skin
Obrion: Strider
Granadure: Wingrunner

Granite
Strength, summoning
Tapped: Powder
through the skin
Obrion: Boulder or
Fast Roller
Granadure: Rumbler

Obsidian
Magnifies innate abilities
Tapped: Powder through the skin
Obrion: Blade
Granadure: Allcarver
Sedimentary

SEDIMENTARY

Limestone
Light
Tapped: Held or worn
Obrion: Solas
Granadure: Solas

Sandstone
Healing
Tapped: Held or worn
Obrion: Healer
Granadure: Healer

METAMORPHIC

Marble
Fire
Tapped: Under the Tongue
Obrion: Firetongue
Granadure: Flameweaver

Slate
Earth
Tapped: Soles of feet
Obrion: Sentry
Granadure: Sapper

Quartzite
Air, Senses
Tapped: Placed in Mouth
Obrion: Pathfinder
Granadure: Longseer

Soapstone
Water
Tapped: Powder swallowed
with water
Obrion: Spitter
Granadure: Water Moccasin

Secret Stones

Diorite
Igneous Stone
Explosive Power
Tapped: Powder
through the skin
Obrion: Unknown
Granadure: Unknown

Porphyry
Igneous Stone
Rage Monster
Tapped: Powder
through the skin
Obrion: Unclaimed
Granadure: Rampager

Anthracite (Blind Coal)
Sedimentary Stone
Aggressive Slipperiness
Tapped: Held or worn
Obrion: Unknown
Granadure: Unknown

Serpentinite
Metamorphic Stone
Sound
Tapped: Unknown
Obrion: Unknown
Granadure: Unknown

NEW STONES!

Chert
Sedimentary Stone
Empathy
Tapped: Unknown
Obrion: Unknown
Granadure: Unknown

Amphibolite Gneiss
Metamorphic Stone
Counters Basalt
Tapped: Powder
through the skin
Obrion: Unknown
Granadure: Unknown

Granite Gneiss
Metamorphic Stone
Counters Granite
Tapped: Powder
through the skin
Obrion: Unknown
Granadure: Unknown

OTHER WORKS BY FRANK MORIN

The Petralist Series

Set in Stone - Book One
A Stone's Throw - Book Two
No Stone Unturned - Book Three
Affinity for War - Book Four (you're reading it!)
The Queen's Quarry - Book Five
The King's Craft - Book Six
Blood of the Tallan - Book Seven

Petralist Origins Stories

When Torcs Fly - Tomas and Cameron
Game of Garlands - Anika
Builder of Intrigue - Aunt Ailsa

The Facetakers Series

Saving Face - Book One
Memory Hunter - Book Two
Rune Warrior - Book Three
Aeon Champion - Book Four

Short Stories

Odin's Eye - Part of *A Game of Horns: A Red Unicorn Anthology*
Only Logical - Part of *Unseen: United! Box Set Anthology* to
    raise funds to fight plagiarism
The Essence - Part of *Dragon Writers: An Anthology*

About the Author

Frank Morin is a storyteller, and he loves great stories wherever he can find them. When not writing or trying to keep up with his active family, he's often found hiking, camping, Scuba diving, or enjoying other outdoor activities.

Frank writes all types of fantasy, from his exciting Facetakers contemporary fantasy / time-travel thrillers, to these popular Petralist novels, and more. Check his website for updates and to sign up for his newsletter to receive the latest on all his releases, scheduled events, and insider information:

www.frankmorin.org.

Or like his Author Facebook page:

www.facebook.com/authorfrankmorin

Frank lives in Oregon with his family, who are his most enthusiastic fans and his most brutal critics. In their home, storytelling is a cherished family tradition that keeps magic alive.